"You're coming to America with me," he said.

"No, Cam."

"I've already booked passage for both of us, Miranda."

"You assumed a great deal."

His thumbs pressed against the back of my neck, his fingers kneading the flesh on either side. I arched my back as his thumbs slid down to press against my spine, stirring the ashes of aftermath, causing them to glow warmer. A honey-sweet languor filled me, spreading slowly, building.

He was leaning over me now, his lips brushing my earlobe, his knuckles running up and down my spine.

"Stop, Cam. Please stop...."

ONCE MORE, MIRANDA

JENNIFER WILDE

BALLANTINE BOOKS • NEW YORK

Copyright © 1983 by Tom Huff

All rights reserved under International and Pan-American Copyright Conventions. Published in the United States by Ballantine Books, a division of Random House, Inc., New York, and simultaneously in Canada by Random House of Canada Limited, Toronto.

Library of Congress Catalog Card Number: 82-90914

ISBN 0-345-38661-5

Manufactured in the United States of America

First Edition: May 1983
Fifth Printing: September 1989
First Trade Edition: July 1993

10 9 8 7 6 5 4 3 2 1

With much love to
Shirlee and Howard Busbee,
who brighten my days

BOOK ONE

Honora

1727–1737

1

THERE IS SO MUCH TO SAY AND SO LITTLE TIME. THERE is so much Miranda must know, so much she must understand, and one day she will, I trust. One day she will be old enough to understand and to forgive. I'd like to take her into my arms right now and explain it all to her in my own voice and let her see my eyes and what is in my heart, but I dare not. I know I would break down and the tears would flow, and that would upset her. At any rate, I doubt she would comprehend it all. She is wise beyond her years, true, far too wise, but there are certain things a girl of nine can't possibly grasp.

No, this way is better. I'll write it all down for her to read when she's a few years older. Perhaps by that time she will have experienced some of the same emotions. Only the good ones, I pray. I pray she knows the burst of happiness that floods the soul with bliss like sunlight, and I pray she never knows the desolation when the sunlight is taken away and darkness pervades those regions once shimmering with brightness. May she never know the grief and the pain and the loss of hope.

I will write it all down and send the papers to the Reverend Mr. Williams. He will, I know, come to my aid. He'll come to London before it's too late and fetch my child and take her back to Cornwall and see that she has the proper upbringing, and, when he feels the time is right, he'll give her these papars so that she might understand. He'll use his influence and see that she receives that which is rightfully hers. You'll do that, won't you, Reverend? I'm writing this for you, too, as well as for Miranda.

She's out now, playing with those wretched children, learning all of their tricks, becoming as sly, as devious as they. I wish there were some way I could prevent it, but there isn't. I haven't the strength. I'm confined to this terrible, squalid room with its brown walls and soiled rug and sour smell, so weak I can barely scribble these words. She has no idea how ill I am. When I realized how bad it was, I resolved to be bright, to be merry, to keep it from her as long as possible. She thinks I'm getting better, and, indeed, when I see myself in the mirror, I do look better. The pallor is gone. My cheeks are a vivid pink, my eyes full of sparkle. I laugh at her prattle. I smile. I'm very vivacious, and when I cough I always use my handkerchief and she never sees the blood.

There has been so much blood. . . .

I shan't go on about my illness. It is God's will, and I have made my peace with him. I'm not sad. I refuse to be sad. Last night I dreamed of Jeffrey. He was standing there on the hillside near the old Roman ruins, and he was smiling. His blue eyes were filled with happiness. His thick golden-blond hair was tumbling in the breeze, and as I climbed the hill toward him he extended his hand to me, and as I took it I could almost feel those strong fingers grasping mine and drawing me to him. I know that I shall soon be with him.

My only concern is Miranda. That horrible Humphreys woman who lives across the hall has already been after me to send the child to the parish workhouse. "You ain't able to take care-a 'er," she claims. "They'll see she 'as food an' a roof over 'er 'ead. They got 'undreds-a kiddies at th' work'ouse."

I know about the workhouses, hellholes of horror for any child unfortunate enough to be sent to one. They sleep twelve to a bed, are beaten, half-starved, shipped off to be treated even worse by the monsters to whom they are apprenticed. A boy of four will be apprenticed to a chimney sweep and forced to perform the most hideous and dangerous tasks. A girl will be sent to one of the factories to work fifteen hours a day at a spindle in a crowded, unventilated room with barely enough light to see by, given barely enough food to sustain her frail body.

The mortality rate of those children confined to the work-houses is shocking, shocking, and no one seems to be concerned about it. Those poor mites deemed unfit for apprenticeship are sent out onto the streets to beg, their poor limbs horribly twisted and mutilated in order to make them even more pathetic. No, no, Miranda will never go to a workhouse, particularly the one here in St. Giles, the worst in all London I hear. You'll see to that, Reverend Williams, won't you? When you read these pages, hear my plea. Please come. Please save my little girl from that fate.

She has changed so much since we were forced to give up the room in Battersea and move here to St. Giles. The merry, mischievous, enchanting child who used to skip down the streets of Lichfield and toss crumbs to the ducks in the pond has grown wily, crafty, sly. Her face is always smudged with dirt. Her dress is always soiled. She's begun to use the most shocking expressions, and of late she's begun to drop her "h's" as well, speaking exactly like those urchins she roams the street with. She never tells me where she goes, what she's been doing. No matter how I question her, she always manages to avoid answering, nimbly changing the subject, refusing to be pinned down.

She's much too clever, much too feisty, far too independent for a child her age. That worries me dreadfully, but I suppose, under the circumstances, it might almost be called a blessing.

Several months ago the money ran out completely, and I feared we would be evicted from even this wretched hovel, feared we would starve, and that was when Miranda began to bring coins home, only a few each day, but enough to keep us in this room, keep us from starving. She claimed that she "ran errands" for people, but when I asked her what kind of errands she ran, she grew extremely evasive.

"Don't you worry none, Mum," she said brightly. "You're gonna get well soon and then you can take in sewin' again and we'll be able to move to a better place. Till then, I'll take care-a us."

"Miranda—"

"I saw the cutest puppy in the street today, Mum. He was all wiggly and frisky, just adorable! When we 'ave a place of our own again, could I 'ave a puppy of my own?"

Too weak to protest further, I began to cough wretchedly, seizing my handkerchief, terribly afraid she would see the specks of blood. Miranda hastily fetched my medicine and gave me a spoonful and then helped me into bed. She held my hand, stroking it tenderly, and later on, when the medicine began to take effect, she read to me from our beloved Shakespeare, reading the sonorous phrases with wonderful ease, pronouncing the most difficult words without making a single error. I drifted off to sleep to the sound of that sweet voice, to the sound of those beautiful phrases.

Ever since that day, Miranda has continued to bring in coins, and now that I am no longer strong enough to go out, she pays the rent and buys all our food and runs to the pharmacist for the ever-more-frequent bottles of medicine. It is as though our positions have been reversed, I the child now, Miranda the devoted parent. She takes care of me, chattering vivaciously, doing her best to make me smile with her amusing, imaginative tales, and I pretend to be stronger than I am, assuring her that I will soon be well.

A week ago the most outlandish creature came to visit me, a woman who called herself Moll. Extremely rotund, she was wearing a shockingly low-cut purple gown trimmed with tattered black lace, and her hair was an absurd shade of orange with jaunty ringlets bouncing on either side of her face. Her plump cheeks were heavily rouged, her mouth a bright scarlet, and her perfume was so overwhelming I longed to throw open the window. Her voice was coarse, husky with gin, but she was wonderfully kind nevertheless. She told me that "Little Randy" had done her "a small service" and she wanted to thank me in person. Before I could protest she thrust some money into my hand and bustled out of the room, her high heels clattering noisily down the stairs.

Miranda grew very cagey when I asked her about the woman. She claimed that the creature had lost her purse and that she, Miranda, had found it and returned it to her. When I asked where the woman lived, Miranda hesitated before answering, finally telling me that Moll lived in a lodging house. I fear it's another sort of house altogether, and I forbade Miranda to see the woman again, however kind she might be. Mrs. Humphreys is a notorious busybody and prides herself in knowing everything that goes on in the neighborhood. She informed me with malicious glee that my visitor is known as Big Moll and that her house is indeed a brothel, one of a string of such establishments owned by someone named Black Jack Stewart.

"That brat-a yours ain't gonna come to no good," she predicted, "runnin' th' streets with that pack-a little 'ooligans, associatin' with a creature like Big Moll. You gotta send 'er to th' work'ouse. Let me arrange it, luv. I know one uv th' nurses 'oo 'elps run it."

"I—I can't send her there, Mrs. Humphreys. Miranda—Miranda is a good child. She wouldn't do anything—"

"Saucy minx, if-ya ask me. Sassin' me every time she gets th' chance, refusin' to answer my questions. Stuck 'er tongue out at me just this mornin' as I wuz passin' 'er on th' stairs."

"She's a spirited child. She didn't mean any harm. She—"

"She ain't gonna come to no good, I tell-ya. If she ain't

caught pickin' pockets she'll end up workin' in that creature's 'ouse, mark my words,"

"I—I appreciate your concern, Mrs. Humphreys, but—I'm not feeling very well just now. I—I think I'd like to take a nap."

"Guess I know when I'm not wanted!" the woman snorted.

She flounced out of the room, slamming the door lustily behind her, but I didn't go to sleep. I was much too worried. I thought about what she had said and realized there was a certain amount of truth in it. What chance did a child like Miranda have in a place like St. Giles? If she didn't end up in the workhouse, she might well end up in even worse circumstances. If only there were some way of saving her. If only I had money. If only there were someone to turn to. Writing to Lord Robert would be futile. I knew, even if my pride allowed me to contemplate such a course. If only . . . it was then that I thought of you, Reverend Williams.

With the money Big Moll gave me I had Miranda purchase this ink, this paper, this quill. I decided to write to you and tell you everything, to ask for your help, to write to Miranda at the same time. . . . You will show her these pages when the time is right, and she'll understand. She'll know who she is. She'll understand at last how we came to be in this squalid slum, with no money and no prospects. By the time she reads this she will, I pray, through your help, have attained her rightful position in the world.

I had a very bad turn this afternoon while she was out. I couldn't seem to stop coughing. The blood. . . . Will I have the strength to finish these pages? Will there be time to complete the job and bundle the pages together and send them off? I must go on. I must find the strength somehow. I can only write a few pages each day, and there is so much to say. . . . Miranda returned with a wedge of cheese, a loaf of bread, a pail of milk. She smiled that beautiful, radiant smile and began to chatter merrily as she sliced the bread and cheese and poured milk into our solitary mug. I wanted to burst into tears. Instead, I laughed and hugged her to me and said we'd pretend the bread was cake and have a party, just the two of us.

I could eat only a few bites. I could hardly swallow the milk. Miranda sat down on the stool and watched me, her lovely blue eyes full of concern, her rich auburn hair spilling over her cheeks in tangled curls, her dress filthy and patched. She hasn't a pair of shoes. My darling is barefoot and wearing rags when she should be wearing velvet. She is roaming wild in the streets when she should be living in a fine mansion with her own governess, her own pony, a private park to ride in. One day, God willing, she will have those things which should be hers, but now . . . now I must write it all down so that she will understand.

When she was smaller she used to crawl into my lap and beg me to tell her a story, and I used to make up fanciful tales to amuse her. Miranda, my darling, I am going to tell you another story. There is a fairy maiden and a handsome hero, a wicked villain as well. There is a little lost princess, too, but this story isn't made up. Every word of it is true.

2

I WAS TWENTY YEARS OLD WHEN I FIRST SAW MOWREY House, and as the carriage moved up the drive I couldn't help but be impressed. It had its own bleak splendor—a great, sprawling place with leaded windows, the pale gray stone bleached almost white by the elements. Cornwall seemed a wild, rugged place after the restrained elegance of Bath, and this aged mansion seemed to blend in perfectly with the wind-swept moors, the crumbling boulders and treacherous cliffs I had seen during the journey. The house was surrounded by wild gardens and great, twisted trees, and as I stepped out of the carriage I could hear the crash of waves in the distance.

A liveried servant showed me into the great hall. Another led me into a vast drawing room all done in faded white and yellow brocade. A man was standing at the fireplace, gazing sullenly into the flames, and though the servant had announced me, he didn't turn. He continued to gaze at the fire for a full two minutes.

I waited, trembling inside. He was extremely tall and so slender that he seemed even taller. His knee boots were of fine black leather, his breeches and jacket of dark charcoal broadcloth, and his jet black hair was streaked with gray, pulled back from his brow and fastened in a short tail in back. It was not powdered. He would disdain such foppery. The Reverend Mr. Williams had told me that Lord Robert Mowrey was a harsh, severe man, and I could sense that harshness already, even before I saw his face.

Another minute passed before he finally deigned to turn away from the fire and acknowledge my presence. I should have curtseyed. I was much too intimidated. His eyes were so dark a brown they seemed black, glowing like dark coals as they examined me. His thin face was pale, pitted, his nose long, his mouth a thin, severe line.

Lord Robert Mowrey. Robert the Devil, they called him in the village. I had heard all about him from one of the serving girls at the inn. The Mowrey pottery works was the mainstay of the village, providing work for the majority of its people, and Lord Robert was a stern employer who paid pitiful wages and couldn't care less about working conditions at the factory. Men were expected to work twelve hours a day in front of blistering open furnaces, with only a short break for lunch. Women and children toiled in stuffy, unventilated rooms that were cluttered and poorly lighted, rooms so hot you wanted to pass out, and there were no facilities, either. If you had to piss or do the other, you had to slip out to one of the stinking wooden sheds in back, and woe unto any employee who didn't do the required quota of work. Out on 'is ear, 'e was, an' no mercy given.

The pottery was pretty enough, the girl informed me, but if you knew what poor souls had to endure in order to produce it—she shook her head and said she'd rather wait on tables th' rest-a 'er days than work in that 'orrible factory. People were always gettin' sick, what could you expect, breathin' that air, them fumes, not a breath-a fresh air. People were gettin' 'urt, too, all them scorchin' furnaces, them clay pits with their flimsy wooden ramps shakin' every time a barrow was pushed over 'em. She'd done her stint when she was a mite, eight years old, packin' pottery in great 'eavy boxes, stuffin' 'em with sawdust. Accidentally tumped a box over one day, broke six plates, four cups and two of them fancy saucers. Thrown out immediately, she was, and no wages either, they went to replace the dishes. Eight years old, bawlin' 'er eyes out and scared Robert the Devil was goin' to 'ave 'er 'ide, but she was one of th' lucky ones—got a job sweepin' up at the inn, eventually started drawin' mugs of ale and 'andin' 'em to the customers. Others weren't so fortunate. . . . Most of the village would starve if it weren't for th' factory. Lord Robert 'ad 'em exactly where 'e wanted 'em, and no one dared complain. They just did their work, sufferin' in silence, makin' them fancy dishes for folks who didn't 'ave to worry where th' next meal was comin' from.

Master Jeffrey, now, 'e was different. Full-a shockin', revolutionary ideas, 'e was, wanted to pay folks more wages, wanted to improve working conditions, put in windows, put in facilities, make things safer, buy new furnaces, stronger ramps. Didn't want children workin' there, either. If you paid their parents enough, children wouldn't 'ave to slave alongside 'em. Robert the Devil wouldn't listen to none of it, called 'is younger brother a fool, a dreamer, so Master Jeff 'ad as little as possible to do with th' factory, wanted to get away from th' place, away from Cornwall, too, for that matter. 'Ad a 'eart, 'e did, 'ad compassion, and there wudn't no place for such lot in a pottery factory, she could assure me, not if you were only interested in makin' more an' more money like Lord 'Igh an' Mighty Mowrey, th' sod.

Gave 'er th' willies, 'e did, she didn't envy me a bit, workin' up at th' big 'ouse. An' another thing, Mollie added, she didn't trust a man who didn't 'ave an eye for th' lasses, and Lord Robert 'adn't the least bit-a interest in the fairer sex. Sure, 'e was married once a long time ago, but his poor wife died not more'n two years after th' weddin', an' 'e hadn't looked at a woman since. All th' daughters of th' local gentry had vied for his attention, for 'e was quite a catch, 'im 'avin' a title an' all, all that money comin' from th' factory, but 'e treated 'em one an' all with utter disdain, not even botherin' to be civil. Lord Robert didn't care for no one on earth but his younger brother. Master Jeffrey . . . oh, a dream, 'e was, kindest man you'd ever 'ope to meet. 'E was a widower, too, poor thing.

I already knew that, for I had come to Cornwall to serve as governess to his four-year-old son.

I thought of all Mollie had said as Lord Robert stared at me with those dark, glowing eyes taking in every detail of my person. His mouth curled at one corner. I grew more and more uncomfortable. He disapproved of me. I could see that. I swallowed, trying to find the courage to speak.

"So you're Miss Honora James," he said.

I nodded, a faint blush tinting my cheeks.

"The curate assured me he knew a suitable woman for the post," he observed in a dry, emotionless voice. "I took him at his word. He sends me a blushing maiden. How old are you?"

"I—I'm twenty."

"You don't look it. You look much younger."

"I assure you, sir, I—"

"You're much too pretty," he said, interrupting me. "I should have gone to London and hired someone myself. I understand the Reverend Mr. Williams is a friend of yours."

"He—he knew my—my parents when he was in Bath. When they died he was very kind. He helped me get into the school. I was twelve years old. He left for Cornwall soon after, but we've kept in touch through letters."

"So you're a poor orphan?"

A sardonic smile flickered on his thin lips. My cheeks flamed.

"Yes," I said, "I'm an orphan, but that has nothing to do with it. Reverend Williams suggested me for this post because he knew I would be suitable. I speak French. I know Latin. I taught geography and spelling to the younger girls, and I intended to become a full mistress at the school. Reverend Williams felt a post like this one would be much nicer for me."

"I see. You've a taste for finer things."

"I'd rather live here than in an attic room in Bath, yes. I assume I would have my own apartment. Reverend Williams said—"

Lord Robert waved my words aside, an irritable expression on his lean, pitted face. I felt a sinking sensation in the pit of my stomach. I would have to go back to Bath, back to that bleak attic room, to those chattering, frivolous girls far more interested in hair ribbons than in spelling, to the condescending smiles of the school authorities who, though always kind, had never let me forget that I was a charity case.

"I expected an older, more experienced person, Miss James. You can understand my position."

"Of course," I retorted. "If you find me unsuitable, I'll return to the inn. Reverend Williams will give me the fare back to Bath."

He frowned, examining me once more with those critical eyes. He seemed to be debating whether to allow me to stay, and I waited for his decision with a cool composure that belied my inner turmoil.

"My young nephew is a willful lad," he said, "full of mischief and bad habits. I'm afraid his father has spoiled him deplorably. The boy's father has been traveling for some time now, and Douglas has become even more unmanageable. Time is of the essence in this case, I fear. He needs stern supervision, and he needs it now."

I maintained my silence, my frosty composure. Lord Robert hesitated before continuing, the frown still digging a furrow between his brows, and then he moved over to one of the windows to pull a bell cord.

"I am summoning Mrs. Rawson, the housekeeper. She will show you up to your rooms and explain your duties. I shall epxect you to teach my nephew some manners, Miss James. I shall expect a decided improvement within a month. Consider yourself on trial."

The door opened. A plump, jovial woman bustled in with much rustling of taffeta. It was garnet colored, extremely plush, and her apron was white organdy. Though her hair was gray, it spilled over her head in outrageous ringlets, a girlish garnet ribbon perched atop in lieu of a cap. Her brown eyes sparkled merrily. Her mouth was small, a bright, unnatural cherry red. She greeted me effusively while her employer stood by with a stony expression. The housekeeper wasn't the least bit intimidated, I observed. Her manner was quite familiar.

"Don't you worry a bit, Lord Bobbie. I'll take care of everything. Come along now, child, I have your rooms all ready. You're quite *young*! I think it's splendid. Dougie is expecting a dragon, he told me so. When he sees how pretty you are he'll take to you right away."

I managed a quick curtsey to Lord Robert before the woman dragged me out of the room, chattering nonstop as she led me up the grand staircase. There was a servants' staircase, she informed me, but *she* certainly didn't use it, nor should I. It was for the maids and the footmen, riffraff like that. She'd been here at Mowrey House ever since she was an infant, long before Lord Bobbie was born. She'd been scullery maid and parlor maid and then ladies' maid to the boys' mother, bless her soul, dear Lady Mowrey, and then she'd become housekeeper, oh, *ages* ago, and "that man" didn't scare her none, far from it. She'd whacked his bottom when he was a baby and wiped pudding from his face when he was a wee lad and he didn't give her no guff, no indeed.

"I keep this house sparklin', that's why. He knows he'd never be able to replace me. He can intimidate the footmen and terrify the maids with his cold, chillin' stare, but me, I pay him no mind. Oh, while I'm at it I'd better tell you about Beresford. He's the butler, luv, stiff as a poker and very taken with hisself, know what I mean? Snooty as all get out. Me, I do my job and do it dandy and he gets uppity with me I give him the finger."

"The finger?"

"La, we've an innocent on our hands. You wouldn't know what I mean, luv. Let's just say I put him in his place. Here's your rooms. Dandy, ain't they? Nice sky blue wallpaper, rose and gray carpet, white furniture. I picked out the furniture myself, took three of the footmen up to the attic and had 'em haul it down and polish it up. That lilac satin counterpane and them matchin' curtains? I made 'em myself, luv, altered 'em from the draperies that used to hang in Lady Mowrey's bedroom. They took quite a bit of airin', I don't mind tellin' you."

"It—it's charming," I said.

"You ain't used to much, I know. I know all about-ja. The curate is a friend-a mine. I ain't religious, mind you, but I occasionally nip over and have a chat with him. I carry him a bottle of port now and then, too. He told me you were little better than a servant yourself at that musty school, said he wanted to get you out of there."

"They were very kind to me," I protested.

"Kind, my ass. Had you doin' chores when you were barely fourteen, had you washin' dishes and scrubbin' floors, that ain't my idea of kindness. Sure, they let you teach some of the younger ones later on, but that's because you're smart as a whip and they was savin' the wages they'd of had to pay another mistress. I know all about it, luv. You'll get better treatment here."

"Lord—Lord Robert seems—rather stern," I said hesitantly.

"I won't deny that. There's lots-a things about the man I don't admire, can't pretend I do, but he ain't so bad if you keep outta his way. He spends most of his time at the factory, overseein' the work, else he's shut up in his office, goin' over accounts with his secretary. He don't get underfoot much, thank the Lord. He's a peculiar one, I readily admit it."

I remembered all the things Mollie had told me at the inn last night, and I saw that the amiable, gossipy housekeeper was more than willing to talk about her employer.

"Peculiar?" I said.

"Almost unnatural, I'd say, though a-course it ain't my

place. Always was a cold, secretive one, even when he was a tot, keepin' to hisself, brooding all the time. Married when he was twenty three—poor woman, she didn't last long. The fever took her away two years after they was married, and I had the impression Lord Bobbie wudn't all that grieved. He ain't worn nothin' but black ever since her death, but theirs wudn't no love match I can assure you. Lord Bobbie never loved anyone but his brother."

I smoothed down the satin counterpane, not wishing to seem too inquisitive, but Mrs. Rawson needed no encouragement to continue.

"The boys' parents died when Lord Bobbie was twenty. Master Jeffrey was a mere tot at the time, barely five. Lord Bobbie devoted himself to that child, raisin' him like he was his own. I always said the only reason he married Lady Betty was because he wanted the boy to have a new mother. Lady B. wudn't interested in takin' on a ready-made son, though. She was interested in parties and frocks and fripperies, couldn't care less about the child. She and Lord Bobbie had some terrific rows about it. He seemed almost relieved when the fever carried her away. It left him more time for the boy."

Mrs. Rawson paused, shaking her head, and then she bustled over to the dressing table to rearrange the crystal bottles and the silver comb and brush set. I assumed she had finished her gossip, but I was wrong. After a moment she sighed and looked at me with bemused brown eyes.

"Ordinarily folks'd say it was admirable for a man to take so much interest in his poor orphaned brother, ordinarily it is, but in Lord Bobbie's case there was somethin' twisted about it. He was jealous, possessive, smotherin' the boy with his love. No mother hen ever watched over her chick like he watched over Master Jeffrey. He didn't want the boy to have any friends, didn't want him to see anyone else, go anywhere without him. Unhealthy. Unnatural. He refused to send the boy to school, hired tutors to come here instead, and Master Jeffrey finally rebelled when he was eighteen, passed all his examinations and went off to Oxford. *Escaped* to Oxford, I always said."

Mrs. Rawson patted her girlish steel-gray ringlets, and a tender look suffused her eyes. "Master Jeffrey, now he ain't nothin' like his brother. He's fifteen years younger for one thing, just turned twenty-five last month, and a finer youth ain't ever walked this earth. He's sensitive, soft-spoken, kind, everything his brother ain't. Always readin' books, he is, always takin' up for the factory workers and beggin' his brother to improve their lot. Handsome, too, like one of them poets, painted in soft strokes, if you get my meanin'."

I didn't, but I was far too intrigued to interrupt her flow of talk.

"He met Lady Agatha in Oxford. An angel, she was, blonde and delicate and eyes as blue as cornflowers. Lord Bobbie liked to had a fit when Master Jeffrey wrote to him and told him he was goin' to get married. Raced off to Oxford, he did, did everything he could to change the boy's mind, said he was too young to get married, said it would be an awful mistake, but Master Jeffrey was twenty years old then, he'd been at Oxford for two years, and he wouldn't listen. Lord Bobbie finally gave his consent on condition they come to Mowrey House to live. They had the weddin' here, and it was somethin' to behold, everybody smilin' and celebratin' and her in miles of white tulle with orange blossoms in that silvery blonde hair. I ain't never seen Master Jeffrey lookin' better. Made my old heart melt, it did, just to see him lookin' so handsome and proud."

She paused, remembering, a tender smile on that plump red mouth, and then the smile faded and her eyes grew sad.

"He got her with child the first rattle outta the box. Master Jeffrey may be sensitive and all, but he's a virile one. I always knew that. He never did chase the girls, but he knew what to do with one and did it good 'n proper, too. Her belly started swellin', and they was both pleased as punch and started makin' plans. She had the nursery redecorated and they was always discussin' names and it was the baby this and the baby that and when the baby comes we'll do such and such and then her time came. It was a breech birth, and Lady Agatha had these real thin hips, she wudn't meant to have children—"

The housekeeper shook her head again and seemed to stare into the past.

"He almost died from grief hisself, the lamb. He didn't want to live after she was gone. Mourned around for months and months—he's still mournin' her and that's a shame. He needs another wife, young Dougie needs a mother. He needs a father, too, for that matter. Master Jeffrey hadn't paid enough attention to the lad, been too busy mournin' and travelin' to ease his grief. He's travelin' now, somewhere in Europe—Italy, I think. Should be back in a few weeks."

"I'm eager to meet the child," I said.

"He knows you're here. Bendin' over the banister peekin'

at you when you arrived. He was in here lookin' at your things when the maid was unpackin' 'em and puttin' 'em away. He'll probably pop in to say hello after a while. You look all tuckered out, luv, and here I've been rattlin' on when you probably want to get some rest. Tell you what, I'll have Cook send some lunch up on a tray. Will that be all right?"

"That will be fine."

"You'll eat in our dining hall. Me and Beresford and Parks, Lord Robert's secretary—we have our own dining hall. The rest of 'em eat belowstairs, as is only fittin'. I'll scurry out now. You want anything, you just let me know. We're goin' to be great friends, luv. The rest of 'em ain't *smart* enough to enjoy a good chat."

Mrs. Rawson smiled her merry smile and left, garnet taffeta skirts crackling, and I sighed, exhausted and still uneasy in my new surroundings. The room was pleasant indeed, luxurious compared to what I was accustomed to, and I had a friend already in the gossipy, exuberant housekeeper, yet my uneasiness remained. I kept thinking of the tall, too slender man with the pale, pockmarked face who had so reluctantly allowed me to remain at Mowrey House "on trial." Harsh, severe, every bit as sinister as the serving girl at the inn had claimed he was, Lord Robert had taken an immediate dislike to me. It was . . . it was almost as though I presented some kind of threat, I thought. How could I possibly present a threat to him? What could he possibly have to fear?

I was to have the answers to those questions all too soon.

It was very late now. I sat at the dressing table brushing my hair, drawing the brush through the long, coppery brown waves. I studied the reflection in the mirror with my customary disapproval. My hair was too red and much too thick. My cheekbones were too high, my mouth too wide, and there was a scattering of pale golden-brown freckles across my cheeks. The girls at school had made fun of me because I was too tall, my bosom was too full, my lips so pink. They had teased me mercilessly, claimed I wore pink lip rouge, said my hair was the color of new pennies and my eyes as gray as the sea.

For years I had longed to be blonde and petite and pink and white, and I was cursed with this bizarre coloring, this tall frame with its embarrassing curves. Yet Lord Robert had said I was much too pretty to be a governess. How peculiar. Did the gentry have a different standard of beauty? I didn't know, but I was certain he hadn't meant the words as a compliment. It was impossible to imagine Lord Robert Mowrey paying anyone a compliment, much less a penniless young woman who had come to seek employ in his household.

I had spent a leisurely day. After lunching in my room, I had explored the nursery and browsed around in the vast, extremely well stocked library downstairs, examining the musty leather-bound volumes with great interest. Later on I had written a short note to the curate, explaining my "temporary" status and adding that I looked foward to lunching with him on Sunday. He had extended the invitation last evening when he met me at the posting station and escorted me to the inn. He had intended to bring me to Mowrey House this morning, but unfortunately there had been a death in his congregation and he had to conduct a funeral, which was why I had had to face Lord Robert alone, with no support.

Putting the brush down, I sighed and stood up, cool in my thin white cotton nightdress. I stepped over to the window and looked out at the night. A mellow silver moon glowed dimly in a pewter gray sky filled with gently moving clouds. The gardens and the woods beyond were etched in black ink, only a few pale rays of moonlight washing the lawns. To my right I could see the great cliffs, half a mile away, beyond the woods, and I could hear the waves crashing against the rocks. The huge old house was silent, the silence merely amplified by the occasional creaks and groans natural to a house this age.

I heard a faint scratching noise behind the wall. Mice? I moved over to the bed and picked up the volume of Shakespeare I had set out earlier. I would read for a while and perhaps sleep would eventually come.

The scratching noise increased as I folded back the bedcovers. I paused, frowning. The noise was coming from behind one of the lilac satin curtains, and as I watched the curtain moved, fluttering visibly. The scratching stopped. I shook my head and started to climb into bed, and then there was a bloodcurdling shriek and the curtain belled out and a figure all in white rushed toward me with the speed of lightning.

"WOOOO! WOOOO! YEEOWWWWWW!"

I stood my ground and calmly plucked the pillowcase off the tiny little boy. He looked up at me with total dismay.

"You ain't scared?" he asked.

"Aren't," I corrected. "Not a bit."

"Hell! It always works on the maids."

"Did you say 'hell'?"

"I sure as hell did."

"I thought so. I shouldn't say it again if I were you."

"Why not?"

"Because if you do, I'll slap you silly."

"You wouldn't dare!"

"Oh, I would," I said firmly. "I wouldn't *like* it, but I'd do it without a moment's hesitation."

"You talk funny."

"I speak correctly, like a lady."

"La de da, you ain't no lady."

"Aren't," I said. "If you say 'ain't' again, you'll get a slap, too."

"You're not so tough!" he blustered.

"I'm very tough," I assured him. "I'm very *nice*, actually, but I can be very tough if I have to be. You and I can be friends and have a grand time together, or we can fight. If we fight, I'll win. Every time."

He grinned. I could tell that he didn't *want* to grin, but he couldn't help himself. He had thick blond hair badly in need of cutting, and his eyes were a lovely slate gray. His cheekbones were broad, his nose already distinctly Roman, and his mouth was a saucy pink. He was very small, stocky and pugnacious and utterly ridiculous in his blue and white striped nightshirt. I wanted to pick him up and hug him, but that would have been a grave tactical error.

"I sneaked in while you were brushin' your hair," he confessed. "You was studyin' your face and didn't see me. I crawled. I should-a waited till you put out the candles to jump out. *Then* you'd-a been scared."

"I doubt it, Douglas."

"I'm Dougie. All the servants call me Dougie. Master Dougie."

"I believe your name is Douglas. I'm not a servant, incidentally. I'm your governess."

"What the he—uh—what the heck is a governess?"

"A governess is a very good friend who tells stories and teaches you all sorts of clever things and slaps you if you're sassy. She teaches you to speak like a little gentleman instead of a young hooligan."

He peered up at me with his head cocked to one side, trying to decide if I was to be taken seriously. After a moment he frowned, shrugged his shoulders and sighed.

"I guess you'll do," he said. "I was expectin' someone *really* mean."

"I'll do very nicely," I replied. "Little gentlemen do not drop their final 'g's,' by the way. They say expec*ting*, not expec*tin'*. I want to hear that final 'g' from now on."

"What's a hooligan?"

"A hooligan is someone who goes around beating people up and stealing their money and getting into all sorts of trouble."

"That sounds like fun."

"It isn't, I assure you. Hooligans invariably end up in Newgate. The constables and watchmen chase them and catch them and lock them up. Newgate is a prison in London, a huge, horrible place where bad people are kept. Some of them have chains on their arms and legs."

"Really?" He was enthralled.

"Yes, indeed. You wouldn't want to end up there, I'm sure."

"I'd bust out," he said. "Who are them constables and watchmen you mentioned?"

"They're—well, they're not much better than hooligans themselves, but they have the authority to catch bad people and lock them up."

"You ever met one of 'em?"

"One of *them*. No, I've never been in London, but I've read all about them. The headmistress at the school in Bath got all the London newspapers. She let me read them after she was finished."

"You're pretty smart," he observed.

"I am indeed. I know lots of fascinating things. I'll tell you more in the morning. Now I suggest you go to your room and go to bed."

"I got an idea," he said. "Why don't I just crawl in bed with you? I get kinda lonely, you see, and sometimes I even get scared when I wake up at night and everything's dark. I wouldn't be any *trouble*," he continued. "I'd be real still and I promise not to kick or hog the covers."

His manner was extremely offhand, his voice quite casual, but I detected the longing nevertheless. The child was starved for attention and affection, that was plain to me. I vowed to give him both, but I had no intention of setting a precedent this first night.

"I'm afraid that wouldn't work," I informed him. "You see,

I *do* kick. I also snore, quite loudly. Your room is right next door to my sitting room, isn't it? I believe there's a connecting door. Why don't we leave that door open and I'll leave *my* bedroom-sitting room door open, and if you wake up in the night you can listen to me snore."

He wasn't overjoyed about it, but he didn't argue. I took him by the hand and led him through the sitting room and on into his own bedroom. He swaggered along beside me, disappointed but stoic. A candle was burning on the night table, the flame casting flickering shadows over the walls. I heaved him up into my arms and swung him onto the bed and tucked him in. He looked up at me with serious gray eyes.

"Are we really gonna have fun?" he asked.

"Loads," I promised.

"I like you, Miss James."

"I like you, too."

I leaned down and gently rubbed my cheek against his, and then I blew out the candle and left the room, leaving the door wide open. Back in my bedroom I sighed and climbed between the crisp linen sheets that smelled faintly of verbena. I might have apprehensions about Lord Robert Mowrey, but I had none whatsoever about his nephew. The engaging young scamp had already stolen my heart.

3

I WAS GIVEN A FREE HAND WITH DOUGLAS FROM THE start, and the two of us got along beautifully. I was nursemaid-companion-teacher-friend, and I found that my experience teaching the younger students in Bath stood me in very good stead. I had learned how to inspire interest and stimulate curiosity and, most importantly, had learned to discipline with a firm but light touch that prompted obedience but never caused resentment. Doug's conduct began to improve almost immediately, and within the week I had weeded from his speech most of the vulgarities and contractions that, while charming, were most unsuitable for a budding young aristocrat. Every time he said "ain't" or "wudn't" or "'em" or such, I refused to speak to him again until he corrected himself, and that was the worst punishment of all for the child who dearly loved conversation.

The nursery was across the hall from our bedrooms—a long, sparsely furnished room flooded with sunlight from the tall windows that looked out over the woods, the sea a misty blue-gray haze visible beyond the treetops. In the cupboard I found paper and colors and scissors, and in the bookshelves there were dozens of books that had been used by generations of Mowreys. Doug and I spent hours at the worktable drawing figures and coloring them, he chatting all the while. We made a tiny theater out of cardboard and colored settings and recreated some of the more suitable plays of Shakespeare, moving the miniature figures we had made across the stage while I told the story of Oberon and Titania and the mischievous Puck. Doug was thoroughly enchanted and insisted we do the part with the donkey's head over and over again.

He was remarkably intelligent for a child his age. I saw no reason why I shouldn't teach him his alphabet. Within days he was reeling off his ABC's with jaunty aplomb, and before the first month had passed he could spell *cat*, *dog*, *Douglas, Honora, Mowrey* and *tree*, adding new words to his repertoire each day. He wasn't nearly so adept with numbers. He could count to twenty without faltering and dimly understood that two plus two was four, but numbers bored him and he obstinately refused to give his attention to them. He much preferred to have me read to him or whirl the great globe of the world around and point out Holland and tell him about windmills and wooden shoes and tulips or show him the vast expanse of America and relate the tale of brave Captain John Smith and the Indian princess who had saved his life.

We didn't spend all our time in the nursery, however. The weather was frequently inclement, the wind roaring, rain lashing the windowpanes, but on fine days we would take long walks after we had finished our studies. Sometimes Cook would prepare a basket lunch for us, and Doug and I would lunch on the edge of the moors, the sky a great airy expanse above, gulls circling against the pale blue like scraps of paper tossed by the wind. The moors lay to the west, rugged and forbidding, covered with grayish brown grass and patches of treacherous black bog. They rose slowly to the hills where Roman legions once had their camps. The village was to the north, the clay pits and the squat, ugly factory with its roaring furnaces beyond, black plumes of smoke spiraling against the sky.

I rarely saw Lord Robert Mowrey. He left early for the factory and spent most of the day there, driving his employees to produce even more pottery, at a faster pace. Once, as I was coming down the stairs to get a book from the library, I heard him reprimanding a footman in a dry, emotionless voice that was far more chilling than noisy anger would have been. On another occasion I heard a parlor maid crying her heart out in a broom closet because she had accidentally broken a vase and feared Lord Robert would dismiss her. He demanded total perfection from the servants, and all of them were terrified of him.

All except Mrs. Rawson, of course. She blithely ignored his stern looks and clipped, icy comments and went merrily on her way, doing her job superbly and defying anyone to say she wudn't a bloomin' treasure. There were plenty who'd love to have her workin' for 'em and u'd be happy to pay her more wages to boot. She couldn't stand Parks, Lord Robert's secretary, and she and Beresford had been feuding for over a decade, but Mrs. Rawson had taken a fancy to me and liked nothing so much as settling down for a nice long gossip when Doug had been put to bed and both of us were free and she could "give my achin' feet a rest and exercise my backside."

Much of her gossip was highly salacious, and I learned a great deal about the Mowreys.

Lord Bobbie never did care much for the women, she confided. He was cold and indifferent to 'em even when he was a buddin' youth. Most young gentlemen hereabouts, they topped a buxom wench or took a whore whenever the itch came upon 'em. Folks expected it, and there was scarcely a squire around who didn't have half a dozen-a his bastards tendin' the fields or pitchin' hay. Not Lord Bobbie. No indeed. No wonder poor Lady Betty'd been so miserable. Who could blame her for seekin' other men? Pretty, flighty young thing like her had to have attention from a man, and if she couldn't get it from her husband, she was bound to go lookin' elsewhere.

"Lord Bobbie never did pay her no mind, and she tried to please him in the beginnin', I'll have to give her credit for that.

She'd get herself all dressed up in a fancy new frock and have her hair all piled up in glossy waves and she'd laugh and chatter and try to amuse him and he'd give her that stern, disapproving look and then just ignore her. She felt she was an intruder, and in a sense she was. He didn't have time for no one but his brother."

"It must have been dreadful for her," I said.

"It was, luv. Lady B. was frivolous and empty-headed, true, but she wudn't bad. I knew she was runnin' out to meet that horny young buck who was stayin' with the Haddens at Hadden Court, sure I did, and I didn't blame her, not after the way Lord Bobbie'd been treatin' her. A woman has needs, too, luv. You'll find that out one day, mark my words. You may be prim and proper and innocent, but there's passion seethin' beneath the surface. It just ain't been tapped yet."

Mrs. Rawson patted her steel gray ringlets and took a sip of port.

"Lord Bobbie didn't shed a tear when the fever carried her off," she continued. "She'd been out to meet that buck—she'd sneak out of the house and meet him on the moors—and one night she got caught in a storm, got drenched to the skin, came in lookin' like a drowned cat. The fever came on almost immediately. The poor thing got worse and worse, coughin' and coughin', her skin on fire—"

The housekeeper shook her head, a pensive look in her eyes, and then she sighed heavily and finished her port.

"Lord Bobbie never visited the sick room, never once, and folks didn't blame him. Folks said she got exactly what she deserved—everyone knew she was carryin' on, you can't keep nothin' secret in these parts. What you sow you're gonna reap, they said, and they sympathized with Lord B. There ain't much compassion in this world-a ours, luv. Folks're eager to blame. Few of 'em ever try to understand."

Mrs. Rawson might not approve of Lord Robert, but she plainly worshiped his younger brother. Master Jeffrey wudn't at all like Lord B. They were as different as night and day. He'd always been quiet and gentle, and he grew even more gentle after Lady Agatha passed on. There was this air of sadness about him that women found irresistible, and there wudn't an unmarried girl-a his own class who hadn't set her cap for him after he was widowed. They all wanted to console him, and no wonder. With those sad blue eyes and those delicate features and that manly physique he was like a storybook prince. His soft voice and beautiful manners made him even more appealing.

"All the women fancy him, and I ain't sayin' he hadn't let one or two of 'em comfort him. A man has to have an occasional piece, they get edgy without it, but he don't tomcat around. There's lots-a lasses who wish he *would*. I was in The Red Lion one evenin' and someone mentioned Master Jeffrey and that brazen Maggie who works there said she'd pay *him* for a roll in the hay."

Mrs. Rawson spoke of such matters with bawdy relish. Three times married and three times widowed, she had had her share of menfolk in the hay and considered herself an authority. I might not think it, but there were some who *still* found her appetizin', that Jim Randall the blacksmith for one. He said she was old enough to know what it was all about and plump enough to make it comfortable, and he wudn't half bad himself, strong as an ox. She whipped up her skirt to show me the red silk petticoat he'd bought for her at the county fair, proudly displaying its gaudy splendor. That man was mad for her, couldn't get enough, and she didn't mind sayin' he was about the best she'd had.

"And believe me, luv, I've had more'n my share."

I couldn't help but smile. Her salty tongue and earthy delight in things of the flesh didn't shock me at all. I was reminded of Chaucer's Wife of Bath, a lady with whom she had much in common.

"Anyway," she continued, "gettin' back to Master Jeffrey, he should be home any day now, and high time, too. All this travelin' he's been doin', it ain't good for him, couldn't be."

"Doug misses his father dreadfully."

"Sure he does. We all do. It's time for him to settle down and put his grief behind him, time for him to start thinkin'-a his son, thinkin'-a the future."

"Do you think he'll marry again?" I asked.

Mrs. Rawson nodded. "Don't imagine he'll waste much time about it, either. Master Jeffrey has a deep need inside him. He'll marry all right, soon, too, and then he'll take his wife and young Dougie and start a new life somewhere else."

"I don't imagine his brother would be too happy about that," I observed.

"He wouldn't like it at all," Mrs. Rawson agreed, "but there ain't much he could do about it. Mowrey House ain't been a happy place for Master Jeffrey—that's one-a the reasons he's stayed away so much. He broke the tie to his brother a long time ago—only Lord Bobbie don't know it yet."

I thought about all these things as she continued to chatter, and Mowrey House suddenly seemed a dark, brooding place full of tragedy and secret passions. Lady Betty and her desperate adulteries. Lord Robert and his strange, unhealthy obsession with his brother. Jeffrey Mowrey and his terrible grief. Had anyone ever been happy here? It was as though the house itself cast some ominous spell over those who dwelled within these walls. Nonsense, I told myself. Nonsense. You're imagining things. Besides...even if it were so, I was merely a governess here, still on trial, and it couldn't possibly affect me one way or another.

I was quite wrong about that, as I was to discover all too soon.

Two days later Douglas and I were returning from a walk along the cliffs, and both of us were in a lighthearted, elated mood. We had tossed bread crumbs to the gulls and watched the waves crashing majestically against the jagged rocks far below, and we had seen a ship on the horizon, a tiny white and brown speck against the violet gray haze. We tramped noisily through the stretch of woods and began to race over the lawns toward the house. Hair flew about my head in a mass of auburn curls that caught the sunlight, and the skirt of my sprigged blue muslin billowed up over ruffled white petticoats. We had already passed the rickety trellises when I spotted Lord Robert standing beside the door to the back hall.

I stopped, clutching a hand to my heart. Douglas darted past me and ran all the faster, yelling like one of the red Indians I had told him about. He didn't see his uncle. He didn't slow down as he neared the house. He yelled lustily and looked over his shoulder to see if I was catching up and collided forcefully against his uncle's legs. Lord Robert caught him by the shoulders and said something with a grim expression on his face, but I was too far away to catch the words. I continued toward the house in a more demure manner, my heart pounding with every step.

"I beat-ja! I beat-ja!" Douglas taunted.

"Go up to the nursery, Douglas," Lord Robert ordered. "I want to speak with Miss James."

"Yes, sir!" the child exclaimed. "See you later, Honora!"

I approached slowly, trying hard to conceal the nervous apprehension welling up inside, trying hard to look cool and composed and unflurried. He was going to discharge me. He was going to tell me my work hadn't been satisfactory. A suitable governess wouldn't race across the lawns with skirts billowing, hair flying, nor would she encourage familiarity with her charge. She would be strict and severe and unsmiling. She would wear drab browns and grays and keep her hair in a tight bun and maintain a lemon-sour expression as she drummed dry knowledge into recalcitrant heads. I felt painfully young and extremely vulnerable as I stopped a few feet away from him, yet I managed to hold my chin high.

He didn't speak. He eyed me with open disapproval, and I was acutely aware of my dress. Although the thin muslin was one of my best, it was three years old and quite snug at the waist. The short, puffed sleeves dropped off the shoulder, and while the bodice had been modest enough when the dress was new, I had grown in the past three years and there was now a distinct cleavage. I could feel a blush tinting my cheeks as he continued to examine me, and I was sure they were as pink as the tiny flowers that sprigged the pale blue muslin.

"You wished to speak to me?" My voice was surprisingly level.

He nodded, still maintaining that icy silence. His brown black eyes were so dark they made his face seem even more pale. It was so harsh a face—nose sharp, cheeks lean and pitted, the mouth a thin slash. Although he had been out all day, his high black boots hadn't a speck of dust. The close-fitting black breeches and black coat accentuated his thin, bony frame and unusual height, bringing a beanpole to mind. Chilly, remote, superior—he seemed bloodless, and I couldn't imagine him smiling, couldn't imagine him feeling any of the warmer human emotions.

"Do you fear I'm going to admonish you?" he inquired dryly.

"I see no reason why you should."

"No?"

"None whatsoever. Children will run and yell, Lord Robert. It's their nature."

"You seem to encourage it."

"It does your nephew good to romp and be high spirited after he's been shut up in the nursery for hours on end."

"Does it indeed?"

"Indeed it does," I retorted.

"You seem to know a great deal about children, Miss James."

"Have you complaints, Lord Robert?"

It was better to brazen it out. It was better to get it over with at once. I wasn't going to let him toy with me. I refused to be intimidated. Lord Robert might dislike me, might disapprove of me, but he couldn't truthfully say I hadn't performed my duties more than adequately. I stood my ground, waiting for the ax to fall.

"I believed you were too young." His voice was flat, emotionless, and his eyes were as critical as ever. "Contrary to my expectations, you have done an excellent job with my nephew."

He paused, waiting for my reaction. I showed none.

"I talked with him at length yesterday when I came in from the factory. Not only has his speech improved one hundred percent, but his manners have as well. I questioned him quite thoroughly and found him to be well versed in a wide variety of subjects. He spent a full five minutes telling me all about Captain John Smith and Pocahontas."

"That's one of his favorites."

"He also told me the plot of *A Midsummer Night's Dream* and brayed noisily when he came to the part about Puck and the donkey's head. It seems he's getting an unusually diversified education."

His words were complimentary enough, but his eyes continued to stare at me as though I were some wretched creature beneath his notice. Perhaps he was merely being sarcastic.

"My brother will be returning to Mowrey House at the end of the week," he said. "I feel sure he'll be pleased with the improvements in his son. When he left, young Douglas was an unruly little savage."

"I look forward to meeting your brother."

"I'm afraid you shan't have that privilege, Miss James."

"Oh?" I didn't understand at first.

"I shall give you a very good letter of recommendation," he told me. "I shall also give you a full year's wages. I don't wish to be unfair."

I turned pale. The ground seemed to vanish beneath me, and it took me a moment to regain my composure. He watched me closely, noticing my reaction, and there was a glimmer of cruel satisfaction in his eyes.

"I'm to be dismissed, then?" I said. My voice seemed to come from a long way off. "May—may I ask why?"

"The results have been satisfactory enough, Miss James, but I find your methods a bit too unconventional. Douglas needs a much firmer hand. He needs a figure of authority."

I didn't reply. I couldn't. He wanted to get rid of me. Why? Why was I his enemy? What had I done to merit that harsh disapproval? Was it merely because I was young? No, no, there was more to it than that. Once again I felt I presented some kind of threat to him, and I couldn't comprehend it. He stared at me coldly, waiting for me to make some objection. I didn't intend to give him that satisfaction.

"I will have your money and a letter of recommendation ready first thing in the morning," he said after a moment.

"Very well," I replied.

"I have also taken the liberty of hiring a coach that will take you directly back to Bath. You'll travel at my expense. You won't have to use any portion of your wages."

"I'll start packing immediately."

Lord Robert stepped aside, and I passed into the dimly lighted back hall. It was very wide and ran all the way across the back of the house, the flagged stone floor covered with rush matting. There was no elegance here. The hall was purely functional, originally designed so that horses could be exercised inside during inclement weather, a feature not at all unusual in houses as old as this. I moved slowly toward the narrow back stairs and climbed them wearily, hardly aware of what I was doing.

Douglas was in the nursery, sitting at the worktable and eagerly studying the figures I had drawn for him that morning on stiff pieces of paper. I had been telling him the story of *The Tempest*, and he had insisted we make cutouts of all the characters and "do" the play in the tiny cardboard theater we had constructed. I had promised him we could color the figures and cut them out this afternoon. He looked up as I entered, his eyes merry with anticipation, a wide grin on his lips. Sunlight streamed in through the windows, burnishing his thick blond hair.

"Here you are!" he exclaimed. "I've been waiting."

"Douglas, there—there's something I must tell—"

I hesitated. How could I tell him? How could I bear to? He had come to depend on me, and he had grown very fond of me, almost as fond as I was of him. My departure was going to shatter him, and from his child's point of view it would be all my fault. I would be deserting him. I cast about for the right words, the right explanation.

"Let's color 'em, Honora!" he insisted, not noticing my mood. "We'll color 'em and cut 'em out this afternoon and tomorrow we'll do the story. I want-a be Calleyban."

"Cal-i-ban," I said. "Want to. *Them*, not *'em*. I've told you repeatedly to pronounce each word fully."

Doug gave an exasperated sigh, very put upon, and then he grinned again and reached for the colors. I sat down at the table, in a trance, it seemed, unable to focus. Later. I would tell him later. I couldn't face it now. I needed to think clearly. I needed time. I took the colors from him and began to color the figures, taking great care, desperately trying to concentrate, and Doug chattered all the while, telling me what color to use on Prospero's hose, informing me that Ariel's tunic should be pink, Caliban's skin green and brown and it might be nice to give him horns as well. When I had finished these, he handed me the drawing of Miranda.

"Her dress ought to be blue, like yours," he insisted, "and let's make her hair red brown. She's going to be beautiful, isn't she? She's going to be almost as beautiful as you are, Honora."

"Douglas—"

"Miranda's a pretty name, almost as pretty as Honora. Prettier, maybe. If I had a sister, I'd want her to be named Miranda. There. Now color her cheeks pink and make her eyes gray, like yours. Mine, too."

I finished coloring the figure. I took the scissors and cut it out, Doug watching with the tip of his tongue between his teeth, fearful lest I make some mistake and spoil what he clearly considered a masterpiece. When I was done, I handed the stiff paper doll to him, and he examined it with thoughtful eyes.

"She looks exactly like you," he said.

I stood up and brushed a heavy auburn wave from my temple, looking around at the spacious, sun-filled room where we had spent so many happy, productive hours. The walls were now adorned with scratchy, brightly colored pictures Doug had done these past weeks—a lopsided green tree, a horse that looked more like a buffalo, a gigantic red apple. I looked at the globe, the pile of picture books, the worktable littered with scraps of paper and colors and cutout figures. We had worked so lovingly on the tiny replica of the Globe Theater that stood amidst the litter. I had indeed been happy here, and for the first time in my life I had felt truly worthwhile as I worked with this child.

"She's my favorite of all," he told me, still examining the paper doll of Miranda. "Know what? I'm going to keep her always to remind me of you. I promise I will."

"It's almost time for your dinner," I said. "You'd better go wash up."

"And we'll do the play tomorrow? Remember, I get to be Calley—Caliban. I love you, Honora."

He hurled himself against me and flung his arms around my legs and hugged me so tightly, so abruptly that I almost lost my balance, and then he scrambled out of the room. A few minutes later I checked his face and hands to make sure they were clean, and when he had passed inspection I sent him downstairs to have his dinner, telling him I wasn't hungry tonight and wouldn't be joining him. The child was puzzled, but he didn't question me. I was grateful for that.

I returned to my own rooms. I would have to ask one of the footmen to bring my trunk down from the attic, but I could do that later. First I would take all my clothes out and put them on the bed. I didn't. Instead, I went into the sitting room and sat down and let the grief sweep over me. I heard a noise outside. It sounded like horse hooves pounding on the drive, but I was too anguished to pay it much mind. Time passed. The room was growing dark. I lighted a lamp, wondering why Doug hadn't come back upstairs. He should have finished his meal half an hour ago.

Perhaps he was with his uncle. Perhaps Lord Robert was sparing me the task of telling the child I was leaving. Would Doug come back upstairs distraught and teary-eyed? I longed to flee this very moment. I heard footsteps on the stairs. They weren't light and pattering. They were heavy, an adult's footsteps, moving down the hall now. One of the servants must be coming up with a message for me, I thought, and I turned to the door.

The most beautiful man I had ever seen stood in the doorway. Jeffrey Mowrey had returned home earlier than expected.

4

MANY HAVE SCOFFED AT THE THEORY OF LOVE AT first sight. Rightfully so, I suppose. It does indeed seem unreasonable, improbable, but I loved Jeffrey Mowrey from the moment I saw him standing there in the doorway, a gentle smile on his lips, his blue eyes smiling, too. I had never seen him before, but he was no stranger. It was as though we had known each other in another lifetime, as though for twenty years I had been unconsciously waiting for this moment, this reunion, and emotions I had never felt before rose within me. I didn't understand it at the time. At the time it took the form of confusion, and I was extremely disoriented. Understanding would come later.

"Miss James?" he said.

I nodded, unable to speak, and he stepped into the room, the smile still curving on that pale pink mouth that was wide and somehow vulnerable. He was tall, though not so tall as his brother, and he had the lean, muscular build of the Greek athletes I had seen in picture books. His hair was dark blond, thick, an unruly wave spilling over his brow. He was a beautiful man. His features were strong and undeniably virile but beautiful nonetheless, the jaw firm, the cheekbones broad, the nose straight, flaring at the nostrils. Beneath smooth dark brows his eyes were gentle, full now of inquiry.

"Are you ill?" he inquired.

I gazed at him, speechless, and it seemed I was seeing him through a haze, as though this were something remembered in a dream, not real at all. He wore a sapphire blue coat and matching knee breeches, white stockings, black pumps. His white satin waistcoat was embroidered with black and blue silk leaves, and a lace jabot cascaded from his throat. The elegant clothes were slightly rumpled from travel, and he smelled of leather and damp silk and perspiration. I passed a hand across my brow, hoping to brush away the bewilderment. He was no dream figure. He was flesh and blood, standing here before me, and no doubt he thought me an utter fool.

"Can I get you something?" he asked.

"I—I'm all right. I—a headache—"

"Perhaps I should summon Mrs. Rawson."

"No. Please. It—it's much better."

"Douglas told me you weren't feeling well. I've been talking with him. Listening to him, rather. He could speak of nothing but 'Honora.' He said he liked you better than anyone except me, and I've the feeling he added that last bit just to be polite."

"He—he should be in bed," I stammered.

"I know, but I have a new horse and he was eager to see it and I permitted him to take a lantern and go to the stables with one of the footmen. I'll not interfere with his routine again, I promise."

I should have made some reply, but no words would come.

"Douglas sang your praises," he said, "and I also spoke to Mrs. Rawson before I came up. She candidly admitted that you're a saint."

"And —and did you speak to your brother?" I asked.

"Briefly. I was too eager to see my son to do more than exchange greetings with Robert. I'm going to join him in his office in a few minutes, but I had to come up and meet this person my son babbled about so enthusiastically. Are you certain you're not ill, Miss James? You're quite pale."

"I'm fine."

"I owe you a great deal," he continued. "I left an illiterate little savage when I departed for Europe. I've returned to discover a chatty young gentleman who can spell his own name and recite the alphabet with lightning speed. He also told me all about *The Tempest*."

"He's a very exceptional child."

"And you're an exceptional young woman to have wrought such changes."

"He learns quickly."

"He obviously has a very good teacher."

The smile flashed again. It would have melted the heart of an ice maiden. He came across the room and took both my hands in his, holding them loosely, and my soul seemed to lift and soar to dizzying heights. I was barely able to draw breath.

"Douglas didn't tell me you were so pretty," he said.

"I—I'm hardly pretty."

"I beg to differ with you."

I blushed. Jeffrey Mowrey laughed quietly and squeezed my hands, closing his fingers tightly over mine in a moment of brief, painful contact that caused my heart to leap.

"It seems you're modest as well. Tell me, Miss James, are there *any* flaws in your character?"

"You'd better ask your brother about that."

"Robert?"

"He dismissed me this afternoon. I'm leaving Mowrey House in the morning. He's hired a coach to take me back to Bath."

His expression changed immediately. A frown creased his brow. He let go of my hands. My fingers still smarted from that moment of crushing pressure.

"Dismissed you? May I ask why?"

"I—I really don't know. He said my work has been satisfactory, but—I really don't know. I—I must ask you to leave me now. I must get one of the footmen to bring my trunk down. I must pack—"

"That won't be necessary, Miss James."

The frown had deepened, making a long furrow above the bridge of his nose, and his blue eyes were dark, disturbed. Jeffrey Mowrey was a sensitive man, I had seen that immediately. There was a tender quality about him, a vulnerability that was enormously appealing, but for a moment, in the dim golden light of the one lamp, I saw another side of him. He would never tolerate injustice, I felt, and if the need arose, he could be utterly unyielding.

"I'll speak to my brother," he said.

"No, please. If—if he doesn't want me here, I should leave."

I had trouble controlling my voice. Try though I might to maintain composure, I was on the verge of tears, and Jeffrey Mowrey sensed it. His frown vanished. He took hold of my arm and gave it a reassuring squeeze, and his eyes, those beautiful, expressive eyes, looked into mine.

"My brother is a very stern man," he said quietly. "He frequently expects too much from people, acts too hastily. I'm sure there's merely been a minor misunderstanding. You're not to worry, Miss James."

"Please. I—I don't want to cause trouble."

"There'll be no trouble," he assured me. "You get some rest now. I'll see you in the nursery in the morning."

He reached for my hands, squeezed them again. Again he smiled, and I felt a strange confusion as his eyes held mine.

In that brief moment I once more had the sensation that we had known each other in some other lifetime, that he was aware of it, too, and then he let go of my hands and nodded gently and left the room. Several minutes must have passed before I finally moved into the bedroom and bathed my cheeks with cool water. I was bewildered, apprehensive, yet underlying it all was a curious elation that was even more disturbing.

Hearing merry footsteps racing down the hall, I went back into the sitting room and managed to assume a severe expression as Doug came tearing through the door.

"Did you see my daddy?" he cried.

"I saw your father," I retorted. "I also heard you running down the hall like a hooligan."

"He said he was coming up to meet you. He has a new horse. He let Bradley take me out to the stables to see it. I carried the lantern myself."

"Indeed?"

"It's a *splen*did, horse, Honora. I'm gonna get to ride it. Daddy said so. He said he'd let me sit up in front of him and hold the reins. *If* I behave."

"Then I suggest you start behaving. That means no more running inside the house."

Doug tilted his head to one side and peered up at me with narrowed eyes. "You look strange," he observed. "I guess you're excited about Daddy coming home, too. He and Uncle Robert are having a talk in Uncle Robert's office. I heard 'em. They were talking about *you*."

"You—you shouldn't have eavesdropped," I scolded.

"Oh, I wudn't. I was just passin' by when I came in from the stables, but Mrs. Rawson, *she* was eavesdroppin'. She was pretendin' to arrange some flowers in a vase on that table in the hall, but she wudn't even lookin' at 'em, and her ear was tilted toward the office door. She shooed me off."

"It's past your bedtime, Douglas. We'd better get you ready."

"Aw, heck."

"Douglas!"

He groaned but made no further protest as I marched him into his room and helped him change into his nightclothes. He said his prayers and climbed into bed reluctantly and told me he knew he wasn't going to sleep, he just knew it, he was much too excited, and it really wasn't fair to him to have to go to bed this early when his daddy was home and it had been so long since he'd seen him. His eyes began to blink and his voice turned groggy and in less than a minute he was sound asleep. I smoothed the wisps of hair from his forehead and tucked the covers around him and returned to my bedroom.

Douglas may have gone right to sleep, but I didn't. Once in bed I watched the moonlight stream through the windows and watched the shadows lengthen on the walls. I listened to the distant murmur of waves and kept seeing that handsome, already beloved face, and I slept hardly at all.

Lord Robert Mowrey summoned me to his office early the next morning, and I went downstairs with considerable apprehension. Pale, weary from lack of sleep, I wore my soberest dress, a long-sleeved sky blue cotton with a white lace fichu and matching lace at the wrists, and I had put my hair up and fastened it in a tight bun in back, hoping to more closely resemble my idea of what a governess should look like. I moved slowly down the staircase, running my hand along the smooth, polished banister, feeling as though I were going to my doom.

What had transpired between the two brothers after Jeffrey Mowrey left my sitting room last night? They had talked, yes, I knew that, but what decision had been reached? Was I to be dismissed? Was the coach even now on its way to Mowrey House? Jeffrey Mowrey had been quite firm, telling me not to pack, not to worry, and there had been a determined set to his mouth, but his brother was utterly inflexible and I couldn't imagine anyone making him change his mind once he had reached a decision.

As I passed the hall table I noticed that the flowers were indeed messed up, jumbled together untidily in the vase. Mrs. Rawson really had been eavesdropping, then, just as Douglas said. I fervently wished there were time to find her and speak to her, for I felt sure she was privy to everything that had been said. I paused in front of the office door and took a deep breath, silently praying for strength. I mustn't let him sense my apprehension. I must be calm and reserved, cool and self-possessed.

I knocked timidly on the door, my heart pounding.

"Come in." The voice was crisp, clipped.

He was sitting behind the enormous desk, examining a ledger opened before him. He didn't look up. He continued to examine a set of figures, apparently unaware of my presence, even though he had ordered me to come in. It was a ploy to make me even more uneasy, to throw me off balance, I saw that, and curiously enough it had just the opposite effect. So transparent a ploy didn't make him more formidable. It made him more the petty tyrant he actually was. He had wealth and power, yes, and many trembled before him, but I vowed I wouldn't be one of them. I had done nothing wrong. I wasn't going to be bullied.

I had never been in the office before, and I examined it calmly while he continued to study the ledger. It was a large room, a rather crudely executed painting of the Mowrey pottery works hanging over the fireplace. Smokestacks reared black and ugly against a blue gray sky, furnace glowing with red orange furor, the clay pits visible in the distance. A shelf on the other side of the room displayed examples of the pottery, blue cups and saucers, blue plates—cheap, easily affordable pottery found in thousands of homes throughout England— along with a set of the more expensive line also produced at the factory, milky white china adorned with pale orange flowers outlined in gold. Adjoining the office was a much smaller office where Parks worked laboriously over accounts and correspondence. He was not there this morning. I assumed Lord Robert didn't want his secretary to overhear what was to be said.

Finally closing the ledger, he pushed it aside and raised his head to look at me. His pale, lean face was expressionless, his brown-black eyes stony. I might have been a stranger to him.

"You wished to see me?" I said.

He didn't reply at once. He continued to stare at me with those dark, stony eyes, and then his thin lips curled with distaste. He lowered his gaze and began to shuffle a stack of papers, ignoring me again. I waited, truly calm now, confident as well. Right was on my side, and I was still young enough to believe that right would triumph in the end.

"My brother was quite distressed when he learned you were to be dismissed," he said. He might have been speaking to himself. "He has insisted you stay on as my nephew's governess."

He didn't look up. He continued to shuffle the papers.

"Has he?" I said.

"I objected, of course. I find it difficult to deny my brother anything, I have a weakness where he is concerned, but I objected most strongly. I informed him that in my opinion you were an unsuitable influence."

"Unsuitable?"

"Too young, too lenient, too lax."

"That isn't true."

"You dress like a whore. You paint your face like a whore."

"That isn't true either, Lord Robert."

He ignored my words, concentrating on the papers, straightening them into a neat pile. His lean face was taut, his lips tight. He was finding it difficult to control himself, I saw. I could sense the anger and hostility seething beneath that cold, austere facade.

"You made an extremely favorable impression on my brother, it seems. He informed me that his son's education is his affair and that you are to be retained. He was quite adamant about it."

"Indeed?"

"He went so far as to say that if you left, he and Douglas would leave, too. He meant every word he said. Under the circumstances I had no recourse but to concede to his wishes. My brother defied me. Deliberately. We've had disagreements before, but he's never openly defied me."

"I'm sorry that you're displeased."

"You're a very clever young woman, Miss James."

"Clever?"

He shoved the stack of papers aside and looked up, and his eyes burned with emotion now, burned with an unalloyed hatred that was chilling in its intensity. Why? Why did this man hate me so? What had I done to deserve it? He stood up, looming there behind the desk so very tall, thin to the point of emaciation, his black suit severe. The burning black-brown eyes intensified the pallor of those lean, pitted cheeks, and I was reminded of some half-demented religious zealot prepared to bring the wrath of God down on his cringing flock.

"I feared something like this would happen," he said. "That's the reason I wanted you out of the house before he returned."

"'Something like this—'" I repeated his words, puzzled. "I don't understand."

"I think you do, Miss James."

"I can assure you, I—"

"I know what you're up to," he told me.

I began to see then. As those hate-filled eyes glared at me I began to understand, and I was stunned. I remembered what Mrs. Rawson had told me about him the day I arrived at Mowrey House, and I remembered the curious feeling I had had that I presented some kind of threat to him. Everything fell into place. I knew why he loathed me, why my very presence was a threat.

"It's my own fault, of course," he continued, and his voice was surprisingly dry, as though he were discussing the weather. "I should never have hired you in the first place. I should have sent you back to Bath immediately."

"Perhaps that would have been best," I agreed. "I've no intention of leaving now."

"No?"

"As long as your brother wants me here, nothing can drive me away."

"You're very brave, aren't you?"

"No, Lord Robert, not brave, just not easily intimidated. I assume you hoped I would decide to leave on my own volition."

"You assumed correctly. If you were wise, Miss James, you would do just that. You would make some kind of excuse to my brother— a sick relative, whatever—and leave within the week."

"I shan't," I said.

He stared at me, thwarted, furious, containing that fury with superb control. I had just made a very dangerous enemy. I understood that, and I was shaken, but I stood my ground with chin held high. Lord Robert picked up the papers he had been shuffling earlier, his face expressionless again, his eyes stony, and when he spoke his voice was utterly flat.

"My brother has informed me that I am not to interfere," he told me. "I shall respect his wishes. His son's education is his affair, as he was so ready to point out. A rather belated conclusion, I might add. He hasn't been too concerned about it until now."

He looked down at the papers, reading the one on top. I waited, certain there was more to come. I was right. After a moment he set the papers back on the desk and gazed at me with frosty eyes.

"One thing more," he said.

"Yes?"

"My nephew's education is my brother's affair, true, but Jeffrey's welfare is mine. He's extremely vulnerable, but I've no intention of letting him be entrapped by a predatory female. I'll be watching you, Miss James, and I strongly suggest you concern yourself solely with your duties in the nursery."

I nodded politely. "Will that be all, Lord Robert?"

"That will be all, Miss James."

I left the office, closing the door behind me and moving resolutely down the hall toward the staircase. I was very pleased with the way I had handled myself. I hadn't allowed him to intimidate me, and I told myself that his scarcely veiled threat didn't frighten me at all. I was going to stay at Mowrey House. That was the important thing. I put Lord Robert out of my mind and thought instead of his brother. Jeffrey Mowrey had said he would see me in the nursery this morning. I moved up the staircase, thinking of him, filled with a joyous anticipation so intense it was almost like an ache inside, an ache only he could soothe.

DOUGLAS WAS RESTLESS AND IMPATIENT, REFUSING to concentrate, refusing to pay attention as we did our math. If two times four was eight, he couldn't have cared less. Sitting at the table with chin in hand, a blond wave dipping over his brow and a surly expression on his face, he fretted, eager to see his father. Jeffrey had promised him that he could see the new horse again today and maybe even ride it, and he could think of nothing else. I gave him my sternest look and informed him in a chilly voice that if he didn't do his lessons I'd tell his father.

"And then there'd be no visit to the stables, I assure you," I added.

"Awright!" he snapped. "Two times two is three—uh—four, and two times four is eight and two times eight is thirteen. There!"

"Two times eight is what?"

"Thirteen!"

"I'm afraid not," I said.

"Fourteen?"

I waited. He frowned and did some mental figuring and

then began to count on his fingers. I glanced out the window, on edge myself, every bit as impatient as Douglas. It was a glorious, sun-spangled day, brilliant rays spilling lavishly through the windows and making pools on the polished hard-wood floor. I could see the sea in the distance, beyond the treetops, and the cry of gulls was a constant, muted background. It was much too beautiful a day to be cooped up here in the nursery like this, but duty was duty.

"Sixteen," he said at last.

"Correct. That wasn't so hard, was it?"

"It was hard as hell."

"Douglas!"

"I'm too little to be learnin' all that hard stuff," he protested. "Why can't we do Calleyban and Miranda?"

"We will, just as soon as we finish our math."

"You look funny with your hair all pulled back like that," he informed me. "I like it better like it was, fallin' to your shoulders. Why don't you pull it back down?"

"You're terribly impertinent this morning, Douglas."

"I wanna see Daddy."

"Your father is probably sleeping late. He had a very long journey, and he was up very late last night."

"I know, talkin' with Uncle Robert."

"We'd better continue, Douglas."

"I'm glad Daddy's home. Do you think he loves me, Honora?"

I was taken aback. "Of—of course he does."

"I just wondered." His gray eyes were thoughtful. "Seems to me if he loved me he wouldn't stay gone all the time. Seems he'd wanna be with me."

He sighed, pensive now, and I wanted to hug him to me and stroke that thick blond hair and assure him that he was indeed loved. Instead, I assumed a severe expression.

"What's two times nine?" I asked.

"Eighteen," he replied promptly.

"Two times ten?"

"Twenty. There. Two times one is two. Two times two is four. Two times three is seven. Two times four is eight. I know it all and it's borin' as hell, so let's do the play."

"Two times three is not seven."

"It is, too!"

"It most assuredly is not."

He began to count on his fingers, scowling, and when he

got to six the scowl turned into a frown and he paused, a puzzled look in his eyes. Then he grinned.

"Six," he said. "I knew it all along."

I gave him an exasperated look, enchanted by his pixie charm but much too sensible to let him know it. Putting aside the math book and papers, I pulled the painted cardboard theater nearer the edge of the table, and Douglas took out the cutout characters we had made to illustrate *The Tempest*.

"I'll be Calleyban and Prospero," he said, "and you be Miranda and Ariel and all them noblemen."

"*Those* noblemen."

"Those boring chaps. Where's Stephano? I wanna be Stephano, too. Now you tell the story and we'll act it out with the paper dolls."

"There was a terrible storm at sea—" I began.

"I wish we had a bucket of water. It'd be more fun, but I guess we'd ruin the dolls if we got 'em wet. There was this terrible storm at sea and the ship with the noblemen and Stephano was wrecked and there was this island—"

"And on the island Miranda lived with her father and—"

"—this ugly monster!" he interrupted, moving the cutout of Caliban across the stage.

He continued to interrupt, finally taking over completely and relating the story himself with great enthusiasm. Bored with Ferdinand, Antonio, and company, he eliminated them completely, doing his own version with considerable imagination and taking much glee in paraphrasing the lines of Caliban and Stephano, the inebriated butler.

"An' I'm gonna have another drink, monster! An' then we're gonna have a big fight!" He lowered his voice to a growl then. "An' I'm gonna *eat you up*, smarty-pants!"

It wasn't Shakespeare, but it was great fun for him, and I told myself it was educational. We were so immersed that neither of us heard Jeffrey Mowrey enter the nursery.

"An' they lived happily ever after!" Douglas cried. "The monster, too. That was *fun*, Honora. Let's do it again!"

Jeffrey Mowrey chuckled. I turned, startled, totally flustered as his blue eyes met mine. Douglas jumped up and raced over to fling himself against his father's legs. Jeffrey Mowrey scooped him up into his arms and slung him over his shoulder as Douglas squealed with delight. I stood up, feeling guilty for some reason, feeling terribly disoriented. Jeffrey Mowrey tossed his son into the air, caught him nimbly, set him on his feet.

"Do it again, Daddy! Do it again!"

"I fear we're outraging Miss James. She looks very severe."

"It's her hair makes her look that way, makes her look prissy. I told her she oughta pull it down."

Jeffrey Mowrey chuckled again and gave his son a friendly cuff on the arm. Douglas beamed, wrapping his arms around his father's right leg and resting his head against it. Jeffrey Mowrey placed one large hand on his son's head and began to tousle his hair. Douglas tilted his head back, looking up at him.

"Can I see the horse again, Daddy? Can I *ride* him?"

"We'll see. You run on down to the stables and find Bradley. I'll join you in a few minutes. I want to talk to Miss James."

"Don't dawdle! Bye, Honora!"

He scampered out of the room. We could hear him running noisily down the hall. I shook my head. Jeffrey Mowrey smiled. His dark brown knee boots were highly polished, his tan breeches snug, fitting calf and thigh like a second skin. His fine silk shirt was a creamy beige, open at the throat, the sleeves very full, gathered at the wrist. Sunlight burnished his dark blond hair, and a heavy wave dipped over his brow. He seemed to bring his own radiance into the room.

His blue eyes gazed at me politely, fondly, and the smile played lightly on his beautifully shaped pink mouth. He was like a storybook figure, a handsome prince whose kiss awakens the sleeping beauty, too handsome, too dazzling to be flesh and blood. He seemed completely unaware of his good looks, and although he had been rowdy with his son, he seemed almost shy now that the two of us were alone.

"He—Douglas is very glad you're home," I said.

There was a slight tremor in my voice. I fought to compose myself, fought to banish those curious, bewildering sensations that stirred inside like tight, tiny buds exploding softly into bloom. I was his son's governess. He was my employer. I must remember that. I assumed a stiff, proper manner, and when I spoke again my voice was suitably grave.

"Ordinarily he's much better behaved. He knows he's not supposed to run in the house. I'll speak to him."

"You needn't apologize for him, Miss James."

Embarrassed, confused, I turned away from him and began to tidy up our worktable. Jeffrey Mowrey moved over beside me and reached down to pick up the paper doll of Miranda.

"You did this?" he inquired.

"I made them all. I thought—I thought it would be nice for Douglas to learn something about Shakespeare. I thought it would be fun if we made a replica of the Globe Theater and—"

"You're extremely nervous, Miss James."

"I—I can't help it," I said feebly.

"You mustn't let me intimidate you. We're going to be good friends."

I made no reply. Jeffrey Mowrey studied the paper doll in his hand.

"She looks remarkably like you," he observed, tilting his head slightly, eyeing the doll. "Her hair is the same rich auburn, her eyes the same lovely shade of gray. You're quite an accomplished artist, Miss James."

"Thank you."

He put the paper doll down and looked into my eyes. "I spoke to my brother," he told me. "Everything is settled. You're to stay on at Mowrey House until such a time as I see fit to dismiss you."

"I—I see."

He smiled again, his blue eyes gently teasing. "I fancy I'll be spending a lot of time in the nursery, observing your work. Have to be sure my son's getting the proper instruction."

"Of course."

I gave him a curt nod, stiff, formal, distant. His lower lip was full and sensual, I noticed, and the skin across those broad cheekbones was taut. I remembered what Mrs. Rawson had told me about him. He might not "tomcat around," as she put it, and his manner with the ladies might be polite and diffident, but Jeffrey Mowrey was a man who savored things of the flesh. I sensed that, inexperienced though I was in such matters.

"You're blushing, Miss James," he said. "Is something wrong?"

I shook my head. I gathered up some books and carried them over to the bookcase. My hands trembled slightly as I set the books alongside the others on the shelf. Jeffrey Mowrey watched me, a thoughtful look in his eyes.

"I guess I'd better go join my son before he drives poor Bradley mad," he said after a moment. "If I don't take him for a ride the young scoundrel will never stop plaguing me. Do you ride, Miss James?"

I shook my head again. "I've never been on a horse."

"Pity. We'll have to take long walks instead."

What did he mean by that? I looked at him, bewildered, and he came over to me and took both my hands in his. He squeezed them gently, and I caught my breath.

"Douglas was right, Miss James. You look much better with your hair down. See that you wear it that way in the future. That's an order."

His voice was low and melodious, making gentle fun of me. He let go of my hands and nodded amiably and then sauntered out of the room. He seemed to take the sunlight with him.

Jeffrey Mowrey visited the nursery the next morning, and the next, and I soon grew accustomed to his presence. Sitting casually on one of the stools, arms folded across his chest, he smiled at Doug's efforts to add and subtract the simplest numbers. He listened attentively when I read the geography lessons. When we "performed" with the cutout figures, he made a most attentive audience. After the first day, Doug was completely at ease in his father's presence, showing off a bit and much better behaved than he ordinarily was, but I was never at ease.

I knew that I loved him. I knew it was a hopeless, futile love and one I must keep carefully concealed. After a while I was able to control all of those beautiful, bewildering emotions that besieged me whenever he was near, and I was able to present a cool, unruffled demeanor, but it was never easy. Once, when we were coloring new figures for the toy theater, I happened to glance up and see him studying me with a curious expression in his eyes. He looked away immediately, but I puzzled over it for hours. There had been admiration in those gentle blue eyes, and there had been something else as well, something I couldn't quite identify.

I told myself I had imagined it.

Douglas and I had planned a picnic for Tuesday afternoon. His father decided to accompany us, and Cook packed an abundant basket with cheese, sausage, chicken, brown rolls, jam tarts sprinkled with powdered sugar and various kinds of fruit. The basket was so heavy I could hardly lift it. Jeffrey Mowrey took it by the handle, thrust a slender bottle of wine among the napkins and led the way across the gardens and onto the moors beyond.

"It seems an eternity since I've been on a picnic," he remarked.

"We have 'em lots of times!" Douglas exclaimed.

"Them," I said. "Speak correctly or don't speak at all."

"Honora's awful mean sometimes," he told his father. "I like her anyway."

"I like her, too," his father said.

He glanced at me and smiled. Silent music seemed to fill my soul, swelling inside, and I seemed to be walking through a silver haze. No love is stronger, more magical than first love, the very newness opening vistas of splendor, allowing one to see with new eyes, and it was as though I had been half asleep before love awakened all my senses. Had I ever fully appreciated the pure, pale blue of the sky, the sparkle of silver yellow sunlight on leaf and stone and grass? Had I ever noticed the faint purple tinge on the brownish gray grass, the streaks of rust and dried green moss on those enormous gray boulders? The moors were beautiful, beautiful. How could I ever have thought them stark and barren?

Douglas raced ahead of us in exuberant anticipation, disappearing around a group of boulders, and Jeffrey Mowrey and I were momentarily alone. He walked in a long, athletic stride, swinging the basket at his side. He was wearing a pair of old brown boots, faded tan breeches, a thin white cotton shirt that was a bit too large, bagging over the snug waistband of his breeches, the very full sleeves ballooning at the wrists. His blond hair gleamed darkly in the sun, unruly in the wind. I felt an uneasy tremor, and there was an aching sensation inside.

Despite the books I had read and the worldly chatter of the older girls at school, despite Mrs. Rawson's frequent and often graphic talk about matters of the flesh, I had only a vague idea of what went on between a man and a woman after the kissing was over and more intimate embraces began. Chaucer was very informative, Shakespeare, too, and the works of Mrs. Aphra Behn revealed much, but the specifics remained a mystery to me. Writers called it the sublime completion, and I understood that I was only half complete now. These new sensations would not cease until Jeffrey Mowrey took me in that intimate embrace and made me whole.

"You're very quiet, Miss James," he said.

"I—I'm afraid I was lost in thought."

"Care to share your thoughts?" he asked.

I shook my head, lowering my eyes demurely. He would never know how I felt about him. I would never dare reveal those feelings by action or word. He was from one of England's finest families, his blood the bluest of blue, and I was the daughter of a greengrocer and his wife. Had the Reverend Mr. Williams not used his influence to get me into the school, I would probably be working in a shop now myself. I could dream, I could revel in his nearness and savor the delight of his presence, but I was doomed to remain incomplete. I accepted that.

Douglas came racing back to join us and declared that he had found a perfect spot for our picnic, leading us to a flat, grassy stretch beyond the boulders. His father agreed that it was an ideal spot. He set the basket down. I took out the large tablecloth and began to arrange things on it. Douglas dashed about, full of high spirits, and his father stretched out on the grass, long, lazy, completely at ease.

"I'm dreadfully hungry," he confessed.

"There's certainly enough food," I replied. "Cook has outdone herself."

"I want one of those tarts!" Douglas exclaimed. "I want it before anything else!"

"You'll have your sweet last," I told him.

"I don't want any of the other things. I'll just eat the tarts."

"I'm afraid you shan't," I said. "You'll sit down and be quiet and eat a chicken leg and a roll and a bit of sausage, and if you eat it *all* you may have a tart."

"The biggest," he added, "that fat one on top."

Jeffrey Mowrey smiled at his son. The sky arched overhead, a pale blue almost white, and sunlight sparkled on grass and rock. The grass rustled quietly in the breeze, taking on a distinct purple tinge in the distance where the ground sloped up to the hillside surmounted by the ancient Roman ruins. I ate very little, nibbling at a piece of chicken, sitting on the grass with my skirts spread out around me in a circle. Douglas ate quickly, eager to have his tart. Jeffrey Mowrey displayed a hearty appetite.

After finishing his tart, Douglas asked permission to go look for colored rocks. It was granted, with the stipulation that he not go so far he couldn't hear me call. The child raced away, free, unfettered, bursting with energy. I watched him pursue a wild rabbit, watched him pause to search the ground, finally stooping to pick up a tiny stone.

"He has quite a collection of colored rocks," I said, "black ones, brown ones, one a deep maroon. One day he found an ancient Roman coin. It was green with age."

"The Romans had a military outpost up there on top of the

hill," Jeffrey said. "The ruins are quite fascinating. I'll have to show them to you one day soon."

"That would be—interesting," I replied.

He took two glasses from the basket and uncorked the bottle of wine, pouring it. It was pale amber, sparkling in the crystal glass he handed to me. I took a sip. It had a sharp, delicious tang, and almost immediately a wonderful glow seemed to steal through me.

"Robert's best. I raided the wine cellar before we left."

I sipped the wine in silence, gazing up at the sky. A brown bird circled slowly, slowly against the blue, growing smaller and smaller as it climbed. The grass rustled. I turned to look at Douglas, far in the distance now, scrutinizing the ground with hands thrust into his pockets. I didn't look at Jeffrey Mowrey, but I could feel him looking at me. I finished the glass of wine, a tremulous feeling inside. The wine helped.

"Another glass?" he inquired.

"I—I'd better not."

It was easy enough to maintain my cool demeanor when we were in the nursery, when Douglas was with us and I was busy with my work, but now that we were alone I was incredibly ill at ease. Several minutes passed in silence, and the silence only made things worse.

"Are—are you happy to be home?" I asked.

"In a way," he replied. "It's good to be with Douglas. I've spent far too little time with him. I've been unfair to him. After my wife died, it was—extremely difficult for me to go on."

I made no reply. Jeffrey Mowrey looked down at the glass of wine he held in his hand, gazing into the clear liquid as though hoping to find some kind of answer there, and then he sighed, raised the glass to his lips and emptied it. I saw the pain in his eyes.

"You've been spending a lot of time at the factory," I said, hoping to distract him from the grief I knew he still felt deeply. "Mrs. Rawson told me you go there almost every afternoon."

He nodded. "Robert insists. I—I suppose I go merely to pacify him. What I see there breaks my heart—the conditions those people work under—men passing out from the heat of the furnaces, women standing on their feet for twelve hours, fainting from exhaustion and lack of fresh air, small children working in squalid, stuffy rooms, packing pottery. They—they don't always have time to get outside to the sheds when they need to—" Delicacy made him hesitate, but I knew what he meant. "The stench is unbelievable. They've been breathing it so long they've become immune to it, but—"

Again he hesitated, his mouth tight.

"Is—isn't there anything you can do?" I asked.

"I used to think so," he retorted. "I begged my brother to make reforms. He laughed at me. 'You can't pamper these people, Jeffery,' he told me. 'You do and they get slack, get impertinent, start expecting even more. You have to use an iron hand and use it constantly. You can't let up or production will go to hell.' I argued with him. He called me a fool, a dreamer, told me I'd best leave such matters to him. I was very young at the time, but—I couldn't get it out of my mind."

He stared into space for a few moments, and when he finally continued there was undeniable bitterness in that gentle voice.

"I continued to think about it all the time I was at Oxford," he told me. "Unknown to Robert, I visited several other factories—not just pottery works, all sorts of factories—and I found conditions there almost as bad. I made a study, and I eventually drew up plans for renovations I felt should be made at the pottery works. Small, stuffy rooms would be consolidated into large rooms with banks of windows to let in the fresh air and sunshine. Facilities would be installed. Dozens of safety precautions would be introduced, new furnaces, conveyor belts to bring the clay up from the pits and eliminate the wheelbarrows and dangerous wooden ramps. My dream factory would be the safest and the most modern in England."

Doug shouted merrily in the distance, chasing another rabbit. The grass rustled. Another bird was circling against the sky.

"It wasn't an idle dream," Jeffrey Mowrey told me. "I spent almost two years working out those plans. I drew up a list of proposals, too. Higher pay would give the workers more incentive and eliminate the need for children working. Various raises for individual industry and accomplishment would give them even more incentive, and shorter hours would actually enable them to work more. Men and women reeling from exhaustion can't produce—" He shook his head, gazing into space again.

"What did your brother say?" I asked quietly.

He didn't answer my question directly. "I obtained a set of the original blueprints for the factory, and a friend of mine from Oxford helped me draw up new ones. He hadn't had any commissions yet, true, but together we were able to draw a set of blueprints incorporating all the renovations with very few alterations to the basic structure. When—after I came back to Cornwall, shortly after the wedding, I gave the blueprints to my brother along with my list of proposals. He was very patient while—while I explained my dream. When I had finished he told me I was still a goddamned fool when it came to business, that I was becoming dangerously radical as well."

"Radical?"

"Pampering the workers, giving them higher wages, shorter hours, renovating the pottery works—it would bring every factory owner in England down on his head. Their workers would demand similar changes, and there would be riots all over the country. Not only would we go bankrupt, we would likely be strung up as well. I—I saw that it was utterly futile. I saw that I would never be able to convince him. He stuck the blueprints and my list of proposals away in the bottom drawer of his desk, and—I guess you'd say I just gave up."

"And now?"

"Robert insists I spend time at the factory. I need to 'learn the business.' He plans for me to take over one day, you see— and Douglas afterward. If I thought there was a chance of realizing my dream, I would—" Again he hesitated, his eyes grim. "Robert would like for me to work with him, yes, but he would always maintain complete control. Fifteen, twenty years from now I would take over, but in the meantime I would—I might help run the factory, but Robert would make all the decisions. I'd have no real say in matters."

"You—you have other plans?"

"I've been giving more and more thought to the diplomatic service. I've made several influential friends in my travels, and I've always been interested in—in performing some kind of real service to my country. I've sent out a few letters of inquiry, but—no, I have no definite plans. Not yet. I go to the factory to keep peace in the family, but I know I shan't stay here. When the time comes I—I'll break the news to Robert some-how. I love my brother and I'm very grateful to him, but he can be—" He paused, searching for the right word. "He can be extremely possessive."

"I see."

"He loves me. He only wants what's best for me, but his ideas of what's best are—they aren't mine. He raised me, you know. I guess you could say he has devoted most of his adult life to me, and—I'm not complaining, mind you, but a—a man has to live his own life. Robert means well, and I don't want to hurt him, but—"

Jeffrey Mowrey cut himself short as though it were too painful to continue. He finally poured another glass of wine, emptying the bottle. I sensed that he was fighting a silent battle inside, and I wished there was something I could do to help. He was silent for a long while, frowning, and when he looked at me again those beautiful eyes were full of determination.

"I'm all he has," he said, "and that's unfortunate. For such a long time there were just the two of us, and that was enough for Robert, but I'm grown now and it—it can't be that way any longer. He's going to have to accept that."

There was another long silence. I thought about all he had told me, understanding better now. The bird was a tiny brown speck against the blue white sky. Douglas was climbing a boulder in the distance. Sunlight bathed the moors with silvery light. Jeffrey Mowrey finished his wine. The frown was gone. He seemed more relaxed.

"Forgive me for going on so," he said. "I—I don't usually talk so much. You've heard about me, Miss James. Now tell me about yourself."

"I'm afraid you'd find it very boring."

"I seriously doubt that."

"I don't know where to begin—"

"The Reverend Mr. Williams told me your parents ran a greengrocer's shop. I understand they were very loving, very devout. He was in Bath before he came to Cornwall, I know, and he said he had known you since you were a little girl. A very bright little girl, he told me."

"You—you asked him about me?"

"Yesterday. I stopped by to see him after I left the factory. He gave me quite a scolding for not coming to see him earlier and added that he expected to see me at services next Sunday. He's a wonderful man."

"He used his influence to get me into the school after— after my parents died," I said. "I worked for them in exchange for the privilege of attending classes."

Perhaps it was the wine, but I suddenly found myself telling him about the school, the students, the classes I eventually conducted. I was the poorest girl there, of course, little more than a scullery maid at first, but I hadn't minded too much. There had been an extensive library, and I had read every single book at least once, stealing extra candles from the pantry so I could stay up half the night, devouring books in my attic room. Several kind ladies in the parish had seen to my clothes, sending parcels of hand-me-downs I was able to alter to fit me.

"It was a hard life," I admitted, "particularly after Reverend Williams left for Cornwall, but—it could have been much worse. I could have been sent to an orphanage. I was eventually given classes of my own to conduct, teaching the youngest girls."

I paused, looking into the past. Jeffrey Mowrey watched me with grave, thoughtful eyes, sincerely interested.

"They wanted me to stay on at the school," I continued after a moment. "I intended to, but then the Reverend's letter arrived and—I decided to become a governess instead."

"I'm very glad you made that decision, Miss James."

His lovely, melodic voice was low, intimate, and I had the feeling he was about to say something more when Douglas came scurrying to join us, tremendously excited about the rocks he'd found and chattering nonstop. I packed the basket, shook out the cloth and placed it on top, and we started back toward Mowrey House.

As soon as we reached the gardens Douglas raced on to the house to show his finds to Mrs. Rawson. His father and I proceeded at a more leisurely pace, pausing beside one of the trellises. Vine leaves rustled with a faint rattling noise and insects hummed.

"I can't remember when I enjoyed a day more," he said.

"It was pleasant," I agreed.

"We'll have to do it more often."

"Douglas would enjoy that."

"I wasn't thinking of Douglas," he replied.

His blue eyes held mine. I felt the familiar confusion and tried valiantly to stem it. What did he mean? Was it possible that . . . that he enjoyed my company as much as I enjoyed his? I put the thought aside. No, no, he was merely being polite to a dull young governess who had told him far too much about herself. It had been foolish of me to talk so much, but I wasn't so foolish that I would allow myself to misinterpret his natural politeness.

"Reverend Williams is eager to see you," he told me.

"I'd like to see him, too," I replied. "He met the coach when I arrived from Bath, but I've not been able to attend services yet. There was no transportation to the village, and—"

"I plan to attend services next Sunday. Why don't you accompany me?"

"I—I'm not sure I should."

"Whyever not?"

I could think of no suitable reply, so I mumbled something about not having a proper dress to wear. Jeffrey Mowrey laughed merrily at this age-old female complaint. He blithely informed me that anything I had would do and added that he looked forward to my company. He took my hand in his, gave it a squeeze and then strolled on to the house, swinging the near-empty basket at his side. I stood watching him as the leaves rattled quietly and the afternoon sun cast pale blue-gray shadows across the lawns.

Several minutes passed. Conflicting emotions held me captive, a wild, unreasonable hope springing alive inside. He *did* enjoy my company, and he wanted more of it. I hadn't imagined that look in his eyes, that inflection in his voice. I gazed at the house, and it was then that I noticed Lord Robert Mowrey standing at one of the windows, staring at me. He turned away, letting the curtain fall back in place.

I wondered how long he had been watching.

6

MRS. RAWSON QUITE AGREED THAT I HAD NOTHING suitable to wear to Sunday services. She went through my wardrobe thoroughly, sniffing disdainfully at the collection of old, altered garments. The puce was much too drab, I should never wear anything so bleak, and gray wasn't my color, not at all, and besides, the nap was beginning to wear. The pink? Pretty enough but too plain. I needed something splendid. The blue muslin was fetchin', real fetchin', but it wouldn't do for church. I'd simply have to have something new.

"I haven't had anything new since I was a little girl," I told her, "and I couldn't possibly buy a dress. Even if I were able to get to a shop, I haven't a pound to my name. Lord Robert hasn't given me my wages yet."

"I didn't mean *buy* somethin' new, luv, I mean we should make somethin'. I'm a whiz with needle and thread, just look at them curtains, that counterpane, and you're mite handy at sewin' yourself. We've got four days. That's plenty-a time to whip somethin' up."

"From an old curtain in the attic?" I asked dryly.

"Don't get lippy, lass. I've a mind to do you a favor, got a bolt of cloth I've been savin' for a special occasion. Bertie Johnson gave it to me last year in return for a little somethin' I gave him in his hayloft one fine evenin'. It would look smashin' on you, that satin. A bit pale for me, ivory's not my color. Give me red or purple any day."

"I couldn't let you—"

"I don't intend to argue with you, time's a wastin'. You stay right here. I'll be back in no time."

She hurried out of the room, returning a few minutes later with a huge bolt of creamy ivory satin printed with tiny, delicate pink and brown flowers, a sumptuous cloth that gleamed beautifully in the candlelight as she unfurled it with a dramatic flourish.

"Just the thing!" she exclaimed. "A mite fancy for an old party like me, told Bertie so at the time. 'Why didn't-ja get red?' I says to him. 'You know I'm fond-a red.' Men don't have no sense when it comes to colors. Me, I'd look plum foolish in an ivory satin frock printed with them exquisite little flowers, but you got the youth and beauty to go with it, lass."

"It's a lovely piece of cloth, Mrs. Rawson."

"There's plenty here for a nice full skirt. Bertie bought big thinkin' it'd be a dress for me. 'Spect we'll have to whip up some underskirts, too. Them old white silk sheets in the trunk'll do nicely, they got real lace trimmin', too. You're gonna look a treat, luv, that's no lie. We'll start workin' tomorrow evenin' soon's you get the brat to bed. I'll be thinkin'-a styles an' such."

We met the next evening in her sewing room. A fire was crackling pleasantly in the fireplace, and her work table was a bright magpie's nest of scraps and ribbons and laces, all jumbled together in a multicolored heap. She set to work immediately, taking my measurements, cutting out a pattern of brown paper, fitting it to me to make certain she'd cut correctly. Her head was tilted to one side, outrageous gray ringlets bobbling, her cherry red lips pursed in concentration.

"We'll start with the underskirts," she informed me. "I washed and ironed them old sheets I was tellin' you about—they look like new, the finest white silk you ever seen. I took all the lace off, washed and ironed it, too, handmade by a bunch-a nuns in France, it was, I remember Lady Mowrey tellin' me. I'll do all-a the cuttin' and we'll stitch together."

Her purple taffeta skirt rustled loudly as she scurried about, fetching scissors and sheets, snatching up a handful of fine Valenciennes lace, kicking a piece of paper out of her way. She cut the silk carefully, the tip of her tongue between her teeth, her eyes narrowed, and soon we were ready to sew.

"You'll want 'em very full," she said. "You want to show off that tiny little waist of yours. Would you believe I once had a waist like that? I did, luv, and everything to go with it, too. The men were fairly wild, they still are, the older ones. It ain't just a fine figure they're interested in, I don't mind tellin' you. I keep 'em hoppin' even though my figure's a thing-a the past."

"You're outrageous," I teased.

"I know what I like, lass, and I don't see no harm in havin' it whenever I get the chance. Keeps the juices flowin'. I could be just as prim and proper as the next one if I was a-mind to, but I don't see much profit in it. Long as they like what I got to offer, I'm gonna enjoy myself. Jim Randall, that blacksmith I was tellin' ya about, he says I'm in my prime and I couldn't agree with him more."

We were sitting in two comfortable overstuffed chairs on either side of the fireplace. White silk flowed luxuriously over her lap as she stitched pieces together for the skirt. I worked on the bodice, the silk cool and slippery between my fingers.

"We'll want to make a lace insert across the bosom," she told me. "Never know who's gonna see it."

"I doubt anyone shall."

"I ain't so sure, luv. I got eyes in my head. I know what's goin' on."

"I—I don't know what you mean."

"You're in love with him, lass, head over heels."

"You're mistaken," I said primly.

Mrs. Rawson smiled and shook her head, gray ringlets bobbing. "I'm mistaken about a lot of things, luv, but when it comes to matters of the heart, I'm *al*ways right. It's my specialty, you might say."

"I—didn't know it showed."

"It's plain as day to someone like me, luv. I expected you to fall in love with him, would-a been surprised if you hadn't."

She paused to rethread her needle, her manner extremely casual. I knew I could trust her with my secret, and in a way I was relieved that someone else knew what I felt. Mrs. Rawson was vastly experienced, and perhaps she could help me understand what was happening to me.

"I didn't intend to fall in love with him," I told her. "It happened all at once, the moment I saw him."

She nodded. "Happens that way sometimes, has to do with chemistry. There ain't much you can do when it hits you like that. It becomes a part of you, in your blood, so to speak."

"That's exactly how it feels."

"He's smitten, too, you know."

I gazed at her, stunned.

"Oh, yes," she said, nodding again. "He's real taken with you. I seen it at once. Guess I know why he's hangin' around the nursery so much."

"He just wants to—"

"Reckon I know what he wants," she interrupted, "but he ain't one for a quick tussle in the broom closet. He takes it real seriously, Master Jeffrey does. He's in love with you, and it's more than just a bit-a fun he's interested in. You want to be careful, luv."

"Nothing—nothing's going to happen."

"I wouldn't count on that. Nature takes its course. What you want to do, you want to be sensible about it. You want to enjoy it while it lasts and not go expectin' the moon."

"I don't expect anything."

"He'll want to marry you," she continued. "That's the way he's made, but of course Lord Robert would never permit that. He'd find some way to prevent it happenin'."

Mrs. Rawson stood up and shook out the silk, a great length of it all sewn neatly together. "Now comes the hemmin'," she said, "and then we'll gather it and fasten it to the waistband, add the lace trimmin' when we've finished everything else. The way I see it, luv, you got two choices. You can resist him when he starts wooin' in earnest, or you can become his mistress and consider yourself lucky to have a man like Master

Jeffrey on them terms, knowin' there'll be heartache later on."

"I still think you're mistaken," I said. "He—he merely asked me to go to church with him."

"And you're goin' to look smashin'," she replied. "When we're done with these new things you're goin' to look like a bloomin' duchess. Here, luv, I'll let you do the hemmin', that part always bores me. I'll cut the satin for the gown."

She said no more on the subject of love, preferring instead to gossip about the household staff. We worked industriously, finishing the underskirts that evening, and we continued to meet in the sewing room each evening, finishing the gown late Saturday night. It had elbow-length sleeves and a low, scooped bodice. The skirt belled out beautifully over the lace-trimmed underskirts. Mrs. Rawson had found some pale coral-pink velvet ribbon and trimmed the bottom of the sleeves and the edge of the neckline with it, three inches of ruffled lace dangling beneath the rim of ribbon. I modeled the gown for her, and she clapped her hands in delight.

"Cunnin'!" she declared. "Just cunnin'! You *do* look like a duchess."

"You don't think it's a—a bit low in front?"

"They're wearin' 'em that way," she informed me. "It wouldn't do for some of them fine ladies to sneeze, they'd pop right out."

"I feel—rather uneasy. I've never worn anything so low."

"With a bosom like yours, luv, you oughta feel proud as punch. Dudn't hurt to show off your assets."

"I just wonder if I should show quite so *much*."

Mrs. Rawson cackled and gave me an exuberant hug, and I thanked her again for her kindness.

"Hadn't enjoyed myself so much in a long time," she vowed. "Lordy!" she exclaimed, eyeing the clock. "It is ten o'clock already? I promised Jim I'd meet him at The Red Lion tonight, and it'll take me a good twenty minutes to get there. I'd better start toddlin', luv."

She bustled across the room, skirts crackling noisily, and at the door she turned, a mischievous grin on her lips.

"He says he's got somethin' to show me," she explained. "I'd be willin' to bet I've seen it a number-a times already!"

I smiled at her ribaldry and later, in my bedroom, hung the gown and petticoat in the wardrobe and thought about our conversation. I wondered if Jeffrey Mowrey would indeed begin to woo me "in earnest." Surely Mrs. Rawson was wrong about that. He was merely being kind to his son's governess. But what if she was right? I knew that any kind of relationship between Jeffrey Mowrey and me could only lead to grief. If he did begin to woo me, would I be able to resist him?

I doubted I would even try.

I was extremely nervous next morning as I went downstairs to meet Jeffrey Mowrey. I had brushed my hair until it gleamed with a rich coppery sheen, and Mrs. Rawson had helped me arrange it in a particularly attractive style, waves stacked artfully on top of my head, three long ringlets dangling down in back. The satin gown made a soft, silken rustle as I moved down the steps. I might not look like a duchess, but I certainly felt like one. It was the most splendid garment I had ever worn.

He was waiting for me in the hall, dressed all in black except for a white lace jabot that spilled over his vest. The knee breeches and coat were a sumptuous black brocade, but the effect was not at all sober. He looked incredibly handsome, young, radiant, a gentle smile on his lips as he took my hand. For a moment it seemed as though I could hardly breathe.

"I see you found a dress," he remarked. "Have you a cloak? I'm afraid the road might be dusty."

"There wasn't time to—" I caught myself. "I don't have a cloak that would go with the gown."

Jeffrey tilted his head slightly, thinking, and then he clicked his tongue. "You'll need one," he informed me. "Perhaps one of mine will do. There's a rather elegant brown silk. It'll be much too large, of course, but it'll keep the dust from spoiling that—uh—most remarkable gown."

He told me to wait and strode briskly down the hall, disappearing and returning a few moments later with a heavy brown silk cloak which he wrapped around my shoulders, tying the laces at my throat. The heavy folds covered me completely, sweeping to the floor. He put on the black silk cloak he had tossed over one of the chairs earlier, and we went outside to the open carriage that was waiting. A footman stood holding the reins.

"It's a lovely morning," Jeffrey said, helping me up onto the seat upholstered in dark blue. "The sky is clear. The sun is shining. Great morning for a drive."

He climbed up beside me and took the reins, clicking them

sharply, and the handsome grays started around the drive. I was acutely aware of his nearness, his leg almost touching mine, and I was fascinated by those strong, beautifully shaped hands that handled the reins with such ease and authority. I was thrown against him briefly as the wheels jostled over a rut. Once we reached the main road to the village the horses clipped along at a steady pace. A vista of great beauty opened up before us.

Far, far ahead the village rested in a fold of the land, looking like a toy village from this distance, gray and brown and rust and tan, tiny green puffs the tops of trees, a tiny copper spire catching the morning sunlight and throwing it back in bright spokes. To our right the land sloped to the edge of the majestic cliffs, the waves slashing at rocks below, and to our left were the moors I had come to appreciate. The only blemish on the landscape was the huge factory that squatted bleak and black and gray beyond the village. Even on this Sunday morning the furnaces glowed a fierce red orange in the distance, and spirals of ugly black smoke rose from the stacks.

"Still interested in seeing the Roman ruins?" Jeffrey asked.

"Very interested," I replied. "I find such things fascinating."

"There were some fierce battles on those slopes," he informed me. "In olden days the Romans had a garrison on top of the hill, and a great wall ran along the top. They were in constant danger from the Druids, never knowing when those blue-painted savages were going to come screeching up the hill with their spears and axes."

"That must have been terrifying."

"I used to love to visit the ruins when I was a little boy," he told me. "I played among the stones and walked along the remains of the wall, pretending I was a Roman legionnaire in breastplate and plumed helmet. Mrs. Rawson made me a fine red cape to wear. Other times I'd streak my face with blue paint and creep up on the ruins with a stone ax I'd made. I felt very savage. Later on, when I was much older, I used to go to the ruins with a knapsack of food and a bottle of wine and a volume of poetry. I'd sit on the stones and read poetry for hours, often aloud, I fear. I loved the music of the words."

"I love poetry, too," I confessed.

"I knew you would," he replied. "I sensed it. We'll visit the ruins this week."

"Douglas will enjoy that."

"Oh, I don't imagine we'll take him along. I want to show them to you properly, and that means a great deal of walking and climbing and clambering over the stones. He'd tire out much too soon, and there's danger of falling when you walk along the wall."

"I see."

He had played among the ruins himself when he was not much older than Douglas, but he clearly didn't want the boy to come along. He wanted to be alone with me, and I knew full well what that signified. As the carriage bowled along behind the spanking grays with their gleaming coats, I had the feeling I was in the middle of a dream. The movement of the carriage, the music of the wheels skimming over the road, the strength and warmth of the man beside me: All seemed part of a romantic dream that must surely evaporate when I awakened.

The village was nearer now. I could make out details of thatched cottages and rows of ancient stone dwellings that had been old when Elizabeth reigned. We were soon moving beneath the oak trees, passing shops and the village green. Jeffrey left the carriage in the yard across from the church, tossing a coin to the flaxen-haired lad who looked after the horses. The church was very old, the rough-hewn brown stones mellow with age, faintly green with moss. Oak trees grew on either side, their limbs casting blue-gray shadows over the walls. There was a walled cemetery in back, the yard in shadow, dingy white marble tombstones visible behind the low wall.

A bell was tolling. People were moving up the flat stone steps and into the dim recess beyond. Jeffrey took my arm and led me inside, removing his cloak and hanging it on a peg, helping me remove mine. Three fashionable young ladies came in behind us, chattering gaily, and the moment I saw them I felt a sinking sensation in my stomach. Their gowns were simple, exquisitely simple, one blue, one gray, one deep pink, all with long, tight sleeves, fine lace fichus covering throat and shoulders. Their hair was worn in high pompadours, no artful waves, no dangling ringlets.

They stared at me and tittered, nudging each other. Jeffrey took my elbow and led me down the aisle to the Mowrey pew. I could feel people staring and hear the whispers that followed in our wake. My dress was all wrong, an outlandish garment worthy only of mirth, and my hairstyle was outrageous. Jeffrey had known that the moment he saw me coming down the stairs, but he had been too gallant and polite to say anything. He helped me into the pew and sat down beside me, giving my hand a reassuring squeeze.

Candles glowed in the semidarkness, golden flames wavering, washing the pulpit with soft light. My cheeks burned, and I desperately longed for the cloak to cover myself. My misery was so intense that I was hardly aware of the service that ensued. The Reverend Mr. Williams delivered an eloquent serman on Christian love, but I heard scarcely a word. When it was over, when we stood up to leave, I felt numb. I knew I couldn't face all those people, not dressed in this ludicrous homemade gown.

"Courage," Jeffrey said.

"You—you knew the dress was wrong."

"*I* think you're beautiful, Honora."

He closed his fingers about my elbow and led me up the aisle. A small crowd had gathered in the vestibule. The three young ladies were standing side by side, mockery in their eyes as Jeffrey took down our cloaks and placed them over his arm. Several people came over to greet him and welcome him back from his travels. He introduced me to each one, his manner extremely casual. It seemed all the gentry in the county had come to service this morning. One of the young ladies laughed shrilly and, nudged forward by her friends, minced over with much rustling of stiff pink taffeta.

"Hello, Jeffrey," she simpered. "It's so nice to have you back."

"It's good to be back, Lucinda. I'd like you to meet my son's governess, Miss James. Honora, Miss Lucinda Carrington."

"Charmed," Miss Carrington said, giving me a cursory glance. "When are you coming to Greystone Manor, Jeffrey? We're ever so eager to hear about your trip."

"I've no idea, Lucinda. I've been very busy since I returned."

"So I *see*," she retorted.

She scurried back over to her friends and all three of them tittered. Jeffrey led me out of the church, his face expressionless. I longed to sink into the ground and vanish. I felt naked. I held my head high and somehow managed to hold back the tears of shame, and then I felt rough, sturdy hands clasping mine and looked into Reverend Williams's warm, beautiful face. He stood at the foot of the steps, greeting people as they came out, and as he looked at me his kind brown eyes were full of warmth.

"Honora, my dear, I'm so pleased to see you again."

"Reverend Williams. It—it was a lovely service."

The curate smiled. "I fear you heard little of it, my child. You seemed to be in a trance."

"I—I feel a bit peaked."

"You need a hearty meal," he informed me. "You and Jeffrey will take lunch with me. Miss Moffat, my housekeeper, is preparing a gargantuan meal, far too much for young Jack and me to eat by ourselves."

"Young Jack?" Jeffrey inquired.

Reverend Williams shook his head and assumed an expression of mock despair. "My nephew. He's destined for a career in the church, and his parents thought it would do him good to spend a few months with me and see the less glamorous side of the church. He's my chief aide and assistant and, I fear, the bane of my existence."

He spoke with great affection, and I could see that he was immensely fond of the lad.

"You two stroll on over to the vicarage," he said. "I imagine young Jack is already there. I'll join you shortly."

"Reverend Williams," I began, "I really don't think we—"

"We'd be delighted to lunch with you," Jeffrey said firmly.

The vicarage was just across the way, a cozy stone dwelling sheltered by oak trees, an elaborate flower garden in back. The housekeeper let us in. She was a tall, bony woman with a put-upon expression and iron gray hair fastened in a tight bun. She wiped her hands on her apron and led us into the large, comfortable study with its shabby furniture and pleasant clutter of books, papers, and plants.

"The boy will be with you shortly," she said brusquely. "I must go back to the kitchen. Company, always company, and he never says a word to me. I'll water the gravy and slice the roast thin!"

Jeffrey chuckled as the woman left the room. "Miss Moffat hasn't changed a bit. She loves to play the martyr. If she didn't have something to grumble about, she wouldn't know what to do."

"Why did you let me wear this dress?" I asked, a catch in my voice.

"It's a lovely dress, Honora."

"You knew I looked ridiculous."

"On the contrary, you look quite lovely."

"They—they were laughing at me."

Jeffrey frowned and stepped over to me, placing his hands on my shoulders. His blue eyes were serious, and when he spoke his voice was quiet, full of conviction.

"You must never worry about what people think, Honora," he told me. "You must never let others dictate to you, let their narrow ideas and opinions influence your conduct. Lucinda Carrington was extremely rude, yes, and she and her little friends laughed at you, but you're worth ten of them."

I looked into those eyes and seemed to drown in them. His fingers tightened on my shoulders, and his wide pink lips parted. I knew he was going to kiss me. My pulse seemed to stop. There was a fraction of a second of sheer panic, and then my whole being seemed to fill with aching anticipation so intense I feared I might swoon. Jeffrey tilted his head slightly to one side and leaned his head down, his mouth inches from my own.

A merry racket sounded in the hall outside. He released me abruptly and stepped back as Reverend Williams's young nephew came into the room, smiling a breezy smile and looking for all the world like a preposterous young dandy. His brown pumps had silver buckles. His white stockings were thin cotton pretending to be silk. His knee breeches and frock coat were brown linen, his waistcoat tan and silver striped satin, and an emerald green neckcloth was tucked plushly beneath his throat.

"I'm Jack," he said, "Jack Jordon. My uncle always has guests to dine after Sunday services and I was hoping it would be you. You're Jeffrey Mowrey. I missed you when you came by before—I was helping the sexton dig a grave, bloody hard work, that! You don't have to introduce me to Miss James. I know her already, just from hearing my uncle talk about her."

He executed a gallant bow that looked utterly ludicrous accompanied as it was with that wide grin. The lad had bright red hair, mischievous brown eyes and a plethora of freckles. His mouth could only be called saucy.

"You look quite spruce," Jeffrey remarked.

"I don't *of*ten get to dress up," the lad complained. "My uncle keeps me horribly busy, digging graves, ringing bells, polishing brass—he takes it all quite seriously! My parents sent me these clothes from London, the second best tailor in the city ran them up, and, truth to tell, this is the first time I've had an opportunity to wear them."

He turned around to display the tails of his frock coat, inordinately proud of his finery.

"My uncle says I'm much too worldly," he confided, "but that's why I'm *here* you see. I'm destined for a career in the church, my parents won't have it any other way, and they thought maybe some of my uncle's goodness and humility would rub off on me if I spent time with him."

"You need a good thrashing," Jeffrey teased.

"That's what my uncle says. I'm really quite devout, though. I'm sixteen years old, and I suspect by the time I'm twenty I'll be reverent as can be and go around with my eyes downcast, praying a lot."

I couldn't help but smile. There had been a moment of acute disappointment when the lad pranced in, interrupting that kiss-to-be, but now I was relieved he had come in when he had. Young Jack Jordon was an absurd, endearing creature, and his bright chatter was just the tonic I needed. The shame and humiliation I had felt earlier vanished.

"I imagine I'll have a very fashionable parish," Jack continued, "preferably in a smart district of London. All the spoiled wives in their fancy gowns will come to me with their problems and I'll be a great comfort to them. Their rich husbands will fill the coffers with gold."

"Which you'll use to do good work," Jeffrey added.

"*Nat*urally!"

"Frivolous scamp," Reverend Williams remarked, strolling into the room to join us. "I'm trying to get all that worldly nonsense out of his head. I fear it's an uphill battle all the way."

He had changed into a simple, roughly woven brown robe with a cord tied loosely around the waist, and he looked as though he should be feeding birds in some remote monastery. Reverend Williams had devoted his life to his fellow man, serving as best he could while his more ambitious colleagues rose in the tightly structured hierarchy of the church. Content to be a humble curate, he seemed to radiate an aura of goodness. A few thin wisps of light brown hair were brushed over his head, and his tan face was pleasantly lined. A smile was always playing on his small mouth, while his gentle brown eyes were true reflections of his soul.

"Miss Moffat is still banging about pots and pans in the kitchen," he confided, "but lunch will be served shortly."

"There're cherry tarts," Jack told us. "My favorites!"

"The rascal has her wrapped around his little finger," Reverend Williams said wearily. "She scolds him and chases him out of the kitchen and pretends to be immune to his crafty charm, but he's cast a spell over her nevertheless. I detest cherry tarts," he added.

Young Jack perched on the arm of a chair, looking very pleased with himself. I had no doubt he would eventually achieve his goal. The smart ladies in their fancy clothes would dote on him, and he would regularly frequent their fashionable salons. Worldly clergymen were always in demand.

Lunch was indeed gargantuan, a lavish repast served grudgingly by the dour Miss Moffat. Although she scowled at him fiercely, I noticed that she gave extra large helpings to the saucy red-haired youth. Conversation was easy and relaxed. Reverend Williams discussed his work in the parish and asked me how Douglas and I were doing. I talked about the progress we had made, and Jeffrey said his son had become a new boy since my arrival. He told us about his journeys in Italy, describing the ruins, the museums, the many splendors of the countryside. Young Jack listened attentively. For all his sass, he was extremely respectful of his elders and clearly worshiped his uncle. I could sense that the lively youth brought much joy into the old man's life.

After lunch Jeffrey expressed interest in seeing the new Latin texts Reverend Williams had recently added to his collection.

"I'll show them to you!" Jack said eagerly. "I read Latin fluently. Already. Greek, too. When I get to Oxford I'm going to amaze them!"

"You're going to Oxford?" Jeffrey inquired.

"You've *got* to go to Oxford to get anywhere in the church," Jack retorted. "You've got to have connections, too."

"Oh?"

"Dean Swift himself's gonna sponsor me. He knows my parents well. Have you read any of his books?"

"One or two," Jeffrey said.

"I think *Gulliver's Travels* is smashing."

"*A Modest Proposal* is more to my liking," Jeffrey replied. "He proposes that certain infants should be eaten at birth. It would not only solve the hunger problem, but it would also help control the population. I wonder if he had you in mind when he wrote it?"

"I was an *enchanting* infant," the youth protested. "Ask anyone."

Jeffrey laughed, slinging his arm around Jack's shoulders and leading him out of the room. Reverend Williams asked if I would like to see the gardens, and the two of us went outside. He fetched an old straw bonnet and a pair of shears from the potting shed and began to fill the bonnet with flowers as we strolled leisurely along the walks.

"You seem to be doing quite well, Honora," he remarked.

"I—I'm very pleased with my position at Mowrey House."

"I wanted to get you away from the school in Bath," he told me. "That was no place for you, but it was the best I could arrange at the time. I had reservations about arranging this position for you, too."

"Reservations?"

Reverend Williams added pale blue flowers to the purple and white blossoms already in the bonnet. "Lord Robert Mowrey is a hard man, a vengeful man, people say, and he can be quite ruthless."

"I—I've heard that."

"You're terribly young and still quite impressionable. I feared you might do something to—" He hesitated, carefully searching for the right words. "To incur his wrath," he concluded.

"Oh?"

"He's extremely attached to his brother, Honora."

"I know that."

Reverend Williams snipped several delicate yellow flowers and added them to the collection. He straightened up and sighed, looking at me with gentle brown eyes that seemed to search my soul.

"You've grown into a very attractive young woman, Honora."

"Thank you, Reverend Williams."

"Your parents would have been very proud of you. I'm proud of you myself. I—" He hesitated again, frowning. "I hope you won't do anything foolish, my child."

I lowered my eyes, waiting for him to continue. He took a piece of string from his pocket and began to bind the flowers together at the stems, making a lovely multicolored bouquet.

"Jeffrey is fond of you," he said. "It's—quite innocent at this stage, you're both fine young people. For your own sake, child, see that it stays that way."

He handed me the bouquet, indicating that the subject was closed, and we went back inside. Jeffrey and I made our departure a few minutes later, Jack and Reverend Williams accompanying us to the carriage.

"Give my regards to Mrs. Rawson," the curate said. "There's a merry sinner I still hope to reform."

"You've a rough job on your hands there," Jeffrey replied. "Our Mrs. Rawson doesn't take to reform."

"She's an excellent woman, good-hearted, full of charity. Weak, alas. I haven't given up on her."

We bade them good-bye and started back to Mowrey House. The sun was shining with a pale, silvery radiance, and floating clouds caused light shadows to move over the land. Jeffrey Mowrey was in a pensive mood, not inclined to talk, and I didn't care to talk either. I kept thinking about that ecstatic moment of anticipation when his mouth sought mine, and I knew that I was weak, too, as weak as Mrs. Rawson ever hoped to be.

I gathered the folds of the brown silk cloak closer about me, gazing at the road ahead without seeing it. I thought of Reverend Williams's words. The gentle old curate had sensed my feelings, too, just as Mrs. Rawson had, and he had tried his best to warn me. I was afraid. For the first time I realized that the man beside me presented a much greater threat than his brother, and the reasons lay inside my own heart.

7

I DIDN'T SEE JEFFREY MOWREY FOR THE NEXT TWO days. Perhaps he had had second thoughts about showing me the ruins. Perhaps he, too, understood the danger and planned to avoid it. It would be far, far better were he to call on Lucinda Carrington or one of her friends and forget all about his son's governess. It would be better for both of us, I knew, yet those two days were torment. Knowing that he was under the same roof yet not seeing him caused anguish I had never dreamed possible.

I kept telling myself that it was for the best, but I had already lost reason where Jeffrey was concerned.

Wednesday was gloomy, the sky a light gray filled with darker gray clouds that floated restlessly across its surface, the sunlight a thin, silvery white. Douglas was in a particularly foul mood, refusing to concentrate on our lessons, and it was with considerable relief that I finally saw to his lunch and put him to bed for his afternoon nap. It was one-thirty. I was alone in the nursery, gazing out at the gloomy sky, feeling desolate indeed. Hearing footsteps in the hall, I turned.

Jeffrey Mowrey stepped into the nursery, carrying a heavy basket covered with a white linen cloth, a loaf of French bread sticking out one side, a bottle of wine visible, too.

"You haven't had lunch," he observed.

"I—I wasn't hungry."

"I haven't eaten yet either. I had Cook fix a basket for us, stole another bottle of my brother's wine."

"You—"

"I promised to show you the ruins, remember? I thought we might as well take a picnic lunch along. The brat's asleep, right? Mrs. Rawson promised to keep an eye on him when he wakes up. I told her we'd probably be gone most of the afternoon."

"But—"

"Don't you *want* to see the ruins, Honora?"

"Of course I do, but—this doesn't seem a particularly auspicious afternoon for it. It's certain to rain."

"Afraid of a little wet weather?"

"I don't relish the idea of getting soaked."

Jeffrey grinned. He was wearing old black boots, faded blue breeches, a ribbed white cambric shirt that had seen much better days, and he looked absolutely beautiful with that unruly blond hair and that grin curling so amiably on his mouth. I was wearing the sprigged blue muslin again, and I fervently wished I had something fresh and lovely to change into.

"I'll fetch a couple of heavy cloaks," he said. "I'll meet you in the back hall in five minutes."

"I really think we should—"

"No arguments," he said with mock sternness. "I'm a gentle

man, true, ordinarily the soul of politeness, but I can be quite ugly when I'm crossed. Argue with me and I'm likely to punch you in the mouth."

I smiled, unable to resist it. He smiled, too, and when I met him downstairs I felt a marvelous elation, as though I had just consumed several glasses of the finest champagne. He had already swathed himself in a heavy cloak of navy blue broadcloth, and he helped me into one of royal blue linen lined with watered blue silk. It completely enveloped me, and I savored the faint smell of perspiration and leather. Jeffrey picked up the basket, took my arm and led me outside.

There was a clap of thunder. The sky was an even darker gray. He held my arm firmly, as though he feared I might try to break away.

"I still think this is a foolish idea," I protested. "We should put it off until—"

"The weather'll enhance the atmosphere of the ruins," he said. "Besides, there's plenty of shelter."

"You—you seem to be in an unusually good mood."

"I'm looking foward to seeing the ruins again, and I happen to be with the most beautiful woman in all of Cornwall."

"You mustn't say such things."

"Why not? It's true, Honora."

"I—"

"Do you realize you've never called me by name? Is it so difficult to pronounce the word 'Jeffrey'?"

"You—you're my employer. I—"

"Honora," he said, "don't you know we're already beyond that? I knew the minute I saw you that ours was not going to be an employer-employee relationship."

"We'd better go back," I said. My voice was shaky.

"Afraid?"

"Yes. Yes, I am. I'm your son's governess. I—"

I couldn't continue. I didn't want to. I fell silent, and Jeffrey was silent, too, leading me across the moors as the grass stirred in the wind and the clouds overhead grew heavier, casting dark shadows over the ground. The land began to slope upward, and we were soon climbing the hill that gradually rose. Mowrey House was far behind us now, and reality seemed to be behind us as well. This wasn't real. It was all a dream: the wind, the darkening sky, the man beside me, the strong fingers that still held my arm in so tight a grip. I was dreaming, and I was afraid, yet the elation was so powerful I was dizzy from it. My blue muslin skirt billowed, lifting, blowing against my legs, and skeins of auburn hair blew across my eyes. Both our cloaks rose behind us like wildly flapping wings.

I was exhausted when we finally reached the top of the hill. It was covered with ancient graystone ruins, fallen pillars, stone-lined pits, part of a building still standing with roof partially intact. The stones were pitted and worn from the elements, streaked with rust, green with moss, and there were thin vines covered with strangely shaped purple wildflowers I couldn't identify. I saw part of the famous Roman wall, several feet high, at least three yards wide on top, and I could imagine Roman legionnaires patrolling it with bronze shields in front of them, spears in hand, their helmet plumes waving as they looked out for the savage blue-painted warriors bent on their destruction.

"Impressive, isn't it?" Jeffrey asked, setting down the basket.

"It—it's lovely."

"I've always had a fondness for ruins. These aren't nearly as spectacular as some of those in Northumberland, but I love them just the same. Want to walk along the wall?"

"Is it safe?"

"If you're careful."

He led me over to the wall, climbed up with nimble, athletic ease and then reached down to help me, encircling my wrists with those strong hands, pulling as I got a foothold on the crumbling stone. He was so very strong, I thought as I stood shakily beside him. He encircled my waist, steadying me, and I felt his warmth, felt those taut muscles. Sensitive he might be, thoughtful and polite and soft-spoken, but he was in superb physical condition.

"You all right?" he inquired.

"Just—just a little dizzy. It's so—so *high*."

The wall stretched for perhaps a quarter of a mile before crumbling into a pile of stones, and standing on it one could look out over the whole countryside. The moors stretched below us, brown and tan and gray, tinged with purple, and one could see the sea, too, a deep blue-gray merging into a misty purple horizon. I gazed, still a bit dizzy. I could see the village far, far in the distance, and Mowrey House was like a tiny dolls' house surrounded by minuscule gardens. The sky was very dark. The wind stopped abruptly, and there was a sullen stillness, as though the earth were holding its breath.

"Careful," Jeffrey said. "It's very uneven here on top of the wall, rough and pitted."

He unwound his arm from my waist and took my hand, holding it tightly as we walked slowly along the wall. Both of us were silent, lost in thought. I wondered if he felt the same delicious strain, the same suspense and feeling of anticipation that gripped me. Nervous though I was, I felt a strange inner calmness as well, a peculiar sense of acceptance. What would happen would happen, and there was nothing I could do about it. All my training, all the words of wisdom and warning were as nothing in the face of these sensations Jeffrey Mowrey aroused. The prim, demure girl had vanished forever, supplanted by a woman who knew instinctively all those secrets denied the girl. Love had indeed transformed me, and I was ready for that final step that would banish the girl forever. Silently, I acknowledged this, silently accepted.

The clouds had almost obscured the sky. The air was still, not a breath of wind blowing, and there was a curious light— pale opal, translucent. It was going to rain soon. We strolled along the wall for several more minutes, silent, and then Jeffrey climbed down and reached up to assist me. He swung me toward him and held me close for a moment before setting me on my feet. He seemed suddenly shy, bothered. He knew as well as I what was going to happen, and he was disturbed by it. Jeffrey Mowrey was no callous seducer of virgins, no amoral rake whose delight it was to despoil. He felt very deeply about me, and he knew those feelings were much stronger than the qualms that plagued him.

It had grown very warm. He removed his cloak, removed mine, looked into my eyes as though to determine whether or not I felt the same way. I reached up to touch his cheek, stroking it gently, and it was perfectly natural, right. I ran the ball of my thumb along the smooth, full curve of his lower lip, looking all the while into those grave, tormented blue eyes. Curiously enough, it seemed I was the more experienced one, the new maturity inside giving me knowledge he had yet to acquire.

"I love you, Honora," he said.

"I know that."

"I think I loved you from the first moment I saw you."

"I know."

"You—" He hesitated, frowning.

"I felt the same way, Jeffrey."

"It—I never thought I'd love again. I never thought it would be possible to feel this way again. It—it just happened."

"It happened," I said.

"I don't want to hurt you. I don't want to cause you pain." I touched his cheek, stroked his temple.

"You're beautiful," he said. "So beautiful. So good. So pure."

"Jeffrey—"

"We should go back. We should go back now."

"We should," I agreed.

"Honora—"

He pulled me to him then and held me tightly, so tightly, and I clung to him, molding my body against his, holding to that strength. There was a distant rumble of thunder. It grew louder, nearer. Lightning flashed, raking at the sky with skeletal silver fingers, illuminating the earth with a blinding silver blue. Jeffrey held me, crushing me to him as the rain began to fall in huge, heavy drops that splattered violently all around us. He released me and grabbed the cloaks and grabbed the basket, leading the way quickly to shelter, the corner of a building still partially covered by a roof.

Jeffrey set the basket down and spread the cloaks over the ground while I shook my skirts and wiped damp auburn tendrils from my cheeks. His blond hair was wet, plastered to his skull, a darker blond wet, and his thin white shirt clung damply to his skin. The rain came down furiously, pounding noisily on the small section of roof, sheets of it swirling only a few feet away from us, blowing wildly in the wind. Jeffrey shook his head and wiped rivulets of water from his cheeks and then looked at me. I smiled and sat down on the cloaks, immediately surprised at how soft the ground was, and then I realized there were several inches of dried moss beneath the cloaks.

A fine spray of mist blew in on us. Jeffrey kneeled down beside me, and I could see that he was extremely nervous. He frowned, his blue eyes so serious, filled with apprehension. He wanted me desperately, and he was afraid, shy now, awkward despite all his experience. I understood the reasons why. I reached up and rubbed the bridge of his nose, erasing that deep frown. Gently, hesitantly, he took my hand and kissed my palm and then leaned down to kiss my cheek, my temple, the curve of my throat. I placed my hands on his arms and ran my palms up and around his shoulders, pulling him nearer.

"Honora," he whispered.

"It's all right, Jeffrey."

"I don't want to—"

"I want you," I said.

"It's—I wish I—"

"It's all right."

He fastened his mouth over mine, and I closed my eyes and sank back onto the cloaks and pulled him down with me. Moss rustled beneath me. The rain pounded. I was oblivious to everything but that mouth, this magic, this marvelous beauty that blossomed inside me as his kiss grew more frantic, frenzied. I writhed beneath him, shifting my position, lifting my skirts, crushed beneath the weight of his body, warmed by his warmth, moaning softly as he raised his head and looked into my eyes and then kissed me again, tenderly, tenderly, trying so hard to restrain the urgency that possessed him.

How did I, who had never loved, know so well how to respond, how to move to those age-old melodies in the blood? He entered me, and I gasped as that smooth, warm hardness penetrated, soft as velvet, strong as steel, and I lifted my hips to meet him, to help him. Flesh caressed flesh, a delicious ache swelling with agonizing intensity, spreading, growing as he stroked, plunging deeper and deeper. There was a moment of excruciating pain as flesh was torn asunder and something burst inside me, and I gripped his back, pulling him closer still as the pain melted and merged into an ecstatic sensation that seemed to wrack my soul, hurtling me into a paradise of unbelievable pleasure.

He gave one final thrust, groaning, rigid atop me, shuddering, then falling limp as fountains of feeling enveloped us both. I held him to me as the fires of love cooled to that gorgeous glow of aftermath. I knew now. Now I was complete, part of a whole, and tears welled in my eyes, spilling over my lashes. Jeffrey saw the tears and kissed them away as I stroked his still-damp hair, running my fingers through those heavy locks.

"I'm sorry," he whispered. "Don't cry."

"I can't help it. I—I'm so happy."

"I love you, Honora. You must know that."

"I love *you*."

We held each other as the rain slackened, and we made love again and it was even better, beautiful, and the rain stopped and the sun gradually began to shine as we adjusted our clothing

and ate the food Cook had prepared for us. We drank the wine
and looked at each other and smiled, and he kissed me again
and held me in his arms, stroking my hair, stroking my back,
silently conveying his love for me. A sweet languor still possessed me, a marvelous ache lingering in my bones, and as I
ran my palms up his back and rubbed his shoulders I trembled
with happiness so blissful it was almost overwhelming.

The sky was clear as we walked slowly down the hillside
and began to cross the moors. It had long since stopped raining,
and the moors seemed to shimmer with late afternoon sunlight.
Our clothes had dried. The grass was dry, too, rustling quietly
in the faint breeze. Jeffrey held my hand, swinging the basket
at his side. Neither of us spoke. There was no need for words.
As we neared Mowrey House he let go of my hand and sighed,
and I turned to look back at those ruins barely visible now in
the distance. I said a silent good-bye to the girl who had existed
before, and her ghost seemed to wave a similar good-bye to
the woman I had become.

HOW CAN I DESCRIBE THE WEEKS THAT FOLLOWED?
Even now I marvel that such happiness could ever be possible
for any woman. I seemed to move in another realm, and even
the air I breathed seemed to take on a marvelous new quality,
inebriating, exalting. I was in the middle of a shimmering,
enchanting dream, yet I was wide awake and alive to every
sensation. The reality I had known before seemed a vague,
distant thing, not real at all. Before Jeffrey, I had been a poor
creature, surviving, existing, but now I was suffused with that
special magic that gives life meaning.

When I was with him, my bliss knew no bounds, and when
I was alone, when I was in the nursery with Douglas or chatting
with Mrs. Rawson, I was acutely aware of his presence nearby.
I maintained a calm facade, cool and efficient with Douglas,

light and jocular with Mrs. Rawson, but always, always my heart seemed to sing: Jeffrey is downstairs in the library, Jeffrey is in the study with his brother, Jeffrey is riding his stallion, now he will be passing through the village, now he will be nearing the factory, in two hours he will be home again.

Try though I might, I couldn't completely conceal my happiness. Often I would pause in the middle of a lesson and gaze out the window and smile to myself. My eyes, I knew, would take on that glow I saw in the mirror when I was thinking of Jeffrey, and when this happened young Douglas would tilt his head to one side and examine me with great interest. Fortunately, these lapses were few, and Doug considered them merely another of the natural eccentricities common to all adults. Mrs. Rawson noticed the change in me, of course. She knew at once what had happened that day at the ruins, but for once she was tactful, giving me an occasional pleased smile and knowing look but maintaining a discreet silence.

Jeffrey continued to visit the nursery, but he did not come as often and he seldom stayed for more than a few minutes. Only rarely did he accompany us on our walks, and then he gave almost all his attention to Douglas, scuffling with him playfully, regaling him with preposterous tales, giving him an occasional stern lecture on the importance of our lessons and an admonishment to "Mind Miss James or you'll wish you had!" I was his son's governess, and his manner was polite and formal, no more. To placate his brother, he spent more and more time at the factory, displaying an interest he was far from feeling, and at least three evenings a week they held long conferences in Robert's office. Jeffrey went over the books. He asked intelligent questions. He detested every minute of it, but it was necessary.

"I need time, Honora," he told me. "I need to—to formulate some kind of plan. I don't want to cause Robert any unnecessary pain. He'll have to know eventually, of course, but—"

"I understand, Jeffrey."

"He mustn't suspect."

"I understand," I repeated. "It must be this way."

"Not for long," he said. "Not for long—I promise you."

On several occasions he donned his best attire and drove to Greystone Manor to visit Lucinda Carrington. I suffered then. Although I knew his paying calls on her was merely part of the subterfuge, I suffered agonies of totally unreasonable jealousy. He didn't care anything about Miss Carrington, didn't even like her, in fact, but she was his kind. She was patrician and she was pretty, exactly the sort of girl people would expect him to pay court to and eventually marry. Jeffrey Mowrey could never marry his son's governess. I was fully aware of that, and I put the knowledge away, refusing to dwell on it.

Lord Robert was not at all pleased with his brother's visits to Greystone Manor and had several sarcastic comments to make about "the empty-headed little fool" who entertained him there. Jeffrey defended Miss Carrington with considerable gallantry and enumerated her charms for his scowling brother. The visits were entirely for Robert's benefit, I knew, and Lucinda was merely a red herring to throw him off the scent, but I suffered nevertheless.

Convinced I no longer presented any kind of threat, Lord Robert seemed to have forgotten my existence. On the rare occasions when I happened to encounter him, he gave me a stiff, severe nod and glanced at me as he might glance at a piece of furniture that just happened to be mobile. That unpleasant meeting in his office might never have occurred. His brother had kept me from being dismissed, true, but not because of any personal interest in me. Jeffrey Mowrey saw me simply as a governess, pretty, perhaps, rather dull but extremely competent, and his older brother had other things to worry about now: drawing Jeffrey into the family business, keeping him at Mowrey House and out of the clutches of Lucinda Carrington.

But Lord Robert didn't know the truth.

He didn't know about those secret trysts late at night after everyone else had gone to sleep. During the day Jeffrey's manner toward me may have been formal and polite, but at night in that small bedroom in the unused east wing . . . at night he was wonderfully passionate and virile, loving me fiercely, straining every muscle to savor my body to the fullest, loving me gently, stroking my flesh, murmuring soft, sweet words, his eyes aglow with love in the flickering light of one single candle. He usually wore only a robe of heavy brown silk brocade, the folds falling loosely, his legs bare, and I wore a nightgown of fine white lawn. We met after midnight, each moving stealthily along separate corridors to the room, and once inside he always embraced me with bone-crushing strength, and I clung to him, trembling, both of us eager to savor the joy awaiting us. Later I returned to my room, he to his, and no one was the wiser. Night after night after night...and during the day a glorious anticipation that made it even more sublime.

It was right. It was beautiful. It was meant to be. I felt no shame. I knew that the world would consider me an amoral woman. I knew that I was going against all my moral training, all my religious convictions, but they meant nothing in the face of my love for Jeffrey Mowrey. I loved him with a rapturous intensity that filled my very soul with shimmering, magical beauty, and Jeffrey loved me, too. It would have to end, I realized that. I realized he would eventually have to abandon me, would eventually marry someone like Lucinda Carrington and take his proper place in society, but I was heedless of the future. There would be pain. There would be heartbreak. I was still sensible enough to know that, but this marvelous now was all that mattered. The future would take care of itself.

And so the weeks passed, weeks of unbelievable beauty, each day filled with delicious anticipation, each night swollen with bliss, and it grew cooler outside and the skies turned a slate gray, filled with threatening clouds that never seemed to disappear. The wind howled across the moors, whistling around the corners of the house, and below the cliff waves slashed angrily against the rocks. The cold outside merely intensified the warmth within and somehow seemed to augment the secret joy that filled my heart.

And then the morning came when I was in the nursery with Douglas, trying to get him to concentrate on his geography. I felt a bit tired, a bit queasy, but I had had very little sleep the night before and I had foolishly eaten kipper for breakfast. Douglas refused to pay attention to the map spread out on the table before us. He wanted to hear about cannibals.

"Do they *really* eat Englishmen?" he asked eagerly.

"I'm sure I wouldn't know, Douglas. Pay attention."

"They *do*. I know all about it. They put 'em in big pots and sprinkle 'em with salt and pepper and then light the fire. They wear beads and colored feathers and dance around the pot waving spears."

"I don't know who has been telling you such tales, but I'm sure they're highly exaggerated. This part over here, the section colored pink, is called Egypt. Many great pharoahs built their—"

"There're lions, too!" he interrupted, paying not the slightest attention to the map. "They *al*ways eat Englishmen, gobble 'em right up and crunch on their bones—"

He cut himself short, staring at me with wide gray eyes full of frightened concern. I gasped, trying to control the wave of nausea that swept over me, and I knew my face must have been the color of chalk. My knees seemed to go weak. I gripped the edge of the table, certain I would have fallen had I been on my feet.

"Is—is somethin' wrong, Honora?" he asked in an anxious voice. "You look real—real funny."

"Some*thing*," I corrected. My own voice was sharp. "How many times have I told you about those final 'g's,' Douglas? Now I—I want you to take this uncolored map here and take this box of colors and—"

I closed my eyes, unable to continue. Everything seemed to go black, and when I opened my eyes Douglas was standing beside me, stroking my cheek, those beautiful gray eyes welling with tears.

"I'll go get Mrs. Rawson," he said.

"No. No, don't do that. I'll be all right in—in just a few minutes. I need—I just need a breath of fresh air. You stay here and color the map, Douglas. I'll take a quick turn in the garden and be right back."

"I'll go with you," he insisted.

I shook my head and stood up, my legs unsteady. I wondered if I would be able to walk. Douglas held on to my skirt, peering up at me with a large tear spilling down his cheek. I patted that unruly blond hair and tried to smile a reassuring smile.

"It's that wretched kipper I had for breakfast," I told him. "I'll be perfectly all right as soon as I've had some fresh air."

"I could use some fresh air myself. We could get some together."

"No more nonsense, Douglas! Color your map."

He turned sulky then and slouched back into his chair and reached for the box of colors. I left the room and somehow made it down the back stairs and into the wide back hall. I paused there, leaning against the wall and staring at the row of windows that looked out over the back lawn. My knees were still weak. My palms were damp. My heart was palpitating now, and I could feel panic spreading. How long? How long had it been? Immersed in my love, going through each day in a kind of blissful trance, I had paid no attention to that monthly cycle.

Straightening my shoulders, bracing myself, I moved across

the hall and stepped outside. It was cool, much too cool to be out without a cloak, but I barely noticed the chill. Folding my arms around my waist, I walked slowly over the lawn. The wind whipped my skirts and lifted my hair, strands of it blowing across my cheeks. It had been six weeks, at least six weeks. I tried desperately to remember. Not this month. Last month? I seemed to recall being late and paying it no mind. Walking beneath the sodden gray skies, I was certain now: I was going to have Jeffrey's child.

The wind rattled the leaves of the vines still clinging to the trellises. I stopped beside one of them, drawing my arms more tightly about my waist as if to protect the life already growing inside me, and the beautiful dream evaporated—shimmering, softly diffused colors torn and tattered by the cold wind of reality. Jeffrey's child, a new life created by the two of us, the product of our love . . . and to the world, a bastard, the product of a shameful, illicit liaison, a child to be pointed at and mocked, a child forced to go through life carrying a dreadful stigma.

Jeffrey would try to do the right thing, to make some kind of arrangement, but the secret would out and his future would be destroyed. Lord Robert would turn on him viciously. The society to which he belonged would laugh at him behind his back and derive much amusement from his little folly, and doors would be closed to him. I couldn't let that happen. I couldn't. I stood beside the trellis and shivered, and the panic continued to grow.

I saw Mrs. Rawson approaching, moving rapidly across the lawn with garnet skirts flapping and girlish gray curls bouncing madly. The wind caught her white lace cap and ripped it off and sent it sailing away, but she paid no heed to it. Her plump face was creased with concern, her eyes full of alarm, and she was puffing as she hurried toward me. I seemed to see her through a haze. She might have been an apparition. Out of breath, cheeks flushed, she reached me and drew me into her arms and hugged me tightly, knowing already, comforting me with her strength and warmth and goodness. For several moments she rocked me in her arms, and then she released me and studied my face with troubled, anxious eyes.

"It's going to be all right, luv. It's going to be all right."

"No. No. It's—"

"Now, now, luv, don't fret. Don't fret. It ain't the end of the world. Here, let's go back inside. You're freezin'. I happened to be glancin' out th' window and I saw you walkin'

~78~

out here, saw th' look on your face, an' then Dougie came runnin' downstairs an' told me you were sick."

"I—I must get back to the nursery—"

"Dougie's with Mary, luv. She's givin' him milk an' cookies, and they're goin' to color maps or somethin' together. You don't worry about him."

"He's my responsibility. Lord Robert—"

"Lord Bobbie an' Master Jeffrey are both at the factory and are likely to be there most of th' day. No one's goin' to accuse you of neglectin' your responsibility. Come along now, luv. No arguin'."

She took my hand and squeezed it tightly and led me back inside the house, making clucking, comforting noises as we climbed the back stairs. I moved as though in a stupor. The nausea had passed now. The palpitations were gone, too, but the panic remained. Mrs. Rawson took me into her cozy sitting room and cleared merry clutter from the sofa and helped me sit down. I looked about me in a kind of bewilderment, not really certain where I was, and the wonderful old housekeeper shook her head and fussed over me and left the room for a few minutes, returning with a clattering tray.

"Here now, a cuppa tea's what you need, luv. A cuppa tea always helps. Just settle back. Let me arrange those pillows. There. I'm going to light the fire and then we're goin' to have our tea and everything'll look better, you'll see."

She put another log in the fireplace and fumbled around with poker and bellows and soon a small fire was crackling merrily. She straightened up and sighed and arched her back and then poured the tea, handing me a cup. I took it and gazed at it as though I had never seen a cup of tea before. Mrs. Rawson patted my shoulder and settled down in the overstuffed chair facing the sofa.

"Drink it, luv. Do as I say."

I drank the tea. It did indeed seem to help. The chill left me, and some of the numbness disappeared. A lump formed in my throat. A tremulous feeling welled up inside, growing stronger and stronger until I was trembling violently. Mrs. Rawson jumped up and took my arms and held them tightly. The tears came, and she gathered me to her as I sobbed. Several minutes passed before I was able to control myself. I dabbed at my eyes with the handkerchief she handed me. I drank another cup of tea, the cup clattering in the saucer as I set it down.

"I—I'm sorry. I didn't mean to give way like that. I—"

"I understand, luv. Besides, a nice good cry's good for you."

"I love him, Mrs. Rawson."

"'Course you do, luv. An' he loves you, too. I seen it at once. I know, luv. I know all about it. Who do-ya think's been changin' them bedclothes in the east wing? Who do you think's been settin' out fresh candles and keepin' things tidy?"

"I—I never thought about it."

"Nor did Master Jeffrey. Folks in love don't bother with such details. Room'ud be in quite a mess if I hadn't been tendin' to things, wudn't it? I guess I should know about such matters, luv. Lord knows I've been in a lotta *rooms* in my day."

"I—I think I'm—" I paused, each word an effort.

"You're in an interestin' condition, luv. Ain't much question about it. I know the signs. I also take care of your underthings, and there ain't been a speck-a red in over two months."

"Two months?"

"Give or take a week or so. Master Jeffrey's an angel and I'd walk over hot coals for him any day, but I could wring his neck for not takin' necessary precautions. He knows about them little sheaths, all right. I found a packet of 'em in his room years ago. There's other ways, too. Kinda clumsy and uncomfortable pullin' it out just then, but—" She shrugged and poured herself another cup of tea. "What's done is done."

"I can't have this child," I said quietly.

"Dudn't look like you've got much choice, luv."

"He loves me, but I—I know he could never marry me. I'm a governess. He's an aristocrat. It—it would ruin his life. I don't want to—to cause him any trouble."

"Bound to be trouble of some kind, luv. It ain't likely he'll marry you, I admit, but Master Jeffrey's got honor. He'll see that right's done, that's the kind of man he is."

"But—"

"You ain't the first humble lass carryin' an aristocrat's bairn, luv, an' you won't be the last, I fancy. A lot of men, they'd turn a lass out in the cold, wash their hands of her, but not Master Jeffrey. He'll find a place for you to stay where no one knows you, see that you get th' proper care, give you enough money for you and the bairn to—"

"He mustn't know," I said.

"He's *got*ta know," she protested.

"There—there must be another way. I've heard of women who—" I hesitated, trying to find the right words. "Some women manage to—they go for bumpy carriage rides and take hot baths and—and mix some kind of powder in their drink. I understand there are midwives who—who aren't really midwives at all, who know how to—"

"You ain't talkin' sense, luv," she said gently. "You're upset, rightly so, but you ain't thinkin' properly. Them things you're talkin' about are dangerous, mighty dangerous."

"You've got to help me, Mrs. Rawson."

"'Course I'll help you. 'Course I will, luv."

"I don't want him to know. He'll—I don't want him to worry."

"I can understand that. You really do love him, I reckon. I reckon you love him like they love in one of them books. Never loved like that myself, always took it a bit more lightly. Easier on the heart that way."

"Do you know one of—one of those midwives, Mrs. Rawson?"

"There's Granny Cookson. She lives in a cottage on the other side of the village. Folks say she's a witch—wouldn't know myself. She's always dryin' herbs an' brewin' potions, has a cat, too. I've heard tell of lasses who went to her for a bit of help."

"Could you get in touch with her for me?"

Mrs. Rawson frowned. Her eyes were dark with worry, and her small red lips were pursed as she toyed with the hem of her apron, silent, thinking about my question. After a few moments she sighed and climbed wearily to her feet, still lost in thought. I got up, too, stronger now, the panic replaced by a hard, tight knot inside. Mrs. Rawson sighed again and looked at me with brow still creased.

"Are you all right now?" she asked.

"I think so. I—I'd better get back to Douglas."

The plump housekeeper studied me with those worried eyes, and then she took my hand and patted it.

"You got a bit of color back in your cheeks now. Don't look so peaked. Tea did that, I reckon. You go back to the nursery, luv, and try not to worry. Everything's goin' to be all right."

"You—you'll help?"

"I'll do what I can, luv. I promise."

~81~

She gave me a hug, and I clung to her for a moment, holding her tightly and fighting back the tears that threatened to reappear. Mrs. Rawson shook her head and clacked her tongue and gently unloosened my arms. She gave me a smile and pointed me toward the door, and I started back to the nursery, still shaken but much calmer than before. I had no idea what was going to happen, but of one thing I was certain—Jeffrey wasn't going to be hurt. I was not going to let this destroy his future. I loved him far too much to let that happen.

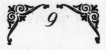

9

THE GRAY HAD GONE, AT LEAST TEMPORARILY, AND this afternoon the sky was a pure pale blue washed with silver sunlight and stretching overhead like a translucent canopy. It was warmer, too, and I wore no cloak over my faded pink cotton frock, a simple, once lovely garment that was not too snug at bosom and waist. The full, carefully mended skirt billowed up over my petticoats as I moved slowly down the narrow, rocky slope that led to the beach below. The ocean surged mightily, restless, relentless, splattering with great foamy spumes against the jagged black rocks. There was a misty violet line on the horizon, and in the sunlight the constantly shifting water must have been a dozen different shades of blue, one melting into another. Gulls circled overhead, squawking loudly as I made my way down the treacherous slope.

I had begun going for long walks every day this past week while Douglas took his afternoon nap, hoping the walks would help combat the terrible depression that had settled over me ever since I had discovered I was with child. I had walked to the outskirts of the village, had explored all the surrounding countryside, and once I had crossed the moors and climbed the sloping hillside to wander through the Roman ruins, remembering, tears in my eyes as I touched the crumbling gray stones of the ruin where Jeffrey and I had retreated from the storm, where, in all likelihood, this child inside me had been conceived. That had been a very bad afternoon indeed, yet I had lingered among the ruins, reliving that first splendor, unable to regret a moment of it even though it had led to my present grief. The walks helped, for I found that if I was very tired I could better conceal my depression when I met Jeffrey in the east wing.

I had never climbed down the cliff before, had never walked along the rocky beach, and as I made my way down the slope I paused, staring down at the great black rocks that rose from the beach like misshapen, prehistoric creatures awash with sprays of foam. Mrs. Rawson had made no reference to our conversation in her sitting room, had carefully skirted the subject whenever I met her. Was she going to help? Was she going to make an arrangement with Granny Cookson? Day after day I waited, and the housekeeper was bright and cheery and kept assuring me that everything was going to be fine, luv, now don't you worry. I knew that she disapproved of the idea of my going to see the witch, and I was leery of it myself, but what else was I to do?

As I stood there halfway up the slope, as the waves crashed, as the gulls circled against the pale blue sky like swirling scraps of white paper, my depression seemed to come to a head, and everything was gray, gray, bleaker by the second. The mental anguish became unbearable, and I stared down at the rocks, thinking how easy it would be to hurl myself down. One single step, one moment of shattering pain, and it would all be over, the anguish, the uncertainty. It would be deemed an accident, and Jeffrey would undoubtedly grieve, but he would be spared another kind of grief. The idea took terrible hold of me as though it were a living thing, urging me, beckoning me, compelling me to take that single step. For several moments I stood in a trance, longing to obey that diabolical summons, and then there was a tiny movement inside me, a sharp, distinct jab in my womb.

I fell back against the rocky wall, closing my eyes, panting. Already the child was a part of me, so much a part that it seemed able to read my thoughts, to protest vehemently, and I knew that I could never, never take that step, could never destroy this life within me. Now, as I brushed my hand across my brow and tried to control my breathing, I was filled with a horrible repulsion at the mere idea. I opened my eyes and gazed at the sky, and by degrees the depression lifted, replaced at once by a new strength and resolution.

I moved on down the slope, carefully now, each step cautious, relieved when I finally reached the bottom. I walked past the gigantic rocks and was soon on a smooth stretch of beach, the cliff looming up at my right, the blue, blue ocean to my left. Waves swooshed over the sand, leaving foamy trails behind as they receded. The sunlight seemed to take on a new brilliance, spangling the water with glittering sunbursts, and the salty air was invigorating, blowing away the last gray vestiges of that terrible depression.

For the first time, I was able to think clearly, and I saw what I must do.

I could not have Jeffrey. For a short while I could continue to meet him after midnight and love him in secrecy, but when my condition became apparent I would have to leave Mowrey House in disgrace. Jeffrey would "do the right thing," as Mrs. Rawson put it, would see that I had money and the proper care, but his future would be endangered and, at any rate, I would probably never see him again. Robert might well cut him off without a penny—he was capable of such a deed—and Jeffrey would remember our love with remorse, would eventually see it as mad folly and see me as the cause of all the unpleasantness bound to occur.

It wasn't going to be that way.

I could not have Jeffrey, no, but I could have his child, a living memento of the beauty and bliss I had known. Already I loved this creature inside me. Already I cherished it with all my heart. I would go away, now, before my condition became obvious. Reverend Williams would help me. I would tell him everything, and although he would be disappointed, would disapprove, he wouldn't censure, wouldn't condemn. He was truly a man of God, full of compassion, and he knew that all God's children were weak. He would help me. I would go away, take a new identity. I would be a "widow," would have my child and somehow provide for it. Reverend Williams would know a place, would know someone who would take me in. I would have to rely on charity for a while, but eventually I would find some kind of work. I was prepared to face any hardship, for no matter how difficult the future might be, I would have my child, a part of Jeffrey to love and cherish for the rest of my life.

I turned, retracing my steps, watching the trails of foam and listening to the cries of the gulls. The depression was gone, but a heavy sadness filled my soul as I moved past the giant rocks and began to climb slowly up the dangerous slope. Now that I was going to give him up, my love for Jeffrey Mowrey seemed to expand, taking on a poignant new tenderness and beauty that was almost unbearable. Tears trailed down my cheeks in shiny rivulets as I thought of leaving him, of never again seeing that beloved face, of never again feeling the warmth and strength of that body. I paused, gazing out at the water, and it seemed my heart was being torn asunder.

I cried for a long time, consumed with sadness that wracked my soul, and after a while I wiped the tears away and continued my climb, depleted, hollow inside, it seemed, moving like one drained of all life force.

I reached the top. He took my hands. He pulled me to him and held me in his arms so tightly I feared my ribs would crack. He held me for a long, long time, crushing me to him, and I sobbed wretchedly, burying my face in the curve of his shoulder. We swayed there on the edge of the cliff, and when finally he loosened his hold and took my chin in his hand and tilted my face up to look into my eyes I thought I would perish with grief and joy. He kissed the tears from my cheeks and kissed my lips tenderly, so tenderly, stroking my hair, gathering me to him again, gently now, as though I were a precious object he must carefully protect.

"I know," he said softly.

"Jeffrey—"

"I know. You should have told me at once."

"I couldn't."

"Honora. My foolish, foolish Honora. Don't you know how happy this makes me?"

"You—it will ruin everything—you can't—"

"Hush," he ordered. "No more."

"Your brother—"

"Do you think I care what Robert says, what Robert does? We're going to be married, Honora."

"It's impossible. You—"

"We're going to be married this afternoon. I've already been to see Reverend Williams. All the arrangements have been made. My carriage is waiting on the road. Mrs. Rawson will meet us at the vicarage."

"She—she told you."

"She told me this morning while you were in the nursery with Douglas. I went at once to the vicarage and talked to Reverend Williams. He agreed to marry us this afternoon. I came back to the house and told Mrs. Rawson to get to the vicarage to help out, and then I started looking for you. I couldn't find you anywhere, and then one of the maids said she'd seen you walking along the edge of the cliff. Honora! Honora! If you knew the madness that possessed me when I thought of you climbing down the slope, possibly falling—I was out of my mind."

He gripped my arms tightly, staring into my eyes.

"I love you, Honora. Didn't you know that? Didn't you know I meant to spend the rest of my life with you?"

"I—I knew you loved me, but—"

"I'm going to marry you. This very afternoon."

"People—your friends—they'll—"

"Nothing in the world matters but you and Douglas. He loves you almost as much as I do. I have a little money of my own. The three of us will go away together and begin a new life, and soon we will be four."

I was trembling. Jeffrey touched my cheek and smiled a tender smile, and as I looked up into those gentle blue eyes I felt a rush of joyous emotion so strong I feared I might swoon. All the dazzling sunlight spilling around us seemed to come from within me, shimmering, radiant, flooding my soul with its incredible beauty. Jeffrey kissed me again, lightly this time, and took me by the elbow and led me toward the road where the carriage was waiting. I seemed to be swimming in sunlight, my feet barely touching the ground, and I found it almost impossible to believe this was actually happening. Surely I was dreaming. It couldn't be real. It couldn't be.

The carriage was real enough, a low-slung, open vehicle of shiny teak with seats upholstered in padded velvet of the palest tan. A groom stood in front, holding the reins as two gleaming chestnuts stamped impatiently in harness. I shook my head to clear it. Jeffrey laughed and squeezed my elbow, and then he helped me into the carriage. It was happening too fast. I was in a daze, unable to relate any of this with reality. I was still swimming in the flood of sunlight, dizzy with elation. Jeffrey took the reins and dismissed the groom and climbed up beside me. He spoke to the horses and clicked the reins and we began to move.

I remember very little of that drive to the village. I gradually came to my senses, gradually realized that this was indeed happening, but I was still shaken. We passed beneath the trees, passed the thatched cottages and the rows of ancient stone dwellings, and villagers paused to watch our progress, most of them nodding respectfully to the handsome young heir of Mowrey House. We drove past the beautiful old church of mellow brown stone, the oak trees tracing shadowy patterns on its walls, and then, a few moments later, we stopped in front of the vicarage.

Young Jack Jordon came tearing outside, a wide grin splitting his mischievous face. He was wearing his preposterous London finery, and his red hair was all atumble. Jeffrey tossed him the reins and climbed down and turned to help me alight. Some moments remain sharp and distinct in memory, as though captured by a master painter and engraved on the mind. This was such a moment, and I can see it now as though I were indeed looking at a glorious painting: the vicarage in the background, mellow and lovely, the porch in shadow, the red-haired boy beside the carriage, grinning, one hand holding the reins, the other resting gently on the mane of one of the chestnuts, and in the foreground, close before me, the handsome young god in dark blue breeches and frock coat, a ruffled white jabot spilling over the top of his embroidered gray waistcoat. His dark blond hair is gleaming. His eyes are full of love. A gentle, loving smile is curving on his full pink mouth, and his strong, beautifully shaped hand is reaching for mine. Can ever an artist have painted so magnificent a scene?

I took his hand. I got out of the carriage. Jeffrey gave my hand a tight squeeze and led me toward the shadowy porch. I was apprehensive now, my pulses leaping. I was going to wake up. Reality was going to intrude. Those terrible gray clouds of depression were going to reclaim me. We paused in front of the door, and Jeffrey sensed my state of mind and leaned down to kiss my cheek, and tears spilled over my lashes once again.

"No tears," he admonished gently. "This is supposed to be the happiest day of your life."

"It is," I whispered. "I—I just can't believe it."

And then the door burst open and Mrs. Rawson grabbed me and hugged me and bustled me into the foyer, her merry brown eyes sparkling with excitement, her small red mouth smiling triumphantly.

"I *knew* it was goin' to work out, I just *knew* it, luv! Mercy, you can't be married in that awful pink frock! I guess it'll have to do," she groaned. "We'll *make* it do! You, Master Jeffrey, don't just stand there lookin' sheepish and pleased with yourself, go on and join Reverend Williams. Do as I say! I'll take charge of this poor lamb. Go on now! We gotta have a few minutes to ourselves."

She hurried me down a short hall and into a tiny room in back of the vicarage. It had hideous flowered wallpaper, a plethora of sickly-looking green plants and a depressing abundance of crocheted doilies and antimacassars. I assumed it was the housekeeper's room, and, sure enough, the tall, dour-faced Miss Moffat stuck her head in the door, eyeing us with great suspicion. Mrs. Rawson bristled visibly, shoved the poor woman back and slammed the door in her face.

"Nothin' but trouble I've had with that one, let me tell you. Wants to take charge of everything, thinks she's the only one who can do anything. If it wudn't for me, we wudn't have flowers, wudn't have wine. I've been runnin' myself ragged, luv, gettin' things ready—Master Jeffrey tells me he's marryin' you and marryin' you this afternoon an' I'm expected to get to the vicarage and perform miracles!"

She picked up a folded piece of lace, shoved me in front of the mirror and, moving behind me, shook the lace out and began to fasten it to my hair. It was very long and gossamer thin, a pale, pale white delicately embroidered with tiny pink and white flowers.

"My own, luv," she confided, "used it three times myself, hope it'll bring you good luck. Turn your head just a little. There. Let's just drape it over your shoulders a bit. Why, look! Them tiny pink flowers are almost th' same color as your dress, make the dress look almost elegant. You're goin' to be the most beautiful bride ever!"

"You told him," I said.

"I had to, luv. I been worried sick ever since you started talkin' about Granny Cookson. I—I couldn't let you do anything like that. Master Jeffrey came in around eleven this mornin' and I met him in the back hall and I guess I blabbed everything."

"He told me," I said quietly.

Mrs. Rawson picked up a bridal bouquet I hadn't noticed earlier. It was obviously her own handiwork, pale white roses and pink-white daisies tied together with delicate sprays of fern, bound with a trailing white satin ribbon. She examined it proudly before handing it to me.

"Had to raid two different gardens, I did," she confessed. "Lucky I had this bit of ribbon on hand."

"It's beautiful, Mrs. Rawson. You—you've done so much."

"Didn't have much time, luv. Haven't moved these old bones so fast since I was married to my second—he was quite a one for a quick chase and topple. Couldn't abide him," she told me. "I always ran like the wind when he got that botherin' notion. Poor soul's heart finally gave out when he was chasin' me around the mulberry tree."

I couldn't help but smile. Mrs. Rawson stepped back to get a better look at me, and then she smiled herself, a genuine, affectionate smile that gleamed in those expressive brown eyes as well.

"You're lovely, luv," she said, "the loveliest bride I ever seen."

"I—I'm frightened."

"'Course you are. Every bride is. Last time I got married I thought I was goin' to pass out 'fore he jammed the ring on my finger. It woulda been just as well if I had—Gordie drank, poor thing, generous to a fault he was, but a greater sot never drew breath."

She shook her head, sighed and then stepped foward to make another small adjustment on the veil.

"There. Perfect. You're goin' to have that happy endin', luv," she said, "just like in one of them fairy tales. You an' Master Jeffrey were meant for each other—I sensed it from the first. He needs you and so does young Dougie and you, you got so much love in your heart, so much goodness in your soul, you need them to lavish it on. The bairn, too."

"I'm going to start crying again."

"Go ahead. All brides cry. It's traditional."

Miss Moffat opened the door and glared at us and informed us in a lemon-sour voice that the others had already left for the church and the reverend was a very busy man and had other things to do besides waiting. *She* was going to stay here at the vicarage and set out the cakes and wine while others were having a good sit-down in a comfortable pew. Mrs. Rawson made a highly unsympathetic reply and, taking my hand, led me back down the hall and out of the vicarage.

"It's just a few steps, luv. Walk'll do you good. I had barely enough time to fetch flowers for the altar, but I hope you'll like what I did. The candles'll help, young Jack an' I stuck dozens of 'em around. He's goin' to provide the music, by the way. Says he's an accomplished organist, whatever *that* means. Guess we'll have to suffer."

We walked quickly beneath the oak trees, the ground dappled with dancing patterns of sunlight and shade, and as we neared the church I could hear the organ music. It was, beyond doubt, the most beautiful music I had ever heard, a strange, haunting piece that was sad and lilting and lovely, as though all the most poignant human emotions had been carefully, delicately transformed into sound. Later young Jack told me it was called Adagio in G Minor by the Venetian, Albinoni. It was the only piece he knew really well, he informed me, and it was supposed to be accompanied by violins, but he thought it would be appropriate even if it wasn't church music.

The music swelled, filling the dim, shadowy church as we stepped inside. Candles glowed soft and gold all about the altar, and there were great masses of white roses. Reverend Williams stood before the altar, prayer book in hand. His weary, beautifully lined face was grave, but his kind brown eyes were full of affection as he saw me approaching slowly down the aisle with Mrs. Rawson at my side. Jeffrey was waiting. He turned. He smiled. The incredibly beautiful music grew quieter, becoming a softly muted background for the short, simple ceremony that followed, and it seemed to express in musical terms all that Jeffrey and I felt for each other, such tender love, such magical emotion.

I remember the pale golden glow of the candles and the fragrance of roses. I remember that sublime music and Reverend Williams's deep, melodious voice, but other details are lost in a blur. Reverend Williams pronounced us man and wife, and Jeffrey kissed me for the first time in front of others. Mrs. Rawson began to sob audibly. Jeffrey kissed her, too, and Reverend Williams took my hands and said he knew I would be very, very happy. Young Jack came prancing down from the organ loft and started explaining about the music. Albinoni was his favorite, he delcared, much nicer than Bach, and Reverend Williams told him to hush and scurry on over to the vicarage and tell Miss Moffat we would be there in a few minutes.

"I'll go with you," Mrs. Rawson volunteered. "Wanna make sure she hasn't poisoned the cakes. Come along, Jack. Albinoni, you say? Must be one of them Eye-talians."

"Jack really is an amazing young man," I said as they moved up the aisle. "I've never heard organ music played so well, and by one so young."

"Oh, he's amazing all right," Reverend Williams agreed. "I fear my nephew will go far. It'll be the ruination of him."

Reverend Williams tactfully disappeared then, and Jeffrey and I were alone there in front of the altar. We looked at each other, silent. His blond hair gleamed in the candlelight. His strong, handsome features were softly brushed by shadow. A smile curved gently on his lips as his eyes gazed into mine. We were married. We were actually married. This marvelous being was my husband, and I belonged to him. As he took me into his arms, as his lips touched mine, I knew a miracle had happened, and I could hardly believe it possible for anyone to be so blessed.

10

THE LOVELY WEATHER DID NOT HOLD. AS WE LEFT the vicarage the sunlight had faded to a pale silver, the pure blue sky turning grayer and grayer as we drove through the village. I had given the veil back to Mrs. Rawson, had given the lovely bouquet to a very surprised Miss Moffat, and saucy young Jack had received an affectionate kiss that caused him to blush to the roots of his hair. He had promised to make a copy of the Albinoni score and send it to me so that I could learn it, and I looked forward to receiving it. We had all eaten cakes, had drunk the wine Mrs. Rawson provided, and I had grown more apprehensive by the moment, dreading the return to Mowrey House.

"It's turning colder," I remarked as we passed the village green. "I can smell rain in the air."

"The weather's always changing in Cornwall," Jeffrey said. "It may storm. I hope not."

"We're about due a storm. This afternoon was most unusual for this time of year."

We had just been married, had only moments ago received Reverend Williams's final blessing, and here we were in the carriage talking about the weather, both of us tense and apprehensive. Jeffrey affected a casual demeanor, clicking the reins lightly, frequently turning to give me a reassuring smile, but I could see that he was as uneasy as I was. He wasn't afraid of his brother, that wasn't it at all, but he knew there was bound to be a great deal of unpleasantness, and a man of Jeffrey's sweet nature detested unpleasantness in any form. He was not a weak man, nor was he cowardly. Jeffrey's strength came from an innate goodness of heart that did not require stern posturing or harsh words or the swaggering braggadocio common with so many men. He was worried, and I knew that his chief concern was that Lord Robert would be hurt.

The sky turned even grayer as we left the village and drove along the road leading to Mowrey House. Far below, the sea was angry, waves crashing mightily against the rocks. The gulls were frantic, circling high, squawking. A brisk wind had blown up, and I shivered in my thin pink cotton dress. Jeffrey noticed it and, handing me the reins, removed his frock coat and draped it snugly around my shoulders. He took the reins back, smiling again. The heavy blue broadcloth had a faint, musty smell, the virile smell of his body. I wrapped it more closely around me.

"I'm sorry there were no rings to exchange," he said. "We'll do that later. We'll have our own private ceremony. I'm going to buy you the most beautiful ring in the world."

"Jeffrey, are—are you happy?"

"You know I am, Honora."

"I'm sorry it happened this way. I never meant—"

"I'm glad. I shouldn't have put it off so long. I should have married you weeks ago, as soon as it—as soon as I knew I could never live without you. I kept mulling it over, trying to think of some way to make it easier on my brother, trying to come up with some plan."

"He's going to be terribly upset."

"That's something I'll just have to deal with."

"Jeffrey—"

"It's going to be all right, Honora."

"I wonder if he's home yet."

Jeffrey shook his head. "There's trouble at the factory. Some of the men are discontent and deliberately slowing down production. They've had enough, you see. They're beginning to rebel. I told Robert years ago it would happen eventually if we didn't—" He sighed. "No need going over all that again, is there? Robert calls them ungrateful malcontents and is determined to deal with them sternly."

"Is he going to dismiss the men?"

"I'm afraid so."

"Won't that—slow down production even more?"

"Not at all. There are dozens of able men in the county who are without work and eager to take their places no matter what the pay and working conditions. Robert believes in very harsh measures. The men he dismisses are going to have a very hard time. Their wives, their children will suffer, too. I tried to reason with Robert, but—" He shook his head again.

There was despair in his voice, and I knew he was thinking of that dream he had told me about, those blueprints and the list of proposals he had given his brother several years ago. Jeffrey had compassion, and there was no place for that in this brutal age when profit was all and human life had little value. We rode in silence for several moments, and I saw Mowrey House in the distance, bleak and forbidding with its bleached gray stone walls and leaded windows. It seemed to loom there like a living, threatening presence, ready to swallow us up and rob us of all joy.

"I wish we didn't have to return," I said nervously.

"Don't fret."

"I—I feel something is going to happen, something terrible."

"Nonsense," he told me.

He turned up the drive, and I stared at the sprawling house surrounded by wild gardens and twisted trees. It grew larger and larger, finally hovering over us in all its monstrous bulk as Jeffrey stopped the carriage in front of the steps. A groom came hurrying around the side of the house to take charge of the horses as Jeffrey helped me down. We moved slowly up the steps, and I had a dreadful premonition, as sharp, as real as a knife stab. I was trembling as we stepped into the great hall.

"Don't, Honora."

"I—I can't help it."

Jeffrey took hold of my arms and looked into my eyes. His handsome face was slightly drawn, skin taut across his cheekbones, and there was a tightness about his mouth I had never seen before, the full lower lip stretched wide. I knew that he felt it, too. I could see it in his eyes.

"Nothing's going to happen," he said.

His voice was firm, his manner stern, but his fingers dug into the flesh of my upper arms with such force that I winced. A few moments passed. Jeffrey seemed to relax then. He released my arms. He sighed, and when he spoke again his voice was carefully modulated.

"I'll speak to Robert tonight, after dinner. You needn't even see him. I'll take him into the study and tell him, and first thing tomorrow morning you and I and Douglas will leave. We're going to London."

"London?"

"I told you I was trying to come up with some plan, Honora. I've written to an old friend of mine from Oxford. He's in the diplomatic service and thinks he might well find some minor post for me in Italy. I didn't want to say anything until I was certain. Wallace hasn't answered my letter yet, but I think he may well be able to get something for me. I met a lot of influential people while I was in Italy. I know the country well."

"Italy," I whispered.

"You'll love it there," he promised. "The sunlight, the vines, the ancient old houses—we'll have our own villa, Honora. I have a little money of my own, I told you that. We might have to struggle a bit in the beginning—we'll have to live in a small village outside Rome or Florence—but I'm sure I can make it in the diplomatic service."

Italy. Our own villa. I could see it in my mind, shabby and run down but cozy, sunlight streaming over the broken flagstones on the patio, gilding the rich green leaves, heat waves rising in the air, the sky a bold, blazing blue. There would be strong wine and coarse, delicious bread and cheese, and Jeffrey would charm the noisy, amiable villagers who would come to love him as everyone who knew him must eventually love him. I clung to the vision, and it helped. My unreasonable dread began to recede a little.

"We're going to be happy, Honora."

I nodded, studying his face, trying so hard to believe him. It was cold there in the great hall, and the wind was raging outside now. I could hear it slamming against the walls, whistling around corners. I still had Jeffrey's coat wrapped around me, but the chill penetrated nevertheless.

"Go on upstairs to Douglas," he ordered. "One of the maids has been keeping him company this afternoon, but he's bound to be sick with worry about you."

"What—what shall I tell him?"

"Tell him that the three of us are going away tomorrow. You might let him help you pack. I'll have Mrs. Rawson pack my things when she gets back. I fancy she'll make a quick visit to her friend Jim Randall before she returns to Mowrey House."

"You'll—"

"I'll speak to Robert after he and I have dined, and then I'll come up to your room."

"Oh, Jeffrey, I'm so—"

"Upstairs with you," he said firmly. "You have a lot of packing to do."

He kissed me and gave me a playful little shove toward the staircase, and I crossed the rest of the hall and began to climb those wide, shabbily carpeted stairs, running my hand along the mahogany railing. It wasn't nearly as secure as it should be, I noted, and several of the banisters were decidedly loose. Halfway up the stairs, I turned, looking back, and I shall never forget the sight of Jeffrey standing there alone in the great hall in his black boots and narrow dark-blue breeches and embroidered gray waistcoat. His hands rested lightly on his thighs, the full sleeves of his fine white cambric shirt belling at the wrists, and a heavy blond wave dipped over his brow. His expression was unguarded now, the lips pressed tightly together, a frown making a furrow above the bridge of his nose, and those gentle blue eyes were full of worry.

Heavy-hearted, I went on upstairs, telling myself that it would soon be over. Tomorrow morning we would leave Mowrey House and be on our way to London, and afterward there would be Italy and the sun-splattered villa and hot, blue skies. Stepping into my bedroom, I removed Jeffrey's coat and draped it carefully over the back of a chair and then moved over to the mirror to tidy my hair. The face in the glass was drawn, pale. The too-pink mouth trembled slightly at the corners. Faint mauve-gray shadows were etched about the lids, and the sea gray eyes were dark with apprehension. I wiped damp auburn wisps from my temples and smoothed back the heavy waves, desperately trying to convince myself that there was nothing to worry about.

I was no longer the timorous little governess. I was Jeffrey's wife now, and there was nothing Lord Robert could do about it. He would be angry. His thin, pitted face would turn even paler than usual, and those black eyes would glow like dark coals, but there was nothing he could do. For a moment I almost felt sorry for him, for Lord Robert loved Jeffrey, too, I realized, and he was going to lose him. His love was dark, twisted, obsessive, "unnatural," according to Mrs. Rawson, but it was genuine nonetheless, and Lord Robert was going to suffer great anguish. He would blame me, of course, but that didn't matter. Jeffrey could no longer live his life to please his brother, could no longer be smothered by that strange, possessive love.

I adjusted the bodice of my faded pink cotton wedding dress and, smoothing down the skirt, turned away from the mirror. Ever since I had arrived at Mowrey House Lord Robert and I had been engaged in a subtle, bizarre struggle, a struggle I hadn't fully understood until now. Now that I had won I felt a genuine pity for him and was genuinely sorry that he had to be hurt. Harsh and rigid he might be, cold, even cruel, but he loved Jeffrey and he was going to lose him. I had almost lost him myself, had given him up in my heart this afternoon on the cliff, and I knew the terrible grief Lord Robert would have to endure.

I tried to put it out of my mind. I crossed the hall and entered the nursery, assuming an expression I hoped would be suitable. The maid, Mary, was sitting by the window, idly leafing through a picture book and looking extremely bored. Douglas was sitting at the worktable, his precious young face a veritable study of sadness. His gray eyes were moist with tears, and there were shiny trails on his cheeks. On the table in front of him lay the figure of Miranda, the colored cutout that so closely resembled his governess. He gazed at it forlornly, a tear brimming over his lashes and following one of the shiny trails to the corner of his mouth.

"You may go, Mary," I said quietly.

Startled, the girl looked up. She got quickly to her feet, put aside the book and, giving me a quick curtsey, hurried from the room, undoubtedly vastly relieved. Douglas stared at me. He straightened up and blinked away another tear. I smiled a tender smile and stepped over to ruffle that thick blond hair. Douglas sniffled and rubbed his eyes.

"What's all this?" I inquired. "Have you been crying?"

"I—yeah, I guess I was. I was—I was 'fraid you weren't coming back anymore. You were gone for so long and you didn't come back and didn't come back and—and no one knew where you were."

"I'm sorry, darling."

"You *never* stay gone that long, Honora."

"Today was—special."

"Don't do it again," he ordered. "I was *sad*."

"I see you've been looking at Miranda."

"It was somethin' to do," he said casually. "That Mary's a bore. She dudn't know any games and can't tell any stories or anything. She's *nice*, I guess, but you're a lot more fun."

"Indeed?"

"I—I'll even do my geography if you promise not to go away anymore."

"What about your math?"

He hesitated, creasing his brow, weighing the matter carefully. "I'll do it, too," he said reluctantly, "but you'll have to help."

I smiled again and mussed his hair and pulled him to his feet. Douglas threw his arms around my legs and hugged them tightly. I felt an overwhelming surge of love for this tiny, preposterous creature who was so outrageous and so endearing. He was my very own son now, and I was going to care for him and cherish him every bit as much as I would cherish the child I was carrying. Douglas wiped his eyes on my skirt and took a deep breath and stood back, affecting a nonchalant pose that didn't fool me for a minute.

"We'd better see about your dinner now," I said. "Afterward I have a surprise for you."

His eyes seemed to light up. "A surprise! What is it?" he asked eagerly.

"If I told you, it wouldn't be a surprise. We'd better go wash your face and hands now."

"You could at least give me a hint," he complained as we left the nursery.

He gobbled his food much too rapidly, eager to hear about the surprise, and I had to scold him quite sternly and force him to chew his meat properly. He devoured the roast beef and the vegetables and actually turned down a second helping of the rich, creamy chocolate pudding he loved so well. I asked a footman to bring the trunks down from the attic and, once we had returned to the nursery, told Douglas we were going to take a trip together, that his father would be coming along, too.

"A *real* trip?" he asked.

"A real one," I replied.

"Not just to the village? Not just to the county fair?"

"We're going to go to London," I said, "And after that we'll probably go to Italy. Italy is the country shaped like a boot, remember?"

"And Daddy's going *with* us?"

I nodded, smiling, and Douglas grew so excited I could barely keep him from dancing around the room. He asked dozens of questions, firing them one right after the other without giving me time to answer, and I thought it better to wait and let his father tell him that we were married, that I was his stepmother. I finally managed to calm him down a little, and we went into his bedroom and packed his clothes, leaving out his pajamas and those garments he would need tomorrow. I allowed him to select a few toys and some books, and we packed those, too. By that time he was so exhausted he could barely keep his eyes open. He was grumpy and surly as I got him into his pajamas, assuring me he wouldn't be able to sleep a wink, but he nodded off almost as soon as his head touched the pillow.

I tucked the covers around him and stroked his warm forehead for a few moments, then went on into my bedroom. The wind was stronger than ever now. There was a threatening rumble of thunder in the distance. It was going to be a bad night. I glanced at the clock. It was shortly after eight. Jeffrey and Lord Robert would be in the dining room now, having their last meal together. Douglas had been a volatile distraction, keeping me thoroughly occupied, but now that I was alone the apprehension I had felt earlier returned in full force.

The footman had left my trunk beside the bed. I opened it and began to take down my clothes, folding them carefully, placing them in the trunk, and time passed, each minute sheer agony. Eight-thirty. They would be finished with their meal by this time. Jeffrey would be asking his brother to step into the study. There was a deafening clap of thunder, then another. Lightning flashed. It began to rain—rain pounding, pounding, lashing against the house in violent sheets. I took down another dress. My hands were shaking. Something was going to happen. Something was going to happen. I could feel it in my blood.

Nonsense, I told myself. Nonsense. This has been the most upsetting, the most bewildering, the most exciting day of your life. Your emotions have been torn asunder, from one extreme to the other, and you're naturally on edge, unstrung. Jeffrey is going to speak to his brother and then he's going to come upstairs and it will all be over. Finish packing. Undergarments now. Shoes. Put them in the trunk. Don't think. Keep busy.

I selected the clothes I would wear tomorrow and, setting them aside, finished packing. On my knees beside the trunk, I smoothed garments down and rearranged things, deliberately killing time, and then I closed the lid of the trunk and stood up. The wind continued to howl. The rain continued to pound and lash, slamming against the windows so violently that they shook in their frames, rattling noisily. That didn't help at all. My apprehension grew, mounting, swelling, and the suspense was almost unbearable. Shrill, jangling emotions battled inside me, clamoring for release, and I felt I was going to jump out of my skin. I stood very still, willing myself to hold on.

It was nine now. Just a little longer. Just a little longer. My face in the mirror across the room was stark white. My gray eyes seemed enormous, staring back at me like the eyes of one gone mad. This was absurd, absurd. I had to get hold of myself. I moved over to the chair and picked up Jeffrey's coat and held it close, rubbing my cheek against the nap of the dark blue broadcloth as a child might nuzzle a worn, familiar blanket. A few moments passed. I managed to still the jangling emotions, at least temporarily, but I knew I couldn't remain in this room a moment longer.

Mrs. Rawson was going to pack Jeffrey's things. I would take the coat to her. She would talk to me and give me something to drink, something strong, some of the port she was so fond of, and I would calm down. Leaving the bedroom, I moved resolutely down the hall, holding the coat close. The noise of the storm was even louder here. It seemed to reverberate down the hall, pursuing me relentlessly. There was a great explosion, a shrieking, splitting sound, a groaning thud. One of the trees must have been struck by lightning, I thought, moving rapidly on toward Mrs. Rawson's quarters.

Candles glowed in her sitting room. A fire burned low in the fireplace. Bolts of cloth were scattered over the sofa. A red petticoat was draped casually across a chair. An untidy bouquet of wildflowers had been tossed on the table, a chipped blue teacup and saucer beside it. I called her name. There was no answer. Of course, she would be in Jeffrey's room, packing. I hurried on. I had never been in his room before, but I knew where it was located. The house seemed to be under attack, the wind howling like a tribe of banshees, the rain hammering on the roof, slamming against the walls. I threw open the door of Jeffrey's room. Mrs. Rawson let out a shriek, dropped a pile of shirts and slapped a hand over her heart.

"Mercy! You scared the wits outta me, luv!"

"I'm sorry. I—here's Jeffrey's coat. I knew you'd want to—"

"Lands! My heart's still beatin' like sixty. It's this storm. I'm always skittish when th' weather's like this, and tonight—"

Mrs. Rawson cut herself short and peered at me with concerned brown eyes. "Lord, luv, you're white as a ghost. Your hands are shakin'."

"I can't help it. I'm so—I thought we could talk. I—I couldn't stay in my room any longer."

"Of course. Of course. Poor child. You're worried about how Lord Bobbie's gonna take the news. I been a bit worried myself, luv, I might as well admit it, but—here now, let me take that coat. You sit down right here in this big chair while I pick up these shirts."

I sat down in the deep brown leather chair and stared at the pale beige walls and the hunting prints and the faded brown and tan and green rugs on the polished hardwood floor. The heavy wardrobe stood open, clothes spilling out, boots littering the floor in front of it. A handsome tweed greatcoat had been flung across the bed. Mrs. Rawson folded up the shirts and put them in one of the two trunks that stood open at the foot of the bed, and then she straightened up and arched her back. She had changed back into her familiar garnet taffeta dress, a white organdy apron tied around her waist, and her frivolous gray curls were untidy.

"I'll finish this later, won't take me more'n a few minutes. Right now I need somethin' to revive me—I was late gettin' back to the house, luv, paid a visit to Jim Randall and he was *burstin'* with energy. Randy as a ram, that one, and he's talkin' again about marryin' me. I told him I just been to th' loveliest weddin' and he said we oughta—Lord, here I'm babblin' like an idiot and you're goin' to pieces. Forgive me, luv."

"I'll be all right. I just—"

"I know. You could use a glass-a port yourself, it'd fix you right up. I don't have any in my room, but I know for certain Beresford had a brand new bottle hidden in the pantry. He likes his nip now and then, too, though he'd go to th' stake before admittin' it. I'll just run fetch the bottle, and then we'll go to my room."

I stood up, dreading the thought of being alone even for a few minutes. Mrs. Rawson saw it in my eyes. She took my hand and gave it a tight squeeze. I felt as though I were seeing her through a mist.

"You *are* in a bad way, luv."

"It's foolish, I know, but all evening I—I've had the feeling something terrible is going to happen."

"You'd better come with me," she said.

Still holding my hand, she led me out of the room and down a narrow hall to the back stairs. The stairwell was dark, and Mrs. Rawson cursed the ne'er-do-well footman who had failed to light the candles. We had to move carefully in the dark, taking each step slowly.

"An' this is your weddin' night, too. Life's barmy sometimes, luv, downright barmy. You an' Master Jeffrey should be with each other right now, snug an' cozy, exchangin' tender words, an' instead here you are traipsin' about in the dark with an old party like me. Mercy! What was *that*?"

The storm stopped, abruptly, so abruptly that the sudden silence was far more alarming than the deafening racket. Everything was still, frighteningly so. Mrs. Rawson and I stood quietly for a moment, both of us unnerved by the bizarre silence, and then we moved down the few remaining stairs and stepped into the wide back hall. A few candles placed at intervals flickered dimly, washing the walls with shadow, intensifying the gloom. Neither of us spoke. Mrs. Rawson's eyes were wide with alarm.

"It's gonna start again in a few minutes," she said finally. Her voice was a nervous whisper. "It'll be worse than ever—

I seen it happen before. Last time it was like this a ship crashed on the rocks below, torn to smithereens it was, all hands lost, hundreds-a cases of fine French brandy washed up on shore next mornin'."

The candles flickered. Shadows leaped on the walls like frenzied demons. The hall was extremely cold, the stone floor icy beneath its covering of rushes. Mrs. Rawson shivered dramatically, but not from the cold.

Slowly, nervously, we moved down the hall, opened a small door and started up the narrow paneled passageway that led to the front hall. Candles burned in elaborate sconces, making warm, golden reflections on the rich mahogany, and a thick Persian runner muffled the sound of our footsteps. We passed along beside the staircase and entered the front hall. A door opened, and Mrs. Rawson clutched my arm in panic.

Jeffrey and Lord Robert stepped out of the study and stood there in front of the door. Neither of them saw us. Jeffrey hadn't bothered to change for dinner. He still wore the black boots, the dark blue breeches and embroidered gray waistcoat and the thin white cambric shirt with full sleeves belling at the wrists. His dark blond hair was untidy. His cheeks were pale, and there were faint smudges beneath those disturbed blue eyes as he looked at his brother.

"It's done, Robert. She's my wife."

His voice was shaky but firm nevertheless. Lord Robert stood very still, tall and beanpole thin in the familiar black suit. His pale, pockmarked face was like the face of a dead man, totally immobile, but those black brown eyes glowed fiercely with emotion—anger and anguish in equal parts. I could tell that he was fighting to control the feelings raging inside.

"She tricked you," he said. "Don't you realize that? It can be fixed Jeffrey. The marriage can be annulled."

"I don't *want* it annulled! I love her. I've loved her from the first. Haven't I made that clear?"

Lord Robert recoiled as though he had been struck. Faint spots of color burned on his cheeks, and when he spoke his voice was a harsh rasp, barely audible.

"I knew there would be trouble. I knew it the minute I laid eyes on her. She's bewitched you. Jeffrey—Jeffrey, you must listen to reason. She'll destroy you. Everything we've planned, everything we've worked for—"

"Everything *you* planned," Jeffrey protested. "I never wanted any part of it. All I ever wanted was—was my freedom. I'm grateful to you, Robert. I'm grateful, but I—I have to live my own life."

Jeffrey swallowed. His eyes were moist. There was a deep furrow above the bridge of his nose. I wanted to rush to him. Mrs. Rawson still gripped my arm. Her face was white. She shook her head rapidly, imploring me not to make our presence known.

"You're all I have," Lord Robert said.

"I'm sorry, Robert."

"If you leave—you can't leave, Jeffrey. A father never loved his son more than I love you. My whole life—I've—it's been for you, Jeffrey. If you leave, I'll have nothing."

"Robert—"

"I'm begging you, Jeffrey. I've never begged before. Don't do this to me. Don't. I—I know I'm not a demonstrative man. I know I seem cold and severe, but I have feelings. I love you."

The last three words were soft, barely more than a whisper. The anger had gone from his eyes, and only the anguish remained. I had never seen such suffering in any man's eyes. Jeffrey looked at his brother and saw the naked emotion. He gnawed his lower lip, hesitating, and then he shook his head.

"I'm sorry, Robert," he said gently. "Honora and I are leaving tomorrow. We're taking Douglas with us. I hope you'll wish us well."

He turned away then and walked slowly toward the staircase. He was suffering terribly, but he held himself erect. He passed not more than ten feet from where we were standing, but he didn't see us. He started up the staircase, moving very, very slowly, as though each step took a great effort. His brother watched, in agony, shaking his head from side to side.

"No!" he cried.

Jeffrey was halfway up the stairs. He didn't turn around. He continued to mount the stairs. Lord Robert cried out again and rushed toward the staircase and leaped up the stairs, taking them two at a time, and I knew, I knew. I broke free from Mrs. Rawson's grip. Lord Robert reached Jeffrey and took hold of his shoulder to turn him around. They were almost at the top.

"I'm not going to let you do this!" Lord Robert shouted.

He whirled Jeffrey around to face him and Jeffrey stumbled and lost his balance. He fell against the railing. There was a terrible splitting noise as it gave, as it broke beneath his weight. Lord Robert tried to grab hold of his brother's arm, but it was too late. I watched in stunned horror as my husband leaned on air for a fraction of a second and then came hurtling down with arms and legs flailing. He landed with a heavy thud. I screamed. I rushed to him, falling to my knees beside him. He looked up at me with dazed blue eyes and tried to move. He couldn't.

"Honora—"

"Don't move. Don't—don't try to speak, darling."

"My—my back—"

"It's going to be all right, darling. It's going to be all right."

"I can't feel—I can't feel anything—"

"Hush. Please. Just—just lie still."

"It's—"

"We'll fetch the doctor. You're going to be fine."

"I—"

"Hush."

"I—love—love you."

"And I love you, my darling. I love you with all my heart and soul."

He looked up at me, and I touched his cheek. I smoothed the heavy blond wave from his brow. He tried to say something else, but no words would come. He twitched violently. The gentle blye eyes seemed to grow dim. I held his hand tightly, tightly, and my tears fell on his cheek. He moaned softly and squeezed my hand in return, and then he gasped and his body went limp and I knew he was gone.

"Jeffrey," I whispered. "Oh, my darling—"

I don't know how long it was before Mrs. Rawson took hold of my arms and gently pulled me to my feet. Tears were streaming down her cheeks, too, and her mouth was quivering uncontrollably. She gathered me in her arms, holding me close. The grief inside me was so terrible, so demolishing that my system refused to acknowledge it. I was totally numb, unable to feel anything whatsoever.

Lord Robert came slowly down the stairs. He turned at the corner of the staircase and moved toward us. He stopped and looked at his brother's broken body, and then he looked at me. I disengaged myself from Mrs. Rawson's arms. She stepped aside. Lord Robert Mowrey and I stood face to face. He looked at me with hatred so fiery, so intense it was like a physical blow, but it didn't matter. Nothing he might do to me could possibly matter now, for Jeffrey was dead and I had no desire to go on living.

11

I LEFT MOWREY HOUSE THE NEXT MORNING. LORD Robert Mowrey summoned me to his study and handed me a bank draft and told me I was never to make any kind of claim on the Mowrey family or I would rue the day. The Reverend Mr. Williams took me in, giving me the spare room at the vicarage, and it was he who helped me through those dreadful days that followed, he and young Jack Jordon and Miss Moffat. Jack was subdued and attentive, doing all he could to make things easier for me, suggesting walks, playing the piano quietly, bringing me bunches of wildflowers, and the dour, put-upon Miss Moffat proved herself wonderfully kind and compassionate.

Reverend Williams talked to me for hours, quoting scriptures and giving me spiritual comfort while employing all his resources to make arrangements for my future. He conducted the funeral services for my husband. I stood beside the grave in that old cemetery behind the church, numb still, barely aware of what was happening. Miss Moffat had dyed one of my dresses black and had given me a heavy black veil. She stood on one side of me, Jack on the other, the two of them supporting me as the casket was lowered into the ground and the sexton began to shovel dirt on top of it.

Lord Robert Mowrey stood on the other side of the grave. Not once did he glance at me. Young Douglas was at his side, and he looked dazed, holding Mrs. Rawson's hand and staring straight ahead. It was not until the service ended that he broke down. He sobbed and called my name and tried to run over to me. His uncle jerked his arm quite brutally and led him out of the cemetery and into the waiting carriage, and that was the last I ever saw of that precious child. Mrs. Rawson visited me several times, slipping over after her duties were done. The child was inconsolable, she told me. He knew that his father had gone to heaven, but he couldn't understand why I had gone away. He cried for me during the night, and all day long he sat in abject misery. If it weren't for him, she would leave Mowrey House herself, but the poor lamb needed her, and Mrs. Rawson felt it her duty to stay and help that darlin' all she could.

Three weeks after the funeral I said good-bye to my friends in Cornwall and was on my way to Lichfield, that sunlit, lovely town where I was to spend the next few years of my life. Margaret Hibbert was sixty-two, a widow, childless. She had a small house on Market Square and for a long time had been looking for a young woman to live with her as a paid companion and help her with her work as Lichfield's leading seamstress. Reverend Williams had gotten in touch with her through one of his former parishioners, had written to her explaining my circumstances, and Maggie had replied that she was willing to give me a try, although she wasn't elated by my "delicate condition."

Lichfield was bustling the morning I arrived, for it was market day. The square was all color and confusion and congestion, farmers selling their produce from wagons, hawkers shouting their wares, housewives bartering vociferously over ribbons and baskets and pans. Chickens squawked. Children darted merrily through the crowd. There was a scattering of black-clad clerics in felt hats as well, for Lichfield was a great cathedral town, the massive, majestic structure with its towering spires rearing up above the green treetops of the close and seeming to shelter the whole town.

Maggie Hibbert was very tall, very thin, with sharp, bony features and large pale-blue eyes that seemed to protrude slightly beneath heavy, drooping lids. Her steel gray hair was pulled back tightly and worn in a bun on the back of her head, and she wore the frailest of muslin frocks in a variety of pastel shades, each sprigged with delicate flowers. Shrewd, intelligent, crusty and outspoken, Maggie was a formidable figure in Lichfield, the terror of impudent children, the scourge of thrifty matrons who tried to haggle over the price of cloth.

Wedged in between a pub and a greengrocer's shop and overlooking Market Square, Maggie's house was charming, tall and narrow with two floors and an attic she had converted into a charming apartment for me "and the babe to be." She showed me up in a brisk, no-nonsense manner, snapped that she trusted I would be comfortable and, during the next days, did everything in her power to see that I was. It didn't take me long to discover that the thorny manner was merely a facade, that Maggie was the dearest soul in the world and very, very lonely. We soon became close friends, and she treated me as she would have treated her own daughter. She fussed over me constantly, deeply concerned about my condition, scolding when she thought I was doing too much, doing her best to cheer me up when depression got the better of me.

Those first months were difficult indeed, despite Maggie, despite the bustle and beauty of that most pleasant of towns. The windows of my attic bedroom looked over the square, and directly across the way I could see the imposing, four-story home of Michael Johnson, the bookseller, the lower floor serving as shop. For hours on end I would sit at the windows, staring out at the activity on the square, remembering, grieving. There were many days when I had no will to go on, when the gray clouds settled and life seemed not worth living. I helped Maggie with her sewing, learning all of the secrets of the seamstress's art, and I pretended to take an interest in fabrics and cutting and invisible stitching, but a turgid lethargy plagued me each day. I had no real interest in anything.

Maggie's nephew Lambert arrived for a short visit in November, coming all the way from London in a chaise. In his early thirties, Lambert had premature gray hair stylishly cut, extremely sincere brown eyes and a smooth, polished manner that must have been very reassuring to the people whose money he handled. Lambert had a green thumb when it came to money, Maggie confided. He had invested her savings very shrewdly, almost doubling it, and he was eager to do the same with the thousand pounds Lord Robert had given me that morning in his study. A thousand pounds was a great deal of money, Lambert told me. Properly invested it could bring in a small, steady income that would provide for me and my child indefinitely. When Lambert returned to London he was my official banker. I was relieved to have someone so capable looking after my affairs.

December was cold but invigorating, a heavy snowfall blanketing everything in white. The children who played so noisily in the square were bundled up in heavy coats and caps, their cheeks rosy as they threw snowballs and shouted in gleeful abandon. Minister Pool froze over, and there was ice skating every afternoon. Maggie insisted I take walks, claiming the exercise would stand me in good stead when delivery time came, and I complied reluctantly, a woolen cloak and two large shawls helping to conceal my condition.

Maggie accompanied me, pointing out the Guildhall and Dame Oliver's School and the Three Crowns Inn, giving me a history of each. We passed Minister Pool and strolled leisurely through Cathedral Close. It was lovely in the snow, the great cathedral looking even more majestic close up. The trees that lined the Dean's walk were encrusted with ice, their limbs glittering in the sunlight. I saw the Palace and the Deanery, the Vicars' Close and Hall, and as we were walking back along Beacon Street Maggie showed me the house of the eccentric Dr. Erasmus Darwin and the Garricks's place nearby. Young Davy Garrick was the liveliest young man in Lichfield, she told me, the handsomest as well. All the lasses were after him, but Davy was more interested in books and getting into mischief with his crony Sam Johnson.

The new year came, and my Miranda was impatient, kicking and stirring, eager to see the world. In February she arrived, squalling lustily, and everything was changed. Into the gloom, into the grayness came this bright, lively, lovely creature who fascinated even in her crib. Maggie was utterly smitten and promptly began to spoil her. Miranda would gaze up at her with those blue, blue eyes, gurgling happily as the old lady stroked her fine auburn hair. Wonderfully healthy, Miranda nursed greedily, and when I took her off the breast she ate her food with equal relish. Was ever an infant so enchanting, so engaging, so little trouble? Has ever a child brought so much joy?

She began to toddle at nine months, was prancing merrily at one. Only a few months later she began to talk, and at two she was babbling nonstop, constantly asking questions, consumed with curiosity. Her auburn hair took on a brilliant, coppery-red hue. Her blue eyes sparkled like sapphires. She was spry, mischievous, captivating, fully aware of her charm and not above using it to get what she wanted. She was deplorably spoiled, yes. How was it possible for her to be otherwise with a grateful, doting mother and an even more doting Auntie Maggie, when total strangers stopped and stared and declared her the most beautiful child they had ever seen?

She had a marvelously vivid imagination, was constantly asking me to tell her stories, would make up stories of her own when I ran dry. At four she was skittering around Lichfield like a ray of sunlight, romping with the other children, spurring them on. She was, I fear, frequently naughty. The children of Lichfield loved to trail after the awkward, ungainly, deplorably unattractive young schoolmaster, Sam Johnson, making fun of his elephant gait and his pale, puffy, misshapen face. Miranda was the ringleader in this taunting. I spanked her quite soundly when I found out and then took her across the square and made her apologize to the unfortunate Sam. Absentminded, befuddled, lost in a world of books and ideas, the bookseller's son blinked in surprise, amazingly unaware that the children had been taunting him.

His companion David Garrick was another matter. He was indeed as handsome as a young god and incredibly magnetic. Davy seemed to draw the sunlight to him, and wherever he was, whatever he was doing, it was impossible to take notice of anyone else. Merry, mercurial, he seemed to burst with vitality, yet one sensed a brooding dissatisfaction beneath the surface, an impatience to explore wider horizons and conquer new worlds. Davy exuded charm and had a special way with children. When she was four years old Miranda declared quite matter-of-factly that she was going to marry him when she grew up. Davy said she was the prettiest little minx he'd ever seen and had promised to wait for her.

Miranda had always loved books and loved to curl up in my lap and gaze at the pictures while I read to her, but at four and a half she was no longer content with merely listening and looking. She wanted to learn to read by herself. She already knew her alphabet and could pick out a few words, but once she decided that wasn't enough, she seemed to learn to read overnight. At five she marched sassily across the square and confronted a startled Michael Johnson, informing him that his books were all for big people and he should sell books that children would like, too.

She was precocious, everyone said so. She adored hearing the stories of Shakespeare's plays, would ask me to tell them over and over, and even though she couldn't comprehend six words out of ten, she wagged the battered volume of plays around with her, pouring over it. She didn't care for math any more than Douglas had, but she took to history and geography with great relish and blithely informed me that she wanted to know everything about everybody, particularly those blood-thirsty kings of old and those beautiful ladies who wore such enormous skirts and had so many jewels.

Captivating, capricious, strong willed and remarkably intelligent, Miranda drove away the shadows, and those years in Lichfield seemed to pass in a golden haze of contentment. I enjoyed my work with Maggie and became a competent seamstress myself, taking on a heavier and heavier load of work as Maggie's strength began to ebb. There were books to read and musical events to attend, for Lichfield's citizens prided themselves on their appreciation of the arts. There was merriment and gossip, exercise and activity and the constant enchantment of my wonderful child.

It ended so very quickly. Maggie came grumbling into the parlor, claimed she'd never be able to get Miss Stewart's bloody tea gown done in time and added that she felt a bit short of breath. She looked rather pale that evening as she told me good night, and I made a vow to make her take it easier for a while. Maggie had always pushed herself much too hard and flatly refused to admit she was getting older. I never had a chance to keep that vow. Maggie died peacefully in her sleep, and all of Lichfield grieved for the gruff but kindly old woman who had been so much a part of the town.

Nephew Lambert was much too busy to come down for the funeral. He sent an emissary instead, a callous young man who went over every inch of the house with a notebook in hand, jotting down estimates. Lambert intended to sell the place, he informed me. All the furniture and goods would be auctioned off. I had two weeks in which to "make other arrangements." It was completely cold-blooded, so much so that I could hardly believe it, but it was true nevertheless. In exactly two weeks everything went under the block. I couldn't bear to stay and watch it. Miranda and I were on our way to London where I would get my money from Lambert, find us a place to live and open my own business as seamstress.

Lambert was very smooth and ever so sincere when I visited his office. He patiently explained the intricacies of investment and showed me why he couldn't put his hands on my money "just yet." As Maggie had provided room and board and had been paying me a small salary as well for the work I did, I hadn't collected a penny from Lambert. Oh, yes, he assured me, my initial thousand pounds had already earned quite a lot, quite a lot. As I had only three pounds left after paying for our fares to London and for our room at the inn upon arrival, Lambert quite generously advanced me enough to rent a tiny apartment and pay our expenses for a few weeks until he could "consolidate" and give me a draft for the full amount.

And that was the first step toward St. Giles, for I was never able to collect a penny from Lambert Hibbert. After months of taking in sewing and saving all I could, I was finally able to pay an advocate's fee and take Lambert before a magistrate, and there I learned what a mockery justice has become in our age. Lambert was crowned with laurels, an altruistic soul who, at great sacrifice, had taken time from much more important business to help a young widow, while I was unreasonable, ungrateful, vindictive and, by rights, should have been thrown into Bridewell for prosecuting such an upstanding citizen. As I was stepping outside after this humiliation I saw Lambert chatting amiably with my advocate. He handed the man some money, and then the two of them sauntered off down Bow Street together.

I was defeated, but I refused to give up. Somehow, some way, I would survive. It would be impossible for me to have my own place of business, but I could take in sewing as I had been doing these past months and hope eventually to build up a clientele. The city was such a large, noisy, crowded place, frightening, heartless—certainly no place for a woman alone with a spirited and curious child. Miranda made friends everywhere, taking to London immediately, loving the noise and excitement, but I was worried about her every minute she was out of my sight.

I worked. I struggled. I tried to take care of Miranda and make a living for us, but my strength began to fail and I was unable to take in as much sewing as before. I felt weak, lethargic, and it took the greatest effort to complete a hem, to trim a bodice. We had to move to cheaper rooms. A few months later we had to move again, then again. I developed a bad cough. I couldn't seem to get rid of it. I made a valiant effort to put on a good front for Miranda's sake, chatting brightly, keeping up with her lessons, having her read aloud to me while I sewed, but I couldn't completely conceal the desperation I felt each day. Things grew worse and worse . . . and eventually we were forced to take this squalid room in St. Giles, and I discovered the first spot of blood on my handkerchief.

Reverend Williams, I am speaking to you directly now. I should have written to you a long time ago, I know, but somehow I couldn't bring myself to do so. You were so kind to me, so kind, but when I left Cornwall . . . I wanted to put everything behind me, Reverend Williams. I wanted to begin a new life, and writing to you would have brought it all back . . . all that I wanted to forget. Maggie wrote to you from Lichfield and kept you informed about me and Miranda, I know. She frequently mentioned the letters. That seemed enough, somehow, and after I came to London I had too much pride. I couldn't write to you, asking for help, not after I had failed to write during those years when everything was going so well. I can no longer afford the luxury of pride. I am desperate, and you are my only hope.

Yesterday I had a terrible siege. It was the worst yet. I couldn't stop coughing, and the blood . . . I was so grateful that Miranda was out and didn't see. Mrs. Humphreys helped me as best she could. She's a querulous woman, malicious and prying, but, in her way, she has been kind to me these past weeks. She detests Miranda, and Miranda is indeed hateful to her, sassing her, making faces, but the woman has taken it upon herself to "look in" on me, and I can't refuse her help. She keeps saying I must send Miranda to the parish workhouse for her own good. She knows one of the nurses. She will make all the arrangements. I can't allow that. I can't. I know what happens to children who end up in those dreadful places, and though I shudder at the thought, I know Miranda would be better off fending for herself on the streets.

Miranda came in very late yesterday, bringing a pail of milk, cheese, two small meat pies. Her rich auburn hair was dirty and sadly in need of a brush. Her face was streaked with dirt. Her bare feet were dirty, too, and her blue dress was in deplorable condition, more gray than blue, mottled with soot, but her smile was as cheerful as ever, her eyes as bright and lively. She chatted blithely about her adventures with the other children. They had played games. She had seen another puppy.

A kind old man had asked her to run an errand for him and, in gratitude, had given her money to buy food. She was making it all up, I could tell that, but I was too weak, too weary to protest.

My daughter has become an adept liar. She is shrewd and crafty and sly, tough and independent and as rowdy as any of those urchins she runs with. She is as dirty, and when she forgets herself she drops her 'h's' and final 'g's' and peppers her sentences with the crudest slang, her voice taking on a peculiar nasal twang. I fear for her. She is so very intelligent, so resourceful and quick, and that makes it all the more frightening. What kind of trouble will she get into if she is not taken from this hideous place?

I sat up in bed, trying to be vivacious, trying to hide my pain, and she poured milk into the cup and watched while I feebly sipped. It was difficult to swallow anything, even the milk, and I couldn't eat a bite. I told Miranda I wasn't hungry, making light of it, but she wasn't deceived. Her blue eyes full of concern, she eased me back onto the filthy pillows and stroked my brow and frowned.

"It's going to be all right, Mum," she promised.

"Yes," I whispered.

"You *are* going to get well."

Darkness fell. Miranda lighted the candle and picked up the battered old volume of Shakespeare and began to read aloud to me. Her voice was rich, melodic, without a trace of the twang. She was reading *The Tempest* and paused to ask me if she had been named after the Miranda in the play. I nodded, smiling, but tears began to spill down my cheeks as I remembered another time, another child, a colored paper doll that so resembled the woman I had been, the woman Miranda would become.

She continued to read and I eventually drifted off to sleep. She was already gone when I awoke this morning, and even as I write these words she is out on the streets, running with her pack of urchins, scavenging, learning things no child should ever know.

You must save her, Reverend Williams.

I am so much weaker after yesterday's spell, so weak I can hardly hold this quill, but I must finish. I don't have long, I know that. A few more weeks perhaps. Perhaps less. I can join my Jeffrey then...I can go peacefully, even willingly, if I know my Miranda will be taken care of. She is a Mowrey, Reverend Williams. She doesn't know that. She knows nothing about Cornwall or her father or Lord Robert Mowrey. I merely told her that her father was in heaven, and she never asked any more questions. I want her to know. When you deem her old enough to understand, I want you to let her read this.

You will take care of her, won't you? Perhaps you will even see that she receives a share of what is rightfully hers. She is my child, yes, but she is also Jeffrey's child, and Lord Robert . . . I can understand why he would hate me, but surely he wouldn't transfer that hatred to an innocent child.

I am weak, so weak. Only a few more words . . .

This morning, after I finished the pages you've just read, I made arrangements with Mrs. Humphreys, and she has promised to get this to you. I am going to wrap these pages up in a neat parcel and address it to you. I've given Mrs. Humphreys money, and she told me she would personally see that the parcel will be on the next chaise to Cornwall. I pray you will receive it. I pray you will come and fetch my Miranda and save her.

I pray you will arrive in time.

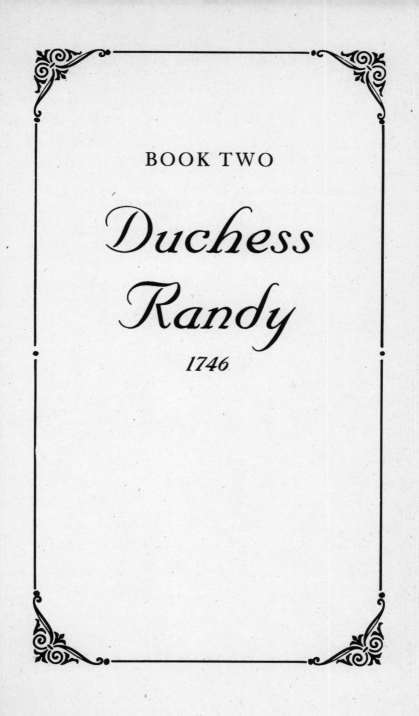

BOOK TWO

*Duchess
Randy*

1746

12

I RUBBED MY EYES AND SAT UP AND STARED AT THE
cat. He was black and scrawny and stared at me with accusing
eyes, as though blaming me for not whipping out a bit of
mackerel and a saucer of milk.

"Sorry, cat," I told him. "If I 'ad milk, I'd drink it meself,
and if I 'ad a bit of mackerel I'd be in 'eaven. Tough life, ain't
it?"

He leered at me and waved his tail arrogantly, prancing over
the great pile of coal and making his exit through the half-open
window. Bloody window. I had forgotten to close it last night.
No wonder I was half frozen. I yawned, gathering the smelly
brown sacks around me and snuggling once more in my cozy
nest of straw. No need complaining. I had the coal cellar all
to myself, didn't have to share it with anyone, and old Hawkins
only charged me a penny a night for the use of it. The cellar
might be tiny and filthy and there might be rats, but it was
much better than those reeking doss houses where as many as
twenty slept in a single cubbyhole—men, women and children
all clambered together on the straw, lice everywhere. Besides,
a girl wasn't safe there.

A girl wasn't safe anywhere in all of St. Giles, not unless
she knew how to take care of herself. I did. I'd been taking
care of myself ever since my mum's death and doing a bleedin'
good job of it, too. I didn't have a twang looking out for me,
bossing me around and smacking my backside when I failed
to bring in enough shillings. I didn't need one. Why should I
go out and sell my tail to strange men and take the money to
some brutal pimp? I was too independent, always had been,
and whoring didn't interest me. A girl might make a living for
a while that way, as long as she was young and didn't get a
disease, but I didn't fancy ending up an ancient crone at twenty,

clutching a gin bottle in some alley and starving to death because my looks were gone.

No, stealing was much easier, as long as you didn't get caught. I'd never been caught, although I'd had a couple of close calls. A thief-taker had grabbed me once, clamping his rough hands on me right after I'd snipped off a fine gentleman's jeweled shoe buckles, but he'd let go soon enough, as soon as I kneed him in the groin. There wasn't a thief-taker or a watchman or a constable in all London smart enough or fast enough to nab me. I was much too nimble, much too sly, and I knew every single hiding place in St. Giles.

The cat crawled through the window again, scampering over the coal and shivering. It was bloody cold out. What wouldn't I give for a nice warm cloak and maybe a pair of shoes? The cloak would be lined with wool and have a fur collar, and the shoes would fit snug, made of kidskin with elegant little heels, and I would admire them as I warmed my feet before my own private fire. I smiled to myself, imagining how it would be. I'd have bread and cheese and a hunk of beef. No, a box of chocolates, each one of 'em wrapped up in a crinkly gold paper. I'd seen a box like that in a shop window once, next to a tray of candied fruit frosted with sugar and looking so tasty I'd almost broken the glass to snatch some.

Fancy people eating candied fruit. And cakes. People ate delicate little cakes with creamy white icing. They ate peaches, too, and lovely grapes and oysters and chickens roasted to a crisp golden brown. I closed my eyes, seeing the table with the feast spread out and me there to eat it all and sip wine from a crystal goblet. I'd eat it all and then wipe my fingers ever so daintily and tell 'em I might take just a smidgin more of the soup and a nice juicy pear. My stomach began to growl. Wasn't any use daydreaming about food. Victuals like that weren't for the likes of me. Folks who lived in St. Giles considered themselves lucky to get a bowl of gruel and a few crusts of bread. Most of them lived on gin, which was cheap as cheap could be, a penny a half quart.

Me, I didn't like gin. Didn't care for the taste, and I didn't fancy what it did to you. Here in St. Giles they mixed it up in foul basements and served it in filthy glasses and you were lucky if you didn't go blind. Children drank it same as grownups and you'd see kiddies of five or six staggering around with eyes all glazed. Helped you forget your misery, gin did, but a girl couldn't pick pockets properly or snip off fancy shoe buckles if she was half out of her mind. I didn't want anything fogging up my senses. An independent thief like me, with no gang to back her up, needed to be as alert as possible.

I yawned. The cat came over to sniff my hair. He mewed in disgust, curling his nose up and moving back to the pile of coal.

"You don't smell like no bleedin' rose garden yourself, mate," I informed him. "One of these days I'm goin' to steal me a bar of soap and get some water and take a proper bath, but I don't see much profit in it. I'd just get dirty again, sleepin' in this coal cellar, roamin' these streets. Besides, bathin' too often ain't 'ealthy."

The cat began to dig into the coal, hoping, no doubt, to find something edible. Poor creature. If I had a scrap of food, I'd give it to him. I hated to see anything suffer, and there was suffering all around you in St. Giles. People dying in basements. Unwanted babies tossed into the gutter. Corpses of dogs and cats slung onto refuse heaps, stinking something awful.

"Tell you what, luv," I said, "I'll find us somethin'. Today's bound to be a good day—there's goin' to be a 'angin' at Tyburn—and I'll make that bleedin' receiver pay me proper this time and I'll buy us a loaf of bread and a big pail of milk and bring it back tonight. That suit you?"

The cat gave a pitiful yowl and continued to burrow into the coal. Cripes. Freezin' cold out and both of us starving and not a penny to my name. Never could get a few pennies ahead, no matter how good I was. That sod at the receiving house cheated you awful—all fences were the same—and you were lucky to make enough to eat on. Two or three bad days in a row and you damn near caved in from hunger. The thing to do was steal food outright, but the sods who kept the stalls were all burly louts with fierce expressions who'd break your neck soon as look at you, and they had sharp eyes, too. You could be hanged for stealing a loaf of bread, strung up on Tybrun Tree same as the wickedest criminal. Only three months ago they'd hung a lad of twelve for the heinous crime of stealing three apples.

I frowned. Didn't do no good thinking about the injustice of it all. Things were the way they were, and there wasn't anything you could do about it. The magistrates and those hired to uphold the law were more corrupt than the criminals, the thief-takers far more savage than the folk they pursued. If you had the money, you could buy your way out of any kind of trouble. You could murder a man and go scot-free if you had the gold to pay a lawyer. He'd hire a couple of straw men to vow you'd been somewhere else the night of the crime and he'd give the magistrate a healthy bribe and you'd saunter out of the roundhouse as free as a bird.

Only the poor swung from Tyburn tree, and the traitors, of course.

They were going to hang a traitor today. One of those poor souls who had fought with Bonnie Prince Charles and managed to escape the slaughter at Culloden only to be tracked down by the vengeful Cumberland. The Duke of Cumberland was the most hated man in England, a bloodthirsty villain who had cut down innocent women and children on the moors of Culloden, and he vowed he wouldn't rest until he had tracked down every single man who had supported the Bonnie Prince. These Hanovers who sat on the throne of England were a bloody lot, stupid and dense, most of 'em, most of 'em not even speaking English half the time, and poor Prince Charlie was a fugitive in Europe when he should have been smiling his charming smile from the throne.

Poor little prince, I thought, snuggling under the rags. I was glad he had fled the field before Cumberland got him, and I shuddered every time I passed the Temple and saw the heads of his followers sticking on the pikes. Cumberland vowed he'd put Prince Charlie's head there, too, after it had been parboiled with Bay salt and Cumin seed to keep the birds from pecking it. The thought made me shiver. It was time to get up, I told myself. No profit in shivering here on the straw with an empty stomach and a body near frozen. It must be at least seven o'clock.

Reluctantly I stirred, sitting up again, massaging my arms and tucking my bare feet under the rags. I ran my fingers through my hair, checking for lice. I hated the beastly little buggers, couldn't abide them. Finding none, I sighed and crawled over to the corner where I kept my possessions: a brush, a broken comb, three candles and the battered Shakespeare book I had snatched up before fleeing Mrs. Humphreys the night my mum died. Picking up the brush, I glanced at the cat and began the morning ritual.

"I may not *wash* me 'air, cat," I said chattily, "but I do keep it brushed properly. Fifty strokes in the mornin', fifty at night, keeps the lice away. Big Moll says me 'air's like red brown fire, says she could warm 'er 'ands from it, says she'd sell 'er soul for a 'ead of 'air like mine. Fat lot-a good it'd do 'er, 'er bein' as big as a barn."

Completely uninterested in my remarks, the cat was far more concerned with the rustling noise behind the wall.

"That's right," I told him. "Rats. Big ones. Why couldn't you 'ave been 'ere last night when that bugger was tryin' to nibble me toes? I must-a chucked a 'undred pieces-a coal at 'im before he gave up and looked for another snack. You catch 'im and I'll bring you *two* pails-a milk."

Putting the brush aside, I picked up the book. It was falling to pieces, I'd read it so many times. Couldn't say I under*stood* it all, but it was nice to read those words and imagine all those kings and princes and fairies and soldiers and unhappy lovers, those castles, those moors, those enchanted forests. I used to read the plays aloud to my mum, I remembered, and she had told me I was named after the girl in *The Tempest*. I flipped through the battered, thumbmarked pages and stroked the watermarked binding that was so sadly torn and ragged, cherishing the volume. It was all I had left of the past.

It would be nice to have more time to read. Folks thought it was barmy, of course. Perhaps it was, but it was so cozy and comforting to light a candle and snuggle up in my nest of straw and forget the dangers and hardships of the day as I read about those enchanted beings who had lovely clothes and lots to eat and sometimes went stark raving mad. Me, if I had a couple of nice gowns and a full belly, I'd never go mad, no matter how ungrateful my children might be. I'd tell 'em to sod off and bring me another meat pasty. Wouldn't kill myself either, just because some silly love affair went wrong. That Juliet really was a ninny, I thought. All those fancy velvet gowns, all those nice things to eat, and she goes and drinks poison because she can't have Romeo.

Bosh! She was out of 'er bloody 'ead.

There'd never been a Romeo in my life, true, and there never would be if I could help it. Men! Who needed 'em? Blustering, bullying sods, the lot of 'em, always out to cheat a girl, always greedy to pop your cherry. I saw 'em lookin' at me, sure. I saw the way their eyes lighted up, saw the way they licked their lips, pantin' to drag me into some dark alley and have their way. Any man stupid enough to put a hand on me got my nails across his cheek, got my teeth sunk into his arm, got a knee in the groin. They called me wildcat, the men of St. Giles, said you don't want to try any tricks with that

bloody Randy, she'll neuter you an' 'ave you singin' soprano.
I'd keep my cherry to myself, thanks a lot, and if I *did* someday
decide to have it popped, it wouldn't be in some filthy alley,
and it wouldn't be in a whorehouse for two pounds, not even
for five. That's what Big Moll assured me it'd fetch.

I put the Shakespeare down. I'd read a lot of other books,
too, stole every last one of 'em. It was easy to steal books.
Folks never thought anyone'd *want* to. I stole 'em and read
'em and then took 'em to the receiving house where the fence
scowled and gave me a couple of pennies and told me I was
out of my bloomin' mind, stealin' books when I could be
stealin' brooches and watches and fancy shoe buckles. Books
weren't worth anything, he grumbled, and I didn't even try to
explain how much they meant to me. I kept on stealin' 'em
and readin' 'em, puzzled sometimes by the words, sure, but
greedy for 'em nevertheless. Once I got hold of a dreary book
of sermons I couldn't make head or tail of, and sometimes
there were dull travel books, but if I was lucky I'd snatch
something like *Moll Flanders* by that chap Defoe. Folks could
call me barmy all they liked, but I 'ad to 'ave my books like
others 'ad to 'ave their gin.

No time to read this morning, though. I wrapped the book
up carefully in a rag and put it back under the loose floorboard
with the brush and comb and candles. I thought of my mum
then. As I kneeled there among the straw and the coal I saw
her face as clearly as though a portrait had materialized on thin
air before me. I saw her as she had looked when we had been
living in the house in that sunny little town whose name I
couldn't remember. I remembered very little about those days.
Everything was hazy and unclear. I seemed to recall a pond
with ducks and a big cathedral with towering spires, and I
vaguely remembered someone called Auntie Maggie, but the
rest was a blur. Once I caught a fleeting glimpse in memory
of a handsome young man who smiled a teasing smile and said
he was going to marry me when he grew up. Davy? Was his
name Davy? The memory flashed in my mind for an instant
and then vanished abruptly.

I remembered my mum, though, and as I gazed at the mental
portrait that materialized before me, it was almost like gazing
into a mirror, for her features were mine. I had the same high
cheekbones and the same mouth, although mine was a bit fuller,
not so delicate. I had the same eyes, mine a deep blue instead

of gray, with faint mauve shadows on my lids, as on hers, and long, curling eyelashes. My hair was auburn, too, like Mum's, but mine was brighter, coppery, leaning more toward red than brown. I might resemble her in a great many ways, but my mum had been a beautiful woman and I was a scrappy, dirty-faced street urchin. The men stared, true, but that was because of my bosom and my narrow waist and my long legs, not because of my face.

The mental portrait gradually began to change, another taking its place, and I was gazing at my mum as she had been that last day. The lovely face had become gaunt, smudges beneath the eyes, deep hollows beneath the cheekbones. Memories came flooding back, bringing the grief that always accompanied them. I would never forget that day. Never. I remembered her gentle smile and the way those sad gray eyes peered up at me as she stroked my cheek with a pitifully frail hand. I remembered the racking cough and those bloodstained handkerchiefs she was always trying to hide under the bedclothes. Mrs. Humphreys came into the room, a horrible woman with shrewd, mean eyes. She was always spying on me, and she was the one who kept insisting Mum turn me over to the parish authorities and send me to the workhouse, saying Mum wasn't able to watch after me, saying I'd be much better off with the other poor kiddies.

"She's goin'," Mrs. Humphreys said tersely. "'Adn't got long now. I 'eard 'er coughin' 'er lungs out last night."

"Get out!" I cried.

"I'm goin' to fetch Jenkins. Jenkins'll know what to do. She's with the parish, Jenkins is, a nurse. She'll see your mum's buried 'an take you back to the parish 'ouse with 'er."

"My mum's not dying!"

Mrs. Humphreys gave me a smug look and tromped heavily out of the room. I held Mum's hand, squeezing it, and she kept shaking her head. Both of us knew it was almost over. Her strength had gone. She was a mere skeleton. I kept wringing a cloth out in water and bathing her brow, and I kept smiling, too, pretending it was just another seizure, pretending she was going to get better. My smile didn't deceive her, nor did her own gentle smile deceive me. I squeezed her hand and bathed her brow, waiting.

"You—you'll be taken care of, Miranda," she whispered. "He—he'll come for you, I know he will. I sent—I sent him a —" She closed her eyes, summoning enough strength to go on. "I told him everything—the whole story, and I know he—he'll fetch you. You'll be—"

Her voice faded. She coughed again, and when she withdrew the handkerchief from her mouth it was covered with blood.

"Don't try to talk, Mum," I said gently. "Don't—"

She murmured a name I couldn't quite hear and told me he would fetch me and take me to someplace called Cornwall and take care of me.

"They—they'll send you to the workhouse, my precious, but it will only be for a—for a little while. He'll come for you and—"

She could say no more. She looked up at me with such pain in her eyes, such love, and the tender smile left her lips and she closed her eyes for the final time. I knew she was gone, even before Mrs. Humphreys and another woman came marching into the room and declared her dead. I fought back the tears as they clucked and chattered, and then Mrs. Humphreys turned to me, eyes glittering with malicious triumph.

"It's a pauper's grave for 'er," she declared, "an' it's th' work'ouse for you, brat! Nurse Jenkins 'ere is gonna take you there."

"Oh no she ain't, you old bitch!"

I grabbed the Shakespeare book and tore down the stairs as fast as my feet would carry me, running through the twisting labyrinth of streets and alleys until I reached Big Moll's. I sobbed and sobbed and begged her to hide me, and the plump, hard-shelled old bawd crushed me to her ample bosom and stroked my hair and told me to shush, told me them bleedin' bastards weren't going to get her little Randy, not bleedin' likely.

Nine years ago that had been, nine long years, yet it was still as vivid in memory as though it had happened yesterday. Big Moll made good her promise, and the parish authorities never did find me, nor did the man who prowled St. Giles for almost three weeks, asking questions, searching for me. Someone told Big Moll he was a man of the cloth, that he'd come a long way to find me. Them clergymen, they were worse'n th' parish authorities, Moll declared. Wudn't one of 'em gettin' 'is 'ands on 'er Randy. The man eventually left St. Giles without finding me. They said he looked very, very sad and worried. Moll said good riddance, them sods were all corrupt. If it wudn't for th' clergy, 'alf th' 'ore'ouses in St. Giles 'ud go broke.

Already an accomplished thief at nine years of age, I quickly became one of the best in St. Giles, fiercely independent, refusing to join a gang, refusing any kind of "protector." Skilled as I was at my trade, I had frequently gone hungry and, even on a good day, barely earned enough to keep body and soul together. They paid a mere pittance at the receiving house for even the finest goods, Black Jack Stewart the only one to make a profit. I was eighteen years old now, still free, still independent and, alas, still hungry.

Putting the loose floorboard back in place and covering it with rags, I stood up straight and yawned. Dim rays of early morning sunlight sifted through the filthy windowpanes, filling the tiny, cramped cellar with hazy white light. I adjusted the bodice of my faded violet-blue dress. The garment was horribly soiled and much too small. My breasts threatened to pop out of the low-cut bodice, and the waist was so tight I could hardly breathe. The full skirt was torn in several places, the ragged hemline swirling at mid-calf.

"One-a these days I gotta get me a new dress," I told the cat, "a pair-a shoes, too. It ain't so bad in the summertime. It's 'ot as 'ell then and shoes don't matter, but on a mornin' like this—"

I shivered dramatically, folding my arms around my waist, but the cat wasn't at all impressed. Nose in the air, tail sticking straight up, he continued his investigations.

"You catch that rat now, you 'ear, luv? I won't forget the milk."

I crept up the narrow wooden stairs and cautiously unbolted the door, opening it as quietly as possible. Old Hawkins let me sleep in his coal cellar for a penny a night, yes, and it was a dandy arrangement for us both, but of late he had the idea that the penny entitled him to something more. As doddering and decrepit as most of the customers who frequented his squalid gin shop, he had taken to lurking in the back hall of a morning, waiting for me to come up. He would engage me in idle conversation and casually stroke my arm, "accidentally" touching my breast. The only reason I hadn't smacked him silly was because I couldn't afford to give up the cellar. I had put the bolt on the door myself, going to considerable trouble to do so, and Hawkins had been quite surprised when he tried the door late at night after the last customers had staggered out.

Men were all alike, even in their dotage. You couldn't trust any of 'em. A girl 'ad a 'ell of a time 'oldin' on to 'er virtue, particularly in St. Giles. I wasn't prudish or prim, but I didn't fancy lettin' any man paw over me. When I finally gave up my virtue it would be on silken sheets, I told myself, and the man who introduced me to those splendid delights would be a man I'd chosen myself. Besides, what was the bloomin' 'urry? I was eighteen, sure, I couldn't deny that, practically an old maid, and half the whores in St. Giles had started sellin' tail by the age of eleven, but I staunchly held on to my cherry. That was one of the reasons they called me "Duchess Randy." They said it in derision, mocking me, but in truth I was rather proud of the title. Who wanted to be like everyone else?

The back hall was empty this morning. Hawkins was probably in a drunken stupor in his quarters over the shop. I crept down the hall and stepped into the alley and made my way nimbly through the piles of refuse. Rats scurried in every direction, diving beneath heaps of rotten vegetables, skittering across the chest of an emaciated old drunk who snored loudly as he sprawled against the wall with an empty gin bottle beside him. A chill wind swept down the alley, and the hem of my skirt billowed up, exposing my bare legs. Jemminy, if only I 'ad me a cloak. It was cold enough to freeze your arse off.

The street outside the gin house was almost as narrow as the alley, almost as filthy, too, lined on either side with shambly, sooty-brown buildings that looked ready to come toppling down at any minute. Lurching, slanting rooftops festooned with black chimneypots leaned out, almost meeting overhead, blocking out most of the sunlight and permitting only a few glimpses of leaden gray sky. Laborers fortunate enough to have work plodded wearily to the crowded, unventilated factories. Dirty-faced, unkempt children played noisily, early though it was, and two shrill old bawds were arguing over a fish one of them clutched by the tail. Life in all its ugliness spilled out onto the pavements.

Sprawling beneath the spire of St. George's, Bloomsbury, St. Giles was a huge, festering slum, a sore on the face of London, "the cesspit of beggary and wretchedness," and the ornate richness of the church that towered so nobly at its entrance merely emphasized the squalor. A dark labyrinth of narrow, twisting streets and alleyways, it was known as "the Rookery," crowded with hideously congested tenements, with brothels and doss houses and gambling dens—every known vice thriving vigorously within its boundaries. Respectable folks dared not step foot in St. Giles, for it was packed with ruffians who would cheerfully slit a throat for a handful of coins. The constables and watchmen who patrolled the slum stepped warily, always in pairs, their chief protection being that they were generally even more corrupt and vicious than the denizens they kept an eye on.

No fine squares and spacious gardens for us in St. Giles, no elegant, majestic buildings and courtyards. It wasn't so bad, though. You got used to it after a while. The overpowering stench didn't bother you, though it would fell a man not accustomed to breathing it in night and day. St. Giles had been my home for almost as long as I could remember—those earlier years seemed like a dream, all nebulous and blurry, not real at all—and I knew every alley, every hidden courtyard and cul de sac, every putrid ditch. It was bleak and ugly, yes, and you had to fight just to stay alive, but there was a raw, raucous vitality in the air and an excitement you wouldn't find in those swell, swank neighborhoods. You knew you were alive in St. Giles, knew if you didn't keep your guard up every minute you'd find yourself in a ditch with your body violated and your head bashed in—or else you'd starve.

I hurried down the street, turned a corner, cut through an alley, heading for Big Moll's. A thin, sallow man in gent's attire came staggering up from one of the opium dens that riddled the slum. I paused, studying him with great interest, my head tilted to one side. He was wearing gent's attire, sure, but the clothes were sadly rumpled and, I decided, his pockets had probably already been emptied by the harridan who kept the den. There'd be much easier pickings at Tyburn, and, besides, folk who spent the night with the pipe sometimes went plumb berserk and had the strength of ten. I let him pass. No need taking unnecessary risks, not unless there was a sure profit in store. Moving on, I passed the tall, tumbling down building where the painted boys entertained gents. Every taste was catered to in St. Giles.

My stomach growled, and I hoped Big Moll was in a good mood. Sometimes when she'd had a good night and wasn't too grumpy she'd give me a cup of coffee and a roll, crabbing all the while, of course, claiming I was eatin' up all 'er profits. It was a long walk to Tyburn, and coffee and a bit of roll would stand me in good stead. Moll was always grumbling and bitching and pulling fierce faces, but she had a heart as big as the rest of her, and there was a soft spot in it for me, had been ever since I'd come to her aid—what?—nine years ago. Yes, Mum had still been alive then, and I had just begun to polish my skills as a thief. I smiled to myself, remembering that day.

Big Moll hadn't been so big then, though she was certainly hefty enough, and her plump face had still been vaguely pretty. She hadn't been managing the house for very long, and she'd been foolish enough to set out for Black Jack's establishment with the night's take in her pocket and no paid bullies to protect her. She hadn't gone fifty yards before two thieves fell upon her, knocking her to the ground and making off with the money. Uninjured, she began to shriek and wail like a stuck pig, claiming Black Jack would have her throat slit if she didn't get the money back. A crowd quickly gathered, laughing and mocking her and throwing refuse, and my eyes flashed angrily as I helped her to her feet, a rotten tomato splattering my cheek as I did so.

"Don't you worry, ma'am," I told her. "I'll get your money back for you. Just see if I don't."

I scurried away then, pursuing the thieves. I had recognized them, and I knew their haunts, knew where they were likely to go. Sure enough, I spotted them in Jacob's Gin Shop, cackling over their success. I sidled up to them and ordered a half pint of gin and, when it came, tripped and accidentally spilled it all over Ted Brown, the burly, pock-faced villain who'd grabbed her money as she fell to the pavement. I apologized profusely and wiped at the damp spots on his coat and then left immediately, Big Moll's money tucked safely in the bodice of my dress.

She had hardly been able to believe it when I returned it to her. Her big brown eyes grew wider. Her plump, painted mouth made a large "O" as she began to count the money. Finding it all there, she clasped me to her and hugged me so tightly I feared my ribs would crack and said I was a bloomin' wonder. She asked me why I hadn't kept the money for myself. I told her the thought hadn't occurred to me. She pounded me on the back and hugged me again and roared that I had a lot to learn about survival in St. Giles and said she'd better start giving me a few lessons, innocent mite that I was. Big Moll was my first real friend in St. Giles and, to this day, the only one I trusted.

Reaching the house, I skipped up the stairs, opened the door and moved down the hall to the parlor, smelling the wonderful aroma of coffee. Three of Big Moll's girls were lolling in the parlor, bleary-eyed, puffy, wearing thin wrappers and very little else.

"Look 'oo's 'ere," Nan said hatefully. "Come to beg a cuppa coffee, I suppose."

I made a face at her. With her stony blue eyes and mousy brown hair, Nan was the least attractive of Big Moll's girls, a skinny, querulous shrew with a sharp tongue and a wretched disposition. Strangely enough, she was also one of the most popular. A lot of men seemed to fancy a snappish whore.

"Pay 'er no mind, luv," Sally said. "She's in a snit. One of 'er regulars passed 'er over last night, chose me instead. 'Ere, let me pour you a cup. We 'ave cinnamon rolls. Fresh, too. The lad from the bakery just brought 'em."

"An' you gropin' 'im in the 'allway 'fore 'e could get away," Nan snapped.

"Up your arse, Nan. You know I never did no such thing. 'E was a 'ealthy-lookin' lad, though. Cheeky as could be."

"Barely sixteen, 'e was."

Sally handed me a cup of coffee and a sticky cinnamon roll. "Pinched my arse, 'e did, just reached out an' gave it a tweak. Gave me quite a turn, I don't mind tellin' you. My rump's still sore."

"Biggest thrill you've 'ad all week," Nan said dryly.

"You're just jealous, luv. Ain't no one wanted to pinch your arse for a long time."

Sally plopped back down on the sofa, plump, jolly, her head a mass of riotous black curls. Her brown eyes were full of merriment, and her soiled pink wrapper scarcely covered her ample girth. I sipped my coffee and took a bite of the roll. Faith moaned from the corner of the room, dabbing at her cheek with a vinegar-soaked cloth. The cheek was terribly swollen and beginning to darken with a bluish mauve bruise. Sally shook her head and frowned.

"Bloody sod! Beatin' up on poor Faith like that. Moll threw a fit when she 'eard Faith squallin', rushed upstairs an' gave 'im what for, told 'im to go to Mother Redcoat's if 'e fancied that kinda play. She tossed the bastard right outta the 'ouse. Black Jack oughta protect us from that sort."

"Black Jack don't give a 'ang what 'appens to us long as 'e gets 'is money," Nan remarked. "What's a battered 'ore to 'im? Plenty more to fill 'er shoes in St. Giles. Understand 'e's openin' a new 'ouse specially for th' gentry and selectin' th' girls 'isself. They gotta be young an' pretty an' virginal."

"Leaves you out, luv," Sally teased.

"I was a virgin for *weeks*," Nan protested. "Moll must-a used up a 'undred of them pellets 'fore th' ruse failed."

I knew the pellets she was referring to, of course. Virgins were in great demand and very short supply in St. Giles. Big Moll and the other madams solved this problem by supplying new girls with a small, easily concealed pellet filled with red ink. Surreptitiously broken at a strategic moment, the pellets covered sheets and thighs with a reasonable facsimile of blood. If a girl was clever enough and a good enough actress, she could lose her virginity over and over again before the customers got wise.

"I 'ad long pigtails," Nan recalled. "That 'elped, an' I cried and carried on somethin' awful. I was a *'uge* success."

Sally raised her eyes heavenward and clacked her tongue. Faith continued to bathe her cheek, whimpering quietly. I finished the cinnamon roll and licked my fingers. A fire had burned down low in the fireplace, the charred logs making a pleasant crackling noise. The parlor with its worn blue carpet and faded, flowered pink curtains was warm and cozy. I dreaded leaving it for the chilly streets.

"'Is men are combin' St. Giles, lookin' for likely girls for th' new 'ouse," Nan continued. "Abductin' any lass 'oo ain't gotta 'arelip and looks like she might still 'ave 'er cherry. You better watch out, Randy."

"I ain't whorin' for no one!" I declared.

"If Black Jack decided 'e wanted ya to, you wouldn't 'ave no choice, Miss 'Igh an' Mighty."

"'E'd 'ave to catch me first."

"That wouldn't be 'ard. Black Jack 'as ways."

I ignored the remark and drank the rest of my coffee. Black Jack Stewart was the undisputed king of St. Giles, the most notorious criminal since Jonathan Wild and certain to come to the same end one day. Until that time came, he would continue to rule the criminal world with an iron hand, keeping tight control over all criminal activity. Every brothel, every gin shop, every gambling house and opium den paid garnish to him, more than half their take in most cases, and anyone who dared defy him or withhold money ended up in an alleyway with throat slit from ear to ear. Black Jack had a private army of murderous ruffians eager to do his bidding, a savage gang even more feared than the vicious Mohocks who had terrorized the populace a few years back.

Black Jack controlled all the receiving houses outright and made an immense profit from the traffic in stolen goods, while the poor thieves who provided the booty were lucky to make ends meet, but we had no other recourse, no other outlet. Any thief who eschewed the receiving houses and tried to sell stolen items on his own met a fate similar to those folk who held out on Black Jack. It was frustrating and bloody unfair. A crafty and accomplished thief like me who took pride in her work couldn't hope to get ahead, but it beat whorin'. Bein' hungry now and then was better than catchin' the pox.

Big Moll came shuffling into the parlor just as I was pouring myself another cup of coffee. Her outrageous wig of bouncing orange ringlets was all askew, her large brown eyes snapping angrily as, hands on hips, she planted her enormous bulk in front of the dying fire and glared at me. Her fat cheeks were generously powdered, and a heart-shaped black satin patch was affixed beneath one corner of her small, vivid red mouth. Her voluminous red taffeta gown had a worn, shiny look, and the fringed purple and blue shawl around her shoulders was decidedly ragged. The bright clothes merely emphasized her considerable bulk.

"'Elp yourself!" she snorted as I set down the coffeepot. "Go a'ead an' eat me outta 'ouse an' 'ome, you bloody little beggar! I don't know why I put up with it!"

I gave her a saucy grin. Big Moll fancied herself a dragon, taking great pride in her surly disposition and razor-sharp tongue, but, alas, she fooled no one but herself. There wasn't a girl in the house who couldn't wrap the corpulent old dear around her little finger.

"Get yourself on up to your room, Faith!" she ordered. "Angie's back with a bucket-a ice. 'Ave you any idea 'ow 'ard it is to find ice, 'ow much it *cost*? She's made-ya an ice pack, an' I want you to put it on that cheek. It'll 'elp the swellin' to go down. Can't earn no money lookin' like you do now. Go on! An' see you stay in bed all day an' 'ave a 'ot lunch!"

Faith left the room, still whimpering, and Big Moll scowled and shook her head, the long orange ringlets bouncing furiously. Sally was munching on another cinnamon roll, and Nan yawned wearily, examining her face in a tarnished hand mirror.

"Poor mite," Moll said. "That sod damned near killed 'er.

If I 'adn't burst in when I did, 'e'd uv done it for sure. Scrawny lookin' bugger, 'e was, looked like a clerk. Them are th' kind to watch out for, th' puny-lookin' ones. They're beat down all day long an' take it out on poor 'ores at night. Mother Redcoat does a brisk trade with them kind."

"Sally said you threw him out," I remarked.

"On 'is arse! Told 'im never to darken my door again. I run a respectable 'ouse, I do, no whips, no peep shows, just good clean toppin'. I 'ave my standards."

"Yeah," Nan said languidly.

"No lip from you, lass!" Moll stormed. "I ain't inna mood for your sarcasm. So what're you doin' 'angin' around this 'our uv th' mornin'?" she asked me. "'Sides stuffin' yourself, that is."

"I'm goin' to Tyburn," I replied.

"Tyburn!"

I nodded. "Ought-a be good pickin's. The gentry always turn up to see the 'angin's, and they're stringin' up a traitor today. One of the men who supported Bonnie Prince Charles."

"A traitor, then," Moll said. She shuddered. "I shouldn't care to see that. What they do to those poor souls—"

"I never watch," I assured her. "I'm too busy minglin' in the mob, pickin' out the likeliest cove."

Hanging alone wasn't considered punishment enough for traitors. They were hung, cut down while still alive, disembowled and subjected to the most hideous tortures before they were finally beheaded. It wasn't a sight for the squeamish, but then there were few squeamish souls in our London. People seemed to relish the most barbaric cruelty, which, indeed, surrounded them on every side in this age we lived in.

"Go a'ead," Moll grumbled, "'ave another cinnamon roll! They'll just get stale, or Sally'll stuff 'erself into a stupor. I wish you wudn't goin' today, Randy. I get uneasy."

"You're always uneasy," I retorted, reaching for the roll. "No need to be. I'm the best there is. I ain't gonna get caught."

"That's what all of 'em say, and all of 'em end up swingin' from Tyburn Tree or rottin' away in Newgate or Bridewell. You've been at it too long as it is, an' your luck's bound to run out soon, if not today then tomorrow or th' day after. I got a feelin' about it."

"Moll's always gettin' a feelin'," Nan observed.

"Shut your mouth, Nan! I *do*, though, an' every time I get a feelin' somethin' bad 'appens, sure as faith. Don't go to

Tyburn today, luv. Stay 'ere. I could use th' company."

"I 'ave my work to do, Moll."

Moll snorted, making one of her fierce faces. "I've told-ya over an' over, you could work 'ere. 'Elpin' me keep things runnin'. You wouldn't 'ave to work on your back, I know 'ow you feel about that. You could run errands for me an' 'elp with th' books an' things like that. It'd be a relief to me, knowin' I 'ad someone on 'and 'oo can read an' write, someone I could depend on."

I merely smiled and shook my head, and Moll snorted again, scowling at me as I ate my second cinnamon roll. She'd been after me to come work for her for four years, at least, and although I appreciated her offer and the kindness behind it, I knew it wouldn't work out. I liked my freedom too much. Moll didn't really want someone to help her run the house. She wanted someone to cluck over and take care of. Fond as I was of her, I didn't fancy the role. Besides, I enjoyed my work. The dangers involved only made it more exciting.

Moll waddled over to the rickety sideboard, opened a bottle of gin and took a hearty swig, belching robustly afterward. Nan stood up, yawned and informed us that she was going to get some sleep. Sally said she guessed she'd go up, too, she'd had a busy night, unlike *some* she could mention. They left the room, Sally taking the rest of the cinnamon rolls with her. Although I was no longer hungry, I could have used a third one just the same.

"I wish you wudn't so bloody stubborn," Moll grumbled, taking another swig of gin. "I been lookin' out after you ever since your poor mum passed over, an' you ain't made it easy, I don't mind tellin' you."

"I don't need anyone to look after me. I can take care of myself."

"Hump! You just *think* you can, missy! You've been lucky, yeah, but you're gettin' too big for pickin' pockets. When you was a tiny mite, it was one thing, no one pays mind to kiddies, there ain't th' risk, but you're too noticeable now, Randy."

"What do you mean?"

"That 'air, that face, that body. Dirty as you are, face smudged with soot an' your dress in rags, you're a beauty. I been watchin' you bloom."

"Rubbish."

"It ain't rubbish! You're too pretty by far to be roamin' th' streets. You don't melt into th' crowd any longer. You attract attention. Th' men're already letchin' after-ya, and there's gonna be trouble. Mark my word."

"I'll do that, luv," I said saucily, "but now I've gotta be on my way. I got a long walk, and there's gonna be a 'uge crowd."

Big Moll frowned, her large brown eyes full of genuine worry. "I got this feelin', Randy."

"You and your feelin's."

"Somethin's gonna 'appen. I feel it in my bones."

"Bosh!"

"You be careful now, pet. Ya-'ear? Promise me you'll be careful."

"I will be, luv. And thanks for the coffee and cinnamon rolls. You're an old darlin', even if you *are* full of nonsense."

Moll snorted, made another fierce face at me and emptied the gin bottle. I heard her titanic belch as I hurried down the hall and stepped outside. The wind was icy and the cobbles chilled my bare feet, but I paid no mind to it. Stomach full, light of heart, I traipsed merrily down the street, anticipating a successful haul at Tyburn and having not the faintest notion that this day was going to alter violently the whole course of my life.

13

THE WIND HAD DIED DOWN AND IT WASN'T QUITE SO cold now, although I was still chilled to the bone as I moved down Plumtree Court Broad Street. Despite the early hour, the streets were thronged. I stepped nimbly to avoid being splattered as a fierce old crone dumped her slops out of a second floor window, but the laborer behind me wasn't so lucky. Instantly drenched with refuse, potato peels draped over his head and shoulders, he gave a violent shout, raised his fist, and filled the air with colorful words. Across the way a mob of people were eagerly plundering the ruins of a tenement that had fallen down, carting off timber that could be sold to washerwomen and clear starchers. All the tenements were in tottering condition and rarely a month passed that one didn't come crashing down, frequently crushing poor wretches to death or maiming them horribly.

Two brawny men were fighting over a pile of timber, fighting viciously, I observed. The blond lout in leather jerkin was trying his best to gouge out the eyes of the black-haired brute. Blood splattered. No one paid the least attention. Such fights were common as dirt in St. Giles. The victor shambled off arrogantly, and more likely the wounded foe was fallen upon by a voracious crowd who rifled his pockets for possible valuables and often stripped the clothes off his body. Violence abounded on every side. It was a way of life and one grew immune to it, as one grew immune to the hideous stench. I still shuddered when I saw the corpse of an infant tossed onto a refuse heap, I still turned away when I saw a maimed, bleeding body sprawling on the cobbles, but I had learned early on that taking care of Randy was the important thing. Compassion could get you killed.

I turned a corner, heading toward the spire of St. George's that towered over the filthy, shambly, multilevel rooftops. A thatch-haired lad who wasn't over ten staggered out of a gin shop, clutching a half pint of the poisonous liquor. His tiny sister tottered out behind him, holding her half pint in her arms as another little girl might hold a doll. Both children were dressed in rags and covered with lice. Both would probably go blind from drinking the swill. There was a horrible, squealing noise as a mud-covered hog came tearing down the street, hotly pursued by a group of shouting women. Fleet Ditch nearby was occupied by hogs that roiled in the slime and fattened themselves on the refuse. Although no one would dare go into the ditch after them, whenever a hog ventured out of the ditch it was fair game for anyone swift enough to catch it. I leaped aside as the hog raced past me. The pack of women almost trampled the children who had come out of the gin shop, knocking the boy to the ground, causing the girl to drop her gin.

I had chased a hog or two in my time, but I'd never been fortunate enough to catch one. A juicy pork roast would be delicious, I thought, moving on down the street, or one of those tasty-looking bacon rolls all smeared with mustard. What heaven it would be to have one right now. Food. One never stopped thinking about it. Fancy havin' enough to eat any time you wanted it. There were people who actually did. I walked on through the crowd, ignoring the din and confusion, passing squalid shops and ragpickers' carts and doss houses, turning another corner to take a shortcut down Half Moon Alley.

A strapping, terrified grocer's apprentice in soiled apron was crouching behind a towering heap of garbage. His brick red locks were all atumble, his brown eyes wide with terror. He couldn't be over fourteen, I thought. Compassion could get you killed, yes, but if you had an opportunity to do someone a good turn without any danger to yourself, you did it. The boy stared at me, trembling all over, and I looked up the alley to make sure that it was empty, then stepped over to him and asked him what was wrong.

"Th' crimps," he moaned. "They've been after it all mornin', snatchin' any lad they 'appen upon. I saw 'em snatch Teddy Bennet, grabbed 'im as 'e was comin' outta 'is 'ouse. I left th' shop to fetch th' cabbage for Mr. Cathcart an' they started chasin' me! They're bound to catch me!"

"Jump over that wall," I told him. "There's a courtyard beyond. The cellar of the building is empty. You can 'ide there."

The boy gulped, muttered his thanks and scrambled hastily over the wall as four fierce-looking men came tearing into the alley. I sauntered on, not a bit alarmed. The crimps who worked for the East India Company weren't interested in abducting girls. The vicious press gangs kidnapped only likely-looking lads to sell to a ship captain short of crew. Although only seamen could legally be impressed, no lad was safe during a "hot press," and the East India crimps were the most brutal of the lot, creating a veritable reign of terror whenever they were on the prowl. The four men thundered toward me, looking left and right.

"You, wench!" one of them called. "You seen a red-'aired boy?"

"'E ran out th' alley!" I cried. "Almost knocked me on my arse, th' bleedin' sod. Go get 'im!"

The four thugs ran out of the alley, footsteps pounding loudly. I wondered how many lads they would kidnap before they were finished. The boys were kept chained up in a foul cellar and horribly brutalized before they were eventually turned over to a sea captain. Nothing was ever done about it. Life was cruel, indeed, I reflected, pleased I had helped the grocer's apprentice avoid a terrible fate. Only the strongest lads survived the scurvy and the floggings and the constant hazards of life aboard ship.

Leaving the alley, I strolled past Critchin's Gin Shop and Mother Redcoat's and a receiving house with windows crammed with plate and brass candlesticks and porcelain clocks. There was a tray of shoe buckles, too, and I recognized those paste-encrusted silver buckles. I'd snipped them off a dandy gent's shoes as he was climbing out of a sedan chair. The grooms had given chase and one of them had almost caught me. A penny I got for those buckles, one penny, and they were genuine fake diamonds and rubies. Bleedin' fences. Robbed you blind every time you brought in your loot.

Lost in thought, I threaded my way through the crowd, utterly at home here amidst the squalor, brash and confident as I passed the toppling buildings and skirted the refuse heaps and took shortcuts down the dark, narrow alleys. Today was going to be very profitable, I told myself. Public executions always brought out a whopping big mob, and with all the noise and excitement and distractions, they were heaven for a pick-pocket. As I neared St. George's, the streets grew a trifle wider. I could see larger patches of gray sky, and thin shafts of dusty yellow-white sunlight slanted through the overhanging rooftops to polish the filthy cobbles. I turned a corner. I could see the magnificent spires and stone archways of St. George's now, towering there like a sentinel at the entrance of St. Giles, symbolizing another world forever closed to the people who dwelled here.

"'Ey, wench! 'Ow 'bout it? I 'ave 'alf a crown to spend."

A husky lout was blocking my way. Gazing at the splendid church, I hadn't seen him. I tensed, giving him a fierce look that didn't faze him at all. He grinned, his lascivious eyes taking in my long legs, my slender waist, the full swell of my breasts straining against the low, tattered bodice of my violet blue dress.

"Up your arse!" I snapped.

"'Alf a bloody crown don't suit you? Well, well, well, looks like we 'ave a bleedin' duchess on our 'ands."

"You'd best keep your 'ands to yourself, mate."

"Saucy, ain't you? Maybe I'll just 'ave it for nothin'."

He moved toward me. I braced myself, eyes flashing, claws ready. Something in my stance warned him. He hesitated a moment, studying me, and then he muttered a curse and shambled away. I was used to such encounters, had learned how to defend myself a long time ago. A kick to the shin, a knee to the groin, nails to the eyes and they let go soon enough. Few of them cared to tangle with a wildcat when a few shillings would get them what they wanted on any street in St. Giles. Tail was too easy to come by to make it worth a fight.

A crowd had gathered at the end of the street, jeering and laughing boisterously as a plump, gin-sodden woman with oily gray hair and pasty cheeks made drunken efforts to defend herself from three filthy youths who were trying to steal the loaf of bread clamped under her armpit. She shouted abuse and flailed wildly, reeling, tottering. The youths were merely amusing themselves, toying with her as a cat might toy with a mouse he has no real interest in devouring. The plump woman slipped on the cobbles and landed on her backside. One of the youths gave her a sharp kick as another snatched the bread. The mob hooted with delight as the third youth grabbed a bucket of slops and poured it over her face. I wanted to kill all three of them, but one didn't interfere. I passed on, turning another corner, and it was then that I saw the two men standing in front of the squalid gambling hall.

One was a muscular giant of a man with a savage face and hair the color of dark honey. He wore muddy boots, tight brown breeches and a leather jerkin over a filthy, coarsely woven white shirt. I didn't recognize him, but I recognized the man with him. I stopped, backing cautiously against the wall. I remembered what Nan had said, and I had no desire to attract the attention of Black Jack Stewart. Tall, skeleton-thin, he wore his customary tall black knee boots, his bottle green breeches and black satin frock coat with dirty gold braid on cuffs and lapel. Tattered white lace spilled from his throat and at the wrists. The king of St. Giles had a great beak of a nose and thin, leering lips, and he always wore a shiny black patch over his right eye.

He seemed to be dressing down his henchman. The blond giant scowled unhappily, nodding. Black Jack gave him some instructions and then turned wearily, a bored monarch disgusted with the inefficiency of his servants. He glanced down the street, idly surveying his domain, and then he saw me leaning against the wall. He stared. I felt a chill in my bones that had nothing to do with the cold. Black Jack stroked his lower lip, reflecting, that one dark eye glittering, never leaving me. He said something to his henchman. The ruffian turned to look at me, squinting. Black Jack asked him a question. The ruffian shook his head. Black Jack wanted to know my name. He wanted to put me in his fancy new house. My heart was palpitating. Fearless I might be, but Black Jack Stewart was another matter altogether.

A baker's apprentice scurried down the street, a heavy bag of flour slung over his shoulder. A skinny lad with bugging gray eyes and a shaggy thatch of white blond hair, he worked for Bullock's, the bake shop near Hawkins's, and his name was Alf. I had spoken to him several times. As he passed the two men, the blond giant seized him roughly by the hair and whirled him around. Alf let out a cry of alarm, dropping the bag of flour. It burst at the seams, flour spilling all over the cobbles. Alf shrieked, even more alarmed now, for he would be held responsible for the flour.

Black Jack's henchman slapped Alf viciously across the face and twisted him around until the lad was facing in my direction. Still gripping Alf's hair, the muscular blond ruffian gave his head a vicious jerk and asked him a question. I stared at Alf, willing him not to give the right answer. The boy gulped, tears spurting from his eyes as the ruffian's fingers wound more tightly around those white blond locks, pulling savagely. Alf spluttered out something. The giant scowled, slapped him across the face again and let go of his hair. Alf tumbled to the cobbles, landing on the shattered bag and causing puffy clouds of flour to explode all around.

Alf hadn't given me away. He hadn't told them my name. I was going to have to thank him for that, but I had wasted too much time already. Black Jack spoke to his henchman again, and the ruffian started toward me. I turned quickly and darted back down the street the way I had come, almost colliding with a hunchback who was carrying a flimsy stick-cage full of squawking chickens. I ran down an alley, climbed a wall, scurried across a yard littered with rotten lumber and into the basement of one of the tenements. Rats scampered in every direction as I padded across the floor and up the rickety stairs. I left the building through a side door, moved up the street at a rapid clip and eventually turned down another alley, arriving back on the street I'd left, only much further up, in the shadow of St. George's.

Keeping well in the shadow of one of the jutting arches, half hidden behind a pillar, I peered cautiously down the street. Black Jack and his henchman were no longer in sight, although poor Alf was still on the cobbles, on his hands and knees, desperately trying to scoop up the flour and get as much as he could back into the split cloth bag. Relieved, I emitted a heavy sigh and strolled on, leaving St. Giles behind me. It had been a scary experience, all right, and I'd been all goose pimples for a moment there, but I put it out of my mind quickly enough. There were hundreds and hundreds of likely girls in St. Giles, far too many for Black Jack to bother trying to track down just one. In the thronging congestion of the slums the chances of my running into him again anytime soon were slim indeed. Life in St. Giles was fraught with danger. One got used to it. No need to worry unnecessarily.

Once beyond St. George's, the whole face of London seemed to change. It was like stepping out of a dark, fetid closet into a spacious and airy drawing room. The streets were wider, with ample room for the wonderful carriages and coaches and sedan chairs, and the shops weren't jammed together so closely. A person could dawdle and gaze into the windows at fine leather goods, at pastries and marvelous china and a veritable garden of beribboned, befeathered bonnets. The pavements were crowded, true, but the people were a marvel to behold: fine ladies in rustling satin and striped taffeta and powdered wigs, gents in splendid frock coats, clerks, grooms, flower girls—a fascinating and colorful parade, constantly shifting, constantly changing. There were squares and parks and gardens—trees everywhere, it seemed—greenery framing fine old buildings of brown and tan and weathered gray. There was dirt, too, of course—everything seemed to be sprinkled with soot—and the smell of the river wasn't pleasant, but after St. Giles it seemed like paradise.

I strolled leisurely, winding my way toward Tyburn, keeping my eye out for an easy mark. I had learned how to size people up a long time ago, and I rarely took chances. That prosperous-looking merchant striding down the street in his sturdy boots and heavy cloak had a mean look to him. He'd be on the watch for pickpockets. That plump housewife with the package in her arms would start squawking if I even got near her, and the thin young clerk with the ink-stained fingers wouldn't have anything on him worth stealing. Those three women in satin gowns who stood chattering in front of the milliner's probably had lots of pickings, but one of them was holding a tiny dog. Dogs nipped your ankles, even tiny, pampered dogs, and a very fine carriage stood nearby, a stocky and sullen-looking groom lounging against it and keeping an eye on the gabbling trio. He'd be on me in a minute if I approached them, would undoubtedly pummel me with his fists and send me sprawling with a well-placed kick.

I sighed heavily and walked on, keeping my eyes peeled for the right opportunity. The three ladies in satin recoiled as I passed by them. One of them gasped and held her nose. I turned and stuck my tongue out at her, and she almost collapsed into the arms of her companions. The sullen-looking groom stood up straight and glared at me, his hands balled into fists. I marched past him with my nose in the air, just like a duchess, and when I was far enough away I made a rude noise and extended a stiff middle finger. He spluttered angrily, but he didn't give chase. He couldn't desert his post just to cuff a saucy street urchin, although he would have liked to lay hands on me. I had seen it in his eyes as I passed. Even in rags, even with my curls all atumble and my face streaked with dirt, I had aroused the brute. It gave one a feeling of power, being able to do that, but such games didn't interest me. Didn't seem fair to trade on your looks when you didn't intend to let 'em paw you.

I moved down Snow Hill and passed over the horrid-smelling Fleet by the narrow stone bridge, hurrying now, for it wouldn't do to be late, and there was sure to be a vast crowd. A public execution was a festive affair, free entertainment for the raucous populace. In a book I had once stolen from one of the stalls I had read that London was called the City of Gallows because you couldn't come into the city by road or by river without seeing at least one. They stood at Putney, at Kensington, in Old Kent Road and Wapping, but Tyburn was the favored spot. There was so much more room for the merry spectators, and all the important criminals were strung up there. The merchants, the stallkeepers, the hawkers and pamphlet-sellers always had a profitable time at a public hanging, as did pickpockets and thieves. Everyone seemed to prosper and have a good time except the poor condemned man.

The crowd had thickened considerably as I moved down Oxford Road. The open country of Marylebone Fields was to my side, the villages of Hampstead and Highgate visible on the high ground beyond. There must be at least five or six hundred people trudging along the road, I reckoned, most of them laughing raucously, singing lewd ditties, waving bottles and eating meat pies and eagerly anticipating the treat in store.

Fine carriages and elegant sedan chairs were caught up in the mob of pedestrians, grooms cracking their whips, shouting abuse, elegant ladies peering around the curtains with alarmed, excited faces. When we reached the junction of Oxford Road and Edgeware Road, near the wall of Hyde Park, I caught my first glimpse of the enormous gallows, so large it could accommodate twenty-one bodies at the same time, and I repressed a shudder. I had been to many executions in my time, but I never watched the proceedings. They were much too grisly, particularly if a traitor was to be executed.

Traitors weren't merely hung. They were cut down while still alive and disembowled, their bowels burst in front of their eyes. They were drawn and quartered next, finally beheaded while hundreds chatted and laughed, ate gingerbread and sipped lemonade, lustily enjoying the splendid entertainment. I found it difficult to understand this thirst for savagery that pervaded our age, for it wasn't something confined to St. Giles and its denizens. Gentry swarmed to executions, noble lords rubbing elbows with costermongers and chimney sweeps, refined ladies devouring chocolates and standing up on their stalls to get a better view.

Tyburn Fields might have been the scene of a fair this morning as I made my way through the thick, jostling crowd swarming around the immense wooden gallows. Mother Proctor's Pews were solidly packed, I observed, the tiers of wooden seats affording a choice vantage point and, incidentally, making a fortune for the shrewd woman who owned the concession and rented them out to the gentry and more affluent merchant class. There were carts and carriages amidst the crush, the rooftops of the latter providing another dandy vantage point. A flock of brightly clad women perched atop one of them, their colored skirts like so many petals fluttering in the breeze as they waved to acquaintances, flirted with men and chattered nonstop. Rowdy revelers of every class thronged the scene, pushing, shoving, cheeks flushed with excitement, eyes aglitter with anticipation. Ancient bawds in filthy shawls guzzled gin and shouted obscenities. Rough laborers reeled about drunkenly, joking with the whores. At least half a dozen fistfights were in progress, and the gallows itself was encircled by a troop of grim-faced soldiers who kept the mob at bay, using the butts of their muskets to discourage the more enthusiastic spectators.

Hawkers shouted their wares, doing a brisk business in gin

and beer, chestnuts and oranges, pasties and tarts and ginger-bread. A husky man with a grinning, amiable face held aloft a rack from which dangled tiny wooden dolls with nooses around their necks, selling the grisly souvenirs at sixpence apiece. "Hear the condemned man's confession!" shouted a pamphleteer, waving handfuls of freshly printed sheets, while others sold lurid accounts of previous executions and even more lurid tales of famous criminals, the life of the infamous Jack Sheppard a perennial favorite. All were crudely written, crudely printed, hastily run up overnight to satisfy the public's lust for such fare. I had read several, fascinated and repelled by the bloodthirsty details and explicit woodcuts.

Alert, cocky, confident, I merged into the crowd, becoming an integral part of the mass of humanity. I was pushed and jostled at every turn and held my own, shoving aside a gin-sodden fishwife who stumbled against me, stepping over a man with a bleeding face who had apparently just lost a fight. A leering youth with a twisted nose smacked my bottom and seized my left breast, squeezing tightly. He yelped in agony and released me promptly when my knee slammed up into his groin. Observers hooted with laughter. I moved on, paying no mind to the incident, savoring the smells of gingerbread and roasting chestnuts and wishing I had a penny to buy some. Horses neighed. Babies wailed. Stray dogs leaped about, snarling and yelping.

Above the din of the crowd the deep bell of St. Sepulchre's could be heard tolling mournfully. It was rung only when a condemned man was on his way to Tyburn. The cart would be arriving soon. The show would begin. I noted a number of my cronies working the crowd this morning, craftily sizing up potential marks, as, indeed, was I. I saw Nimble Ned edging closer to a fat merchant who foolishly had a gold watch fob dangling across his paunch. Jaunty, freckled Ned stumbled clumsily against the merchant, apologized profusely and brushed the man's lapels, disappearing quickly into the mob with the fob safely tucked into his pocket. Effective, I thought, but my own technique was much more subtle, and I was cagier, never making my snatch without a clear avenue of escape. Better to find a mark on the edge of the crowd, where it would be easier to make a getaway. Better, too, to wait until the execution began and there would be more distraction.

The crowd stirred, moving en masse as a great clatter of horses sounded. An elegant coach was approaching, flanked on either side by fierce-looking soldiers holding pikes aloft. "Make way! Make way!" those in the lead shouted, and the whole procession headed directly into the thick of the crowd, heedless of bodies blocking the way. There were anguished screams and cries as people tried to get out of the way. Men, women and children were pushed back, shoved, trampled as soldiers and carriage moved forward to the space cleared in front of the gallows by the other soldiers.

"Cumberland!" someone yelled. "It's th' Bloody Duke! 'E's come 'isself to watch th' fun!"

I had already moved back to an elevated stretch of ground on the outskirts of the crowd, and I had a good view of the activity before the towering gallows. The soldiers stopped, dismounted. The door of the white and gold carriage bore the royal insignia. Coachman and grooms wore the royal livery. A hush fell over the crowd as the door was opened, white steps let down and a grotesquely corpulent figure in powdered wig clambered out. His bloated, puffy face had a vile expression, the tiny piglike eyes squinting, the fat mouth curling petulantly. He wore white leather pumps, white silk stockings, pale lime-green satin breeches with a frock coat to match. Lace cascaded frothily from throat and wrists, and diamonds flashed brilliantly as he moved ponderously to speak to one of his men.

It was my first sight of royalty. I wasn't the least bit impressed. Like thousands of other loyal Englishmen, I had utter disdain for the stolid, German-speaking Hanovers, as dense, dimwitted a lot as ever sat on the English throne, and William Augustus, Duke of Cumberland was the most despised, the most feared man in England. Known as "The Bloody Butcher" after his brutal and bloodthirsty campaign against Bonnie Prince Charles in Scotland, he was his father's favorite son and un-doubtedly a superb commander, utterly ruthless, completely cold-blooded, but he was also a coarse, foul-tempered slug. The Scots hated him with passionate intensity, quite naturally, but he was scarcely less hated by his own countrymen, who felt he was trying to undermine the position of his brother Frederick, Prince of Wales, heir to the throne.

A special seat had been arranged for him near the gallows. He waddled over to take it, puffing heavily, propping his chin on his fat hand and scowling impatiently. Subdued at first, distinctly hostile, the mob decided to ignore his presence and were soon as rowdy as before. I saw a man and a woman, shopkeepers from the look of them, carrying the limp, bloodied body of a small child out of the crowd. The woman was sobbing uncontrollably. The man's face was ashen with grief and rage. The child was obviously one of the victims of the trampling when Cumberland's troops forced their way into the midst of the crowd. Such incidents, common enough, hardly endeared the Bloody Duke to the populace.

The bell of St. Sepulchre's had continued to toll all the while, and now the condemned man's cart could be seen approaching, followed by yet another troop of soldiers carrying pikes. The hangman sat up in front on top of the coffin, the prison chaplain behind him, while the prisoner stood in back, bareheaded, chin held high, his wrists tied behind him. He was a young man, surely no more than twenty, a handsome lad with windblown raven locks and clear blue eyes, and there was something undeniably noble about his profile. He wore a plum-colored velvet frock coat and breeches, rumpled and dusty from prison. I noted that his white lace jabot was tattered and smeared with dirt.

The crowd roared, making way for the cart, but there were some people who stood as silently as I. Perhaps they felt as I did. A grievous sadness swept over me as I watched that handsome youth step down from the cart, calm, dignified, facing a hideous death with incredible bravery. It wasn't right. He was so young. He had merely been supporting the man he believed the rightful king. A man shouldn't die for that. No man should have to die the way this youth was going to die, in unspeakable agony. I turned away, sick, detesting the rulers who condoned such savagery, detesting the people who flocked to watch, relishing every moment. Sometimes the human race seemed downright despicable. Tough I might be, primarily interested in my own survival, but a person had to have *some* feelings, even though they were bothersome and made life so much more complicated.

Bracing myself, ignoring the gleeful noise as the prisoner climbed up the steps to the gallows, I put feelings aside and set about my business. I had come to pick pockets. Pick pockets I would. The crowd was concentrating on the forthcoming spectacle now. The time was perfect. Now, to find a likely-looking mark. I strolled casually on the outskirts of the crowd, observing, speculating, selecting my victim with great care. I had already discarded a number of possible candidates when I spotted the two gents standing together on a slight rise of ground, immediately behind the mob.

Perfect. The thin chap in black didn't look very promising, but the big blond looked like he'd have prime pickin's, and I had a clear getaway if anything went wrong. I moved a bit closer, inspecting them without seeming to do so, idly patting an unruly auburn wave. Both men were tall, the blond, heavily built, strong and solid, agreeably husky without being in the least overweight. He wore rust velvet knee breeches and frock coat, white silk stockings and wonderful brown leather pumps with tempting silver buckles. His broad face was open and pleasing, the chin cleft, the wide mouth sensual. Under other circumstances the dark brown eyes would undoubtedly be twinkling amiably, and the tousled golden blond hair added a boyish touch. He looked a good-natured sort, a wealthy idler who probably spent his time at the gaming tables and in the company of beautiful, compliant women.

His companion was a good two inches taller, six feet three if an inch, and he was extremely lean, with broad, bony shoulders and the strong, wiry build of an athlete. He stood very straight, blue eyes fiery, his long hands balled into tight fists. He seemed to literally crackle with tension, and one sensed great violence just beneath the surface, barely repressed. His hair was shiny jet black, thick and straight, one heavy wave slanting across his brow, his face lean, handsome and intimidating. His black pumps were the worse for wear, I noted, the pewter buckles not worth a farthing. His thin black cotton knee stockings had been clumsily darned, and though elegantly cut by a fine tailor, his black breeches and flaring black frock coat had a slight greenish tinge, the unmistakable sign of age.

A dangerous number, that one, I thought. Penurious, too, it would appear, although that sharp, finely chiseled face had a distinct aristocratic stamp. Not one to tangle with, him. His friend, though . . . bound to have a fancy pocket watch, maybe even a purse full of gold coins, and those silver buckles. . . . If only he were alone. If only he weren't with the scowling, fierce-lookin' chap with the murderous blue eyes. Instinct told me to move on, find another mark, but the pair presented a definite challenge.

I continued to watch them, debating whether or not I should take the risk. Alone, the husky, pleasantly attractive blond would have been the perfect mark. Even if he caught you, even if one of those powerful, well shaped hands clamped around your wrist, a pitiful, craftily worded sob story would induce him to let go. He reminded me of a sturdy, sleek, overgrown

~146~

puppy, even though his expression was suitably grave at the moment. If the blond was a puppy, his companion was one of those lean, vicious German dogs, a Doberman, tense and bristling and ready to spring. He had the killer instinct, that one, and if I were wise I'd give him a wide berth.

The crowd was impatient as the chaplain spoke a few words to the prisoner, piously holding his Bible and no doubt contemplating the profits he'd make when he published his own version of the condemned man's confession. The young man shook his head, foregoing his opportunity to speak the traditional final words to the assemblage. The Duke of Cumberland leaned forward in his chair, watching avidly as the chaplain stepped back and the hangman dropped the noose over the handsome youth's head, settling it about his throat and giving it a quick, professional twist. The husky blond took his companion's arm, indicating that they should leave. The man shook the hand away fiercely, spitting out harsh words I was too far away to hear. I sensed that he knew the prisoner, that there was a close tie between them.

I told myself he'd be too intent on the proceedings to pay mind to anything else. I'd sidle up to the blond, make my snatch and be long gone before either of them knew what had happened. Confident of my skills, much too confident for my own good, I wasn't one to turn my back on a challenge. And so, brushing a fleck of soot from my faded violet-blue skirt, I took a deep breath and sauntered idly toward the two men and straight into the arms of a relentlessly tempestuous future.

14

ROWDY, RAUCOUS, THE CROWD WAITED IMPATIENTLY
as the hangman made a final adjustment, stroking the thick rope almost lovingly. The youth in plum velvet stood very still, staring straight ahead, seemingly oblivious to the noose around his neck. Cumberland leaned forward in the plush, gilded chair

that had been provided for him, gripping the arms with fat hands, a greedy, rapacious gleam in those tiny pig-eyes. Behind him, the swells in Mother Proctor's Pews smiled and chatted, some of them standing to get a better view of the proceedings. The hangman clicked his tongue and nodded, satisfied the drop would insure the maximum pain without breaking the neck. Hanging was a fine art that required the most skillful touch. If done properly, by a master, the victim could dance on air for almost twenty minutes, gasping and gurgling and enduring unspeakable agony before death finally freed him.

"I think we'd best leave now, Gordon," the large blond man said. He had a lovely voice, deep yet soft and soothing. "It's madness, subjecting yourself to this horror, and the lad your first cousin."

"He was a damned fool. They all were, both my brothers as well, following that inept, irresponsible young idiot. Oh, the Bonnie Prince has charm enough, I'll grant that, but if he ever had two brain cells that functioned at the same time it would be a miracle. That's what I told them when they asked me to give my allegiance."

The words were harsh, spoken in a cold, clipped voice that sent shivers up my spine. The blond looked uneasy, a worried frown creasing his brow.

"You're bitter, Gordon. You've a right to be, both your brothers slaughtered at Culloden, your family estate confiscated, you forced to eke out a living on Fleet Street pandering to the vilest public tastes. It's enough to turn a man sour, I admit, but this obsession you have—"

"I'm a Scot, Bancroft. Perhaps not a loyal Scot. The majority of my countrymen consider me a coward for not taking to arms like my brothers, consider me a traitor for writing that article exposing the Bonnie Prince for the nitwit he is—"

"Thank God, you did," the blond interrupted. "If you hadn't penned the article, if you hadn't made your stand quite clear, if you hadn't already been living in London and—"

"But I'm a Scot nevertheless," the tall, lean man continued, ignoring his companion's interruption. "I can't stand by and see my kin slaughtered, can't see my home wrecked and looted, my property confiscated without vowing to do something about it. I'm just grateful my parents weren't alive to see the destruction."

He spoke the words in that same chilling voice, and it somehow made them doubly effective. His lean, not unattractive face was devoid of expression, but the clear blue eyes burned fiercely with all the emotions he so sternly repressed. I could sense the cold rage, the pent-up violence, the thirst for revenge seething just beneath the surface. Wrestling with a private demon, that one, I told myself, edging a step nearer. The blond in brown velvet rested his hand lightly on his friend's arm.

"You're a Scot, true, and a good one, but—it's over, lad."

"It isn't over for Angus. Not yet. I thought he had more sense than the others, and now—" He cut himself short, grimacing. "Would that he'd died on the moor with Ian and Davy."

"Your cousin has already shown himself a noble youth. He's going to die a brave death. There's no need for you to watch it, to torment yourself this way. It can only add fuel to your—to this insane obsession. I shouldn't have permitted you to come. Dammit, I should have drugged you, should have locked you in a wardrobe, bound you hand and foot."

"You're my friend, Bancroft," the Scot said coldly, "the only friend I have in this bloody, barbaric country. I'd hate for you to do something that would spoil our friendship."

"Aye, mate, I know what a thorny, bristly, surly chap you are. I also know the fine, sensitive fellow who dwells beneath that savage facade. I fear no man, but I wouldn't dream of riling you. I saw you in that fight at the Three Boars, saw what you did to the bloke who shoved you. I don't *think* you'd turn on me, but I'd risk like treatment if I thought it'd help rid you of these crazy ideas you're nursing."

"You're a good person, Bancroft. A good friend."

"I try to be. It's hard with a savage like you."

"He's going to pay," the Scot said calmly. "If it takes me the rest of my life, I'm going to see that Cumberland pays. Look at him, leaning forward, eyes glittering. The sod's actually licking his lips."

"Gordon!" his companion warned. "Remember yourself. Those words could get you arrested."

He glanced around nervously to see if anyone had overheard, but those in front of the two men were too intent on the show to have paid any attention to the reckless words, while I, a few feet away, wore an expression of the utmost innocence, totally unaware of the blond gent and his friend. The crowd roared as the ground vanished beneath the feet of the condemned man, as the rope tightened around his neck and he began to swing. There were loud cheers as he twitched, struggling in spite of himself, kicking out in agony. The hangman rubbed his hands, extremely pleased. Cumberland continued to lean forward in his chair, almost toppling out of it as he savored the spectacle.

"Jesus," Bancroft muttered.

The tall, lean Scot at his side showed no emotion whatsoever now, standing perfectly straight. Those sharp, harsh features might have been sculpted from the hardest flint. I moved a bit closer, ever so casual. Bancroft winced, not wanting to watch, unable to tear his eyes away. I was standing not more than a foot away from him now, a little to his rear, waiting for the ideal moment. He was sure to have a gold pocket watch, maybe a purse. I longed for those silver buckles as well, but I'd lost my penknife two days ago and hadn't had time to steal another one. The people directly in front of the two men were stamping and hooting, stumbling a little, and one man reeled back, almost crashing into the blond. Perfect. Hand like air slipped into the plush velvet pocket, closing around a small, round metal object, brought it out, tucked it into the bodice of my dress. Easy as could be. Nothing simpler. Now for the purse. Must be in the other pocket.

I shifted position, standing behind the man now, to his right. I waited a second or two, and then my hand drifted foward like the lightest feather and floated into the other pocket, feeling the chamois bag, feeling the delicious weight of the coins within. I clasped my fingers around it carefully so there would be no warning jangle and then withdrew my hand. Iron bands clamped suddenly around my wrist, squeezing so hard I feared the bone would snap. A pair of fierce blue eyes burned into mine. The Scot stared at me with cold, venomous hatred, his thin lips stretched into a tight, vicious smile.

"Lemme go!" I cried. "Lemme go!"

"Caught you, you little vermin. Thought you were being clever, didn't you, slut?"

"Ow! You're 'urtin' me!"

I tried to pull away. He gave my wrist a savage twist that almost brought me to my knees. Hercules himself couldn't have broken free of that grip, and I was a poor, hungry street urchin. I dropped the bag. It clattered at my feet. Bancroft turned, bewildered, only now aware of what was happening. I cried out as the Scot gave my wrist yet another twist and needles of terrible pain shot up my arm.

"What's happened?" Bancroft exclaimed. "What's going on?"

"She filched your purse. Filched your watch, too."

"Bleedin' liar! I never! Lemme go!"

Holding me firmly with his right hand, he plunged his left into my bodice, fingers digging roughly between my breasts to fasten around the watch. He took it out and held it up as though it were a trophy. Bancroft shook his head slowly, gave a curious little smile and, taking the watch, dropped it back into his pocket. The Scot continued to stare at me with those chilling blue eyes, mouth curled up at one corner now, the heavy black wave spilling over one side of his brow. He looked as though he'd like nothing better than to beat me senseless, and I had the feeling he'd do so at the least provocation. I didn't struggle. I didn't dare. He held my wrist at a crooked angle, fingers twisting savagely, and the least movement on my part brought excruciating pain.

"Well, well, well," Bancroft said amiably, examining me. "What shall we do with her?"

"If I had my way, I'd break her bloody neck. It's scum like this who are responsible for making London the cesspool it is. Thieves, pickpockets, cutthroats—the lot of 'em should be rounded up and hung."

"She's terribly young," Bancroft remarked idly.

"And a hardened criminal already."

He gave my wrist a brutal jerk. I stumbled, falling to my knees, tangled auburn hair spilling over my face. He jerked me up, swung my arm out and took a step to one side, twisting the arm behind my back, jamming my wrist high between my shoulder blades. I screamed, tears springing unbidden to my eyes. He slung his free arm around my throat, his forearm pressing tightly against my windpipe.

"I say, Gordon, no need to be so rough. She's little more than a child."

"Adult enough to steal your watch, lift your purse."

His voice was cold, steady, with a harsh, metallic rasp, a voice to send chills down your spine. I found it difficult to breathe with that bony forearm held so firmly against my throat. I dared not move, knowing full well he would strangle me brutally without the slightest hesitation. I was a fighter, yes, quick with tooth and nail and knee, but I had sense enough to know when I was out of my league. This Scot had the killer instinct. I'd seen that immediately, and I sensed that he was far more dangerous than the most brutal denizen of St. Giles.

Bancroft picked up his thin chamois purse, jangled the coins inside, then put it back into his pocket. Those good-natured brown eyes examined me closely, amusement in their depths, and I knew that if I was to get out of this it would be through his grace. I contrived to look extremely pitiful, grimacing with pain as the Scot gave my wrist a slight turn. Both men seemed to have forgotten the execution, the man dancing on air even now, and I saw that Bancroft, at least, was relieved by the distraction I had provided.

"Shall we drown the wench?" he asked. "The river's nearby. You could hold her under."

"Nothing would give me more pleasure," the Scot retorted.

"Wenches drown in the Thames every day," Bancroft continued in a teasing voice. "I wager there'd be no hue and cry. I doubt seriously if anyone would even miss her."

"Oh, *please*, sir," I wailed. "Please don't."

Bancroft smiled. It was a lovely smile, warm and friendly, the kind of smile to melt your heart. He was a soft touch, big and handsome and amiable, and I felt sure he'd not allow anything terrible to happen to me. After all, it was *his* pockets I'd picked, not the bloody Scot's. Tears spilled down my cheeks, attractively, I hoped. I sobbed, gulping a little as the Scot's arm tightened a fraction of an inch. Bancroft studied me, eyes twinkling, not at all perturbed by my thwarted crime.

"I—I 'adn't ever done nothin' like this before," I lied, looking up at him with welling eyes. "It—I was so 'ungry, you see. I 'adn't 'ad anything to eat since—for two 'ole days, an' I was starvin'."

"She's lying," the Scot said coldly.

"I ain't!" I protested. "It's true, every bleedin' word!"

"You were hungry?" Bancroft inquired.

"It wudn't so much for me, it was—it was for my wee baby brother and my mum. My mum's sick, sick somethin' awful, and I don't 'ave no pa, an' my poor baby brother just—just wails. 'E 'as th' fever. I was desperate. I 'oped to take 'em some food and get some medicine for my poor wee brother."

"Touching," the Scot said dryly.

"Lemme go, you brute! You're breakin' my arm!"

"You're breaking my heart," he retorted.

He jammed my arm up a bit higher, almost wrenching it out of its socket. I cried out, but his arm cut off the sound, brutally tightening, trapping the cry in my throat. I could feel the blood rushing to my head, felt a strange dizziness as black clouds slowly enveloped my brain.

"I say, Gordon, give the wench some air. You're choking her. You're upset, mate. You're in a foul mood, seething with anger, consumed with a thirst for revenge—I can understand that, but you needn't take it out on this pathetic little street waif. It's not Cumberland you have in that stranglehold."

"Would that it were," the Scot snarled.

I was sinking into unconsciousness when he relieved the pressure around my throat. The misty black clouds receded. I coughed and spluttered, my face all flushed and warm and my arms and legs felt numb. Th' bleedin' sod would 'ave killed me if it 'adn't been for th' gent. Although the arm was looped loosely now, resting lightly across my windpipe, his fingers still held my wrist with brutal tightness, keeping my arm locked high behind me so that I was in constant pain.

"Please," I whispered. "Please let go of my arm."

"Shut up."

"You're hurtin' me awful."

"I'm glad to know that."

"Really, Gordon, there's no need to torture the wench. No real harm has been done. What do you say we tan her bottom and let her go."

"You can't give these vermin the least quarter, Bancroft. You let them get by with something like this and it only encourages them."

"I'll never do it again," I promised. "I swear I—"

He wrenched my arm again, tightening the bar across my throat. "I told you to shut up," he said.

"What do you propose we do?" Bancroft asked.

"Find a constable. Turn her over to him."

"They'll clap her in prison. The wench might even hang."

"Hang enough of 'em and the rest will think twice before slitting a throat and lifting a watch."

The Scot was dead serious. Bancroft looked perturbed. All this while the Scot's cousin had been swinging from the gallows, his every twitch accompanied by hoots and cheers from the merry, rapacious mob. There was a great roar now as he was cut down and stretched out on the wooden platform. A physician took his pulse, rested his ear against the man's chest and declared him still alive. The mob applauded wildly. A bucket of water was hurled into the man's face to revive him. A fire was lighted in a huge black pot. The flames began to crackle immediately, a plume of dark black smoke curling up to the sky.

The Scot stiffened, momentarily forgetting me, although he still held me in that brutal lock. I could sense the tension in him, could almost feel the anger and anguish that charged through his veins. Bancroft frowned. He clearly wanted to get his friend away before the second stage of the execution began. The condemned man was pulled to his feet. He stared about him in a daze, water dripping from his head and shoulders. He saw the crowd, saw the soldiers, saw the flames leaping lustily in the huge black pot. He closed his eyes and straightened himself up, determined not to cringe.

"Look, Gordon," Bancroft said nervously, "I—I really don't think I care to stay for this. You've seen enough, mate. No need tearing yourself apart. It can only—" He hesitated, groping for the right words. "We have to dispose of this wench," he continued. "We'd never find a constable in this mob. There's a roundhouse a mile or so from here. What do you say we take her there and discuss the matter on the way."

"There's nothing to discuss," the Scot said dryly. "I don't intend to let her go."

"It wudn't *your* pockets I picked!" I protested.

"Wench has a point there," Bancroft agreed. "If charges are pressed, I'll have to press them, not you."

"You will, if you value our friendship."

"You're a hard man, Cam Gordon."

"And you're forever good-hearted, Bancroft. It's going to get you into a lot of trouble one of these days."

Bleedin' bastard. Brutal sod. The milk of human kindness never flowed in *his* veins, not for an instant. As a child he probably took pleasure in slaughtering small animals, probably beat up other boys and felt good as he bloodied their mouths. How I'd love to kick him in the balls, kick him so hard he'd be neutered for life. How I'd love to rake my claws across those lean, hard cheeks and bring the blood, make the sod squeal. Maybe I'd have a chance. Maybe on the way to the roundhouse he'd drop his guard and loosen his hold and I could break free without having my arm torn off. I hadn't given up hope yet, not by a long chalk. In St. Giles you learned to keep right on hopin' till they finally threw the dirt into your face.

"Shall we leave?" Bancroft asked.

"Very well. Come along, slut."

I didn't have any choice. He started walking, wrenching my arm, forcing me to march ahead of him, his arm still looped around my throat. Every step I took was agony, for those fingers clamped relentlessly around my wrist, twisting it, holding my arm at that excruciating angle. Sod didn't care at all. Wasn't his arm bein' pulled out at the roots. We left Tyburn Fields, heading toward Oxford Road, and the noise of the mob gradually began to recede, fading to a dim, muted roar.

"You're really determined to turn the wench in, aren't you?" Bancroft said idly.

"Damned right I am."

"She's a pretty thing beneath all that dirt."

"Smells like a refuse heap," the Scot snarled.

"I wish you'd reconsider, Cam. Pity to see a wench so young rot in Bridewell or dangling from a gibbet."

"Why all this concern for a thieving little whore, Bancroft?"

"Something called compassion. I'm cursed with it. Guess it's never bothered you much."

"It's never bothered me at all."

"I ain't a whore!" I exclaimed. "I ain't never let any man top me, never once, no matter how much I was offered. I still 'ave my cherry, you bleedin' liar!"

Both men ignored me. They might have been taking a casual stroll together. Although he held me firmly, forcing me along in front of him, I had a feeling the Scot was hardly aware of me, that I didn't exist for him as a human being. We passed Marylebone Fields, Hampstead and Highgate in the distance, gray and brown under the bleak gray sky. A few stragglers hurried past us on their way to Tyburn, worried that they'd miss everything, but there were no carriages, no carts or sedan chairs. A cow grazed nearby. A dog barked. This part of London seemed curiously deserted, all activity concentrated on that field far behind us now. The roar of the crowd was barely audible, a mere buzzing in the background.

My arm was practically numb now, the burning, tearing sensation dulled to a throbbing ache. He held me firmly but without pressure, his arm looped loosely around my neck. If only I were wearing shoes, I could rear my foot up and slam the heel down on his instep, then swing my elbow back into his ribs and bang his balls with the side of my hand. That'd do it. He'd let go for sure, but I was barefoot, and instinct told me this one would maim me savagely before I made the first move. No, if I was going to get out of this, I'd have to use my wits. I stumbled deliberately as we moved over the stone bridge that spanned the Fleet. The Scot gave my wrist a jerk, pulling me up. I began to sob.

I sobbed quite beautifully, quite pathetically, sobbed so softly and so wretchedly it should have melted the hardest heart. The Scot paid no attention whatsoever, the bastard. I forced tears into my eyes. They spilled over my lashes and streamed down my cheeks in shiny rivulets, and my sobs grew even more mournful. Who could resist such pathos? Bancroft was beginning to grow very uneasy, I could see that. At least *he* had a heart. I gulped and swallowed, trying valiantly to control my sobs, but they merely increased in volume, growing louder and louder and even more pathetic.

"Stop that hideous caterwauling," the Scot ordered.

"Go play with yourself, you scurvy son of a bitch!"

Bancroft looked appalled, and then he chuckled, delighted. Damn both of 'em! All that beautiful sobbing, all that brilliant acting, all that energy wasted. Insensitive clods! Didn't care a jot about me or my poor sick mum or my wee baby brother burnin' with the fever. I thought I had Bancroft on my side, almost *did*, in fact, until my blasted tongue gave me away. Damn! I was furious with myself, even more furious with Bancroft who was laughing heartily now.

"Laugh, you bastard! You ain't th' one bein' drug to the roundhouse. It ain't so bleedin' funny to me!"

"Has a tongue on her, Cam," Bancroft said merrily. "Has a lot of spirit, too. Never thought I'd see the day when someone called Cameron Gordon a scurvy son of a bitch and lived to say anything else."

Cameron Gordon made no reply. He wasn't amused. The sod probably never laughed in his life unless he happened to step on a baby chicken. Solemn as a grave, that one, grim as the plague. Bloody Scot! So what if his two brothers were killed at Culloden and he lost his property and his first cousin was even now having his entrails roasted in front of his eyes. That didn't give him the right to torture a poor, innocent girl who was just trying to keep body and soul together as best she knew how. He had a right to be bitter and angry, sure, but he didn't have to take it out on me.

We were nearing the roundhouse now, one of many of the temporary gaols in the city where thieves, felons, forgers and other miscreants rounded up by the constables and Bow Street Runners were kept until they were sentenced and sent to pillory, prison or the gallows. They were hideous holes, all of 'em, filthy and rat infested, prisoners all crowded together in dank, dark basements, the stench so bad you could smell it half a street away. The putrid fumes filled the air like a fog, and many prisoners died of jail fever, a virulent form of typhoid that cheated many an executioner of his sport. I had heard all about the dreaded gaols. The subject frequently came up in my profession.

"Wonder what they'll do to her?" Bancroft inquired.

"Hang her, probably," Gordon replied.

"Maybe they'll just put her in the pillory for a couple of days and cut off her hand," Bancroft said chattily. "I understand they do that to thieves on occasion if the magistrate has had a good breakfast and is in a good mood when he passes sentence."

His voice was teasing, but I wasn't at all amused. Many miscreants preferred hanging to being locked in the pillory, a large wooden plank with holes for the victim's head and hands. The pillory was always set up in public so the people could be reminded of the wages of sin, and the rowdy populace took savage delight in pelting the poor soul with sticks and rocks, mud and buckets of excrement and rotten fruit and vegetables. Many a person suffocated from the mud and filth splashed on his face, clogging mouth and nostrils. Others were blinded or sustained fatal injuries from the stones. A forger might have his nostrils slit and ears cut off as part of the sentence, a pickpocket have a hand lopped off and the stump seared with a hot iron. It was barbarous and inhuman, and I could see why some preferred the gallows.

"Pity to see a pretty thing like her lose a hand," Bancroft continued in that same chatty vein, "maybe an eye in the bargain—the mob can turn quite vicious, I understand. Tormenting a pilloried man seems to be one of the people's chief pastimes."

"They have to have something to do," Gordon replied.

"Maybe they'll simply hang her," Bancroft said.

And I thought he was a good-natured chap, a great, friendly pup! He was as bad as the Scot.

"By the way, Cam," he said, "you ever replace that skinny, frightened little titmouse you had working for you, living in the maid's room?"

"She left me. Sneaked out in the middle of the night without even bothering to ask for her pay. I can't seem to keep a maid."

"And no wonder, the way you treat 'em. Always yelling and hurling things at 'em, expecting 'em to polish your boots and darn your stockings and fetch your meals and keep that pigsty of a place in order, threatening to throttle 'em if they

~157~

make any noise while you're working. How many have you had now, six?"

"Eight," Gordon confessed. "Ungrateful wretches, every one of them."

"They'd rather face starvation on the streets than face the devil every morning in the shape of Cam Gordon. Can't say I blame 'em."

"Fine friend you are," Gordon said dryly.

"I've seen how you treated the poor creatures."

"I paid them generously. I gave them a comfortable room. I never laid a hand on a single one of them."

"Browbeat 'em, tongue-lashed 'em, threatened to boil 'em in oil if they so much as touched your precious manuscripts, kept them in a constant state of terror. You *can* be a demon, Cam, particularly when you're working on one of those bloody novels you're always churning out."

"It's called artistic temperament."

"Oh, is that what they're calling it nowadays? Called it surly boorishness when I was a lad. Seems to me working for you'd be about the worst punishment that could be wished upon a girl."

"What are you getting at?" Gordon asked sharply.

Bancroft assumed an air of hurt innocence. "Nothing," he said, "nothing at all. I had an idea, but it probably wouldn't work. I'm always thinking of the comfort and well-being of my friends."

"That's one of your most grievous faults."

"No one appreciates me," Bancroft complained.

Leaving Oxford Road, we turned down a narrow street lined with mellow tan and gray brick buildings, painted wooden signs hanging over the pavements. An aproned man was selling apples from a cart. A knife sharpener was busily turning his wheel, sharpening a pair of scissors for a plump matron in blue bonnet. Sparks flew. Pedestrians thronged the pavements, but no one paid the least attention to us. A tall, lean, dour-faced gent in black restraining a filthy urchin in violet blue rags wasn't at all an unusual sight, it seemed. A carriage rumbled down the street, the horses leaving a steaming deposit on the cobbles. A nimble street sweep with straw broom scurried to sweep it aside. We passed a shabby square, turned again, started down a narrow, shadowy street of old brown shops, the dusty windows cluttered with yellowing prints and folios and discarded furniture.

Gordon had relaxed his grip on my wrist somewhat, holding my arm loosely behind my back, and the pressure against my throat was feather light. Could I make it? Could I break away from the demon? I knew I could out run him if only I could get out of his clutches. I tensed myself, bracing for the attempt. His fingers clamped tight around my wrist, jerking upward. His forearm pulled back against my throat.

"I wouldn't advise it," he said harshly.

Bloody sod could read minds as well!

"Please, sir," I pleaded. "I didn't mean no 'arm. I don't want to 'ang. I don't want to 'ave my 'and lopped off. I—I just wanted to be able to buy food an' medicine for my mum and my wee baby sister."

"It was your wee baby brother a few minutes ago."

"Bleedin' scum. 'Ave a memory like an elephant, don't you? So I picked 'is pocket. I was 'ungry. I 'adn't eaten in two days. 'E ain't squawkin'. 'E 'as his watch an' 'is bloomin' purse back. Why don't you let me go? You don't want to 'ave my death on your conscience, do you?"

"If I ever had a conscience, I fear it atrophied a long time ago."

"Bugger you, then! I 'ope you fry in 'ell!"

Bancroft looked mightily amused, brown eyes twinkling, a wide grin curling on his full pink mouth. This was all a merry lark to him, dragging a poor girl to her doom. In his way he was even worse than Cam Gordon, and I could expect no help form that quarter. I realized that now, and there was a terrible sensation in the pit of my stomach as the full enormity of my situation struck me for the first time. It was going to happen. I was going to be thrown into the roundhouse. I wasn't going to be able to break away, and I wasn't going to be able to talk my way out of it.

I didn't panic. I didn't cry. I didn't struggle, not even when I saw the roundhouse up ahead, brown and bleak and forbidding, a large gray cart in front of it, two Runners loitering on the steps and looking far more vicious than any of the ruffians in St. Giles. The smell was awful, noxious fumes emanating from the sooty brown stones and hanging in the air like a poisonous cloud. Bancroft made a face, whipping out a handkerchief to hold to his nostrils. Ignoring the surly Runners, Cam Gordon marched me up the steps and into the building, Bancroft trotting along behind. The corridor was dim, the yellowed plaster walls speckled with brown stains. The stench was so strong I thought I was going to faint.

A beefy constable with a square, florid face and dark, blazing eyes sat behind a desk. He looked up angrily, bristling with belligerence. Cameron Gordon told him what had happened in a cold, indifferent voice. The constable glared at me as though I were the most despicable vermin. He took out a ledger and began to ask questions, scribbling in the book with considerable effort. The Scot released me. A gaoler came shuffling down the corridor with a ring of jangling black keys at his waist. I rubbed my arm, glancing around, weighing my chances of escaping. It was hopeless. The odds were against me. The constable fixed those belligerent black eyes on me and demanded my name.

"Mi—Miranda," I stammered. "They call me Randy."

"Last name?" he barked.

"I—I ain't sure. My mum's name was James. I never knew my pa."

"Figures. Miranda James," he said, writing awkwardly in the ledger. The ink splattered. He cursed under his breath.

"What's your mum do? Whore?"

"My—my mum's been dead for nine years. She wudn't no whore. She was a fine lady."

"Yeah. Yeah. You gotta place-a residence?"

"I sleep in a coal cellar. In St. Giles."

My voice was quavering. My cheeks were burning after his implication about my mum. I had never felt so lonely, so lost, so vulnerable. I wanted to cry, but I wasn't going to. I held my chin high, trying my best to maintain a shaky dignity. The Scot looked bored. Bancroft looked exceedingly uncomfortable, his mouth turned down at both corners.

"Any livin' relatives?" the constable asked.

"I ain't go no one," I replied.

He asked more questions and made more scribbles in the ledger and handed a sheet of paper to Bancroft. Bancroft studied it for a moment with dubious eyes, and then he signed. The constable gave him the name of a magistrate, told him he would be expected in court at three the next afternoon and nodded curtly to the gaoler. The gaoler took me by the arm and led me away. I heard Bancroft say something to the Scot. He sounded terribly distressed. The gaoler took me down a long corridor and unlocked a heavy door at the end of it. He shoved me inside and clanged the door shut behind me. I heard a key turning in the lock and the sound of his footsteps receding.

I stood at the top of a flight of wide stone steps gleaming with patches of moisture. A few thin gray rays of sunlight streamed in from a single barred window set very high in one wall, well above street level, but they merely intensified the gloom. The steps led down into a huge black hole, and as my eyes grew accustomed to the dark I could discern dark forms shuffling restlessly below. A coarse voice called out, ordering me to come on down and join the party. There was a cackle of laughter and the sound of someone urinating on the stone floor. An enormous rat scurried up the steps, sniffed at my bare feet and made a squeaking noise before disappearing into the shadows. I had never known such terror. I began to tremble, gnawing my lower lip. Several moments passed as I struggled to control the trembling.

You ain't dead yet, Randy, I told myself. They 'aven't chucked that dirt into your face. Buck up. Idn't goin' to do you no good to stand 'ere cowerin' like a baby. You ain't really afraid. You can take care of yourself. Remember who you are.

"Come on, luv," the coarse voice called. "All-a us down 'ere 're eager to make your acquaintance."

I squared my shoulders. I took a deep breath. Slowly, defiantly, I started down the filthy stone steps.

15

I SAT HUDDLED IN THE CORNER ON THE DAMP, FILTHY hay that was strewn over the icy cold flagstone floor. I was wary, alert, not daring to close my eyes no matter how much I longed to sleep. How many hours had passed? Thirty? Forty? Morning had turned into afternoon, afternoon into evening, and then, after hours of total darkness, thin rays of sunlight had begun to slant through the barred window again like ghostly fingers reaching down to torment all the doomed souls locked up here in hell. The other prisoners prowled around like caged animals, snarling and spitting, striking out viciously, but no one bothered me, not after I made my stand.

They had surrounded me immediately as soon as I reached the bottom of the steps, a whole pack of them, leering and laughing and ready for sport. It was traditional for a new prisoner to pay "garnish" to those already in gaol, but I had no coins, no valuables, nothing but the ragged dress I stood in. One of the men roared with delight and declared he'd take his garnish in flesh, and I smiled at him and looked delighted myself and told him he'd catch the pox, the worse case of pox in th' 'ole bleedin' country, but I assured him it would be worth it, what was the clap compared to havin' Duchess Randy? No whore at Big Moll's was ever more brazen, more provocative. The man backed off, convinced I was riddled with the dread disease. I laughed, taunting him, and then I put my hands on my hips and offered myself to any man who had a few pence to spend on paradise. It worked. There were no takers. I was not going to be brutalized and raped repeatedly by every man who still had the strength to do so. I called them names, playing my part with gusto, and all the while I was shaking inside, so frightened I could hardly breathe.

The women were not so easily put off. They continued to crowd around me, vile, vicious and, I knew, far more dangerous than the men. An ancient crone with stringy gray hair spat at my feet and jabbed my arm with her finger. I doubled up my fist and drove it into her stomach with all the force I could muster. She crashed to the floor, shrieking like a banshee. When she tried to get up I hit her again, slamming my fist into her jaw. A hefty woman with pockmarked face and short-clipped black hair grabbed me and tried to pull off my dress. I fought like a wildcat. I kicked and clawed and used my teeth. I was much smaller than she was and not nearly as strong, but after five minutes she crawled away, cursing and bleeding and vowing revenge.

I was a pariah after that, a savage, diseased whore, and the other prisoners kept away from me, soon finding new diversion as other poor souls came down those slimy brown steps after the door clanged shut behind them. I picked out the corner, brushed as much hay as possible into it and sat down, glaring like a tigress whenever anyone dared come near. My arm and shoulder were still sore from the Scot's manhandling of me. One of my legs was badly scratched from the fight, and the roots of my hair stung from the brutal pulling. I felt bruised and battered, but I had come through the initial ordeal with great success. I wanted to curl up and sob my heart out. I folded my arms across my knees, not daring to let down my guard for a single minute.

Through the haze of semidarkness I saw the pockmarked woman muttering to two of her friends. The three of them stared at me, making plans. I made a face at them and extended a stiff middle finger. Had they known how weak, how tremulous, how terrified I really was, they would have been on me in a minute, would have beaten me senseless, but they didn't quite dare. They'd wait until I fell asleep. And so I hadn't slept at all. All night long I'd kept my vigil as the rats scurried and squeaked, as prisoners slept and snored and coupled on the stone floor like farm animals. I nodded now and then, true, but never for more than a few minutes at a time. The ticks and fleas and lice would have made real sleep impossible at any rate.

In the morning the gaoler had brought in a basket of stale bread and buckets of thin, tasteless gruel. I tried to eat. I couldn't. Those prisoners with a few coins were able to purchase meat and cheese and fresher bread, but most of them bought gin instead. All morning long various prisoners were shackled and taken out to be sentenced on Bow Street and new prisoners were brought in. The ancient crone I had knocked down was led away, shrieking in anguish. The gaoler dragged her up the steps as those below hooted and laughed and applauded. Two men got into a bone-crushing fight. A pale girl with lank blonde hair took on three men in exchange for a hunk of cheese and a pint of gin. Scenes of horror abounded on every side, and I knew that this was just a taste of what one would experience in a real prison like Newgate or Bridewell.

Would I be sent to Newgate? To Bridewell? Would I be pilloried? Hung? Anything could happen. It all depended on the magistrate. Any prisoner with access to money could hire an advocate and, if enough money passed hands, sail away from court free as a bird, no matter how serious his crime. The advocate would gather up three or four straw men and "prove" his client's innocence. A hundred or so men always loitered around Bow Street, the straw stuck into their shoe buckles indicating their readiness to be a friendly witness for a minimal fee. An advocate could step outside and gather up half a dozen of them for no more than a sovereign or two, and the straw men would solemnly swear that the prisoner had been elsewhere at the time the crime had been committed. The magistrates were quite accustomed to seeing the same witnesses appear before them over and over again, but there were very few men more corrupt than those who passed sentence on Bow Street, and the appearance of straw men meant the prisoner had money, most of which would end up in the worthy official's own pockets. The system worked beautifully for all concerned.

But I had no money nor any way of obtaining any. Like thousands of other penniless souls I would be totally at the mercy of the magistrate, my sentence depending on his whim, his mood. There were laws, of course, dozens of bulky journals crammed full of decrees and edicts and stringent regulations covering every eventuality, but few of the magistrates who dealt with criminals on Bow Street ever bothered to consult them. As I huddled in the corner, bruised and hungry and terrified, I knew I might well be sentenced to hang, and I knew that in all the world there wasn't a single person who would really care. Big Moll might shed a tear or two, true, but then she'd sigh and shrug her shoulders and get on with life. I had no one, no one at all.

Ain't goin' to do you any good feelin' sorry for yourself, Randy, I told myself. Ain't goin' to do any good at all. You're a fighter, not a whiner, and you ain't givin' up. When they march you into that courtroom you're goin' to 'and that bleedin' magistrate a story that'll 'ave 'im bawlin' in 'is beer. You're goin' to break 'is bleedin' 'eart. Before you're through 'e'll probably pin a bloomin' medal on you.

Ever the optimist, I consoled myself with these fancies, but a small voice deep inside told me I was whistling in the dark. My sob story hadn't worked with the Scot, hadn't moved him a bit, and Bow Street magistrates were hardly celebrated for their compassion. It took a certain kind of individual to sentence other men to hang or undergo the most hideous and inhuman tortures, and that kind of individual wasn't likely to be moved by a dirty little pickpocket caught red-handed at her craft. I plucked a flea from my scratched leg and ran my fingers through my hair, refusing to listen to that inner voice, refusing to give up hope. Once you did that you were sunk for sure.

The gaoler came for me a short while later. He pulled me to my feet and snapped shackles on my wrists, two tight iron bracelets with a heavy length of chain dangling between them. He gave me a shove and told me to climb up the steps. The pockmarked woman spat at me as I passed. I didn't even bother to give her the finger. I marched up the steps with the gaoler close behind me. He unlocked the door and shoved me into the hallway. One of the Runners I had seen out front yesterday was waiting, a stocky lout with coarse black hair, a broken nose and glowering black eyes. His trousers, vest and coat were a noisy green and brown check, ill-fitting and worn, his stock a hideous shade of yellow.

"'Ere she is," the gaoler growled.

"Fletcher's court?" the Runner asked.

"Fletcher it is. 'E'll be waitin' in 'is wig, ready to pass sentence on 'er, an' I 'ear 'e's in fine fettle today. Already sentenced four to 'ang an' two to th' pillory an' one to be publicly flogged—woman caught cheatin' 'er customers at the fish stall."

"'Ow many lashes?"

"Fifty."

The Runner grinned. "Don't wanna miss that 'un. Oughta be fun to watch. You, wench," he continued, "you can come along without givin' me any trouble or you can make it 'ard on yourself. What's it gunna be?"

"I won't give you any trouble," I said meekly.

"Should-a shackled 'er ankles, too, Bullock," he snarled. "Why th' 'ell didn't-ja shackle 'er ankles?"

"Pitiful-lookin' lass like this 'un too much for you to 'andle?"

"I can 'andle 'er, all right. She gives me any trouble, I'll break both 'er legs for 'er. 'Ear that, lass? You give Jim Elsom any trouble an' 'e'll make you wish you 'adn't."

"I 'ear you, Jim."

"Don't give me no lip, neither! Come along!"

He took hold of my arm and led me down the hall and past the deck and out of the building. Although it was dim enough, the sunlight was blinding after the darkness in the roundhouse. I blinked, stumbling a little. Jim Elsom muttered a curse and dragged me along the pavement, shoving aside any pedestrian who happened to get in his way. He walked briskly, jaw thrust out, expression menacing, and I trotted along beside him. The rusty iron bracelets were pinching my wrists. The chain rattled, banging against my knees every step I took. Elsom gripped my arm just above the elbow, his fingers digging tightly into my flesh, pulling me on.

We moved down Long Acre with its stretches of shambly

houses, its small shops and the huge sheds that housed carriage makers and wheelwrights. I was weak physically and emotionally drained and so hungry my stomach seemed to be squeezing together. As we passed the Church of St. Anselm and the sooty, rundown cemetery in front of it, I knew it would be futile to try and escape. I'd never make it weak as I was, with these bloody heavy shackles, and Elsom would be on me like a vicious bulldog. We crossed Bow Yard and started down Bow Street. It was narrow and dingy, brown and gray and green, and everything was stained with soot. Carriages and carts rumbled down the street, coachmen cursing, cracking their whips. The pavements were thronged with villainous-looking men who loitered outside the shops and alehouses. The din was deafening, the air foul, the atmosphere threatening.

Elsom dragged me toward a squat, ugly building with brown wooden beams and yellowing tan plaster marbled with soot. The gray slate roof was oppressive, giving it a top-heavy look, a forest of crumbly orange brick chimneys and thin black chimney pots crowning it. Other buildings pressed close on either side, squeezing it tightly. Elsom took me up the steps and into a large, dusty foyer and turned me over to a skinny clerk in black. His face was pale, pinched-looking, shadows of weariness beneath his sullen brown eyes. His peruke was gray with stale powder and slightly askew, his bony fingers ink-stained.

"'Ere's th' James wench," Elsom said, handing the clerk the key that unlocked my shackles. "I 'ear th' old man's in rare form."

The clerk sniffed disdainfully. "I wouldn't know," he said in a thin, prissy voice. "They're in chambers."

"Bugger you," Elsom growled.

The two of them led me to a set of double doors at the end of the foyer. The clerk rapped on the rough wooden panel. A burly constable threw open the doors, took hold of my arm and pulled me inside. Elsom and the clerk retreated. The constable closed the door and led me down a narrow aisle between two rows of heavy benches. At the end of the aisle was a low wooden railing, beyond it a cleared area with chairs and a ponderous table littered with musty, leather-bound tomes and rolls of paper tied with dusty ribbon. The wall behind was paneled in dark wood, a low door leading into the chambers beyond.

The courtroom was empty. It smelled of sweat and smoke

and fear. Candles flickered dimly in tarnished brass wall sconces. Plaster was flaking from the low ceiling, and the heavy wooden beams were worm-eaten. It was a stifling, oppressive place, the foul air stagnant. The constable stood at my side in front of the railing, holding my elbow firmly. My knees shook. I felt they were going to give way beneath me. Several long moments passed. The skinny clerk entered, gave the constable the key and then, opening the gate in the railing, took his place in a flimsy chair beside the table.

The door to the chambers opened. The magistrate came out followed by Bancroft and Cam Gordon and a fourth man whom I took to be an advocate, though he was much better dressed than those usually seen on Bow Street. He and the magistrate spoke together for a moment in low voices, the advocate very smooth, the magistrate snappish and impatient. Bancroft and Gordon came on through the gate and sat down on one of the benches. Gordon looked bored. Bancroft looked very pleased with himself. He winked at me. After a few more moments of conversation, the advocate joined the two men on the bench and the magistrate settled himself importantly behind the table.

He was quite old, sixty at least. His face was very thin, grayish yellow, deep pouches beneath his cold gray-blue eyes, flesh hanging loosely about his jaw. His nose was long and sharp and humped, his thin lips colorless, and his long white wig seemed much too heavy. He shuffled some papers, spoke irritably to the clerk and then fixed his icy gaze on me. My knees were still shaking, and I could feel all hope evaporating. Magistrate Fletcher looked as though he would relish pulling the wings off a fly before crushing it under his thumb. I took a deep breath, valiantly trying to still the trembling.

"Miranda James," the constable announced.

"Yes. You may go, Peters," Fletcher snapped.

"Have him take those bloody shackles off her first," Bancroft insisted.

Fletcher shot a freezing glance at the large blond and then nodded to the constable. The shackles were removed. There were large red welts on both my wrists. The constable left. I stood alone in front of the railing, staring at the man who was to decide my fate. The magistrate cleared his throat and shuffled some more papers, pursing his thin lips as though he had just been sucking a particularly sour lemon.

"Miranda James, you have been found guilty of a grievous

crime," he began in that parchment-dry voice. "It is my duty to pass sentence upon you, and the penalty for thievery is grave indeed. If crimes such as yours were permitted to go unpunished, this great country of ours would soon be uninhabitable—"

He droned on, speaking by rote, repeating words he had said so many times that they had lost all meaning. I stood very still, holding my chin high, and the stuffy, oppressive room seemed to whirl slowly, dark panels moving around, candle flames blurring. The dry, indifferent voice seemed to come from a very great distance. I closed my eyes, willing myself not to pass out.

"—hung by the neck until dead," he concluded.

I stared at him. I was going to hang. I felt nothing.

"However," he continued, "you are a very fortunate young woman. I have made a generous and very unusual concession in your case."

"Con—concession?" I stammered.

"These gentlemen have interceded on your behalf. We are not without compassion," he said, pompously employing the royal "we." "After due consideration we have agreed to make an exception in your case."

"I ain't goin' to 'ang?"

"You have been sentenced, instead, to a period of seven years of indentureship. Ordinarily indentured servants are transported to the colonies to be sold at public auction, but in this instance other arrangements have been made."

"I—I don't understand."

"Your article of indenture has been assigned to Mr. Cameron Gordon, and you are officially bonded to him."

"You—you mean I be*long* to 'im? Like a bleedin' slave?"

"For a period of seven years," Fletcher said.

"Bloody 'ell!"

"Should you displease him at any time, should you attempt to flee his premises and resume your old life of crime, you will be turned back over to the court and the original sentence will be duly carried out."

The weak, dizzy feeling vanished. The room was still now, and I could feel the color flooding back into my cheeks. A fine kettle of fish! Th' bleedin' sod would do anything to keep a housemaid! I brushed damp auburn tendrils away from my temples and adjusted the bodice of my grimy violet-blue dress, a flood of relief sweeping over me. I wasn't going to 'ang! I wasn't going to be pilloried! I wasn't even going to be sent to prison.

"Do you understand this arrangement?" Fletcher inquired.

I nodded. "I'm 'is," I said. "If 'e finds me unsatisfactory, 'e runs me back to court and I swing."

"You should be extremely grateful."

"Oh, I *am*," I assured him. "I'm so bloody grateful I could dance a jig. Thank you, your 'onor. You 'ave a 'eart big as a 'ouse."

Bloody bastard would 'uv 'ad me strung up in a minute if 'is pockets 'adn't been padded good an' proper. How much 'ad it cost 'em? Twenty pounds? Thirty? More than that, probably. Maybe as much as a 'undred, and they'd have to pay that fancy advocate, too. They? No, Cam Gordon wouldn't spend a penny to save me from 'angin'. It was the blond, Bancroft. This was 'is idea. That was why 'e'd jabbered on about maids an' such when they were takin' me to the round-house yesterday. Bless 'im! 'E was a sport, all right.

The clerk stood up. "Court is now adjourned," he announced in his prissy voice. The magistrate said something to him, and then they both went into the magistrate's private chambers, closing the door behind them. I sighed, feeling feisty now and so hungry I could eat a horse. The three men stood up. Bancroft shook the advocate's hand, patted him on the shoulder and told him he'd see him soon. The advocate left. Bancroft winked at me again and grinned. Cam Gordon still looked bored.

"Well, lass," Bancroft said, "how do you feel?"

"'Ungry as 'ell," I retorted.

He chuckled, those brown eyes dancing with amusement. I longed to give him a great big hug. He crooked his arm, offering it to me just like I was a bloomin' lady. I tucked my hand in it, and he escorted me up the aisle and into the dusty foyer, Gordon trailing silently behind us. Three Runners and their prisoners crowded the foyer. Poor wretches, I thought. Weren't any of 'em goin' to be as lucky as I was. The three of us stepped outside, me still holding on to Bancroft's arm. His velvet sleeve was ever so soft. He smelled like a bloomin' garden. Wind ruffled his dark golden locks as he moved to the edge of the pavement and raised his arm in signal.

"I hope you're satisfied, Dick," Gordon said dryly.

"Oh, I am. You should be, too. Look at it this way, Cam,

my lad, your domestic problems have been solved and you're not out a single penny. Your friend Richard Bancroft has done you a great service."

Cam Gordon looked at me with cold speculation. "I'm not so sure of that," he retorted.

"I'm goin' to be th' dandiest maid you ever 'ad," I told him, lying through my teeth. "I'll fetch your meals an' darn your stockin's and polish your boots an' keep your 'ouse so tidy you'll 'ardly recognize it."

"And if she doesn't, you can beat her," Bancroft promised.

"Don't think I won't."

Probably enjoy it, too, the bastard. Not that 'e'd 'ave the chance. This lass wasn't about to be a bodyservant to Mr. Cam Gordon, no indeed, but I'd play along with them for a while, at least until we got out of this neighborhood with so many constables and Runners about. A grand carriage pulled up in front of us, all polished teak with brass trimmings, two spanking bays in harness. A liveried groom popped down jauntily and opened the door for us. Bancroft handed me inside with mock gallantry. Soft tan leather upholstery. Amber brown velvet curtains. It was bloody wonderful, fit for a queen. Bancroft sat across from me, and Gordon was forced to sit beside me. He wasn't any too pleased about that, sniffing audibly.

"She smells like a goat stable," he said as we drove away.

"Nothing a good scrubbing won't take care of," Bancroft replied.

"She probably has lice as well."

"I 'aven't!" I protested. "I'm very careful about lice!"

"This is a wretched idea, Bancroft. I should never have let you talk me into it."

"You needed a maid, Cam."

"Quite true. A maid, not some vicious little guttersnipe who'd gladly slit my throat for a handful of pennies."

"You *afraid* of her?" Bancroft teased.

Cam Gordon didn't deign to reply to such an outrageous suggestion. He sat with his arms folded across his chest, those clear blue eyes without expression. His face was all sharp planes and angles, the forehead high, the cheekbones broad and flat, jawline firm. It really wasn't an unattractive face, too sharp and severe to be handsome, of course, but undeniably striking, and that thick straight hair was glorious, black as ebony and glossy as could be, one heavy wave perpetually slanting across his brow like a lopsided 'V' with the point an inch or so above his right eyebrow. Men would be leary of Cam Gordon, would give him a wide berth, and certain women would find him wildly intriguing.

"I must say," Bancroft remarked, "Old Fletcher was easy enough to manage. Soon as he caught a sniff of all those gold sovereigns Hampton mentioned he was ready to do anything we wanted. Lass could have been an ax murderess, wouldn't have mattered a bit."

"They're all corrupt, worse than the felons they sentence. Fletcher's no exception."

"Hampton assured me it'd be a snap. He had all the papers drawn up before we even went to Bow Street."

"I know, Dick," Gordon said dryly. "I was there. Quite reluctantly, I might add. I still think the whole idea is pure folly, but one indulges one's friends."

"Hampton made himself a nice fee, Fletcher collected a fat bribe, you have yourself a permanent servant."

"And you're seventy pounds poorer."

"What's money when one has a chance to do a good deed?" Bancroft inquired eloquently. "No need to be so morose, Cam. You wouldn't have the poor child hang, would you?"

"At the moment it would give me considerable pleasure."

"You don't mean that. Your bark's much worse than your bite, Gordon. I've been on to you for a long time. Look at her," he continued, "pale as a ghost, weak as a kitten, covered with scratches and bruises. You're frightening her to death with all this scowling. She's your property, man. You own her now, lock, stock, and barrel."

"I'm less than enchanted."

"You shouldn't look a gift horse in the mouth, Cam," Bancroft said breezily. "This little lass is going to work her fingers to the bone for you. She's going to be your adoring, obedient slave. Aren't you, lass?"

"Oh, yessir!" I assured him.

"See? You've won her heart already."

Gordon made a snorting, disdainful noise. He was wearing the same clothes he'd been wearing the day before: the worn pumps, the poorly darned black stockings, the black breeches and coat and tattered maroon silk neckcloth. He smelled of leather and sweat and damp linen, and I noticed that the fingers of his left hand were lightly stained with ink. He was left-handed, then, like me. Although he wasn't nearly as tense and wrought-up as he'd been yesterday, one still sensed the energy and violence pent up inside. If, yesterday, he'd been like a dangerous animal, taut, ready to spring, today he was indolent, no longer on the prowl. But just as dangerous, I told myself, remembering the way he'd handled me.

"By the by," Bancroft said, "how is the beauteous Lady Evelyn? She still haunting your humble abode?"

"With irritating regularity."

"I suppose she still wants to save you from the squalor and whisk you away to the splendors of Grosvenor Square. Wish *I* had a savior like that, gorgeous and experienced and rich as Croesus. Widows are always your best bet, I hear, and Lady E.'s panting to make an honest man of you."

"I'm well aware of that."

"Trouble with you, Cam, is you don't like women. After you've laid 'em you can't get rid of 'em fast enough."

Cam Gordon didn't disagree. "I've never met a woman who didn't bore me to distraction after an hour or so. Their minds are full of frippery. Their chatter is inane. They're good for one thing only, taking care of men, seeing to their needs. If it weren't for biology, I'd have made a good monk."

Or a Grand Inquisitor, I said to myself.

"Where—where are we goin'?" I asked in a pitifully meek voice.

"Holywell Street," Bancroft replied. "Delightfully raffish neighborhood. Lincoln's Inn Fields and the Courts of Justice are nearby, and Fleet Street's just around the corner. You get draymen and costermongers, publishers and printers, down-at-heels actors, journalists, penmen, writers by the score—most of 'em mad, of course. Never met a scribbler who was sane."

Cam Gordon didn't rise to the bait. He continued to stare into space with clear blue eyes focused on interior scenes. Perhaps he was thinking about one of 'is bleedin' novels. The elegant carriage had slowed down considerably. We were inching down a narrow, congested street, and as I peered out through the sparkling glass pane I saw a whole group of food vendors hawking their wares on the pavement. A plump, jovial fellow was handing a bacon roll to a grand lady in stiff pink taffeta. It was a luscious-lookin' roll, dripping with mustard. I clutched my empty stomach, eyes full of longing.

"I—I think I'm goin' to faint," I moaned. "Them bacon rolls—"

Richard Bancroft immediately tapped on the window above his head and told the coachman to stop. He opened the carriage door and hopped out. Traffic was forced to a standstill.

"You want a bacon roll, a bacon roll you shall have," he said jauntily.

"You might get me a twist of them boiled shrimp, too, and some chips 'ud be 'eaven."

"Anything else?" he inquired.

"I think I see 'em sellin' lemonade."

Whips cracked. Horses neighed. A burly drayman with a cartload of barrels filled the air with some splendidly inventive curses, but our coachman refused to budge. Cam Gordon clamped his fingers around my wrist, his eyes still gazing into space. Thought I was goin' to leap out of th' coach. Wudn't a thing further from my mind. I 'ad to get some of my strength back before I did anything like that. Three street urchins came running up to peer into the interior of the coach, standing on tiptoes to gaze through the windows.

Bancroft returned, shooing the urchins away. His arms were laden with a marvelous array of food. He handed me a bacon roll and took his seat, careful not to spill the lemonade as the coach started to move again. I devoured the bacon roll—sheer bliss with great hunks of bacon and globs of tangy mustard rolled up on a bun. I devoured the chips next, eating them by the handful, and then I quickly laid waste to the plump pink shrimp twisted up in a piece of paper. The lemonade was delicious, sweet and tart and ever so satisfying. When I finished it, Bancroft handed me a big, crisp apple. I sank my teeth into it, crunching noisily.

"Greedy little baggage," Gordon remarked. "It'll cost me a fortune to feed her."

"Poor thing was starving," Bancroft told him.

"Ain't never 'ad such a fine meal," I said.

Dropping the apple core onto the floor of the carriage, wiping my hands on the hem of my dress, I settled back contentedly against the soft leather padding. Amazin' what a good solid meal could do for you. Except for a few aches and bruises I felt fit as could be and saucy as ever. Fancy me ridin' in a swell carriage like this, just like a real duchess, a 'andsome gent grinnin' at me an' pullin' a surprise sack of sugared almonds out of his pocket. I gave him a dazzlin' smile and began to plop the almonds into my mouth. If it was Bancroft, now, I'd settle right in with 'im an' polish 'is boots without a single complaint.

"You live on 'olywell Street, too?" I asked him.

"Heavens, no," Bancroft replied in mock horror. "Patrician chap like me would be a fish out of water in such a disreputable milieu. I have swank bachelor quarters on Leicester Square, as befits the second son of an earl."

"Jemminy! You're an *earl*'s son?"

"Afraid so," Bancroft admitted, "not that it does me much good. Forced to toil in the fields of Mammon, alas. My brother's lord of the manor now and has an amazingly fertile wife. Four brats already she's spawned, all of 'em male. Algernon considers me the blackest of sheep, washed his hands of me a long time ago. I have to work for a living like poor Cam here."

"You write books, too?"

"Perish the thought. No, I'm an upstanding employee of the Bank of England, investments my specialty. You ever want to double your money, give it to me. I'll invest it in a Peruvian gold mine or a cannon factory in Germany and make you a wealthy woman. I seem to have this magic touch where money is concerned. Beats me why I should."

"Fancy workin' in a bank."

"Nothing fancy about it, I fear, and I spend as little time as possible in those hallowed halls. Much prefer to rag about with my unsavory friends, chaps who write blood and thunder epics and live on Holywell Street."

"Are we almost there?"

"Almost. We're on Fleet now. Incidentally, Cam," he added, "I had my man purchase a few things for her and take 'em to your digs. Shoes and stockings, petticoat, frock—I told him she was about my Cousin Lucie's size. If they don't fit, we'll send him for more."

"Thoughtful of you."

"Can't have her running about naked. Catch her death of cold."

Shame about the clothes, I thought, but duds like them would only get me into trouble in St. Giles. Wouldn't Big Moll's eyes pop out of 'er 'ead when I told her about my adventures, and wouldn't the girls turn green when I told 'em about Richard Bancroft and his velvet suit and the sack of sugared almonds. They'd never believe the carriage and the coachman and groom in tan velvet livery with gold braid. Wouldn't believe it myself, come to think of it. Leaning against the plush upholstery, my stomach full, I sighed, enjoying myself immensely.

Through the window I could see booksellers' shops and

printers' establishments and cozy-looking coffeehouses, wonderful places with fancy brick fronts and plate glass windows. Archways led into intriguing courtyards. Harried-looking chaps with flapping coattails and windblown hair dashed about waving papers or carrying armloads of books. Plump, distinguished gents in gray wigs and sensible frock coats stood in front of the coffeehouses, arguing ardently over some heated literary subject. Critics and publishers. Poets and journalists. Newsboys waving the latest editions. This was Fleet Street, the famous thoroughfare that daily provided the city with a flood of words, dozens of newspapers and journals, a barrage of broadsheets, books by the score, an unending cascade of printed matter. Heaven it was. I'd have to explore it one of these days, maybe steal some of those books settin' out there on tables on the pavement.

The carriage turned off Fleet onto Holywell and a few moments later halted in front of Number Ten, a great, shambly building four stories high with an archway in front leading into the courtyard. Ancient yellow brick. Fancy wooden balconies strung across the front. High pitched rooftops and tall chimneypots. A chophouse, a tavern and a butter and cheese shop on the ground floor. Folks who lived at Number Ten wouldn't have to go far for victuals. Through the narrow archway I caught glimpses of a pump and strings of washing billowing in the breeze. Looked wonderfully cozy, I thought. Nothing like it in St. Giles. More's the pity.

The groom opened the carriage door. Bancroft climbed out and reached in to take my hand. I alighted, sweet and submissive as could be. Gordon joined us, stern, wary. I smiled at him. Bancroft let go of my hand. Gordon reached for me. I seized his hand in both my own and sank my teeth into his palm. He let out a roar. I tasted blood. Quick as a wink I let go of his hand, slammed my fist into his breadbasket and, when he doubled over, clipped him on the jaw for good measure.

"Take that, you bully!"

And then I started running. I ran fast as the wind, feeling a wild elation as my bare feet slapped the pavement. Both men took off after me. I could hear them behind me, boots pounding. I laughed, darting around a corner, flying down another street, leaving them far behind. They weren't about to catch me. Duchess Randy wudn't about to be no one's property. No indeedy. Bloody Scot 'ud just 'ave to find 'imself another slave.

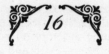

16

DARK ORANGE RAYS SLANTED DOWN ACROSS THE
rooftops, spreading thick shadows over the streets. It was growing darker by the minute, colder, too, and I was eager to get
back to my coal cellar. I could see the spires of St. George's
up ahead now, the top parts gilded a blazing orange-gold, the
lower deep blue, shadowy. I was vastly relieved. I had eluded
my pursuers easily enough—after chasing me a few minutes
they lost sight of me completely—but in doing so I had lost
my way, and it seemed I had been wandering about unfamiliar
streets for hours. I was on home ground now. I hurried along,
shivering as an icy cold wind swept down the street.

The spires of St. George's had lost their gilt when I finally
reached the church, the majestic stones shrouded with thick
blue-black shadows, the faintest glimmer of white marble visible. Beyond, St. Giles crouched like some gigantic brown
beast with jaws wide open, ready to swallow me up. I'd be
safe in the belly of the beast. Bloody Scot'd never be able to
find me. As I scurried past the church I heard a rustling noise.
Someone stepped out from behind one of the columns, moving
quickly toward me.

"Randy? Is that you?"

It was Sally, plump, jolly Sally with the riotous black curls.
She didn't look very jolly now, though. In the dim, fading
light her round face was drawn, her large brown eyes full of
fear. She was wearing a tattered pink cotton frock, a flimsy
gray wool shawl thrown loosely around her bare shoulders and
half-naked bosom. Glancing around apprehensively, she took
hold of my arm and pulled me into the shadows.

"Sally!" I exclaimed. "You look like you just seen a ghost."

"'Ere, get be'ind this column with me. Jesus! I been waitin'
for 'ours an' 'ours. Waited yesterday, too, all afternoon long
an' 'alf th' evenin', an' then Nan spelled me."

"You—you've been waitin' for *me*?"

Sally nodded, black curls bouncing. She pulled me deeper into the shadowy recess behind the column, cautioning me to silence as someone walked past. When the footsteps died away, she heaved a deep sigh of relief.

"Big Moll sent us, said you'd 'ave to pass by St. George's to get 'ome an' said for us to stop you. 'Don't let that child step foot in St. Giles,' she ordered. ''E—'e's after you, Randy."

"'E? What're you talkin' about, Sally?"

"Black Jack Stewart. 'E seen you yesterday mornin', found out who you were an' started askin' questions. 'E—'e found out where you sleep, an' 'e knows you come to see Big Moll. 'E 'as men stationed both places, waitin' for you to turn up. 'E—'e wants you."

I was silent, shivering again, and not from the cold.

"'E came to th' 'ouse 'isself, 'e did. Slapped Big Moll around, askin' 'er questions about-ja. All 'is men 'ave a description of you, an' they're turnin' St. Giles upside down, lookin' for-ya. 'E—'e told Big Moll you were goin' to be 'is main girl, said 'e was goin' to break you in 'isself."

I remembered the tall, skeleton-thin figure in the bottle green breeches and black satin frock coat with dirty gold braid. I remembered the great beak of a nose, the leering lips, the shiny black patch over his right eye, and I remembered the way he had stared at me with his one good eye. That eye hadn't missed a thing. Alf, the baker's apprentice, may not have given me away, but it hadn't taken Black Jack long to find out who I was. I shivered anew, thinking of that stare and what it meant.

"'E means to 'ave you," Sally said in a shaky voice.

"'E idn't," I replied. "'E ain't about to."

"Black—Black Jack, there ain't a man in Lun'on powerful as 'e is. When 'e sets 'is mind to 'ave somethin'—"

"'E ain't 'avin' me!"

"Big Moll, she's awful worried. She says you can't come back to St. Giles, Randy. It ain't safe. 'Is men're combin' it right now, like I told-ja. You're in terrible trouble."

"I know," I said.

My voice was calm now. I knew what I had to do. It wouldn't be pleasant, but it'd be a 'ell of a lot better than workin' on my back for Black Jack Stewart. Sally gripped my arm, pulling me close as someone else passed in front of the church. The last dark orange rays had faded now. I peered at the narrow alleyways of St. Giles, a few flickering yellow lights beginning to shine amidst the black brown squalor. I smelled the stench. If I entered that filthy labyrinth I knew so well, Black Jack's henchmen would nab me for sure.

"What're you goin' to do, Randy?" Sally asked.

"I'm skippin'," I told her. "I met a man yesterday. 'E's a bad 'un if ever there was one, but—it's a long story, an' I 'aven't time to go into it now, luv."

"You're goin' to this man?"

I nodded. "Give—give Big Moll my love, Sally. Tell 'er I'll miss 'er."

"We're all gonna miss you, too, Randy," Sally said. Her voice was quivering with emotion. "You—you've been like one uv th' family. You take care-a yourself, you 'ear."

She gave me a big hug. Her cheeks were damp with tears. I squeezed her tightly, wanting to cry myself, and then I sighed and squared my shoulders and told her good-bye. Sally stayed huddled behind the column as I hurried away into the darkness, away from St. Giles, away from a life of bondage far worse than that awaiting me on Holywell Street. Cam Gordon was going to be surprised when I turned up on his doorstep, would probably give me a dreadful beating, but I'd be safe with him, far from the clutches of Black Jack and his crew, and I could always run away from him again when things calmed down a bit.

Damn, I thought, trudging along the pavements, retracing my steps. Life was bloody 'ard sometimes. I thought of my beloved Shakespeare book, hidden beneath the floorboard in Hawkins's coal cellar. I hated leaving it behind. It was my only link with the past, with my mum. I really wanted to cry now. I wanted to bawl. It was rough, bein' a fighter, bein' strong and self-sufficient all the time. A scruffy-lookin' gent in a dark topcoat gave me the eye as I passed an alehouse. He started after me. I whirled around and tole 'im to shove off if 'e didn't want a dose of th' clap. A girl couldn't let 'er guard down for a single minute, couldn't even walk down th' street feelin' sorry for 'erself without 'avin to play the fierce alleycat. Men! Bugger 'em all! Who needed the bleedin' sods? World 'ud be better off without 'em.

It took me over an hour and a half to find Holywell Street again. A man in the chophouse on the ground floor of Number Ten told me sure, he knew Cam Gordon, chap came in lots-a times, surly bloke, always scowlin', never 'ad a kind word to say to anyone. He lived on this side of th' courtyard, on the top floor. He would, I thought, climbing up the stairs. The stairwell was poorly lighted, the wooden steps creaky. I could smell cabbage cooking. A baby was squawling in one of the flats. A light-looking blond in frilly skirts was tussling with a muscular chap on one of the lower landings, giggling merrily as he thrust his hand down her bodice. Nice place, this. It wudn't all that different from St. Giles after all, just cleaner an' not so dangerous.

I found the flat. I stood in front of the door, panting a little after all those bloody steps. I could hear voices within. Gordon wasn't alone. Perhaps he was entertaining the beauteous Lady Evelyn, I thought. No, both voices were male. I caught my breath, straightened my hair a bit and then knocked smartly on the door, bracing myself for the worst.

He opened it. He stared at me. He had removed his frock coat and the maroon neckcloth. His white silk shirt was thin, rather threadbare, open at the throat. The sleeves were full, gathered at the wrists, the tail tucked loosely into the waistband of his snug black breeches. His right hand, I noticed, was bandaged. He held a pewter mug in his left.

"'Ello," I said pleasantly. "I've come 'ome."

"You have, have you?"

"I wudn't really runnin' away," I explained. "I just wanted to tell all my friends good-bye."

"Who is it?" Bancroft inquired. He was out of sight, but I couldn't fail to recognize that voice.

"Guess," Gordon said.

Bancroft got up and came to the door, standing just behind Gordon. I gave him a smile. He looked utterly dismayed, then delighted. Cam Gordon looked extremely perturbed, and I couldn't really blame him. When I bite someone I bite hard.

"Ain't-ja goin' to ask me in?" I said.

Cam Gordon grabbed my arm with his bandaged hand, jerked me into the room and slammed the door so hard the walls shook. I wasn't alarmed. I expected a bit of rough treatment.

"I say, this *is* a surprise," Bancroft remarked.

"She's going back!" Gordon thundered. "First thing in the morning I'm taking her back to Fletcher and telling him to hang her!"

"Easy, mate. No need to get carried away."

"Little savage! The doctor said I might be infected. He smeared medicine all over my hand before he bandaged it. Smarted like hell."

"I ain't rabid," I assured him.

"Shut up! She's going back, Bancroft. First thing in the morning."

"What are you going to do with her in the meantime?"

"I'm going to tie her up so tight she can't move, cram a gag down her throat and lock her in the wardrobe."

"Why don't we have another mug of grog first?" Bancroft suggested.

"I should never have agreed to this ridiculous scheme of yours, Bancroft! You and your goddamn good deeds!"

Richard Bancroft grinned, not in the least disturbed by his friend's heated state. He'd obviously seen Gordon this way a number of times before. Mouth curling merrily, brown eyes amused, he sauntered across the room to pour himself another mug of the mulled wine. It smelled delicious. A fire crackled in the dusty gray-brick fireplace. The room was very large, incredibly messy. Clothes were strewn everywhere. Books and papers littered every available surface and spilled over onto the floor. There was a skylight with cracked panes, stars visible in the sky above. Beneath it, a large wooden table was cluttered with paper, quills, a huge pot of ink, more books. There were cobwebs, balls of dust, stacks of dirty dishes. No wonder 'e couldn't keep a maid!

"Here, Cam," Bancroft said, taking Gordon's empty mug, replacing it with the one he'd just filled. "Calm down. After all, the wench *did* come back. I think you should give her another chance."

"I'm going to strangle her!"

Bancroft glanced casually around the room. "I'd wait a day or two," he said, "let her clean the place up first."

Gordon snorted and flung himself into an overstuffed green chair with the padding coming out through a split in one arm. He drank his mulled wine with an angry furrow between his brows, chucked the empty mug aside and looked at me with fiery blue eyes. I moved over to warm my backside in front of the fire. Bancroft perched lazily on the arm of a disreputable blue sofa with sprung button, watching us both with amused eyes.

"You're going to work your tail off!" Gordon told me.

"Yessir," I said meekly.

"You're going to obey my every order."

"Yessir," I said sweetly.

"Is that quite clear?"

"Clear as can be."

"Take off those filthy rags. Toss 'em in the fire."

"Up your arse, you bleedin' lecher! You ain't seein' my teats an' my tail, not bleedin' likely! No man's ever laid eyes on 'em, and you ain't about to be th' first!"

He got out of the chair. He stalked across the room, flung open the door of an enormous wardrobe, pulled down a rumpled maroon satin dressing robe. He marched over to me, thrust the robe into my hands and said he'd give me exactly sixty seconds to take off those stinking rags.

"Turn around," I snapped.

He scowled. He turned around.

"You, too," I told Bancroft.

He looked very disappointed, but he turned his back, too. I peeled off my ragged violet-blue dress and the filthy petticoat beneath and tossed them both into the flames. Naked as the day I was born, I slipped on the robe. It was much too big, of course, and it smelled of dust and camphor, but the satin was delicious-feeling against my skin. I knotted the sash around my waist, pushed the long sleeves up over my elbows and told the men they could peek now.

Cam Gordon seized my wrist and dragged me roughly into another room, a kitchen of sorts. A huge, ugly fireplace with hooks for big black pots to hang over the flames. An immense cupboard, doors hanging loosely on the hinges. A wooden table heaped high with dirty dishes, cheese rinds, empty bottles, a hunk of sausage dried up hard as leather. The dark, smoky walls were adorned with mildew patterns. A large tin bath set against one wall. Gordon pointed it out to me, eyes flashing blue fire.

"There's the tub! There's a pump in the courtyard. Take those kettles over there down and fill 'em up with water. Bring the water back. Heat it. Fill the tub. Scrub yourself until every layer of grime is gone."

"I couldn't go down to the courtyard like this," I informed him, ever so reasonable.

Blue flames flashed. Mouth tightened. Hands looked as though they longed to fly at my throat. I smiled sweetly, meek and submissive. Cam Gordon didn't explode, not quite. He took the kettles down to the courtyard himself, and Bancroft helped me drag the tub into the other room and place it in front of the fireplace. Much too cold to bathe in the kitchen, we explained when the irate Scot returned. The water was heated, poured into the tub. Gordon gave me a hunk of soap, a towel, then brought in the clothes Bancroft's man had brought earlier on.

"Bathe!" he ordered.

"You an' th' other gentleman'll 'ave to leave the room."

"Jesus! I'm going to do it. I'm going to kill her!"

"Look, Cam, why don't we pop over to The Red Doe and have something a mite stronger than this wine. You could use a few, mate. We'll leave the wench to perform her ablutions in private. You can lock the door behind us."

Gordon agreed reluctantly. He would have preferred to stay and choke the life out of me. They left. I heard a key turning in the lock. I whipped off the robe, grabbed the hunk of soap and climbed into the tub. The water was deliciously warm. I scrubbed and scrubbed, reveling in the luxury of sweet-smelling soap and thick, foamy lather. Layers of grime vanished. Skin began to take on a lovely glow. The flames crackled in the fireplace. An old brass clock on the mantle tick-tocked lazily. I continued to scrub, losing track of time. I washed my hair, rinsed it, washed it again, and when I finally stepped out of the tub over an hour had passed.

Naked, curiously content, I dried off and idly examined the clothes Gordon had tossed onto a chair. Wonderful soft-blue kid slippers with heels two inches high. Fine white silk stockings so thin they were almost transparent. A white silk petticoat, thicker silk, rich and creamy, the skirt like billowing petals. A muslin frock, pale lime green sprigged with tiny, darker green leaves and tiny blue flowers. Jemminy! Must-a cost a bleedin' fortune, an' brand new! I fondled the garments, rubbing the glorious silk against my cheek, stroking the soft leather, hesitating a long time before daring to put them on.

The petticoat clung to my bosom and waist like another skin, caressing me softly, the skirt flaring out wonderfully. The frock had a low-cut bodice and short, puffed sleeves, and it was a bit snug at the waist. The very full muslin skirt belled out over the one beneath, both of them rustling as I whirled around like a dancer. If th' girls could only see me in such duds! Real silk! Sprigged muslin! I danced around for a few minutes and then settled on a chair to pull on the stockings. They were, alas, too large, and Bancroft's man hadn't purchased any garters. The shoes were too small, pinching my feet dreadfully. Who needed shoes and stockings anyway? I put them aside and sat happily in front of the fire, letting my hair dry. It felt soft and feathery as the heat did its work.

Imagine me sittin' 'ere snug as could be in front of a fire, wearin' silk an' muslin. It wudn't to be believed. The logs had all burned down, glowing orange and red, flaking into ash, coals glowing, too, glowing like rubies, the heat warming me all over. I ran my fingers through my hair. All dry now, feeling like silk itself. Wonder if 'e 'ad a brush? I got up and wandered into a third room, larger than the kitchen, not nearly as large as the one I had left. A gigantic bed with ornately carved headboard and posters, another wardrobe, a dressing table, both carved like the bed. Old wood, blackened with age, lovely just the same. More books. More dust. More litter.

There was a brush on the dressing table. There was a huge mirror hanging on the wall above it. Blimey! Who was that stranger? Who was that girl with fresh, glowing skin and radiant blue eyes and hair shinin' like dark coppery-red fire? Couldn't be Randy. Couldn't be. I gazed at the reflection, amazed at what I saw. It was a bloomin' aristocrat with them high cheekbones, that straight nose, those full pink lips. I tilted my chin haughtily, lowered my lids, made an exaggerated curtsey. Beat anything I ever seen, it did, and the street urchin stuck her tongue out at the snooty miss in the glass.

I brushed my hair until it fell in rich, lustrous waves that gleamed with dark highlights. Putting the brush aside, giving the stranger a final glance, I went back into the front room, heated the mulled wine and, fetching the pewter mug Gordon had chucked across the room, filled it with the warm, cinnamon-spiced grog. It was heavenly, made me feel all cozy inside, made me feel kind of dreamy and drifty and nice. I sat down on the disreputable blue sofa. The springs twanged. Dust flew as I settled back on the plump blue cushions. The lazy brass clock over the mantel continued to tick. It was after ten o'clock. Bancroft and the Scot must be enjoyin' themselves at The Red Doe, brawlin' an' carousin' with th' wenches, probably, just like all th' other men.

I yawned, dreamy as could be, ever so snug nestling against the cushions. I had a delightful glow inside from the wine and longed for another mug, but I was much too comfortable to get up and fetch it. Leaning my head back, I gazed up at the skylight, the sky a velvety black beyond the glass, stars blinkin' an' blurry. You're a lucky lass, Randy, I told myself. It idn't goin' to be so bad 'ere. You'll 'ave clothes to wear an' food to eat an' a nice warm place, an' if it don't work out, you can always go back to your trade. Th' Scot's mostly 'ot air, mostly bluff an' bluster. 'E ain't really so fierce.

My eyelids were growing heavier and heavier. I fell asleep, waking with a start an hour later at the sound of footsteps pounding on the stairs. I sat up and rubbed my eyes as the key turned in the lock. Bancroft came in first, looking flushed and merry and not entirely sober. His fine velvet coat was rumpled, his neckcloth loose. Dark gold hair unruly, brown eyes sparkling, he burst into song, bellowing out an extremely bawdy ballad with great gusto. Cam Gordon came in behind him, slammed the door, scowled and clamped his right hand over Bancroft's mouth.

"Jesus, Bancroft, you'll have me evicted! A man who can't handle his port should never touch the stuff."

Bancroft removed the hand from his mouth, gave Gordon a surly look and told him he was an uncouth bastard who didn't appreciate fine music. Gordon frowned, not nearly as put out as he pretended to be. He gave his friend a rough shove that was more affectionate than anything else and, when Bancroft started to topple over, grabbed his arm and held him upright.

"Man's a bloody financial genius and can't drink a few glasses of port without losing his head," Gordon grumbled.

"I haven't lost my head! I just feel good. Wouldn't hurt you to loosen up a bit yourself, you dour, bloody Scot! Always scowlin', always mutterin' threats and makin' fierce noises. Bosh! You don't fool anyone."

"You're drunk, Dick."

"Secret meetings with those other Scots, hatchin' dangerous plans—you'll get yourself hung yet, Cam Gordon."

"Shut up."

"There isn't a Scot alive who wouldn't love seein' Cumberland blown to bits, but most of 'em have enough sense to just—"

"Shut *up*, Dick!"

His voice was thunderous. Bancroft was immediately contrite. Gordon shook his head, exasperated, then helped his friend into a chair and stalked into the kitchen and began to bang pots around. Bancroft rubbed his eyes and blinked and after a moment looked up and saw me sitting on the sofa. His eyes widened. He rubbed them again, unable to believe what he saw, then took another look.

"Cam!" he yelled.

Gordon came tearing back into the room, alarmed.

"What is it!"

"You tell *me*," Bancroft exclaimed, pointing.

Cameron Gordon looked at me. No expression whatsoever registered on that sharp, angular face. He might have been looking at a stick of furniture. Bancroft shook his head as though to clear it and climbed unsteadily to his feet, brown eyes alight with appreciation.

"Venus herself has stepped down from Olympus to grace your humble abode, man. Have you ever *seen* such a vision?"

"You need coffee, Bancroft. I'll make us some."

"Look at that hair, it's like dark copper fire. Look at that face, sheer perfection, man, and the *body*! I know I had 'em assign the article of indenture to you, Cam, but I've changed my mind. I want her myself."

"You already have a maid, Bancroft."

"Who's talking about a maid? I want her for my *bed*, man!"

"You ain't 'avin' me, you blitherin' sot!"

Bancroft grimaced as though in pain. "Ow! That voice. Do you think we could cut her tongue out, Cam?"

"Ain't nothin' wrong with my voice!"

"Sounds like a cat screechin'," Bancroft said. "Such noises coming from such a lovely throat. Let's do it, Cam. Let's cut out her tongue, then I can take her to the best places and pass her off as a duchess."

Gordon gave him an exasperated look and returned to the kitchen. Richard Bancroft grinned at me. I stood up, smoothing down my skirts, preening just a little for his benefit. I didn't like what he'd said about my voice, hurt my feelin's real bad, it did, but it was impossible to be angry with him. He was a great, amiable pup, full of nonsense and handsome as could be in a jolly sort of way. A girl could certainly do worse, I thought.

"Shoes an' stockin's don't fit," I told him. "Shoes're too small, stockin's too large, an' there ain't no garters."

"The dress fits divinely," he assured me. "You're a raving beauty, lass. Who'd have thought it under all that grime."

"The dress is completely inappropriate," Gordon said, returning with a pot of water and a tin of coffee. "I don't know what your man could have been thinking. She's going to scrub floors, scour pots, empty slops, not decorate a drawing room."

"A delightful decoration she'd be, too," Bancroft said. "*My* drawing room could use a little sprucing up, as a matter of fact."

He set the pot of water on the glowing coals and placed the tin of coffee on the edge of a table, then turned to look at me with a close, scowling scrutiny, eyebrows pressed together, blue eyes fierce, the heavy black wave dipping over his brow like an inverted 'V.' He wasn't at all pleased by my transformation, I could see that. For some reason it disconcerted him, made him uneasy. Peculiar chap, this one, full of dark moods and contradictions, impossible to figure out.

"You didn't empty the bath water," he said curtly.

"I'll do it first thing in the mornin'."

"You're going to work hard, wench."

"I—I know that, sir. I will, too. Just wait an' see."

"I should take you back, let them hang you."

"I'm sorry I bit your hand," I told him.

"You're my property now, wench, my responsibility. You try anything like that again and I'll take my belt to you. I mean it."

He did, too. His voice was cold and flat and scary. I lowered my eyes demurely, trying to look repentant. I could feel the force of his stare, and I could feel something else, too, something I couldn't define, a strange, disconcerting sensation that was bothersome but not at all unpleasant. I raised my eyes, looking into his. They were a cold, harsh blue, and I felt extremely uncomfortable under that gaze, all the sass and fight gone out of me.

"I—I'll make the coffee," I said nervously.

"I'll do it. You go to bed."

"I—don't know where I'm supposed to sleep."

He stepped across the room and opened a door I hadn't noticed before. A short flight of steps led up to a small attic room perched atop the roof, one of the windows looking down over the skylight, another looking out across the courtyard. I followed him up. Moonlight spilled through the windows, revealing a small brass bed, a rickety dressing table with chipped porcelain chamber pot and jug, a chair. There was a candle in the pewter candlestick that set on a small table beside the bed. Cam Gordon opened a drawer and took out a match, lighting the candle. The room filled up with soft golden light, and I saw the quilted white counterpane, the shabby pink rug, the delicate pink and blue patterns on the white chamberpot and jug.

"It's small," he said gruffly, "but the others found it satisfactory enough."

~186~

It was heaven. It was clean, too, not messy like the rooms downstairs. I gazed around with a sense of wonderment. A room like this, all to myself, with a real bed, a real rug on the floor, however shabby. I couldn't hide my wonderment, and Cam Gordon, seeing it, scowled again.

"Go to bed," he said. "You'll be getting up very early tomorrow morning. We'll have to get you suitable clothes—a cotton dress, an apron, a cap, shoes that fit. I suppose you can keep this finery—" He hesitated, the scowl deepening. "Shop probably wouldn't take it back anyway."

He turned and left abruptly, closing the door at the foot of the stairs. I still felt strange, changed somehow, as though something beyond my ken had happened to me. Probably comin' down with a fever, I told myself. Wouldn't be at all surprised after traipsin' all over th' city in th' cold. I took off the dress and draped it carefully over the chair, then blew out the candle and removed the petticoat and climbed into bed. A real bed, soft as feathers. Sure beat a pile of rags in the coal cellar. Moonlight streamed through the windows, silvering the walls. Shadows danced on the ceiling. Tired as I was, I expected to fall right to sleep. I didn't. I couldn't seem to sleep at all.

Wrapping the counterpane around me, I stepped over to the window that overlooked the skylight. Peering down through the lead framework of cracked, sooty panes, I could see a section of the room below, the door, the fireplace, the old green chair. Bancroft was sitting in the chair, drinking a mug of coffee and listening none-too-attentively as Cam Gordon held forth. The Scot paced about restlessly, now in sight, now moving out of my line of vision. He seemed to be declaiming, making broad gestures like an actor on a stage, his expression quite savage. Bancroft yawned sleepily, as though he'd heard this particular tirade a number of times before.

What a strange, unusual man, I thought, returning to bed. Tense. Tormented. Angry. Wrestling with a private demon. Yet I suspected there was another Cam Gordon behind that hostile facade. Bancroft was genuinely fond of him, and he was bound to have good reason to be.

The moon vanished behind a cloud. The room filled with black, although there was a faint yellow glow coming up through the skylight. I closed my eyes, really comfortable for the first time in memory. I could hear noises from below—voices, footsteps, muffled by walls. Wind swept over the rooftops, whistling loudly, and me snug in my own bed, warm as toast under the covers. Who'd 'uv believed it this mornin' when I was huddlin' in gaol. A feather mattress. Clean linen sheets. Two blankets. It was amazin', that's what it was. Amazin'.

Drowsy, I thought of all that had happened to me these past two days. Was it only yesterday morning I had awakened in the coal cellar with the cat prowling hungrily, looking for food? Seemed weeks and weeks ago. Hadn't a penny to my name then, and now I owned a brand new dress and a silk petticoat, and I was going to have another dress as well and shoes that fit. I'd have plenty to eat, too. Wouldn't have to steal for it. I'd have to work hard, of course, and cope with that bloody, temperamental Scot, but the prospect didn't disturb me at all. It seemed . . . somehow exciting, strangely pleasant. Instead of dreading morning, dreading my next encounter with him, I seemed almost to be looking forward to it. Curious . . . Curious as could be.

The noise woke me up. I opened my eyes, disoriented, confused. A door had slammed loudly. Footsteps were moving below. The door to this room was opening now, a tiny golden glow widening, spreading as Cam Gordon came up the steps with candlestick in hand. Bancroft had finally gone and now th' bleedin' Scot intended to 'ave 'is way with me. I made a soft, moaning noise, pretending to be fast asleep, watching him cautiously through lowered lashes. He stood at the foot of the bed, holding the candlestick high, looking down at me, and his eyes weren't at all hostile now. They were, instead, extremely thoughtful.

Softly brushed by candlelight, his lean, sharp face didn't seem nearly so harsh. Without that scowl, that deep furrow above the bridge of his nose, without that tight grimace on his lips, he seemed younger and curiously vulnerable, a man wounded by life, nourishing his grief in private. Unguarded, those clear blue eyes were sad, beautiful, and the heavy black wave falling over his brow gave him a boyish look. Cam Gordon gazed at me for a long time with thoughtful eyes, and then he frowned and the furrow reappeared and the harshness returned. He hesitated for a moment, torn, battling with himself, and then he turned and went back down the steps, closing the door quietly behind him.

I was bewildered. Bothered, too. I lay there in the darkness, trying to figure it all out, trying to understand this trembly feeling inside. I was relieved, sure, I had to be relieved, bloody Scot was as strong as a stallion an' fierce as a tiger, could 'uv 'ad my cherry easy as pie, but what was this other feeling underlying the relief? Why did I feel . . . almost disappointed? Must be mistaken. Must be comin' down with th' fever. I tried to go back to sleep, but sleep was a long time in coming, and when it did it was filled with dreams unlike any I'd ever had before, delicious dreams, disturbing dreams, dreams that brought a blush to my cheeks when I recalled them the next morning.

17

EMPTY THE SLOPS. FETCH THE WATER. CARRY THE coal. Up the stairs, down the stairs and don't you dare tarry. I soon learned to hate that bloody stairwell and those endless flights of creaky wooden steps. I knew 'em all. The third step on the second flight screeched like a cat when you stepped on it. The fifth step on the fourth flight groaned like a bogeyman, gave me quite a turn the first few times I put my weight on it. Most people simply tossed their slops out the window, a sensible thing to do, but that didn't suit Mr. Cam Gordon, no indeed, his new slavey had to carry 'em down and empty 'em in the gutter, a shockin' waste of energy. How many buckets of water did I fill in the courtyard and lug up the stairs each day? I soon lost count. I came to loathe the sight and smell of coal, great ugly black chunks that weighed a ton when you had to carry 'em by the pailful. Fragile thing like me shouldn't 'ave to carry coal, but 'is bloody 'ighness wasn't about to lift 'is 'and doin' anything so mundane.

No, he was too bleedin' busy sittin' at the table scowlin' an' mutterin' and makin' almost indecipherable ink tracks on page after page of blank paper. He'd scribble for a while, curse, wad the page up, glare at the wall and then reach for another page, dippin' his quill in the pot of ink. He kept at it for hours on end, temper gettin' shorter, curses gettin' louder, and me expected to scrub the floors and wash the windows and fight the dust and keep as quiet as a mouse while doin' it. How can you dust books quietly? You 'ave to slam 'em together real smartlike—bang! bang! bang! Dust fairly flies. He yelled like a red Indian when I did that, hurled a candlestick at me, and when I was cleanin' out the kitchen cabinet and stumbled and dropped a stack of tin plates he came tearin' into the room like a wild man, black hair bouncin', blue eyes blazin'. Thought he was goin' to kill me for sure that time.

There were other times when, lost in his work, the whole place could have fallen about his ears without his noticing. His quill fairly raced across the pages then, ink splattering, a lot of it staining the fingers of his left hand. The pile of finished pages on the right side of the table grew admirably tall, all neatly stacked together with a lopsided pewter owl perched on top to keep them in place. When, after a day like this, he finally put quill aside and stood up, stretching his arms, arching his back, he was invariably in a good mood. Cam Gordon in a good mood meant he was merely sullen and quiet, meant he didn't stalk around like a caged tiger and slam things around and fill the air with horrible threats against bloody publishers who expected bloody miracles and could take their bleedin' demands and shove 'em up their noses—only he rarely said "noses."

I got up in the morning, lighted the fires, fetched water for coffee, and put the kettle on to boil. I popped around the corner to fetch fresh rolls, buttered them, carried rolls and coffee in to him on a tray. He scowled and yawned and sat up, quite, naked under the sheets, and muttered a sullen good-mornin'. After he'd had his breakfast—I took mine in the kitchen, all the rolls I wanted, sweet rolls with butter, at least two cups of coffee—he had to have water for washing and shaving and it had to be warm, not hot, woe unto the poor bond servant who brought him water too hot. Dressed, still sullen and grumpy, he either left for Fleet Street to harangue his publisher for more money or else settled down to work, the latter always with great reluctance.

In my neat black shoes, thin white stockings, plain cotton petticoat, and pink cotton dress, white apron tight around my waist, frilled cotton cap atop my head, I set about my tasks, cleaning, scrubbing, straightening. It gave me great satisfaction to see the grimy windows shine like diamonds after I finished with them, to discover that the kitchen floor wasn't brown at all, was, in fact, a rich, dark-gold wood gleaming after I scoured it and washed it with soap and water and lemon juice. What satisfaction to see the kitchen cabinets all neat, everything in place, tins aligned, dishes clean. I took pride in my work from the first and bitterly resented it when, after I'd cleaned his bedroom and had everything looking smart and respectable, Cam Gordon came marching in to change and in a matter of minutes had it looking like a cyclone had blown through.

Dust and dirt and litter were my enemies, and I waged a battle against them. It was a perpetual battle, for London was a filthy city full of smoke and soot and grit, and it seeped in and settled on windowsills and walls no matter how hard you tried to keep it out. And having someone like Cam Gordon underfoot so much of the time didn't make things easier, either. Didn't know things had a proper place, that one. Didn't know clothes belonged in the wardrobe, dishes in the kitchen, books on the shelf. He'd leave a hunk of cheese in a saucer, leave the saucer on the floor beside the sofa. Might as well send the mice engraved invitations. He'd leave his boots in the middle of the floor, his neckcloth on the table, his frock coat tossed over the arm of a chair. I picked up and picked up and picked up and put things back in their proper places and then he'd yell because he couldn't find whatever it was he happened to want at any given moment. It was frustrating and often infuriating, but it was never dull.

I shook the rugs out in the courtyard. I lined the cabinets with paper. I polished the furniture with beeswax. I swept and mopped and scrubbed, and although it was wearying, it was strangely exhilarating as well. I was determined to please him, but you might as well expect blood from a turnip as praise from a dour, sullen Scot. Sure, he was aware how hard I was working, couldn't help but be, but that was what I was supposed to do, work like a bloody slave, and he never deigned to express approval. He never addressed me at all unless it was to complain about something or vent his rage on a poor, 'elpless slavey who 'appened to be on 'and to absorb his wrath. He never came up to my room again after that first night, and, in fact, he hardly seemed to notice me at all most of the time. I was there for his convenience, a kind of machine whose only purpose was to make things comfortable for him—to clean his flat, do his laundry, polish his boots, darn his stockings, fetch his meals. Bleedin' sod! Took all the restraint I 'ad to keep from tellin' him what for several times a day.

At noon I brought his lunch in to him on a tray—cheese, buttered bread, sausage, a bunch of grapes, another mug of coffee—and most of the time he just grunted when I set it down on the table where he was working, never said a word. Other times he'd start, mutter a curse and glare up at me with murderous eyes because I'd interrupted him and broken his chain of thought. I longed to dump the whole tray in his lap then, longed to tell 'im 'e wudn't so bleedin' special, but I never did. I was as meek and 'umble and timid as a mouse, though I had to bite my tongue. It was a kind of game, ever so amusing. I was playing a part, and I wondered how long red-'aired Randy with her wicked tongue was going to be able to keep it up without tearin' into him.

Around four every afternoon Gordon changed and went out, rarely came back until late. He took his evening meal at one of the eating houses, leaving me to fend for myself. I'd either find something in the kitchen or pop down to the chophouse for something a mite tastier. Gordon left money for household expenses in an orange and white ginger jar that set on the mantel beside the lazy brass clock, and I was expected to purchase all the necessary provisions. It wasn't that he trusted me, it was just that he believed he had me thoroughly intimidated, believed I wouldn't dare do anything that would cause him to send me back to Bow Street. I wouldn't think of takin' any of the money in the ginger jar for private purposes, but an occasional juicy chop or a tasty meat pie for Randy were necessary provisions if I was to maintain my strength to do his bleedin' work.

When he was gone and I had the place to myself I could rest a bit, prowl around, investigate. To my credit I must say that I spent much of that time darning his stockings, brushing his coats, polishing his boots, trying my best to make his shabby wardrobe as spruce as possible, but I wasn't above snooping. I was naturally consumed with curiosity about the book he was writing, but who could read his handwriting? It'd take you hours to decipher those small, messy black hen-tracks—his publisher, I knew, screamed and raged about that unreadable script and had to hire an extra man whose sole job was to figure out the words and make a decent copy for the printers. I gave up after a few extremely bothersome attempts, couldn't make out one word in ten, and with all the other books in the place, who needed to read something written by such a thorny Scot? Probably wudn't worth readin' anyway.

Those other books I had dusted so carefully and arranged so neatly were a bitter disappointment. Books about warfare. Books about weapons. A book on medieval torture with gruesome woodcuts. A History of Public Executions. Military books telling you how to kill your enemy with knife, gun, garotte or bare hands. Books about soldiers, pirates, bloodthirsty Roman emperors, and a whole collection about Famous Criminals and their foul deeds—nothing I'd care to curl up with for a cozy read. They were all thumb-marked, well read, several of them with little strips of paper stuck between the pages to mark special passages. When he was working he'd frequently fetch one of the books, open it to the pages marked with the paper strips and read with great concentration, a deep frown creasing his brow. He would jot down notes, nod, put the book down and go on with his work. If he wrote books like the ones he kept around him, it was just as well I couldn't read his hand-writin', I thought, wishing I had my beloved Shakespeare to pour over.

There were, in addition to the others, several books written by someone named Roderick Cane, and they looked brand new, hadn't been read at all, the pages fresh and crisp, the bindings still smelling of glue. Unlike the rest of the books, these were novels, thundering tales of blood feuds and furious revenge. They were written, I discovered, with great verve and dash, exploding with incident. The heroes were always bold, ruthless scoundrels charging through adversity with bloodthirsty relish and a singular disregard for human life. Villains were dispatched on every side, their deaths described in vivid detail. This fellow Cane seemed to delight in violence, the bloodier the better, and the books were littered with corpses. Women, when brought in at all, were invariably treacherous creatures who tricked, entrapped and deceived before getting their just deserts.

Although I could see why the books would appeal to Cam Gordon—all that bloodshed, all those murders—Roderick Cane wasn't to my taste at all. Who wanted to read about the no-bleman-turned-outlaw who lured his wicked kinsmen into dark alleys and whipped a garotte around their necks, smiling as he strangled them to death? Who wanted to read about a soldier-turned-assassin who tracked down foes of Good Queen Bess and slit their throats with a knife, sometimes torturing them beforehand to get information? No, they didn't delight me at all, but they were the only books on hand besides those grue-some histories and military books. At least this Cane knew how to hook his readers and make 'em keep turnin' the pages, however appalled they might be by the action described.

I was curled up on the delapidated blue sofa late one afternoon resting my feet and finishing *The Curse of Hesketh*. The
hero had just dumped the deceitful Lady Hesketh in an oubliette
and, ignoring her cries, was waiting for the villainous Lord
Hesketh to return, planning to drag him to the dungeon and
give him a taste of the rack upon which the hero's brother had
been broken in an earlier chapter. Caught up in the story in
spite of myself, I didn't hear the footsteps on the landing, didn't
hear the door opening.

"I say," Bancroft remarked, "the wench is *read*ing."

I jumped, startled out of my wits. Bancroft and Gordon
stood just inside the room, the door still open behind them.
Bancroft was splendidly attired in dark green velvet breeches
and frock coat, silky white lace spilling at wrists and throat.
This was the first time I'd seen him since that night three weeks
before when I'd first come to Holywell Street. He looked delighted to see me. Cam Gordon looked livid.

"I—I done my work," I said defiantly. "I was just restin'
a bit before fetchin' my meal. I—I didn't think you'd be back
so soon."

"That's obvious," Gordon retorted.

"I 'aven't 'urt your bleedin' book. See, it ain't damaged at
all."

"*The Curse of Hesketh*," Bancroft read, peering at the title.
"Hmmm. Interesting."

"Where'd you learn to read?" Gordon demanded.

"I've been readin' ever since I can remember. Your boots
an' breeches are all splattered with mud," I observed, trying
to change the subject.

"That's why I came back. Damn coach splattered me all
over. I have to change before Bancroft and I go out to dine.
So you can read, can you? Understand all the words?"

"This bloke Cane uses words anyone could understand.
Nothin' fancy or poetic about 'is prose."

Bancroft chuckled, giving his friend a sly look. Mischief
danced in his dark brown eyes as I stood up, putting the book
aside.

"I polished your other boots this mornin'," I said. "There's
a pair of clean black breeches in the wardrobe."

"You enjoying the book?" Bancroft inquired.

"'Ardly," I replied. "Nothin' but blood an' thunder, just
like all th' rest of 'is books. Th' characters ain't real at all—
'eroes just dash about killin' foes, don't 'ave no genuine feel-

in's, an' th' women are sticks, not a one of 'em believable. This Cane fellow knows 'ow to tell a story all right, but 'e dudn't know diddle about 'uman nature."

Cam Gordon hadn't left the room. He looked even more livid, mouth tightening, eyes like blue ice.

"Looks like we have a literary critic on our hands," Bancroft said, "a very astute one at that."

Gordon ignored him. "Roderick Cane happens to be one of the most popular writers in London," he informed me in a chilling voice. "His readers clamor for more. His publishers can't keep him churning them out fast enough."

"That dudn't make 'im a *good* writer," I said airily. "It just means a lot uv people 'aven't any taste."

"I suppose *you* do?"

"I know a good book when I read one. *Moll Flanders* for example. Fellow who wrote it knows 'ow a woman *feels*, an' 'er 'ardships an' 'eartaches are all the more movin' because Moll's a real, livin' person. We care about 'er, want 'er to find 'appiness. If she was a stick like them women in Cane's books, we wouldn't even bother finishin' th' book."

"Bravo!" Bancroft explained. "The wench has a *brain*, Cam. Who'd have thought it?"

"She'll be quoting Shakespeare next," Gordon snapped.

"'E's my favorite," I confessed. "I've read all 'is plays dozens-a times, 'is poetry, too."

Cam Gordon clenched his hands, longing to wring my neck. Richard Bancroft found it almost impossible to contain his mirth. Gordon gave him a threatening look, longing to wring *his* neck, too. Bancroft perched on the arm of the green chair, mightily amused, though I couldn't rightly tell why.

"What would *you* suggest 'this fellow Cane' do to improve his books?" Gordon asked. His voice was vicious.

"Well," I began, "'e may be popular, but I'd bet my bottom most of 'is readers 're men. Lots-a-ladies like readin', too, an' if 'e were to put in a little romance an' some tender feelin's, 'e'd appeal to th' ladies, too. 'Is 'eroes are monsters. If they genuinely loved some fair 'eroine—not one of them evil trol-lops 'e's always creatin'—an' if they 'ad moments of weakness an' doubt, if they felt remorse about 'avin' to kill so much, they'd be appealin' to both sexes. Cane could double 'is read-ership."

"I *say*," Bancroft said.

"Do you know this Roderick Cane?" I asked him.

"Oh, I know him very well indeed, wench."

"Bet 'e's a bastard," I said. "Bet 'e's cold-blooded as they come."

"Unquestionably," Bancroft said.

I turned to Gordon. "Do *you* know him?"

"Intimately."

"Dudn't surprise me at all," I said. I couldn't resist it.

He stormed out of the room then. I could hear him slinging things about in the bedroom. A boot slammed into the wall. A vase crashed to the floor. The wardrobe door slammed so loudly I jumped. Couldn't figure out why he was so mad. He'd asked my opinion. I'd given it. Bancroft was laughing merrily, just like it was the grandest joke ever. I frowned, looking at him, and then I looked at the writing table and the pile of finished pages settin' there so neatly with the pewter owl on top. I could feel the color leaving my cheeks. Jemminy! I should 'ave guessed!

"'E—'e—," I stammered.

"Right you are, lass," Bancroft chuckled. "He's Roderick Cane. Wouldn't dream of publishing that rubbish under his real name."

"Lord," I whispered. "'E'll murder me for sure."

Cam Gordon didn't murder me. He came storming out of the room in clean boots and breeches and told me in thunderous tones that when he came home he expected to find the other breeches dried and brushed, the dirty boots shining and that bloody mess in there cleaned up or he'd have my hide. I nodded meekly, not daring to speak. Bancroft grinned. Gordon shoved him viciously toward the door, and I could hear the big blond's hearty laughter long after Cam Gordon had slammed the door behind them.

I was particularly cheerful the next morning when I brought his breakfast in to him. The rolls were generously buttered. The coffee had an extra spoonful of sugar. There were kippered herrings as well. Gordon grunted sleepily, sat up, shoved the hair out of his eyes and took the tray without so much as looking at me. He seemed bothered when he finally settled at his writing table, but I was convinced it had nothing to do with me or what I had said the night before. He wasn't even aware of my presence. He sat there moodily, staring at the empty paper, the familiar frown making a deep furrow above the bridge of his nose.

I soon learned what was on his mind, for later that morning

a Mr. John Beaumont came to call, a stout, fussy, officious man with thinning brown hair and a cheery smile that wasn't reflected in his cold gray eyes. Mr. Beaumont was the associate of Mr. Sheppard, Gordon's publisher, and handled all those tiresome business matters which had nothing to do with books or writing but kept Thomas Sheppard & Co. financially prosperous. Toying with the gold fob dangling across the expanse of his flowered waistcoat, Beaumont cheerily reminded Gordon that the new Roderick Cane novel was to have been delivered to his publisher two months ago, that a substantial amount of money had been advanced for it and that, if the book weren't delivered by the end of the month, every penny of that money must be returned.

Gordon was civil. Barely. He reminded Mr. Beaumont that Thomas Sheppard & Co. had made a bloody fortune from the Roderick Cane novels and were still reaping a hefty profit from same. He told the little man that writers were not clerks, that books depended on a creative process that couldn't be regulated by the clock and added that, if Thomas Sheppard & Co. were unhappy with his work, he would be delighted to take future Cane epics to any one of a dozen other publishers who would be damned pleased to get them, on time or not. Unfazed, Mr. Beaumont gently reminded the errant author that there was a little matter of personal loans advanced periodically on the strength of projected future earnings, said loans not yet fully repaid by said earnings. With a subtle reminder that debtor's prison might not be entirely out of the question, Mr. Beaumont took his leave.

Gordon didn't rant and rave as I had expected him to do. He sank deeper into gloom, muttering inaudible phrases under his breath and completely unable to work the rest of the day. I wondered why, if the Roderick Cane books were so popular and made so much money, the man who wrote them had to live in run-down lodgings on Holywell Street and why he had only three frock coats to his name. All those loans, all those advances—what had happened to them? The pseudonymous Roderick Cane should be living in splendor, living like a prince, and instead he lived like the humblest scribbler with ink-stained fingers. That question was answered the next night when Richard Bancroft came to call. I was in my attic room, darning stockings by candlelight, but I had left the door partially open and could clearly overhear everything the two men said in the big room below.

Gordon heatedly described Beaumont's visit, angrily re-
counting all that had been said, then launched into a loud and
lengthy tirade against publishers, publishers' assistants and the
whole bloody business in general, employing a few choice
words I hadn't even heard in St. Giles. Bancroft listened patiently and, when his friend had finally run down, casually
remarked that ranting like a madman wasn't going to help
matters at all.

"You might break a few sticks of furniture," he added. "That
sometimes works, I hear."

"What am I going to *do*, Dick? The vultures are closing in.
I wouldn't put it past Beaumont to actually have me thrown
into debtor's prison. I owe Sheppard over a thousand pounds.
I owe *every*one, as a matter of fact."

"As your banker, old chap, I'm fully aware of your financial
embarrassment. I know where every penny of it has gone."

"I have two widowed sister-in-laws, Dick, two young nieces
and four nephews who were left penniless. I had to make
provisions for them."

"And you did so, most adequate provisions. With the trusts
I've set up in their names, none of them should want."

"It was the least I could do."

"And your aunt and spinster cousin—"

"I couldn't let them starve!" Gordon said defensively. "When
my uncle was killed they—"

"I know, I know," Bancroft interrupted. "You sent them
the money to open a tea shop, and I've no doubt they'll make
a grand success of it. I'm not begrudging you the money you've
lavished on relatives, Cam—I quite admire you for it. It's the
money you've given to this—this secret organization of unruly
Scots."

"It's my business, Dick."

"Hundreds of pounds they've milked from you. Hundreds
of pounds, Cam, and most of the men with prices on their
heads, most of them on Cumberland's list of traitors to the
crown. You realize, mate, that if your financial aid to them
was ever discovered—"

"You know too bloody much!"

"You needn't have confided in me. You needn't have trusted
me."

"I'd trust you with my life, you amiable bastard. I'd kill
any man who so much as hinted that Dick Bancroft would ever
betray a friend. Ever since we were at Oxford together you've

been like a brother to me, much closer than either of my real brothers ever were, and—"

"Careful, Cam," Bancroft said lazily, "you're growing dangerously close to expressing genuine affection for another human being. It isn't your style, mate."

"Go to hell!"

"You've paid your dues, Cam. You refused to fight for Prince Charles on principle—principle that took a lot of courage for a Scot whose whole family passionately supported him. Your own kin considered you a traitor and disowned you. And now, after it's all over, you turn around and join this pack of rabble who—"

"Be careful, Dick. You may be my friend, but—"

"—who plot and scheme to pull off some wild act of retribution that's certain to get you all killed. Cut your ties with that lot, Cam. I feel as you do about Cumberland, you know that. He'll go down in history as one of the greatest military butchers of all time—rightfully so—but let history settle the score. Give up this madness, mate. It's destroying you. It's already gotten you into dire financial straits, and before it's over—"

Bancroft cut himself short and emitted a weary sigh. "I might as well talk to the wall as talk to a thorny, stubborn, obstinate Scot! Pour me another mug. I desperately need it."

Needle still now, the stockings limp in my lap, I listened to the sound of pewter clinking against pewter, of wine splashing. I was learning a great deal about my Scot tonight, things that explained much that had been puzzling me. The candle flickered in its holder, the yellow orange flame dancing wildly and casting nimble shadows on the walls. Cam Gordon paced back and forth, I could hear those restless footsteps, and Richard Bancroft sighed again, his velvet frock coat rustling as he shifted position in his chair.

"You still haven't answered my question," Gordon said. "What am I going to *do*, Dick?"

"The way I see it, you have three choices."

"What are they?"

"First of all you can finish this bloody book you're writing, finish it as quickly as possible, then write another one just as fast. Sheppard is a greedy bastard, but he'd gladly turn loose a sizable chunk of money if he had one Roderick Cane book in hand and the assurance that another was on the way."

"My second choice?"

"You can forget all about writing and marry Lady Evelyn Greenwood. The lady would be delighted to keep you in luxury for the rest of your life, you know. She has an awesome passion for you—beats me why she should—and she happens to be one of the richest widows in London."

"Evelyn Greenwood doesn't want a husband. She wants a pet Scot who can keep her amused during the day and bang hell out of her at night."

"She's terribly fetching," Bancroft said idly. "A bit ripe, perhaps, a trifle bruised, but there's not a man I know who wouldn't love to put his boots under her bed. Tell me, Cam, is she really as good as they say she is?"

"She's good," Gordon said. His voice was flat.

"And so rich! There's your answer, man."

"What's my third choice?"

"You can always slit your throat."

"You're a great help, Bancroft!"

"I try, mate. I try."

After Bancroft left that night, Cam Gordon went back to his writing table, working till dawn. He worked almost nonstop for the next three days, pausing only to wash, shave, catch a few hours of sleep. He ate very little. The food I brought to him on trays remained untouched for the most part, but he consumed cup after cup of coffee, couldn't get enough. He was scarcely aware of my presence, and I realized that he was in another world. The flat, my movements, the noises coming up from the courtyard, the bells of St. Clement Dane's—London itself had ceased to exist for him, and nothing was real but the violent world he created on paper.

Shortly after noon of the fourth day, Gordon reached for another blank page, dipped his quill in ink, scribbled two paragraphs and then emitted a great sigh of relief. He jotted down two more words—"The End"—beneath the paragraphs and, lifting the pewter owl, placed the page on top of the by now huge pile of finished pages. He stood up. He seemed to be in a stupor. He looked weak, so exhausted he could barely stand, and his face was terribly drawn, deep shadows under his eyes. He looked pale, too—complexion a waxy white, the heavy black wave dipping crookedly across his high forehead. He glanced around the room as though he'd never seen it before, looked at me as though I were a stranger.

"You look ill," I said.

"Just—just tired—" His voice was hoarse, barely audible.

"You 'aven't 'ad anything to eat. I'm goin' to fetch you some 'ot soup an' you're goin' to eat all of it an' then you're goin' to sleep. Workin' all night an' all day for four days—it ain't 'ealthy."

"Can't—can't sleep. Have to take the manuscript to Sheppard."

"You ain't leavin', not in th' shape you're in. You'd never make it down th' stairs, you'd fall an' break your bloody neck. *I'll* take the manuscript to your publisher an' I'll stop by th' chop'ouse on th' way back an' fetch some soup."

Gordon stared at me, trying to look stern. "I give all the orders around here, wench."

"Not today you don't."

Cam Gordon didn't argue. He was dazed, not himself at all. I led him into the bedroom. He sat down on the bed. I asked him where Thomas Sheppard & Co. was located. He told me. I left him in the bedroom, went up to the attic and washed my face and brushed my hair and changed into the silk petticoat and sprigged muslin frock. I wrapped the manuscript in brown paper and tied it with string and then stepped back into his bedroom. He was sprawled out on the bed, already fast asleep. Clutching the manuscript tightly, fully aware of its value, I left Number Ten and headed up toward Fleet, feeling very important and businesslike.

Fleet Street was as exciting as I remembered from glimpsing it through the carriage window. Ragged newsboys waved their sheets, shouting about Scandal in Surrey and the latest "'Orrible Crime." Journalists thronged the pavements, hurrying here and there and breathlessly exchanging snippets of news with each other as they dashed. Booksellers arranged their wares in shop windows, and learned, loquacious gentlemen argued volubly as they left the coffeehouses. The torrent of words poured forth with bustle and bravado, the whole street charged with a tense, hurried atmostphere that was marvelously stimulating. It was an exhilarating business, this makin' of words, and me almost a part of it, 'urryin' along like everyone else, carryin' a book that, soon as it was printed, would be read by 'undreds an' 'undreds of people.

Thomas Sheppard & Co. was only five streets down from Holywell on Fleet, a short walk. Brown brick, squeezed in between a tan brick printers' establishment and a dun brick stationer's, it had plate glass windows in front with the name of the firm in gold across them. A bell jangled sassily as I stepped inside. This front part was a book shop, shelves lined with gorgeous new books, a glorious smell of leather and fresh ink and glue filling the air. A clerk in black scurried over to assist me. I told him I had to see Mr. Thomas Sheppard on Very Important Business. He looked doubtful. Putting on my haughtiest expression, I told him I was Miss Miranda James, Cameron Gordon's assistant, and 'e'd better move 'is arse if 'e didn't wanna loose 'is bleedin' job. He looked stunned. Hesitating only for a moment, he hurried through an archway and then down a long hall, returning a few moments later to lead me to one of several offices in back.

It was ever so grand, the grandest room I'd ever been in. Dark green velvet curtains hung at the windows, and the walls were a rich golden-brown wood, panels gleaming. Chairs were covered in soft brown leather, just invitin' you to sit in 'em, and thick, elegantly patterned rugs were scattered over the parquet floor. Mr. Thomas Sheppard's desk was as big as a 'ouse, mahogany surface smooth as a lake, silver and onyx inkwell catchin' a sunbeam and makin' glittery spokes. The bookshelves behind it contained beautiful volumes bound in red and brown and gold leather. I longed to touch 'em. Jemminy! Imagine Duchess Randy in a room like this!

Mr. Thomas Sheppard sat behind the desk, a tiny, dried-up lookin' man who, when he stood up, wasn't nearly as tall as I was. No wonder I 'adn't seen 'im at first. His sandy hair was thin, sprinkled with gray, and his skin was like old parchment. Large blue-gray eyes twinkled amiably behind gold-rimmed spectacles. He bowed, polite as could be, and small as he was, he looked extremely dapper in his wonderfully tailored leaf brown frock coat and green silk neckcloth.

"Miss James?" he said.

I nodded, still haughty and grand, not about to be intimidated. The publisher came around the desk to shake my hand. I carried it off as though I'd been shakin' 'ands all my life. Mr. Sheppard indicated one of the big leather chairs and asked me if I'd care to sit down. I shook my head. Those friendly eyes examined me with considerable appreciation, me in my finery, my hair all brushed an' shinin'.

"I wasn't aware Cam had an assistant," he said. "I must say I envy him having one so young and attractive. What can I do for you, Miss James?"

"I 'ave 'is new book 'ere," I said.

Sheppard blinked. He seemed taken aback at the sound of my voice. Couldn't imagine why.

"Uh—uh—you have the new Roderick Cane?"

"Right 'ere," I said, "an' it's 'is best. 'E's been workin' night an' day to finish it so you can 'ave it printed up an' sell 'undreds an' 'undreds of copies an' make a bleedin' fortune."

"Cam's books are extremely successful," he admitted, "far and away the most successful we publish."

"An' 'im practically starvin'," I snapped.

"Oh?"

"Ain't fair, 'im workin' so 'ard an' that Mr. Beaumont comin' and threatenin' to put 'im in debtor's prison. 'E was dreadfully upset, 'e was, an' all them people waitin' for th' new Roderick Cane book. It's a bloody wonder 'e got it finished at all."

"I—uh—wasn't aware Beaumont was quite so severe," Sheppard said.

"'E was an arse'ole, 'e was. Sheppard an' Company makin' a bleedin' fortune from 'is books an' treatin' 'im like 'e was a criminal 'cause 'e 'appened to be a few weeks late."

"I'll speak to Beaumont," Sheppard promised.

The blue-gray eyes were twinkling now behind the gold-rimmed spectacles, and a tiny grin played on the publisher's lips. He liked me, I could see that. I liked him, too. Wudn't at all like that prissy Beaumont.

"'Ere's th' book," I said, handing him the parcel. "'E's already started th' next one," I lied, "started it last night, an' 'e wants two 'undred an' fifty pounds in advance."

Sheppard was taken aback again, his eyes widening. "Two hundred and fifty pounds! We've never advanced *that* much."

"'E 'as to buy paper," I said matter-of-factly. "'E 'as to buy ink, too, an' quills, an' 'e 'as to pay 'is rent an' buy food an' 'e needs new clothes. 'E can't work if 'e's worried about things like that."

Sheppard didn't reply. He looked concerned, and not about the welfare of his top writer.

"This book you 'ave in your 'ands is gonna make a lot, idn't it?" I asked crisply.

"It—I imagine it will make enough to completely clear Cam's debt to us. If it sells like the last one, I'm certain it will."

"An' th' next one'll sell like that, too, won't it? 'Is share uv th' profits oughta be a lot more than two 'undred an fifty pounds."

"Undoubtedly. Much more than that."

"So?" I said.

Sheppard hesitated, looking at me with doubtful eyes, and then, after a moment, he began to grin again. I maintained a tough, stubborn demeanor, determined to argue some more if necessary. It wasn't. The publisher shook his head, chuckling, and then he put the parcel down on his desk and took my hand in both of his, squeezing it affectionately.

"I've no idea where Cam found you," he said, "but I hope he realizes what a treasure he has. He'll have his two hundred and fifty pounds. He'll have it before the end of the week. You drive—uh—an extremely hard bargain, Miss James."

"*Some*body's gotta look out for 'im," I said.

Thomas Sheppard himself escorted me down the hall and to the front door. He was still grinning, delighted by our encounter and, for some reason, vastly amused. These publishin' blokes weren't so 'ard to deal with, I told myself. You just 'ad to know 'ow to 'andle 'em. The bell jangled as the head of Thomas Sheppard & Co. opened the door for me. He took my hand and said he certainly hoped to see me again. I said it'd been enchantin', cool and dignified as could be. You'd 'uv thought I was one of th' bloomin' gentry.

"Don't forget about 'is money now," I cautioned.

"I'm not likely to forget a—uh—single moment of this most remarkable interview, Miss James."

"Well, ta ta for now."

Sheppard was grinning again as I stepped out the door.

I fairly danced down Fleet Street. Th' bleedin' Scot was goin' to 'ave quite a surprise when he got 'is two 'undred an' fifty pounds. He was goin' to be pleased, too. 'E might even thank me, might even start noticin' me an' treatin' me like a 'uman bein'. It was barmy, I know, but I was actually beginnin' to . . . to *like* workin' for 'im. I looked forward to seein' 'im each mornin', looked forward to waitin' on 'im an' makin' 'im comfortable, and when he looked at me with those harsh blue eyes I got a peculiar feelin' inside, a feelin' I couldn't quite understand. It was kind of scary and kind of thrillin', and it was kind of pleasant as well. Beat anything I ever 'eard of, it did. It just beat all.

18

WHEN HE FINALLY WOKE UP WELL AFTER NOON THE
following day, Cam Gordon had no memory of what had transpired between us after he scribbled those final words on the
paper. After he had washed, shaved, dressed and eaten the
lavish lunch I carried in to him, he sauntered idly into the front
room to examine the manuscript before carrying it to the publisher. Finding it gone, he turned pale. I cheerfully explained
what had happened. Horrified, he flatly refused to believe that
he could have done anything so wildly improbable and foolhardy, and, convinced I was up to some diabolical mischief,
he seized my shoulders, shaking me viciously, interrogating
me in a savage, trembling voice.

I protested my innocence. I assured him I had delivered the
book to Thomas Sheppard himself, that he, Cam Gordon, had
given me the publisher's address. He shoved me away from
him so forcefully that I stumbled and crashed onto the sofa.
He tore out of the flat, thundering down the stairs. My upper
arms were hurting where he had gripped them. My neck and
head still felt wobbly. I'd cracked the back of my leg on the
edge of the sofa when I fell. Bloody savage! You try to be
good, you try to be 'elpful, an' what does it get you? Screamin'
an' shakin' an' sore arms. I hoped th' bleedin' sod was run
down by a carriage or, even better, one of them great 'eavy
lorries loaded with barrels of ale. Serve th' brute right, it would.

He was in quite a different mood when he returned two
hours later. Cool and self-possessed, he strolled idly into the
kitchen where I was washin' 'is bleedin' dishes and informed
me in an indifferent voice that he owed me an apology. Face
streaked with coal dust after lugging a bucket upstairs, hair all
damp and tumbling over my brow, arms up to the elbows in
warm, soapy water, I resolutely ignored him, pretending he
wasn't there. I scrubbed a plate, dipped it into a second tub of

hot water to rinse it, set it aside for drying, and then I started on a cup, giving it my undivided attention.

"You needn't sulk, wench," he said.

"I 'appen to be a 'uman bein'!" I snapped. "I 'ave a name. It's Miranda. I—I ain't a 'wench'!"

He elevated one brow. "Oh? I beg your pardon."

"Shakin' me like that! Yellin' at me! My 'ead still dudn't feel like it's on right. I'm goin' to 'ave bruises on my arms where you gripped 'em!"

"You're going to have bruises on your backside if you continue in this particular vein."

"Go on! Threaten me! I'm littler 'n you are an' weaker, too. You can afford to play the bully, you sod!"

"Bancroft's right. You do have a tongue on you."

"I ain't afraid of you, Cam Gordon!"

The faintest suggestion of a smile flickered on his lips. "You're not?" he said. "What have I been doing wrong?"

I turned my back on him, plunging my arms deeper into the soapy water, grabbing a greasy pot and scrubbing it vigorously. I could feel his presence there in the doorway behind me, could feel him watching me with thoughtful eyes. Why didn't he leave? Scots! Bullyin' sods, th' whole lot of 'em! I rinsed the pot and washed a pan and then, finished with the washing, dried my hands, took up a fresh cloth and began to dry the dishes.

"Sheppard was quite impressed with you," Gordon said.

I didn't 'ear 'im. 'E wudn't there.

"He said you were extremely persuasive, and, I must say, I was quite startled to learn I was going to be two hundred and fifty pounds richer. I've never had an advance that generous before. If you don't put down that cloth and listen to me," he continued, "I fully intend to grab you by the throat and squeeze your lights out."

His voice hadn't changed by a single inflection. It was calm and reasonable, almost polite. I hurled the cloth down and, whirling around, glared at him with blazing eyes.

"Then who'd do your bleedin' dirty work!"

"You have a point there," he admitted. "Perhaps I shouldn't squeeze your lights out. Perhaps I should just choke you into insensibility. Your neck would be sore for a while and your voice would be quite hoarse, but you'd still be able to perform your duties."

His voice dry, his manner detached, he looked at me with those cool, indifferent blue eyes, and again a hint of a smile played on his lips. He was teasin' me. Th' sod was actually teasin'! I could hardly believe it. Assuming an irritable expression, I brushed damp ringlets from my cheeks and continued to dry the dishes.

"He congratulated me on having so remarkable an assistant," Gordon said.

"'E did, did 'e?"

"I was, naturally, quite surprised. I owe you an apology, Miranda."

"You sure as 'ell do," I snapped.

"You needn't get snippy about it. I'm trying to be decent."

"Dudn't come easy for you, does it?"

"Listen, goddammit—"

"Go on, yell at me again."

"Women!"

He whirled around and stormed off, and I smiled to myself, curiously delighted with this exchange. He left shortly afterward and didn't come back until very late, long after I'd retired to my attic room. He was in an extremely sullen mood the next few days, moping around, staring into space or else reading one of those gruesome books, scowling, jotting down notes. I went about my duties as quietly as possible, and he seemed hardly aware of my presence. I might as well have been invisible. On the fifth day, after an inordinate amount of moody staring, he suddenly slammed shut the book in his lap, moved resolutely over to his writing table and began to scribble furiously, filling page after page with those indecipherable black hen-tracks.

The new Roderick Cane novel seemed to be coming with remarkable ease, I noted four days later. Gordon had gone out early in the afternoon, the first time he'd left the flat since beginning the book, and I had made myself a cup of tea. Sipping it contentedly, I picked up the pile of finished pages and began to examine them. The hero seemed to be someone named Burke, James Burke—squinting, I could make out that much—and he'd been deprived of his inheritance by a wicked uncle and had taken to a life of crime, becoming a notorious underworld figure incredibly like Black Jack Stewart, only Burke was tall and handsome and women were always trying to seduce him. Burke had no use for them, treated them with shocking rudeness, was interested in nothing but making a fortune and eventually having his revenge on the uncle and his four vicious cousins.

My tea had grown cold. I set the cup down, still holding the last page, and it was with amazement that I realized I'd actually been able to read his handwriting. I had struggled at first, squinting and frowning, and then, without my even being aware of it, the crazy black tracks had suddenly begun to make sense, shaping themselves into recognizable letters and words. Caught up in the story, I had read on, oblivious to paper, scrawls, tea. It was a bloomin' miracle, that's what it was. The tiny, squeezed-together scratches made perfect sense now, easy as pie to read. Picking up the cup of cold tea, I felt very pleased with myself. It was kinda thrillin' to read a book in progress, long before anyone else saw it, and I had to admit that this new Roderick Cane was excitin' indeed, even if some of the details about receivin' 'ouses were wrong. I wondered if I should mention it to him . . . and then it happened.

I turned to take the cup of tea into the kitchen. I stepped on the edge of a rug. I slipped, stumbling back into the table, and the cup flew out of my hand and great streams of cold, mahogany-colored tea rained down on the pile of pages, soggy leaves tumbling after. For a moment I was paralyzed with horror, and then I whipped up my skirt and began to dab at the pages before the ink ran too much. Ten minutes later I had the pages seperated and spread out over the table, limp, splotchy, barely legible.

I wondered how he would do it. Would he hurl me out the window and send me crashing to my death on the courtyard below? Would he choke me? Would he smother me with a pillow? More than likely he'd seize the poker and beat me to death with it. Run, Randy. Flee for your life. Get away now while you still 'ave the chance. You can't go back to St. Giles, not with Black Jack Stewart on the prowl, but London's a big city, you can lose yourself in it, an' you can always take up your old trade.

Panic gradually subsided. The pages were beginning to dry, wrinkling up as they did so, mottled with blurry, gray splotches where the ink had run and orange splotches from the tea. I carried them over to the fire two at a time and held them up until they were thoroughly dry, and when all of them had been dried this way I piled them back up in order, a crinkly, uneven pile. I cleaned the table off and straightened everything up, and then I sat down in his chair, reaching for the pot of ink, a quill, a clean sheet of paper. I placed the first page of manuscript beside the clean sheet, dipped the quill into the ink, shaky, my nerves all ajangle.

A foggy haze seemed to fill my mind, shutting out everything else, and this haze was gradually penetrated by a curious golden light, and I saw a little girl in pink frock and white muslin pinafore, long auburn ringlets bouncing as she turned to look up at the lovely woman who so resembled the woman I was now, her eyes a serene gray instead of blue, her hair more brown than red. It was my mum, and we were in a room with blue wallpaper and sunlight was streaming through the window. I was impatient, eager to take some crusts of bread and toss them to the ducks, eager to be with my friends, but first I had to practice my handwriting, had to copy two full pages from the book opened on the desk while my mum supervised. "No, no, darling, that won't do. Start over again. Each letter must be clear, must be elegant. A lady's handwriting is a thing of beauty...." And I sighed with exasperation and started over again and the haze returned, the scene evaporating, merging with the haze.

I began to copy the first page. My hand was shaking. The ink splattered, making jiggly black dots all over the paper. I started again, forming each letter carefully, linking it smoothly with the next, gradually getting the hang of it. How long had it been since I'd written anything? Couldn't remember. Must've been years an' years ago, but 'andwritin' wudn't somethin' you forgot. After I finished the first page I examined it carefully. Clear, real clear, elegant, too, almost like copperplate, just a mite shaky because I'd been so nervous. I copied the page over again, and this time it was indeed a thing of beauty. Wonderfully pleased with myself, I reached for another fresh sheet and the second page of manuscript.

The afternoon sunlight faded as I worked. I got up to put another shovelful of coal on the fire and another log. I lighted the candles, my back aching just a little, my left hand feeling stiff and cramped. I flexed my fingers and sat back down and continued to work and almost before I knew it the candles had burned down and I had to get new ones. The old brass clock on the mantel ticked lazily. It was after ten. The fire had died down, coals glowing in a bright red-orange, log charred and flaky, and through the skylight overhead I saw a black, black expanse lightly sprinkled with stars. My back felt as though someone had driven a knife into it and my hand seemed ready to drop off at the wrist, but I just had a few pages left to copy now. I longed for a bite to eat or a cup of tea, at least, but I didn't dare take time to fetch it.

I had two pages left to copy when the door opened and Cam Gordon came in. I turned in the chair, looking up at him guiltily, quill still poised over the page. He was wearing his black breeches and frock coat and a lovely blue neckcloth a few shades darker than his eyes. His face looked drawn, pale, the heavy black wave slanting crookedly over the right side of his forehead. He shut the door and looked at me and I started to tremble, my nerves snapping at last, tears welling.

"May I ask what you're doing?" he inquired.

"I—I—"

I started sobbing then, and the tears splattered and somehow I managed to tell him what had happened, sobbing miserably all the while, tears blinding me, streaming down my cheeks, and he stood there like a statue, icy cold, immobile, his face expressionless, and I told him he could kill me if he wanted to, I didn't care, I didn't care, it was an accident, an accident, and he was awful, awful, cold and cruel and I tried so hard, so hard to please him and I was just a bleedin' machine to 'im, not 'uman at all, not someone who 'ad feelin's, and he marched across the room and pulled me out of the chair and held me, smothering my face against his shoulder, his arms crushing me.

"Get hold of yourself," he said. "Get hold of yourself."

"I can't 'elp it! I didn't mean to—it was an—"

"Hush!" he ordered.

I continued to sob, continued to tremble, and then, when it seemed I could sob no more without tearing myself apart, I shuddered and grew still in his arms and grew painfully aware of that tall, hard body, those arms holding me so tightly, the wonderful, musky smell of sweat and silk and leather and tobacco. I felt an altogether new sensation, felt faint as well, felt I would surely crumple to the floor if he didn't hold me. I caught my breath. My cheek was resting on his chest, just below his shoulder, the black broadcloth rough against my skin, and I tilted my head back and looked up at him.

"Your eyes are swollen," he said gruffly.

"I'm sorry."

"Your face is dirty."

I brushed my cheek with my fingertips. He was still holding me tightly. I could hardly breathe. I didn't want to. I wanted to keep on feeling this magical sensation that filled my being, a strange and marvelous ache that was like silent music throbbing in my veins. I didn't fully understand it, but I didn't want it to stop. It had something to do with that body, those arms, the smell, that harsh, handsome face inches from my own. I frowned, disturbed. Cam Gordon released me and stepped back, frowning himself.

"I'm not a monster, Miranda," he said.

"Yes, you are. You're 'orrible, 'orrible."

"Did you actually believe I'd kill you merely because you spilled tea on the manuscript?"

"I felt pretty sure you'd try."

"How did it happen?"

"I—I was readin' it, an' I got caught up in th' story an' then—then it just 'appened. I—I was scared. I knew I 'ad to do somethin' so—so I copied it all over. I still 'ave two pages to go—"

Cam Gordon picked up one of the freshly copied pages and idly examined it, his face betraying no emotion whatsoever. It might have been a mask, sharp and lean and curiously beautiful.

"You did this?" he inquired, his eyes still on the page.

"I—I tried to make it neat as I could. It ain't perfect, I know, but at least a person can read it."

"You have a beautiful hand," he said.

"My writin' ain't bad either."

"You know, of course, that Sheppard has a man on the payroll whose sole job is to decipher my handwriting and make a legible copy for the printer. His salary is deducted from my share of sales. As of today that man is out of a job."

"What do you mean?"

"I mean that you have just become my copyist."

"You expect me to copy everything you write?" I exclaimed. "You expect me to do that on top 'uv everything else! It's bleedin' 'ard work, it is! My 'and near dropped off. My back's near broken, an' I 'ave dots dancin' in front of my eyes from strainin' to read them bleedin' 'en tracks! I ain't doin' it! I 'aul your water up all them bloody stairs an' I empty th' slops an' bring up th' coal an' light th' fires an' fetch your meals. I clean this flat, scrub th' floors, wash th' windows, darn your stockin's an' polish your bleedin' boots, but if you think—"

"You'll do it," he informed me.

"Like 'ell I will!"

I started the next afternoon, carefully, lovingly copying everything he had written during the day, and when he returned that evening I proudly displayed my handiwork. His spelling was awful, I told him, you spelled soot with two 'o's, them simple words tricked you every time, and he grew testy and asked me where I learned to spell and I told him it was somethin' that just came naturally, maybe because I read so much. Some people could spell and some people were good with addin' an' subtractin' an' things. Me, I was bewildered by numbers, but I 'ad a gift when it came to spellin'.

"You'll be writing the goddamn things for me next!" he predicted.

"Not for a while," I replied. "I 'aven't got th' knack uv it yet, but I probably will after I've studied it enough. I'm beginnin' to see 'ow you do it. You set th' characters an' get th' story rollin' an' then—"

"Jesus!"

"Dudn't seem so 'ard," I said airily.

"I've never murdered a woman. I've wanted to, God knows, I've been strongly tempted on more than one occasion, but—but—" He cut himself short, glaring at me with blazing blue eyes. "That you're breathing at all is one of the great miracles of our time!"

"You're terribly touchy," I told him. "I guess maybe all writers are. By th' way, you made a mistake about th' receivin' 'ouses. James Burke wouldn't demand a tariff from th' owners, 'e'd own 'em 'imself an' 'ave 'is men runnin' 'em for 'im. That's 'ow Black Jack Stewart does it."

"Oh?" His voice was laced with sarcasm. "I suppose you know the notorious Stewart personally."

I shook my head. "I ain't actually met 'im, but 'e knows me, knows who I *am* at least. That's th' only reason I'm 'ere right now."

"What's that supposed to mean?"

I hesitated, realizing I'd said too much. Cam Gordon waited, those eyes demanding an answer to his question. Reluctantly, I told him about that frightening encounter the morning of the execution. I described the way Black Jack Stewart had stared at me and told him everything Sally had said that evening in the shadows of St. George's. I cautiously admitted that if Stewart hadn't been looking for me, I would never have returned to Holywell Street. Gordon showed no reaction to this confession, might not even have heard it.

"He meant to abduct you?"

"Still would if 'e could. 'E probably still 'as 'is men out lookin' for me. It ain't been all that long."

Gordon said nothing, but he looked angry, that familiar frown cutting a deep furrow above the bridge of his nose.

I had forgotten all about this conversation early the next afternoon as I strolled back to Holywell Street with my arms laden with packages. Noticing that my stocking had a run in it, that my one work dress was getting a bit bedraggled, Gordon scowled, took two pound-notes out of the ginger jar and told me to go buy some new things. Elated, I left on winged feet and had an enchanting two hours spending the money. I bought not one dress but two, a lovely blue cotton printed with small purple flowers and a pale orange-pink cotton with scooped neckline and puffed sleeves. I also bought a violet silk shawl with shiny silk fringe, a heavy dark-blue woolen cloak lined with gray silk, four pairs of stockings and the loveliest kid leather shoes, dark purple with heels two inches high. They fit, too.

You 'ad to know 'ow to go about it, I thought, traipsing down the street with a smile on my lips. Some folks'd take th' two pounds an' go to a shop an' buy all new stuff, one dress maybe, maybe a skimpy cloak, but that didn't make sense when you could get things second 'and, good things, too. I'd bargained furiously with the old bawd who ran the secondhand shop. She'd wanted extra for the shawl, extra for the shoes. I told her she could take 'er bleedin' rags an' stuff 'em an' I'd take my two pounds an' spend 'em elsewhere. She backed down rapidly, though she claimed I was robbin' 'er as she wrapped the things up. When I got back I'd launder the clothes carefully, 'ang 'em out to dry in the courtyard and then iron 'em with the heavy flatiron I used on 'Is 'Ighness's shirts an' things. They'd be good as new then.

It had been a long walk to the secondhand shop, and I was still quite a way from Holywell Street when I got a funny feelin' on the back of my neck, a feelin' difficult to describe but so strong it was almost physical. Someone was watchin' me. Sharp instincts developed from years on the streets told me I wasn't mistaken. I slowed my step, dawdling, and I could feel it between my shoulder blades now. I dawdled even more, finally pausing in front of a shop window to admire a collection of

~213~

dusty porcelain vases and ornate brass pots. The pavement was extremely crowded, people passing behind me, carriages rumbling noisily up and down the street.

Casually, ever so casually, I turned, looking back the way I had come, trying to spot the culprit who'd been sizin' me up. Not those bustling matrons with their baskets of produce. Not the red-faced gent with lopsided hat, tipsy smile and red cheeks. Not the Italian organ-grinder with his scrawny, outrageously attired monkey. There must 'uv been 'alf a 'undred people comin' an' goin', movin' purposefully, more comin' out of th' shops. Not a soul in sight who looked a bit suspicious. Maybe I'd been imaginin' it. No, no, Randy uv St. Giles 'ad th' instincts uv a cat. She wudn't a prim, skittish lass with jumpy nerves. Someone had been watchin' me, all right, followin' me probably, maybe for some time. I continued to search the street, eyes sharp.

There! That big bloke in the dark leather jerkin, loitering a bit too indolently in front of the butcher shop, right shoulder resting against the wall, his arms folded, head turned away from me. I couldn't see his face, just the back of his head. His hair was thick and shaggy, the color of dark honey, and he was at least six feet four, shoulders broad, legs powerful in the tight brown breeches. As I watched, a stout gent in pale blue satin frock coat and powdered wig walked past the butcher shop. The blond brute stood up straight, stumbled, fell against the gent, almost knocking him down. The gent muttered a curse, straightened his wig and moved on in my direction. The blond slipped a glittery gold watch with a heavy chain into the pocket of his jerkin and sauntered off, his back still to me. I never did get a good look at his face, but it didn't matter now. Bloke spotted me with all these packages and thought I'd be an easy mark, followed me for a bit and then decided the gent in pale blue would yield better pickin's.

Putting the incident out of my mind, I hurried on back to Holywell Street to find Cam Gordon still hard at work. I didn't have time to launder my new clothes. I had to make him a cup of coffee, find him a certain book, build up the fire and get more coal, pop down to the butter and cheese shop for a hunk of cheddar, pick up a fat, juicy link of sausage with crackling skin and carry a dinner tray in to him, since he didn't intend to go out. He stopped work around seven, had another cup of coffee and, while I copied what he'd done, moodily researched methods of torture in Renaissance Italy which Burke might be able to use.

I washed the clothes early the next morning while he was still asleep, hung them up on a line in the busy, bustling courtyard. Children played noisily with a ball. Dogs yapped. Women gossiped cheerily at the pump. It was a sunny day, cold and clear, and the clothes were dry by noon. I heated the iron up over the fire and slowly, carefully pressed each garment. Imagine me owning four dresses, two pairs of shoes, my own cloak, lined with silk, and a silk shawl, too. It was heaven, that's what it was. Almost made up for havin' to deal with a churlish, temperamental Scot who spent his time scowlin' and scribblin' bloodthirsty tales of vengeance. As I put the clothes away in my tidy attic room, it suddenly occurred to me that I was happy, actually happy for the first time in memory.

Gordon was still working furiously at four o'clock, and I had a pot of stew started. Onions and chunks of beef were bubbling in broth in a big pot over the kitchen fire while I busily peeled carrots and potatoes. I didn't know anything about cooking, always popped out for victuals, but anyone, it seemed, should be able to make stew. I dumped the carrot and potato peelings into a large, round pan of water, plopped the cut-up vegetables into the bubbling pot and frowned as I smelled the aroma. Maybe I shouldn't've put in both them big pieces of garlic, I thought. Maybe some more salt an' pepper 'ud 'elp tone down the garlic. I merrily added more seasoning, feeling quite creative. 'Is 'Ighness was goin' to 'ave a tasty meal cooked with my own two 'ands.

I peeked into the front room. The Scot was writing industriously, gritting his teeth as he did so. Probably killin' off one uv th' cousins, I told myself. Someone knocked at the door. Gordon ignored it. The knocking continued. Gordon didn't hear it. Hastily wiping my hands on a cloth, I scurried across the room and opened the door and stared in silent amazement at the tall, glamorous creature who stood before me. She was several inches taller than I, with a round, ripe figure that was a bit too fleshy but undeniably voluptuous. Her hair was thick and glossy and dark gold, elaborately arranged in waves on top with long ringlets dangling down in back. Her complexion reminded me of a bruised white rose petal, and her emerald eyes glittered darkly.

"And who might you be?" she asked haughtily.

"I might be Eleanor of Aquitaine," I retorted, "only I ain't. I 'appen to be Mr. Cam Gordon's assistant."

The woman arched one dark, perfectly formed brow. Her mouth was large and plum red, greedy-lookin', and she had a heart-shaped beauty patch affixed just below the right corner. Provocative. Definitely. She smelled of crushed violets, a heady perfume, and she was wearing a green and cream striped satin gown. The bodice clung to her like a second skin, exposing most of her bosom, leaving her shoulders bare, and the skirt belled out in scalloped flounces that separated to reveal the ruffled cream lace underskirt. She wore long emerald velvet gloves, a chunky diamond-and-emerald bracelet on one wrist, diamonds glittering at her earlobes as well. At least thirty-five, probably much nearer forty than that, she had long since lost the bloom of youth, yet she exuded a powerful allure. Those worldly, experienced eyes had seen a lot of ceilings. That lush, well padded body had seen a lot of service.

"Who is it!" Gordon called irritably.

"Don't rightly know," I said.

I did, though. This couldn't be anyone but the much-discussed Lady Evelyn Greenwood who, according to Bancroft, was as rich as Croesus and had an insatiable yen for my Scot. The lady pushed haughtily past me and strolled over to Gordon, lace and satin rustling, perfume filling the air, jewels flashing with shimmering green and silver fires. I closed the door noisily. Fancy wearin' jewels in th' middle of the afternoon. Couldn't be good taste. Downright ostentatious if you asked me. Gordon looked up at her, scowling mightily, not at all delighted to see her.

"What do you want, Evelyn?" he asked.

"Cam, darling, you *know* what I want. It's been so long."

"I've been busy," he snapped.

She ran her fingers through his hair, smiling a languorous smile, enchanted by his foul humor and the challenge it presented. I longed to stay and watch the action, but Gordon shot me a threatening look and I scurried back into the kitchen. I left the door open a crack, though. I might not be able to watch, but I fully intended to hear. Gordon muttered something I couldn't quite make out, and Lady Evelyn laughed huskily, her skirts rustling again. I could smell her perfume all the way in here, even over the garlic.

"I *do* wish you'd abandon these sordid lodgings, Cam," she complained. "I know you're a mad, eccentric writer—that's why I adore you, darling—but living like this is absurd. That hideous courtyard—dogs barked at me, a wretched child made a face, I had to *weave* my way through lines of washing to get to the door. And those stairs!"

"No one asked you to inconvenience yourself, Evelyn."

"Don't be ugly to me, Cam, darling," she said in a pouty voice. "*Why* must you be so difficult? I've told you over and over again that I'd be delighted to put you up in swank bachelor quarters."

"And I've told you over and over again that I'm not a male whore."

"You're so un*rea*sonable! You won't let me buy you presents, you won't let me find you a decent place to live—I would have to fall in love with a man of principle. It's so boring! I've missed you dreadfully," she continued, lowering her voice provocatively.

"I really don't have time for this, Evelyn," he said wearily. "I've just started this book. It's imperative I finish it within two months."

"Poo! You work much too hard, darling. You need a little distraction."

Gordon was silent. I tiptoed over to the door and peeked cautiously through the inch-wide crack I'd left open. Gordon was still sitting at the table, turned away from his work, glaring up at her with eyes that gleamed a dark, threatening blue. He was seething inside, growing angrier by the minute, and Lady Evelyn was absolutely enchanted, deliberately baiting him. She smiled, reaching a hand out to run her index finger lightly down his lean cheek, touching the sullen curve of his mouth. Gordon scowled, tense now, a panther ready to spring.

"I want you, darling," she purred.

"You've made that abundantly clear."

"You want me, too. You know you do."

He stood up so abruptly that the chair crashed to the floor. His eyes were flashing violently now. He seized her wrist. Lady Evelyn blanched, thrilled to the core. He stormed toward the bedroom door, dragging her along with him. Her high heels clattered noisily on the floor. Gordon kicked open the bedroom door and gave her arm a savage jerk, slinging her into the room. Lady Evelyn let out a cry, half in terror, half in ecstacy.

"All right!" he thundered. "You're going to get what you came for, and then you're going to get *out*!"

"Cam! You're so masterful!"

The bedroom door slammed so hard a framed print fell off the wall, glass shattering. Such carryings-on! It was scandalizin'! I opened the door wider in order to hear better, and the things I heard! Such thumping, such banging, such squeaking of springs! It was enough to make you blush all over, it was. The bed was actually scooting across the floor, legs bump-bump-bumping on the hard wood. Lady Evelyn made noises like a drowning cat, totally uninhibited, and then there was a scream and a clattering explosion as the slats gave way and springs and mattress thudded to the floor. The Scot was certainly vigorous, I reflected.

Silence. Then a sigh I could hear all the way in the kitchen. Rustling noises. I closed the door again, again leaving a crack to peek through. Five minutes or so later the bedroom door opened and Lady Evelyn stepped out, smiling a gloriously contented smile. Her hair was mussed, her bodice awry, satin and lace skirts rumpled. She glanced back into the bedroom, blew her energetic lover a kiss and then pulled the door shut. She moved over to the mirror, adjusted her bodice, fastened a wave back up with a pin and smoothed down layers of satin and lace, smiling the whole while.

She left then, gems flashing, skirts rustling, perfume wafting behind her. Oh, she was an elegant lady all right, elegant as could be with her fancy gown and velvet gloves and haughty voice, but there wudn't a girl at Big Moll's anywhere near so brazen. 'Ad th' morals uv an alleycat, she did. Needed somethin' to cool 'er off. I glanced at the large pan of water on the drain board, carrot and potato peelin's floatin' on top. You shouldn't, Randy, I told myself. You shouldn't even *think* it.

I carried the pan of water out onto the landing and down to the end of the narrow hallway. Resting it carefully on the edge of the windowsill, supporting it with my stomach, I pushed open the window. It was directly above the doorway leading from courtyard to stairwell, and anyone entering or leaving this section of the building had to pass through it. Gripping the pan, hoisting it up a bit, I leaned out the window, waiting. Slut was sure takin' 'er time. She was probably weak in th' knees after all that exercise.

A full minute passed before she sauntered out onto the cobbles. I turned the pan over, merrily dumping the contents out, wishing it was slops instead of just dirty water an' vegetable peelin's. Lady Evelyn let out a shriek that must've been 'eard in 'Ampstead as it drenched her. She flailed her arms in the air and continued to shriek as I ducked back in and carried the empty pan down the hall. That was *wicked* of you, Randy, I scolded myself. You oughta be ashamed of yourself.

I wasn't. I was grinning all over.

It was at least an hour before Cam Gordon returned to his writing table. I heard him rumbling around, putting the bed back together, cursing volubly, and a bit later I heard water splashing as he washed. When he finally came out, white shirt tucked loosely into the waistband of his breeches, jet black hair hastily brushed but still unruly, he wore a savage scowl, blue eyes daring me to make a single comment. I assumed an air of the utmost innocence, sweetly inquiring if he was ready for his dinner now. He examined my words carefully to see if they might contain some impudent double meaning. Finding none, he gave me a curt nod and sat down.

"Imagine you 'ave quite an appetite," I observed, then scurried quickly on into the kitchen.

My stew was a disaster. Cam Gordon took one taste and let out a roar that shook the walls. I took a spoonful and candidly admitted that it might be just a trifle salty. He made several rude comments at the top of his voice, hurt my feelings dreadfully, then ordered me to get my backside down to the chophouse and fetch a decent meal and be damn quick about it. I took money from the ginger jar and left, deliberately dawdling as I moved down the stairs. I felt extremely pleased with myself, hurtful comments or no.

The sun was going down as I stepped outside, the courtyard brown and shadowy, streaked with fading dark-orange rays. The children had gone inside now. The pump stood empty, water dripping slowly over the rim of the wooden bucket someone had left beneath it. A large black and white dog gnawed a bone, looking up at me as I passed. I crossed over the cobbles and sauntered under the archway that led to the front of the building. It was dark here, purple gray, walls coated with layers of shadow. A large carriage stood on Holywell, directly in front of the archway. The horses stamped impatiently. The coachman wore a heavy cloak with the collar pulled up around his face, and he gripped the reins tightly, as though ready to take off at a second's notice. Probably waiting for someone, I thought. A man loitered in the nest of shadows before the entrance, leaning against the wall with only his boots and sturdy. brown-clad legs visible, the rest hidden by shadow.

I'd get a nice, tasty meat pie and a tankard of ale for 'Is 'Ighness, sausage and a twist of chips for me. I'd buy another loaf of bread, too, and some cheese and a pail of milk, just in case he decided to work late and needed something to nibble on in the wee hours. I stepped out from under the archway, so near the carriage I could have reached out and touched it. Footsteps shuffled behind me. I turned. The man who had been loitering in the shadows approached me. He was big and blond and wore a leather jerkin.

My heart seemed to stop beating. I was paralyzed.

"You—you *were* followin' me—" I whispered.

He grinned, nodding. "Knew you were on to me. Picked that bloke's pocket to throw you off th' scent. Worked right nicely, it did. Followed you on 'ome without a 'itch."

"You—you're—"

"Black Jack's been waitin' for you, Randy," he said. "'E's been waitin' a long time."

Before I could run, before I could cry out, the carriage door flew open behind me and dark, smelly cloth smothered me and I was lifted and hurled into the carriage. They'd thrown a cloth bag over me. I kicked, struggling. Strong arms held me. There was deep, masculine laughter. The carriage springs creaked loudly as the second man climbed inside. The door slammed. A whip cracked. The carriage moved rapidly down the street.

19

I MUST HAVE PASSED OUT. I WAS STRUGGLING UP through layers of darkness, trying desperately to breathe. Something horrible and smelly was smothering me, covering me, stench filling my nostrils and mouth, thickening, making it difficult to inhale. I struggled, sank, the darkness claiming me again, vaguely aware of the jostling movement, rocking, bumping, of the pressure of arms holding me tightly. Where was I?

What had happened? The questions flashed in my mind, melted away, and I could feel myself going limp as the darkness swallowed me up.

"Better take th' bag off 'er, Matlock," a crude voice said. It seemed to come from a great distance, barely audible. "We don't want 'er to smother. 'E wouldn't be too 'appy if we 'anded 'im a corpse."

I was shoved upright. Dazed, barely conscious, I felt the cloth rubbing my cheeks as it was pulled up. A bag. A bag. They'd thrown a cloth bag over me. Two men. A carriage. I was being abducted. I coughed, reeling with dizziness, gasping as the bag was removed and I was able to breathe again. I was completely disoriented for several moments, blinking, and then panic swept over me and I tried to jump up, tried to scream. A brutal hand was clamped over my mouth, my head jerked back against a shoulder. I struggled viciously. The man holding me chuckled, curling his free arm tightly around my waist, his hand crushing my lips and bruising my chin.

"Regular wildcat, ain't she?" he said.

"She's a wild 'un, all right. I 'eard all about 'er."

"I like 'em a bit wild. Makes it more interestin'. Ain't no fun when they're all weak an' willin'."

I kicked. I slammed my heels into shins. I threw back my arm, fingers finding hair. I yanked with all my might. A sharp chin dug into my shoulder, a rough cheek pressing against my own. The arm around my waist grew tighter, tighter, cutting me in two, while the rough palm forced my head back until I felt sure my neck was going to snap. I had the sense to grow still. There're times to fighting, sure, but there're also times when you've gotta use your 'ead. Th' brute could tear me into little pieces without even exertin' 'imself, an' 'e would, too. I let myself go limp, relaxing against him.

"That's better," he said.

He cautiously removed his hand from my mouth, ready to clamp it back over my lips if I started to scream. Both his arms were wound around my waist now, holding me close against him. I could smell sweat and skin, damp cloth and old leather. The carriage rocked and bounced, the wheels skimming noisily over the cobbles, horse hooves pounding. The blond brute was sitting on the opposite seat, his hands on his knees, his brows lowered, his mouth a wide, brutal slash of dark pink. The man who was holding me was almost as large as the blond. Tilting my head back, I could see that he had dark red-brown hair and mean brown eyes and a nose that had been broken at least twice.

"Think you can 'andle 'er, Matlock?" the blond taunted.

"Yeah, Grimmet, I can 'andle 'er. Me an' 'er 'as an understandin'. We're gonna be real good friends."

The blond snorted, folding his arms across his chest. The redhead chuckled and turned me around until I was facing him. The brown eyes gleamed darkly with lust in the dimness of the carriage. One arm moved up, curling around the back of my shoulders. The thick lips parted. My heart pounded wildly, and I tensed, ready to gouge his eyes out. He might kill me, yes, but I intended to do an awful lot of damage before he did. He chuckled again and started to lower his lips over mine.

"I wouldn't, Matlock!" the blond warned.

"You can 'ave 'er after I get done, Grimmet. There's plenty-a time."

"Let go of 'er," Grimmet ordered.

The redhead turned to glare at his colleague. It was clear that the two men detested each other, working as a team only because they'd been ordered to do so. I squirmed in Matlock's arms, trying to pull free, and he wasn't even aware of my struggles as his anger mounted.

"You tellin' me what-ta do, Grimmet?"

"That I am, mate. Anything 'appens to 'er, it's my ass as well as yours."

"'E ain't gonna—"

"They say she still 'as 'er cherry. Black Jack plans on takin' it 'isself. 'E finds out you beat 'im to it, 'e's gonna slit your throat, mine, too, for lettin' it 'appen."

"I ain't afraid of 'im!"

"No?"

The question was flat, without inflection. Matlock hesitated for a moment, then scowled and let me drop back against the cushions. I caught my breath, and my heart continued to pound wildly. I closed my eyes, moving as far away from him as I could. The panic was still there, shrieking silently inside me, ready to burst its bounds and turn me into a jibbering madwoman like those poor, pathetic creatures they kept chained up in Bedlam. I couldn't let that happen. I couldn't. I had to gather my wits, use 'em. I wudn't gonna be raped, not yet. For the time being I was perfectly safe unless I did something foolish like trying to jump out of the carriage.

Pull yourself together, Randy. Calm down. Stop tremblin' inside. It ain't gonna do you no good. You gotta use your 'ead. You've been in bad scrapes before. You're gonna get outta this one.

The panic didn't go away, but somehow I managed to contain it. I took several deep breaths and straightened my skirts, sitting up in the corner of the carriage. Matlock sat beside me, a huge, angry hulk, and Grimmet watched me with narrowed, suspicious eyes, not trusting me for an instant, ready to spring if I made the least movement.

"'Ow—'ow did you find me?" I asked. There was a quaver in my voice.

"Wudn't no trace uv you in St. Giles," he told me. "Couldn't find 'ide nor 'air of you, but Black Jack wudn't about to give up. 'As a real letch for-ya, 'e does, 'as 'ad ever since 'e saw-ya that mornin'. 'E kept us lookin' for you all them weeks, then 'e finally decided you might-a been pinched. 'E 'as connections on Bow Street, checked it out, learned you'd been bonded to this bloke Gordon, an' th' rest was easy, just a matter uv findin' th' right opportunity to grab-ya."

"You—you're takin' me to 'im?"

Grimmet nodded. "'E 'as a special 'ideaway in St. Giles where we're breakin' in th' girls for th' new 'ouse. 'E's expectin' big things from you, Randy. 'Magine you'll be 'is number one 'ore."

Like 'ell I will, I thought. Anger was beginning to stir, eclipsing the panic. I wudn't no weak, whinin' maiden snatched out of some fancy girls' school. I was Duchess Randy, schooled on the streets, more than a match for these two brutal oafs. I might not 'ave th' brawn, but I 'ad brains, an' th' two of 'em together didn't 'ave th' intelligence of a peahen. I gazed at the blond, forcing back the anger, summoning a shaky calm that gradually grew more stable. Black Jack Stewart was just going to 'ave to find 'imself another whore.

I couldn't get out of the carriage, no, but when we got to th' 'ouse I'd 'ave an opportunity to get away. I'd make one. I wudn't scared. Not any longer. Not much. I was calm now, calm an' crafty. I 'ad brains an' determination, an' I 'ad incentive. . . . 'E'd be gettin' restless now, getting surly, wonderin' where I was, wantin' 'is dinner. Bleedin' Scot. Beautiful, bleedin' Scot. I'd grown used to 'im. I'd grown fond of 'im, crazy as that seemed, maybe more than fond. Feelings I had never dared examine too closely stirred inside now, now that I was in danger of losing him, and my determination solidified, hard, cold, supplanting everything else. Nothing was going to keep me from him. Nothing. I'd face Black Jack Stewart and 'is whole bleedin' army, and I'd win, too.

No longer afraid, I sat calmly in the carriage with my two abductors, biding my time. Through the windows of the carriage London was dark gray and brown, mottled with black shadows as darkness fell, a few lights making blurry yellow-orange splotches against the dreary expanse. I could smell the river, a combination of mud and moss and water, salt and the stench of refuse. A church bell tolled solemnly. Matlock and Grimmet were silent, Matlock still brooding angrily, Grimmet still watching me with narrowed eyes. Another smell assailed my nostrils, an unmistakable smell that I knew so well, that seemed even stronger now that I'd been away from it for a while. Like the lair of some filthy animal, St. Giles exuded the odor of the beast.

We passed St. George's, marble and masonry gleaming a dull gray white among the shadows. We drove through the labyrinth of narrow, congested streets, and I made a note of each familiar landmark, composing a mental map that would guide me back to my Scot. The brothels, the doss houses, the opium dens and gin shops and sordid tenements were just as they had been, but they seemed alien now, seemed even filthier and more squalid now that I had come to know another world. I had been a part of St. Giles, a product of these streets and alleys, shaped by them, but that had changed now. Already it had changed, and I was a stranger. The carriage moved down Half Moon Alley, pathetic whores and swaggering ruffians and gin-soaked bawds thronging the pavements, dirty, tattered children darting about noisily. A scrawny little girl in pink rags taunted a fishmonger, hands on hips, her hair tangled, her face streaked with dirt. As the monger cursed her she seized a scaly haddock from his cart and dashed away, disappearing into the mob. I might have been witnessing a scene from my own past. That child might have been me just a few short years ago.

"Won't be long now," Grimmet said gruffly. " 'E 'as everything ready, 'as a room for 'er. Don't lose 'eart, Matlock. Maybe 'e'll let you 'ave a turn at 'er when 'e's broken 'er in."

"To 'ell with 'im!"

"That attitude's gonna get you in a lotta trouble, mate."

"Mind your own soddin' business, Grimmet!"

Grimmet smiled a taunting smile. Matlock glared at him. They were like two bulls in a pasture, stamping the ground, ready to charge at each other. Grimmet was obviously the chief henchman, Matlock his underling, a situation that clearly galled him. The redhead turned to look at me with a combination of hatred and vicious lust, as though I were somehow responsible for his lack of stature in Black Jack's organization. I repressed a shudder, knowing full well that were it not for Grimmet's presence I would already have been savagely raped. Both of them were brutal animals, but they were like playful pups compared to their leader, the man who intended to "break me in."

I refused to think of it, refused to let panic and fear get another hold on me. We drove deeper into the labyrinth, turning down first one street, then another, moving through the darkest, most dangerous section of St. Giles, a neighborhood avoided by all but the hardiest, most corrupt denizens of the slums. I recognized Wormwood Alley, a narrow, dingy passageway barely wide enough for the carriage to pass through, and a few moments later we stopped before two crumbly brick pillars with a heavy iron gate between them. A burly lout shouted at the coachman. The coachman gave some kind of password, and the gate was unlocked at once, creaking audibly as it was swung back.

The carriage moved into a small, closed courtyard and stopped with a rocking jolt. Matlock shoved open the door and scrambled heavily out. Grimmet followed, reaching back to take my arm, pulling me roughly onto the cobbled ground. The carriage turned around and moved back down Wormwood Alley. The burly giant swung the heavy iron gate shut with a bang and snapped the padlock in place. Night had fallen completely now, and the courtyard was a nest of darkness, thick black shadows cloaking the decrepit three-story gray frame house surrounded by overgrown shrubbery and tall trees. Moonlight sifted through the tree limbs, and I could see that the courtyard was entirely surrounded by a huge stone wall at least ten feet high, the barred gate providing the only access. The place was a bloomin' fortress, I thought, frowning. Climbin' that wall wudn't goin' to be no lark, but I'd climb one twice that 'igh if need be.

Grimmet clenched my arm firmly, leading me up three broken marble steps and into a huge, empty foyer with a bare gray wood floor and faded blue paper peeling on the walls. Candles burned in a pewter candelabra sitting on a rickety wooden table. Open archways led into the other large rooms, equally bare, and a once stately staircase curved up into darkness, a tattered violet runner covering the steps. Matlock followed us in, banging the door shut behind him, and a raven-haired ruffian in black breeches, gray blue shirt and thin black leather jerkin came up a flight of steps that apparently led to the basement. He carried a tray, and he examined me as though I were a side of meat.

"I see you brung 'er," he said coldly. "Any trouble?"

"Easy as pie," Grimmet retorted. "Never 'ad an easier snatch. 'Ad a bit uv trouble with Matlock 'ere, though. 'E wanted to bang 'er 'fore Black Jack 'ad 'is fun."

The dark-haired man looked at Matlock, and then he set the tray down on the table, jerking his head back toward the basement steps.

"Fat blonde down there still 'adn't made up 'er mind to cooperate. Refused to eat 'er meal. Reckon we'll 'ave to let 'er starve a couple-a days. She'll be willin' enough to work then."

"'Ow 'bout th' one upstairs?"

"Oh, she's purrin' like a kitten. 'Ad 'er myself a while ago. Fast learner, that 'un. Get 'er washed up an' in a fancy gown, she'll bring 'em in like a magnet. 'Bout ready to leave, 'er."

They continued to talk, Grimmet keeping a firm grip on my arm, Matlock sulking, and I learned that there were five girls stashed away in various parts of the house, being "trained" for their new line of work by Black Jack and his men. Grimmet, Matlock and Hogan, the black-haired man, were the only ones on duty tonight, although Black Jack and two others would be arriving later on. That made six, seven counting the lout guarding the gate. It wudn't goin' to be easy gettin' away from seven of 'em.

"When's 'e arrivin'?" Matlock asked sullenly.

"Wouldn't know," Hogan said. "'E don't tell me 'is plans, just said 'e'd be 'ere sometime tonight."

"Any gin left?"

"Plenty-a gin left, but I suggest you keep away from it. 'E dudn't like us 'ittin' it when we're watchin' th' wenches."

"Sod off, 'Ogan!"

Matlock shambled down the foyer and disappeared into one of the back rooms. Hogan and Grimmet exchanged glances. Hogan shook his head.

"That 'un's gonna find 'imself outta work. Mistake givin' 'im any kind 'uv responsibility. You go on and get yourself a bite to eat, Grimmet. I'll escort this 'un up to 'er room."

Grimmet released my arm. I rubbed the flesh where his fingers had squeezed. Hogan examined me again, silent, clearly not finding me to his taste. I sensed that he was even more important than Grimmet, perhaps Black Jack's top lieutenant. His face was an impassive mask, his eyes a stony blue-gray, his lips thin and cruel. Wouldn't think nothin' of drivin' a knife through my 'eart, that one, wouldn't even blink an eyelash. He jerked his head toward the staircase, indicating that I should precede him, and I found his grim silence far more intimidating than the others' rough treatment. Hogan didn't need to resort to brutality to get his message across. Just lookin' at 'im chilled you to the marrow of your bones.

I went up the staircase to the second floor, the hallway as bleak and deserted as the foyer below. Hogan motioned for me to continue on up to the third floor, and I obeyed silently, still outwardly calm but beginning to feel shaky again inside. The full enormity of my plight, of what they planned for me, struck me with sudden force, and I paused a moment, gripping the banister. No, no, I wudn't goin' to think about it. It wudn't goin' to 'appen. Not to me. I moved on up the stairs, knowing that if I allowed one chink in my armor, I'd be utterly lost and a prey to every fear. Other girls might 'ave 'ysterics, might faint, might cry an' cringe an' beg for mercy, but not me.

When we reached the third floor, Hogan moved in front of me, opening a door a short way down the hall. He stood in the doorway, waiting for me to enter. I moved past him, silent. We hadn't exchanged a single word. The room was large and surprisingly well furnished, a floral-patterned wine-and-gray carpet on the floor, wine-colored drapes at the windows, a chair upholstered in royal blue sitting in front of the gray marble fireplace. A fire burned low, the dancing blue-orange flames reflected in the polished headboard of the large brass bed that dominated the room, an elegant royal-blue counterpane covering it. A bottle of wine was chilling in the silver bucket that sat on a low table, two fine crystal glasses beside it.

Hogan tilted his head toward an open doorway and addressed

me for the first time, his voice as cold and expressionless as his face.

"In there you'll find a bath. I 'ad one of th' wenches 'eat the water an' bring it up just a while ago. Bathe yourself. Do a thorough job uv it, understand? You'll find a brush, comb, paint for your face—everything you need to make yourself fetchin'. There's a gown. Put it on. I'll be back up 'ere in an 'our to check on you. Be ready. Black Jack may not show up for some time, but you be ready."

There was no overt threat, but it was there nevertheless, every word laden with icy menace. I didn't want to admit that he frightened me, but he did. He scared th' 'ell outta me. No use denyin' it. He stared at me for a moment with stony gray-blue eyes, then turned and left the room. He closed the door, locked it. When the sound of his footsteps had died away, I moved over to the door and examined it. Solid oak. Steel lock. I bent down to peek through the keyhole. He had taken the key with him. In the adjoining room I found a hairpin, and I spent at least twenty minutes trying to pick the lock, finally realizing it was utterly futile. I'd need a packet uv explosives to get it open.

The windows were all barred. Sure, they would be. Heavy iron bars, impossible to pry loose. I was as much a prisoner here as I'd been in the bowels of the roundhouse. I stood very still in the middle of the bedroom, trying to come to terms with the situation. All right, Randy, you can start gettin' all panicky again, start tremblin' an' feelin' sorry for yourself, or you can use your 'ead. Use your 'ead. Play along with 'em. Make 'em think you're resigned, an' wait for your chance. It'll come. You're goin' to get out uv 'ere. Keep calm.

Half an hour must have passed since Hogan left, and he would be coming back soon. Better do what 'e said. Better bathe and "be ready." I went into the adjoining room and removed my clothes and bathed quickly. The soap had a subtle, provocative scent, a faint suggestion of wild violets. It was smooth and creamy, elegant. Must've come from France, I thought, rinsing myself. I climbed out of the tub and dried myself with a large, soft towel. Nothin' but the best for Black Jack. I slipped on the petticoat of frail black lace, the skirt swirling in billowy layers. The gown was rich red silk brocade embroidered with tiny jet-black flowers, and the cloth made a delicious rustle as I put it on.

None uv th' girls at Big Moll's ever 'ad a garment like this un, I thought as I stood in front of the full-length mirror. The elbow-length bell sleeves were very full, dropping off the shoulder, and the snug, form-fitting bodice left half my bosom bare. The sumptuous brocade skirt was extremely full, belling out over the lacy underskirts. The fit was surprisingly good, although it was a bit tight at the waist, and the high-heeled red satin slippers might have been made for me. Well, Randy, I told myself, you certainly look the part. You look exactly like a very expensive whore. I brushed my hair until it fell in thick, lustrous waves, and then I examined the face paints, disdaining them all. I didn't need lip rouge and powder and the rest. An old 'ag like Lady Evelyn might 'ave to paint 'erself an' put on patches to make a man notice 'er, but I wudn't pushin' forty.

Returning to the other room, I prowled around restlessly, growing edgy again despite myself. Ten minutes passed, twenty. Hogan should already have been back up here. What was I going to do? If only I had some kind of weapon, something I could crack him over the head with. I glanced around the room. No vases, no heavy books, no poker or shovel by the fireplace. There wasn't anything I could use, unless . . . I hurried over to the table and pulled the bottle out of the bucket. Ice tinkled loudly. French wine, judgin' from th' label, probably cost a bleedin' fortune, not that Black Jack would've paid for it. Holding it firmly by the neck, I lifted the bottle like a club. It was plenty 'eavy enough, so 'eavy you could crack a man's 'ead wide open.

I smiled to myself, feeling better now. They weren't quite as smart as they thought they were. I'd knock Hogan unconscious and, somehow or other, sneak downstairs and out of the house without any of the others seeing me. Maybe there was a back staircase for servants. Most big 'ouses 'ad 'em. I'd slip out and climb that bloody wall—it wouldn't be easy, but I'd do it—and I'd be long gone before they knew it. I waited, tense, and it seemed an eternity before I finally heard footsteps in the hallway outside. Don't get jumpy now, Randy. Relax. You got surprise on your side. 'E ain't expectin' anything. 'E thinks you're a 'elpless female.

Gripping the neck of the bottle tightly, concealing it in the generous folds of the red brocade skirt, I took a deep breath as the key turned clumsily in the lock. Sure was takin' 'im long enough, I thought as the key continued to rattle in the hole. There was a loud click. The door was pushed open slowly, stealthily. It wasn't Hogan. It was Matlock. He'd been at the gin after all, reeking of it as he stood there holding the door back, brown eyes burning with malevolent lust. I stared at him coldly, calmly.

"You an' me 're gonna 'ave us some fun, slut."

"Think so?" I said.

He grinned. He lurched toward me. I swung the bottle up as high as I could and slammed it against the side of his head. Matlock stared at me for half a second, shocked, stunned, and then he toppled to the floor with a heavy thud, arms and legs akimbo. The bottle hadn't even broken. Amazin', I thought, still holding it tightly. I stepped over Matlock's body and moved quickly through the door and into the hall, red brocade swirling, swaying, rustling with the sound of dry leaves.

I almost bumped into Hogan. He stepped onto the landing just as I was darting past the stairwell. I whirled, startled. He looked at me without expression. I swung the bottle. He seized my wrist, twisting it brutally. I dropped the bottle. It rolled down the stairs, clanking loudly on each step, still not breaking. I doubled up my fist and drove it into Hogan's jaw. He saw the blow coming, turning his head quickly so that my knuckles merely grazed him. I kicked his shin and tried to get at his groin with my knee. He released my wrist, grabbed my shoulders and hurled me against the wall. My head banged against the wood and lights seemed to explode, orange-yellow-red. Black clouds claimed me an instant later, shrouding my brain. I was dimly aware of the rustle of silk as I slid to the floor, and then there was nothing but darkness.

I moaned. The sound came from a great distance and seemed to echo inside my head, distorted, dying away. The black clouds billowed like smoke, thick, dense, gradually thinning, black melting into gray, and I was swimming through them, moving upward, reaching for the light that shimmered on the surface. I could see it clearly now, lovely light, softly diffused, growing brighter and brighter as gray clouds evaporated. The light touched my eyelids, golden white, burning brightly, and I opened my eyes and stared at the ceiling for several moments, disoriented, still groggy.

I was in the bedroom. I was on the bed with the royal blue counterpane, my head resting on a satiny pillow. I sat up, resting on my elbows. The back of my head ached dreadfully, but no serious damage had been done. I blinked a few times and things gradually came into focus. They'd taken Matlock's body away. I wondered idly if I'd killed him. Hoped so. Bloody bastard. The door was closed and locked. The fire had burned down completely, pink gray ashes glowing dimly. The candles in the wall sconces had burned down, too. Only short wax stubs were left, the flames dancing wildy. I must have been unconscious for at least two hours, maybe more. It must be well after midnight, I thought, climbing shakily to my feet. My legs wobbled slightly as I moved over to the window.

Holding back the drapery, I peered through the bars at a sky black as ebony, faintly streaked with silvery gray blurs of moonlight. The moon was a thin, white disc, almost transparent. I let the drapery fall back into place, feeling weak, dispirited, all bravado gone now. I wanted to curl up in a corner and cringe and cry, but I had too much self-pride to allow myself to do that. No tears for Duchess Randy. Tears were for cowards. I could feel them welling up in my eyes nevertheless, and I fought them back, scolding myself for such weakness. You're down, Randy, an' you're dispirited, but you ain't about to give up.

Time seemed to drag, each minute stretching out interminably, and the tension mounted. Why didn't 'e come? I couldn't do anything till 'e got 'ere. Locked up 'ere like this, 'elpless, I 'adn't a thing to do but think, building up th' dread in my mind, growin' more an' more skittish. Me, I was made for action. Face to face with danger I was quick-witted, nimble, able to cope, but this waitin'.... I folded my arms around my waist, pacing the room. One of the candles spluttered out, then another. Wonderful! 'Alf an 'our more an' I'd be in total darkness, an' that'd be just dandy. 'Elp a lot, it would. I'd probably start screamin' my 'ead off.

I heard noises coming from downstairs—loud, thudding noises as though furniture was being banged about, only there was no furniture. I frowned, then tensed as I heard footsteps pounding up the steps. In a 'urry, 'e was. After all this time th' bastard was in such a 'urry 'e was racing up the stairs, couldn't wait. Almost without thinking I grabbed the silver ice bucket, emptied the icy contents onto the floor and raised it high, ready to hurl it at his head. Th' sonuvabitch might 'ave me, but 'e was goin' to 'ave a fight on 'is 'ands. 'E'd 'ave to kill me, an' I fully intended to do everything in my power to kill 'im first. A furious rage filled me, driving away doubt, driving away fear, and I was truly like a wildcat now, fierce and cornered and as dangerous as Black Jack Stewart ever hoped to be.

He pounded on the door. What'd 'e think I was goin' to do, open it for 'im? Bloody sod 'adn't even bothered to stop for th' key. 'E was bangin' 'is shoulder against the wood now, 'e was goin' to break a bone, 'e was. I gripped the silver bucket tightly, holding it over my head, ready to sling it with all my might. My eyes were flashing. My blood was racing. He was kicking the door now, his boot making a duller thud. The door shook, giving. He kicked it again. It flew open and slammed back against the wall. I threw the bucket. Cam Gordon ducked, raven hair bouncing, the skirt of his black frock coat swirling. The bucket crashed into the door frame, splintering wood.

"Jesus!" he cried.

"Cam!"

I flew to him, flew into his arms, and he held me in a crushing grip against his chest. I buried my face in the curve of his shoulder and began to sob uncontrollably. His arms tightened even more, squeezing the breath out of me, and I wrapped my arms around his back and clung to him and a thousand questions popped into my mind, but they weren't important now. He'd come. Somehow he'd found me and he was here and he was holding me and that was all that mattered. There was more noisy thudding from below, shouting as well. Cam Gordon took my shoulders and held me away from him, frowning.

"Bancroft seems to be having some trouble. I thought we got them all. More of 'em must have come in."

"Ban—Bancroft's 'ere, too?"

"Later," he said gruffly.

He pulled me toward him and slung an arm around my shoulders and led me out of the room and down the hall to the staircase. We started down the steps, and I let out a cry as I saw Black Jack Stewart climbing toward us. He was wearing the same bottle green breeches and black satin frock coat with dirty gold braid, tattered white lace at throat and wrists. His face was ashen, making the shiny black eye patch seem even darker, and his thin lips curled in a lethal smile as his one good eye glittered darkly. He had a knife, gripping the hilt so tightly his knuckles were white. The blade gleamed, catching the light.

Cam shoved me behind him. I stumbled, falling on my behind, red brocade skirt rustling loudly. Gordon stood very still, utterly calm. One hand rested on the banister. The other hung loosely at his side.

"It—it's 'im!" I exclaimed. "It's Black Jack!"

"Shut up, Miranda."

"Cam! Cam, be careful—'e's a killer!"

Black Jack moved slowly up the stairs toward us, the blade gleaming, the thin lips smiling that horrible smile. He was twelve steps below us now. Ten. Nine. He paused, drawing the knife back and forth in front of him.

"I don't know who you are," he said in a dry, hoarse voice, "but you're going to die. The woman is mine."

"On the contrary, she happens to be my property."

Gordon's voice was perfectly level, almost pleasant. He might have been discussing the weather. Black Jack moved up one more step, swishing the knife, slicing the air, his eye glittering with evil relish. He paused again, and I caught my breath as I saw him tense, that tall, wiry body coiling tightly for the attack. Gordon didn't move a muscle. Legs spread wide, he stood there on the step below me, perfectly still. There were more banging, thudding noises from below, another shout. My throat was dry. My heart seemed to bang against my rib cage. Black Jack let out a cry and lunged forward, charging up the remaining steps.

Gordon whipped back the skirt of his frock coat, pulled the pistol out of his waistband, aimed, fired. There was a deafening explosion, a puff of smoke. A red blossom burst into bloom on Black Jack's forehead, just above his eyes, spreading, spurting. He jerked, whirled, crashed against the banister, tumbled over it, his legs kicking in the air before they disappeared from sight. His body made a horrible thunking sound when it hit the floor at the bottom of the stairwell. I stared at the empty air where Stewart had been only seconds before, stunned, shaken to the core of my being. Cam Gordon blew on the barrel of the pistol, slipped it back into the waistband of his breeches and turned to look at me with cool blue eyes.

"Are you all right?" he asked.

I nodded. He pulled me to my feet and ordered me to stay behind him and we continued down the steps. The noises from below grew louder, more violent. A heavy object crashed against a wall. Something fell heavily. A body was sprawled on the second-floor landing. Hogan. His head sagged to one side at an impossible angle. His neck had been broken. His mouth was open, and a thin stream of blood trickled from one corner. His eyes seemed to bug out of their sockets, staring in sightless horror at the ceiling above.

"Did—did you do that?" I stammered.

"With a great deal of pleasure," he told me.

I shuddered, following him down to the foyer. Richard Bancroft was battling vigorously with two of Stewart's henchmen I'd never seen before. Dark gold hair tumbling over his brow, brown eyes alight with excitement, he threw himself into the fray with considerable zest, grinning a merry grin as he slung one man to the floor and planted a booted foot on his throat. He drove a powerful fist into the second man's stomach and, when he doubled up, grabbed him in a headlock. The man on the floor thrashed, flailing his arms, kicking his legs, making dreadful gurgling noises as Bancroft bore down on his throat with his full weight. Something cracked. The man grew still. Still holding the other man in the headlock, Bancroft raced across the room with him, slamming his head against the wall. When he released his hold, the man crumpled to the floor like a limp rag-doll.

"Finished?" Gordon inquired.

"Thanks for all the *help*, lad."

"You seemed to be doing nicely without it."

Bancroft brushed the golden locks from his brow and looked at us with twinkling brown eyes, his cheeks pink, the merry grin still playing on his lips, and I was reminded of a great, jolly pup who had just had an invigorating romp.

"That all of 'em?" Gordon asked.

"There was a chap with an eye patch, came in with these two a couple of minutes after you went upstairs."

"He won't be bothering us," Gordon said.

Bancroft straightened his emerald green silk neckcloth and brushed a speck of dust from the skirt of his rich brown velvet frock coat.

"Haven't had such a rousin' good time in I don't know when," he remarked. "We oughta do this more often, Gordon."

"There—there were two others," I said in a shaky voice.

"One of 'em's in the next room," Bancroft informed me, "big red-haired lad, side of his head smashed in. Somebody clobbered him good. I think he's breathing, though. The other's outside in the courtyard with the chap who was guarding the gate. They're—uh—resting comfortably."

"Dead?" I asked.

"Chap guardin' the gate isn't. I just knocked him out. Can't say about the big blond lad friend Gordon here was questioning. His arm's broken, I know that, and his voice was soundin' awfully funny when he finally told Cam which room you were in. You kill him, Cam?"

"Afraid so."

"Pity," Bancroft said.

I passed a hand across my brow, beginning to feel faint again. "There—five other girls are bein' 'eld prisoner," I said. "We—we've gotta set 'em free."

"Imagine this'll do the job," Bancroft said, pulling a ring of keys from his pocket. "Took this off the gatekeeper."

"You might have mentioned it," Gordon said dryly. "I damn near dislocated my shoulder breaking down that door."

"You didn't give me time, lad. Went tearing into the house like a madman soon as you dropped the blond chap. Carriage with three others pulled up not more than a minute later. Any idea where these girls are?" he asked me.

"One of them's in the basement. I—I don't know about the others."

Bancroft moved cheerfully toward the basement stairs, and Gordon took my elbow and led me outside. The night air was cool. Leaves rustled faintly in the breeze. The sky was a soft black now, beginning to lighten, black fading into a deep gray. I shivered. Cam Gordon removed his frock coat and wrapped it around my shoulders, and then he wound his arms around my waist, holding me loosely in front of him. I rested the back of my head against his shoulder and closed my eyes, tears streaming down my cheeks now.

"It's over, Miranda," he said.

"You—you came," I murmured.

"Of course I came. When someone steals my property, I retrieve it."

"'Ow did you know—"

"A little boy across the courtyard saw it happen, finally got around to telling his mother about it a couple of hours later. She hurried over to inform me. I knew it must have been Black Jack's men who took you. Bancroft showed up then, hoping to talk me into a night on the town. We had one, all right."

"'Ow—'ow did you know where to come?"

"We came directly to St. Giles and made a few inquiries. We had to use some rather forceful persuasion to get the information."

Shadows stirred all around us. Flecks of moonlight danced at our feet. Cam Gordon tightened his arms around my waist, drawing me closer. That strong, solid body was like a pillar behind me, and I rested against it, safe, secure, feeling his warmth, smelling his smell, enveloped by him. He had risked his life to get me back, had killed two men. I must... I must mean something to him. Bleedin' sod would never admit it, but I must be more to him than... than just another servant. I reveled in his nearness, and several long moments passed before he spoke again.

"At least this solves one problem," he said.

"What's that?"

"The ending of my book. I wasn't sure what I was going to do. Now I've decided. A rival gang lord will abduct Angelica, take her to a house like this one, and Burke will come charging to the rescue."

His book. All this time he'd been standing here in the moonlight, holding me close, and he'd been thinking about his bloody book! At least th' evenin' wudn't a total waste. I tried to pull away from him, but he held me fast. I thought I heard a soft chuckle.

"After all this, you're going to have to work twice as hard, you know," he informed me.

"Oh?"

"I fully expect to see a decided improvement."

"Bugger you, Cam Gordon," I whispered.

20

DAWN WAS BREAKING AS THE CARRIAGE TURNED DOWN
Holywell Street, the pale gray sky streaked with misty pink

and soft orange banners, the city below still clothed in night shadows. I was so sleepy and weary I could hardly keep my eyes open, and I only vaguely remember getting out of the carriage and walking under the archway to the courtyard beyond. Cam Gordon opened the door for me, and when I looked up at all those stairs I knew I'd never make it upstairs. I gave a soft moan, shaking my head. Gordon sighed in disgust and swept me up into his arms and began to mount the steps. I was too weary to comment. I wrapped my arms around his shoulders and nestled my head against the curve of his neck and closed my eyes, drifting off to sleep before we even reached the first landing.

When I opened my eyes the sky was a much darker pink stained with apricot and deep gold. I was on my bed in the attic room, still wearing the red brocade gown and black lace petticoat, both sadly rumpled now, and I was ravenously hungry. I sat up, rubbing my eyes. That wudn't dawn streakin' th' sky. It was sunset, and I'd slept all bloody day. No wonder I was hungry. As the dying rays of sunlight streamed through the windows I got up and washed my face and brushed my hair. He had brought me upstairs and dumped me on the bed, hadn't even bothered to put any cover over me, and it was cold. I shivered, smoothing out the skirts, puffing up the crushed bell sleeves, my stomach making ominous noises. I hadn't had a bite in over twenty-four hours, not since noon yesterday, and I'd gotten used to eating these past weeks.

The Scot was at his worktable when I went downstairs, his quill flying over a page already half-covered with messy black tracks. Lost in his work, he didn't hear me, even though I stumbled over a pile of books he had left in the middle of the floor. The place was an incredible mess—books, papers everywhere, his coat over the back of a chair, a platter of food on the floor in front of the sofa. I spied bread, cheese, sausage, half a baked chicken—heavenly manna at the moment—and, plopping down on the sofa, I tore into it with great relish, tearing a drumstick off, stripping it of meat in record time. Sod musta gone out for food 'imself. Fancy that. They probably charged him double, held him up proper. He might write books, but he didn't know anything about shoppin' for food, as 'elpless as most men when it came to mundane matters like that.

He cursed loudly, tore up the page he'd been working on, seized a new sheet and jabbed the quill viciously into the pot of ink. I sighed and finished up my meal and then went to the kitchen to make a pot of coffee. The kitchen was in a dreadful mess, too. It was hard to believe he could create such chaos in such a short time. He'd spilled something on the floor. Looked like soup. The coffee canister had been turned over, beans everywhere. He'd even fetched his own water, I noted, seeing the half-full bucket on the drain board. Good. I didn't feel like 'andling all those stairs just yet. I put water on to boil and ground up the beans and, a few minutes later, poured the marvelously aromatic brew into a heavy blue cup, adding a generous spoonful of sugar.

"I'll take a cup!" he roared.

I poured one for him and carried it to him and took my own over in front of the fire, sipping it slowly as the crackling flames warmed my backside. He continued to work, finishing one page, starting another, pausing to consult a book open on the table beside him. He was wearing scuffed black leather slippers and, over old black breeches and a thin white shirt, a once-splendid navy blue dressing robe, the shiny satin worn thin in several places and slightly frayed at one cuff. He really did need a new wardrobe. All his things were falling apart. But it was more important for his kin to have decent clothes, I thought, remembering the conversation I had overheard between him and Bancroft. The Roderick Cane books made a fortune, yet, what with needy relatives in Scotland and the contributions to the band of rebels, their author barely had enough to live on.

"How do you spell 'heritage'?" he asked gruffly.

"H-e-r-i-t-a-g-e. You spell cat c-a-t."

"Don't get lippy!"

I finished my coffee, had a second cup and then began to straighten the room. Gordon paid me no mind. He got up once to fetch a book, the skirt of his dressing robe making a soft, swishing noise. He had a faraway look in his eyes, still living his story as he searched for the book. The heavy black wave slanted across his brow. His face looked a little pale. I wondered how much sleep he'd had. Standing in the middle of the room, oblivious of my presence, he read a page or so and tossed the book onto the sofa and moved back to the table. I made an exasperated face, fetched the book, put it back in its proper place. Once the room was sufficiently tidy, I went into the kitchen, put all the food away, washed the dishes, and mopped up the sticky mess on the floor.

"Damnation!" he cried.

I hurried back into the front room. "What's the matter?"

"I just broke the bloody quill. It's my last one. Run fetch me a batch of new ones."

"It's after eight. The shop closed hours ago."

"Why the hell didn't you buy some last time you were at the stationer's? I can't be expected to keep track of things like that! I've got work to do, important work!"

"I'm not your nursemaid, Cam Gordon! I don't even get wages. Don't yell at me just because you got caught unprepared."

"I'm right in the middle of a *very* big scene. I wanted to get it finished tonight. I've been working most of the day. Damn! Damn, damn, *damn!*"

"No need gettin' in an uproar," I told him.

"Listen, goddammit, you don't understand the first thing about creative—"

"I 'ave an extra quill in my room," I said patiently.

"Why in *hell* didn't you say so!"

"You didn't give me a chance. I shouldn't've even told you, should've let you stew in your own juices."

He glared at me, brows lowered threateningly, eyes snapping blue fire. "One of these days, Miranda, one of these days—I swear to God, I'm going to lose control and choke the life out of you."

"Yeah, an' I'll scratch your eyes out 'fore you even get started good."

"Get upstairs and get that quill! Now!"

I made a face at him. He clenched his fists, looking murderous, and I moved airily past him and went upstairs, feeling curiously elated. Sod was as 'elpless as a baby, really. 'Ad no idea 'ow 'e ever got along without me. 'E was full of bluster, always yellin', always makin' vicious threats, but in many ways 'e was a little boy. I got the quill and carried it back down to him, and he took it with a sullen look, pouting. I smiled to myself, longing to run my hand over that thick black wave and brush it off his forehead. He jabbed the quill into the pot of ink and was soon immersed in his work again.

I put another log on the fire and wandered into his bedroom to straighten up in there. The odor of Lady Evelyn's perfume still hung in the air like a cloying, invisible cloud. I opened the windows and waved a cloth, trying to get rid of the noxious scent. He'd managed to put the bed back together, I noted.

The slats were all in place, the bed shoved back into its proper position. Remembering those noises and the look on her face when she came out of the bedroom, I angrily jerked the bed-clothes off and wadded them up for the hamper. I fetched fresh sheets and put them on, carefully smoothing down the fine old linen that had been carefully mended a dozen times, the cloth thin with age. Taking out the spare counterpane of quilted tan brocade, likewise aged but wonderfully clean, I spread it out over the bed and fluffed up the pillows in their matching bro-cade cases. The room was better now that fresh air had driven away the perfume and there were no traces of the recent guest. Leaving the windows partially open, I sighed and went back into the front room.

Gordon continued to work, scribbling away industriously as the old clock on the mantel ticked away. Fetching a book, I curled up on the sofa and read a few pages without any great enthusiasm. I wasn't interested in German military tactics. Bloody boring, if you asked me. I was going to have to filch some money from the ginger jar and go to one of those dusty old stalls where they sold secondhand books and bring back something worth reading. Maybe I'd even be able to find a volume of Shakespeare to replace the one I had had to leave behind in the coal cellar.

Putting the book aside, I glanced idly about the room, so snug and cozy with the fire burning low, the worn, comfortable furniture. Old wood gleamed. Faded pastel colors soothed the eye. The Scot worked in his aged navy blue satin robe, the quill scratching, making a noise like mice in the wainscoting. I gazed at him, studying the serious, intent profile, nose sharp, lips held tight, the heavy black wave tumbling forward. He paused, sighing, then flexed his arms, his broad shoulders rolling beneath the dark satin. He read a few lines, frowned, crossed out a word or two and started to work again, lost in that world he was creating on paper. How wonderful it must be to be able to do that, I thought. How marvelous to leave the real world with all its cares behind and step into another, more vivid, more vital, alive with fascinating characters whose lives you alone control.

Wouldn't mind writin' a book myself one day. I was cer-tainly learning all about the craft, observin' the Scot, copyin' his work. There was a knack to it, definitely, and without that knack you 'adn't a prayer, but it seemed to me that the main thing was the ability to work and work and keep on workin' even when it got rough and the words refused to come and the characters refused to speak and move about. Cam Gordon raged then, grew surly, ground his teeth, cursed a lot and wadded up quantities of paper, but he kept right on working until something clicked and the words began to flow again.

It was well after midnight when he finally put the quill aside and stood up and stretched. He looked about the room in surprise, as though startled to find himself in London, in the flat on Holywell Street. He seemed surprised to find me sitting on the sofa as well. He stretched again and stepped over to stand in front of the fire, relaxed now, in an unusually benign mood. His work must have gone very well indeed.

"Finish your scene?" I inquired.

He nodded. "Finished an entire chapter."

"Have—have you been working all day? Did you get any sleep at all?"

"I slept a few hours this morning. I was awakened somewhat rudely by an unexpected visitor. She was very unhappy."

"She?"

"The lovely Lady Evelyn. It seems that when she left yesterday someone deliberately drenched her. Ruined her hair, ruined her gown, and her gown cost a small fortune. She'll never be able to wear it again."

"What a shame," I said, ever so concerned. "Who'd do a thing like that?"

"Who, indeed? There were filthy, soggy carrot and potato peelings all over her, she claimed. If I'm not mistaken, there were carrots and potatoes in that abominable stew you tried to poison me with."

"Seems to me there were."

"What happened to the peelings, I wonder?"

"I wonder," I said.

The faintest suggestion of a smile flickered on his lips. He wasn't at all perturbed.

"What—what did you tell the lovely Lady Evelyn?"

"I told her that if she insisted on visiting such disreputable areas of the city, she'd have to suffer the consequences. She didn't like that in the least, had quite a few choice words to regale me with."

"I can imagine."

"I had no idea she knew such words."

"Dudn't surprise me one bit."

"She was extremely irate. Accused *me* of drenching her, said I was a villain, a heartless brute, an unfeeling monster and a stubborn son of a bitch to boot. I agreed with her, of course, and then I threw the baggage out."

"Good!"

"Why did you do it, Miranda?"

"I—I just 'ad an urge. Couldn't resist it. Comin' 'ere with all them airs uv 'ers, actin' like she owned you, actin' like a—a cur in 'eat. A woman like 'er—she'd ruin a man."

"She's already ruined quite a few, I fear."

"You—you ain't mad?"

"On the contrary, I'm grateful to you. Lady Evelyn was becoming something of a problem."

"If she was so bloody much trouble, why'd you put up with 'er in th' first place?"

"The flesh is weak," he told me, "and a man has needs. Lady Evelyn was all too willing to take care of them."

"I see. What-ja goin' to do now that she's gone?"

"I suppose I'll just have to look elsewhere," he replied.

He gave me a long look that I found extremely disconcerting, those blue eyes dark with something I'd never seen there before, and then he strolled over to the small, warped cabinet and opened one of the lacquered doors. He pulled out a bottle of wine I didn't even know we had, poured a glassful and sipped it thoughtfully, looking at me over the rim of the glass. I felt something tremulous stirring inside of me, felt suddenly skittish and ill at ease. I fooled with one of the bell sleeves, puffing it back up, trying to avoid those eyes, but when I glanced up again he was still looking at me with that intense gaze.

"I—you must be 'ungry," I stammered, getting to my feet. "I'll get you a bite to eat."

"I'm not hungry, Miranda."

"Some coffee, then. You'd like a nice 'ot cup uv—"

"I don't want coffee. I'm drinking wine. You look as though you could use a glass yourself."

"No—no, it—it'd go right to my 'ead."

He poured a glassful nevertheless and brought it over to me. I hesitated a moment before taking it, and when I did my fingers touched him and I felt a shock go through me. My hand shook, wine swirling in the glass. Cam Gordon placed his hand over mine, steadying it, and I thought surely I was going to swoon

~242~

then, me, who scoffed at such namby-pamby foolishness. I was trembling inside, absolutely terrified with a new kind of terror I'd never experienced before.

"What's the matter?" he asked in a low voice.

"Nothin'—just—just let me 'ave my wine."

Again the hint of a smile curled on those thin pink lips. He let go of my hand, and I raised the glass to my lips and took a great, greedy gulp of the wine and then a second one. It was like tart liquid velvet, smooth and tangy, warming me all over. I took another gulp, wishing desperately that he wasn't standing so close, those blue eyes dark and smoky now, half hidden by heavy, drooping lids. Didn't 'e 'ave somethin' else to do? Did 'e 'ave to keep starin' at me like that with lips slightly parted? I knew what was on 'is mind, all right, I knew full bloody well, and it scared the bejesus out uv me. I gulped down the rest of the wine, trying to be casual about it.

"More?" he inquired.

"Not bleedin' likely. I—I'm already beginnin' to feel woozy."

"You're supposed to sip it slowly."

"Took your time tellin' me, didn't you? I—I ain't one of your bleedin' gentlewomen who 'ave wine an' pheasant every day. I ain't never 'ad it before, if you wanna know th' truth."

"Relax, Miranda."

"'Ow th' 'ell am I supposed to relax when you're standin' so close, breathin' down my neck."

"Does it bother you?"

"It bothers th' devil outta me."

"Why?"

"You know bloody well why. I ain't like your precious Lady Evelyn."

"You're certainly not."

"I—I 'appen to be a—a good girl, whether you believe it or not, so you can just—just get that look outta your eye and get them ideas outta your 'ead, Cam Gordon."

"Those ideas have been in my head for quite some time," he admitted. "I've been wrestling with them for weeks."

"You keep right on wrestlin'," I retorted.

He looked deep into my eyes for a moment, then took the empty glass from me and carried it back over to the cabinet and set it down. I heaved a sigh of relief. Couldn't breathe properly when he was standin' so close. Couldn't think clearly. Still couldn't. My head was all muddled and my heart was palpitating and I felt flushed all over. It was too bloody 'ot in 'ere, yet the fire had almost burned down. Several of the candles had spluttered out, and the room was a dim, cozy lair, pale golden light alternating with soft shadows and creating an intimate atmosphere that didn't help matters at all. The bell of St. Clement's Dane tolled in the night, deep and sonorous. Through the panes of the skylight the sky was a misty blue-black, shimmering with moonlight.

He turned around and folded his arms across his chest, resting his buttocks against the cabinet and studying me with those hooded eyes. In the dim glow of candlelight his navy blue robe had a deep, silky sheen, and his face was brushed with shadow, looking leaner, looking lovely. I could handle the testy, hot-tempered Scot who yelled at me and made threats and threw things—I found it quite stimulating, in fact—but this sleepy-eyed, seductive Cam was another matter altogether.

"I—I guess I'd better get busy copyin'," I said nervously. "I ain't a bit sleepy. I can probably get all of it done tonight. You—you go on about your business. I'll just relight them candles an'—"

"Be still," he said.

"I've gotta get that copyin' done. Otherwise I'll get be'ind an' then you'll start yellin' at me an'—"

"Stop prattling," he ordered.

I obeyed. I looked at him. I wanted him, I wanted him desperately, and he wanted me, too, and I'd never been so skittish, never been so shaky and defenseless. I seemed to be standing on an invisible threshold. I longed with all my heart to cross over it and enter the magical new world I knew awaited me, yet at the same time I fervently longed for things to stay the same. How many times had I nourished secret fantasies in those drowsy, dreamy moments in the wee hours of the night before sleep finally claimed me? Some of them had brought a warm blush to my cheeks, yet during the day I refused to acknowledge them, pretended they'd never occurred.

"I see you're still wearing that dress," he said.

"I—I didn't think to change. I was 'ungry an' I came downstairs an' then I got busy an'—"

"Take if off," he said.

"Right—right now?"

"Right now."

"Not bloody likely! I ain't strippin' in front of you! I—"

"Do as I say!"

His voice was stern, scary. Hands shaking, I reached behind me and tried to undo the tiny hooks. I couldn't. Cam Gordon crossed the room and moved behind me and rested his hands only on my bare shoulders. I arched my back, shivering now, cold all over, and I seemed to drift away into space as his fingers gently caressed the side of my neck. I was no longer standing in the shadowy room. I was floating, floating, and incredible sensations filled me, tight buds of sensation bursting softly into bloom, blossoming, spreading. He stroked my throat and shoulders and then began to undo the hooks, carefully, expertly, as though he'd had a great deal of practice.

I felt the bodice loosening, the rich red brocade no longer pressing snugly against my breasts. When he undid the last hook the bodice fell forward, held up only by the sleeves. He ran a fingertip down my spine. I closed my eyes, my knees so weak I felt certain they were going to fold under me. The sensations continued to blossom, exploding now, filling my blood with a tingling ache that was a delicious torture. He caught his thumbs in the bands of the sleeves and pulled down, silk sliding free. Moving around in front of me, he placed his hands on my hips and, kneeling, pulled the gown all the way to the floor, a bright circle of silk at my feet. I stepped out of it, kicking the gown aside, stepping out of the shoes as well. Cam Gordon straightened up and moved back a step or two, gazing at me with dark blue eyes.

"Please," I whispered. "Don't—don't do this. Let things be."

"I want you, Miranda. I've wanted you from the first."

"It ain't—ain't right."

"I find this primness out of character," he said.

"I—I ain't bein' prim. I've never—"

"You want it as much as I do."

"That might be true, but this—this'll change everything. We 'ave a—we get along an' there's no—"

"You're beautiful," he said harshly. "God, you're beautiful."

"Cam—"

"There's not a woman in all London to compare with you."

Wearing only the frail black lace petticoat with its skirts billowing like layers of finest black gossamer, I looked into his eyes, trembling. A force beyond my control compelled me to take the final step that would carry me over the invisible threshold, yet I held back, afraid even as that glorious ache swelled inside, demanding release, demanding fulfillment. No longer was I my own being, a separate entity, sufficient unto myself. I was but part of a whole, and only this man could make me complete.

"We'll burn the gown," he said, "the petticoat, too."

"Yes. I—I could never wear it again. I should—should have burned it already."

"I'll buy you a new gown, Miranda, much finer than this one. I'll buy you a dozen."

"No," I whispered. "That—that isn't what I want from you."

He took hold of my shoulders and hooked his thumbs under the thin straps of the petticoat, tugging at them, and my breasts swelled beneath the cloth, straining, satiny white mounds and firm pink nipples barely veiled by the fragile black lace. He caught hold of the cloth, ripping it asunder, and in moments the petticoat was at my feet, in shreds, and I was completely naked. He wrapped his arms around me, drawing me to him, and the nap of his satin robe was cool and silken against my skin. A curious languor stole through me, rendering me helpless, even as newer, stronger sensations exploded silently inside.

"I've fought this," he said. "For weeks I've been fighting it, telling myself I couldn't possibly be attracted to—to a savage little street urchin with the face of an angel and a tongue that would make a stevedore blush. You've bewitched me, wench."

"Da—damn you, Cam Gordon. If you feel that way—"

"You come into my life like a starving alleycat, hissing and scratching and wreaking havoc at every turn, and I longed to strangle you, longed to dump you in the trash bin and toss you out with the rest of the garbage, and then, damn you, you made yourself indispensable, made me wonder how I ever got along without you."

"You—you ain't exactly 'eaven yourself. You're 'orrible lots uv times, an'—"

"If I had any sense, I'd still do it, I'd dump you in the trash bin and toss you out before it gets any worse, but I fear I've already taken leave of my senses."

"Let go of me, you—you sod."

He tightened his grip, looking down into my eyes. His own

were a dark, dark blue now, glowing with desire, half hidden by the drooping lids, and his mouth was inches from my own. This sweet torture couldn't go on much longer, couldn't, or I would swoon. He held me with his right arm curled around the back of my shoulders, and his left hand moved down my back, the palm sliding over the curve of my bottom, strong fingers curling around the flesh, squeezing. He parted his lips. I felt a violent tremor shake me.

"I've never known anyone like you," he said.

"I—I ain't so unusual. I—I just—"

"You're an original, a marvelous original—and all mine. Last night, when I thought I might lose you, I almost went out of my mind. I realized then I couldn't possibly do without you."

"Do—do we 'ave to talk so much?"

He smiled then, and I placed one hand on the back of his neck and lifted the other to smooth back that heavy black wave that spilled over his brow. He covered my mouth with his own, kissing me for a long, long time, his neck muscles working as his tongue thrust forward, the tip jabbing the wall of my throat. He crushed me to him, and I could feel the tension in that long, lean body as he forcibly restrained himself and fought the urgency that threatened to overcome him. He freed my lips and raised his head, his features taut, almost harsh. Lifting me up into his arms, he carried me into the bedroom and pulled back the bed covers and placed me on the bed.

The room was cool as fresh air came in through the partially opened windows, but neither of us noticed. My whole body seemed to be melting with a warmth that burned like a sweet fever beneath my skin. I stretched on the cool linen sheets, writhing, waiting, and Cam stood at the side of the bed, looking down at me with an inscrutable face. The curtains stirred softly in the breeze, making a faint, whispering sound. The room was a bower of deep blue-gray—dark, velvety shadows brushing the walls, and pale shafts of moonlight slanted through the windows. I was bathed with silver, and it seemed I could almost feel the moonlight caressing my body.

Cam unfastened the sash of his dressing robe, pulled the robe off, tossed it onto the foot of the bed. He sat on the side of the bed, and the mattress sagged slightly and I reached up to stroke his back as he removed first one slipper, then the other. What luxury, what bliss to be able to touch him freely, to feel warm flesh beneath the thin white cloth of his shirt. He stood up again, peeling off the shirt, dropping it onto the floor. I was in the middle of a dream. This was yet another fantasy, and surely I would awaken in my attic bed and it would evaporate into half-remembered vestiges of chimerical bliss, but I could feel linen beneath me and moonlight did indeed caress my skin and my Scot padded across the room to close one of the windows, naked himself now, a tall, lean Grecian statue come to life, warm flesh instead of marble.

He returned to the bed and I lifted my arms and curved them around his back as he leaned down to kiss the hollow of my throat. His lips were warm and moist, lightly brushing my skin. I closed my eyes, spiraling into an oblivion of sensation as he kissed my breasts, the nipples tight, taut, threatening to burst as his tongue touched them. I gasped, clutching his back, and the springs made a groaning noise and the mattress sagged yet again as he climbed over me, looming there just above me, palms supporting him. Both of us were bathed in moonlight now, and then a cloud obscured the moon and blue black darkness covered us. He lowered himself onto me, his body heavy, pinioning me beneath him, my own a warm cushion for his weight.

A moment of purely instinctive panic shot me back to the surface of reality, and I struggled, trying to push him off, and he was rough and stern, holding me firmly, parting my legs. I cried out as I felt the warm, hard, velvety soft tip of his manhood seeking entry, and then that rigid shaft thrust deep into the sheath of my flesh and met an obstacle and thrust again, again, harder, deeper, and panic possessed me entirely and there was a tearing, searing pain that made me cry out again and then the pain miraculously melted into a blissful ache as secret fountains sprang into being, flooding me with an ecstatic pleasure that grew and grew, swelling inside, exploding, again, again, yet again as he drove deep, rending me asunder, it seemed. His entire body grew taut, stretched on a rack of pleasure, and he plunged one more time, thrusting mightily with all his strength. He shuddered convulsively, as did I, and there was a final explosion and sensations shredded into soft sparks that burned out slowly inside and left me stunned, shaken, broken and breathless on the sweet shores of aftermath.

He slept then, and I slept, too, awakening later when moonlight brushed my lids. The room was gilded with silver again, and his head was heavy on my shoulder, one arm clutching me to him, one leg thrown over mine. He grunted irritably in his sleep as I ran my fingers through his hair and moved my palm over the strong curve of his shoulder. He groaned, opening his eyes, pulling me closer, and we began to grapple again and he took me lazily and there was no pain this time, no panic, and the pleasure was intense, incredible. When we were done, when he was dead weight atop me, still inside, spent, I smiled and held him, lashes damp with happy tears I hadn't known I'd shed.

I was in the kitchen at eleven o'clock the next morning and coffee was boiling and filling the place with a marvelous aroma and brilliant sunlight splashed through all the windows and streamed down through the skylight and I was smiling again as I arranged sweet rolls on a plate. Cam was sleeping still, but I'd been awake for hours. I had bathed and brushed my hair and put on the blue cotton frock printed with small purple flowers I had bought at the secondhand store. Wrapping the fringed violet shawl around my shoulders, I had gone off to the bakery, selecting the most delicious rolls for his breakfast, and all the while there was a warm, wonderful glow inside me. I felt marvelous. I felt magnificent. My blood seemed to sing and I wanted to laugh aloud in sheer joy.

I was still a bit sore down there, true, and my body felt bruised, felt pulverized, as though I'd taken a beating, but it was a glorious feeling all the same and I cherished every ache. Church bells tolled as I took the coffee off the fire and poured two cupfuls, placing them on a tray along with the plate of rolls and a spoon and a small white sugar bowl with pink posies and a tiny pitcher of cream that matched. I heard him stumbling about noisily in the bedroom, heard water splashing and boots banging, and then he came into the front room and I met him with the tray and a smile.

"Mornin'," I said.

"Good morning!" he snapped.

"My, grumpy this mornin', ain't we?"

"I'm always grumpy in the morning!"

"I know, not fit to live with until you've 'ad at least two cups of coffee. 'Ere it is, nice an' 'ot, and I fetched your favorite cinnamon rolls, an apricot one for me. Sit down."

He sat. He scowled. I smiled. He drank his coffee and glared at me, and I fetched the pot and poured him another cup and added sugar and cream, stirring it for him, waiting on him as though he were an indolent pasha and me his happy handmaiden. He was wearing boots and black breeches that clung tightly and a fine white lawn shirt that was much too old and needed to be mended. I watched him proudly, possessively, and he finally finished his coffee and rolls and I took the things away. He was standing in the middle of the room with his arms folded when I returned, sunlight spilling all around him from the skylight above. His face was impassive, and, when he spoke, his voice was flat, utterly without inflection.

"I owe you an apology for last night, Miranda. I don't know what came over me."

"I know what came over you, an' last night was wonderful. I wouldn't've missed it for anything."

"Why didn't you tell me you were a virgin?"

"I did. I've told-ja that a number uv times, but you never believed me."

"If I had known—" He paused, frowning, looking very stern now. "I don't make a habit of deflowering young girls. I never meant to touch you. You're my responsibility, and—"

"Cam," I said, "darlin' Cam, you don't 'ave to apologize. I'm glad. I wanted you to deflower me. I—I've wanted it to 'appen for ever so long, an' I feel glorious."

"Damn," he said, uncomfortable now.

"Somebody 'ad to be th' first. I'm 'appy it was you. I'm yours now, all yours, and you're mine."

"Jesus!"

I laughed at his alarm and went to him and put my arms around him and tilted my head back and looked up into his eyes, and for a moment he looked exactly like a terrified boy, and then he sighed and shook his head. Merry noises rose up from the courtyard below. Children were playing. Dogs were barking. Women were gossiping at the pump. I gave him a tight hug and then stepped back and cocked my head to one side and told him it was time for him to start work.

"What the hell have I gotten myself into?" he asked miserably. "I give the orders around here, and don't you forget it!"

"I won't," I promised.

"You're even more beautiful this morning. That hair, that face, that incredible body. I have half a mind to skip work this morning. I'm in no mood to start a new chapter. I'd much rather—"

"I know," I said, "but you ain't goin' to. Not—not till you've done at least ten pages."

"Life is hell," he groaned.

No, it isn't, I thought as he moved sullenly over to his worktable. As I watched him sit down and take up his quill and open the bottle of ink I realized fully and for the first time just how wonderful life could be.

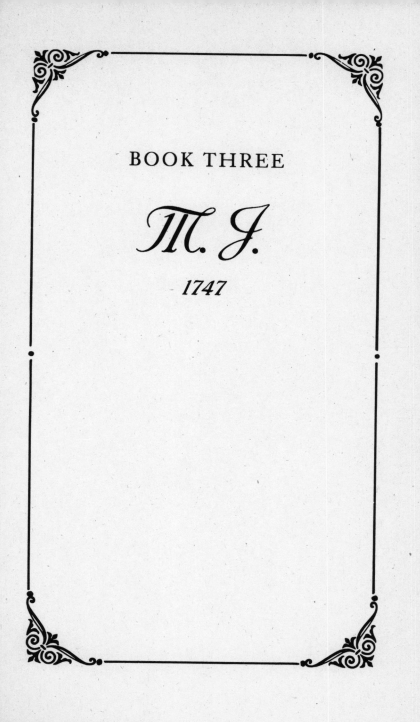

BOOK THREE

M. J.

1747

21

IT WAS THE MIDDLE OF APRIL AND SPRING WAS DEF-
initely here, a glorious spring, I thought, the loveliest I could
remember. You didn't pay much attention to seasons in St.
Giles—it was either hot or cold, always uncomfortable—but
now, as I sauntered back home from marketing, I savored the
soft air that seemed to caress you and the wonderful smells of
sap and soil and blossom. Under a sky of the palest blue-white
the parks and squares were a haze of delicate green and yellow
green as tiny leaves budded open. Daffodils nodded jaunty
golden-yellow heads in the gentle breeze, while purple and
blue hyacinths stood like stout beflowered pixies peering between their tall emerald leaves. Swinging my basket, heavily
laden after an hour of haggling at the market, I turned down
Fleet Street and, passing Holywell, moved on toward Greenbriar Court.

We had moved three weeks ago, after the first printing of
Gentleman James sold out. Sold out two days after it appeared,
it did, and there had been four more printings already. James
Burke seemed to be taking the reading public by storm, and
the new Roderick Cane was far and away the most successful
yet. For the first time in years Cameron Gordon was out of
debt, actually had a bit left over, he did, even after leasing the
house and buying me an entire new wardrobe. No more secondhand clothes, he insisted, and he was very firm about it. I
was his "amanuensis" now, and I couldn't go around looking
like a ragbag. Amanuensis, I discovered, was just a fancy word
for secretary. I was that, all right. I was also maid, housekeeper,
body servant, errand girl and bed partner as well, but you
wouldn't catch me complaining, no indeed, particularly about
that final role. We might be living in sin, not respectable at
all, but those amorous assaults on my body—morning, noon

or night, whenever he happened to fancy a bit of frolic—were deliciously satisfying.

We still squabbled a lot. That hadn't changed one bit. His temper hadn't improved at all, and he now accused me of being bossy and uppity, said I was an aggravating shrew with the soul of a bourgeois housewife just because I scolded him for his messiness. He yelled and made threats and threw things, same as always, and I sassed right back and we usually ended up in a wrestling match, tussling violently on the floor, under the table, in the hallway, going at it outrageously and without a single inhibition. Cam was a wildly passionate lover, tempestuous and tireless, shockingly greedy, too. Never knew when he was going to hurl down his quill and start chasing me through the house.

Sauntering down Fleet, I smiled, thinking of his voracious appetite, loving him so much I feared my heart might burst. I suspected that he was fond of me, too, although, being Cam, he naturally never said so. Any expression of sentiment was anathema to him, and Cam Gordon would face a firing squad before admitting affection for another human being, but there were deep feelings there nevertheless. Behind that brusque, thorny, querulous facade was a man as tender and thoughtful as any alive—he just wasn't going to let on about it. Complex and mercurial he might be, often infuriating and always enigmatic, but I wasn't planning to trade him off for a more traditional model. There'd never be another man quite like Cameron Gordon, and there'd never be any other for me. I knew that already.

These next ten days were going to be rugged, I reflected, for he had departed for Scotland yesterday morning and I was going to miss him dreadfully, just as I had yesterday. Hadn't been able to sleep a wink last night, skittish as a kitten I was, restless as could be. We'd been sharing a bed for three months now, and I'd grown used to snuggling up to that long, lean body, as close as I could get, his arms around me, his warmth warming me. I'd grown used to his snorting in his sleep and thrashing around and pulling all the covers off me, and without him the bed seemed bleak and cold and unnatural. Wouldn't tell me the real reason he was going to Scotland, the sod, made some feeble excuse about seeing his kin, but I knew it had something to do with those bloody rebels he was in cahoots with. He was on some sort of "mission"—he'd let the word slip out inadvertently—and that worried me a great deal.

He spent far too much time with that motley crew of fanatics, and I didn't hesitate to tell him so in no uncertain terms. Slipping off to secret meetings two or three times a week, always at a different location, plotting, planning, giving them funds—it was insane. Dangerous, too. Extremely dangerous. Cumberland was still actively searching out the rebels—there'd been four more executions since Cam's cousin rode to Tyburn—and it was just a matter of time until this group of subversives was discovered. I begged him to give it up, sever all ties with them—Bancroft did, too—but, stubborn Scot that he was, he refused to listen to us. The war was over, I kept telling him. Bonnie Prince Charlie had been routed and the past was the past, but Culloden had to be avenged, he declared. Cumberland had to pay.

They had some crazy idea about assassinating Cumberland. I knew that much. Assassinate Cumberland, indeed! The Bloody Butcher never stepped foot out of the palace without a whole retinue of guards, never went anywhere in the city without a troop of soldiers in tow. Their chances of getting to him were about as likely as my being invited to tea at St. James's Palace. And if by some miracle they *did* get to him, what then? They'd be cut to shreds, hacked to pieces by Cumberland's men, the fiercest, most brutal band of soldiers in English history. It was nonsense, all of it, and I suspected that they realized that, too, and were playing at being rebels like little boys played with wooden swords. The secret meetings assuaged their wounded pride, made them feel less defeated and were probably no more than an opportunity for them to let off hot air, but that didn't make them any less dangerous.

As soon as Cam got back from his "secret mission" to Scotland we were going to have it out again, I vowed. Dick Bancroft and I would gang up on him and make him see reason, and if that didn't work, I'd hit him over the head with a skillet. In the meantime, there was no point in my worrying about it. Nothing I could do. Ten days without Cam! They weren't going to be easy. I'd see Bancroft a couple of times—he'd promised Cam to stop by and "check on me"—but what was I going to do the rest of the time? Lord John and Lady Cynthia might help, I thought as I crossed the street, although I was already beginning to grow terribly impatient with *that* pair.

Passing Drake's Coffee House and Messrs. Kenyon & Blake, Booksellers, I finally reached the narrow, cobbled passageway that led to Greenbriar Court, brick walls pressing close on either side. It was barely wide enough for a fair-sized cart to pass down, and you'd miss it in a blink if you didn't know it was there. Down the passageway that smelled faintly of horseflesh, and there you were, the bustle of Fleet Street muffled by the buildings that surrounded the tiny, hidden court. Three old houses with minuscule lawns looked upon the circular, cobbled yard. The one on the east side was a pale, faded yellow with white shutters and pitched gray slate roof bleached near-white with age. I had no idea who lived there. It had been empty ever since Cam and I moved in. On the north side, facing the passageway and the backsides of the brick buildings on Fleet Street stood a large, rather decrepit gray house with two small, gorgeous flower beds in front, one on either side of the short walkway leading to the front steps. A Major Barnaby lived there with his wizened crone of a housekeeper. Retired from the military life now, the major was writing his memoirs and rarely saw the light of day, coming out only to tend his flowers.

Our own house sat on the west side, directly opposite the yellow house. It was small and unpretentious, only two stories, but as charming as could be with its mellow tan walls and old white shutters, the small pear tree in front abloom with delicate white blossoms that filled the air with a lovely fragrance. Thomas Sheppard had found the place for us. It belonged to one Benjamin Mortimer, an aged writer of travel books who, wishing to spend his declining years with a spinster sister in Kent, was eager to lease. Sheppard published Mortimer's books, and he made all the arrangements for us, obtaining the lease at a wonderfully reasonable price. We took the place furnished, bringing only one or two pieces of furniture from the Holywell Street flat. There was a tiny vegetable and herb garden in back and, luxury of luxuries, our own private pump. No more trotting up and down endless flights of stairs for water.

It was absolute heaven, I thought, crossing the yard with its rough, uneven cobbles a golden gray-brown in the sunlight. Greenbriar Court was serene, quiet as a churchyard, tucked away here in the middle of the noisy, clanging city, and Fleet Street only fifty yards away down the narrow brick passage. The court wasn't so quiet this afternoon, though. Curious yapping noises came from the yellow house, and I noticed that the window curtains were pulled back to let in the sun. Its mysterious owner must have returned, I observed, unlocking the front door and stepping into the cool, sunny foyer.

There were only three rooms downstairs—a large, comfortable sitting room, a formal dining room we had never used and in back, a charming old kitchen, copper pots and pans hanging on the walls along with dried herbs and strings of onions. There was a large fireplace, a gigantic black iron stove that filled me with terror, a huge hutch filled with dishes and a heavy, battered oak table with matching chairs. Sunlight bathed the dull-red brick floor. Hell to polish, that floor. I kept it gleaming nevertheless. Blue and green canisters sat on the drain board, and a wonderful row of heavy oak cabinets filled the wall above it.

I set my basket down on the table and began to put the provisions away in the cabinets — apples, oranges, carrots, bread, two hard sausage rolls, a creamy wedge of cheese wrapped in cloth to keep it moist. I had picked up a pot of mustard and two meat pies as well. Plenty of food in the house now, and I could always make a jaunt to the eating house around the corner from Fleet and bring back some chops or slices of that delicious pink roast beef. One of these days I was really going to have to learn to cook, I mused, closing the cabinet door, but Cam wasn't particular about what he ate and I'd much rather go out for victuals than try to cope with that great, frightening stove.

Pausing to glance out the windows at the small, sunny walled garden in back, I moved back down the hall to the front of the house. A narrow staircase led to the second floor. There were just two rooms upstairs, a bedroom overlooking the garden and a second bedroom in front that Cam had converted into a workroom, books and papers littering the place, a gigantic desk replacing the old worktable. Impossible to keep straight, that room, but I made a valiant effort, endlessly tidying up after him. Glancing at the slender grandfather clock that stood in the hall in its polished mahogany case, I saw that it was just two o'clock in the afternoon. What to do with the rest of the day? I was restless, at a loss without Cam underfoot to keep me occupied. I'd spent the whole morning cleaning the house. It was spotless. Laundry was all done, too — extra sheets and bedclothes neatly folded in the chest at the foot of the bed, put away with tiny bags of dried verbena to make them smell nice. No darning to do, either. No books to read.

Might as well stop stalling, Randy, I told myself. You started it. You got yourself into it, and you've either got to tear up those pages and forget you ever wrote 'em or else get in there and get back to work. Sighing wearily, frowning a very unhappy frown, I trudged reluctantly into the sitting room. Benjamin Mortimer had simple, exquisite taste, if somewhat limited means, and the room was cozy and charming with its pale cream walls, light gray marble fireplace and the faded, rather shabby gray rug patterned with sky blue flowers. Draperies of ancient lime green silk hung at the windows. The sofa and two matching armchairs were covered with worn sky-blue velvet. Everything had been selected with loving care a great many years ago and had the soothing patina of age.

In front of one of the windows stood a small, beautifully fashioned secretary of rich red-brown mahogany, the wood gleaming, and it was here that I did my secret work. Sitting down in the delicate yet sturdy mahogany chair with seat of sky blue velvet, I opened the secretary, its front projecting to make a desk surface. I took out the old silver ink pot, the quill I'd nipped from Cam, the stack of finished pages. Just fourteen of 'em, and I'd been working on the book for two whole weeks, writing on the sly when Cam was out of the house or else immersed in his own work upstairs. Fourteen pages. Two weeks. That was just a page a day, I thought miserably, and on a good day Cam could turn out fifteen or twenty. I was a novice, sure, but you'd think I'd be able to do better than a page a day, particularly when you considered the hours and hours I spent at it.

I had left Lady Cynthia waiting at the old manor, her husband safely away on a trip to France, and Lord John had just come in, admitted by the trusty old servant who had nursed Lady C. since birth and was in on their secret, abetting them in their romantic intrigue. Placing a clean page in front of me, dipping the tip of the quill in ink, I stared at the page, thinking hard. The ink dried. I toyed with the feather as brilliant rays of sunlight spilled through the window, making a sunburst on the silver ink pot. Lovely sunburst, I thought, tiny golden spokes reflecting on the empty page. Another three or four minutes passed before I finally dipped the quill in ink again and wrote eight words: *Lady Cynthia watched Lord John climb the stairs.*

Abject, I stared at the sentence. Boring. Lifeless. I couldn't see either of them, couldn't *feel* anything. The words conveyed nothing, and my noble characters were mere names, not flesh and blood. This wasn't nearly as easy as I had thought it would be when I started the bloody book. I thought it would be fun, thought it would be exciting, and rarely had I known such anguish. There was a knack to it, all right, and I obviously didn't have it. Looked so easy when you watched someone doing it. Seemed a snap when you read what someone else had already written. Nothing to it, you thought, and then you tried to do it yourself and suffered the agonies of the damned. Frowning deeply, I crossed out the words and started again.

Lady Cynthia watched ... All right, she's watching, but how does she feel about it? She's happy. She's elated. She's nervous, too, because this is the first time she's seen him since their violent quarrel and wasn't *that* torture to write! I added the words *with trembling heart*. Does a heart actually tremble? Sounds like she has some kind of disease. I crossed out *trembling* and wrote the word *joyous* and added an *a* before it. *Lady Cynthia watched with a joyous heart as Lord John climbed the stairs*. We see Lady Cynthia, know how she feels about it, but Lord John's still dull as ditch water, no life at all. I stared at the page some more, utterly abject, and then I smiled and crossed out the last three words and added *bounded eagerly up the stairs*. *Lady Cynthia watched with a joyous heart as Lord John bounded eagerly up the stairs*. That was better. That was more like it, yes, and it had only taken me forty-five minutes to write that one bloody sentence. At this rate I'd be seventy-three years old before I finished the first section.

Nevertheless, I forged ahead, and after a while the words seemed to come a bit easier. I continued working until the sharp, stabbing pain in the small of my back made further work impossible, and then I scooted the chair back, emitted a heavy sigh and looked at what I'd done. One and a half pages, all crossed out and marked over and looking far more messy than anything Cam had ever turned over to me for copying. Not nearly as much as I would have liked to have done, but I had fifteen and a half pages now and that was better than nothing. Would I ever be able to write a complete book? Seemed impossible at the moment, but I wasn't going to give up. I felt a sense of satisfaction as I stacked the pages together and fastened the top back on the ink pot. Me, Miranda, actually writing a book. Beat all, it did. Who'd uv thought it?

Closing the secretary, I got up and stretched, throwing my shoulders back to alleviate the pain in my back, and I could hear tiny bones popping. Hard on your back, this writing business. Didn't know how Cam stood it, sitting hunched over like that for hours on end. No wonder he was so grumpy and irritable. I didn't intend to tell him about my own writing.

Wouldn't dream of it. No telling what he'd say. If I kept at it long enough I was bound to get better, and if I did, if I was finally able to write something that wouldn't make him hoot with laughter, then I might let him see some of it. Sure wished he was here right now. I missed him something awful, and him just gone thirty-six hours.

Standing there in the sitting room with the afternoon sunlight making bright patterns on the floor, I thought of all the changes that had occurred in my life these past months, and it was amazing. Didn't seem quite real. Half a year ago I had been sleeping in a filthy coal cellar, picking pockets for a living, going without food much of the time and freezing my arse off on the streets, and here I was in this lovely house with plenty of food on hand and plenty of money tucked away in the ginger jar I still kept on the mantel beside the lazy old brass clock. I had been all alone in the world without a living soul to care whether I lived or died, with the possible exception of Big Moll, and now I had someone of my very own. Sometimes, when I really thought about it, it was almost scary, too good to be true. I had the feeling I was in the middle of a glorious dream, and I feared I might wake up at any minute and it would all disappear and I'd be back in St. Giles again, desolate and alone.

A peculiar scratching noise broke into my reverie, and I cocked my head, listening. It seemed to be coming from the front door. Someone scratching on the door. Didn't make sense. Why wouldn't they knock? The noise continued, scratch, scratch, scratch, and then there was a thin, shrill yapping sound. Stepping into the hall, I opened the front door and looked out. No one there. Something small and fluffy brushed against my skirts then, and tiny paws pattered merrily on the hall floor as my visitor explored eagerly. Startled, I watched the tiny ball of pale golden-brown bouncing around, ears flopping, tiny puffed tail wagging vigorously.

"Who're you?" I inquired. "And where did-ja come from?"

The preposterous creature paused in his exploring and tilted his head to one side, considering my questions gravely, and then he yapped at me and dashed into the sitting room. I had left a newspaper on one of the chairs. My visitor made an energetic leap, caught the edge of the paper in his mouth and then raced down the hall with it, the newspaper flapping noisily, ten times the size he was. I watched with consternation and amusement as he dropped the paper, backed off a few steps and then attacked it, happily tearing it to shreds.

"Really!" I exclaimed. "That ain't at all polite. You're messin' up my 'all!"

He turned, gave me a sassy yap, then continued to shred. He couldn't possibly be more than six inches long and four inches high, if that, and he firmly believed he was a great, fierce mastiff. He growled as he demolished the paper, though his growls sounded more like gurgles. Finally bored, he stopped, eyed the mess he'd made and then cocked his head at me again, tail wagging like mad. His eyes were dark brown and enormous, and his fur, I decided, was the color of champagne.

"Pleased with yourself?" I asked.

He yapped again, and I could have sworn he nodded.

"What kind of dog *are* you, anyway? You're no bigger than a mite, much too small to be payin' calls without a chaperone."

Head still cocked, he began to sniff audibly, and then he spun around and trotted into the kitchen quick as a wink. When I joined him, he was sitting up and staring at the cabinets, tail thumping. He began to yap again, although in an entirely new tone. The yap was full of entreaty now, and his eyes never left the cabinets.

"You 'ave a good nose on you, mutt," I told him. "You smelled my sausage, didn't-ja? Expect me to give you some. Regular little beggar, you are. Very well, I'll cut some up for you."

He waited patiently and, to my relief, silently as I took down the sausage, cut a few slices and chopped it up into small bits, placing them on a saucer for him. When I set the tidbits before him he sniffed them, backed away in disgust and started that shrill, distressing noise again. He looked at the cabinets and then looked at me and then back at the cabinets again, informing me in no uncertain terms that what he wanted was yet to be served.

I sighed, sliced one of the meat pies, put some on a saucer and tried that. He looked at me as though I had insulted him. Desperate, I took out one of the carrots. He began to bounce up and down eagerly, tail wagging so hard I feared it would fall off.

"This is absurd!" I said. "Dogs don't eat carrots."

His eager leaps and whirling cartwheels assured me that I was quite mistaken about that. I peeled the carrot, washed it and chopped some of it up. When I set the third saucer down he bounded toward it with such zest that he overshot the saucer and did a flip, rolling about like a fluffy acrobat. Finally getting his legs back, he greedily devoured the ambrosia and licked the saucer clean, doing it with remarkable speed.

"Full?" I asked.

He looked at me with appreciative eyes, glanced disdainfully at the two other saucers and pranced back into the hall just as frantic knocking sounded on the door. His owner, no doubt, I thought, hastening to the door. When I opened it, my visitor started yapping again, quite loudly, and the woman standing before me gave a cry of relief.

"Thank goodness! Naughty, naughty, *naughty*!" she exclaimed. "Gave me such a fright, he did, running off like that and this our first day home! He's just two months old, got him in York three weeks ago. I've been touring, my dear, and I don't mind telling you it's a relief to get back to London. They *adored* us, of course, I sometimes think the provincials are far more appreciative of the arts, they're so starved for it. It was one triumph after another every stop along the way and that's very gratifying but, my dear, the wear and *tear*!"

She fanned herself, pantomiming exhaustion, and I fear I stared at her with total dismay. Plump and fleshy, though pleasingly so, she wore a pink silk gown with long sleeves, squeezed-in waist and preposterously full skirt, a white lace fichu draped over the shoulders and fastened in front. Her face was powdered and rouged, her mouth a vivid red. Her lively blue eyes were lined with black, the lids a dark mauve, and her painted black eyebrows were arched in perpetual surprise, giving her a startled look even in repose. She wasn't quite as tall as I was, but her towering, powdered pompadour made her seem much taller. It had to be at least a foot high, I thought. A bright pink silk bow was affixed atop it, and three long, girlish ringlets dangled down in back. Although it was impossible to determine her age behind all that paint, she had to be fifty and was probably much older than that.

"I'm Marcelon Wooden, my dear," she said, pronouncing it "Maw-suh-lun." "I live in the yellow house across the way and, I must say, I'm delighted to have a new neighbor. Benjamin was a dear but, frankly, a bit tedious, always wanting to talk about his travels and in the *dreari*est monotone. Put me right to sleep soon as he opened his mouth. Major Barnaby's even worse. Fine figure of a man like that tending flowers, writing his memoirs, never going out for a bit of fun. A bachelor, too! Needs a good woman to look after him at his age, and I don't mean that hideous creature who skulks around like a demented deaf-mute. Couldn't keep a house if her life depended on it. You, Brandy! Come to Mother! Shame on you, giving me such a turn."

She scooped the dog up into her arms, and it flicked out a tiny pink tongue to lick her chin.

"I've tried and tried to be neighborly," she continued before I had a chance to speak. Her voice was rich and rolling, extremely dramatic. "I took him a cake, took him a bottle of port, invited him out to dine, invited him to the theater, my treat, and you'd have thought I was trying to *kid*nap him. Brusque, bristly, I've never seen such rudeness in all my born days! I don't care if he *is* straight and tall and ever so distinguished with that sandy gray hair and those piercing gray eyes and that mustache, there's no excuse for treating a kind, concerned neighbor so rudely. Practically *marched* me out of the house, the brute!"

Lips pursed, she shook her head. The towering white pompadour was beginning to list a little to one side. Brandy snuggled against her bosom, gazing up at her with adoring eyes.

"What kind of dog is that?" I inquired.

"He's a poodle, my dear, I *do* hope he'll grow a little. Rambunctious as all get out, this one, much more so than Pepe or Sarge were at that age. They're his older brothers, you'll meet them. When I discovered he'd slipped out of the house I flew into a positive tizzy, my dear, hurried over here to see if you'd seen him. Someone told me that Roderick Cane had moved into Benjamin's house and I must confess I haven't read any of his books but I admire anyone who writes and I must say, he's certainly suc*cess*ful, isn't he? You must be his wife."

"'Is—'is name ain't really Roderick Cane. 'E just uses that name for 'is books. 'Is real name is Cameron Gordon, 'e's a Scot, an' I'm Miranda James."

Now it was her turn to look dismayed. The blue eyes widened, and the painted black brows arched even more. Her mouth formed a round, scarlet 'O'. The pompadour listed perilously to the left, ringlets bouncing.

"My *dear*!" she exclaimed. "We're going to have to do something *about* that!"

"'Bout what?"

"That hideous voice, my dear. You're positively charming,

~265~

loveliest creature I've seen in years, sweet and warmhearted, too, I can tell that—we're going to be great friends, my dear—but that voice! That shrill, discordant screech! It has to go, no question about it. And you drop your h's,' too! It's inexcusable! Sends shivers up my spine. We'll change all that soon enough! I've done quite a bit of coaching in my day, and it'll be a joy working with you. Give me something to do while I'm resting." I'm resting."

"Restin'?"

"Between engagements, my dear, a situation that occurs all too frequently in my autumn years. I'm an actress, didn't I tell you? You must come over for tea. I was just setting things up when I discovered Brandy had disappeared. We'll have a long, lovely chat and get to know each other and you can meet Pepe and Sarge. I fear things are in a bit of a mess, I'm terribly disorganized, always was, and I'm without a maid at the moment, but we'll manage."

"I—I ain't sure you—you understand."

"Understand what?"

"My situation. Cam an' I ain't married."

"La! We of the theater understand such things, my dear. I wasn't married myself for ever so long, wouldn't have married Mr. Wooden if he hadn't been so terribly stuffy about such things. He wasn't in the business, you see. Owned a fleet of fishing boats, he did, but he was a dear, kind man just the same, much too good for me. Passed on ten years ago, the angel. Stop licking Mother's chin, dearie, you're spoiling my powder. Come along, Miranda dear, I'm longing for some company, it's always so dreary when you get back from a tour. I didn't offend you, did I, speaking about your voice that way?"

"I—I know I ain't got a refined voice, but—I'd *like* to speak better."

"So you shall, my dear. So you shall! We'll have you speaking in an elegant lilt in no time at all. We'll work on the *grammar*, too."

Mrs. Wooden reached up to adjust the listing pompadour, which I now realized was a wig, and, closing the door behind me, I followed her across the cobbled yard to the old yellow house. She was a fantastic creature with her outlandish attire and nonstop chatter, her dogs and her painted face, but there was something immensely engaging about her just the same, even if she *had* made all those comments about my voice. I wondered if she really could teach me to speak properly. Now that I was living with Cam I longed to make him proud of me, and wouldn't he be pleased if I suddenly started talkin' like a lady.

Opening the front door, Mrs. Wooden set Brandy down, and he scurried down the hall, yapping blissfully. Another dog joined in, barking much more maturely. We followed the tiny poodle into a large salon cluttered with beautiful battered old furniture and absolutely awash with books. They were stacked on the mantel, piled on the floor, crammed helter-skelter into shelves that covered two walls floor to ceiling—books of every shape, size and description, leather bound, cloth bound, dusty and enchanting. My eyes fairly boggled. A small black poodle leaped about with frantic abandon, barking fiercely now, and another poodle, small and white, curled lazily on a faded rose brocade sofa, looking immensely bored.

"Sarge!" Mrs. Wooden cried, clapping her hands together. "Hush! You, too, Brandy! They encourage each other, I fear. Sarge is seven years old now, but ever since I brought Brandy home, he's been acting just like a pup himself, showing off something awful, vying for attention. Behave yourself! Pepe, now, he's ten and an absolute darling, sweetest disposition you could hope for. Mother's favorite baby, aren't you? You just sit right down, Miranda dear. I'll run bring in the tea cart."

She fluttered out of the room, and I sat down on the sofa, a bit dazed. Pepe looked up at me with vaguely suspicious eyes and after a moment, deciding I was a friend, moved over to snuggle next to me, resting his head on my leg. I stroked his long silky white ears while Sarge tore about the room with a much-chewed red ball and tiny Brandy burrowed under a stack of newspapers. Crowded, cluttered and dusty, the room was an enchanting place, full of character. A huge piano stood in one corner, its case gleaming a dark, dull gold, the varnish peeling. Small, beautifully framed paintings were arrayed on top of it, all of them of Mrs. Wooden at various ages and in unusual costumes. One of them depicted a radiantly lovely girl in Elizabethan ruff and bejeweled skullcap, her features only vaguely resembling those of my hostess. She must have been acting for a very long time, I reflected as Pepe sighed and nuzzled my skirt.

Above the elegant but soot-streaked white marble fireplace with its peacocktail brass screen hung an immense painting of a very handsome young man. The bottom part of its heavy, ornate gold frame was half-concealed by the books piled on the mantel. Against a stormy gray background, the man in the painting moodily contemplated the human skull he held in one palm, and I knew at once that the man was an actor, portraying Hamlet, and the skull was that of poor Yorick whom, alas, he had known well. Dressed all in black, a black velvet cloak lined with gray silk falling from his shoulders, the actor had unruly gold hair and the features of a young Adonis. The pink lips were full and sensual, the nose Roman, the brow undeniably noble. The eyes were dark and brooding, and as I gazed at the painting I had the curious feeling that those eyes had once gazed into mine, full of merriment, that this pale, godlike youth was someone I had once known. That was absurd, I knew, but the feeling persisted.

"Mr. Garrick," my hostess said, wheeling in a noisy wooden cart laden with a sumptuous array of food. "I was his very first Gertrude, and he was a marvel, my dear. There's never been a Hamlet like his, never will be again. Such soul! Such emotion! Such magic! Davy Garrick is a genius, one of the miracles of our age, and I consider myself fortunate to have been on the same stage with him."

Davy? The name seemed to touch a distant chord of memory, but I wasn't able to pin it down. Davy Garrick with merry mouth and dancing eyes, said he was going to marry me one day.... The memory flashed in my mind for half a second before submerging in gray. I couldn't possibly have known anyone like him, and he certainly wouldn't have promised to marry me. I decided my mind must be playing tricks on me.

"The press and the public went mad over him as Hamlet," Mrs. Wooden continued, pouring tea into exquisite china cups. "Unfortunately, I didn't fare quite so well. Colley Cibber wrote that 'As Gertrude, Mrs. Wooden gave a performance befitting her name,' and ever since, when an actor isn't up to his role, they say he gives a 'Wooden' performance. Oh, the slings and arrows! The humili*ation* of it all. I *would* like to be remembered, my dear, but certainly not for that! Colley Cibber's a brilliant man, I can't deny that. He's Poet Laureate, and he was manager of the Drury Lane for a long spell, but, *entre nous*, he's a perfect beast to work with. Have you read his book?"

"I'm afraid not."

Mrs. Wooden handed me a cup of tea. "*An Apology For The Life of Colley Cibber*," she said, "came out six years ago.

I'm mentioned in it several times, and the little worm certainly *should* apologize. I'll lend you a copy."

"All these books," I said, gazing around the room. "There must be thousands of 'em. It—it's like bein' in 'eaven."

"My brother left them to me. He was a dear man, quite the scholar, his nose always in a book. Spent a fortune on them, he did. He'd go without food to buy a book. I like having them around, but I must confess I don't read all that much myself. Haven't the time. I read *plays*, of course. I have them stashed all about the house. Always looking for an interesting new part."

Mrs. Wooden began to regale me with marvelously colorful anecdotes about her forty years in the theater—witty, amusing, frequently touching stories peppered with exciting names I felt I should have recognized. As she talked she kept refilling my teacup and plying me with the most delicious treats: small slices of bread spread with a creamy past of cheese and chopped walnuts, tiny anchovies on top, a helping of coral-colored smoked salmon, squares of buttered bread covered with watercress and, to top it off, a rich plum cake soaked in apricot brandy. I had never eaten such wonderful food nor listened to such fascinating talk.

"More cake? No? You're certain? Another cup of tea, then. No, nothing for you, Sarge! You had your snack earlier on. Go play with your ball! Pepe adores you, my dear. He *never* takes up with strangers like that. See, he's licking your hand. They always know whom they can trust, unlike us poor humans who are always kicked in the *derrière* because of our blind faith. So you see, my dear," she continued in that grand dramatic voice, "I was never a *name*, but I worked with all of them and had steady employment while some of your glittering names were waiting for the right vehicle and being forgotten by the fickle public."

"It—it must have been terribly exciting, Mrs. Wooden."

"You must call me Marcie, my dear, all my friends do. No one calls me Marcelon, and I'm 'Mrs. Wooden' only to my public. It *was* terribly exciting, I'll not deny it, but there's been a heap of heartache and grief as well. Always is in the theater. Still, I wouldn't have missed a minute of it. Things are a bit sketchy at present—not many roles around for a ripe old party like me, and when you're forced to tour—" She clacked her tongue, a sad and thoughtful look in those expressive blue eyes.

"But you're marvelous," I said, touched. "I just know there's going to be a wonderful role coming up soon."

"Davy keeps promising he'll find one for me. We've remained extremely close all these years—he gave me that painting, said there was no one in London he'd rather have have it. Put his friend Sam Johnson's nose quite out of joint, that did. Johnson wanted the painting himself. *Dread*ful man, Johnson. The manners of a bear, the disposition of a bull, but a marvelous talker, holds you absolutely spellbound at the dinner table or in a coffeehouse."

"Is he an actor, too?"

"Oh, no, my dear. He's not much of anything yet. Wrote a magnificent poem, 'London,' and a very fine book called *The Life of Richard Savage*, a bit wordy to my way of thinking. Mostly he's a drudge, churning out articles for *The Rambler* and *The Gentleman's Magazine*, but he has this grand scheme of compiling a dictionary of the English language. He's the most brilliant man in London, I suppose, certain to be famous one day. He's coarse and boorish and gruff, ugly as sin, too, by the way—sometimes I wonder what Davy sees in him, but then they grew up together and came to London together and I guess that counts for something."

"You certainly know some interesting people," I remarked.

"One does meet them in my profession, that's one of the rewards of being in the theater. But here I've been rattling on for over an hour, my dear, talking about myself, and I want to know all about *you*! How is it that a lass so lovely and charming and refined-looking has such a horrendous voice? Where do you come from, and how did you come to be the companion of such a famous, successful writer?"

"I—actually I'm 'is bond servant," I admitted.

Her eyes widened, brows shooting up. "Oh?"

"I—I was pinched, you see. I was pickin' 'is pocket an' 'e caught me an' I was tossed in th' round'ouse an'—are you sure you want to 'ear this?"

"My dear," she drawled, "I'm all *ears*! Start at the beginning. Tell me *every*thing."

I hesitated, uncomfortable now, reluctant to go on, but as she poured herself more tea I began to tell her about my mum, about St. Giles, about Big Moll and all that had happened to me up until the time we moved to Greenbriar Court. Mrs. Wooden listened with rapt attention, absolutely fascinated, the cup of tea growing cold in her hand. Once I started to talk it

~270~

seemed I couldn't stop, and for some reason I found myself telling her things I had never told another living soul. I told her of my hopes, my fears, my dreams, my desire to make something of myself, make Cam proud of me, and when I finally fell silent Mrs. Wooden was visibly moved.

"My dear," she said, "I—I've never heard such a tale. Why, you're re*mark*able!"

"Me? I don't see 'ow you figure that. Ain't nothin' remarkable about me. I just—just wanna *do* somethin' with my life. I wanna accomplish things an'—an' be somebody worthwhile."

"And so you shall, my dear!" she exclaimed. "So you shall! You're bright and intelligent, far more intelligent than you realize, I suspect. You're young, engaging, perfectly beautiful—why, you're a *diamond*, my dear, a genuine diamond in the rough!"

She was growing very excited now. You could hear it in her voice and see it in her eyes. Brandy scampered across the floor and scratched at her pink skirts. She scooped him up onto her lap. Sarge began to race around the room in a frenzy, cavorting with the red ball, demanding attention. Pepe sighed again and looked up at me as though to disassociate himself from such boring antics. Mrs. Wooden gave me a thrilled, excited look.

"I *need* a project at the moment, and, my dear, you're *it*!"

"What—what do you mean?" I asked, rather alarmed by her enthusiasm.

"We're going to polish you, my dear. We're going to work and work and turn you into the person you were meant to be. What fun we'll have! You're going to shine, my dear. You're going to dazzle them! Before we're finished you're going to set this town on its ears!"

"Me?"

"You. Miss Miranda James! What a lark it will be, bringing you out, giving you polish! What a challenge! It'll be *very* hard work, of course, my dear, but, oh, how rewarding!"

"I ain't afraid of work," I assured her.

"Am not," she corrected.

"In the meantime, I was just wonderin', could—could I borrow some of them books?" I asked timidly.

"*Those* books!" she cried. "My dear, I in*sist*!"

22

CAM WOULD BE RETURNING TOMORROW. IN ONE SENSE
it seemed he'd been gone forever, the nights so long, so lonely,
yet the days had clipped right by, full to overflowing with
activity, thanks to Mrs. Wooden. I'd never worked so hard in
all my life, but how thrilling, how exciting, how challenging
it all was. Nine days we'd been working, and already I was
making distinct improvements. Mrs. Wooden declared herself
delighted with our progress, then sternly added that we must
redouble our efforts. She was a marvelous teacher, patient,
persistent, encouraging, always colorful, given to breathless
outbursts and flights of fancy I found wonderfully amusing.
She was an outlandish creature, true—chatty and overdra-
matic—but she had a huge heart and, beneath the frippery, a
kind, compassionate nature rare as unicorns in this day and
age. I felt myself blessed to have such a fascinating new friend.

Standing in front of the full-length mirror in our upstairs
bedroom, I wondered if Cam had missed me as much as I had
missed him. Probably not, probably hadn't given me a single
thought, the sod.... No, no, I wasn't going to start backsliding
already. A well-bred young lady *never* called anyone a sod. It
was *shock*ingly vulgar. A well-bred young lady didn't even
know such words. *Bloody* and *bleedin'* were forbidden, too,
and I must never make mention of arse, my own or anyone
else's, nor refer to certain bodily functions and the product
resulting from same. Such a lot to remember. I'd never make
it, I thought, brushing a heavy auburn wave from my temple.

I'd never even *look* like a lady, I admitted, gazing at my
reflection with a critical eye. Ladies were soft and pink and
blonde and ever so delicate. I was too tall, my waist too slender,
my bosom too full, and my coloring was much too vivid: eyes
too blue, lips too pink, hair a blaze of coppery red-brown.
Fragile and frail and elegant I'd never be, though at least I had

high cheekbones and a patrician nose. The ragged, filthy street urchin had vanished completely. Skin glowing from my bath, hair aglow with shiny highlights, I was wearing a frock of brown and cream stripped linen, the cloth very fine, the stripes thin. The elbow-length sleeves were tight, ending in white ruffles, and the bodice had a modestly low scooped neckline. The full skirt swelled in two puffed flounces that parted in front to reveal the ruffled white underskirt. Well, Randy, I thought, you may never be a lady, but at least you ain't a St. Giles ragamuffin any longer.

Aren't a ragamuffin. A well-bred young lady never said *ain't*, under no circumstances, and she said isn't, not *idn't*, doesn't, not *dudn't*. She knew when to say *them* and when to say *those* and, if not, simply kept her mouth shut. She carefully pronounced her final 'g's,' never dropped her 'h's' and spoke from her diaphragm, dra-a-a-a-w-ing the words up and giving them resonance and shape. She didn't speak through her nose and squawk like an agitated duck. Mrs. Wooden could be quite succinct in her criticisms. I *never* sounded like a duck, I protested. She calmly begged to differ with me.

Giving my hair a final pat, I turned away from the mirror, picked up the book I had borrowed and hurried downstairs. It was after ten already, and Mrs. Wooden would be waiting. It was marvelous of her to be devoting so much time to me. She airily brushed away any protests on my part that she surely must have better things to do. *I* was doing her a favor, she insisted and then candidly confessed that when you were down on your luck in the theater your friends had a habit of vanishing into the woodwork, except for a rare, rare few like Davy Garrick, bless his generous soul. Mrs. Wooden had not performed in London in over four years, and the tour she had just completed was with a distinctly third-rate repertory company that couldn't get a theater in the metropolis if they worked for free. Some, like that dreadful Colley Cibber, claimed that Mrs. W. was past her prime, but she staunchly refused to believe such nonsense and patiently waited for the right role that would place her back into the thick of things.

Glorious morning sunlight splattered the worn cobbles as I crossed the court to the old yellow house. Major Barnaby was tending his roses this morning, I noted. Straightening up to his full six feet, lean and ramrod stiff, he gave me an extremely hostile look as I knocked on Mrs. Wooden's door. In his early sixties, well preserved and handsome in a stern, bristly sort of way, he stood beside the bed of opulent salmon-pink roses with clipping shears in hand, piercing gray eyes aglitter. His sandy gray hair was cut short, his mustache neat and rather jaunty. He was indeed a fine figure of a man, I thought, remembering Mrs. W.'s description, but I couldn't imagine why he was so belligerent this morning. He had always been civil, if reserved, whenever I'd seen him before.

A chorus of shrill yaps and noisy barks sounded in the hallway when I knocked a second time. The door flew open. Brandy leaped at my skirts, yapping joyfully. Sarge whirled and cavorted like a small black tumbler. Mrs. Wooden gave me an effusive greeting and then stared dramatically past my shoulder at our neighbor, her chin held high, her eyes full of haughty disdain. Pulling me inside, ordering the dogs to hush, she slammed the door with considerable emphasis, as though she were slamming it in the major's face.

"I see that *dreadful* man is still out there," she exclaimed, "puttering in his precious rose beds! I suppose you *heard* the ruckus this morning? They must have heard it in Tower Yard. *Such* a tempest! Such an uproar, and that man actually threatened to use his riding crop on poor Sarge. I gave him a sizable piece of my mind, believe me!"

"What happened?" I asked.

"Sarge got out, my dear. I saw Major Barnaby working on his roses and thought I'd take a bit of fresh air in front of the house and Sarge nipped out as soon as I opened the door and darted *straight* for the major's roses. He hoisted his hind leg and watered one of the rosebushes and I thought the major was going to have a seizure! His eyes blazed. His cheeks flamed pink. He began to snort and shout, carried on like a madman! I naturally rushed over to rescue my baby, and that horrible man addressed me in the *most* unflattering terms!"

"What'd he say?"

"Never you mind, my dear. It doesn't bear repeating. I told him exactly what I thought of him, I did, told him what I thought of his roses, too! A man handsome as he is, puttering about in a rose bed! If he weren't so unfriendly and standoffish, he just might find something *better* to do. He isn't even sixty-five yet and as healthy as a horse. Full of vigor! There's no excuse for a man so eligible closing himself up like a hermit."

I smiled to myself. Mrs. Wooden's real bone of contention with the major was quite transparent. Brandy and Sarge preceded us down the hall, scampering merrily into the long, spacious room at the back of the house that served as Mrs. Wooden's "studio." Sunlight splashed in through a bank of windows overlooking her back garden, making patterns on the golden brown hardwood floor. A number of framed theatrical posters hung on the walls, and there was a rack of costumes she kept in perfect condition. A tall golden harp stood in one corner, and a long worktable sat beneath the windows, cluttered with books and papers. Several tall, lovely screens stood about, from India, she informed me, called Coromandel screens, their colors rich and glowing. Pepe was curled up on the long pale-blue sofa, lifting his head lazily as we entered the room.

"Did you read the grammar book I lent you?" Mrs. Wooden inquired.

"I read it twice," I told her. "It—it's peculiar, but when I'm reading I'm always aware of proper grammar—if the author makes a mistake, I spot it instantly and know what word he *should* have used. I always use the right words when I write, too. It's only when I speak that I make mistakes."

"They're really not mistakes," she said generously, "they're merely habits you've adopted. Everyone around you said 'them apples' so you said it, too, even though you knew it was wrong."

"Maybe so."

"You obviously received excellent early training, Miranda—from your mother, I assume—and then, when you moved to St. Giles you gradually took on the colors of its inhabitants, in your speech, in your mannerisms, until, on the surface at least, you were indistinguishable from them. What *we* are attempting to do is remove the St. Giles's influences."

"I see."

"And you're making excellent progress, my dear! We've just about restored your final 'g's,' but we have a lot of work on your 'h's.' We'll concentrate on them this morning."

I groaned. 'H's' were 'ell. Seeing my reluctance, Mrs. Wooden clucked and informed me that we must *forge* ahead. She was wearing a lovely yellow silk frock with a white lace fichu, a yellow silk bow atop the towering, powdered pompadour. Although it was still morning, her makeup was as vivid as ever—lips bright red, cheeks rouged, eyelids mauve, a heart-shaped black satin patch on one cheekbone. Extending her left arm out in a florid gesture, she told me to repeat after her: "How horrid to have herring."

"'Ow 'orrid to 'ave 'erring," I said.

"*How* horrid to *have* herring!" She corrected. 'Huh! Huh! Huh! Sound those 'h's!' Watch my lips! Huh-ow huh-orrid to huh-ave huh-erring."

"Huh-ow 'orrid to huh-ave herring."

"That's better. Again!"

"*How* huh-orrid to *have* herring."

"A little better, a little better, but you're not bringing the words *up* and shaping them. You're speaking from your nasal cavities, not from your chest, my dear. There's an absolutely lovely voice there, I know there is, it's just been warped and distorted by lazy speech habits and unfortunate associations."

"It 'urt—huh-urts—when I try to speak deep like that."

"That's your imagination. You're just not accustomed to using those muscles when you speak. Again now—draw them up, roll them, give them texture."

"How—horrid—to—'ave—herring."

"*Have* herring!"

"Have herring," I croaked.

"I want you to say that sentence twenty-five times now, slowly and carefully and from the chest."

I groaned, but I obeyed, and after I'd said it ten times or so it seemed to come a bit easier, seemed to sound better and didn't huh-urt so much. I was gettin'—get*ting*—better, getting the hang of it. Maybe it wasn't hopeless. Maybe I really could sound like a lady, and wouldn't Cam be proud then. Concentrating mightily, I "dre—e—ew" the words up and shaped them.

"There!" Mrs. Wooden cried, interrupting me. "My dear, that was *lovely*."

"It was?"

"You sounded almost human. Try not to *strain* so much. Relax. Let the words come up naturally."

I finished the twenty-five repetitions, exhausted. Never knew it was so hard to speak properly. Mrs. Wooden declared herself pleased with my progress and ordered me to say "Hannah has happy holidays" ten times, which was even more difficult to do. Hadn't said it five times before I detested the name Hannah. Hurt like the devil, saying that word, pronouncing both 'h's.' Hadn't got one out good before you had to do another. There was a loud knock at the front door just as I finished the tenth repetition. Brandy and Sarge barked lustily, tearing down the hall, and even Pepe lifted his head to give a bored "ruff-ruff."

"Who could *that* be!" Mrs. Wooden exclaimed, clasping a

hand over her heart. "I wonder if that dreadful Major Barnaby has come to apologize? You stay here, my dear. I'll just run see who it is."

She left the room, and I sighed with relief, stepping over to examine one of the Coromandel screens, turquoise and coral pink and silver birds and flowers marvelously inlaid in black panels bound with silver. I heard the front door opening, and then Mrs. Wooden gave a cry of surprise as Sarge and Brandy continued to vocalize with gleeful abandon. There was hearty male laughter and an exchange of words I couldn't make out over the racket of the dogs. Mrs. Wooden seemed to be protesting something, her guest insisting.

"Be *quiet*, Sarge! You, too, Brandy! There! See how you've stirred them up? Of course I'm delighted to see you. I'm thrilled, in fact, but you can't come in right now. I—I'm terribly busy, and—"

"Is this any way to treat an old and adoring friend? I *know* you, Maw-suh-lun. You're hiding something. What is it?"

"I'm not hiding anything!" she protested. "It's just—it's just that, well, I've only been back a few days and the place is in a dreadful shambles—"

"Doesn't matter in the least. I came to have some of your famous plum cake, my darlin', and I don't intend to leave until I get it. Besides, I have some extremely interesting news to relate. Come along, we'll chat in your studio."

"No! No—I mean, the salon's much more comfortable. If you insist on barging in like this, we'll use the salon."

"Ah ha! You *are* hiding something. I knew it!"

Purposeful footsteps strode down the hall, followed by the clattering rat-tat-tat of high-heeled slippers. The most gloriously beautiful man I'd ever seen burst into the room, followed by a very flustered Mrs. Wooden and two capering dogs. I stared in confusion as Mrs. Wooden made frantic gestures behind the man's back.

"And who is *this*?" he inquired, moving toward me.

"Don't open your mouth, Miranda!" Mrs. Wooden cried. "Do you hear me? Don't open your *mouth*."

I gulped and nodded, clamping my lips tightly together. The man paused a few feet away from me and clasped his hands behind his back and leaned forward, examining me with narrowed eyes as he might examine a painting, looking for flaws. Paralyzed, I watched with considerable apprehension as he stepped nearer, studying my hair, my complexion, nodding with distinct approval as his eyes took in my bosom. I swallowed, lips still clamped.

I recognized him immediately, of course. He was a few years older than he had been when he had posed for the Hamlet painting, and, now in his early thirties, his face was even more interesting, a lived-in face, attractively lined, mobile and expressive. It wasn't that he was all that handsome, not really. On closer inspection his looks weren't remarkable at all, but he had an incredible magnetism that took one's breath away. He seemed to gather all the light to him and send it back in dazzling rays, seemed to radiate vitality and zest and virile energy. Never had I seen such remarkable presence, and, what was even more remarkable, he seemed completely unaware of it, his manner jaunty, relaxed and totally unassuming.

On stage David Garrick might be attired in great splendor, but this morning he looked almost unkempt. His dark gold hair seemed a bit oily, as though it might need a good washing, pulled away from his face and tied with a bit of old string in back. His black leather pumps were scuffed, his white cotton stockings were clearly aged, and his dark maroon knee breeches were frightfully creased. Over a white lawn shirt with frilly white jabot he wore a disreputable forest-green frock coat with tarnished silver buttons, the skirt wide and flaring, the cuffs rather frayed, the cloth itself shiny with age. It was the sort of garment a pirate might wear, I thought, yet the overall effect was utterly disarming.

My heart thumped as he continued to examine me, and then he moved back a pace and gave an emphatic nod.

"Exquisite!" he declared. "Positively exquisite! Exactly the type I've been looking for. What's your experience, my beauty? Have you worked in London? Not that it's terribly important, I'll be using you primarily for ornamental purposes. Nothing too demanding at first."

"She's not an *ac*tress, Davy!" Mrs. Wooden protested.

"With that face, that body, she doesn't have to be. I'll put her in velvets and satins, use her as stage dressing."

"She's not interested!"

"Why don't you let her speak for herself?"

"She can't."

"Mute?"

"Not exactly."

"A hideous speech impediment?"

"She—she has a *terrible* case of laryngitis—yes, that's it,

~278~

she has laryngitis and her physician has ordered her not to say a word for at least two days or there might be *dreadful* consequences. Isn't that right, Miranda?"

I nodded, swallowing again. Davy Garrick tilted his head to one side, looking at both of us with grave doubts. My lips were beginning to hurt from staying clamped so tightly. I parted them, exhaling a great gust of breath. Mrs. Wooden gasped, alarmed, and I quickly clamped them together again. Garrick stroked his chin with his index finger, sensing a mystery and wondering how far he should pursue it. I longed for him to leave so that I could breathe normally again.

"If she's not an actress, who *is* she?" he asked sternly.

"She—she's my niece."

"Didn't know you had any brothers or sisters. Thought you were an orphan."

"I was—I mean I *am*. Miranda's my niece by marriage—the daughter of the late Mr. Wooden's brother. She's been living in Chester all these years and—and I've brought her to London to keep me company."

"I don't believe a single word you've said, Maw-suh-lun, luv. I'll let you off the hook for the time being, gentleman that I am, but I want you to know that I intend to get to the bottom of this eventually. I shall, rest assured. You haven't promised her to some other manager, have you?"

"Of course not!" she exclaimed, outraged. "I told you, Miranda's not an actress. She's never been on a stage in her life, has no desire to be. She's—wait a minute! What do you mean, some *other* manager?"

"That's my news, ducks. I've just become manager of Drury Lane. Co-manager, actually, with Lacy, but I'll be in full control."

"*Davy!* How marvelous! I thought you were going to continue at Covent Garden under Rich's management. I never dreamed—oh, this is *splen*did! You'll be able to mount your own productions, pick your own *casts*! Tell me quickly, who have you engaged?"

"Haven't engaged anyone yet. The season won't begin till September, and the entire theater has to be redecorated, walls torn down, new mortar put up, hundreds of alterations made. Place has hardly been touched since Sir Christopher Wren designed it over seventy years ago."

"Who are you *think*ing of engaging?"

"Haven't given it a whole lot of thought, luv. Peg, of course."

"I thought that was *over*," Mrs. Wooden said.

"It is, alas, leaving me older and sadder if not much wiser. Darlin' Peg may have the morals of a terrier and the manners of a sow, but she's still a damn fine actress and I bear no grudges. I shall probably engage Mrs. Cibber—"

"Of *course!*" Mrs. Wooden interrupted. "She's *very* good." Her enthusiasm was less than genuine.

"Mrs. Pritchard, too, no doubt, don't want to play favorites. I'll round up a superlative company, ducks, the best the city's ever seen."

Mrs. Wooden was clearly crestfallen. "I'm sure you will," she replied.

Garrick smiled a teasing smile and, sauntering across the room, flopped down on the long blue sofa and stretched his legs out. Brandy and Sarge romped over to sniff as the actor dug into one of the huge pockets of his frock coat and, seemingly by accident, pulled out a handful of doggie tidbits. Sarge leaped up onto Garrick's lap, wildly excited. Too small to master such a titanic feat, Brandy pawed at the actor's leg and yapped mournfully. Above such demanding antics and already snugly ensconced on the sofa, Pepe merely wagged his tail a couple of times, convinced justice would be done. Garrick casually distributed morsels to all three dogs as he continued to chat.

"Don't know who else I'll engage," he said, "but, naturally, when the right role comes along I'll consider engaging my roguish old Marcie. We're going to open with *A Merchant of Venice*, luv, and, alas, I fear you're a bit ripe for Portia."

"*Merchant!*" she said, disgusted. "Shakespeare's been *done* so much. I don't know why you don't open with a nice, rousing Restoration comedy. I *shine* in Restoration comedy."

"I know, ducks, and I'll keep that in mind. That's all, mutts. Greedy little buggers, aren't you? I'll bring more next time. Now, Marcie, the least you can do is give a poor, famished genius a cup of tea and some of your famous plum cake with apricot brandy. I've been thinking of nothing else for days."

"I declare, Davy Garrick, you're as audacious as ever! You *will* find a role for me, won't you?"

"Of course I will, ducks. You don't think I'd forget my old sweetheart, do you? Marcelon Wooden will shine again, I promise."

"Restoration comedy is *so* much more amusing. I never felt comfortable playing all those dreary Shakespearian queens, if you want to know the truth. Give me something with a bit more dash, a bit more elan. Give me something I can—"

"Give me some cake and tea at once!" he demanded.

Mrs. Wooden threw up her hands in mock disgust and scurried blissfully out of the room. David Garrick smiled a radiant smile and watched her departure with fond eyes. He was an audacious rogue, scattering charm in every direction, as comfortable with his fame as he was with his old clothes, perfectly natural in everything he said and did. With our hostess out of the room, he turned that charm on me, giving me a grin that was even lovelier than his smile.

"Enjoying London?" he asked.

I nodded.

"Much more exciting than—where was it? Chester? I should imagine you're quite overwhelmed by the sights and sounds of our great metropolis. I know *I* was when I first arrived from Lichfield. Bowled me over, it did. For days I couldn't do anything but gaze and gape. Have you ever *thought* about going on the stage?"

I shook my head, terrified I'd slip up and let him hear my voice.

"When you get over this distressing infirmity you'll have to get Marcelon to bring you around to the Drury. It'll be full of workmen hammering and sawing and slapping up plaster, but I'd love to show it to you just the same. Magical place, a theater. I still get goose-bumps every time I walk backstage— all those ropes, all that dust, all those painted flats, that mystery, that excitement. Nothing in the world like it. Have you ever been to the theater?"

I shook my head.

"Never? Amazing! We'll have to do something *about* that. I don't know what Marcie has in mind for you, my beauty, but she isn't going to be able to keep you under wraps for long, I assure you. Once the bucks in London get a glimpse of you they're going to pursue you in droves, but they'll have to get up before breakfast to beat out Davy Garrick. I've first dibs, my beauty, and don't you forget it."

"What kind of nonsense are you prattling now?" Mrs. Wooden demanded, wheeling in the old tea cart.

"I've been telling yon beauty that I have plans for her, Marcie luv. I intend to sweep her off her feet."

"You might as well forget it, Davy," she said, slicing cake and placing it on saucers. "Miranda's a *good* girl. She'd never have anything to do with an *ac*tor, I can tell you that right now. Besides, she's going back to Chester first thing next week. Isn't that right, Miranda?"

I nodded. Davy Garrick made a mournful face. Mrs. Wooden poured tea and carried a cup to the actor along with a slice of cake. She served me next, and I sat down on one of the straight chairs nearby, holding myself very rigid, hardly daring to breathe, much less eat cake and sip tea. Garrick downed his tea and tore into the cake with gusto, holding out the empty saucer a few moments later. Mrs. Wooden gave him a second slice.

"Always were fond of my plum cake," she declared. "I remember how you used to eat it backstage when we were doing *Hamlet*. How's your good friend Sam Johnson, by the way? Boorish as ever, I assume."

"All involved with his grandiose plans for the dictionary," Garrick replied. "He's signed a contract to do it now and can't talk of anything else—I take that back. He *can* and does, interminably, but the dictionary's his chief subject nowadays. Holds forth about it in all the coffeehouses."

"Insufferable man," Mrs. Wooden said, "but fascinating. I'll have to admit that, even if I can't abide him."

"Sam's quite fond of *you*, luv," Garrick told her.

"He *is*?"

Garrick grinned, forking another bite of cake. "He says you remind him of a painted maypole. Says he feels like breaking into a jig every time he sees you."

"He *would* say something like that, and I'm not at all sure I like it. I wish him well on the dictionary, at any rate. It's bound to be a herculean task, and if anyone can pull it off, Samuel Johnson can."

Teacup and saucer of cake balanced in my lap, I sat with my back as straight as a ramrod, listening to them discuss the eccentricities of the irascible writer. Garrick had a marvelous voice, rich and melodious, a lovely lilt that was soothing to the ear yet completely unaffected. Finished with tea and cake, he set the cup and saucer on the floor and lolled back against the cushions, stretching his legs out even more. They were very well shaped, I observed, long and muscular. Garrick had the physique of an athlete in superb condition, and he moved with jaunty grace as natural with him as breathing. What an impression he must make on the stage, I thought.

"Yon beauty has a faraway look in her eyes," he said. "I fear we're boring her with all this talk about Sam."

The remark startled me out of my reverie, startled me so much that I darn near dumped the cup of tea onto my lap. Very, very carefully I got up and took the cup and saucer of cake over to the worktable, setting them down. Garrick watched me, studying my movements. I was extremely self-conscious, felt clumsy as an ox under that amiable, speculative gaze. Resuming my seat, I folded my hands in my lap and tried to look pleasant, convinced I looked like an idiot. Garrick casually stroked Pepe, who had snuggled up against him in a small white ball. Sarge was begging his mistress for a taste of cake, and Brandy was now curled up on top of a stack of papers, fast asleep.

"What exactly does your ravishing young niece *do* in Chester?" Garrick asked. "Besides chatter nonstop, I mean."

Finally relenting, Mrs. Wooden gave Sarge a bite of cake. "Oh, she does a lot of things—embroidery, needlepoint, a bit of watercoloring, a dab of botany, keeps herself quite occupied."

"Sounds frightfully dreary. You really should persuade her to stay in London, luv."

"Oh, her parents would never allow *that*. I had a difficult enough time persuading them to let her visit this long."

The actor stretched his arms out and rested them along the back of the sofa, the skirt of his forest green frock coat falling back to reveal a worn black silk lining. Head tilted to one side, he looked at his hostess, one dark brow slanting up in a quizzical arch. Mrs. Wooden busied herself with the tea things, clattering cups and saucers nervously. She was not a skillful liar, and her guest clearly knew her well enough to know when she wasn't telling the truth. An amused grin curled on his lips, and he stood up and ran a hand through his thick dark-golden hair.

"There's a mystery here, ducks," he declared. "Would that I had time to pursue it, but, alas, I have several more visits to make this afternoon—must spread the good news, you know."

"It's been lovely seeing you, Davy. I do hope you'll come again."

"You can be sure of it."

He gave her a vigorous hug that caused her to gasp and caused her pompadour to tilt alarmingly. She shoved him away from her with mock disgust and quickly adjusted her head piece, her cheeks flushed with pleasure. David Garrick strode over to my chair, took my hand and pulled me to my feet. I looked up at that dazzling face with apprehension. He smiled a lovely smile, eyes gleaming.

"It's been a pleasure, my beauty," he crooned.

He squeezed my hand then, and then he lifted it slowly to his lips and turned it and kissed my palm. I was speechless. Under the circumstances, it was just as well.

"I don't believe any of this nonsense Marcie has been telling me about you," he said. "You're the most enchanting vision I've laid eyes on in many a day, and I have a feeling you and I are going to see each other again. Until then I shall dream of the fair Miranda."

That was quite enough to turn a girl's head, but then Davy Garrick was a professional charmer and he probably talked that way to all the girls, even the ones who squinted. Full of blarney, he was, audacious as could be, yet I coudln't help but feel flattered. Cam Gordon had certainly never talked to me like that. Never would, either, dour, undemonstrative Scot that he was. Garrick gazed into my eyes a moment longer and then released my hand. Mrs. Wooden led him to the front door, and as he left he seemed to take all the sunlight with him.

"Jemminy!" I exclaimed as Mrs. Wooden returned. "It was 'ard as 'ell, keepin' my mouth shut all that time. I didn't think th' bleedin' sod was *ever* gonna leave."

Mrs. Wooden winced, appalled by my words and the voice in which they were spoken, but she was much too enraptured by the actor's visit to scold me. She beamed with pleasure, patting her pompadour, her eyes all aglow.

"I *knew* Davy wouldn't fail me. Manager of the Drury Lane! And him so young! To think it was just ten years ago that he came up from Lichfield to go into the wine business with his brother."

"Lichfield?" I said.

"His birthplace," she explained. "He and Sam Johnson grew up there. Eager to get away from the place, both of them. Eager for broader horizons."

"Does—" I paused, frowning. "Does this Lichfield have a cathedral?"

"I believe so. Seems I've seen an engraving of it."

"Does—does it 'ave a pond? With ducks?"

"*Have*, Miranda. Huh huh huh. Pronounce those 'h's!'"

"Does Lichfield *have* a duck pond?"

"I wouldn't know, my dear. I've never been there myself. What a peculiar question, though. Why do you ask?"

"I—I just wondered," I said.

Mrs. Wooden shrugged, far too full of the visit to be distracted by my questions. Voice rolling dramatically, she regaled me with information about the actor.

"Not quite six years ago it was that Davy made his first real appearance on the English stage. October 19th, 1741, a historic night it was, too! He played Richard III at Goodman's Fields—no one had ever heard of him, no one expected anything, the doorman only took in thirty pounds that evening, a paltry take, let me assure you. He stepped on stage, and before he uttered a single word Davy *was* Richard—he didn't rant, he didn't orate, he didn't proclaim, he simply *was* the wicked hunchback. He set a new standard in acting that night, Davy did. No actor in history has received such an enthusiastic reception."

"Were you there?"

"Indeed I was—pure chance, my dear. I was between engagements and I hadn't seen *Richard III* in a while, and so I went to Goodman's Fields—an out-of-the-way theater, quite *déclassé*, looked down upon by the West End snobs. I was there for Davy's debut, and I knew immediately that here was a genius the likes of which we had never seen before—and probably won't see again."

"'E—he's—that good?"

"He's amazing! Incredible! Words can't express, my dear. In that one night he established himself as our greatest tragedian, and then he astonished everyone by turning to comedy just to prove his versatility. There's no role he can't play with absolute perfection—a villain, a fop, a fool, a brooding romantic hero, a scheming merchant, a bumbling oaf. He's sheer magic."

"Who's this Peg you were talkin' about?" I asked.

Mrs. Wooden made a face. "Peg Woffington," she replied, settling down on the sofa with much rustling of yellow silk skirts. "A great tall girl with large, irregular features—ugly as a mud fence, actually, but when she's on stage you never notice it. A brilliant actress—hurts me to say it, but it's true. Abounding vitality. Incomparable zest. She excels in comedy and has a penchant for roles allowing her to masquerade as a boy—when she appeared as Sylvia in *The Recruiting Officer*, masquerading as Jack Wilful for half the play, they said such exuberance hadn't been seen on stage since the death of Nell Gwynn."

Sarge trotted over to the sofa with the red ball in his mouth, his black tail wagging. Mrs. Wooden took the ball and tossed it. Sarge darted after it. Brandy woke up and scampered after him with a blissful yap.

"Many say Peg's the reincarnation of Nell," Mrs. Wooden continued. "She has the same careless brio and, I might add, the same deplorable morals. Drinks like a fish, swears like a trooper, takes lovers by the score. I can't abide the creature myself, but neither can I deny her talent. Davy was head over heels in love with her, of course. It was quite a tempestuous relationship—such fights, such jealousy, such clashing of wills. He's just now getting over it, poor lamb. Quite the ladies' man, Davy is, an outrageous flirt, but he was *serious* about Peg."

Gathering Pepe onto her lap, she began to stroke his soft white fur. "I must say, my dear, he certainly was smitten with *you*."

"Was he?" I said casually.

"Completely smitten. Mystified. Intrigued."

"Ain't gonna do him much good," I retorted.

"Miranda! Young ladies don't—"

"*Isn't* gonna do him much good," I corrected myself. "A chap like that, all charm and dazzle—a girl'd 'ave to be crazy to 'ave anything to do with 'im."

"Huh huh huh! Your 'h's!'"

"I'll never get it," I said woefully. "I try and try, but I keep slipping up. It's so huh-*hard*. Who wants to speak like a bleedin' duchess, anyway?"

"You do," she assured me, putting Pepe aside and climbing to her feet. "You mustn't be discouraged, my dear. We've made remarkable progress already, and in a very short while you'll be speaking in a voice as elegant as can be."

"It'll still hurt," I complained.

"It won't hurt at all. Once you learn to use the proper muscles you'll speak quite naturally, won't even be aware of it. Let's get back to work, my dear. You were doing quite well earlier. Hannah has happy holidays."

"Hannah has hap—do we *have* to do this?"

"We have to. No arguments now. Get to work!"

Mrs. Wooden drove me with stern but amiable determination, and after a while I found that 'h's' weren't really all that difficult once you got the hang of saying them. I worked with renewed enthusiasm, and Mrs. Wooden was elated, declaring me a superb pupil. When I finally went home late that afternoon I was quite pleased with myself. I had a bite to eat and settled down at my secretary and labored on the book for a while, but thoughts kept distracting me and it was almost impossible to concentrate on the boring Lord John and the insipid Lady Cynthia. Try though I might, I couldn't make them breathe today.

Finally putting the quill aside, I stared through the window at the yard and the lovely old yellow house across the way. Sunlight faded, dark yellow-gold on the cobbles, and shadows were beginning to thicken. I thought of David Garrick, so handsome, so charming, so overwhelming. I couldn't get over the feeling that I had known him before. An elusive memory seemed to flicker around the edges of my mind, never quite clear enough for me to grasp it. Lichfield. A great cathedral. A pond with ducks. Handsome young Davy with the merry grin and lively blue eyes. Could I have lived in Lichfield when I was a little girl?

The room grew dim as sunlight vanished, and a curious melancholy took hold of me as I realized just how little I knew about myself. I vaguely remembered a small town, and I remembered my mum, of course, saw flashes of her in memory, but everything else was a misty blur besides the years in St. Giles. I had no idea who my father may have been and wasn't even certain of my name. Had Mum married someone named James, or was I a love child? It didn't matter, I told myself, lighting the candles. It didn't matter at all. I was Miranda James and I lived on Greenbriar Court and I was the luckiest girl alive, for I had Cam. Davy Garrick might dazzle and charm, but compared to my Scot he faded to insignificance.

I had my Scot and he was returning tomorrow. One more night in my lonely bed and I would be in his arms. There could be no greater bliss.

23

SIX O'CLOCK IN THE MORNING IT HAD BEEN WHEN HE
finally came home. Six o'clock in the bloody morning, sunlight
streaking the sky in cool pink strokes, shadows evaporating,
him staggering up the stairs and coming into the bedroom
looking worn and haggard, pulling off his clothes, climbing
into bed without a word, falling asleep almost immediately.
Damn him to hell. Back from Scotland two weeks now and
going out almost every night to his bloody secret meetings with
his bloody conspirators, leaving me all alone. You'd think I
was still his bleedin' maid, think I was just a piece of furniture
for all the attention he'd given me. Sod hadn't even brought
me a present from Scotland. Wouldn't have hurt him. Hell, a
simple bit of purple heather would've done, would've said
something, would've meant the world.

It was one o'clock in the afternoon now and he was still
asleep and I longed to march upstairs and grab him by the feet
and drag him out of bed so forcefully he'd crack his head on
the floor. I'd enjoy that. Maybe I wouldn't drag him out of
bed. Maybe I'd take a pan of ice cold water and dump it over
his head. Serve the sod right, it would. Ignoring me, treating
me like I wasn't there, neglecting his book and traipsing all
over London to plan and conspire with those bloodthirsty rebels
when he knew how I felt about it, knew how scared I was.
The bastard hadn't even noticed my elegant new voice. Never
dropped my final 'g's' anymore, carefully pronounced each
'h,' spoke with a lovely resonance. Like dark velvet, Mrs.
Wooden said it was, said it was a blooming miracle, one day
I'm squawking like an agitated duck and the next I'm speaking
in a soft, refined drawl that would put a duchess to shame.
Still needed work, of course, a few burrs here and there, but
a miracle all the same, and Mr. Cam-sodding-Gordon was so
preoccupied I might just as well have been jabbering in Hindu.

Sleeping away upstairs he was, in the middle of the day. Downright immoral, and me with my hair just washed, thick and soft as silk, gleaming like molten copper with shiny red highlights. I was wearing one of my nicest frocks, too, lovely sky-blue silk with deep sapphire stripes that matched the color of my eyes, skirt belling out over my petticoat, waist snug, bodice cut modestly low with the puffed sleeves off the shoulder. Why bother to make myself attractive for him? I might as well be dressed in rags for all the good it did, might as well have dirty hair and a face streaked with soot.

Damn him! Two weeks he'd been back and four times he'd slept with me. Slept? Much too dignified a term. Grabbed me, banged away lustily, rolled over and then *he* slept while I fumed. More like rape, it was, all four times, and I wasn't Lady Evelyn, I wasn't a whore conveniently on hand to serve him when he felt the need to release some of his pent-up anger. Things were going to change. They were going to change this very day, I vowed, or else . . . or else I'd know the reason why. I wasn't going to drag him out of bed, no, and I wasn't going to dump water over him, much as I longed to. Well-bred young ladies didn't do such things, and I was going to be a lady if it killed me.

Fuming, I sat at my secretary in the front room and stared at the half-filled page before me, utterly stymied. I had written thirty-three pages now, two and a half chapters, and my lovers were locked in an embrace and as dry as dust, as lifeless as two corpses. What had ever possessed me to think I could write a novel in the first place? It was unmitigated torture, every word an ordeal, and who would want to read such artificial folderol anyway? The plot was trite. The characters were stiff, the dialogue stilted, the whole thing a tremendous waste of time. What did I know about noble lords and ladies and elegant mansions and love in high places? Might as well destroy the evidence of my folly and leave the writing to Cam, I decided, and I was stacking the pages together when someone knocked briskly on the front door.

Abandoning the pages, I hurried into the hall lest repeated knocks awaken the slumbering Scot. When I opened the door Mr. Thomas Sheppard blinked, looking most ill at ease away from the snug confines of his office. Somehow one didn't visualize him in the open air, in the bright afternoon sunlight. Indeed, he seemed vastly relieved when I showed him inside and closed the door. Leading him into the sitting room, I smiled politely, trying my best to hide my surprise.

"Mr. Sheppard," I said, "what—what an unexpected pleasure. I didn't know you ever left your office."

"Rarely do," he admitted, "but in this instance—" He hesitated, his large blue-gray eyes showing discomfiture behind the gold-trimmed spectacles.

"Is something wrong?" I inquired.

Again he hesitated, looking rather like a dried-up little pixie in his neatly tailored tan breeches and coat, his brown and cream striped waistcoat and neckcloth of palest green. His thin sandy hair looked slightly more gray than I remembered, an errant lock splayed across his brow and adding an incongruously boyish touch. I gave him an encouraging smile.

"May I help you in some way, Mr. Sheppard?"

"I—uh—I'd much prefer to discuss it with Gordon. Is he in?"

It was my turn to hesitate. "He—actually he is, Mr. Sheppard, but he isn't awake."

"Oh?"

"He's been working so late, you see. Didn't stop until after six this morning, and then he was absolutely exhausted—I can awaken him, of course, if it's really necessary."

"Working, eh?" he said.

"Terribly hard," I lied.

"I take it *The Spoils of Dowland* is nearing completion, then?"

"I—I don't imagine it will be long now."

Lying through my teeth, I was. He'd done exactly three chapters, and those not his best work. Hardly took quill in hand these days, much too busy skulking around London on mysterious errands that weren't going to do anyone any good and might well cause a great deal of trouble.

"I'm very glad to hear that," Mr. Sheppard said. "He hasn't delivered those early chapters he promised, you see, and with a June fifteenth delivery date I was beginning to grow—well—a bit perturbed, I might as well confess it. Cam hasn't always been the—uh—the most de*pen*dable writer I've dealt with."

"June fifteenth delivery date," I said, frowning.

"That's what he agreed to when I gave him the advance. Largest advance I've ever made, incidentally, but after the success of *Gentleman James* it seemed reasonable enough. He promised *Spoils* for the middle of June, said he'd deliver it in batches so my printers could get a head start setting up the type. I want to bring it out in September, you see, and—"

He hesitated again, looking extremely uncomfortable now, looking doubtful when he saw the expression on my face. I quickly concealed the shock and dismay I was feeling and gave him another, very reassuring smile.

"I'm afraid it's largely my own fault," I confessed, groping for words. "I do all his copying, you know, and—well, I've gotten terribly behind. Cam didn't *tell* me he was supposed to deliver the manuscript in sections—he's been working so hard I—I guess it slipped his mind."

Slipped his mind to tell me about the advance, too. Largest advance Thomas Sheppard & Co. had ever paid one of their writers, and I had a rather good idea where every penny of it had gone. Not into the ginger jar and certainly not into the bank. Not to his relatives and not to some deserving charity. No indeed. It had gone straight into the hands of those wretched rebels to finance that secretive venture he had obliquely hinted about once or twice. Could I possibly stab him in his sleep and get by with it? Could I plead self-defense?

"I'll do my best to make amends, Mr. Sheppard," I said, light and charming as could be.

"I quite understand," he replied.

"You'll receive the first chapters as soon as possible, and I can assure you they'll be well worth waiting for. *Spoils* is Cam's very best book, even more exciting than *Gentleman James*. His readers are going to love it."

If they ever saw it. June fifteenth was less than a month away. He'd have to work night and day to meet that deadline, and he'd shown no inclination whatsoever to get to his worktable of late. It was dishonest, taking all that money and making no effort to keep his part of the bargain. If he didn't deliver the book on time, Sheppard & Co. could well take him to court—serve the bastard right, it would—and he couldn't possibly repay the money. Visions of debtor's prison loomed, Cam in a dark, damp cell, cheeks sunken, eyes haunted, chains rattling as he moved on the wet, filthy straw scattered over the cold stone floor.

But I was forgetting my duties as hostess. Hoping to appear warm and hospitable, I asked Mr. Sheppard if he would care for a cup of tea. He shook his head, studying me closely with amiable blue-gray eyes.

"Forgive me," he said. He smiled a thin, dry but charming smile. "I was staring, I know, but—you seem different somehow."

"Do I?"

"The feisty, engaging, and—uh—quite alarming young woman who came to my office a few months ago seems to have vanished."

"Indeed?"

"Replaced by an elegant young woman who speaks in a cultured voice and has all the social graces."

"I'm still working on the voice," I confessed, "and I'm gradually learning the social graces. A friend is giving me lessons in both. Yesterday, after we finished our vocal exercises, I learned about forks and spoons, which ones to use when."

"Admirable," he remarked.

"It's very hard going sometimes," I told him. "When I'm not repeating my vowels or setting a mock table, I'm walking across the room with books balanced on my head and learning about French wines. Mrs. Wooden is very thorough."

"Wooden? Would that be Mrs. Marcelon Wooden?"

"You know her?" I asked.

"I once saw her give a—uh—most remarkable performance as *The Duchess of Malfi*. It was an unforgettable evening," he added dryly.

"She lives across the way, you know. She's determined to make a lady out of me."

"I should say that she's doing a very good job of it," Sheppard replied, very gallant. "I only hope Gordon appreciates the efforts you're making. He's an extremely fortunate man—I said that after our first encounter, when you made your somewhat—uh—alarming appearance at my office."

"Was—was I really so awful?"

"You were enchanting," he assured me, "also a most astute business person. You drove a very hard bargain indeed. Brains, beauty, vitality—I must confess, if I were thirty years younger, Gordon would have some heavy competition for your favor."

"If you were thirty years younger, Cam wouldn't have a prayer."

Sheppard chuckled, eyes twinkling with delight behind the gold-rimmed spectacles. He straightened the lapels of his frock coat and brushed the errant lock of sandy hair from his brow.

Glancing around the room, he noticed the secretary and the stack of pages I had been on the verge of destroying.

"Work in progress?" he inquired.

"In—in a manner of speaking," I said, uneasy. "It's—nothing, really."

Sheppard moved over to the secretary and picked up the top page, examining it idly. "Quite a boon to us, your copying all of Gordon's work. Saves us ever so much time. Hmmm. This isn't his usual style."

"It—it's not his."

"No? You're working as copyist for someone else, too?"

I shook my head, horribly uncomfortable. Sheppard looked up from the page, his eyes full of inquiry.

"I—I'm afraid it's my own work," I admitted. "I had the—the absurd notion that I might be able to write a book myself. It was just—just an experiment. Quite foolish, of course."

Sheppard read a few more lines. I gazed miserably at the floor, wishing it would open beneath me and swallow me up.

"Cam—Cam doesn't know anything about it," I said. "I was ashamed to mention it to him. It's quite awful, I know that. I was just about to tear it up when you knocked on the door."

"I'm glad you didn't," he told me. "Would you mind if I took this back to my office?"

"I—you don't really want to read it, Mr. Sheppard. It's dreadful, every word of it."

"Why don't you let me be the judge of that," he suggested, gathering up the pages. "I publish a great many books and quite a number of magazines. We're always looking for new writers, not nearly enough of them to go around, you know. Fierce competition on Fleet Street these days."

I nervously assured him that it would be a complete waste of time, but Sheppard was politely—and firmly—insistent and, five minutes later, left the house with the manuscript in a large brown envelope I had reluctantly provided. I felt strangely vulnerable, as though a secret part of me had been violated. Mr. Sheppard was a kind man. He had promised not to say anything to Cam, and, tactful as he was, he probably wouldn't say anything to me, either. After reading the pages and seeing what a hopeless botch they were, he would doubtlessly be diplomatic and never refer to them again.

Glancing at the clock, I saw that it was nearing two. Sod

couldn't sleep all day, could he? He'd want coffee when he woke up, and he'd be hungry, too. I went into the kitchen and lighted the stove and put water on to boil and sliced bread for toast and took down the marmalade. Waiting on him hand and foot, taking care of him like he was a helpless little boy—it was demeaning, that's what it was. I was no longer the ragged little street urchin he'd manhandled so brutally that day of the execution. I was a different person, and I deserved to be treated differently. Technically I was still his bond servant, of course, but that piece of paper no longer signified. Sod had no right to take me for granted and treat me like I was merely a convenience.

Coffee done, bread toasted, fire banked down, I left coffee and toast on the stove to keep warm and went upstairs, skirts making a soft, silken rustle. High time for him to get out of bed it was, high time for me to give him a piece of my mind, too. Tossing money around like it was paper when *Gentleman James* came out, getting himself out of debt for the first time in heaven knows when, then spending, spending, spending, more debts, bigger debts, and me not at all perturbed because *Spoils* was bound to make even more money. Then I discover that he's already taken a hefty advance from Sheppard and the book hardly begun. . . . It was infuriating. It was frightening as well. Brilliant he might be, with a dazzling mind, yet he was so blind in other ways. Those damned rebels, plotting, planning, taking his money. . . . It had to stop.

I stepped quietly into the bedroom. The curtains were closed. The room was hazy with shadows. He was asleep, sheets all tangled about his legs, chest bare, one arm clutching a pillow as though it was a foe he had in a vicious death lock. He was restless these days, unable to sleep well, too much on his mind, disturbed and preoccupied ever since he returned from Scotland. I stood at the foot of the bed, watching him, and the love inside me swelled until it was almost unbearable. I loved him too much, far too much, so much that life without him was unthinkable. I wasn't really alive when he wasn't near, was merely in a state of suspension as I waited to see his face, hear his voice, feel his touch.

He stirred, clutching the pillow tighter, muttering something in his sleep. He ground his teeth, squeezing the pillow in the crook of his arm, and then, after a moment, he gave a heavy sigh and relaxed, breathing heavily but evenly. I watched his chest rise and fall and moved quietly around the bed to smooth back the heavy ebony wave that had fallen across his eyes. He muttered again and made a face, and I gently stroked his lean, taut cheek and the curve of his lower lip, loving him so, filled with a rapturous emotion that was almost frightening in its intensity. He was surly and sullen and infuriating, prey to dark moods, and he had a savage streak that was undeniable—I'd seen that on the day of the execution, when he had treated me so brutally—but none of this deceived me. I knew the real Cam, the sensitive, vulnerable man who hid behind the savage facade, and one day, I vowed, he would trust me enough, love me enough that he would no longer need to hide.

Moving away from the bed, I stepped to the windows and parted the curtains. Afternoon sunlight streamed into the room in pale yellow-white rays that banished the shadows. Cam moaned, releasing the pillow and slinging an arm over his eyes. He was completely naked, the sheets twisted, leaving one leg bare, the edges just covering his upper thighs and private parts. I longed for him, longed to remove my clothes and climb into bed with him and tease him awake and taunt him into a state of passion and relish him to the full, but I had my pride, and I was still angry with him. This longing, these tender feelings shimmering inside me must be sternly repressed. Sod needed a stern reprimand, needed to know I wasn't going to take much more of this wretched treatment.

"Ohhhhh—," he moaned.

He moved the arm away from his eyes and blinked in the sunlight, curling his thin lips irritably.

"Do we have to have all that bloody sunlight?"

"It's two o'clock in the afternoon, you swine."

"Two?"

"You've been sleeping all day."

"Do I smell coffee?" he asked sleepily.

"Wouldn't know. Do you?"

"Jesus, you're in a charming mood."

"I was in a charming mood last night, too, waiting for you to come home, waiting and waiting and waiting, worried sick the whole time, not knowing what might have happened to you."

"You gonna start in on that again?"

"I don't like it, Cam."

He sat up against the headboard, pulling the sheets up to his waist. He shoved hair from his brow and rubbed his eyes. I picked up his breeches and his shirt and draped them over a chair, picked up his boots and hurled them none too gently into the open wardrobe. He scowled, displeased with my mood, tightening up defensively.

"Be a luv," he said, "go fetch me a cup of coffee."

"Fetch your own bloody coffee!"

He looked at me for a long moment with frosty blue eyes, facial muscles all taut, mouth tight. I stood my ground, glaring at him defiantly and watching the invisible wall go up around him.

"You want to fight," he said, "is that it?"

"No, Cam, I don't want to fight. I want—I want to be treated like a responsible human being, not a piece of furniture, not a piece of tail for you to grab whenever you happen to grow horny."

"My, my, we do have a lot of grievances this morning, don't we?"

"You—ever since you got back from Scotland, you've hardly acknowledged my presence."

"I've had a lot on my mind."

"I know that. I've tried to understand. I know how you feel about Culloden, Cam. I know how you feel about the deaths of your brothers, about losing the family estate, about the execution of your cousin. I know what it's done to you, how it's warped you. That first day at Tyburn—you were ready to kill, and I can understand that, but—"

"It's none of your affair, Miranda."

"Isn't it?"

"It has nothing to do with you."

"I live in this house. I share your life. Anything that effects you concerns me a great deal."

He didn't answer. He climbed out of bed, calmly removed his breeches from the chair and pulled them on. I watched as he dressed, bristling, determined to have this out once and for all. Cam ignored me. He might have been alone in the room. Tucking his shirt into the waistband of his breeches, he sat down on the bed and pulled on his stockings. They needed darning again, I noticed. Sod was death on stockings, couldn't keep a decent pair.

"Mr. Sheppard was here," I said icily.

"Oh?"

"You were asleep. I didn't want to awaken you."

"Thoughtful of you."

"He told me about the advance, Cam, said it was the largest amount Sheppard and Company has ever paid for a book."

"Quite true," Cam replied.

He stepped over to the wardrobe, moving past me as though I weren't there. He dug around, looking for shoes, finally coming up with a pair of badly scuffed black pumps with tarnished silver buckles. His lips tightened. His eyes were a steely blue.

"Goddamn!" he exclaimed. "These are scuffed, caked with dirt. I thought keeping my things in order was part of your job."

"And copying your manuscript and cooking your food and warming your bed and picking up after you and—"

"Shut up, Miranda. I'm not in the best of moods. I might just say or do something both of us would regret."

"I'm not in the best of moods, either. Mr. Sheppard told me the book is due in less than a month. You've hardly begun it. You—"

"I'm warning you," he said.

"What did you do with the money, Cam?"

"You really want to know?" he asked.

"I want to know."

"I used it to rent a very elegant house in the country, just outside London. I took a three-month lease—that should be long enough, I figure. The rest of it went for perfume, a number of elegant satin gowns and eight barrels of gunpowder. Are you satisfied?"

"I—I don't believe you."

"Believe what you like," he said.

He stalked out of the room. I heard him go downstairs, heard him banging about in the kitchen. I stared at the empty bed awash with sunlight, a terrible hollow feeling in my stomach, an aching pain in my heart. I wanted to give way to tears and revel in my misery, but I was too stubborn. I steeled myself, took a deep breath and went down to the kitchen. He was sitting at the table, moodily sipping a cup of coffee.

"What's happening, Cam?" I asked quietly. "You promised me you'd give up this insane nonsense. You—"

"I made no such promise."

"I don't intend to put up with this," I said.

He set his coffee cup down very carefully and turned to look at me with hard blue eyes. He was cold, remote, a stranger.

I felt a chill, and all my instincts warned me to let it drop, let it be, but I couldn't do that. He stood up, resting his hands lightly on his thighs.

"And what will you do?" he inquired.

"I'll leave," I said.

"Indeed. And what would you do, take up your old profession? Aren't you afraid you might have lost your touch?"

"I don't think I'd need to pick pockets, Cam."

"No?"

"I don't imagine it would be too difficult to find another man to take me in."

"You'd do that, would you?"

"In a minute," I lied.

He moved across the floor with the speed of lightning, four quick strides and he was in front of me, his eyes a fiery blue, blazing with fury. I took a step backward, flinching. He raised his arm, slammed his hand across my cheek with such force that I fell against the wall. He struck me again, again, each blow fierce, savage. I cried out, my ears ringing, my face afire. He grabbed my throat and began to throttle me, and I kicked his shin and raked my fingernails across his cheek. He let go of my throat. I sank to the floor, gasping and coughing. He seized my hair, yanked me back up, crushed me into his arms and slammed his mouth over mine.

I pounded his chest and shoved at him, desperately trying to break free. He released me, panting. I doubled up my fist and drove it into his stomach with all my might. I kicked him again, and this time he cried out. I darted across the kitchen and seized one of the pans hanging on the wall and hurled it at him. He ducked. The pan crashed against the wall just above his head. I grabbed another. He leaped toward me and seized my wrist and gave it a brutal twist and the pan clattered to the floor.

"You son of a bitch!" I cried.

"Leave me, would you! Take up with another man!"

"Damn right I would!"

"Not bloody likely, my girl!"

"Let go of me!"

"You belong to me, you little wildcat!"

"I belong to no one!"

"I'd kill you before I'd let you—"

"Try, you sod! Just—"

He stopped me with his mouth, seething with passion now,

tense, fully erect in his breeches. He kissed me with a vengeance, punishing me with his mouth and tongue, and then he swept me up into his arms and carried me down the hall and dumped me onto the sofa in the sitting room. I tried to get up. He shoved me back and whipped up my skirts and fell on me and took me with an unbridled lust that left me bruised and breathless. Tears spilled over my lashes, and, spent, he frowned and kissed away the tears and cradled me to him, gently stroking my hair.

I cried silently, clinging to him, and Cam held me close, his hand moving over my hair, smoothing it. He lifted it, caressing the back of my neck, and I tilted my head back, looking up at that sharp, lean, beloved face. There was a deep furrow above the bridge of his nose, and his lips were pressed tightly together, turned down at the corners. I could tell that he was shaken by what had happened, by what he had done to me. He pulled me closer and I buried my face in the curve of his shoulder and he held me very, very tightly, as though he feared he might lose me. I rubbed my palms over his back, feeling warm skin beneath the thin cloth, feeling the strong curves of muscle, and his arms tightened even more, telling me what he could never bring himself to tell me in words, reassuring me of emotions he would never admit. We were closer then than we had ever been, and it was worth the pain, worth the humiliation to have this silent affirmation of his love.

I leaned back against the cushions, his body heavy atop mine, his face inches from my own. I lifted my hand and touched the four thin red streaks where I had clawed him. He winced. I kissed his cheek, kissed his chin, kissed those thin, cruel lips, and he shifted his weight, curling an arm around the back of my neck and touching my throat with his fingertips. My throat was sore and both my cheeks still burned from his blows. My whole body felt bruised and broken, yet I was filled with a marvelous languor, a delicious glow that streamed through my veins, warm and wonderful and tantalizing.

"I—I shouldn't have said that," I whispered.

"You shouldn't have," he agreed.

"I could—could never leave you, Cam."

"I wanted to kill you."

"You almost did."

"The thought of another man touching you—"

He scowled and kissed me long and hard and I squirmed beneath him, trying to alleviate the pain of his weight bearing down on me. He parted my lips with his and thrust his tongue inside my mouth and waves of sweet agony swept over me and I was drowning in sensation. Cam raised his head and looked at me again and scowled again, strong and stern and in command and not about to show any sign of weak, unmanly emotion. He took me again, slowly, deliberately, giving me the pleasure he had denied earlier, and for all his control there was tenderness in every stroke, the final, brutal thrust plunging me into a shattering oblivion of bliss. He shuddered and went limp, using my body as a cushion, and the glorious ashes of aftermath warmed us both.

Later, much later, we were back in the kitchen and Cam was at the table eating the food I'd prepared for him and I was wearing another dress and my face was clean, my hair newly brushed. He'd brushed his hair, too, and it gleamed a dark blue-black and he looked very sober as he devoured the food. Worked up quite an appetite, I thought, smiling to myself. Cam glanced up and saw my smile and gave me a grim, reproving look. Lovely, savage Scot, not nearly as fierce as he pretended to be, and I gave as good as I got. There was a nasty bruise on his shin, and those claw marks were going to be on his cheek for several days. Good thing I hadn't *really* tried to hurt him.

"Finished?" I inquired.

"Delicious," he said, "particularly the cake."

"Mrs. Wooden sent it over. It's her specialty."

"You've been spending quite a lot of time with her, haven't you?"

I nodded, removing the dishes from the table and setting them on the draining board. Cam moved his chair back and folded his arms across his chest, slouching indolently with his shoulders resting against the back of the chair, his long legs stretched out in front of him. Chin tilted down, the heavy black wave slanting across his brow, he raised his eyes, watching me as I stacked the dishes. He looked like an indolent pasha, I thought, well fed and pampered. What a pleasure it was to pamper him.

"I assume she's the one who's been teaching you to speak properly," he said.

"So you *have* noticed?"

"Couldn't help noticing, could I?"

"You didn't say anything."

~300~

"Didn't think it was necessary."

"She's giving me all sorts of lessons. I'm learning how to walk properly and how to use tableware and how to select wines. Last week I learned the proper way to eat an artichoke. Seems an awful lot of trouble for so little satisfaction, all those leaves you have to pull off. We've set up a reading program, too. She owns thousands of books."

"And what's the purpose of all this?"

"Why, to make a lady out of me."

"That's what you want to be? A lady?"

"I—I want to be someone you can be proud of, someone you wouldn't be ashamed to be seen with."

"I've never been ashamed of you, Miranda," he said quietly.

"I know, but—"

"I like you just the way you are."

"A person has to grow. A person has to—"

"You're utterly unique," he said, looking at me with hooded lids. "You're also extremely appetizing in that pale pink dress."

"It's not as pretty as the one I had on earlier."

"Your cheek's a bit swollen. There are faint bruises on your throat. I really gave you a beating, didn't I?"

"I—suppose I provoked you."

"You're a most provoking wench. You ever talk about leaving me again and I'll beat you twice as hard. You'll be black and blue for a week."

"You—like having me around, then?" I asked cautiously.

"If I didn't, I would have thrown you out months ago."

"Cam—"

He frowned, afraid I was going to turn sentimental and demonstrative. Cam Gordon would face a pack of armed robbers without turning a hair, would stand in front of a firing squad without the slightest display of emotion. He feared neither man nor beast, yet he was desperately afraid of any overt display of affection, any expression of tender sentiment. Grim, thorny, he carried Anglo-Saxon restraint to an absurd degree and would go to the stake before admitting that he felt as other men did. It was part of his enigma and, strangely enough, one of the things that made him so endearing and vulnerable.

"What time is it?" he asked.

"It must be almost seven. You—you aren't going out again, are you?"

"Not tonight," he said. "I have—everything under control."

There was a slight hesitation in his voice. We were on dangerous ground again, but I wasn't content to let the matter drop.

"You won't be seeing your rebel friends, then?"

"Not for a while," he replied.

"It—it's just that I worry so."

"You don't need to worry, Miranda."

"You didn't really buy gunpowder, did you?"

"I had to tell you something."

"All that talk about renting a house, buying perfume and satin gowns. You were trying to make me think you had another woman."

"Maybe so," he drawled lazily.

"I'd scratch her eyes out."

"Would you?"

"I certainly would!"

He liked that. His thin lips curled in a lazy half-grin, and his eyelids were heavy, half-veiling his eyes as he studied me. The eyes told me clearly what was on his mind. I felt a purely feminine satisfaction, a sense of power that only that look in a man's eyes can give.

"Come here," he ordered. There was a husky catch in his voice.

"What do you want?"

"I want an encore."

"You hardly touch me for two weeks, and suddenly you can't get enough of me."

"We have the whole evening before us. I'm going to take you upstairs and show you a few new wrestling holds."

"Not tonight you're not," I said.

"No?"

"You're going upstairs, all right, and you're going to work on *Spoils*."

"Am I indeed?"

"And if you're very, very good, if you do at least ten pages, I may permit you to show me those holds."

"I have a powerful yen, Miranda."

"Sublimate," I told him.

"Jesus! Where'd you learn that word?"

"I've learned a lot of new words."

"Can't say I care for all this learning. It's mucking you up, making you altogether too cocky."

"Get to work, Cam."

"Making you bossy, too. I'm boss around here, remember."

"Ten pages," I said. "At least."

He gave me another fierce look, but he went upstairs and he took out the manuscript and started to work. Content, glowing with happiness, I read downstairs in the sitting room, finally putting the book aside and thinking about the day and all that had happened, nourishing the love that shimmered inside, as inebriating as the headiest wine. How lucky I was, how very lucky. He wasn't easy to live with, no. He was an impossible man, moody, enigmatic, violent, full of faults, but he was mine and I loved him beyond all reason.

He was still working when I went upstairs. The quill was fairly flying across the page, and there were several wads of paper on the floor and he was gritting his teeth, eyes flashing dark blue as he visualized the scene he was committing to paper. I went into the bedroom and removed my clothes and climbed into bed, falling asleep soon after, and several hours must have gone by before the mattress sagged and the springs creaked and I awoke to find him crawling in beside me. He pulled me into his arms and I sighed, only half awake, and he covered me with his body and nuzzled my throat with his nose and I wrapped my arms around his smooth, naked back and wound my legs around his.

"Ten pages?" I asked sleepily.

"Twenty," he told me.

His body was warm and heavy and the skin across his shoulders was moist and he smelled faintly of perspiration, a delicious, virile musk as potent as the strongest aphrodisiac. The room was in darkness, only a few shimmering silver-gray moonbeams stealing through the windowpanes. He caught my earlobe between his teeth and I struggled and we tussled for a moment and he applied one of his wrestling holds and trapped me flat beneath him and I was helpless, his willing captive. He spread my arms wide and pinioned them to the mattress and stretched over me, our stomachs pressing together.

"Twenty pages," I whispered. "Guess you're entitled to your encore."

"Two," he murmured.

"Sure you're not too tired?" I teased.

"I'm raring to go."

"You're raring, all right."

"You noticed."

"I noticed. Oh, Cam—"

"Number one," he said.

24

THE CLERK SHOWED ME DOWN THE HALL AND RAPPED
lightly on the door and opened it for me. A lot politer than
he'd been to me the first time, he was, treated me like I was
someone important. I thanked him in my grandest manner and
stepped nimbly into the office, clutching the manuscript as
though it were the most valuable of art objects. The office was
as grand as I remembered—that rich golden wood gleaming
like dark honey, the green velvet drapes ever so elegant, soft
brown leather chairs inviting—and this time Mr. Thomas Sheppard popped right up and hurried around the enormous mahogany desk to greet me.

"Miss James," he said. "This is an unexpected pleasure."

I nodded politely, all dignity, very conscious of my new
polish and poise. I was Miss Miranda James now, elegantly
attired in a lovely silk frock of the palest cream with thin bronze
stripes, my hair artfully arranged in upswept copper waves,
three ringlets dangling in back. Took me forever to get it pinned
up, it did, and the ringlets were hell, but I felt quite the young
lady of fashion. Mr. Sheppard smiled, and there was a definite
twinkle in his eyes. Did he find my new mode and manner
amusing?

"I told you I'd bring you the early chapters, Mr. Sheppard,"
I said, employing my most refined tones. "I have here almost
two hundred pages of *The Spoils of Dowland*. He should easily
have it finished by June fifteenth."

"You think so?"

"I intend to *see* that he does."

Sheppard smiled, relieving me of the manuscript and placing
it on the smooth surface of the desk beside the silver and onyx

inkwell. He was dressed in a pale tan suit, a mustard silk neckcloth at his throat. His large blue-gray eyes still twinkled, and those old-parchment cheeks were flushed a faint pink. He was quite pleased to see me, and why not? He had half of Cam's book in his hands now with every expectation of receiving the rest within the next two weeks.

"Apparently you're a very good influence on him," he said.

"I try to be."

"Gordon has rarely worked so well. He's usually shockingly late turning in his manuscripts."

"He has some very bad habits. I'm trying to break him of them."

"Oh?"

"It's a tremendous task," I admitted.

"Won't you sit down, Miss James? Could I have my clerk bring you a cup of tea?"

I was honored. He would never have offered Duchess Randy a cup of tea. I shook my head nevertheless, eager to be gone. Nervous as all get-out, I was, a tremulous feeling inside despite my admirable poise.

"I know how valuable your time is, Mr. Sheppard, and I won't take any more of it. I just wanted to bring the manuscript myself. I wouldn't trust none of them—uh—any of those messenger boys with it. It's much too precious."

"I'm eager to read it."

"It's terribly exciting. Got quite caught up in it when I was copying it. A bit too much torture and bloodshed for my taste, but his readers seem to love it."

"They do, indeed," Sheppard agreed. "*Do* sit down, Miss James. I want to talk to you about your own book."

Here it comes, I thought, a sinking sensation in the pit of my stomach. I had been jittery about it all morning, had dawdled on Fleet Street, building up my courage, hoping against hope he'd have the tact not to mention it. Thoroughly miserable, I sat down on the edge of one of the deep leather chairs and folded my hands primly in my lap, trying to look casual. I didn't dare sit back in the chair, afraid I'd sink into the soft leather. Back straight, my expression composed, I gazed at the spines of the lovely books displayed behind his desk, dreading what I knew was to come.

"I read it," he said.

"Did you?"

"I read it twice, in fact. I took notes the second time."

"It—it was awful, wasn't it?" I said glumly.

"I'm afraid it was, Miss James."

"I told you it would be a waste of time."

"Not at all," he said.

I stared at him, puzzled. Mr. Sheppard smiled, looking for all the world like a dapper, dried-up little pixie. I adjusted the long ringlet that dangled over my shoulder. It was beginning to grow limp, and the waves were beginning to slip, too. What ever had possessed me to attempt such a pretentious style? I must look as ridiculous as I felt.

"What—what do you mean?" I asked.

"You have a great deal of talent, Miss James."

"The book was awful. You just said so."

"Indeed it was—stilted and contrived and artificial—but the prose style was quite vivid. I could *see* your characters, dreary as they were, and I could see the park and the manor house, although I must say you botched up a number of details. It's quite obvious you've never been in a grand ballroom, never heard a lady issue instructions to one of the servants. 'Run put the kettle on, Meg,' gave me quite a chuckle."

A blush tinted my cheeks. Why didn't he just take out a knife and stab me in the heart? It would have been kinder. Quicker, too. He clasped his hands behind his back and paced slowly back and forth, warming to the subject.

"It was perfectly clear that you were writing about something you knew absolutely nothing about, a society you've never even glimpsed in passing. The plot was preposterous—what there was of it—and the transitions were most unwieldy. I could hear the wheels grinding."

Wheels? Bloke wudn't even makin' good sense.

"The characters were doing what *you* wanted them to do, not what they would do themselves—had they been real enough in the first place to have motivations and wills of their own. I could feel the author in the background, putting them through their paces."

"So you think I should give up writing," I said.

"Quite the contrary."

"Maybe I could go into a convent and do penance."

Sheppard chuckled, delighted. Whatever made me think he was a nice man? I stood up, cheeks a bright pink now. I might have the appearance of a young lady of fashion, but Duchess Randy lurked dangerously near the surface. Took all the control

I could muster to keep from tellin' him what he could do with his fancy criticisms.

"I'd best be on my way, Mr. Sheppard."

"Writers," he said, shaking his head. "They're all so sensitive. I once made the mistake of telling Gordon one of his chapters needed a small revision. I thought he was going to murder me."

Pity he didn't, I said to myself.

"He turned pale and banged his fist on the desk and ranted for a good twenty minutes. Gave me quite a turn. Artistic temperament, I suppose it's part of the magic. I suspect you have your share of it."

"I knew the book was bad, Mr. Sheppard," I said heatedly. "I didn't want you to read it in the first place. Unless my memory fails me, you practically *wrested* it out of my hands."

"That I did, and I'm very glad."

"Everyone needs a few chuckles."

"I want you to write a story for me, Miss James."

I gazed at him, utterly startled.

"I should be drawn and quartered for attempting a novel, and you want me to write a *story*?"

Sheppard nodded, ever so pleased with himself.

"You're not ready for a novel yet, that's—uh—a little beyond your scope just now, too ambitious an undertaking, but you have a very genuine talent and I would like to be the one to develop it."

I sat back down, slumping against the back of the chair and forgetting all about poise and posture.

"Genuine talent?" I said. "Me?"

"I have the feeling that, were you to attempt something a little less difficult and were to write about a subject familiar to you, you could write a very good story indeed."

"You *do*?" I'm afraid it was a squawk. Mrs. Wooden would have thrown her hands up in horror.

"I do, indeed. Would you be interested in trying?"

"I dunnow. Writin's 'ard as—writing is very difficult, an'—and I'd be scared to death, knowin' you were going to read it."

"Nonsense," he said.

"The whole idea's scary."

"As I believe I told you, I publish a number of magazines. Have you ever seen *The London Reader*?"

I shook my head, still dazed. Mr. Sheppard moved behind his desk, opened a drawer and took out three of the most recent issues, bringing them over to me. I took them reluctantly, as though I were afraid they might bite.

"*The London Reader* comes out twice a month," he explained, "and each issue contains stories concerning various aspects of life in the metropolis. I'd like for you to read the stories in these issues and get an idea of how they're done, then write one yourself."

"About London?"

"There are stories about shopkeepers, stories about chimney sweeps, stories about dockhands and barristers and actors—about all kinds of people who live in the city."

"I don't know anything about shopkeepers or chimney sweeps."

"Then write about what you *do* know," he said. "The stories are relatively short, no more than fifteen or twenty pages. I'd be most interested in seeing what you come up with, Miss James."

"Even after readin' my novel?"

He smiled. "Even after that."

I stood up again. One of my fancy waves had come loose, spilling across my brow. I shoved it back and, plucking out a pin, pinned it back in place, dignity quite gone.

"You'll try?" he asked.

"I ain't makin' any promises," I said, forgetting every single thing Mrs. Wooden had taught me.

I took the magazines home, however, and that night, while Cam toiled away in his study upstairs, I read several of the stories. *The London Reader* was an attractive, if unimpressive, magazine, printed on inexpensive paper and lavishly illustrated wtih woodcuts and engravings. Some of the stories were good indeed, some merely passable, some so tedious I couldn't read more than one or two paragraphs. All of them featured a central character whose work or mode of living illustrated something about city life, and when I finally put the magazines aside, I knew I couldn't possibly write anything Mr. Sheppard would find suitable. Shopgirls who sold ribbons and were swept to the altar by handsome bucks who discovered them behind the counter, chimney sweeps who were taken in by kindly old gentlemen, fishmongers who slit open oysters to find pearls and moved to the country—fairy tales all, written to please the public and, in my opinion, every bit as artificial and contrived as the novel I'd begun.

The only London I really knew anything about was St. Giles, and there were no happy endings there, that was for bloody sure. Wouldn't do me much good to write about *that*, would it? Pickpockets and whores, ruffians and beggars, children who starved or went blind from gin—not exactly the stuff fairy tales were made of. Mr. Sheppard meant well and I appreciated his interest, but I would be much better off copying Cam's work, helping him with his spelling and putting all ideas of writing out of my head. For the next few days I did just that. Cam was working so hard and producing so much that it was all I could do to keep ahead of him, making legible copies of those messy, scrawled-over pages. No sooner had I finished with one batch than he handed me another.

Nevertheless, a worrisome seed had been planted in my mind, and I kept remembering the two small children I had seen coming out of the gin shop that day when the wild hog had left Fleet Ditch and came charging down the street pursued by a mob of women. Both children had been blond, the little girl holding her half pint of gin as though cradling a doll, and the mob of women had almost trampled them. I remembered the look on the little girl's face when she dropped the bottle, and as the days passed it seemed to haunt me. A story gradually began to take shape, of its own volition, it seemed, for I didn't dwell on it and was much too busy to give it any real thought. When I least expected it, when I was working with Mrs. Wooden or changing the bed linens or copying Cam's work late at night, bits and pieces came to me, snatches of dialogue materializing, vivid images flashing in my head. I knew that little girl. I knew her history. I knew her fate. I had to write about her.

A week went by, and one Thursday morning I opened my secretary and sat down and stared out the window. Mrs. Wooden had gone out to do some much needed shopping, so we would not be working, and Cam was fast asleep after working all night long. It was a gray day, the sky wet and threatening, the courtyard dim and shadowy without sunlight. Reluctantly, I took out paper and ink pot and quill. I sharpened the quill, delaying the inevitable. I straightened the paper, examining the watermarks as though they held immense fascination for me. I polished the paperweight and studied my fingernails and, finally, when I could delay no longer, I sighed heavily, dipped quill in ink and wrote a title across the top of a page: "The Gin Girl."

My little girl was ten years old and her name was Betty and she lived in a foul basement with her adored younger brother, her vicious, gin-sodden parents and two other families. It was Betty's job to fetch the gin each morning, and she vowed that someday, somehow she was going to get away from St. Giles, take little Joey with her and make a better life for them. The gin she carries to the basement every day symbolizes to her all the evil and despair of the life around her. She refuses even to taste it. Despite the horror and squalor that are her daily lot, she is full of hope, her love for little Joey sustaining her. When, one morning, her parents send Joey to the parish house to be apprenticed to a chimney sweep and inform Betty that she's going to have to earn her keep as best she can, she takes her first sip of gin.

I wrote rapidly, without even thinking of it, the words seeming to spill from the tip of my pen. I lived the story. I saw the rats scurrying over the floor, saw the damp brown mildewed walls of the basement and smelled the stench and heard the shrill voices brawling. I felt the pain when Betty's mother hit her, and I felt that hopeless, bleak despair when she finally relinquished hope and lifted the bottle of gin to her lips. The story wrote itself—I was merely the medium through which it flowed—and five hours later I put quill aside and brushed the tears from my eyes. Shaken, depleted, I stacked the seventeen pages together, pushed them back and closed the secretary.

Cam was awake. I could hear him moving around upstairs. He would be hungry. I went into the kitchen and made coffee and prepared food, and he came in looking fresh and rested. Seeing my expression, he paused, frowning, then asked me if something was wrong. I shook my head. I tried to smile. I continued to put food on his plate. His frown deepened, and he came over to me and I set the plate aside and threw myself into his arms and he held me close, crushing me to him.

"What's all this about?" he asked gruffly.

"It—it's nothing."

"You've been crying, haven't you?"

I nodded. "No—no reason. It's just been such a gloomy day and I've been working so hard and—" I let the sentence dangle.

"I've been driving you."

"You've been driving yourself."

"Almost done now. Another week, a week and a half at the most, and it'll be all finished."

"I never realized what writing—what writing did to you, what it took out of you. I know now why you're so moody and irritable, why you're so distracted and remote."

He arched a brow. "Oh? And what brought on these amazing insights?"

"I was just—just thinking about it, trying to understand."

"Poor Miranda," he said in a deep voice. "You have a lot to put up with, don't you? Moody, irritable, distracted, remote—and that's not the half of it. We writers are a miserable bunch."

"I'm not complaining," I whispered.

"That's a relief. Usually you do nothing else."

"That's not true."

"Usually it's nag, nag, nag, all day long," he teased.

"Liar."

"I have a lot to put up with, too, keeping you in line."

"You're lucky to have me, you sod."

He grinned and tilted his head and lowered it and kissed me, and then he sat down at the table and began to eat, forgetting all about me. There was a faraway look in his blue eyes as he thought about the chapter he was working on, and when he finished his food he got up and wandered out of the room without so much as a word, going directly upstairs to his work. After what I had experienced earlier in the day with my own writing, I was able to understand him much better, and I vowed to be more patient with his moods.

The sun was shining brightly ten days later when I left the house to take the final chapters of *The Spoils of Dowland* to Thomas Sheppard. Having worked nonstop for almost forty-eight hours, poor Cam was in bed and claimed he had no intention of getting out for at least a week. I had been working almost as hard myself, copying the pages, feeding him, keeping him supplied with paper and fresh quills and constant cups of coffee, but I felt a wonderful elation as I went down the narrow passageway and stepped into the brightness and bustle of Fleet Street. He had done it. He had finished the book on time, and he had not left the house a single evening to meet those horrid conspirators. I told myself that he had finally seen the light of

~311~

reason, that giving them that huge sum of money had been his final act, his last contribution to a hopeless, dangerous cause.

Sunlight sparkled on the cobbles and reflected in the windows of all the shops. Carriages and lorries rumbled down the street, horses neighing, hooves clattering noisily. The color and vitality of Fleet was as invigorating as always, and I hurried along as briskly and purposefully as anyone else, carrying priceless pages that would soon be read by thousands, carrying seventeen more that would never be read at all. I had made a neat copy of "The Gin Girl," and I would give it to Mr. Sheppard and he would be utterly appalled and that would be that. Writing the story had been a form of release for me, a means of expressing things that had been pent up inside for years. I had written about what I knew all right—the horror, the despair, the hopelessness endured by almost half the population of London—but I was quite realistic and knew people didn't want the truth. They wanted pretty fairy tales or thundering, violent melodramas like the ones Cam wrote so adroitly.

The bell tinkled merrily as I opened the door. The clerk greeted me effusively and kept me waiting for only a moment as he hurried to inform Thomas Sheppard of my arrival. I gazed at the shelves of lovely new books, longing to read them all, then followed the clerk back down the hall to the office. Sheppard smiled, took the manuscript from me, set it on the desk and took my hands and squeezed them tightly.

"I knew you wouldn't fail me," he said. "My printers are waiting. The presses will soon be turning. The binders will be working overtime. Thousands of Roderick Cane readers will soon be devouring his new book."

"And Thomas Sheppard and Company will be raking in coins," I added.

"Quite true. Why do you think I'm so elated?"

He grinned a pixie grin and squeezed my hands again, and I couldn't help but smile. He told me that I looked exceptionally attractive. I thanked him. I was wearing a simple frock of deep blue cotton, and my hair fell in lustrous coppery waves. No elaborate coiffure today. No foolish airs. Sheppard said that a celebration was in order and asked if I would have a glass of wine. I shook my head.

"I'd better not, Mr. Sheppard."

"I intend to send a case of the finest French to Gordon this very afternoon—must make a note of it. A little token of my appreciation. And how is he, by the way?"

"Utterly exhausted. He claims he's going to sleep for a week."

"And then, I trust, he'll hop right out of bed and start working on yet another novel."

I smiled again. "You're incorrigible," I teased.

"Merely greedy," he replied, "and you, Miss James, how are you doing? Did you read the magazines?"

"I read them, yes, but I'm afraid I could never write the kind of story you want, Mr. Sheppard."

He looked surprised, disappointed as well.

"I—I did do a story," I said hesitantly, "just to see if I could. I wrote it very quickly, much too quickly, but the words just seemed to pour out and—I should have thrown it away, I know, but I made a neat copy and brought it along just—just to show you how wrong you are about me."

"You brought it?"

"It's there, on top of Cam's chapters."

Mr. Sheppard stepped over to his desk and cut the string and removed the brown paper and lifted the story from the large stack of paper. I immediately panicked. He wasn't going to read it now! I glanced apprehensively toward the door, and Mr. Sheppard became very stern and businesslike and ordered me to sit down in a voice that brooked no nonsense. I sank into one of the deep leather chairs, vowing never to step foot inside this office again. Cam could deliver his own manuscripts—he'd done so before, hadn't he? I would never be able to look Mr. Sheppard in the eye after he read those seventeen pages I had copied so carefully. He was reading them now, sitting behind his desk, a grim, critical expression on his face as his eyes moved over the pages in hand. He was going to hate it. He was going to detest every word.

I tapped on the arm of the chair. I brushed imaginary lint from my deep blue skirt. I counted the books on the shelves and watched sunlight slanting through the windows and suffered acute agonies as he read page after page and finally set the last one aside and looked up at me. He didn't say anything. He removed his fine gold-rimmed spectacles and took out a large white handkerchief and dabbed at the corners of his eyes. He was crying. Jemminy! Was it *that* dreadful.

"I don't know what to say, Miss James."

"You needn't say anything," I assured him.

He dabbed his eyes again and put the handkerchief back into his pocket and put on his spectacles. He stacked the pages neatly together and looked down at them and shook his head.

"It's one of the most moving stories I've ever read," he said.

"Moving?"

"It's full of compassion, full of anger as well, and it obviously comes straight from the heart. You know St. Giles. You know what life is like for those who dwell there. You've brought it all vividly to life. I've rarely read anything so graphic, so convincing."

"You—you *like* it?"

"I'm overwhelmed, my dear."

He stood up and came around the desk, clasping his hands behind his back and pacing slowly in his habitual way.

"I'm simply amazed," he said.

"So am I."

"I can hardly believe it was written by one so young."

I gripped the arms of the chair, leaning forward. "I wrote every bleedin' word of it myself!" I cried defensively. "Cam 'adn't even seen it. 'E dudn't know anything about it!"

Sheppard grinned, amused by my outburst. "I know you wrote it, Miss James. I merely meant that it's a—uh—remarkable feat."

The publisher talked on and I gathered myself together and tried to recoup some vestige of dignity, irritated with myself for losing my composure and forgetting my speech, irritated with him for making me do so. He informed me that "The Gin Girl" wasn't at all appropriate for *The London Reader*, was, as a matter of fact, much too good for that particular magazine. He would feature it instead in the next issue of *The Bard*, a far more prestigious publication, and he would pay me the generous sum of two pounds for the privilege of doing so. My ears pricked up at that.

"Two pounds?" I said.

"I'll sign a voucher and have my clerk pay you immediately."

"You really like the story?" I asked.

He assured me that he did, that it was an amazing, remarkable piece that he would take great pride in publishing. I stood up and brushed a heavy coppery-red wave from my temple and smoothed down my blue skirt. Sheppard continued to praise the story, and when he finished I told him that since it was so good, so remarkable, he'd better pay me five pounds instead of two.

His eyes widened in shock. He enumerated all the reasons why it would be absolutely impossible for him to pay such an outrageously high price for such a short piece of fiction, and I smiled again and politely enumerated all the reasons why I couldn't possibly accept less. Ten minutes later, worn, flustered, wearing an expression that could only be called martyred, he signed a voucher and his clerk gave me five pounds.

"This is robbery," he complained.

"I know," I said, "but next time you can pay me ten."

"Ten!"

Mr. Sheppard shook his head and informed me that all writers were in league against him, plotting his downfall, planning to bankrupt him. He was turning gray, growing old before his time, all because of these unreasonable and unruly creatures who plagued him, and he would undoubtedly end up in debtor's prison. His tirade was quite delightful, going on at length, and when he finally finished I gave him a mischievous smile. He sighed in disgust and adjusted gold-rimmed spectacles and, finally, grinned.

"Shameless creature. Baiting me like that."

"Do you really think readers will like my story?" I asked.

"I expect it to cause a sensation. I imagine I'll have to run off twice my usual number of copies of *The Bard*."

"Then five pounds wasn't so steep, was it?"

"A bargain," he confessed. "You know, behind that very charming exterior there's a very tough young woman. I'd as soon negotiate with Genghis Khan, I assure you."

I smiled again, considering his words a compliment. "I've had to be tough most of my life," I told him. "It was a question of survival. Old habits die hard."

Mr. Sheppard took my hands again and squeezed them, then opened the office door for me. I moved past him with a soft rustle of skirts, and he escorted me down the hall.

"You're going to be a very successful writer, Miss James," he told me.

"Oh, I don't know that I'll ever be able to write anything else. 'The Gin Girl' just—just happened. It was something I had to do. I don't imagine I could ever be a real writer, like Cam. It'd be much too difficult, I'm sure."

"Writing is in your blood, my dear. You'll write more. You won't be able not to write. By the way, we still haven't settled the question of your name."

"My name's Miranda James. Thought you knew that."

~315~

"No, no, I mean the name we will use on the story. We couldn't possibly publish it under a woman's name."

"Why not?" I inquired.

"Women don't write," he explained cautiously. "Women cook and sew and take care of men or else they become old maids. They're an inferior sex, you see, quite necessary and often decorative but incapable of thinking about anything weightier than hair ribbons. A few bluestockings turn up now and then, it's true, but they're freaks of nature and have the distinction of thinking like men."

We were in the front shop now, standing beside a table of books, and I was on the verge of making a very heated rejoinder when Mr. Sheppard hastily assured me that these weren't *his* sentiments, far from it, but reflected the prevailing attitudes of society. If "The Gin Girl" were published under my own name, it would not be read, for no one named Miranda could conceivably write anything that would interest readers of *The Bard*. Though I was loath to admit it, I was realist enough to see his point.

"I wouldn't want to use my own name anyway," I said. "I—I'm not sure how Cam would react if he found out I'd written something. He's so sensitive, and—I fear he shares the prevailing attitudes about the 'inferior' sex. As far as Cam is concerned, women were created soley to satisfy his domestic and sexual needs."

Mr. Sheppard blushed slightly at my use of the word "sexual," prim bachelor that he was. He nervously brushed at the lapels of his frock coat and began to suggest a number of masculine pseudonyms. I didn't like any of them at all and told him I didn't *feel* like a Michael Jordon or a Malcolm Johnson and asked if we couldn't simply use my initials. "M.J." would be rather intriguing, I thought, and it certainly wouldn't betray my gender. Worn down, looking martyred again, Mr. Sheppard wearily agreed.

"I'd like to say that it's been a pleasure doing business with you," he said dryly.

"I've enjoyed it immensely," I assured him.

"Please give Gordon my best regards. Tell him I'm eager to discuss the next Roderick Cane with him."

"After this afternoon I have the feeling it might be more profitable for him if you discussed it with *me*," I teased.

The publisher turned pale, and then, seeing my grin, he sighed and shook his head again and grinned himself. The bell jangled merrily overhead as he opened the door for me. He said he certainly hoped I would be bringing him another story before long, and I told him we would have to wait and see. I fairly danced down Fleet Street. I was a writer! Me. Randy from St. Giles, pickin' pockets for a living less than a year ago. I had written something that was actually going to be published in a magazine, and I'd been paid for it, too. Five pounds! Five whole bloomin' pounds! It was the very first money I had ever earned honestly, and it seemed like a bleedin' fortune.

I longed to rush home and wake Cam up and tell him all about it, but I couldn't do it, of course. Cam was the creative one, the temperamental artist, a role he relished and frequently played to the hilt. He wouldn't take kindly to having another writer under the roof. I was certain of that. Sod would probably think I was trying to compete with him, and that wouldn't do at all. No, men being what they were—Cam in particular— "The Gin Girl" and its true authorship would have to remain my secret.

25

IT WAS BY FAR THE LOVELIEST GOWN I HAD EVER SEEN, a deep, deep sapphire blue, the satin sumptuous, wonderfully luxuriant. Me, in a gown like this, it beat everything, but Cam had said I was to buy something fancy to celebrate his finishing the book and I hadn't felt like arguing with him. Mrs. Wooden had helped me pick out the cloth—shrewd shopper that she was, she had taken me along to a drapers who specialized in stuffs for theatrical costumes, buying it at a tremendous savings—and then she had marched me to a seamstress who created the gown especially for me, charging next to nothing. The hat I had bought to go with it had actually cost more than the gown, but even so I hadn't used all the money Cam had so generously provided.

I stood in front of the mirror downstairs, preening without shame, admiring the creature in the glass: complexion radiant, blue eyes sparkling, coppery hair gleaming with rich highlights. The elbow-length sleeves were puffed, worn off the shoulder, and the snug, form-fitting bodice was cut shockingly low, exposing an inordinate amount of bosom. Mrs. Wooden had assured me it was quite the style, adding that when you had a splendid set like mine you might as well show them off, so forget the fichu. The full skirt swelled out over six black lace underskirts, the shimmering sapphire folds making a soft, swishing music when I moved. I felt elegant as could be and just hoped I didn't catch a bad cold exposing so much smooth, creamy flesh.

Cam had purchased a new outfit, too, at my insistence, and he was dressing upstairs in the bedroom now. Richard Bancroft would be calling for us in half an hour. We were going to go to the park and promenade with all of the swells, something I'd been longing to do, and then Bancroft was taking us to dine at one of the better coffeehouses. It was an occasion, the first time Cam and I had ever gone out together socially, and I was elated, eager to have him see me in the gown, eager to watch the swells and see the interior of one of the popular eating places. He was certainly taking his time, I reflected. I had hoped he'd be done in time for us to have a glass of wine together before Bancroft arrived.

The lazy brass clock ticked on the mantel. Getting a little nervous now, I was. I could use a glass of that lovely wine Mr. Sheppard had sent over as promised. We'd drunk only two or three bottles these past two weeks, Cam immersed in books about Japan, of all places, furiously jotting down notes as he poured over rare, exotic volumes he had scoured the city to find and purchased at great expense. He had accidently stumbled across a volume entitled *Travels In The Interior of Japan and Some Curious Histories of A Strange and Barbaric Country, By An Englishman* and, fascinated, had driven all the booksellers into a frenzy, demanding they find more books on the subject for him. Engrossed in his research, he had been moody and distracted of late and hadn't paid the least attention to me, hardly aware of my presence except when he had that familiar yen. Then he was *most* attentive.

Impatient now, afraid he might be having trouble with his stock, I went upstairs and stepped into the bedroom. Cam was standing in front of the mirror, scowling irritably, doing his best to fold the neckcloth properly. His new clothes were splendid indeed, and he looked like an angry young Adonis as he fumbled with the heavy silk. Standing silently just inside the doorway, I watched lovingly as, unaware of my presence, he continued to struggle with the sky blue silk.

His new pumps were a glossy black with fine silver buckles, his stockings were the finest white silk. His knee breeches were a dark maroon, as was the frock coat, both garments expertly cut to show off his broad shoulders, narrow waist and long, muscular legs. The coat had a flaring skirt and deep cuffs, frothy cream lace spilling over his wrists. His waistcoat was heavy cream satin with deep sapphire stripes. Tall, lean, as lithe and graceful as a panther, he had never looked so handsome, the elegant clothes enhancing his virility and somehow emphasizing that aura of ruthlessness I had noted the first time I saw him at Tyburn Hill. Finally satisfied with the fold of the sky blue stock, he emitted a heavy sigh and turned around, seeing me for the first time.

"It's still not right," I said.

"What's not right?"

"The neckcloth."

"Damn thing drives me crazy. Can't see the use of 'em. Pure folderol, serves no purpose."

"Here, let me fix it for you."

I moved over to him and fingered the heavy silk, adjusting the folds, and Cam stood very stiffly, gritting his teeth and looking exceedingly impatient. I finished and stood back and nodded with satisfaction, and then I touched his lean cheek and brushed back the ebony wave that slanted across his brow. Cam made a face, refusing to be humored. Surly Scot! Hadn't even commented on my gown. I moved back over to the doorway and turned around, giving him an exasperated look. I wasn't really irritated, just mildly provoked. Sod was probably still thinking about Japan and those fierce sam-ur-something warriors in their funny silk robes. Writers!

"What's the matter?" he asked.

"Not a bloody thing!"

"Shrewish minx. Need a good thrashing."

"Go grab yourself."

"I'd rather grab you," he said.

He was noticing me now, the randy brute. His eyes took in

~319~

my bare shoulders and the swelling expanse of bare bosom, that familiar and not unflattering reaction occuring down below and spoiling the line of his breeches. I repressed a smile.

"What are you smirking about?"

"You."

"I feel like a tailor's dummy in this rig. Damned uncomfortable. The breeches don't fit right."

"They did a while ago."

"Know what I'd like to do?"

"Bancroft will be here in a few minutes, so just put those gamy ideas out of your mind."

"Damn!"

He tugged at his neckcloth in despair. It came unloose. Realizing what he'd done, he looked utterly helpless, then murderous.

"You'll have to do it yourself," I said blithely.

"You're going to pay for this!"

I made a face and went back downstairs, delighted. Might not be attentive and courtly like some men, my Scot, and he might not lavish me with compliments and words of endearment, but I had no real complaint. A veritable stallion he was, unbridled and uninhibited, and had we not been expecting a guest in a matter of minutes, he would have paid me the ultimate compliment with fierce, lusty action far more satisfying than words.

He still hadn't come down when Bancroft arrived a few minutes later. Bancroft gave me a long, approving look as I led him into the sitting room.

"I can hardly believe it," he said. "Is this the ragged, dirty-faced urchin who picked my pocket last winter? You look positively radiant, by far the loveliest creature I've seen all day."

"Thank you, sir."

"Heavens! It talks differently, too. What happened to that shrill squawk that sent shivers up my spine?"

"I've been taking lessons," I said grandly, "and my voice was never *that* bad to begin with. Besides, a gentleman shouldn't remind a lady of her past imperfections."

"I beg your forgiveness, milady. I may be a hopeless boor, but I am, I assure you, a most ardent admirer."

"Bugger you, Bancroft."

He grinned a broad grin and sat down. Big and blond and jovial, he looked handsome and dapper in knee breeches and

~320~

frock coat of soft brown velvet, frothy white lace jabot and beige brocade waistcoat embroidered with brown leaves. His dark brown eyes were warm and playful, his full pink mouth designed for smiles, and his lively, sportive manner was wonderfully engaging. As he leaned back and spread his arms out over the back of the sofa I was reminded more than ever of a great friendly pup.

"Shame on you," I scolded, "staying away so long. It's been weeks since we've seen you."

"I've been frightfully busy, alas, jaunting about the country, looking into possible investments, making heaps of money for those people who're fortunate enough to have me handling their affairs."

"Modest as ever, I see," Cam said, entering the room.

"I say! You look quite the dandy today."

"I feel like an idiot. Tailor insisted on this color, this cut. I'd like to tie him over an ant bed."

Bancroft and I exchanged smiles, and I poured wine for all three of us. I noticed that Cam's neckcloth still wasn't quite right. He gave me a surly look as I handed him his wine.

"This is good wine, Bancroft," he said. "Sheppard sent over a whole case when I delivered the final chapters of *Spoils*."

"Finished it, did you? Phenomenal! Never known you to be so productive. I suspect the lovely Miranda has had something to do with it."

The lovely Miranda sipped her wine demurely, and Cam ignored the remark and began to tell Bancroft of his plans for the next Roderick Cane.

"The coffers are almost empty, and I figure I'd better churn out another one as quickly as possible. What do you know about Japan?"

"Absolutely nothing. Somewhere near China, isn't it? But I *do* know the coffers are almost depleted. I've been meaning to talk to you about it. You have approximately twenty-three pounds between now and starvation, and—"

"Don't be tedious, Dick! Anyway, I ran across this amazing book written by a chap who spent seven years in Japan, and it's full of the most fascinating material. The Japanese are very inventive when it comes to torture. The things they can do with bamboo would chill your blood, and the whole mystique of the samurai warriors is—"

Bancroft groaned, preparing to endure a long harangue, and I excused myself and went upstairs to put on my gloves and hat. The gloves were of frail black lace in a delicate floral pattern, the hat of black velvet with a very broad brim, a huge sky-blue satin bow on one side, white, sky blue and lushious sapphire plumes spilling down the other. It was an exquisite creation, marvelously complimenting my gown, and I felt wicked to have paid so much for it. Could have stolen the thing easy as pie while the clerk stepped into the back room, had it for nothing, but Marcelon would have had apoplexy and those days were behind me.

"—so my hero will have spent twenty years in Japan, an English samurai, and when he returns to England to win back his inheritance, he'll use all his knowledge of the deadly arts to get his revenge. Dealer I know is trying to locate a genuine samurai sword for me, thinks he'll be able to find one before too long—I want to get the feel of one, authenticity, you know—and I've discovered that bamboo will grow quite nicely in English soil. I have a torture scene in mind—"

My bloodthirsty Scot was still going full blast, while the good-natured and genteel Bancroft listened with a combination of amusement and horror. I glanced at the clock, cleared my throat and rudely interrupted.

"I really don't think Richard is interested in hearing all the gory details, Cam," I said.

"On the contrary," Bancroft protested. "I find it utterly absorbing. If the book is half as exotic and violent as it sounds, it'll be wildly successful. One thing about Gordon, he knows his readers and always gives 'em exactly what they crave."

"I was promised a trip to the park."

"And I have a carriage waiting on Fleet," Bancroft said, climbing to his feet. "I must say," he added, "that chapeau is stunning!"

"Thank you, sir."

"Jesus!" Cam exploded, noticing it for the first time. "No wonder I'm going bankrupt!"

"Come along," I said irritably. "You certainly know how to make a girl feel appreciated."

It was a lovely summer afternoon, sunny and warm but not too warm, London wearing its most amiable face with mellow old buildings brushed with shadows and church spires gleaming in the sunlight and pigeons frolicking under trees in the squares. Bancroft was all affability, treating me with a teasing mock-gallantry, and, while hardly affable, Cam was less taciturn than usual. He generously informed me that my chapeau was indeed stunning and added that he'd wring my bloody neck if I bought another one.

"It's that Marcelon Wooden," he grumbled as the carriage turned into the park. "The woman's a dreadful influence."

"Wooden?" Bancroft said. "The actress?"

"She lives in the yellow house across the court," I told him. "She's the one who's been giving me lessons. Do you know her?"

"I've never had the honor of meeting her, but I have seen her—uh—act. Must have been ten years ago—I was a mere lad, of course. Saw her in *Tis A Pity She's A Whore*."

"And?"

"Twas a pity," he said.

We left the carriage in the designated area, Bancroft gave instructions to the driver, and the three of us strolled leisurely up the shady pathway to the promenade. The rhododendrons were in full bloom, blazing pink and white and pale blue-purple on either side of the pathway. Bees droned lazily. The trees cast cool gray-blue shadows over the lush green grass, and leaves rustled pleasantly in the breeze. The promenade was a veritable parade of wonderfully attired men and women taking the air, ambling at a snail's pace the better to show off their splendor, while open carriages moved slowly up and down the roadway adjoining, their occupants in even more splendid attire. I was agog as we took our place in the procession and found it difficult not to gape. Jemminy! So many swells! So many velvets and satins and plumes! It was a pickpocket's paradise, but a plethora of stalwart soldiers and guardsmen assured one that this rarified air wouldn't be contaminated by the undeserving poor or the raffish hoi polloi.

You've come a long way from St. Giles, Randy, my girl, I told myself as I sauntered along in my satin gown and fancy new hat. My gloved hand rested in the crook of Cam's arm, and Bancroft strolled beside me on my left, attentive as could be. Two handsome gentlemen, and me looking just as grand as any of these haughty ladies with their chins so high. Beat all, it did. Big Moll and the girls would hardly believe it. I could hardly believe it myself. If I 'adn't—*had*n't gone to Tyburn that day, I'd still be in rags, lifting pocket watches and snipping off shoe buckles to keep body and soul together. Bless my good fortune, and bless my Scot, too, for he was responsible for it all.

"I say, Cam," Bancroft remarked, "here comes an old friend

of yours. Lady Evelyn Greenwood herself—a vision in watered green silk and black egret feathers."

"God! Where?"

"Luxuriously ensconced in that carriage approaching. Elegant rig, isn't it? Must have cost her a fortune."

Cam peered uneasily as the grand open carriage moved slowly toward us on the roadway, two gleaming ebony steeds prancing in harness. Lady Evelyn was indeed a vision, her green silk gown cut daringly low, diamonds and emeralds sparkling at wrists and throat. The wide-brimmed green silk hat atop her dark gold waves was literally awash with midnight black egret, the feathers sweeping dramatically. The young man at her side was strikingly handsome with dark brown hair, roguish brown eyes and the build of a champion pugilist. Modishly attired in the finest male plumage, he couldn't be older than twenty or so, and his dewy youth made his patroness seem even riper than she was.

"Who's that with her?" Cam asked.

"Her head footman, I believe. Lad named Todd. I didn't recognize him at first without his livery."

"When would *you* have had occasion to see her footman, Bancroft?"

"Oh, after you tossed her aside Lady E. developed an inordinate passion for yours truly. She came to discuss investments and invited me to come home with her. The flesh is weak, I fear."

"I'm shocked, Bancroft! I had no idea you went in for that sort of activity."

"I went in, all right. Lady E. was mad for me for all of seven days. It was the most exhausting week I've spent in years."

As the carriage drew nearer both Cam and Bancroft assumed sheepish expressions and averted their eyes. Lady Evelyn looked livid. I gave her a radiant smile and nodded ever so warmly, would have given her the finger if I weren't a well-bred young lady now. Two bright pink spots blazed on her cheeks as the carriage moved on past. I felt glorious. Lady E. might have a title and jewels and fancy carriages, but I had Cam, and I wouldn't trade places with her for all the wealth in England.

"Sticky, that," Bancroft sighed. "The lady still hasn't gotten over your cruel abandonment. I, alas, was just a passing fancy. *You* she wanted to marry."

"She'll get over it," I said.

"She frequently *did*," Bancroft retorted.

I smiled at his wit, but Cam turned all stiff and sullen, not one to appreciate that kind of humor, particularly if he happened to be the butt of it. Bancroft delighted in teasing him almost as much as I did, and I suspected that few were allowed such liberty. At the moment he looked as though he would enjoy murdering both of us.

Cam's humor wasn't improved when, a short while later, a troop of militia came into view, their scarlet coats vivid in the sunlight, their powerful white horses pacing impatiently under the restraint imposed upon them. The soldiers rode in front and in the rear of a dazzling white open carriage with a coat of arms emblazoned on the side. Everyone on the promenade stopped dead still. A buzzing of whispers filled the air, for the carriage contained the Duke of Cumberland and the most spectacularly beautiful woman I had ever seen.

Fat, sluggish, pouting, his tiny pig eyes squinting, the Bloody Duke wore white satin breeches and frock coat with diamond buttons, fine white lace cascading from his throat and wrists. His white satin waistcoat strained around his girth like an exquisite sausage skin, and his puffy hands clutched a silver-headed cane propped between his knees. His powdered wig was slightly askew. His numerous chins shook with the movement of the carriage. Plump mouth curling disdainfully, he looked neither left nor right and seemed to be miserable despite the presence of the woman at his side.

She wore a gown of pale pink satin, simple and elegant in style, the skirt spreading out like the petals of a rose. Her complexion was flawless, her features those of a goddess. The fragile, beautifully shaped pink lips seemed to droop sadly, and the lovely blue eyes were decidedly pensive. Her dark raven hair gleamed with lustrous blue-black highlights, worn in an unpretentious arrangement of waves and ringlets. One might have expected her to be wearing a fortune in diamonds, but she wore no jewels whatsoever. She needed none. I fancied that Helen of Troy must have looked like this, absolutely breathtaking, so lovely she scarcely seemed real.

"Who *is* she?" I whispered.

"Lady Arabella Dunston," Bancroft told me, "impoverished widow of the late, unlamented Lord Peter Dunston. Because of Lord Peter's mounting debts and his inability to stay away from the gaming tables, the Dunstons retired to the country over eight years ago—at the King's request. Some claimed that Cumberland's interest in Lady A. was a contributing factor."

"They were—" I hesitated.

"Oh, no," Bancroft said. "Young Cumberland was eager, but Lady A. was most unwilling. The King was eager to avoid a scandal, as well as remove a gentleman who was becoming an open embarrassment to the court. Dunston went to his reward two years ago, and Lady A. has only recently returned to London. Cumberland lost no time in renewing their acquaintance."

"And the King no longer objects?"

"There's a vast difference between a thirty-year-old widow without a penny to her name and the demure young wife of a dissolute but exceedingly blue-blooded nobleman. Besides, Cumberland has long since ceased to pay heed to his father's wishes."

During this exchange Cam had been standing as rigid as a statue, seething with hostility that seemed to crackle in the air around him. His hands were balled into tight fists, knuckles white as chalk, and his eyes were a frightening, steely blue. As the first band of scarlet-coated soldiers rode past us, he forced himself to relax, assuming an impassive, inscrutable expression. The gorgeous white carriage came nearer, only yards away now, the coat of arms in gold and ivory, gleaming. Cumberland stared straight ahead. Lady Arabella looked directly at Cam, their eyes meeting, holding. Subtly, almost imperceptibly, she nodded. Cam gave no indication that he'd seen it. The carriage passed on, another band of soldiers bringing up the rear.

Did he know her? Had the nod been merely a gracious gesture? A dozen questions popped into my mind, but instinct told me I'd best not ask any of them. Deeply disturbed by seeing the hated Cumberland, Cam was in a dangerous mood and was likely to remain so for some time. Playful surliness and mock ferocity and artistic temperament were one thing, easy to deal with and frequently stimulating, but this mood was the real thing, the kind of mood he had been in at Tyburn: cold, contained, lethal. Bancroft and I exchanged looks, and he quickly suggested that we move on to Green's Coffee Shop.

"I'm famished," he confessed. "I could eat a whole side of beef all by myself."

"Me, too," I said.

"You'll like the place, Cam. It's just recently opened and already the literati have taken over—place is packed with poets and novelists and journalists. Food's the best in London, coffee's the strongest, the atmosphere wonderfully convivial. I picked it with you in mind."

"It sounds marvelous!" I exclaimed.

"Stop trying to humor me!" Cam snapped. "Both of you!"

We returned to the carriage, and though Bancroft and I chatted amiably, Cam remained grim and silent as we drove through the city. Bancroft talked about the new Corn Exchange just built in Mark Lane and the fortunes to be made there if one invested shrewdly. The smell of fish was overwhelming as we passed Billingsgate, and there was a delay on the Strand due to an overturned lorry. Whips cracked. Horses neighed. Angry voices cried out. We finally moved on, and the carriage stopped in Covent Garden Square a few minutes later. Bancroft dismissed the driver, and we began to stroll through the area, stepping over cabbage leaves and wilted marigolds as we passed the stalls that were closed for the night.

It was growing late. Shadows were gathering. The sky was a pale gray with spreading stains of pink and gold. I admired the mellow, majestic old buildings built by Inigo Jones over a hundred years ago as Bancroft led us through a twisting labyrinth of narrow passageways and alleys until we finally reached Green's. Located in a cul-de-sac impossible to reach by carriage, it had a crumbling Tudor front with soot-blackened oak beams and tan plaster. It was unprepossessing, looked almost disreputable, in fact, but Bancroft led us inside with jaunty confidence and considerable pride at his discovery.

I tried to conceal my excitement as a be-aproned proprietor greeted us rather gruffly and led us toward a choice corner table. I had never been inside a coffeehouse before, had never eaten in a public eating house, although I'd fetched plenty of victuals and carried them back home. What luxury to sit down at a table and have someone wait on you, even if the table was plain oak rubbed smooth with age, the utensils heavy tin, the mugs common pewter. Nothing fancy about Green's, I noted. The flagstone floor was sprinkled with sawdust. The dark oak walls were adorned with battered copper plates. Candles burned in wheel-shaped wooden fixtures suspended from the ceiling, yet the room was still dim.

Filled with smoke, too, it was. A great many men were smoking tobacco, only a few taking snuff, and all of them seemed to be talking at once, angrily, exuberantly, arguing about poetry and philosophy and publishers. Manuscripts abounded, their merits being heatedly discussed, and many tables were littered with the books and pamphlets and newspapers the patrons had brought along with them. I noticed with some alarm that I was the only woman in the place, with the exception of three buxom, jovial barmaids who scurried about pouring drinks and fending off advances.

"I thought this was a *coffee*house," I remarked. "Everyone seems to be having ale or port."

"Coffee's served during the day, coffee and delicious cakes, cheese and bread," Bancroft explained. "In the evenings regular fare is served and we have coffee afterward. Shall we start with oysters on the half shell?"

I nodded, terribly stimulated, drinking in the atmosphere and the wonderful smells of beer and pickles, sawdust and smoke, roast beef and freshly baked bread. The men at the next table were arguing loudly about Christopher Marlowe, comparing him to Shakespeare, and at another table nearby a thin-faced poet with unkempt hair was reading his latest sonnet to a group of shabbily dressed journalists with ink-stained fingers. Cam was sullen and uncommunicative, but Bancroft ignored his mood, intent on showing me a good time. I was uneasy about the oysters. Never had any before. Didn't know how to eat them. Bancroft grinned, squeezed lemon on one, speared it with a fork and twisted it out of its shell. I followed his example, and as the first oyster slid down my throat I had to admit to myself that I'd had greater gastronomical thrills. I forged ahead nevertheless until my plate contained nothing but six pearly, empty shells and a squeezed lemon rind.

"How were they?" Bancroft asked.

"Delicious," I lied.

"They're an acquired taste," he admitted.

"We—we're not having artichoke by any chance, are we?"

"Hadn't planned on it," he told me.

Thank goodness, I said to myself.

The roast beef that followed was marvelous, pink and tender and dripping with natural gravy, the green peas and potatoes lavishly buttered, the bread coarse and crusty and wonderfully tasty. The men drank port with their meal, but I suspected it wouldn't be ladylike for me to have any, so I took off my black lace gloves and placed them in my pewter mug, an action that caused Bancroft to grin again but brought no comment. He insisted that I have the custard for dessert, and it was a revelation, thick and creamy, served with a delectable sauce of brandy, butter and brown sugar poured bubbling hot over the custard.

"I've never had such a meal," I confessed. "I didn't know it was possible to eat so well."

"Ordinary fare," Bancroft said, "though superbly cooked. You'll have to dine at a really grand eating house — gooseliver paté, pheasant, nightingale tongues."

"*Nighting*ale tongues?"

Bancroft nodded gravely, but the merry look in his eyes told me he was teasing. Dark blond hair burnished by candlelight, full pink mouth curving into a grin when I reproved him, he was the most engaging dinner companion imaginable, unlike Cam who had scarcely said a word since we sat down. One of the buxom barmaids came back to the table with a bottle of port, but the men both shook their heads and my black lace gloves still rested limply in the pewter mug. The girl shrugged her shoulders and sauntered away, heavy hips swaying. Our dessert dishes were removed a few minutes later, small plates set before us, and cheese, biscuits and an enormous platter of fruit were brought to the table.

"It was so kind of you to bring us here, Dick," I said.

"The pleasure's all mine. It's not often that I have the privilege of dining with such delightful company."

"Some of us are more delightful than others tonight."

"Excuse me," Cam said abruptly, "there's a chap over there I need to see."

He left the table and moved across the room to speak to a lean, sharp-faced man with rich red-brown hair, frosty blue eyes and thin lips. Sitting all alone against the wall, wearing brown, the man looked to be in his early thirties and, for some reason, reminded me of a fox. He seemed tense, disapproving, and he was almost as sullen as Cam. They exchanged a few words, and then Cam sat down at the table and they huddled together, discussing a very grave matter from the looks of it.

"He's been impossible," I said. "I—I apologize for his rudeness."

"Oh, I'm quite accustomed to Cam's moods, pay no attention to 'em. I learned a long time ago just to ignore him when he turns all silent and surly."

"Seeing Cumberland this afternoon upset him dreadfully."

Bancroft nodded, gazing across the room at the red-haired man with such harsh features.

"I wonder who that can be," I said.

"Probably another scrivener," Bancroft replied. "They're probably comparing notes on bamboo torture. Want some grapes?"

I shook my head. "Do—do you think it could be one of the rebels?"

"Chap does look like a Scot," Bancroft admitted, "that red-brown hair, that sharp, dour face, but not all Scots are blood-thirsty conspirators. I've known one or two who were actually quite genial."

"I think—I think Cam's broken with the rebels."

"Indeed? High time, I should think. Dangerous business."

"He gave them an awful lot of money."

"I know," Bancroft said, reaching for a pear. "I tried to reason with him, but he wouldn't listen. Broke my heart, it did, seeing all that money going to that lot."

"He hasn't gone out at night for a long time—no secret meetings. I just hope he's come to his senses."

Bancroft picked up a knife and began to peel his pear. I watched the two men across the room. The dour redhead had taken out a piece of paper, and both of them were studying it. So he *was* a writer, after all, showing Cam a poem or a page of manuscript. I turned back to Bancroft, relieved, eager to talk to him in private now that we had a chance.

"You should try one of these pears," he said. "They're delicious."

"I couldn't eat another bite. I—there's something I—I'd like to discuss with you, Dick."

"At your service."

"I—I'm a writer, too. I wrote a story. It's going to be published in *The Bard*. Cam mustn't know about it," I added hastily. "You have to promise me you won't tell him."

"*Pas un mot*," he said.

"What?"

"Not a word, milady. You're secret's safe as houses with me. What's your story about?"

I told him about "The Gin Girl" and how I had come to write it and how it was to be published with just my initials. He listened intently, not at all dismayed, and when I had finished he congratulated me and said he wasn't surprised that I should have brains and talent along with so much beauty. I thanked him for the compliment and glanced around apprehensively, afraid Cam might be returning. He and the red-haired man were still sitting at the table across the room, talking intently.

"It's about corn," I said, returning my attention to Bancroft. He looked startled. "Corn?"

"What you were talking about earlier, in the carriage—the new Corn Exchange and the fortunes to be made. That's what I wanted to discuss with you. Mr. Sheppard paid me five whole pounds for the story and I want you to invest it for me."

"Five whole *pounds*?" He sounded amazed.

"And there'll be more, too. I have another idea for a story, all about a little boy who becomes a pickpocket and part of a gang and gets caught and thrown into prison. I should get even more for that one. Seven pounds maybe. Maybe even ten."

"Ten? Incredible."

"I thought I'd turn all my earnings over to you and let you invest them for me. I—I'm sure you get some kind of commission, but that's all right with me. You have to make a living, too."

"Would that all my clients were so understanding," Bancroft said.

He smiled to himself, amused for some reason, and then he shook his head and assured me that he would study the market and invest my money as shrewdly as possible.

"Rely on me, lass. I'll make a wealthy woman of you."

Visions of riches filled my head, and I saw myself riding in a fine carriage I'd paid for myself, wearing lovely clothes I'd purchased on my own. I would buy all the hats I wanted, and I'd buy new furniture, too, and presents for Cam and Mrs. Wooden. Imagine havin' your own money, makin' it yourself, not havin' to rely on anyone else. I'd have my very own ginger jar and would never have to ask Cam for anything. All this from scribbling stories. . . . I vowed to write the story about the pickpocket as soon as possible and then do another and yet another and another after that.

"I'm so glad we came today," I said. "Cam's been so engrossed in those books about Japan I was afraid he'd refuse."

"Refuse?" Bancroft looked surprised. "It was his idea."

"*His* idea?"

"I sent him a message saying I'd like to take the two of you to Green's whenever it was agreeable. I expected him to put me off. He didn't. He replied almost immediately, suggesting we come this evening. He added that you had been wanting to see the promenade, suggested we go there before dining."

"I thought—" I paused. "I thought you had to insist."

"Not at all," Bancroft replied, cutting another slice of pear. "I was surprised, frankly. He's not usually so amenable."

He certainly isn't, I thought, and I frowned, a niggling suspicion beginning to grow. *Cam* had chosen today for our outing, yet he had led me to think it was a terrible inconvenience, a cause for much grumbling and complaint. He reluctantly tore himself away from his books, reluctantly donned his fine attire. He could easily have put Bancroft off until he had completed his research, and yet... Why had he chosen today? Why all that pretense? Was there something I didn't know about?

I turned to look at the two men across the room. They were standing now, the red-haired man preparing to leave. He hadn't ordered a meal, I saw, just a glass of ale. Could... could he have come here especially to meet Cam, the "casual" meeting carefully prearranged? That piece of paper they'd been studying so closely, could it have something to do with the plot to assassinate Cumberland? Could Cam have known beforehand that Cumberland would be at the park today with Lady Arabella? No, no, the whole idea was ridiculous. The red-haired man was undoubtedly a poor scrivener, as Bancroft had said, and Cam would never have gone to the promenade if he had even suspected Cumberland would appear. The mere sight of the Bloody Duke had put him in the blackest of moods.

"Is something wrong?" Bancroft asked.

"I—I was just thinking."

"Frowning, too."

"Please forgive me. I was being—quite foolish."

Cam returned to the table a few moments later. The fruit and cheese were replaced by a plate of tiny iced cakes and large brown cups filled with steaming hot coffee. It was rich and strong and delicious. Cam was in a much improved humor as we drank it, talking with Bancroft and actually making an effort to be agreeable. Foolish indeed to have entertained those suspicions, I thought. He had made a great to-do about going out today, yes, grumbling and carrying on, but Cam loved to dramatize himself and was frequently disagreeable just for the sake of being disagreeable, hoping to aggravate me. It was a kind of teasing, a game both of us enjoyed and played to the hilt. He had had no ulterior motives in choosing today for our outing. I had been terribly unfair to him, thinking those thoughts,

~332~

but I would make it up to him when we got home, I vowed, and he would never know what brought on the sudden amorous onslaught.

He looked so elegant in the maroon frock coat and striped waistcoat and sky blue neckcloth. The neckcloth was still a bit crooked, bunched up under his chin. The harsh, handsome face was all lean planes, sharp and formidable, a face that would intimidate strangers, fascinate women. The frosty blue eyes gleamed with intelligence as he talked to Bancroft, and somehow the heavy ebony wave slanting across his brow emphasized that air of ruthlessness. Not exactly a charmer, my Scot, not warm and amiable and engaging like Bancroft, but I wouldn't change a thing, I decided. Watching him, proud and full of love, I was eager to get home, eager to tease him and cause that bulge in his breeches again and engage in another of our passionate wrestling matches that he always won.

"More coffee?" Bancroft asked.

"None for me," I told him, reaching for my gloves.

"Nor me," Cam said. "We'd better leave, Dick. I want to make some more notes tonight."

"You're really enthused about this Japanese book, aren't you?"

"I want to start it as soon as possible, write it as quickly as I can. I need to replenish the coffers."

"Won't argue about that, mate."

We got up to leave. Bancroft went over to pay the bill and speak to the proprietor as Cam led me toward the door. The candles flickered, casting wavering yellow-gold light over the dark oak walls. The place wasn't nearly so crowded now, not nearly so noisy. As we reached the open area beyond the tables, the front door opened and two men came in, one of them stout and grumpy, wearing a shabby, poorly fitting navy blue coat and a dirty gray wig like a barrister's, the other man tall and blond and magnetic, laughing at some remark his companion had just made. He turned. He saw me standing there with Cam. His wonderfully expressive eyes filled with surprise, then delight, and my heart seemed to leap as he hurried over.

"The fair Miranda!" he exclaimed.

Cam bristled. Oh, Jesus, I thought. Bancroft sauntered over to join us, one brow arched in inquiry.

"We meet again," Garrick said.

I nodded. I tried to smile. I couldn't. David Garrick looked at me, looked at Cam and Bancroft, sizing up the situation.

~333~

His eyes were full of speculation now, full of mischief, too, and a smile played on those marvelously chiseled lips. He was wearing dark blue velvet breeches and matching frock coat. Both had seen better days, and the lace that spilled from neck and wrists was definitely tattered. One sleeve was badly ripped, and flakes of dried plaster were sprinkled across his shoulders. Looked as though he'd put in a hard day of manual labor, he did, and he smelled of sweat and dust and wood shavings, yet David Garrick seemed to carry his own radiance along with him. Although the room was still dim, I had the feeling that we were all bathed in light.

"Fancy meeting *you* here," he said. "Thought you were going back to—Chester, was it?"

I felt my cheeks coloring. "I—I changed my mind."

"She *can* speak! Lovely voice, too. Sam! Sam, come over here. I want you to meet the lass I was telling you about a few weeks ago."

His companion lumbered over, heavy, cumbersome, looking extremely unsociable. His great jowly face was pasty pale and pockmarked. His fleshy lips were petulant, his nose enormous, and his huge, myopic eyes seemed to stare right through me, shrewd and critical and missing nothing. The long, elaborately curled gray wig was greasy, and his dusty navy blue coat was at least two sizes too large. His black silk stock was threadbare. The famous Sam Johnson did indeed resemble a great, disgruntled bear, I thought. Garrick introduced us. Johnson grunted.

"Was I not right?" Garrick asked. "Is she not the fairest creature you've ever feasted your eyes on?"

Johnson studied me, scowling, and several moments passed before he finally passed judgment.

"Passable," he growled. "I've never trusted a woman with red hair. Invariably shrewish, every last one of 'em. I want my poached salmon and mutton with red currant jam, Davy."

"I've heard a great deal about you, Mr. Johnson," I said in an angelic voice. He stared at me as though amazed I would have the effrontery to address him.

"None of it was highly flattering," I continued. "I fear I must agree that you *are* the rudest man in London."

"Touché, Sam! Touché! Isn't she a joy?"

"Impertinent wench, if you want my opinion. It's that red hair."

"Not impertinent, Mr. Johnson," I said sweetly, "merely

unintimidated by your impressive reputation and your boorish manner. I've read several of your pieces and enjoyed them immensely. I found them full of warmth and wit and wisdom."

"Did you, indeed?" he snorted.

"Qualities sadly unapparent in their author," I added.

Johnson blanched, at a loss for words. The surly old bear was clearly unaccustomed to such impertinence, particularly from the lips of a snip of a girl like me. Constantly assured by colleagues and cronies that he was a Great Man of Letters with a tremendous future ahead of him, he took them at their word and played the role with carefully cultivated eccentricity. He was unquestionably a great writer—I had loved his poem "London," had been deeply moved by his account of the life of Richard Savage—but he was also a posturing old fraud.

"Touché again, Sam!" Garrick cried, delighted. "Seems you've finally found someone to call your bluff."

"Bluff, indeed!"

"Sam, you see, is actually the kindest, gentlest of men," Garrick explained. "He lives in constant fear that the world will find him out."

"His secret's safe with me," I said.

Garrick grinned. Johnson glowered, but he looked at me with a new interest, and I thought I detected a tiny gleam of amusement in those shrewd, myopic eyes. Cam was stony-faced. Bancroft was finding it hard to conceal the merriment he felt. There was a moment of awkward silence, and then, remembering Mrs. Wooden's instructions on how to make a proper introduction, I introduced Cam and Bancroft to the other men. Johnson grunted. Garrick made an exaggerated bow.

"Mr. Garrick's an actor," I said.

"That's obvious," Cam snarled.

"I've seen you perform," Bancroft said. "I understand you're forming a new company."

"That I am, and I hope to persuade the fair Miranda to sign up with me. Such beauty would illuminate any stage she cared to grace."

"Miranda is not interested in the stage, Garrick," Cam told him.

"No."

"Not in the least."

Garrick turned to me. "Your uncle, I assume?"

"I'm Miranda's protector," Cam said coldly.

"I'm just a friend," Bancroft added.

"Protector?" Garrick said, eyes twinkling. "It seems our Marcelon was prevaricating quite outrageously that day. I must give her a severe scolding, and *you*, my beauty, must come to the Drury Lane and see what I'm doing with the place."

"I'm afraid Miranda won't have an opportunity to accept your invitation, Garrick," Cam said. His voice was steely. "She's going to be far too busy, I assure you."

Garrick ignored these remarks and, taking my hand, lifted it to his lips and said that seeing me again had been an overwhelming pleasure. Cam tensed at my side, but Garrick was totally unperturbed by the Scot's open hostility. Releasing my hand, he told me that he hoped to have the pleasure again quite soon, and then he took the grumbling Johnson by the arm and led him toward a table in the back of the room. Bancroft said that our carriage would be waiting at Covent Garden Square and tactfully suggested that we move on. Cam nodded curtly, and I felt a strange exhilaration as he took my elbow and marched me outside. He was jealous, actually jealous. You couldn't be jealous unless you cared. I wanted to skip back inside and give Davy Garrick a big hug for bringing this about, but under the circumstances it would have been most ill-advised.

26

MR. SHEPPARD SIGHED WEARILY, ADJUSTED HIS SPECtacles and reluctantly agreed to pay me twenty pounds for the two stories. "Pockets" was the story I had described to Bancroft at Green's three weeks ago, and "The Wages of Sin" was all about a very young prostitute forced to go on the streets at the age of nine, wasted away by disease and drink at fourteen, finding relief at last when she leaps from Tower Bridge and drowns in the Thames. Not happy stories, neither of them, but they reflected the life I had known in St. Giles, and both

~336~

characters were typical of thousands who struggled to survive in the slums of London. Like "The Gin Girl," they seemed to have written themselves, words coming in great torrents. I had spent an afternoon on each.

"You're going to bankrupt me," Sheppard grumbled as he wrote a voucher. "Ten pounds a story! If my other contributors ever found out—" He shuddered at the thought and waved the paper to dry the ink.

"I'd be happy to submit the stories elsewhere," I said sweetly. "After 'The Gin Girl,' I feel sure there are other publishers who would be interested in M.J. Might even pay me more than ten. Might pay twelve. If it's such an imposition—"

"Don't even consider it!" he protested. "You wait here. I'll go fetch the money myself."

I had to smile as the dapper, flustered little man scurried out of the office. Sheppard might grumble as a matter of course— I suspected that all publishers grumbled from habit as much as anything else—but he wasn't going to risk losing me, not after "The Gin Girl" had proved to be such a tremendous success. The issue of *The Bard* that contained it had come out three days after our dinner at Green's, and it had sold out within hours, had gone back to press not once but three times, all because of "The Gin Girl." The story seemed to have taken literary London by storm, the chief topic of conversation in all of the coffeehouses, the true identity of the mysterious M.J. hotly debated. Several minor scriveners had modestly implied that they were responsible for the piece, though none could provide proof, and Sheppard refused to provide so much as a hint as to the author.

I had been amused to hear that many claimed Samuel Johnson had written it, an allegation the old bear had hotly denied. It was a remarkable piece of work, he declared, worthy of Defoe at his best, gripping, powerful, written in vigorous, moving prose, but he couldn't take credit for it, much as he might like to. The author was obviously middle-aged, he added, for the story reflected half a lifetime of observation of the human condition. The feeling and compassion in the piece indicated that the author might well be a man of the cloth, which would explain the pseudonym. While compassionate, "The Gin Girl" was grittily realistic and would cause the powers that be to look askance at any clergyman who had penned it. Johnson concluded by saying that he would greatly like to meet

M.J. and treat him to dinner. I wondered what his reaction would be if I rapped on his door and told him I had come to accept his invitation. Apoplexy, probably.

Sheppard had conveyed much of this information to me, Mrs. Wooden the rest, for I couldn't resist sharing my secret with her. It was very exciting to have caused such a furor, to be the subject of so much speculation, but it seemed an awful lot of fuss over such a simple little story, and, besides, I was much too busy copying Cam's new book and keeping the household going to pay much mind to it. Occasionally I would take my copy of *The Bard* from its hiding place and gaze at it, and each time I felt that same wonderment I had felt when I had first seen it. I turned the sleek, expensive pages. I read the beautifully printed words and studied the Hogarth engraving especially commissioned to illustrate my story, and the wonderment swept over me anew, yet somehow it didn't seem to have anything to do with me, Miranda, living on Greenbriar Court.

Just as well, I thought ruefully. One writer on the court was trouble enough. Cam had begun *The Stranger From Japan* the morning after our evening with Bancroft, and he had been working furiously ever since, working like a man possessed, driving himself deplorably, almost as though he were in some kind of race with himself. For some reason he felt he had to finish it before the end of July, and in three weeks he had already done three hundred pages. Written at white-hot speed, the pages were charged with passion and filled with thundering action, the most exciting he'd ever done, and those exotic details about Japan and barbaric Japanese customs added a new spice that was going to enchant his readers. Jeremy Hammond, the English samurai warrior who wreaks havoc in stately homes, was Cam's most vivid hero, and he had never employed the revenge motif more powerfully . . . or with such violence. Dispatching villainous foes with samurai sword or spread-eagling them over razor-sharp bamboo stakes, Hammond was sure to delight all those Roderick Cane readers who relished such bloodthirsty fare. Lurid, thundering melodrama the book might be, but it was written with great vigor and undeniable panache.

Working so furioulsy, often going without sleep for forty-eight hours at a time, Cam had been in an unusually volatile mood, flaring up at the least provocation, throwing things about, yelling, or else he was grim and silent, brooding, reminding me of a keg of gunpowder about to explode. I had had my hands full, no question of that. Feeding him, fetching things for him, picking up after him had kept me hopping, and copying the flood of pages that came from his pen took up the rest of the time. I had barely been able to squeeze in my daily lessons with Mrs. Wooden, and the fact that I had been able to write two stories of my own still amazed me. The mysterious M.J. might be the current sensation of the coffeehouses, but Miranda James had precious little time to indulge herself with fantasies about fame and fortune. I was too busy coping with Cam Gordon and his alter ego.

I stood up as Thomas Sheppard came back into the office with my money. His large blue eyes were martyred as he handed it to me, woeful as he watched me take out a small chamois bag and drop the money inside. Drawing the string tight, I carefully tucked the bag away in the bodice of my sprigged muslin frock. Sheppard's cheeks flushed a bright pink.

"Isn't that a—uh—rather unusual place to keep your money?"

"Could be," I admitted, "but it's safe. No one's going to be able to pinch it from me, not unless they plunge a hand between my teats. It'd take a brazen thief to do *that*, wouldn't it?"

"I—uh—suppose so." His cheeks grew even pinker.

"I'm on to all their tricks," I said chattily. "I used to be a thief myself, you know. I wouldn't dream of carrying money in a pocket or purse. That's like asking to be robbed."

"You're an amazing young woman, Miranda."

"I don't see anything so amazing about knowing how to watch out for myself. I'd be a bloody—I'd be an idiot if I hadn't learned something from all those years in St. Giles."

Sheppard shook his head and moved behind his desk, idly fingering the stories he had just purchased.

"I'd say you learned a great deal from those years," he said. "These stories are superb. I hope you'll do more—as quickly as possible."

"I have a couple more in mind," I confessed, "but they have to gestate a while before I'll be ready to commit them to paper."

Sheppard smiled. "'Gestate'? Your vocabulary is certainly growing."

"I try to learn five new words a day. Mrs. Wooden helps me. We select a word, and then I have to use it in ten sentences, five spoken, five written. It's not easy, I can tell you for sure, but after all that the word's yours for keeps."

"And how long will these stories have to gestate?"

"I never can tell. I thought about 'Pockets' for several weeks before I sat down to write it. 'Wages' just popped into my mind one morning. I seemed to see the whole thing all at once. I wrote it the next day, soon as I could get to it. Copying Cam's book keeps me busy as can be."

Sheppard frowned, thinking. "You know," he began hesitantly, "it might not be a bad idea if we went back to our old arrangement with Cam."

"Old arrangement?" I was puzzled.

"Hiring a copyist to decipher his manuscripts. We'd pay him ourselves," he added hastily. "That would leave you free to do your own work. You could do twice as many stories."

"But—"

"You're going to be a very important writer, Miranda. I don't think you have any idea how good you are. You're that rare and unusual phenomenon, the natural writer. You were born with a remarkable gift, a gift you're just now beginning to develop, and one day—one day quite soon, I feel—you're going to be even more valuable to Sheppard & Co. than Cam is."

"Nonsense," I said. "Cam's the writer. I—I just scribble."

"Cam is a very competent novelist. He knows what his readers want. He delivers it. He does it extremely well. You, on the other hand, write from the heart, from the soul. You—"

"You're just trying to flatter me because you want more stories," I interrupted. My voice was light, teasing, but I was worried by what he had said and didn't want to hear any more. "I'll go on copying Cam's manuscripts, Mr. Sheppard. He—he'd be terribly upset if we changed things, particularly now that he's working so hard."

"You love him very much, don't you, my dear?"

"I suppose I do."

"I hope you're not hurt too badly."

"What—what does that mean?"

Sheppard hesitated, and then he shook his head again and forced himself to smile and assumed a false, breezy manner that didn't deceive me for a minute.

"Nothing," he said cheerfully. "I'm delighted with the stories. I'll publish 'Pockets' in the next issue of *The Bard*, 'Wages' in the issue after that. I'll commission Hogarth to make more engravings, one for each story. Which reminds me, I have a gift for you."

"A gift?"

Sheppard nodded and opened his top desk drawer and took out a piece of heavy paperboard with a tissue-thin sheet hanging over it. He handed it to me, and when I lifted the tissue I beheld the original Hogarth illustration for "The Gin Girl." There was my Betty coming out of the gin shop, several bottles clutched to her bosom with one arm. She was holding Little Joey's hand, and her eyes were full of grief. The proprietor of the shop was leering at her through the window, while a sodden old bawd sprawled on the pavement at the side of the steps, clutching an empty bottle. It was a scene I had witnessed daily in St. Giles, drawn to the life in all its squalor, all its sadness.

I had known little about Hogarth before *The Bard* appeared. Mrs. Wooden had eagerly filled me in, letting me know what an honor it was for him to have done the illustration. Although scorned by critics and connoisseurs of art, Hogarth was one of the most popular and certainly the most controversial artists of the day. *The Rake's Progress*, a series of engravings finished in 1735, had caused a sensation, so critical were they of English society, and another series, *Marriage à la Mode*, just completed last year, wittily and savagely depicted the mating customs of the aristocracy. Hogarth was devoting more and more time to portrait painting of late, Marcelon had informed me and declared that the portrait of Garrick as Richard III he had painted two years ago, in '45, was Davy's favorite by far. Hogarth might be arrogant and egotistical, despised by the art world, but she, for one, considered him a wonderful artist.

"I—I don't know what to say, Mr. Sheppard," I told him, gazing at the beautifully executed illustration. "Hogarth is— he's a very famous artist. Mrs. Wooden told me all about him."

"He's famous, all right," Sheppard agreed, "but for the wrong reasons. I've known him for years—chap's far more temperamental than any of my writers. He's grateful for the little commissions I throw his way, 'finger exercises,' he calls 'em, although he doesn't hesitate to charge an exorbitant fee."

"This—this must be very valuable," I said.

"Probably will be one day. I wanted you to have it."

The publisher smiled and patted my hand. What a perplexing man he is, I thought. He looked like a timid, dried-up little pixie, yet he was one of the shrewdest, toughest men on Fleet

Street. He played the martyr and grumbled about paying me twenty pounds, and then he turned around and gave me an original Hogarth that must be worth several times that amount. I was deeply moved and found it difficult to express myself.

"Thank—thank you very much, Mr. Sheppard."

"Consider it a bribe," he said as he led me out of the office. "Sheppard and Company want all the stories you can produce, and we want that novel, too—the novel you're going to write in a year or so."

"Oh, I've given up on novels. Lord John and Lady Cynthia were enough to convince me I've no knack for it. Stories are one thing, but a novel—I'll leave that to Cam."

"We'll see," he said.

"Thank you again for the Hogarth, Mr. Sheppard."

"I'm very fond of you, my dear," he said, opening the front door. The bell jangled merrily. "And not just because you're going to make a tremendous lot of money for us. You're a bewitching creature, and you've brought a freshness and vitality into this stuffy old firm that was sorely needed. I thank *you*."

"You're quite welcome," I told him, "but the next story is *still* going to cost you twelve."

Sheppard made an exasperated noise and shoved me playfully through the door, closing it behind me. I smiled to myself and walked blithely on down Fleet, holding the Hogarth carefully against my bosom. I'd have to hide it, of course. Couldn't have Cam finding it and asking a lot of questions. I would wrap it in brown paper and put it in the bottom drawer of the secretary, along with my copy of *The Bard* and the original manuscripts of my stories. He never looked in the secretary, considered it my territory. It'd be safe as houses there. Me, owning an original Hogarth and twenty pounds snugly tucked between my breasts in a soft chamois bag, money I had earned myself. Honestly, too. Life was downright amazing, that's what it was.

Dodging a noisy newsboy, moving around a stout gentleman examining the books on a table in front of one of the shops, I looked at the lovely, soot-streaked row of buildings—brown, tan, dusty orange brick, all marvelously ornate with plaster molding, multilevel roofs projecting a forest of chimneypots— and I marveled at this incredible, bustling city where so much could happen so quickly. The dirty-faced urchin who had been lifting pocket watches a year ago was now the talk of the coffeehouses, albeit pseudonymously. I had met the celebrated

Samuel Johnson. David Garrick wanted me to go on the stage. I was living with Roderick Cane, famous in a way—infamous, alas, in literary circles—and Thomas Sheppard wanted me to write a novel myself. It was a wonderment.

I hadn't told Sheppard the truth about my writing a novel, not exactly. Lord John and Lady Cynthia *had* been an ordeal, it was true, and I had decided I hadn't the knack, but that was before I wrote the stories. I'd never be able to write a pretty, fashionable romance for the ladies to while away their hours with, lapdog in lap, bonbons nearby, for I knew nothing about that kind of life, but a novel about a young girl who grows up in St. Giles and manages to rise above her environment . . . a novel, in fact, with plot line closely following my own life, with necessary changes . . . that was a different matter altogether. I'd call it *Duchess Annie* and my hero would be a painter, not a writer, and . . . I'd probably never write it, much too ambitious, much too scary to think about undertaking, but the idea was there, just the same, gestating away like crazy in my head. Who had *time* to write a novel, anyway? Snatching a few hours to dash off a story was one thing. Undertaking a major project like a novel . . . it was merely a foolish dream. Just as well I'd kept my mouth shut in Sheppard's office. Wouldn't have done to go blabbing away about such a silly idea.

Lost in thought, I stepped off the pavement and moved across the street without bothering to look. A huge lorry almost ran me down, the burly driver waving his fist and cursing me roundly. Instinctively I made a face and extended a stiff middle finger, quite forgetting for a moment that I was a well-bred young lady. He gaped and almost dropped the reins, probably because I was wearing an elegant pink frock and seemed so refined. A man on the pavement looked stunned, too. I smiled sweetly at him and moved on toward the narrow passageway leading to Greenbriar Court. The saucy urchin hadn't been completely exorcised yet. I was going to have to work on that. Shooting the finger was definitely not done.

And then I walked directly into the woman in the violet silk cloak, almost knocked her down, I did, stumbled myself, dropped the Hogarth, let out a "Bloody 'ell!" that startled the pigeons roosting on the eaves above. Tottering, I slammed my hand over the spot where the chamois bag rested beneath my bodice, ready to scratch and kick if she tried to snatch it. Hussy might be gorgeously attired in a dark blue silk gown and that long, hooded cloak, but you never could tell.

"Are—are you all right?" she asked.

"I ain't 'urt! Where's my drawin'?"

The woman picked up the Hogarth from the pavement. I snatched it out of her hand, and I recognized her then. The hood of her cloak had slipped back over the lustrous blue-black waves. A soft pink flush suffused those creamy magnolia-smooth cheeks, and the blue, blue eyes were full of concern. Close up, Lady Arabella Dunston was even more beautiful, so beautiful I could hardly believe it.

"I fear it was my fault," she said. Her voice was soft and low, a lovely voice. "I was—preoccupied. I wasn't watching where I was going."

"Oh, no," I protested. "It was my fault. I charged right into you, almost knocked you down."

Lady Arabella smiled a gentle smile and pulled the hood back up around her face. The deep violet silk made her eyes seem violet blue. I marveled at the long, curling lashes, the lids faintly etched with pale mauve shadow, the smooth, perfectly arched brows. She emanated compassion and kindness, an aura of gentility and goodness that was as intangible as perfume and just as real. There was quiet sadness, too, in her eyes, in her manner, and I found it hard to believe this woman was the mistress of the treacherous Cumberland. No hard, calculating courtesan, this, no haughty, high-born trollop with the instincts of a guttersnipe and a heart of stone.

"Are you certain you're all right?" she murmured in that low, musical voice. "You look rather stunned."

"I'm fine. I—I must apologize for sayin' what I said. Sometimes I forget myself."

"No apology is necessary. I've heard that expression used quite often, though never with such quaint inflection. Is your drawing undamaged?"

I lifted the sheet of tissue up. Protected by the stiff paper-board on which it was mounted, the Hogarth hadn't been harmed. I sighed with relief, smoothing the tissue back down. When I looked back up at her, Lady Arabella averted her eyes, and I had the fleeting impression that she had been studying my face, that she knew who I was. That was absurd, of course. How could she possibly? There was a moment of silence, and then she smiled again, nodded and moved past me. I turned, watching her as she walked on down Fleet to where a dusty, undistinguished coach stood waiting, obviously a common hackney hired by the hour. Glancing around apprehensively, as though fearing surveillance, she pulled the hood closer about her face, opened the door of the coach and climbed inside.

The coach drove away. I stood there, only a few yards from the passageway to Greenbriar Court, puzzled by the incident. What was the gorgeous Lady Arabella Dunston doing on Fleet Street at this time of the afternoon, and why had she been wearing a long, concealing cloak on such a warm summer day? Why would the acknowledged mistress of the Duke of Cumberland be riding in a dusty, mud-splattered coach? Her manner had been . . . almost furtive. It was a puzzlement indeed. Fine ladies didn't skulk around London on their own in hired coaches unless . . . unless there was a very good reason for wanting to go undetected. Some man was probably involved, I thought. Could the Duke's mistress have a secret lover, someone she had met in one of the coffeehouses on Fleet? That would explain the cloak, the coach, the furtive manner.

Who could blame her? I thought, strolling down the narrow brick passageway toward the court. She might be the Duke's mistress, but I didn't imagine she had much choice in the matter. A widow alone and penniless would have no defense when the King's son decided he wanted her. I suspected she had been totally unwilling, yet unable to put off a man so very powerful. Those lovely eyes had been so sad that afternoon I had seen her in the carriage, sad today as well. If she had a secret lover—some young man as impoverished as she, probably—I wished them well. How horrible to be in the clutches of a man like Cumberland, a victim of his lust. Gave me the shivers just to think about it. Poor Lady Arabella. I certainly didn't envy her.

Cam was still upstairs in his study when I got in. I hid the Hogarth in the secretary, hid the money, too. I'd have to give it to Bancroft the first chance I had. He had already invested the five pounds I had earned from "The Gin Girl" and told me it was sure to double itself before long. Glancing at the clock, I saw that it was almost five. Time to start thinking about Cam's dinner. There was half a beef pie in the pantry. I could heat it up for him, or I could pop around to the chophouse and bring him back something more substantial. He hadn't eaten any lunch today, had irritably shooed me out of the room when I went up to ask him what he wanted. He was working too hard, not eating properly. He was going to have a proper meal tonight, I vowed.

He wasn't working when I entered the study. He was standing at the window with arms folded across his chest, staring moodily out at the court. Something was bothering him, I could see that as soon as he turned to face me. His eyes were a dark blue, a deep crease between his brows, and his facial muscles were taut. The afternoon light spilling through the window behind him created deep blue highlights in his jet black hair. He moved over to the desk, sullen, displeased to see me. He looked leaner, I thought, looked drawn, faint smudges beneath his eyes. I longed to go over to him and brush that heavy wave back and stroke that lean cheek and comfort him, but he had thrown that invisible wall up again and I knew I couldn't reach him.

"Is something wrong, Cam?" I asked quietly.

He shook his head and picked up the lopsided pewter owl that perched atop the pages he had written today. A sizable stack, I observed. He stared down at the pages, but something told me he wasn't thinking about the book. After a moment he set the owl back down, scowled and looked up as though surprised to find me still standing there.

"I came to see about your dinner," I told him. "There's some beef pie I could warm up, or I could go round to the chophouse and—"

"I won't be eating in tonight, Miranda."

"You're going out?"

"Bancroft came by while you were gone. I'm meeting him at the club, and after we dine we'll probably make a night of it. I've no idea how late I may be out."

"I—I see."

"I want to finish this chapter before I leave. I'll leave the pages on your secretary. You can copy them after I'm gone."

His manner was cold and remote. He was clearly dismissing me. I turned and left, livid. He might have something on his mind, might be bothered, but that was no reason for him to treat me like I had some highly contagious disease. Me so concerned about him, wanting to get him a proper meal, and him dismissing me like I was a bothersome servant. Sod him! I was on the sofa in the sitting room, reading, when he came in shortly before eight. He was wearing his handsome new maroon frock coat and breeches, his striped waistcoat and the sky blue neckcloth. His face was still drawn. He looked tense. The smudges beneath his eyes seemed even more pronounced.

He glanced at me, set the pages on top of the secretary and left without a word. A real charmer, he was. If he thought I was going to work my ass off copying his bloody manuscript while he enjoyed a night on the town, he was sadly mistaken.

I copied it, though, every single page, working late into the night. The house was still, lonely, and Greenbriar Court was very quiet. It was well after midnight when I finished, the candles burning low, casting pale golden shadows on the wall. Restless, I prowled around the rooms, wishing he would come back, feeling lost and adrift without him in the house. I had grown so accustomed to having him around—to nag, to scold, to tease, to wait on, to love—that even a temporary seperation like this left me feeling empty and disoriented. Hours might pass without my seeing him, true, him shut up in his study, me busy with my own work, but just knowing he was there gave me a sense of security. Without Cam around I felt incomplete, as though some vital part of me was missing.

I went to bed and hours passed and I watched the moonlight playing on the ceiling, making mottled silver-gray patterns, and I listened to the creaks and groans of the house settling and strained to hear the sound of his footsteps on the cobbles, and finally, exhausted, I went to sleep and woke up with that long, lean body sprawling over me, one arm curled around my shoulder, one leg slung heavily over both mine. His nose was buried in my throat. His sleek jet hair touched my cheek. He had slung his coat over a chair. His neckcloth and shirt dangled over the side, and his stockings and breeches had fallen onto the floor. It must have been dawn when he came in, I thought, for the moonlight had almost vanished when I had closed my eyes for the final time. Bright morning sunlight gilded the ceiling now.

I could hear the pigeons cooing and hear the sounds of traffic on Fleet. A church bell tolled. Ten o'clock. Time for me to be up. Mrs. Wooden would be expecting me. I stirred, trying to disentangle myself from him. Cam made a noise in his sleep, pulling me closer. I pushed at him. He held me tighter and I fretted and he opened his eyes and scowled and pulled me beneath him and pinioned me with the weight of his body and I could feel his manhood growing warm and rigid. I made a valiant effort to throw him off, remembering my anger, remembering the way he had treated me, but he was much too strong, much too determined. He entered me exuberantly, with amazing strength, and I forgot my anger, forgot everything but the glorious torment of the moment and the bliss that mounted with each savage thrust.

Cam went out with Bancroft several more times during the next two and a half weeks, and I didn't complain, though I missed him dreadfully each time. He and Bancroft had business, he explained, for Bancroft was going to invest the money Cam had received for *The Stranger From Japan* and this necessitated many long conferences, always in the evening, always at Bancroft's club, and they always went out on the town afterward. I told myself that Cam needed the relaxation, for he was still working as one possessed—the book was almost finished now, only three more chapters to go—but that didn't make the lonely nights any easier to endure.

I kept wishing that Bancroft would come by the house and visit awhile before they went out so that I could sneak him the twenty pounds for investment, but he never did. I hadn't seen him in weeks, and I was beginning to grow terribly impatient. Twenty pounds was a tremendous amount of money. No telling what it could be earning if it was properly invested. Cam went out with Bancroft on a Wednesday night, and the next afternoon I decided to take matters into my own hands. It was well after three, I had finished my copying duties, and Cam was working away busily upstairs after sleeping until almost noon. I changed into my brown and cream striped linen frock, brushed my hair and stepped into the study to tell Cam I was going shopping. He scowled and waved me away impatiently, so immersed in his work that he probably hadn't even heard me.

The Bank of England was located on Threadneedle Street, a nice long walk, but it was a pleasant afternoon and the sights and sounds of London were endlessly fascinating, as always. The bank, I knew, had moved from Grocer's Hall in 1734, its new building on the site of the house of Sir John Houblon, one of the first directors of the bank. It had been hemmed in by the Church of St. Christopher le Stocks, three taverns and several private houses, but these had been pulled down, new offices added onto the original house, and the courtyard of the church now served as the central garden of the bank. It was an imposing, intimidating building—all that money in those vaults, all those guards, all those important deals being made— but I marched across the courtyard and walked right in just as though it was something I did every day.

My courage left me when I got inside. There were so many

tables, so many desks, so many clerks scribbling in ledgers, so many men coming and going and looking so important. I didn't know where to turn. A tall, soberly dressed man finally came over to me, his pale blue eyes full of suspicion. Almost totally bald and thin as a rail, he had a smug, officious manner that put me off immediately. He asked if there were something he could do for me. I told him I was Miss Miranda James and needed to see the Honorable Richard Bancroft immediately. He smirked and said that that wouldn't be possible unless I had an appointment. Him so patronizing and me with twenty whole pounds tucked away in my bodice—made my blood boil, it did. I informed him in my haughtiest voice that an appointment wouldn't be necessary and added that if he knew what was good for him he'd move his ass or find it in a sling.

The man turned pale. He staggered backward. He stared at me in stark horror for a moment and then scurried away like a scared rabbit, disappearing around a corner. Bleedin' sod! Treatin' me like I was his inferior, and him a lowly employee. I tapped my foot impatiently, waiting for him to come back. He didn't. Five minutes later a rather stocky young man with muscles bulging beneath his coat came and told me to follow him. He had sleek blond hair and a tough but pleasant face and seemed amused as he led me down a long hallway in one of the new wings. Probably a guard, I thought. Did they think I was going to rob the place? He finally stopped in front of a door, rapped on it jauntily and showed me into Bancroft's office.

"That will be all, George," Bancroft said.

The young man grinned. "You want I should stand guard outside in case she gets violent?"

"I'll call if I need help."

"I'd be careful," the youth advised him. "She looks down-right dangerous to me."

Bancroft chuckled as the muscular blond left and closed the door behind him. He was wearing black pumps and white silk stockings, forest green velvet knee breeches and a thin white lawn shirt with the sleeves rolled up over his forearms. His velvet frock coat and a lovely silk neckcloth were hanging over the back of the chair behind his desk. The desk was piled high with papers and ledgers and official-looking documents with seals attached. Here in this fancy office with windows over-looking the garden, Bancroft exuded an air of confidence and authority that was most reassuring.

"What on earth did you say to Tanner?" he asked. "He was convinced you were a madwoman, refused to go back and fetch you himself, told me I'd better send a guard after you."

"Sod wasn't going to let me see you. I told him he'd better move his ass. Thought he was going to faint."

"I'm surprised he didn't. He's currently in the cloak room, trying to recover from the shock. You're looking wonderfully radiant this afternoon, Miss James. To what do I owe the pleasure of this unexpected but highly diverting visit?"

"If you mean why am I here, I'm here on business."

"Oh?"

I leaned forward, plucked the chamois bag from between my breasts, took out the money and handed it to him. He seemed as surprised as Sheppard had been at my place of concealment and watched with considerable interest as I stuffed the empty bag back between my breasts, yet he was visibly impressed when I told him there was twenty pounds there and I wanted him to invest it for me. He was all business then, counting the money, making out a receipt, looking very serious as he signed it. His dark blond hair was tousled, and his brown eyes were twinkling again when he handed me the receipt. I folded it up and put it with the chamois bag for safekeeping, an action he watched with not the slightest lessening of interest.

"And what kind of morning did *you* have?" I asked.

"A rather frantic one, I fear. Things were popping in Change Alley. I was there by nine, bartering with the dealers. Sugar has suddenly become a very big item. I invested in several cane fields."

Dealers in stocks and shares in the trading companies had met in the Royal Exchange until 1698, I had learned, and then they moved to Jonathan's Coffee House in Change Alley, and it was there that the London Stock Exchange had come into being. Bancroft spent almost as much time in the Alley as he did in his office here at the bank. Some called it the financial center of the world, activities there on any given morning affecting all Europe.

"Cam slept till noon," I said.

Bancroft rolled down his sleeves, fastened them and slipped on the forest green velvet frock coat. "Bully for him," he said, smoothing down the lapels. "Wish I could have."

"It must have been difficult for you to get up so early after staying out so late last night. What time did you get in, three? four?"

"I was in bed by eleven, lass. I'm virtuous as can be these days. It's frightfully boring."

"You—you weren't out with Cam last night?" I asked carefully.

"Haven't seen him in weeks," Bancroft replied.

He picked up the pale yellow-tan neckcloth, fastened it around his neck and stepped over to a mirror, skillfully folding the cloth. I felt a leaden sensation in my stomach. My pulses seemed to have stopped dead still. Bancroft brushed his hair back, neat and resplendent now, a grin on his lips as he turned to me.

"I've worked quite enough for one day. Since you're going to be one of my major clients, the least I can do is take you out for tea. I'll ply you with tiny iced cakes and watercress sandwiches and—" He paused, looking at me closely. "Are you ill, Miranda?"

I shook my head. I told him I felt fine. Bancroft took me by the shoulders and sat me down in one of the comfortable chairs. I felt as though I were in a trance. There were glasses and a crystal decanter on a table beneath one of the windows. He poured brandy and forced me to drink. It tasted horrible, burned my throat going down, burned my insides, but I began to feel better almost immediately. I could feel the color returning to my cheeks, and I gave Bancroft an apologetic smile.

"I—I guess it was the long walk. It's terribly warm out, and—I'm all right now, Dick. Stop looking as though you were staring into an open grave! You're depressing me."

He continued to fuss over me, and I had a difficult time convincing him I was not going to keel over in a swoon. I was hardly the type. He insisted on taking me back to Greenbriar Court in his carriage, and although I would rather have been alone in order to think, there was no way I could refuse. Hovering over me like a mother hen with a fragile chick, he helped me into the carriage he had had brought around to Threadneedle Street. Those warm brown eyes were full of concern, and he spoke in a hushed, careful voice as though I were already sinking into that final sleep. When he took my hand in his and patted it I could no longer restrain myself. I jerked my hand away and told him that if he didn't stop clucking over me he'd soon be singing soprano. He chuckled then and relaxed his vigilance.

When the carriage stopped in front of the passageway on Fleet he helped me out, and I told him I would prefer he didn't see me to the house. Bancroft protested. I gave him a look that should have turned him to stone. He shook his head, grinning, then gave me a hug and climbed back into the carriage. With considerable relief, I watched it drive away and I stood there for several long moments, trying to pull myself together. Fleet was as bustling as ever, carriages bowling along the cobbles, newsboys shouting, journalists scurrying, but I was totally oblivious to it. I no longer felt dazed, no longer felt the shock and hurt and disappointment. I felt, instead, a hard, cold anger and a steely determination that nothing could shake.

He had been lying to me. All this time he had been lying to me. He was as deeply involved with the rebels as ever. He was one of them, had been all along, and nothing but disaster could come of it. That trip to Scotland—he had lied about that, too, I was certain of it—and that "accidental" meeting of the red-haired man at Green's had been carefully prearranged. They had been meeting secretly for months and months and months, ever since Culloden, working out some diabolical plot, and instinct told me that things were coming to a head. That was why Cam was so eager to finish his book. At long last they were planning to make a definite move. Thinking they could go against someone as powerful as Cumberland—it was insanity! Cam Gordon was a goddamned fool, and somehow, someway I was going to have to save him from the disaster he rushed so blindly to meet.

27

WORKMEN SAWED, HAMMERED, TROWELED ON PLAS-ter, the entire theater a bustling beehive of activity, a chaos of banging, slapping, shouting, yet there was a curious order involved. As David Garrick led us down the main aisle, proudly pointing to the newly plastered and beautifully gilt ceiling, I wondered how anything was accomplished amidst this confusion, but the results were already beginning to show. A fleet of upholsterer's apprentices were busily ripping the old covers from rows of seats, dust flying, while the upholsterer argued vociferously with a plump merchant who unfurled bolt after bolt of blue velvet, none of them satisfactory, it seemed. On the great bare stage, workmen were uncrating an enormous chandelier, crystal pendants tinkling loudly.

"Blue and gold and pale ash gray," Garrick was saying. "The seats and curtain will be a rich, deep royal blue, the walls covered with sky blue brocade embossed with gold fleurs-delis. Ivory marble pillars, gold gilt, ash gray velvet hangings —I'm bored with red, bored with garish trappings. Subdued elegance and harmony of color, that's what I'm after."

"It's going to be gorgeous, Davy," Mrs. Wooden exclaimed. "It must be costing a fortune."

"It is," Garrick confessed. "My first season damn well better be a roaring success. Careful with that chandelier!" he cried. "Nothing but the finest velvet, the finest brocade, genuine gold leaf gilt—the gilt work's being done by a group of Italian artisans especially brought in for the job. All the structural changes have been completed, walls torn down, foundations reinforced, new staircases put in, boxes added—what you see going on now is the dressing up. Once the seats are covered, the chandeliers hung, the walls recovered and the carpets laid, this place is going to knock your eyes out."

"The Drury Lane is going to be the most dazzling theater in England," Mrs. Wooden declared.

"In the *world*," Garrick corrected. "It's also going to be the best. Come on, I'll take you up on stage. Watch those ropes. I'm delighted you could come, Miss James. I'd given up hope of ever seeing you again."

"Marcie insisted," I said.

"Actually, I told her if she showed up without you, I'd strangle her on the spot," he told me. "I've had plenty of practice, playing Othello so often. Do you like what you see?"

"You seem to be doing a magnificent job, Mr. Garrick."

"Davy. Here, give me your hand, these steps are a bit tricky. Actually, I haven't done anything myself, just hired the very best men available. A bit of a problem organizing things, but I'm good at that—good at bossing people about and getting results. Terrorize 'em, that's my philosophy. Works with artisans and laborers as well as actors. I'm a perfectionist, I fear, believe in driving 'em till they drop."

"Every word he says is true," Mrs. Wooden assured me.

"Working with Davy is *exhausting*. Exhilarating, too, of course! He brings out the very best in a person."

"Excuse me for a moment, ladies," Garrick said. "I've got to go speak to those chaps with the chandelier. Be right back."

He sauntered off, leaving us standing in the wings. His walk was a vigorous, bouncy stride, shoulders rolling, arms swinging. He seemed to generate vitality and zest, carrying a crackling excitement along with him. His dark blond hair pulled back and tied with a string, his face aglow, one cheek smudged with dirt, he looked handsomer than ever. His thin white cambric shirt was loose and moist with perspiration, the full sleeves rolled up over his forearms, the tail tucked carelessly into the waistband of his tight gray knee breeches. His white cotton stockings were in deplorable condition and his black leather pumps sadly scuffed, the silver buckles tarnished, yet all this only emphasized the splendor of the man. He looked like a prince in disguise, I thought, watching him confer with the workmen across the stage.

"Isn't this exciting?" Mrs. Wooden said breathlessly. "Oh, to be back in a real theater again! Can't you *feel* the magic? Davy's promised to get me back in harness soon. He's going to mount a Restoration comedy this season, and I'll have a splendid part—something showy and full of panache. He's looking for the right play. Mrs. Cibber is a competent Shakespearian actress, I admit that, providing you don't mind that placid, bovine expression and spiritless delivery, but she could *never* do comedy. I can't understand why he ever signed her. Audiences find her comforting, I suppose. She reminds them of a sweet-faced, white-haired grandmother. Dull woman. Dull as ditch water."

Marcelon rattled on, a spectacular sight in rust and cream striped taffeta. If the gown was outlandish, the hat she wore with it was even more so—fluttery rust ostrich plumes spilling in profusion over the wide cream taffeta brim, the crown stovepipe tall. Face painted, eyes full of animation, she was an outrageous and endearing figure, generating her own special magnetism. I felt as drab as a sparrow beside her in my simple muslin frock.

"—needed to get *out* for a spell," she was saying. "I've been quite worried about you, my dear, I may as well confess it. These past two weeks you've been—distracted, preoccupied. Something's been worrying you, I can tell. It isn't like you to be so listless."

"I—I've been working very hard."

"Much too hard," she declared. "All that writing, all that copying. You need some *amuse*ment, Miranda. You stay cooped up in that house, working like a slave for that awful man—he *ter*rifies me, my dear, so dour and scowly, so volatile. He's handsome, of course, in a lean, ruthless sort of way, but he doesn't ap*prec*iate you."

"You don't know him, Marcie," I said quietly.

"I know what he's *do*ing to you, my dear. Men! How complicated they make our lives. How much better off we'd be without them! Did I tell you I had another run-in with Major Barnaby?"

Mrs. Wooden launched into her account of the latest spat with great enthusiasm, and though I appeared to listen, my mind wandered. Two weeks it had been since I had learned of Cam's deception, since I had vowed to do something about it, and I had done nothing but worry myself sick. He hadn't gone out even once during all that time, had devoted every waking hour to his work, and I tried to tell myself that I had overreacted, that there was some other explanation for those nights when he had supposedly been with Bancroft. With any other man I would have suspected another woman, but in Cam's case that would be absurd. He was a thorough misogynist, actively disliked women, distrusted them. They were a necessary evil, and as long as he had one at home to take care of all of his needs, he wasn't about to seek the company of another. No, I knew in my heart he was conspiring with the rebels, and I had merely been procrastinating, keeping quiet because I so dreaded a major confrontation.

I wouldn't be able to put it off much longer, I knew that. He was almost finished with the book, had been working on the last chapter when I had finally gone to bed last night. Once the book was finished, he would devote all his energy to the conspiracy, and that disaster I dreaded would be upon him. I had to do something, but what? For two weeks that question had plagued me. It was always there, making it impossible for me to relax, to sleep properly, to concentrate on my work. I had hoped my coming to the theater with Mrs. Wooden this afternoon would prove distracting and get my mind off things, but it didn't seem to be working out that way.

"And I was absolutely dumbfounded, my dear! I couldn't believe he was actually asking me to dinner. *He*'s going to do the cooking—he says my plum cake with apricot brandy can't hold a candle to his almond delight—and later we're going to play cards. He was very dry and fussy about it, said he was asking me over just to get me off his back, but I know he secretly longs for company. A good-looking man like that has no *business* being alone."

I smiled, making an effort to be cheerful. "I'm sure you'll captivate him, Marcie," I said brightly.

"Oh, my dear, I have no desire to do *that*!" she protested. "I'm just being kind to a poor, lonely old man."

"Of course."

"I'm an ar*tiste*, my dear. I've no time for romance."

Garrick rejoined us and showed us samples of the deep blue velvet that had been selected for the curtains and pointed out the elegant gilt work on the proscenium while workmen continued to bang and bustle and shout. The great chandelier tinkled as it was carried off the stage, pendants shimmering, crystal ropes swaying. Garrick wiped his brow and looked about him with satisfaction, visibly pleased with the wonders he had wrought. Mrs. Wooden made exclamations and said she'd never seen anything like it and it would be a joy and *honor* to act in such a theater, and then, abruptly, she cut herself short and stared as a middle-aged woman in pink approached us from across the stage.

The woman was plump, with a round, moon face and great dark eyes and fluffy white hair pulled away from her face and fastened in a bun in back. She had the placid, sweet expression of a contented cow, I thought, yet there was an undeniable warmth about her, a curious allure that made one feel cozy inside just seeing her. Her pink silk gown was exquisitely simple, her pleasant face free of makeup. As she drew nearer Mrs. Wooden bristled, a bright, false smile forming on her lips.

"Mrs. Cibber!" she cried. "How *lovely* to see you!"

Mrs. Cibber smiled sweetly and took Marcelon's hands and squeezed them and said the pleasure was all hers. She had left a script in her dressing room, she explained, had come back to fetch it and had heard her dear old friend's voice coming from the stage. Mrs. Wooden winced at the "old" and smiled all the more and gave the plump actress a hug. Garrick introduced us and Mrs. Cibber said I was enchanting and asked if I was going to join the company. Her voice was very soft, reminding me of mellowed old velvet.

"Miranda doesn't act," Mrs. Wooden said quickly, sounding quite shrill in comparison. "You already have your dressing room? I imagine it's very grand, isn't it? I'd *love* to see it, my dear."

"Davy's been very generous," Mrs. Cibber told her. "I don't know how I'll ever adjust to so much luxury and space after years of changing in those drafty old broom closets we used."

"How well I remember," Mrs. Wooden sighed. "Mildewed walls, the smells of stale powder and grease paint, a rack of mothy old costumes abandoned by the previous occupant, and the mirror was *al*ways too small and murky as mud. They were always freezing cold, too, those dressing rooms. How many times did I go onstage with chilblains, shivering in an elegant velvet costume."

"My new dressing room is nothing like that. Come, I'll show you."

"I wouldn't *miss* it! I'll join you in a few minutes, Miranda."

The two women left, the one so serene, the other so animated. Davy Garrick watched them depart with a thoughtful look in his eyes, a half-smile playing on his lips. His clothes might be disreputable, his face smudged, and that thick blond hair might be a bit too oily, but he was still the most attractive man I had ever seen, the unpretentious attire somehow enhancing that virile charm and personal radiance. As Marcelon and Mrs. Cibber disappeared, he turned to me and gave the smile full play.

"Poor Marcelon," he said. "She's so transparent."

"You *are* going to find a part for her, aren't you? You—you aren't merely stringing her along?"

"Would I do that?" he asked teasingly.

"I've no idea, Mr. Garrick."

"Do you think you could possibly call me Davy?"

"I don't know you that well."

"We'll have to do something about that, my beauty."

"Getting back to Marcie—"

"I'm planning a revival of *The Way of the World*. Marcelon isn't the greatest actress in the world, but in the right role, one suited to her own particular talents, she's capable of giving an amazing performance."

"She'd be perfect as Lady Wishfort," I said.

"You know the play, then. Congreve might have written Wishfort with Marcelon in mind—it's pure Marcie, all flash and fireworks and frippery. She'll be sensational. I haven't mentioned any of this to her yet, don't want to get her all stirred up until everything's definitely set."

"I won't say anything," I promised. "She's going to be thrilled when she finds out, though. It's very kind of you to—to take such an interest in your friends."

"It's my nature," he confessed. "I'm the kindest, most thoughtful, most lovable chap in London—don't believe all those stories you hear to the contrary."

The smile was still curving on those full pink lips, and he was looking into my eyes with a disconcerting intensity. David Garrick had sexual allure that was almost overwhelming in its power, and even though I was immune to it, I could feel its potency. As those dark, gleaming eyes looked into mine I realized that he would like to sleep with me, and that took me aback. Loving Cam as I did and so totally immersed in that love, I was incapable of thinking of any other man in that way, even one as glorious as David Garrick. I lowered my eyes, not really perturbed. I felt he was paying me the ultimate compliment, but I didn't want to give him the wrong impression.

"Come," he said lightly, "I'll show you the Green Room."

He led me backstage, a dim, cavernous area full of dust and shadows, ropes dangling down like vines, old crates stacked haphazardly, painted flats leaning against the walls in tattered sections. He took my arm, holding it lightly just above the elbow and guiding me around the various obstacles. Holding back a section of mothy red velvet curtain, he led me down a narrow corridor that smelled of metal and rust and peeling paint. The bustle and noise out front seemed distant, sound muted, and the air here was cool and rather clammy. I had the feeling we were being observed by the ghosts of all those famous performers who had thronged here in days of yore. It was an eerie sensation, discomfiting but not at all alarming.

"All the improvements and embellishments have been made out front," he explained, "where they will show. Backstage the Drury's the same old barn, vast and drafty, though I've redone the principals' dressing rooms. Wouldn't want to tamper with the atmosphere back here. The ghosts might get me."

"Ghosts?"

"Place is full of 'em," he said. "Didn't you see that weeping lady in her pointed hat and medieval veils? Wringing her hands as we passed her, longing to play Guinevere just one more time. I'll probably haunt the place too some day. Couldn't think of a nicer way to spend eternity. Be careful of these steps. I fear they're a bit uneven."

The Green Room was cozy and comfortable and had obviously not been tampered with. Everything was slightly worn and mellow, fabrics a bit threadbare, woods gleaming with the soft patina of age. Candles glowed warmly, and the low tables in front of the sofas were littered with old programs and yellowing handbills and discarded scripts. The room wasn't green at all. The walls were covered with old rose silk that had faded to a pale gray-pink, adorned with the portraits of actors and actresses of days gone by in ornate but tarnished gold frames. An ancient purple velvet cloat trimmed with false ermine hung in a tall glass display case. Garrick told me that it was said to have belonged to the great Richard Burbage, worn by him the night he first performed *Lear*.

"Just think," I said, truly impressed. "Shakespeare himself might have handled it, might even have tried it on."

"Quite likely," Garrick agreed. "You know Shakespeare?"

"I grew up on him," I replied. "I know all the plays, know parts of some of them by heart."

Garrick smiled and opened the glass case, carefully removing the aged, once sumptuous cloak, the purple velvet nap worn, the ermine sadly yellowed. Stepping behind me, he placed the cloak over my shoulders and reached around to fasten it at my throat. I was amazed, in awe, too, as the heavy folds engulfed me, falling to my feet. Me, Miranda, wearing a cloak that might once have been worn by the greatest writer of all time. It made me feel terribly humble, made me feel nervous, too. Garrick took my hand and led me over to a long mirror so that I might see myself.

"It suits you," he said softly. "You look very regal, like some sad, lovely princess."

He was standing behind me, a little to one side, and I could see him in the mirror, tall, handsome, smiling a gentle smile as his eyes met mine in the glass. I turned to face him. His eyes were glowing with open admiration, and there was desire as well, subtle, good-natured, yet unmistakable.

"I wish you'd reconsider joining my company," he said.

"I'm not an actress, Mr. Garrick."

"I could make an actress of you, Miranda. You have intelligence, it shines in your eyes. You have sensitivity and soul as well, and, most important of all, you have remarkable presence."

"Indeed?"

"You're one of the most beautiful women I've ever seen, and you have a special magnetism that is extremely rare. You must know that. You must have seen the way men look at you."

"I appreciate your interest, but—" I hesitated.

"You're not tempted?"

"I'm afraid not," I said quietly.

"That's a great pity—a great disappointment, too. Personally, I mean. I find you utterly fascinating, Miranda. I'd like to know you—much better."

The husky, caressing tone of his voice left no doubt as to what he meant by that. How many women would have given anything to become the mistress of the famous David Garrick? Hundreds. Thousands. And he wanted me, Miranda, late of St. Giles and still not entirely free of that environment. I wasn't the woman he believed me to be, but somehow I felt my background would make no difference whatsoever to him. He was an amiable man, kindhearted, generous—totally unaffected for all his fame. Virile, charged with energy, he would be a wonderfully passionate lover—playful, considerate, showering his woman with attention and robust affection. I sensed all this, and I was almost sorry my heart irrevocably belonged to another.

"I hate to see you wasting yourself, Miranda," he said.

"Wasting myself?"

"On a surly, volatile writer of cheap fiction who is utterly incapable of appreciating you. I know all about Gordon. I made it my business to find out about him. The man's little better than a thug, obsessed with violence."

"That isn't true."

"You wait on him hand and foot. He treats you like a chattel. He's unworthy of you."

I carefully removed the cloak and handed it to him. "That may be so," I replied, "but I happen to love him."

Garrick gazed into my eyes for a moment longer, and then he smiled and shook his head and replaced the cloak in its case. There was no tension whatsoever between us. Closing the glass door, latching it, he turned to look at me with fond eyes. I suspected that he had rarely, if ever, been turned down, but he was handling it with wonderful aplomb.

"The human heart is mysterious indeed," he observed woefully.

"And mine belongs to Cam Gordon."

"Alas! Would that it were not so. I'd like to dress you in velvets, cover you with jewels, smother you with attention."

"Oh?"

"I'd spoil you deplorably, Miranda."

"I don't doubt it."

He stood there with his arms folded across his chest, his head cocked to one side, a gentle, thoughtful smile on his lips. His dark eyes gleamed, still fond, disappointed as well. Tall, with the lean, muscular build of an athlete in superb condition, he exuded energy and good nature and sexual allure in his worn, shabby attire. David Garrick was golden, touched with genius, one of the great men of our day, and I felt something very like regret as I gazed at him. He sighed, running a hand over his sleek blond hair, and when he spoke his voice was wonderfully persuasive.

"Why settle for crumbs, Miranda, when you can have a kingdom?"

"You're offering me a kingdom?"

He nodded slowly. "All that I have. I think it's quite likely that I'm in love with you."

"You don't even know who—who I am."

"I'd like to spend the rest of my life finding out."

"I'm sorry, Mr.—" I hesitated, smiled gently. "I'm sorry, Davy."

He sighed again, heavily this time, quite dramatically. The mood lightened. He looked utterly crestfallen, playing the rejected suitor with just the right touch of exaggeration.

"I intend to suffer," he told me, "but I shan't do it in silence. I shall pine for you, Miranda."

"No doubt you will."

"And I shall wait," he added.

It was mere badinage, I knew, light and playful repartee that came easily to a man like him, but I was flattered nevertheless. Garrick grinned and led me out of the Green Room and chatted pleasantly about the further improvements he hoped to make and the production of *A Merchant of Venice* that would inaugurate his reign as manager of the Drury Lane. Mrs. Wooden joined us on stage a few minutes later, enthusing volubly about the wonders of Mrs. Cibber's dressing room, stoutly declaring that she was positively thrilled for her friend's good fortune and adding that *no* one was more deserving of it than that dear, sweet, relatively competent actress.

Garrick put us into a carriage, and Mrs. Wooden continued to chatter nonstop as we rode through the city. Her stiff taffeta skirts crackled as she shifted position. The rust plumes on her preposterous, endearing hat billowed. Gazing out the windows of the carriage, I only half-listened to her. Sunlight gilded the dome of St. Paul's, turning it a bright silver-gold. Pigeons fluttered against the pale blue sky like scraps of gray silk. Noxious fumes assailed our nostrils as the carriage drove past a row of squalid tenaments. I was in a thoughtful, rather pensive mood when we finally turned down Fleet. Why settle for crumbs when you can have a kingdom? he had asked. Was that what I had done? Jewels, velvet gowns, things of that sort meant a lot to some women, but I was content with the kingdom in my own heart. As long as I had Cam I needed no such fripperies.

It was almost five o'clock when we got back to Greenbriar Court. The poodles were barking lustily in the front hall of the yellow house, eagerly awaiting their mistress's return. Mrs. Wooden gave me a hug and then hurried across the cobbles to open her front door. The dogs spilled out onto the doorstep, leaping joyfully, hurling themselves against her striped taffeta skirt. She scolded them and shooed them inside, gave me a wave and disappeared behind the door. I was rather apprehensive as I opened our front door and stepped into the small foyer. We had been gone much longer than I had thought we would be, and Cam was sure to ask questions. Knowing the way he felt about actors—David Garrick in particular—I hadn't told him I was going to the Drury Lane. Our encounter with the actor at Green's Coffee House had put him in a foul mood indeed, and I knew that he would be furious if he found out I'd seen the man again.

I smiled to myself as I went upstairs. Cam Gordon might be thorny and gruff, might never woo me with tender words or mention the word love, but he was extremely possessive and wanted me completely under his thumb. Though he would never admit it, he had a violently jealous nature. Perhaps I'd tell him where I had been after all, just to stir him up. We hadn't had a real rousing quarrel for quite some time. We would fight, we would make up, and then . . . and then he would be in a conciliatory mood and I would bring up the matter of the rebels that had been plaguing me all this time. My smile vanished. I should have brought it up immediately, as soon as I returned from the bank, but he had been working so hard, and he was always so testy when he was in the final stages of a

~362~

book. If he worked at all well today, he should have the book finished by this time. He had been working on the final pages when I left.

The study was empty. Cam was gone. The house was very still. I hadn't noticed before. Books were scattered over the floor and piled on the chairs in untidy stacks. The samurai sword he had purchased from a dealer rested on the window ledge, its ornate brass hilt wound with an intricate pattern of leather, its long, lethal blade glittering in the sunlight. Wads of paper littered the floor around the desk, but there were no pages under the lopsided pewter owl. The inkwell was open, a broken quill beside it. I put the stopper back into the inkwell, frowning. Where could he be? Had he finished the book? If so, where were the pages? Worried, distracted, I went into the bedroom, removed my muslin frock and put on a violet blue cotton work dress with snug waist and low-cut bodice.

I tidied up the study, straightened up the desk and then went downstairs to the kitchen. Rays of late afternoon sunlight wavered through the windows, polishing the dull red brick floor and making silvery sunbursts on the copper pans that hung on the wall. I lighted the huge black iron stove and put coffee on and broke eggs into a large blue bowl. He'd be hungry when he got back. I'd make an omelet. Cooking was still not my forte—it made me terribly uneasy—but I had learned to make an omelet after much practice and a number of disastrous failures. Beating the eggs thoroughly, I added cream and spices and sprinkled in parsley flakes and put it on to cook slowly in a generously buttered skillet. Chopping up sausage, I placed it on top of the batter once it had begun to firm up, then carefully folded the sides over. This part was always tricky. If the batter hadn't cooked long enough, it always tore and got runny and then you had a buttery mess on your hands. Success. I flipped the omelete over to brown slowly.

Wasting my time, probably. You had to eat an omelet hot if it was going to be any good, and I had no idea when Cam might be back. Nothing worse than a cold omelet. Where could he have gone? The man was going to drive me insane, that's what he was going to do. Why couldn't he be sensible and normal and uncomplicated like most men? Why did he have to be so complex, so temperamental, so obstinate and infuriating? Scots! The whole lot of 'em must be mad. Maybe it had something to do with the climate. Going out like that, me not having an inkling where he was, when he'd return, worrying myself silly. Why did I have to love him so much? Why did I have to care so desperately? Life was so much easier when you were your own person, when all your happiness didn't depend on the whim of a bloody, thoughtless, stubborn Scot.

I turned. Cam was standing in the doorway. I gave a start, dropping the turner I was still holding.

"Jemminy! You scared the bloody 'ell—you gave me quite a turn! I didn't hear you come in."

"I didn't mean to startle you," he said dryly.

He was wearing his old black broadcloth breeches and frock coat, a maroon brocade waistcoat, a steel gray silk neckcloth. His thick black hair was neatly brushed, the sleek, heavy wave slanting over his brow, and his blue eyes were cool. He was so long and lean, much too lean, his features sharp, foxlike, wonderfully handsome to my eyes. I picked up the turner and brushed an auburn wave from my cheek, affecting a calm indifference I was far from feeling. Sod could at least have let me know he was going out and given me some idea when he would be back.

I flipped the omelet over again. It was beginning to turn a light golden brown.

"Is that coffee I smell?" he asked.

"It's fresh. Do you want a cup?"

He nodded. I poured a cup and put in sugar and stirred it and handed it to him. He sipped it slowly, thoughtfully, watching me over the rim of the cup with a curious speculation, as though I were some rare species he was trying to figure out. I didn't like that look at all.

"Did you finish the book?" I asked.

"I finished it around two."

"I'm eager to read the pages."

"Same old formula, same thundering climax awash with blood. The English samurai gets his revenge, gets his inheritance, gets the heroine. He finds out she's a treacherous bitch after his money, shoves her away from him in disgust and books passage back to Japan."

"A typical ending, I see, full of cynicism and bitter irony. I don't suppose it ever occurred to you to end a novel with a happy embrace."

"Never," he replied.

"I didn't see the pages on your desk."

"I took them to Sheppard," he said.

"Oh?" I was surprised and not a little worried.

"I brought them downstairs first, intending to leave them on your secretary. I opened all the drawers, looking for a paperweight."

He took another sip of coffee, looking at me, watching for my reaction. My heart seemed to stop beating. I felt very cold.

"You—opened the drawers?"

"Found some interesting things," he replied. His voice was casual, much too casual. "Three stories in your handwriting. A copy of *The Bard*. An original Hogarth. You really should have it framed, Miranda."

"You know, then," I said.

"Sheppard told me everything—he did so under considerable duress, I might add. After he'd given me all the details, he relaxed somewhat and spent the next half hour enthusing about your remarkable talents. You're going to be one of the best, he assures me. I read the stories. I'm inclined to agree."

"Cam—"

"I also agree that you're much too gifted, much too valuable a talent to be wasting your time copying my rubbish. You should be spending that time creating your own masterpieces."

"You—you're angry, aren't you?"

"Because you're a far better writer than I could ever hope to be? Because I took you in off the streets, fed you, clothed you, gave you protection and a roof over your head and you go behind my back and undermine me with my own publisher? Don't be absurd."

"It—it wasn't that way, Cam. Damn! My omelet!"

I grabbed a plate and whisked the omelet onto it. Butter was burning in the skillet. I jerked the skillet off the stove and scorched my hand and slung the skillet into the sink and cursed. Cam calmly sipped his coffee as I waved my hand and blew on it. The skin was just lightly scorched and it wasn't really all that painful, but the bastard didn't have to be so bloody superior about it. I scowled and placed the omelet on the table and began to take down plates and silverware.

"It'll be rather crisp," I said, "but I'm sure it's still edible. Shall I slice some cheese and bread? I could—"

"That's another thing," he interrupted, his voice still infuriatingly casual. "You shouldn't be wasting your time cooking and cleaning house and taking care of a hack like me. Your time is much too precious."

"I'd like to know who else you think's gonna take care of you? If it wudn't for me, you'd bloody well—"

"You're losing your fine veneer, Miranda. The guttersnipe's beginning to show through."

"You—you resent my trying to better myself, don't you? You'd like me to be a simple-minded little slavey, worshiping the ground you walk on, nourishing your—"

"Careful. You're losing control."

"Sod you, Cam Gordon!"

"You're quite attractive when you're angry. Your eyes are a flaming blue, your cheeks a lovely pink. Tongue's a bit salty, though. You may no longer be my property, but I'm still quite capable of slapping you senseless."

"What do you mean, no longer your property? I'm bonded to you, you son of a bitch, and—"

"Not any longer," he said calmly. "I've given you your freedom, and it's been officially recorded in the books—I attended to that little detail when I left Sheppard's. You're a free woman, Miranda. There's nothing whatsoever to hold you here any longer."

"You had no right to do that! I—"

"You served only a small portion of your allotted time, granted, but I assured the court that you're a thoroughly reformed character, self-supporting and no longer the least threat to decent society. I signed a statement to that effect, had it duly witnessed. It cost me two pounds to have everything recorded, another twenty in bribes to have it taken care of promptly, without the customary rigamarole and delays, but it's done now."

I stared at him, silent, fighting to control the conflicting emotions that swept over me. He was so cool, utterly unperturbed, standing there sipping his coffee as though we were discussing the weather. A wild panic was building up inside me. I forced it back, willing myself to be calm when the very floor beneath my feet seemed to have vanished.

"I guess I'm supposed to be grateful," I said.

"You're entitled to a life of your own, Miranda."

"My life is with you, you bastard."

"Indeed?"

"I happen to love you."

"That's your misfortune," he said coldly.

"Just try throwing me out!"

Cam took a final sip of coffee and set the cup down, still cool and unperturbed and frighteningly remote, bearing no resemblance to the passionate lover who took me with such fierce abandon, who needed me far more than he would ever acknowledge.

"If you wish to stay, you may, of course," he said. "I'll see to it that you receive a salary commensurate with the services you perform."

"Goddamn you, Cam, I—"

"And I'd advise you to watch your mouth. I demand respect and total obedience from my servants. Step out of line and I'll beat hell out of you."

"Yeah, and lose both your eyes tryin'!"

Someone pounded on the front door then, startling both of us. Cam cocked his head, listening, a deep, angry furrow creasing the flesh above the bridge of his nose. The pounding continued, echoing down the hall, loud, persistent, urgent. I hesitated a moment and then moved lightly past him and hurried down the hall to open the door.

The red-haired man who had been at Green's Coffee House stood on the doorstep, his fist raised to pound against the wood again. I stared at him in surprise, completely taken aback. He was very tall, very thin, his lean, foxlike features somehow familiar, as though I'd seen them many times before. His rich red-brown hair fell across his brow, a heavy wave slanting down to a point just above his right eyebrow, just as Cam's did. His lips were thin, his blue eyes hostile. He wasn't at all handsome, raw-boned where Cam was sleek, crude where Cam was elegant, but the family resemblance was so striking I was amazed I hadn't noticed it that night at Green's.

"May—may I help you?" I asked.

The man shoved past me, slamming the door as though he feared hot pursuit. He looked about anxiously, ignoring me completely.

"Now just hold on!" I protested. "You can't—"

"Where's Cam? I must speak to him immediately!"

"He—he's—"

"I'll take care of it, Miranda," Cam said, moving down the hall. "You go on back to the kitchen."

"But—"

"Go!" he thundered.

I obeyed, turning in time to see Cam seize the man's arm and march him into the sitting room. I heard him loudly berating the man for daring to risk coming here in broad daylight, and the man replied just as loudly that it was imperative and then their voices grew quiet and all I could hear was a low, conspiratorial murmur coming from the sitting room. I looked at the omelet, cold now. Dinner was spoiled. Everything was spoiled. I threw the omelet out and put things away and washed dishes and straightened up, deliberately keeping myself busy, holding anger and hurt and curiosity at bay.

Half an hour must have passed. The kitchen was spotless. The sun was going down, dark orange rays slanting through the windows, fading as soon as they touched the floor. He couldn't expect me to stay here all night, cowering like a prisoner. I braced my shoulders and stepped into the hall just as they came out of the sitting room. I stepped back, listening.

"Skinner's warehouse," the man said, "by the Thames, eleven o'clock."

"It's too damned risky, Ian! At this stage we have to—"

"There's no avoiding it. Next Thursday, she says. We have to make final plans."

"Goddammit, it's too soon. We need—"

"We have no choice," the man snapped.

He left then and Cam closed the door behind him and stood there in the shadowy hallway with a worried look in his eyes. He had forgotten all about me and our argument. I could tell that. He shook his head and frowned, staring at the grandfather clock without seeing it, and then he heaved his shoulders and started upstairs. The house was filling with deep blue-gray shadows. I lighted candles, calm now, determined, knowing what I must do. Cam came downstairs shortly after eight and left without a word. I put aside the book I had been pretending to read. I could feel the tension begin to build.

Skinner's warehouse. By the Thames. I had only a vague idea where it was, but I was certain I could find it. At nine-thirty I went upstairs and fetched a heavy cloak and left the house myself. It was a long walk to the warehouse district, and I wanted to allow myself plenty of time.

28

MISS MIRANDA JAMES WITH ALL HER READING, HER
well-bred manner and her cultured voice would have been terrified to be out alone at night without masculine protection,
but the streets of London held no terrors for Duchess Randy.
It was the tough, street-smart urchin who moved along so
purposefully now, alert and defensive, though Randy had never
owned such a fine violet-blue cotton frock, such a warm purple
cloak. I could have hired a coach, of course—they were easy
enough to flag down on Fleet—but under the circumstances it
would be unwise. The driver might remember me, might remember taking me down to the waterfront, you never could
tell. No, it was better this way, even if there was a certain risk
involved. I wished I had a blunderbuss with me so I could
blow the brains out of any rogue who might accost me, but,
unarmed, I'd have to rely on my own resources.

London at night was a dark, dangerous jungle full of savage
beasts ready to maul, maim and murder without the slightest
remorse, and the savagery wasn't confined to slums like St.
Giles, either. Criminal gangs like those organized by Black
Jack at least had a purpose, did their foul deeds with profit in
mind, but the city was full of vicious amateurs who roamed
about making mischief simply for the sport. It was almost
impossible to get a conviction for rape, particularly when the
age of consent was twelve, and bands of well-born dandies
frequently prowled en masse, drinking, carousing—any woman
they encountered in danger of brutal gang rape. Finding no
easy prey, these men of gentle birth often raided brothels,
wreaking havoc, leaving the place in shambles, often setting
torch to it in order to watch the blaze. Malicious, amoral,
sometimes murderous, these high-spirited aristocrats were far
more dangerous than those who turned to crime for a living.

Thieves, cutthroats, white slavers, villains of every description thrived in this savage age when human life had little or no value, when public executions were festive events, when even the most upright citizen merely shrugged his shoulders at murder and accounts of vicious cruelty. How many lives were brutally snuffed out on any given night in London? How many people were beaten senseless, left for dead? How many children were tortured, women violated, men waylaid and robbed? And who really cared? Certainly not the so-called officials. It was a way of life and you took your chances and there wasn't anything you could do about it. Respectable society, such as it was, put stronger bolts on its doors and windows and never ventured out at night without gun, sword or a bodyguard of burly servants.

Jesus, Randy, you're scaring yourself, I thought, quickening my step. You never used to let things like that bother you, accepted 'em just like everyone else. No use dwelling on 'em now. I turned a corner, passed a gambling house ablaze with lights, shouts and raucous laughter spilling through the windows. Three drunken bucks stumbled down the steps, holding onto each other for support, powdered wigs askew, satin frock coats stained with wine. One of them yelled at me, fell flat on his face when his companions let go of him, hitting the pavement like a sack of potatoes. His two friends laughed with glee, delighted with the spectacle, even though the man's nose was bleeding furiously and might well be broken. Such sights were so commonplace as to be unworthy of notice, and I moved on without turning a hair.

Carriages bowled down the street, many of them surrounded by footmen who ran alongside bearing torches, panting for breath. The flames flickered wildly in the night, leaping and waving like frenzied red-orange demons. I passed an alleyway, a dark, fetid tunnel of darkness. Dull, thudding noises issued from its depths accompanied by agonized cries. Footpads beating their victim or a couple of bucks taking their sport. Someone whistled at me. I ignored it, hurrying on past another gambling house, a number of taverns, an elegant brothel with slender white pillars, velvet curtains at the windows, gorgeously attired creatures capering inside with wealthy old men as music played. A savage-faced footpad gave me the eye as I crossed the street. I gave him the finger. He grinned, taking me for a whore, one of his own kind and therefore safe from his attentions.

"'Ave a good night, luv!" he called.

"'Ave a stroke, you bleedin' sod!"

He laughed hoarsely and took off after the two drunken bucks who had abandoned their dazed, bleeding companion and were reeling along the pavement with arms linked. They'd be lucky to reach the next street without being assaulted and robbed. Easy marks. Fools. Begging to be victims. Anything that happened to 'em served 'em right. I turned down another street, noisy life spilling out onto the pavements in a kaleidoscope of violent color. I walked briskly, with the hostile, confident air that had served me so well in St. Giles, a bristling manner that warned all not to mess with this 'un. Leaving the populous street, I moved past a darkened square and down another street clothed in darkness, thieves and prostitutes lurking in the murky shadows, and here I assumed a provocative manner, glancing casually about for a potential customer. You didn't need a blunderbuss if you knew how to conduct yourself. No one was going to rob a whore, and any man who laid a hand on me with rape in mind would find himself clutching his balls and squealing in agony.

Cautious, ever alert, I made my way toward the waterfront, trusting luck to guide me to Skinner's warehouse. I had no idea what I would do when I got there, had no sort of plan in mind, but I would worry about that later. I wasn't going to burst in on a band of dangerous rebels and demand they cease their activities, nothing so dramatic as that. I wanted information, and maybe I'd be able to conceal myself somewhere and eavesdrop. I knew now that trying to reason with Cam would be a waste of time, would only anger him and make things worse. I had tried to talk to him about it before, as had Bancroft, and neither of us had made the least dint in his fierce determination. No, talk would be futile at this point, but if I could somehow learn what they were planning to do next Thursday, I might be able to prevent Cam's participation, if not to thwart the plan entirely.

Bloody, foolhardy Scot! Would he ever come to his senses? Probably not, I realized. Cam was Cam and I really didn't want to change him, I just didn't want him to get his silly head blown off or see him swinging from the end of a rope. As I plunged on through the dark streets I thought about our encounter in the kitchen this afternoon. Nothing to worry about, I assured myself. His pride had been sorely wounded, yes, and he'd been angry. He felt I had deceived him, gone behind his back and made a fool of him somehow, but he'd get over it soon enough. It was absurd for him to feel threatened by my writing, and

Cam would surely see that. He was one of the most successful writers in the country with a vast, loyal following who eagerly awaited his next book. I couldn't hope to compete with him, nor would I dream of trying. Poor, darling Cam, he was so terribly sensitive beneath that harsh, thorny facade.

I was nearing the waterfront now, a dark, sinister area at night, a labyrinth of gloomy warehouses and seamen's taverns, bridges spanning the Thames, ghostly ships bobbing on their moorings. I could smell tar and salt and canvas, fish and hemp and the horrid stench of the water itself. The Thames was always awash with refuse and garbage, and bloated corpses were not at all uncommon. No wonder there was so much disease in the city, I thought. Heavily armed night watchmen patrolled some of the warehouses, their swinging lanterns like fireflies in the distance, and bawdy maritime ballads were raucously sung in the taverns. I moved through the labyrinth, anxious now, worried about the time, wondering how I was ever going to find Skinner's in this darkness.

A swollen silver-gray moon rode high in an ashy sky filled with ponderous black clouds while below everything was pitch black, the light spilling out of the taverns only intensifying the gloom. I reached the docks, at the water's edge now. Waves sloshed noisily against the hulls of the ships that rocked in a tightly packed row, only a few feet between them, their masts soaring up in the night like thin, skeletal fingers. A great bridge spanned the river nearby, and I heard giggling and panting noises as a prostitute entertained a customer against the stone railing. I strolled along apprehensively, the wooden planking uneven beneath my feet, water slapping, sloshing, ships creaking and groaning as though in agony.

A church bell tolled in the distance, one, two, three ... eight, nine, ten, eleven times. It was eleven o'clock! They'd be there now. Lusty cries and the sounds of smashing furniture and breaking glass broke the silence as a fight broke out in one of the taverns downriver. I stopped, standing beside a huge barrel that smelled of tar, a coil of rope atop it. What to do? This was absolutely futile. I could wander around in the darkness all night long ... if I didn't have my throat slit or wasn't gang-raped by a pack of drunken sailors. My nerve was disappearing fast. A trembling was beginning to stir inside. No one was entirely fearless, not even Duchess Randy. Whatever had possessed me to take such an insane risk?

Footsteps approached. I cringed, and then I scolded myself

and drew myself up, fierce, hostile, prepared to knee and claw and wound. Miranda James might cringe, but Duchess Randy had been in dozens of situations a hell of a lot worse than this. A lantern swung, the dim yellow-orange rays swirling in a slowly moving circle that illuminated sections of wooden planking, a pair of scuffed brown boots, legs clad in navy blue and the skirt of a heavy navy-blue jacket. The rest of the man was in shadow. He was humming a ditty to himself and stumbled now and then, the lantern swinging in wide arcs. I heaved a sigh of relief. One of the watchmen, clearly the worse for drink. I stepped from beside the barrel, directly into his path. He jumped and gave a hoarse cry, frightened out of his wits.

"Evenin'," I said amiably.

The man backed away, raised his lantern and stared at me with wide, terrified eyes. Broad-shouldered, stocky, he had a fleshy, pockmarked face and shaggy black hair streaked with gray. Finally realizing I wasn't a murderous ruffian intent on plunging a knife into his heart, he gulped, shook his head and took a hefty swig of rum from the bottle he carried in his free hand. I smiled a friendly, reassuring smile.

"Didn't mean-ta spook ya, luv," I said.

"Jesus! My 'eart near leaped outta my chest. You shouldn't oughta pop out at a soul like that, wench. You ain't one of th' regular girls, are you? 'Adn't never seen you 'round 'ere before."

"Come down 'ere to meet a bloke. Said 'e'd be waitin' in front-a Skinner's ware'ouse, but I ain't familiar with th' waterfront. 'Fraid I'm lost, luv. Think you could 'elp a poor workin' girl find 'er way?"

The watchman grinned. "You're way off course, wench. Skinner's ain't on th' docks. It's back be'ind these ware'ouses, near dry dock. Walk back to th' bridge, go up th' street till you pass a yard with boats settin' up on blocks. Skinner's is right beyond it, one uv a row-a ware'ouses, alleys between 'em. 'As a big white sign over th' front. Ya can't miss it."

"Thanks, luv. You're a sweet'eart."

"Watch yourself, wench, Lotta unfriendly types wanderin' around 'ere at night."

I blew him a kiss and hurried back toward the bridge and followed his directions. Less than five minutes later I passed the boatyard, and there was just enough moonlight for me to discern the white sign hanging over the windows of one of the warehouses across the way. No lights were burning, at least not in front. I approached the warehouse and started down the narrow alley that separated it from the warehouse on the left. A cat yowled, leaping out of the darkness. I gasped, paused, my heart pounding. It was terribly dark here, blacker than black, and I could hear rats scurrying in the garbage that littered the ground in great piles. Far away, at the very end of the alley, a dim yellow glow shone into the darkness, coming from a window set high up in the wall, a mere slit of light, barely visible from here. Taking a deep breath, I moved on down the alley toward the light, rats darting in every direction, garbage scattering.

The window was small, at least eight feet from the ground, several old crates piled haphazardly along the wall beneath it. It was open to provide a bit of air to those inside, but the curtains were drawn, the light streaming from an inch-wide slit where they hadn't quite come together. Hearing a murmur of voices, I hesitated only a moment, then nimbly but cautiously climbed up until I was crouching directly in front of the window. Crates wobbled precariously beneath me as I changed my position and peered through the slit in the curtains.

There were seven of them, sitting around a table in the center of the large, cluttered room that was apparently some kind of office, and another, a tall, husky blond youth, stood in the shadows just beyond the misty circle of light shed by a single lamp sitting in the middle of the table. Cam sat beside the man named Ian, their faces grim, deeply shadowed. The man sitting on Cam's right had broad, rugged features and thick yellow-red hair, a nasty scar on his cheek, and the other four were turned away from the window, only their shoulders and heads visible from where I crouched. Several papers and a large map covered the surface of the table.

"—set, then," Ian was saying. His voice was harsh, only one side of his mouth moving as he spoke. "We'll go over it one more time."

"Do you really think it's necessary, cousin?" Cam said dryly. "Everyone here knows his role, knows what he's to do."

His cousin. Of course. That explained the family resemblance. Cousin Ian bristled, his blue eyes full of hostility.

"You may have financed most of this, Cam, but I happen to be in charge. I'd appreciate it if you'd keep that in mind."

A faint, ironic smile played on Cam's lips. The two men clearly detested each other, perhaps because they were so much alike, but while Cam's bitterness and hostility was held in check

and contained behind a cool, civilized facade, his cousin had
no such polish. Violence might seethe beneath the surface, and
he might be harsh, but Cam was not a vicious man. Ian was,
vicious as any cutthroat who roamed the streets, a testy, fiery,
violent man as dangerous as a rattlesnake and as quick to strike.
I sensed that at once, and a cold shiver seemed to move down
my spine.

"We'll start from the beginning," he said harshly, baring
the teeth on the right side of his mouth. "The house is here"—
he pointed to a spot on the map—"two miles outside of London,
a charming retreat surrounded by woods and conveniently iso-
lated. Cousin Cam rented it for Arabella as soon as they returned from Scotland. She's spent very little time there, but
she's spoken of it with great fondness to Cumberland, saying
that she'd love to spend some time there with him, far away
from the bustle and strain of court."

"We know all that," the man with the scar said impatiently.
"She has an apartment at the palace, luxurious quarters generously provided by The Butcher, but she's shy, demure, hates
being on public display. She'd prefer to stay in the country
house and have him visit her there, but he has refused to
consider it. And now—"

Ian shot him a savage look, cutting him short, then continued
in the same harsh, matter-of-fact voice.

"She has finally persuaded him to spend a few days with
her there. They will leave next Thursday—after Cumberland's
men have checked the place out. They'll find nothing, for the
eight barrels of gunpowder have been stowed away in a hidden
cache in the wine cellar, behind a stone wall that opens only
when you press a secret lever. A 'priest's hole,' I believe it's
called."

He paused, looking at the other men, enjoying himself.
Words rang in my mind. I had asked Cam what he had done
with the money Sheppard had given him for *Spoils. I used it
to rent a very elegant house in the country, just outside London. . . . The rest of it went for perfume, a number of elegant
satin gowns and eight barrels of gunpowder. Are you satisfied?*
I hadn't believed him. I had thought he was taunting me. Every
word had been true. Lady Arabella was one of the conspirators.
Cam had brought her back from Scotland—she must have gone
there after her husband's death—and she had come to London
with the express purpose of fascinating Cumberland and win-
ning his confidence. Her great beauty and the Duke's previous

interest in her had made her task quite simple. Financed by Cam, wearing the perfume and the satin gowns he had bought her, she had easily seduced the Duke of Cumberland, and now she was going to lead him into a trap.

"Cumberland's the most hated man in England," Ian continued. "He never appears in public without a heavy guard, never travels without a troop of his private soldiers. The sod lives in fear of assassination and has taken every precaution—that's been our problem. Till now there's been no way we could possibly get to him. For over a year we've had to cool our heels, plan after plan worked out, discarded—"

There was a loud, rustling noise in the garbage nearby, followed immediately by a dull thud on the crate next to the one on which I crouched. Turning my head away from the window, I peered at the crate. There was just enough light for me to see a furry gray form as large as a grapefruit, a long, scaly tail writhing to and fro. My blood ran cold. I started. The crates wobbled noisily, threatening to collapse. The enormous rat dove into the garbage and scurried away.

"What was that!" one of the men exclaimed.

"Probably a cat," Cam said calmly. "I heard one yowling when I arrived. The alley's full of plump, savory rodents."

"I don't like it! Maybe we should—"

"Shall we get *on* with it!" Ian snapped. "I don't care to be here half the night. Relax, MacLeod, it was just a cat. After the house has been thoroughly checked out, Cumberland and Arabella will leave London, traveling with ten handpicked men. Cumberland's personal cook, his valet, and two of his menservants will have gone on ahead to prepare things, a very small staff for the king's son, but Arabella has stressed that she wants privacy, as few servants as possible. The cook will prepare a lavish meal. The menservants will serve it in the dining room. The valet will be upstairs, turning down the bed, laying out the Duke's linen nightshirt and his sleeping cap—"

"Do you have to tell us every bloody detail!" The man with the scar said impatiently.

Ian gave him a vicious look, impatient himself, aggravated by these interruptions. Cam leaned back in his chair, arms folded across his chest, a bored expression on his face. The husky, good-looking blond youth was no longer visible, must have stepped back into the shadows. Still shivering from the sight of the rat and the fright he'd given me, I balanced myself carefully on top of the crates, craning my neck as I peered through the slit in the curtains. The alley seemed to be full of sinister noises now, but I forced myself to ignore them, forced myself to concentrate on what was happening inside. Ian continued to talk.

"After dinner, after Cumberland has gone upstairs to prepare for bed, Arabella, kind, thoughtful creature that she is, will carry four bottles of excellent French wine out to the men standing guard around the house, said wine to be shared among them. The gracious lady will see that each man has a glass of it, to make their long vigil a bit less unpleasant, and half an hour later all of them will be sleeping like babies. The drug's very potent."

"What if she slips up?" MacLeod broke in. "What if she makes a mistake and gets the wrong bottles of wine? We'll go charging in and—"

"The bottles are clearly marked!" Ian snapped. "I placed them there in the rack myself. Arabella knows exactly where they are. She's no fool, MacLeod. She has as much to lose as we do. She's not going to muck up. Just be sure *you* don't!"

"Up your arse! What makes you think you're so goddamned superior? I for one could do without your smug, condescending manner, treating the rest of us like we're dolts, bossing everyone around!"

"You want out?" Ian asked. "You're perfectly free to get up from this table and walk out."

"Yeah, and you'd put a knife in my back, wouldn't you, you sod?"

"Right between the shoulder blades!"

"Are we going to massacre each other," Cam asked dryly, "or are we going to get on with things?"

"I don't know why *he* has to be in charge!" MacLeod protested. "You're the one who put up the money for all this, Gordon. You should be directing it, not him."

"I was under the impression we were all in this together," Cam said. "After Cumberland has been disposed of, it would give me considerable pleasure to watch you and my dear cousin cut each other to shreds, but until then I suggest you both cool down."

MacLeod mumbled something I couldn't make out, and although his back was to the window, I could imagine his expression. Ian's clear blue eyes were full of hatred as he stared across the table, his sharp, lean face a chilling mask with the

~377~

heavy red-brown wave slanting across his brow. Several moments passed. The tension that crackled in the air inside was almost visible. The other men were uncomfortable, shifting about uneasily in their chairs. Cam still leaned back with his arms folded, bored, above it all.

"Arabella will distribute the wine," Ian went on irritably, "then go upstairs and keep The Butcher occupied. At precisely eleven o'clock we'll leave the Green Oak Inn, which is approximately half a mile from the house Cam rented. We'll go to the house, slip in, overpower the four servants and bring the eight barrels of gunpowder up from the cellar. They'll be placed in the sitting room directly below the bedroom. Arabella will join us. The fuse will be lighted, we'll all scurry out into the woods, the house will go up like a tinderbox and Cumberland will be blown to kingdom come."

"How do we know he won't hear us bringing up the barrels?" the man with the scar asked. "How do we know he won't wake up, and—"

"He'll be sound asleep," Ian assured him. "Arabella will persuade him to drink some of the wine, too."

"The servants—we gonna leave 'em in the house?"

Ian nodded, eyes cold, without feeling. "We'll garotte them before bringing up the barrels. They'll have seen our faces. We can't afford to let them live."

I crouched there on top of the crates and listened with mounting horror as he talked about the murders of four innocent men in such a cold, matter-of-fact voice. How could Cam possibly be related to such a monster? How could he possibly be a part of such a diabolical plot? I shivered. I had heard enough. I carefully climbed down from my precarious perch and stood in the alley for a moment, shaken to the core. Rats scurried in the garbage, filling the alley with scratchy, rustling noises, and shadows seemed to move in the darkness, blacker than black, surrounding me, closing in. A dark form approached slowly, stealthily, moving along the wall.

Get hold of yourself, Miranda, I scolded. You can't lose your nerve now. Get out of this stinking alley. Get back to the house.

I turned and started cautiously toward the street that separated the warehouses and the boatyard. Someone was following me. I could hear footsteps behind me. He was getting closer, closer. I could feel his eyes boring into the back of my neck. Nonsense. Nonsense. It's just your nerves. A rat skittered across my foot. I froze, panting, afraid I'd pass out. The walls of the warehouses on either side of the alley seemed to close in on me like towering black waves that would topple at any moment, swallowing me up.

He took another step. I whirled around. He was almost upon me. I couldn't see his face, only a tall, dark form. I gasped. He leaped toward me, and I swung at him and kicked and tried to knee him in the groin, but he was nimble, agile, despite his size, and two strong arms wrapped around me, holding me up, my legs kicking in air. I reared back, fighting furiously, and he dropped me and I scrambled in the garbage and he reached down for me and I caught hold of his hand and tried to sink my teeth into it, but again he was too quick, jerking me to my feet, slinging a warm, muscular arm around my throat.

"Easy, easy," he crooned, "I don't want to hurt you."

I kicked his shin, reached back, trying to claw his cheek, and his forearm pressed steadily, almost gently against the side of my neck. I felt myself growing dizzy, growing weak, a pleasant lethargy stealing over me as that pressure continued. Everything grew hazy. I began to drift into a warm, cozy oblivion, sleepy, so sleepy, limbs growing numb. "Relax," he crooned into my ear, "that's right, just relax, lovely, lovely...." Then I disappeared into that pleasant, welcoming haze.

"—in the alley, huddled up on top of those crates under the window and peering in at us."

The voice seemed to be coming from a long distance, soft and blurred, not at all unpleasant. I blinked, my head resting back against a broad shoulder, two strong arms curled loosely around my waist, holding me up.

"Don't think she could possibly be a spy," the voice went on, deep and melodious. "Probably a waterfront girl. Fought like she knew what she was doing. I got her in my stranglehold, didn't choke her, just applied a little pressure against the side of her neck. She passed right out."

I opened my eyes. Everything was foggy, softly blurred, but I could see the flickering light and the men around the table, on their feet now, looking at me. The light hurt my eyes. My head ached dreadfully. The husky blond held me almost tenderly in front of him. I moaned and peered up at his face. It was young and fresh and not unattractive, the lips full and pink, the dark brown eyes gentle. He couldn't have been much older than twenty.

"You all right, lass?" he inquired.

His Scotch accent was pronounced, a pleasant blur as though he caressed each word with his tongue. I nodded and stood up straight, and he unwound his arms from around my waist and rested his large hands on my shoulders with just enough authority to let me know who was in control.

"How much did you hear?" Cam's cousin asked sharply.

"I—I heard everything," I murmured. "I know what you're planning to do. It's—"

"Shut up!" he commanded.

"What are we going to do with her?" one of the men asked.

"We'll have to kill her," Ian said calmly.

"Now hold on!" the youth protested, tightening his grip on my shoulders. "Killing Cumberland is one thing, and it may be necessary to kill his servants, too, though I still think we can get around that, but murdering a girl in cold blood is—it's every bit as bad as what he did at Culloden!"

"She has to die."

"Robbie Bruce isn't going to stand here and—"

"We have no choice," Ian snapped, cutting him off. "You're quite adept with that stranglehold of yours, Robbie. Slap it on her again, hold it a bit longer, a bit tighter. It'll be over in less than a minute."

"I'm no killer! I—"

"Killed your share of Englishmen during the late conflict, though, didn't you? Young as you are? Killed a number of them with your bare hands if I'm not mistaken."

I was in the middle of a nightmare, standing in a murky room with bare brown wooden walls brushed with the elongated shadows of the men who stood around the table, the single lamp shedding a flickering circle of misty yellow light. It was a nightmare, yet I could smell sawdust and sweat and rat droppings and feel Robbie's fingers gripping my shoulders tightly and feel the blood coursing through my veins. I could see the faces of the other men—Ian's fierce, determined, Cam's bored, indifferent, as though he had never laid eyes on me in his life.

"This is different!" Robbie protested. "She's not the enemy. She—"

"No?" Ian asked. "She's seen all of us. She knows what we plan to do. You're going to let her saunter out of here?"

"We don't have to kill her. We—uh—we can tie her up, keep her prisoner until it's all over."

"Then turn her loose?" Cam's cousin smiled a chilling,

deprecatory smile. "So that she can identify each and every one of us after the fact? You want to be drawn and quartered? Strangle her, Robbie. Show us your technique. Do it!" he ordered.

"I'm not going to!"

Ian sighed wearily. He shook his head. He reached into the pocket of his leaf brown frock coat and pulled out a long, thin cord with a knot in the middle. Wrapping an end around each hand, he jerked it, testing its strength, and it made a loud, snapping noise like the crack of a whip. My knees gave way beneath me. I would have fallen had Robbie not slung an arm around my waist, supporting me. Cam's face still had that cool, indifferent expression. The scar-faced man was scowling. The others looked tense, uneasy.

"I'm afraid I haven't your particular skills," Ian said calmly. "I use a garotte. It's quite painful, I understand, much more painful than your method. Shove her over here."

"That won't be necessary," Cam informed him.

Ian whirled around to face him, the cord taut between his hands, and Cam looked at him with bored blue eyes.

"Put it down, Ian," he said.

"You're going to kill her yourself?"

"I intend to take full responsibility for her. She won't give us away, I assure you."

"How can you be sure of that? She's your woman, yes—I recognized her at once, of course. It's your fault. She must have followed you here. You were careless, Cam. Clumsy. Your little whore is going to pay for it."

Cam flipped the tail of his jacket back and pulled out the long black pistol crammed into the waistband of his breeches. He pointed it at the spot directly between his cousin's eyes, just above the bridge of his nose. His manner was utterly calm, his eyes still bored, but not a man in the room believed he would hesitate to pull the trigger. He cocked it. The noise sounded like an explosion in the silence. Ian paled, his sharp, bony cheekbones turning as white as chalk.

"Drop the cord, cousin, or I'll splatter your brains all over the wall."

Ian dropped the cord, his eyes gleaming with hatred. Robbie gave a heavy sigh of relief, his breath brushing my cheek. The man called MacLeod, a tall, sturdy Scot with unruly brown hair, chuckled, delighted to see Ian so effectively put down.

Ian looked more than ever like a vicious fox.

"You're making a grave mistake, Cam," he said in a thin voice.

"I'll take that risk."

"You're risking *our* lives as well!"

"Miranda isn't going to say a word to anyone, before or after."

"I still think—"

"No one gives a ruddy sod what you think!" MacLeod told him. "Let's get the bloody hell out of here. We'll meet late Thursday afternoon at The Green Oak."

"Right!" Robbie said.

He released me. I was still weak, doubtful that I could walk, and that nightmare feeling persisted, none of this quite real. Cam thrust the pistol back into the waistband of his breeches and came over to me and took my wrist in a firm grip and led me out of the room and into the vast warehouse and I stumbled along beside him, my cloak swirling behind me. I could smell cotton and hemp and something that might have been whale oil as Cam moved purposefully toward a door in the rear, undeterred by the darkness.

The night air seemed cool after the stuffiness inside, and there were a few thin rays of moonlight now, just enough to gild surfaces with a pale silver sheen and intensify the shadows. I could see Cam's face now and it might have been chiseled of pale marble, hard, immobile. The blond youth caught up with us as we moved down the dark street in back of the warehouse.

"That was touchy, Cam," he said quietly, striding along beside us. "Ian and MacLeod going at each other like that, you having to show your pistol. I don't like the feel of it. Sometimes I think Ian's gone off his head, getting worse and worse these past months. I can hardly believe he's your cousin."

"Distant cousin," Cam replied. "We share the same bloodlines, but the relationship is tenuous. He was at Culloden. He witnessed the butchery. It may well have unhinged him."

"I was at Culloden, too," Robbie reminded him, "in the thick of it, in my kilt and tam, lost my weapon early on, had to use my hands, bloody carnage all around, and it didn't unhinge me."

"You're young, Robbie. Resilient. The young don't scar so easily. Got your lorry?"

"In the yard over there. Littered with wilted cabbage leaves and onions, I'm afraid. I deliver produce to Covent Garden," he explained to me. "Sorry I had to manhandle you in the alley, ma'am. You were like a wildcat."

I made no reply. I was still in the middle of the nightmare. We crossed the street, and Cam lifted me up onto the flat wooden seat of a wagon that stood in a dark, littered yard. He climbed up beside me. Robbie Bruce swung up on the other side, grabbing the reins and clicking them smartly. The sharp, sweet odor of onions stung my eyes as the wagon pulled out of the yard. I could hardly see the two sturdy horses. They moved at a steady plod down the street, and the wagon bounced and swayed, rocking me from side to side. Cam wrapped an arm around my shoulder and held me tightly, his profile immobile in the pale moonlight, his eyes staring straight ahead. As we passed a brightly lighted tavern rowdy sailors spilled out onto the street, yelling at us. Robbie Bruce pulled a long whip out of its holder and cracked it in the air over their heads. They fell back, filling the air with noisy obscenities.

How long did it take us to reach Fleet? Fifteen minutes? Thirty? I lost all conception of time as we drove through the night, away from the waterfront, past the dark squares, past the gambling halls and brothels. Robbie had to use his whip several more times, and once Cam pulled out his pistol, leveling it at two ruffians who rushed us and tried to seize the reins. One look at his face and the gun and they scurried back into the shadows. Fleet was deserted, looking bare and bleak in the thin gray moonlight. Cam swung down, reached up to help me alight, thanked Robbie for the ride and jerked his head curtly, indicating that I should precede him down the passageway.

The court was silent, but lights were glowing in all three houses. I had left candles burning in the sitting room and the bedroom upstairs, flames protected by glass globes. Mrs. Wooden's bedroom windows upstairs were soft yellow squares, and hazy light streamed from the windows of Major Barnaby's study. The leaves of the pear tree rustled quietly as I opened the front door. Everything was calm, quiet, peaceful, but the nightmare quality persisted. I turned in the hallway to watch Cam come in. He closed the door behind him, locked it and stared at me for a moment before stepping into the sitting room to pour himself a brandy. He hadn't addressed a single word to me all night. That lethal calm was terribly unnerving. I stood in the hall for a few moments, watching him drink the brandy, his eyes staring at nothing, his face totally devoid of expression, and then I went upstairs to the bedroom.

I took off the long purple cloak and hung it in the wardrobe. I was surprised to find my hands were trembling as I shut the wardrobe doors. I closed my eyes. I could feel my nerves being pulled taut, tauter, tauter, threatening to snap. When they did I would fly apart. I couldn't let that happen. I took several deep breaths and stepped over to the mirror and studied my face in the glass. My cheeks were pale, and faint mauve-blue shadows tinted my lids. Candlelight burnished my hair, making it seem a darker red, glinting with coppery gold highlights, and my eyes were a very dark blue, the eyes of a stranger.

I heard him coming up the stairs. I turned, willing myself to hold on to some semblance of calm. He stopped just inside the doorway, looking at me. He had removed his jacket, his neckcloth. His white lawn shirt was opened at the throat, the full bell sleeves gathered at the wrist. The long pistol was still thrust into the waistband of his snug black breeches, the butt jutting out. He didn't say a word, just stood there in the doorway with one hand resting high up on the sill, the other lightly touching his thigh. The heavy black wave slanted across his brow, and his blue eyes gleamed with speculation, as though he couldn't quite decide what to do with me.

We were silent, and that was appropriate, for none of this was real, it was part of a dream. The lean, handsome man standing in the doorway, the pale woman in her violet blue dress, hair gleaming red gold, the bedroom with its faded lavender walls, shabby blue-gray rugs with pink and green patterns, the heavy dark-oak wardrobe and the huge four-poster with its worn blue satin counterpane—all were insubstantial, wavering in the misty silver-gold light of the candle. The tears filling my eyes made everything blurry, and I brushed them away and forced myself to grasp reality. Cam Gordon gazed at me thoughtfully, and I bit my lower lip, numbness leaving now, emotions sweeping over me.

"Go ahead," I said. "Get it over with."

"You shouldn't have meddled, Miranda," he said calmly.

"You shouldn't have been there in the first place. You're a goddamned fool, Cam. You're going to get yourself hung."

"Don't try to change the subject."

"That cousin of yours—he's mad. He wanted to kill me. I thought you were going to let him."

"Perhaps I should have," he replied.

I groped behind me, found a hairbrush, closed my fingers

around the handle. I hurled it across the room at him as hard as I could. It crashed loudly against the doorframe just inches from his head. Cam didn't blink an eye.

"You're not going to say a word about any of this," he said.

"I'm not going to let you get yourself killed, you sod! I'm not going to stand by and—"

"You won't say a word," he interrupted, his voice quite firm, still calm. "You'll forget everything that happened, everything you heard."

"Like hell I will. If you think you're going to—"

"I'll take any measures I deem necessary," he continued. "If I have to keep you prisoner in this house, tie you up, gag you, I will. I don't imagine that will be necessary."

All the anger went out of me then. I felt weak, helpless, utterly defenseless. Cam bent down to pick up the hairbrush and took it over to a table. The full white lawn sleeves billowed as he moved. He put the hairbrush down, turning to look at me with lazy nonchalance.

"It's insanity, Cam, absolute insanity."

"I don't care to talk about it any more, Miranda."

He took the pistol from his waistband and placed it on top of the table. The long barrel gleamed silver black in the candle-light.

"You might as well kill me now," I said. My voice was trembling. "You're going to get yourself hung, and I—I couldn't live without you. If anything happened to you, I'd have no reason to go on living. I—I love you, you son of a bitch, and—"

"Hush, Miranda," he said quietly.

He came over to me and attempted to take me in his arms, and I slapped him across the face so hard my wrist almost snapped. Cam flinched, but his expression never changed. My palm stung painfully. My wrist was sore. A vivid pink handprint burned on his right cheek. He pulled me into his arms and covered my mouth with his and I struggled for several moments and then sobbed and clung to him desperately. Cam lifted his head and looked into my eyes, his own gleaming darkly. He kissed me once more, warm lips caressing mine with a new tenderness that gradually grew urgent. He scooped me up into his arms and carried me over to the bed and everything was lost then, lost in the cruel splendor of love that was my salvation and my glory, my torment and my fate.

29

THE SKY SHOULD HAVE BEEN WET AND GRAY AND OP-
pressive, the city dark, shrouded in gloom this Thursday afternoon, but it wasn't that way at all. The sun was shining brightly,
radiant rays splashing through all the windows, filling the house
with silver white light, and a bird had the temerity to warble
throatily in the pear tree out front. The sky was a pure pale
blue. The air seemed to sparkle. It was, in fact, a glorious
summer day, this Thursday, and even now Cumberland's men
were checking out the house in the country outside London
while, at the palace, the Bloody Duke and his gorgeous, demure
mistress were making preparations to depart. Others were making preparations, too, and there was nothing I could do to
prevent it.

There should have been a clap of thunder. Lightning should
have streaked across an ominous black sky. The bird trilled
merrily. The poodles barked as Mrs. Wooden brought them
outside for a romp in the court. I turned away from the sitting
room window and listened to the lazy brass clock ticking on
top of the mantel. It was four o'clock now, and Cam still hadn't
come back. He had left shortly after twelve, informing me that
he had "business" to take care of and would be back as soon
as possible. I knew that he planned to leave for the Green Oak
Inn at seven in a hired coach . . . three hours from now. Only
three more hours. I tried to hold the panic at bay, tried to hold
on to some vestige of calm.

These past five days had been strange indeed, so quiet, so
uneventful, and had it not been for the dark cloud hanging over
them—the knowledge of what he planned to do—they would
have been wonderful. It wasn't necessary to tie me up, to gag
me, to keep me prisoner in the house, for he knew I wouldn't
say anything. I couldn't. It would mean his death, along with
the deaths of the gentle Robbie Bruce and all the others. A

new Cam had been my companion since the night Robbie brought us back from the waterfront. The harshness, the surliness, the scowls, the moody silences and angry outbursts had vanished as though by magic. He had been kind, attentive, tender, if somewhat remote, treating me with a quiet courtesy he had never shown before.

The days had been serene, and the nights . . . the nights swollen with passion, the room a haze of blue gray darkness, the ceiling speckled with moonbeams that danced like lazy silver sprites as on the bed he took me again and again, caressing me, stroking me, cherishing me, our bodies moving in a dance as lazy, as lovely, as that of the moonbeams. The fierceness, the furor of my demon lover gave way to a new consideration, a gentle concern for my own pleasure, as though I were a treasured instrument and he a master musician bent on drawing forth the sweetest sounds. Strong, skilled, superbly controlled, he gave, where before he had taken, and the splendor of those nights seemed to shred my senses and carry me to new heights of ecstacy. Weight, warmth, sweat, smells, hands exploring my body, lips caressing my skin, manhood probing, probing, deeper, yet deeper, uniting us with each stroke, unleashing waves of sensation that drowned us both in taut, tormenting, unbearable bliss that went on and on and on until, exhausted, entwined, we watched the moonbeams give way to the soft, rosy glow of dawn. He never mentioned love, no, he was too proud, too stubborn, too stoic to let that word pass his lips, but words were not necessary.

Yet underlying all this was the sure knowledge that, come Thursday evening, he would leave the city and join his countrymen in a suicidal mission. It was almost as though he sensed that . . . that these were the last days we would ever spend together, that, like me, he had a premonition of disaster and wanted to leave me with memories to cherish. How could I savor the splendor, knowing what was to come? How could I welcome the tenderness, the compassion, when it was to be taken from me so soon? Better a thorny, churlish, temperamental Cam who was not going to participate in this wild folly. Better blows and angry words and surly silences than gentle caresses from a man who was going to abandon me and charge headlong toward almost certain disaster.

Calmly, without emotion, he had explained everything to me, and now I understood much better the motives behind the planned assassination. It wasn't merely for revenge, although that played an important part. Cumberland's death would, they felt, be a strong political statement, an ultimatum that would make the King reconsider and revise his policies toward Scotland and those Scots who had supported the Bonnie Prince. He would declare a general amnesty, would restore all the properties that had been taken over by the Crown...or else he would meet the same fate as his son. Couldn't they see that Cumberland's death would only make matters worse, would strengthen his resolve to totally crush all those involved in the "treason" led by Charles Edward Stuart, the Young Pretender? When I tried to point that out to him, Cam merely replied that I didn't understand such matters.

I knew now, too, why Lady Arabella Dunston had thrown her lot with the rebels. Unbeknownst to Cumberland, the lovely Arabella had Stuart blood and was, in fact, distantly related to the Bonnie Prince. Though raised and educated in England, she was Scottish by birth and after her husband's death had returned to Scotland to live with relatives as impoverished as she. One of the few to know of her heritage, and knowing of the Duke's former interest in her, Cam had gone to Scotland to persuade her to join them. Hating Cumberland already, embittered by what he had done to her countrymen and fiercely loyal to the distant cousin whom she believed to be the rightful king, Lady Arabella had promptly consented to do anything she could to help squash the Hanovers, dreaming like so many others of a day when Prince Charlie would make a victorious return.

While the others might possibly escape undetected, Lady Arabella's participation in the conspiracy would be obvious to everyone, and there was no way she could remain in England after Cumberland was killed. A closed carriage would be waiting in the woods tonight to take her directly to Dover where at seven in the morning a boat would carry her across the Channel to France, and there she would join the Bonnie Prince in his ignominious exile and wait for that glorious day when Justice was Done. Lady Arabella Dunston would be commemorated in Highland legend and poetry along with Flora MacDonald as one of the heroines of her country...unless her neck was broken by the public hangman.

As I stood there in the sitting room, listening to the poodles yapping merrily as they romped about the court, the premonition I had felt for so long grew stronger still. They had worked everything out down to the finest detail, yes, but something was going to happen...something unexpected, unforeseen. They were all going to be killed or captured. Something was going to happen. I was certain of it. The premonition grew, taking shape like a huge black cloud that swelled overhead, blotting out the sunlight, shadowing my soul. I couldn't let him leave. I couldn't. There was nothing I could do to help Lady Arabella or Robbie or any of the others, but I had to save Cam. Somehow I had to keep him from leaving. I couldn't persuade him with words. He was much too strong for me to be able to overpower him. I could hit him over the head with something, perhaps, but what if I hurt him, what if I cracked his skull? There had to be some way...there had to be.

I heard Marcelon calling after the dogs, scolding them, and I suddenly remembered something...what was it? It was there, just at the edge of my memory. We had been talking about sleeping and...Lady Arabella was going to give the soldiers wine laced with a drug that would put them to sleep immediately. Mrs. Wooden sometimes had trouble getting to sleep, she had confessed, it was one of the signs of age, alas, loath though she was to admit it, she used to drop right off, but now.... The pharmacist was so dear, so adorable, so understanding, and he gave her this marvelous drug. Three or four drops in a glass of wine and she slept like a baby. *Three or four drops in a glass of wine....* I knew then what I had to do.

Marcelon was quite surprised by my visit. She had brought the dogs in and was feeding them, chopped liver for Sarge and Pepe, chicken bits for Brandy, who had grown remarkably these past months, three times the size he had been when he first came begging for carrots, though still considerably smaller than his brothers. They barked and pranced, Brandy devouring his food and trying to eat Pepe's as well, Sarge growling ominously when the prissy upstart approached his bowl. I ignored their antics, trying to control my pounding heartbeat, trying to appear casual and offhand. Marcelon chattered vivaciously, leading me into the study, telling me about the latest spat with Major Barnaby, and it was a good ten minutes before I could bring up the drug. I was having a little trouble getting to sleep, I explained—there'd been so much on my mind recently, I had been so busy—I would like to try her potion.

She looked worried. She looked dubious. I was far too young

to need to rely on any kind of drug, she informed me in a stern voice, and then she launched into a lecture and I was almost in tears before she finally cut herself short and peered at me closely and left the room abruptly, returning with a small bottle of inky-looking fluid. No more than three or four drops, she warned me, and I was to return the bottle first thing in the morning. She took my hand and squeezed it and said she hoped I knew I could come to her any time, no matter what problem I might have. I was like a daughter to her and would never know the *lift* I had given her these past months. She had been so *low*, and. . . . I hugged her quickly, assured her that I would be fine and hurried back home.

Cam returned half an hour later. He looked weary, distracted. He gave me a light, perfunctory kiss and went on upstairs. I took out the last of the bottles of wine Sheppard had sent, fine French wine, the best—thank goodness there was one left. I hesitated a moment, listened to make certain that Cam was still upstairs and then uncorked the bottle. Three or four drops in a glass. How many in a bottle? I didn't dare wait until I poured the wine to put the drops in. He might see me. I would drug the whole bottle and then only pretend to drink the glass I poured for myself. How many drops? I removed the stopper from the tiny bottle and dumped a third of the fluid into the wine. It made blurry gray-black streaks in the light rose. I recorked the bottle and shook it and the streaks gradually disappeared, blending with the rose. The wine looked slightly darker now, but I felt sure he wouldn't notice.

A final glass of wine, I would say. A final glass of wine before you go. It will relax you. My hand trembled as I hid the tiny bottle behind the ginger jar and put the bottle of wine back where it belonged. What if I had added too much? Dear God, what if I poisoned him? No, no, that was absurd. He was only going to have one glass. I took several deep breaths, pulling myself together. I had to remain calm. I couldn't let him suspect. I stepped over to the mirror and brushed back my thick auburn hair. My eyes were a dark, worried blue, my cheeks flushed a faint, soft pink, and the corners of my mouth were drooping sadly. I mustn't let him know what I was feeling. I must put on a brave front and smile and . . . and pretend I understood.

I went upstairs. Cam was in the bedroom, taking clothes from the wardrobe, putting them into a long, fat leather bag with handles that fastened in the middle. It was as large as a small trunk but would be much easier to handle. Why was he packing? Did he plan to flee the country after it was all over? Did he plan to desert me? I caught my breath. He turned, saw me standing in the doorway, saw my expression, and, putting down the waistcoat he had been folding, came over to me and placed his hands on my shoulders.

"It's merely a precaution, Miranda. I need to be prepared for a hasty departure in case—in case something goes wrong."

"But—"

"Nothing is going to go wrong, but I'll carry the bag with me just the same. All of us are. It's just good sense."

"Where—where would you go?"

"I'd go to France, with Arabella. The boat will be waiting for her, and if something should happen, the rest of us—those of us who can make it—will sail with her."

"Cam, I'm so worried. I—"

"Nothing is going to happen," he assured me. "Arabella will be driven to Dover and the rest of us will separate and return to our respective homes and no one will be any the wiser. We've spent months working this out."

"I don't care. I feel—"

"Are you going to fall to pieces on me now?" he asked quietly.

I looked into his eyes. They were stern yet tender, hard yet full of concern. His fingers gently kneaded the flesh of my shoulders. I could feel his warmth, his strength. I wanted to melt into his arms and cling to him and sob, but I didn't. I looked into his eyes for several long moments and held back my tears and, finally, shook my head.

"I—I'm not going to fall to pieces," I said.

Cam squeezed my shoulders. "Good girl," he said, and then he released me and went back to his packing.

"You're making a dreadful job of that," I told him. "Look, everything's all crumpled, jammed in any which way. Let me do it."

Cam looked relieved and stood back and watched with that particular look of male helplessness while I emptied the bag, refolded the clothes, put them back in. Shirts, breeches, waistcoats, frock coats, a heavy cloak, two pairs of boots. Neckcloths, shaving equipment, brush and comb. I was finished in twenty minutes, everything neat and tidy, the bag completely full. Cam took out a flat leather purse thick with money, put it on top of the clothes, then shut the bag and snapped the clasp.

"I went to the bank today," he said, "had a talk with Bancroft, withdrew all my money."

"Oh?"

"I opened an account in your name, Miranda, transferred some funds into it to—" He hesitated, frowning. "I wanted you to be provided for in case something—merely another precaution."

"You didn't have to—"

"Let's not discuss it," he said sharply. "It's five-thirty. I suppose I'd better start getting ready."

"Cam—let's—there's no hurry. Let's have a—a glass of wine together first."

He seemed pleased. He smiled an indulgent smile and then slung his arms around me, glad that I was taking it so well, glad that I wasn't going to make a scene. He tilted my head and gave me a long, lazy kiss that turned into something more than he had planned. I could feel his erection swelling as he held me against him. He had a voracious appetite, my Scot, greedy as could be. A veritable stallion, he was.

"Damn," he said, holding me away from him. "I didn't plan on that. You bewitch me."

"Is it—"

"It's throbbing for you. There's no time. I'll just have to suffer. Tonight, though, when I get back—" He paused and grinned an evil grin. "You'd better eat a hearty dinner. You're going to need a lot of energy."

"I hate for you to go—"

"Go on. Get out of here. Your beguiling presence only makes it harder—to bear, that is. Go get the wine ready. I'll change and join you downstairs in a few minutes."

I was extremely nervous as I brought the wine and two crystal glasses into the sitting room. The sunlight that had been splashing through the windows streamed in lazily now, thin yellow-white rays aswirl with infinitesimal motes of dust. The sky was a darker blue-gray, and hazy purple-blue shadows were beginning to gather in the court. The tray rattled as I set it down on a table. The wine looked terribly dark. Would he notice? The room seemed warmer than usual, although the windows were open and a gentle breeze stirred the pale lime draperies. My cheeks were flushed. My hair felt damp. I adjusted the bodice of my rust and cream striped dress and smoothed down the skirt with hands that fluttered like butterflies.

It was six o'clock when he finally came downstairs, carrying the heavy bag with him. He set it down in the hall beside the old grandfather clock and came on into the sitting room. I was standing by the secretary, composed now, calm as could be on the surface. He was wearing his oldest black breeches and frock coat, nap shiny and worn, an aged waistcoat with steel gray and black satin stripes. A large black silk neckcloth was knotted loosely around his neck, hanging in an uneven triangle. He gave me a fierce look and pulled the cloth up over the lower part of his face, only his eyes, brow and hair visible. Pulling out his pistol, he looked exactly like a savage bandit, blue eyes menacing above the black silk.

"Effective?" he inquired.

"Extremely," I said. "You—you look quite sinister."

He jerked the neckcloth down and smiled. "Good. All of us will have our faces covered when we enter the house. The four servants will take us for bandits, won't be able to identify us. No need to kill them. We'll simply overpower them, tie them up good and tight and dump them out in the woods, then go on about our business."

"I—I'm relieved. Your cousin—"

"Ian's a mite too bloodthirsty even for me," he admitted. "He has a distinct taste for violence, as, indeed, do I, but I'm able to sublimate my darker urges with my charming epics. Ian has no such outlet. He'd gladly garotte all four of them himself and relish every minute of it."

"He frightens me, Cam."

"After this is all over, the rest of us are going to have to do something about Cousin Ian. Ship him off to the colonies, I imagine, unless severer measures are called for. He's too hotheaded, too impetuous. He represents a danger we can do without. I'll be glad to see the last of him."

"Are all Scots so violent?" I asked.

"Not a bit," he replied. "As a whole we're the most lovable race on the face of the earth, gracious, outgoing, friendly to a fault with our bagpipes and kilts and our quaint old customs. It's only rarely you find bad apples like Ian and me."

There was an almost jaunty air about him as he moved over to the mantel, a sense of suppressed excitement, of barely contained energy. He was a man about to prove his manhood in a bold, reckless act of derring-do, and that gave him a curious elation that was purely male and as old as time. After months and months of vicarious adventure spun out at his worktable, he was going to experience the real thing. It was serious business, true, deadly serious, yet there remained a certain thrill that gave him that jaunty air and made him restless, impatient to be off. The crusaders must have felt that elation when they set off to reclaim the Holy Land, I thought. Soldiers certainly felt it when they went off to war with such swaggering aplomb. It was only later that the glow vanished and grim reality intruded.

"It's almost time," he said.

"We have nearly an hour, Cam. Re—relax. Here, let me pour you a glass of wine."

"You're being very good about this, Miranda."

"I'm trying," I said.

I poured the wine. My hand wasn't shaking at all. I handed the glass to him with lowered eyes, demure, resigned.

"I know how worried you've been about all this," he continued, "and I understand. It's something I have to do."

"Of course."

"I'll make it up to you. When this is over, I intend to—to show you how much I appreciate you."

He took a sip of wine, looking at me with thoughtful eyes. He took another sip, apparently finding nothing unusual about the taste.

"I realize I'm not the easiest man in the world to live with," he told me, "but you've been extremely patient. You've been supportive and helpful and I'm afraid I haven't always seemed grateful."

"You—you don't have to say these things, Cam. Finish your wine."

"There've been times, it's true, when I've longed to throttle you, but over all it's been—it's been the best year of my life. There, I've said it. I may be a writer, but I'm not very good when it comes to expressing my feelings."

"I've noticed that."

"I guess what I'm trying to say is that you're the only woman I've known who has never bored me."

"And?"

"When this is over I'm going to do something about it."

He finished his wine and set the glass down. The drug was having no effect whatsoever. I could feel panic beginning to grow. What if it didn't work? Marcelon had been extremely perturbed by my request. She had been out of the room a long time. What . . . what if she had substituted the drug for . . . for colored water? Don't panic, Miranda. Don't panic. He's not leaving this house. If you have to hit him over the head with an andiron, you will.

"Have some more wine," I said calmly.

"I don't suppose another glass would hurt. You're not having any?"

I refilled his glass and handed it to him. "I'm not thirsty. How—how do you feel?"

"Determined. Cumberland's death will do a lot of good for a lot of people, Miranda. This isn't some harebrained, hot-headed scheme dreamed up by a pack of firebrands. It's been carefully—thought—out—" His voice was beginning to slur ever so slightly. It was taking him longer to pronounce his words. "We've worked—everything—out. It's taken us— over—a year to come—come up with this plan—and— and—"

He set the glass down so abruptly that the wine splattered over the rim and made a puddle on the table. He looked at me with wide eyes, realization dawning as the drug began to cloud his mind. I gazed back at him calmly.

"You—you—" His voice was thick.

"I couldn't let you go, Cam."

"Trea—treacherous bitch!"

He stumbled across the room toward me. He swung his arm back, hand tightened into a fist, ready to hit me across the jaw with all his might. His eyes seemed to glaze over then and he lurched forward, toppling like a felled oak. I caught him around the waist, almost falling myself as I caught the full weight of his body. His head lolled across my shoulder. His arms hung limply at his sides. His legs might have been rubber. I tugged and heaved, trying to support him and almost breaking my back in the effort. Straining, panting, I somehow managed to guide him over to the sofa, and when I let go of him and gave him a shove backward, he fell so heavily that one of the springs broke with a noisy twang.

I lifted his legs up onto the sofa and straightened him and put a cushion behind his head and smoothed the hair from his brow, a worried frown creasing my own. Dear God, had I killed him? No, no, he was still breathing, somewhat heavily, and his pulse seemed normal enough. My own was leaping, and my heart was pounding. I sat down in the large chair across from the sofa, the enormity of what I had done sweeping over me. He'd never forgive me. Never. I had betrayed him, yes, but I couldn't let him go. I couldn't lose him. He would be furiously angry, rightfully so, but he . . . he would see, he would understand why I had to do it.

I told myself that, and I tried to believe it as the sunlight grew fainter and the shadows grew longer and the lazy brass clock ticked on and on like some weary but persistent cricket. The room filled with a soft blue haze that gradually turned purple, darkening, and darkness fell and I could barely see him stretched out there on the sofa. The moon came out and a blurry silver seeped in, banishing the purple black. Nine o'clock. Ten. I sat very still, listening to his breathing, trying not to think of what was happening at that house surrounded by woods. Eleven. Eleven-thirty. Twelve. Cam mumbled something and flung an arm out. It dangled over the side of the sofa. He snorted in his sleep and continued to breathe deeply, evenly.

Coffee. He would need lots of coffee when he finally woke up. When would that be? How much of the drug had he taken into his system? Would he sleep until morning? He mumbled again. The drug must be wearing off. I got up and began to light candles, banishing moonlight and shadows. Twelve-fifteen. He was scowling in his sleep. He looked like a great, limp doll stretched out there on the worn sky-blue velvet sofa. I gazed at him for several long moments before going into the kitchen to light the fire and put the coffee on. It was soon bubbling in the pot, filling the room with a rich, tangy aroma.

Food. He hadn't eaten. He would be hungry. I sliced bread and cheese and sausage, keeping myself busy, hoping to still the panic that was building up inside again. He would understand. He . . . he would be angry, he would probably beat me, but . . . I heard him stirring in the front room. I hastily poured coffee into one of the heavy blue cups and hurried to him. He was sitting up on the sofa, his cheeks flushed, his hair damp, spilling across his brow. He brushed it back and looked up at me with eyes that seemed to stare right through me.

"What time is it?" he asked.

"It—it's almost one. Here—I—I thought you would want some coffee."

He took it without a word. He drank it slowly, his normal color returning. I brought the pot in and poured him another cup and set the pot on the mantel, a tremulous sensation rising, threatening to overcome me. I forced it back, forced myself to remain calm. I had done it and I was glad and I would face the consequences without flinching. The house was very, very still. I could hear leaves rustling in the pear tree outside. Cam finished the coffee and set the cup down and wiped his brow again. He stood up. His legs seemed shaky.

"What was it?" he asked.

"It was a—a sleeping potion. Mrs. Wooden gave it to me. I told her that I was having trouble sleeping. She—she had no idea what I planned to use it for. I suppose you—you're terribly angry."

He didn't reply. He tugged at the hem of his waistcoat, straightening it, brushed the lapels of his coat. He might have been alone in the room. The silence was dreadful. I couldn't endure it.

"Say something!" I cried.

"There's no need for words, Miranda."

"*Do* something! Hit me if you want to, but—"

My voice broke. Tears filled my eyes. I stared at him, and he gazed at me as he might gaze at some faintly bothersome stranger who had entered his sitting room by accident. He looked away, and my whole body seemed to go cold. I could take his anger, take his blows, but this calm indifference terrified me. Tears spilled over my lashes as he stepped into the hall, moving past me as though I weren't there.

"Cam!"

I rushed after him. I caught his arm. He took hold of my fingers, pried them away.

"It's over, Miranda."

"You must understand! I had to do it! I—"

There was a commotion in the courtyard. Heavy footsteps rushed across the cobblestones toward the house. Someone pounded on the door. I leaned against the wall as Cam opened the door and Robbie Bruce rushed into the hall. He was out of breath. His blond hair was dark with perspiration, his clothes sweaty. He had clearly been riding at the greatest possible speed and under tremendous stress. One sleeve of his coarsely woven white shirt was torn and there were powder burns on his snug tan breeches, a dark smudge across his right cheekbone. His old leather jerkin was unlaced, flapping, stained with blood. Cam grabbed his upper arms and held him in a tight grip, and the youth took several deep breaths, sweat running down his brow.

"What happened?" Cam demanded.

"We've got to flee, Cam! We can't lose a moment! The redcoats—"

"What happened, man!"

Robbie was near hysterics, incapable of coherent speech. Cam slapped him across the face, a brutal, determined blow that caused the youth to cry out in dismay. He gnawed his lower lip. He shook his head, making a valiant effort to pull himself together, and after a moment he swallowed and looked up at Cam with stunned brown eyes.

"You—you didn't come. We waited and waited and—and finally Ian insisted we go on. We—we were half an hour behind schedule, and everyone was edgy and—and out of sorts. They— Ian was in charge, but we all—the rest of us considered you our leader and when you didn't show up—" He caught his breath again. "Everything went wrong—from the beginning everything went wrong."

Cam released him. Robbie wiped sweat from his eyes, pushed the wet blond locks from his brow.

"The guards were out cold, littering the ground all around the house, and we went in and found the servants and—I *told* Ian we were supposed to cover our faces but he—he—we overpowered them and tied them up and then he took out his garotte and told us to go on and bring the powder up from the cellar. The powder—we got six barrels up without any trouble and then MacLeod—" He shook his head, his eyes filled with grief and pain. "MacLeod dropped a barrel in the hall and it burst open and Campbell was right behind him, carrying a candle. He—Cam, he slipped in the powder! The candle—both of them were blown to pieces. The whole house shook. It—it started burning."

"Arabella—"

"She—she was still upstairs. She hadn't been able to get Cumberland to drink any of the wine. He—he hadn't heard us before, but when the explosion went off he started screeching in terror. He scrambled out onto the roof and screeched for the guards. I raced upstairs and got Arabella and took her out into the woods and then—then the redcoats came. The relief, Cam. The relief! We didn't know—we didn't plan on a relief guard. They arrived minutes after the explosion and all hell broke loose. They—Ian and MacGregor were cut to ribbons, Malcolm was shot and—and they took Burns and Cochrane alive. They got Cumberland down from the roof, and he kept screeching 'Find the woman! Find the woman!' and then—redcoats everywhere, Cam! They were charging through the woods, looking for Arabella—"

"Did you—"

"I got her into the coach, watched it drive away. Two redcoats charged me. I wrested the sword from one, drove it through his chest, grabbed the other one by the throat, broke his neck. I had left my wagon in the woods—good horses, not the nags. I drove them like mad. We've got to leave at once, Cam. If we hurry, we can make it to Dover before the boat leaves."

Cam nodded, grim. Robbie caught his breath and wiped perspiration from his brow.

"Burns and Cochrane won't tell them about the boat," he said, calmer now, "but Cumberland has—has ways. He'll have them tortured until they reveal the names of all the other conspirators. It may take hours, it may take days, but we—we've got to leave the country at once."

"You're right," Cam said.

"The wagon's on Fleet, right outside the passageway. There—there's nothing more we can do, Cam. We've botched it. If you had been there, maybe—maybe things would have gone differently. We would have been there half an hour earlier, you would have taken charge. Maybe we could have blown the house up and made our escape before—before the redcoats—"

Robbie cut himself short, his large brown eyes full of pain. The lad was on the verge of tears. He frowned, squaring his shoulders, fighting to control the unseemly, unmanly emotions that gripped him.

"Why weren't you there, Cam?"

"Later. I'll explain later. Go on to the wagon. I'll join you in a minute."

"No," I said.

Robbie nodded and left, and Cam turned to look at me. I leaned against the wall beside the grandfather clock and shook my head, silently pleading with him. He picked up his bag.

"Take me with you," I whispered.

"Cumberland's men will eventually come here," he said. "They'll question you. You know nothing about it. You're merely my servant. Do you understand? Go to Bancroft first thing in the morning and tell him what happened. Bancroft will stand by you."

"Cam—"

"I've provided for you generously. You'll have no problems."

"Take me with you. Cam, take me with you. I—you can't leave me behind. I can't—I couldn't go on without—"

"You don't understand, Miranda," he said calmly. "You're responsible for this. You're responsible for the deaths of all those men."

"That isn't true! I—"

"I should kill you for what you've done. I won't. I'm too goddamned weak to do it. You've made me that way. I rue the day I met you, Miranda. I never want to see you again for the rest of my life."

He might just as well have plunged a knife into my heart. It would have been quicker. It would have been kinder. He looked at me for a moment longer with cold, unfeeling eyes, and then he left. I was numb, absolutely paralyzed. My system rejected the pain. No one could endure pain like that. I heard his footsteps moving across the court. I heard them echo as he moved down the passageway. He was taking my life with him, leaving behind a mere shell of a woman, without soul, without spirit, without reason for being.

Something snapped inside me. I flew to the door and flung it open, raced across the court and down the passageway, hardly aware of what I was doing. I stumbled onto the pavement and saw the wagon disappearing around a corner and cried out. Fleet was empty and silent, black and gray and bathed in pale moonlight. Cam was gone. I would never see him again. I stood there in front of the passageway. The cold night air chilled my bare arms and shoulders, tore at my hair, but I felt nothing, nothing whatsoever. Cam was gone. I was dead inside. I would never be able to feel again.

It was over now. Cumberland's men had come to the house two days later and Bancroft had been with me and I had been wearing my oldest cotton dress and a shabby dust cap and spoke in my coarsest St. Giles accents as he had instructed. He assured the men that I was merely a housekeeper, but they bombarded me with questions nevertheless, and I stammered and squawked and cursed them roundly for tearing into the house like a band of red Indians. Convinced I was an ignorant slavey who knew nothing, they ransacked the house, finding nothing whatsoever that could possibly link Cam with the rebels, and then they concentrated on Bancroft, an acknowledged friend of the traitor.

Bancroft was thoroughly shocked by the accusations against his friend, certain there must be some dreadful error. He told them quite frankly that Cam had come to the bank three days before and withdrawn all his funds. He was planning to leave for Plymouth immediately, where he intended to sail for the colonies on the next boat. Bancroft candidly admitted that he had been startled by this sudden decision, but Gordon had told him he was disillusioned with England, with his hack work, and was going to grow tobacco in Virginia. Bancroft considered it the wildest folly, but his friend was stubborn and unstable and once he made up his mind to do something nothing could deter him from his course.

After several hours of intensive search and brutal questioning, the men departed, as convinced by Bancroft's performance as they had been by my own. That had been four days ago, and now Cam's things were in storage and all of the furniture had been covered with dust sheets and my trunk was packed and waiting in the hall downstairs. Thomas Sheppard would soon be arriving to drive me to the cottage he had rented for me outside Stratford. It was on the river, he had informed me, the lawn sloping right down to the bank. There were willow trees and swans, and I would have the peace and serenity I so desperately needed. I would be able to rest, to forget, he said, and he hoped I would eventually be able to write.

Mrs. Wooden would be coming to spend some time with me—the poodles would *adore* the country—and Sheppard would drive down periodically to check up on me and Bancroft would probably visit, too. The three of them had arranged my life admirably, and, listless, I had let them, making no protests, making no suggestions, showing no interest whatsoever. I was going to Stratford and I would sit on the lawn and look at the willows and the swans, but I wouldn't forget, I would never forget, and I would never write another word either. The mere thought of picking up a quill filled me with lethargy.

I was upstairs in his study, bidding a final farewell to the room where he had spent so much time these past months. It looked bleak and bare now, nothing of Cam remaining. His books, his papers, the samurai sword, the pewter owl, all his personal effects were stored in Bancroft's attic, the chair and worktable covered with a shabby gray-white sheet already beginning to collect dust. Late morning sunlight slanted through the windows, making pale yellow-white pools on the bare hard-wood floor. He had toiled so hard on *The Stranger From Japan*, determined to finish it before . . . I knew why now. Every penny he had received for the book had been invested with Bancroft in my name, and it was already beginning to earn.

Cam had provided for me generously indeed. Sheppard had paid a small fortune for the last Roderick Cane novel. Bancroft assured me I would soon become a wealthy woman. It meant nothing to me. How could money possibly matter? As I gazed at the empty room, as the pools of sunlight spread, making sparkling reflections on the ceiling, I felt the pain welling up and I sternly repressed it, refusing to feel. You can give way to it, Miranda, you can let it destroy you, or you can fight it. You can sob and moan, give in, give up, or you can try to survive. You've always been a fighter, I told myself. You're not a weak, whining, defenseless maiden. You've acquired a cultivated voice, a certain amount of polish, but beneath all that you're still Duchess Randy, raised on the streets of St. Giles and beholden to no one.

What are you going to do? I asked myself. Are you going to let that bloody sod destroy your life? Are you? Several moments passed, and I could feel something hard and cold building up inside. I welcomed it, clung to it with all the strength I could muster, knowing full well it would be my only salvation.

How could he have done it? How? Damn him. Damn him to hell. I loved him with all my heart and soul, but I hated him, too, and the bitter resentment made the anguish easier to bear. I wasn't going to cry. I wasn't going to weep and wail and make a spectacle of myself. No. No. I refused to do that. I was going to Stratford and somehow . . . somehow I would survive. Mrs. Wooden informed me that I was young and beautiful, that there were dozens of men who would be delighted at the opportunity to help me forget Cam Gordon— Davy Garrick leading the pack—but there would be no more men. They hurt you. They abandoned you. They broke your heart.

There were footsteps and voices downstairs. Sheppard's manservant was carrying my trunk out. Sheppard and Mrs. Wooden were talking in quiet voices, cautious and concerned, as though I were some fragile creature unable to look after herself. They had both been wonderful, Bancroft, too, and I was grateful to all three of them, but they needn't worry about me. I wasn't going to throw myself into the Avon. I wasn't going to fall apart. I was going to suffer, yes, suffer terribly, but I was much tougher than any of them suspected, and that toughness would come to my aid now that I needed it.

"Miranda! Miranda, dear, we're ready!" Mrs. Wooden cried cheerfully from the foot of the stairs.

"Coming," I called.

I said good-bye to the room. I said good-bye to the life I had known. Calm, beautifully composed on the surface, suffering terribly inside, I went downstairs and smiled at my friends and began the business of surviving.

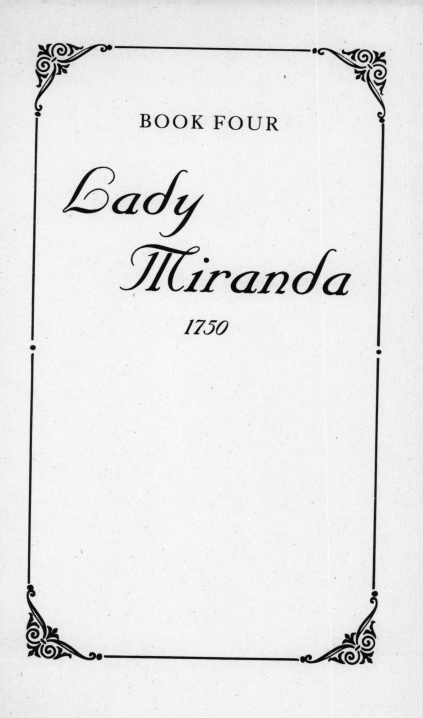

BOOK FOUR

Lady
Miranda

1750

30

LORD MARKHAM'S PEACOCK SCREAMED SHRILLY AS IT strutted regally across the lawn of Markham House, by far the most elegant mansion on the ultraelegant Grosvenor Square. Bloody peacock, I thought, glancing out the window. He was beautiful with his tail feathers all spread out like that, sure, but I'd still enjoy shooting him. Always shrieking and squawking, that bird, frequently pecking on my windowpane and peering in at me with arrogant eyes. I was fortunate indeed to be able to lease Dower House, a small gem of a house Lord Markham had built in back of his property, to the right side of the big house and separated from it by a spacious sweep of lawn, but that bleedin' bird was a constant irritation. Drove all the neighbors crazy, he did, but the powerful Lord M. was deaf to all complaints.

Originally built as a wedding present for Lord Markham's daughter, then engaged to a polished young nobleman with the bluest of blood, Dower House had its own drive, its own small garden, and it was truly exquisite, with drawing room, dining room, kitchen and pantry on the ground floor, a small spiral staircase in the foyer leading up to the bedroom and sitting room above. Although the rooms were small, each was tastefully and magnificently appointed in the most luxurious style, the grandeur subtle, scaled-down, an elegant, unobtrusive background lovingly created for the soon-to-be newlyweds. Alas, Lord M.'s daughter failed to appreciate her father's efforts. Wantonly tossing aside her aristocratic fiancé, she had run off to Rome with a handsome but impoverished Italian painter, eventually succumbing to the fever. Dower House had been carefully kept up for twenty years, but it had remained vacant until Lord M. decided to lease it to me on a yearly basis.

Seventy-eight years old, querulous, cantankerous, wildly

eccentric, Lord M. had taken particular delight in thumbing his nose at his haughty and aristocratic neighbors by leasing Dower House to the celebrated, notorious M.J., author of those scandalous stories and the even more scandalous *Duchess Annie*, the most shocking, the most successful novel in years. The other residents of Grosvenor Square were absolutely appalled at having such a creature in their midst, for it was well known that *Duchess Annie* was largely autobiographical, that I had grown up in St. Giles, had been a pickpocket, the mistress of the rebel Cam Gordon and God *knew* who else. When the novel had come out two years ago, it had been impossible to keep my identity a secret, and the gentlemen of Fleet Street had written reams about the saucy waif who had sprung from the slums to pen the most popular book of the day. I had been totally frank with them from the first, and they had been utterly enchanted, deeming me the most fascinating personality in London, a Great Beauty, more elegant and refined than the highest born damsels, filling the papers, in short, with florid and flattering nonsense that intrigued the public, delighted my publisher and amused me mightily.

Me, Miranda, a celebrity. It did indeed beat all. People stared and whispered on those rare occasions when I went out in public—Hogarth's portrait of me, done shortly after the novel appeared, had been reproduced in all the papers and thousands of prints of it had been sold in stationers' shops all over London. I was a phenomenon, a freak, and famous hostesses bombarded me with invitations, vying with each other to show me off in their salons, but I staunchly refused to be lionized. I led a very quiet life, rarely going out and devoting almost all my time to *Betty's Girls*, the novel I would soon be finished with if that screeching bird would just shut up.

It squawked again, nearer the house now. I was tempted to open the window and hurl my inkwell at it. Damned nuisance, that creature, and me laboring on the very last chapter of the book. Another noise! What was this? Was I destined to be driven out of my mind? Betty had died and the brothel had been besieged by a band of roistering aristocrats who raped the girls and set torch to the house. Molly and Jill had been abducted by Big John Cantrell and forced to work for him, and Nancy, Mary and pathetic little Belle were left alone to face the freezing winter cold. Closer than sisters, they were, lost without Betty's loving protection, clinging together like.... More noises! Banging about upstairs, footsteps clattering down the stairs, rap-tap-tapping on the black and white marble tiles of the foyer. What in *hell* was going on?

"Law, Miss Miranda! You still sittin' there at that desk, coverin' them pages with words, and it's already after six! What can you be thinking of?"

"Precious little in all this racket," I retorted. "What are you *do*ing here, Millie?"

"Mrs. Beresford sent me over, said you wuz entertainin' tonight, said I wuz to get your bath ready an' help you dress. Cook's preparin' the *dan*diest meal, ever so fancy. Bob an' Tom are bringin' everything over at seven-thirty an' Pearson is goin' to serve."

"Damn! I'd forgotten Sheppard and Bancroft were coming tonight."

"You'd forget your own head if it wudn't fastened on good," Millie said tartly. "If you didn't have us to watch over you, no tellin' *what* would happen. Put them pages away now. You gotta get bustlin'."

I groaned. Not five full feet tall, her freckled face stern, a white mobcap askew atop carroty red curls, Millie was as bossy and officious as ever, a pint-sized, green-eyed tyrant. Needing little attention himself, spending most of his time traveling abroad, Lord Markham nevertheless maintained a full staff of servants. Convinced they hadn't enough to do, considering them a lazy shiftless lot to begin with, he had decreed that they should take care of Dower House and its tenant in addition to their other duties. Left alone in the big house nine months out of twelve while their employer journeyed from spa to spa nursing nonexistent infirmities, the staff of Markham House overwhelmed me with constant attention and loving care. I was their adored pet, which definitely had its disadvantages when I was trying to work.

"I didn't realize it was so late," I said, putting my quill aside.

"I should think not! Sun already beginnin' to go down, light gettin' dimmer an' dimmer an' you strainin' your eyes. I don't know why you want to spend all your time cooped up in here anyways—it ain't healthy. All them beautiful gowns hangin' in th' wardrobe upstairs, that dashin' Mr. Garrick always beggin' you to go out with him, an' you writin' books all th' time—I could understand it if you wuz old an' ugly, Miss Miranda, but—"

I groaned again, getting to my feet. For all her sass and

bossiness Millie would gladly have gone to the stake for me, and there were many times when I would gladly have lighted the kindling. This was one of them.

"I've got your bath all ready, water hot an' scented, soap an' towels all laid out. I've selected a gown for you, an'—"

"I'm perfectly capable of selecting my own gown, Millie," I informed her in icy tones. "You may go now. I won't be needing you any more."

"Yes, you will," she retorted. "I'm goin' to do your hair."

"Jesus!"

"No one does your hair like I do, you gotta admit it. I have a touch. You run on and have your bath, an' I'll tidy up down here and be up to do your hair in half an hour or so."

"Don't you dare touch my manuscript!" I warned.

"Wouldn't dream of it, missy. The last time I moved one of them pages you screamed and carried on for a week."

I gave her an exasperated look and went on to my bedroom, passing through the small, elegant foyer with its black and white marble floor, pale, pale blue silk walls, molded white ceiling and small but sumptuous chandelier, the crystal pendants glittering like diamonds. The walls of the bedroom were covered with the same pale silk, the blue of a light summer sky, and there was a white marble fireplace. French windows opened onto a miniature balcony with white marble balustrade. Through them I could see the green sweep of lawn, spread with shadows now, and part of the square.

The water was indeed warm and wonderfully scented, and I luxuriated in the glory of it, so relaxing after endless hours at my desk downstairs in the drawing room. I smiled at Millie's scolding. Why did I stay "cooped up" and refuse to go out except on rare occasions? Why was I "writin' books all th' time?" Because that was what I wanted to do. Writing had been my salvation when Cam Gordon fled to France, leaving me behind, and during that year in the tiny cottage outside Stratford I had learned just how much it meant to me. It was something all my own, something no one could take away from me, and stepping into that world that I created on paper made the real world with its grief, its anguish, its sorrow and disappointments much easier to bear.

Millie wouldn't be able to understand that, of course. Few people would, I thought, stepping out of the porcelain tub, drying myself off. I had something special that few people were blessed with, and it...it was marvelous compensation for all those things that were missing in my life. I might not be happy, true, but only fools expected to live in a rosy haze, a perpetual state of happiness. I was content, pleased with my life, proud of my achievements, and if there was no bliss, there was no turbulence, no torment either. The serenity and calm in which I passed my days had been hard won. I was alone, but I was independent as well, beholden to no one. I was sad on occasion, but I was a success, and I had done it on my own. How many women in this day and age could say the same?

Millie had laid out the bronze brocade gown, a gorgeous creation I had never worn. I put on the frail, leaf-brown petticoat that went with it, the bodice form-fitting, cut extremely low, ten skirts belling out from the tight waist and swirling in gauzy brown layers. No more secondhand clothes for Miranda. No more bargain gowns for the notorious M.J. Madame Valentina created all my clothes, incredibly lovely gowns, beautiful frocks, and, unlike the duchesses and countesses and highborn dames who flocked to her establishment, I paid my bills promptly. Clothes and books were the only thing I indulged myself with, though I had few occasions to wear the former and, busy with my own, precious little time to read the latter.

Sitting at the elegant dressing table, I gazed at my reflection in the silvery glass. The woman who gazed back at me bore little resemblance to the naive, vivacious girl abandoned by Cam Gordon three years ago. The sauciness was gone, that radiant glow of youth replaced by the smooth patina of maturity. The sapphire blue eyes that had flashed with anger and sparkled with joy were full of new wisdom, observing the world without illusion, and the full pink mouth had a soft, sad curve that was new as well. A Great Beauty, the papers claimed, cool and poised with high sculpted cheekbones and patrician nose. What nonsense, I thought, lifting the brush to the rich coppery-red waves that gleamed gold in the candlelight.

"*I'll* do that," Millie exclaimed, bustling into the room. "You just sit there an' relax an' look lovely. Such hair, like molten copper. Where are the pins? Where's my curler? You're going to look gorgeous, Miss Miranda."

I sighed wearily and let her have her way, and Millie worked happily with brush and comb and curlers, stacking smooth, heavy waves atop my head in a marvelous arrangement, leaving three long ringlets to dangle in back. The candles glowed softly, filling the room with an amber haze. Night had fallen outside, and a cool evening breeze blew across the balcony and stirred the silk curtains hanging at the opened French windows.

"There!" Millie declared, giving the ringlets a final pat. "Looks lovely, dudn't it?"

"You're a marvel, Millie."

"Bob an' Tom've brought the dinner over, keepin' it warm in all those silver dishes with candles burnin' under 'em. Pearson's downstairs, lookin' prissy an' important in his best black velvet coat. Here, I'll help you into your gown."

I slipped it over my head and smoothed it down, and Millie began to fasten the tiny, invisible hooks in back. The luxurious bronze brocade was embroidered with floral patterns in darker bronze-brown silk, the cloth shimmering richly as I spread the full skirt out over the gauzy leaf-brown underskirts. Madame Valentina was an artist in her own right, creating a special style for each of her clients. Disdaining the long, tight sleeves, the lace fichus, the flounces and the paneled skirts currently in fashion, she insisted on elegant simplicity for my gowns. The short, narrow sleeves were off-the-shoulder, the bodice cut extremely low, skirt swelling from a narrow waist.

"You look—you look just like a vision," Millie declared, stepping back a few paces. "Ain't never seen anything lovelier, an' I mean it."

"Thank you, Millie."

"Shame to waste it all on that dried-up old gentleman an' that hefty blond toff who handles your business. Cocky, that one. Altogether too playful. Know what he did last time he was here? Pinched my backside, he did, reached out and gave it a whoppin' pinch as I was showin' him in."

"Oh? And what did you do?"

"Grinned at him," she confessed. "Can't help likin' him, even if he ain't all that proper. What I meant, though, is you should be dressin' up for a lover, Miss Miranda, not your publisher an' your banker."

"That will be quite enough, Millie."

My voice was crisp, sternly informing her that she had gone too far, but as I moved down the lovely white marble staircase I repressed a rueful smile. Millie wasn't half as saucy as I had been a few short years ago, and her impudence was prompted by a genuine affection and concern for my welfare. Pausing for a moment in the foyer, I observed the cool, patrician woman in the sumptuous, shimmering bronze gown that left shoulders bare and bosom half-exposed, the form-fitting bodice, tight waist and swelling skirt emphasizing her tall, slender build. Who was she? Not Duchess Randy. Not the lovesick girl of Greenbriar Court. Others might see her a celebrated, scandalous creature who was wildly successful in her chosen field, but that glamorous image had nothing to do with the woman who spent hours and hours each day toiling at her desk with ink-stained fingers and tumbling hair.

If I wasn't Randy or naive Miranda nor the notorious M.J. imagined by the public, who . . . who was I? A lonely, hard-working woman of twenty-two years, though much older in spirit, at heart. Lonely? Yes, I admitted to myself as I moved on into the drawing room. I was lonely at times, but I had my friends and I had my work and I was . . . I was much better off than I had any reason to expect. I had no lover, true, but that was by choice. Any number of men would be delighted to assume that role, and one in particular had been ardently wooing me for three years, though in vain. I didn't *want* a lover. Mrs. Wooden grimly predicted I would become a dried-up old maid if I didn't mend my ways and described that state to me in horrific detail, but was it so dreadful, so tragic, for a woman to lead her own life? I didn't need a man to support me, to take care of me, to rule my life.

You've become far too introspective of late, Miranda, love, I scolded myself, probably because the book is coming to an end and you haven't yet begun thinking of the next. You'd be much better off planning a third M.J. than moodily examining your soul. You're damned lucky, and don't you forget it. If something is missing from your life, you've got far more than you deserve, so buck up and stop being so bloody pensive!

There were voices in the foyer, and a moment later a sober-looking Pearson in black velvet coat stepped into the room to announce the "Honorable Richard Bancroft" in sepulchral tones. Dick came bustling in behind him, full of energy and hearty good cheer. A bit heavier than he had been three years ago, he was wonderfully attractive in his soft brown velvet breeches and frock coat, a wide grin on his lips. Warm brown eyes atwinkle, dark blond hair gleaming in the candlelight, he more than ever resembled a sleek, prosperous pup. He seemed to bound across the room and gave me a hug that almost cracked my ribs.

"You're not on a playing field, Dick," I complained, brushing back a lock of hair his hug had dislodged, "and I'm not your opponent. Look what you've done to my hair."

"Looks better that way," he informed me. "Lord, Miranda, that gown you're wearing is—are you sure it's legal to show that much flesh?"

"Madame Valentina assures me the ladies in France show much more."

"I must pop over to Paris soon as I can, see for myself. That miserly old fogy hasn't arrived yet? Probably in his office counting the profits *Duchess Annie* and the book of stories are still bringing in."

"You're terribly hard on poor Sheppard," I said.

"Have to be. Once I became your business manager, he became the enemy. I have to keep an eye on him. Bloke'd rob you blind if I didn't. Are you going to be a proper hostess and offer me a glass of wine, or are you going to let me perish of thirst while we wait for him to come tottering in?"

I made a face at him and stepped over to the enameled white cabinet to get his wine. Hands thrust into his pockets, rocking slightly on his heels, he exuded energy and confidence and good cheer, and the drawing room with its beige and white walls, white marble fireplace and beautifully molded white ceiling seemed much too small to contain him. My collection of Hogarth engravings hung on the walls in simple black frames and pale blue mats, each one illustrating a scene I had written, and his portrait of me hung over the mantel. Bancroft examined it as he sipped his wine.

"Chap did a magnificent job with that portrait," he remarked. "Never can get over how lifelike it is."

Hogarth had painted me sitting at my desk, quill in hand. I was wearing a deep blue frock, and my hair was slightly disarrayed, my blue eyes thoughtful as I examined the manuscript before me. The background was done in misty shades of blue, gray and black, depicting, on my left, a sordid street in St. Giles and, on my right, slightly below the other, a bustling section of Fleet. The rich blue of my frock, the brilliant coppery red of my hair, the pink of my lips and the creamy flesh tones seemed to glow all the more against the sober hues behind me. The painting had created a sensation when the artist exhibited it, and I had had to bid viciously against David Garrick in order to obtain it. Cost me twice what it should have and would have cost even more had he not finally, reluctantly given in.

"And how *is* the ardent Mr. Garrick?" Bancroft inquired. He must have been reading my mind.

"Performing commedia dell'arte at the Drury Lane—*Queen Mab*, to be exact. He's a most impressive Harlequin, all verve, vitality and audacious dash. Johnson calls him the greatest Harlequin of the century."

"Still pursuing you?" Bancroft asked.

"I—I see him occasionally, not nearly as often as he would like. I'm extremely fond of him, as you know, but—Davy's not content to settle for a close friendship."

"Can't say that I blame him, not if you sashay around before him in gowns like the one you're wearing now. Everyone in London knows he's pining for you, perishing with unrequited love."

"Mr. Garrick loves to play a role, and at the moment it amuses him to play the forlorn suitor. He sees other women much more frequently than he sees me. In fact, he's quite taken with Lady Burlington's young protegé."

"That Austrian dancer?"

"Mademoiselle Violette—that's a stage name, of course. Her real name is Eva Maria Veigel, and I understand she's quite charming. Lovely, too."

"Doesn't hold a candle to you, lass. I saw her dance. She's pretty, all right, if you like 'em plump and winsome, but no one would give her a glance if you were in the same room."

"You're a loyal friend, Dick."

"Also a damned good judge of female pulchritude. I've had a lot of experience along those lines."

Bancroft finished his wine, set his glass down and gave me a long, searching look, his warm brown eyes serious now. I knew that he longed to talk about the past and all that had happened three years ago, but there was a silent understanding between us that Cam Gordon's name would never be mentioned. I felt sure that the two men had kept in touch ever since Cam fled the country—Bancroft had subtly intimated as much on more than one occasion—but I refused to question him. I wanted only to forget.

"I worry about you sometimes, Miranda. You're too much alone."

"I'm quite content with my lot, Dick."

He frowned. "I know. That's what worries me. You've become more and more reclusive, more and more set in your ways. You're *young*, Miranda—what? twenty-two? twenty-three?—and you might as well be forty. I can understand why you don't want to become too seriously involved with a chap like Garrick, but—" He hesitated, searching for words, extremely uncomfortable.

"I appreciate your concern, Dick," I said lightly, "but—you're not to worry. I'm the luckiest woman in London, thanks largely to your shrewd management."

"Just doing my job," he muttered.

"Making me a very wealthy woman," I added, "and, incidentally, driving my poor publisher to desperation. You're a darling, Dick, the most amiable of men, but when it comes to business you're a—a veritable shark."

"Have to be. You've gotta go for the throat when you're dealing with someone like Sheppard or he'll eat *you* alive. When you asked me to take over your business affairs, in addition to handling your money, and when I saw what he was doing to you—"

Bancroft scowled and shook his head, and I smiled to myself. Having successfully changed the subject, I offered him more wine. Thomas Sheppard arrived a few minutes later, looking dapper and unusually sober in blue black broadcloth, a white silk neckcloth providing a touch of relief. Sandy hair a bit thinner, complexion like old parchment, he greeted me with a warm smile and adjusted his gold-rimmed spectacles. When he saw Bancroft standing in front of the fireplace the smile vanished and he assumed the weary, put-upon expression he always wore when my jovial but hard-as-steel business manager was present. Bancroft nodded politely. Sheppard emitted a martyred sigh.

"Bancroft," he said.

"Sheppard."

"Come to bully me some more, I see."

"Hadn't planned on it, Thomas."

"You're half my age and twice my size, Bancroft. I should think you would be ashamed to terrorize and victimize a fragile old party like me, taking advantage of my frail health and failing memory."

"You're about as frail as a barracuda, Thomas, and as for your memory—you can account for every penny you ever earned from a hapless writer and relate in detail how it was invested. Rubbing your hands as you do so," he added. "You may not carry a knife, but you're as greedy as any cutthroat in London and probably even more vicious."

"I resent that!" Sheppard protested.

Both men enjoyed these sparring matches tremendously and found them wonderfully stimulating sport. Though bitter adversaries on the surface, each secretly nourished a fond regard for the other, and each received all the respect due a worthy opponent. When Bancroft took over my business affairs he had made a thorough study of the publishing business, and then he had gone to Sheppard with a revolutionary and—to Sheppard—absolutely scandalous proposal. It was standard practice on Fleet Street for an author to receive a lump sum for a book, the amount based on past success and projected sales, and, after that amount was paid, the author never received another penny, no matter how successful the book might prove to be. Bancroft refused to take a lump sum for *Duchess Annie*, insisting, instead, that I receive a percentage on each copy sold. Sheppard shrieked wildly in protest, claiming such a precedent would threaten the very foundations of Fleet, but in the end Bancroft had won, the agreement had been signed and I had become the wealthiest writer in London.

"Miranda's almost finished with *Betty's Girls*," Bancroft remarked. "I've read what she's done. It's remarkable."

"I don't doubt it."

"It's going to create another sensation. She has the temerity to suggest that whores have heart, have soul, feel pain and grief and anguish like the rest of us. She dares to imply that they're frequently the pathetic victims of society instead of its scourge. It's going to sell even better than *Annie*."

"You're going to start twisting my arm," Sheppard groaned. "I can see it in your eyes. You're going to tyrannize me and—"

"We let you rob us with *Annie*, Thomas. We agreed to accept a measly fifteen percent on each copy sold. For *Betty's Girls* I fully expect twenty-five. You're going to make thousands of pounds, hundreds of thousands, if it sells as well as I think it will, and I intend to see that my client—"

Sheppard's cheeks had paled. Bancroft's voice had taken on a brutal edge, and his eyes gleamed with cruel delight as he watched his victim squirm. Sheppard took a deep breath, squared his shoulders and readied for the fray. I reminded them gently that this was a social occasion and no time to discuss business. Both looked disappointed, as though I had interrupted them in the middle of a particularly rousing game of chess, yet both were as amiable as one could wish as we went into the dining room.

Lord Markham's cook had surpassed herself tonight. There was oxtail soup, a marvelous fillet of sole, a rack of pink, juicy lamb and tiny quails cooked to a golden, buttery brown, with vegetables and wine suitable to each course. For dessert there was a sumptuous pudding with brandy sauce *flambé*, wickedly delicious. Served by the officious but impeccable Pearson, with Tom and Bob standing by in their best livery, it was a superb meal, the conversation as satisfying as the food, and both my guests were in a mellow mood as we returned to the drawing room.

"By the way," Sheppard said as I served him a glass of after-dinner brandy, "I've been seeing quite a lot of one of your friends."

I handed Bancroft his glass and turned around. "Oh? Who might that be?"

"Mrs. Marcelon Wooden. She came into the shop about two weeks ago for extra copies of *Duchess Annie* to give to some actor friends and, for some reason, felt that, as she was your oldest and dearest friend, she shouldn't be required to pay for them. I happened to be passing through the shop while she was arguing with my clerk and she—uh—pounced."

"That's our Marcie," Bancroft observed.

"She told me she was delighted to see me again—I had just met her that one time, when we were—uh—when you left for Stratford—so I told her I would be delighted to give her a few complimentary copies of the book and she felt obligated to give me complimentary tickets to her play and—well, one thing led to another and we've—uh—been seeing each other fairly often. She's a remarkable woman."

"She is indeed," I agreed.

"Absolutely intolerable ever since *The Way of The World*," Bancroft added. "She stole the play, you know. Poor Mrs. Cibber, Garrick himself hadn't a prayer of being noticed once she flounced onstage and started shooting off her fireworks."

"She was marvelous, Dick!" I protested.

"Didn't say she wasn't. I'm just saying she's been intolerable since she became 'The Sensation of The Season,' to quote the journals. I handle her finances," he explained to Sheppard, "and, let me tell you, she has some very eccentric ideas about banks."

"You adore her," I told him.

"I'm also turning gray. Watch yourself, Sheppard. She thinks it a crime for any man over twenty to be unmarried. Poor Major Barnaby had to flee the country to get away from her."

"He went back to India to refresh his memory and gather material for his memoirs," I corrected.

"Had him in her clutches, she did. Poor man made his escape in the nick of time."

"Pay no attention to him, Thomas. Marcie's a darling. I don't know what I would do without her."

Sheppard seemed slightly uncomfortable at the turn the conversation had taken, but there was a wry little grin on his lips nevertheless as he thought of the exuberant and colorful creature who had come storming into his life and threatened to disrupt his staid, fussy bachelor habits. Marcie's success was a source of great delight to me. Ever since her dazzling performance as Lady Wishfort in the Congreve play, she had been in constant demand by managers eager to mount productions tailored for her unique talents. No one had any illusions about her acting abilities—she was, in truth, an atrocious actress, as critics were quick to point out—but she had an outrageous, audacious, larger-than-life quality that enchanted audiences and had made her one of the great personalities of the English theater, ardently adored by the multitudes who packed the house whenever she performed.

"It's growing late," Sheppard remarked, glancing at the clock. "I have a manuscript to finish reading tonight. I'd better take my leave, Miranda."

"I have my carriage out front, old man," Bancroft said. "I'll drop you off."

Sheppard looked dubious. Bancroft grinned. "No strong-arm tactics, I promise. We won't even discuss business."

"Well—"

Bancroft slung an arm around the tiny little man's shoulders and gave him a hearty squeeze.

"Come along, Thomas. Miranda looks a bit weary. It's been a lovely evening, love. Food delicious, hostess enchanting, conversation stimulating. I enjoyed it."

"Me, too," Sheppard said as Bancroft half-dragged him out of the room. "I'll be in touch."

"So will I," Bancroft called.

I stepped outside with them and we made our final farewells. The lawn was brushed with pale silver. The square was black and silver and blue gray, misty golden lights glowing in windows. Bancroft and Sheppard walked toward the waiting carriage, two black silhouettes against the silver, and I stepped back into the foyer. Pearson appeared to inquire if I would be needing anything else. I shook my head and thanked him and, after he had departed, put out the candles downstairs and went wearily up to my bedroom.

Millie had turned back the bedcovers and laid out my nightgown. The French windows were open. A soft evening breeze caused the thin silk curtains to billow. They made a whispering sound as I took off the bronze gown and its matching petticoat and hung them up in the lovely Boulle wardrobe. Slipping on the frail, creamy beige gauze nightgown, I sat at the dressing table and took down my hair and brushed it. The curtains whispered. The clock ticked quietly. It was after midnight now. Six and a half hours until dawn. It was coming over me again, that melancholy that always came over me when I was alone in the evening. The days were fine. The days were filled with work and there wasn't enough time to accomplish all I wanted to accomplish, but the evenings . . . the evenings were filled with a subtle, persistent sadness that, while never acute, was always there, waiting to claim me.

Blowing out all the candles except those on the bedside table, I climbed into bed and settled back against the pillows and picked up the final volume of *Tom Jones*. When it had come out last year it had created almost as great a sensation as *Duchess Annie*, scandalizing readers and selling enormously well. Its author, Henry Fielding, had been a magistrate on Bow Street for the past year and a half, and, in poor health already, he was virtually killing himself trying to establish a respectable police force and clean up the corruption in our legal system. Dedicated, compassionate, he was making tremendous reforms that would benefit every man, woman and child in England, and he wrote his "foolish little epics" merely for relaxation. I suspected that the novels he considered such trifles would be read long after his work on Bow Street was forgotten.

Although I adored the book and was reading it now for the second time, the rollicking adventures of Fielding's gamy young foundling could not distract me tonight. I set the volume aside and blew out the candles and gazed at the silvery flecks that began to dance on the ceiling. The curtains billowed, in and out, in and out, whispering, and the sadness swept over me once again. The bed was large and cool and there was no body beside mine to cling to, to caress. I was but half, and the man who had once made me whole was...was out there in the world somewhere and I would never see him again.

I was over him. Yes, yes, of course I was. I had hardened my heart. The wounds had healed. The pain, that terrible anguish, had eventually disappeared, and I could think of him without that wrenching, tearing sensation, but the sadness still came, and...and the longing, even now, even after three years. I gazed at the ceiling and watched the silvery flecks of moonlight dancing on the blue black and the memories came, try though I might to resist them. Don't, Miranda, I warned myself. Don't remember. Don't. Think about the book. Think about ...Damn him. Damn him. Why couldn't I hate him, as I had tried so often to do? Why couldn't I forget? Why? The memories came and finally I slept and memories merged into dreams.

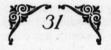

31

BRANDY BARKED LUSTILY AS MADAME VALENTINA'S assistant came in with the gowns over her arms. The celebrated and terribly exclusive couturier forced a thin smile on her lips and made a comment about how adorable the little creature was. Marcelon beamed proudly. Brandy cavorted across the plush carpet, reflected in the multiple mirrors. The assistant grimaced. Pepe was curled up on a bolt of blue velvet, sleeping soundly, and Sarge was busily destroying a piece of discarded lace Valentina had given him. She clearly detested the poodles and would have loved to toss them out of her grand fitting room, but even Valentina didn't dare offend the famous and beloved Mrs. Wooden whose patronage brought in a great deal of business. Besides, Marcie and I were two of the very few customers who paid promptly and in cash.

"Scrumptious!" Marcelon exclaimed as the assistant handed Valentina one of the gowns and hung the other up. "Absolutely scrumptious! *Do* be quiet, Brandy! I had hoped he'd calm down with age," she confessed, "but he's still as frisky as ever. Go play with your little brother, darling."

Valentina smiled another forced smile, waved the assistant away and helped me into the sumptuous honey-colored velvet trimmed at bodice and hem with glossy black fox fur. Tall and thin with a pinched, painted face and improbable silver blonde hair piled atop her head in messy waves, Valentina invariably wore black, a pair of stunning emerald earrings her only adornment. Shrewd, sharp, snobbish and rapacious, she was a superb businesswoman who had struggled for years to attain her position in the world of fashion and would fight like an alleycat if it were threatened. She was, unquestionably, the best couturier in England, better than many in France, and she charged accordingly.

"It's a dream, Miranda!" Marcie assured me as Valentina finished hooking the gown in back. "That velvet—I've never seen its equal."

"Especially imported," Valentina told us. "Only the one bolt. The Duchess of Hartford was determined to have it, said she *must* have a gown made from it. I told her it was reserved. She said she didn't care, said she would pay double for it. I finally convinced her it wasn't her color."

"Shouldn't think so," Marcie remarked. "She has a complexion like a lemon."

"The bane of my existence," Valentina sighed, stepping back to observe me. "She insists on dressing like a twenty-year-old—pink silk, pale blue, ruffles and sashes and lacy garlands. She's pushing seventy, poor thing. It takes all my tact to keep her from looking like a gaudy maypole. Perfect, Miranda," she said, squinting her shrewd green eyes. "*Almost* perfect. I don't usually care for long sleeves on you, but these are just right."

I studied myself in the mirrors. Although I loved buying these exquisite creations, fittings were always an ordeal. Standing around interminably while someone tugged and pulled and draped and poked pins into cloth wasn't my idea of bliss. The gorgeous honey-colored velvet seemed to glisten with a rich golden-brown sheen. The long off-the-shoulder sleeves fit glove-tight, and with its snug, low-cut bodice, tight waist and swelling skirt, the gown was undeniably a masterpiece, the glossy black fur edging the bodice and skirt hem adding a luxurious touch.

"Something is missing," Valentina complained, squinting

still. "It's stunning, of course—primarily because of *you*, Miranda, dear. It's such a joy to work with someone who has so magnificent a form—but it needs—" She made a clicking noise with her tongue and nodded briskly. "More fur, the cuffs should be trimmed with fur like bodice and hem. Don't you agree, Mrs. Wooden?"

"Definitely," Marcie said. "*Do* stop that, boys! They're fighting over the piece of lace. Let him have it, Brandy! There. They're really being unusually naughty today. I must apologize."

"Perhaps one of the girls could take them out for a walk," Valentina suggested with another forced smile.

"Heavens, no! There's far too much traffic."

"I hadn't thought of that," Valentina lied.

Brandy and Sarge settled down, Pepe continued to snooze and Valentina made a few minor adjustments to the gown and helped me out of it. Brandy growled at her as she carried it back to the workroom. Marcie shuffled about in her chair, blue and gray striped taffeta crackling. Pulling her black lace shawl closer around her shoulders, she sighed and looked at me with fond eyes. Considerably plumper than she had been three years ago, she still wore her towering powdered pompadour, adorned today with tiny black velvet bows, and her face paint was as outrageous as ever: bright pink lips, pale blue eyelids, far too much rouge and powder, a heart-shaped black satin beauty mark on one cheek.

"I really should buy a couple of new gowns myself," she confided. "I've been going out *quite* a lot of late, and you'll never guess with *whom*."

"Thomas Sheppard," I said, brushing the skirt of my cream silk petticoat. "He and Bancroft came to dine last week. He told me about it."

"He did? My dear, what did he *say*?"

"He said that you were a very remarkable woman. I've a feeling he's smitten, Marcie."

"Really? He's a love, my dear, so shy and attentive and thoughtful and so *rich*. He's much too *short*, of course, I feel like a giantess beside him, but I must confess I'm terribly fond of him. He brings me chocolates in fancy boxes, sends flowers backstage, is so *sweet* to me—not at all like that detestable Major Barnaby."

"Thomas is a dear. And a confirmed bachelor," I added.

"Not for long, my dear. I have *designs* on him, I might as

well admit it. A man like that has no business being a bachelor, and I'm growing a bit weary of my single state. I have my career, of course, and it's wonderfully satisfying—I don't know what I'd do without my work—the applause, the laughter, all that love pouring across the footlights—but a woman needs something *more*, my dear."

"Indeed?"

"You'll discover that soon enough, if you haven't already. Writing books is all very well, but—"

"Don't start in on me, Marcie."

"Davy's *mad* about you, and when I see that dreadful little Austrian dancer moving in on him—" She shook her head, pompadour tilting. "She's already giving herself airs, thinks she's going to snare him. He'd give her the gate in a minute if you gave him the least—"

"I adore you, darling, but sometimes your mania for match-making drives me to distraction."

"I just want you to be happy, Miranda."

"I *am* happy," I protested.

"You're content, my dear. There's a vast difference."

Marcie adjusted her pompadour as Valentina returned and helped me into the second gown. Brandy was happily shredding the piece of lace Sarge had abandoned in order to admire himself in one of the mirrors. He barked. The poodle in the glass barked back. Sarge scurried under Marcie's skirts, peeked out from under the taffeta and growled menacingly at the mirror. Valentina grimaced and pretended to be as amused as the mutt's mistress was.

"This silk comes from Lyons," she told me, "and I have it on the best authority that Pompadour herself had her eye on it. It's gorgeous, and with your hair—" Valentina clicked her tongue to indicate bliss.

The cloth was indeed gorgeous, a rich creamy beige with pencil-thin orange and pink stripes and, between them, rows of tiny brown, pink and rust flowers, the colors soft and subtle against the beige. The gown had full puffed sleeves worn off-the-shoulder, a low, heart-shaped neckline and form-fitting bodice. I turned this way and that, and the extremely full skirt belled out, rustling with a lovely silken music.

"I thought about burnt orange velvet bows," Valentina said, "or perhaps a brown velvet sash, but no, no, I told myself, the cloth is so rich and spectacular anything else would distract.

Pompadour's dressmaker would festoon it with garlands of silk flowers and rows of lace and all sorts of gewgaws. The French have never really understood fashion—simplicity! That's the key!"

"Lord!" Marcie exclaimed. "You're absolutely breathtaking, my dear! I've never seen you look so lovely. It's your masterpiece, Valentina, no doubt about it. Would that *I* could wear such a creation."

"You have your own style," Valentina assured her.

"Alas, I'm all too aware of that. Long sleeves, lace fichus, must hide the neck, cover the arms. Oh, to be twenty again. Oh, to be fifty, for that matter. Time does take its toll."

"A few minor alterations, Miranda. I want to take the waist in just a fraction more and realign the hem in back. Both gowns should be ready in a couple of days. I'll have them delivered."

I removed the gown and put on the simple blue silk I had worn to the shop, and a few minutes later Marcelon and I were driving away in her elegant closed carriage, driver and footman in golden brown livery. Pepe curled up in my lap, occasionally giving my hand a sleepy lick. Sarge perched his forelegs against the side of the coach and peered out the window while Brandy surreptitiously chewed on the edge of Marcie's black lace shawl.

"Such gorgeous gowns," she sighed. "and what will you do with them? You'll hang them up in the wardrobe with all the others and no one will ever *see* you in them. It's still early, my dear, and I don't have to be at the theater until seven. Why don't you come back to Greenbriar Court with me for tea? There's my plum cake, as usual, and that girl I have working for me makes marvelous cucumber and watercress sandwiches."

"I—I'd rather not, Marcie."

"I've been trying for months to get you there. You wouldn't recognize the place, white wainscoting throughout, thick blue carpets, mirrors in gilt frames and *such* chandeliers, my dear. Pink and gray striped silk curtains, chairs upholstered in the same silk. I've discovered a marvelous furniture maker, Thomas Chippendale. He opened his workshop in Long Acre a few years ago, and he's going to become the rage, just wait and see. Such simplicity, such elegance of line! You *must* come, Miranda."

Marcie sighed and gave me a disgusted look, but she didn't persist, understanding all too well my reasons for not wanting to return to Greenbriar Court. I knew I couldn't move down that narrow brick passageway, couldn't see that mellow gray house with the peach tree in front without a flood of memories sweeping over me. The grief, the anguish that had almost destroyed me those first months had finally been controlled, contained, locked away inside me, and I didn't dare risk re-opening the wounds.

All three dogs barked with delight as I unlocked the front door and let them into the house. They danced down the foyer and scampered into the drawing room, eagerly awaiting the delicious snacks they always received at Miranda's. Not only did they visit two or three times each week, but I always kept them when Marcelon went on tour with one of her plays. Millie hurried over from the big house when she saw us arrive and, fifteen minutes later, appeared with a heavily laden tray: a silver pot of tea, two delicate porcelain cups, scones, strawberry jam, Devonshire cream, bread and butter sandwiches, slices of ham, slices of tongue. The poodles were in ecstacy.

"You do spoil them so," Marcelon complained. "They're absolutely impossible for hours whenever they get back from your house."

"They were deplorably spoiled long before I ever met them. Here, precious, have another bit of tongue. You two, too. No carrots, Brandy. You're going to have to settle for this."

Marcie piled thick clots of cream and strawberry jam on her scone. "Started your new book yet?" she asked.

I shook my head. "I just finished *Betty's Girls* last week— I'm still in a state of exhaustion."

"Thomas says it's even better than *Duchess Annie*. He says it's going to be a phenomenal success."

"He's rushing it to press as soon as possible. I suppose I'll be besieged by journalists again, by painters wanting to do my portrait and readers wanting me to sign their books and society hostesses wanting to show me off in their salons. I may run away."

"Being in the public eye has its disadvantages," Marcie agreed. "I often have to *fight* my way out of the theater, all those adoring hoards jumping about, craning their necks for just one more glimpse. I always blow kisses," she confessed.

"You love the attention. I detest it."

Marcelon shook her head and piled jam and clotted cream on another scone. "I'll never understand you, Miranda. All this fame, all this critical acclaim, all this wealth you've acquired, and you keep yourself shut up like a prisoner. You're so *young*, so lovely, and you're letting life pass you by."

"I've had quite enough of life," I informed her. "I prefer my work and my—my own amusements. I have books to read and friends to see and a charming place to live and—"

"You've got to get over him," she said flatly.

"I don't know what you're talking about."

Marcelon set down her teacup and put on a very severe expression. "You know very well what I'm talking about. I'm talking about Cam Gordon. I know you don't want any of us mentioning his name, but I think it's high time you face the truth."

"And what, pray tell, would that be?"

"The truth is you're ruining your life over a man who was never worthy of you to begin with. He treated you abominably, he used you deplorably, he was surly, temperamental, violent, *never* appreciated you. He kept you around because you were a convenience to him, and—"

"That will be quite enough, Marcelon."

"And then, after you saved his life, he *blamed* you for it, abandoned you without a qualm."

"He had to get out of the country immediately. He—"

"Of course he did," she interrupted, "and he could easily have taken you with him. I'm glad he *did*n't, naturally, but if he had truly loved you, he would never have—"

"I don't care to talk about it!"

"And I don't give a hang whether you do or not. He's never tried to get in touch with you, never tried to send a message of any kind, and—"

"He's a rebel. There's a price on his head. He wouldn't dare step foot on English soil."

"He's done it a number of times," she informed me.

"What—what do you mean?" I asked. My voice was barely a whisper.

"You don't want to talk about it," she said airily. "I'll just finish my tea and be on my way."

The peacock squawked outside. The dogs barked. Marcelon lifted the cup of tea to her lips and looked at me with great self-satisfaction. I longed to hurl the silver pot at her head. Instead, I calmly picked up a knife and began to cut up the tongue into even smaller strips. All three poodles hurried over and pawed my skirt anxiously. I fed them the tongue, ignoring their smug mistress.

"He's been in touch with Bancroft," she said.

"Has he?" I was terribly indifferent, concentrating on the dogs.

"Dick told me all about it when we had lunch the other day. He's received several letters over the past three years. Gordon always used a false name in case Dick's mail was being watched."

I finished feeding the tongue to the poodles and then got up and went over to one of the windows. Holding the curtain back, I peered out at the sweep of lawn, sun-brushed now, dark green grass tinged with silver. Marcelon chattered on, and though I pretended not to listen, I absorbed every word, grateful to her for breaking the silence at last. I had desperately wanted to know about him, rarely a day passing without my wondering where he was, what he was doing, but pride had always prevented me from asking Bancroft for information.

"Prince Charlie has his own little court in France," she told me, "surrounded by his loyal supporters. He's something of a thorn to the French, an embarrassment they could easily do without, but they welcomed him with open arms and continue to tolerate his presence, albeit begrudgingly. Apparently the Bonnie Prince is a royal pain in the ass, neither bright nor brave and far from being the heroic figure his countrymen believe him to be. He's spoiled, stupid, arrogant, and a wretched coward—it's fairly common knowledge. Anyway, Gordon and his friend Robbie Bruce spent precious little time at the court of the Bonnie P."

She paused, and I could hear the rustle of taffeta and the clatter of china as she poured herself another cup of tea. The peacock strutted slowly across the lawn, tail feathers spread. The big house cast soft blue-gray shadows over part of the grass. Two of Lord Markham's footmen idled near the back door, making eyes at one of the parlor maids who was dusting a rug.

"They were there less than three months," Marcie continued, "and then set sail for the American colonies—under assumed names, of course. Lady Arabella Dunston went to Rome at about the same time. Seems she met an Italian nobleman who was young and rich and handsome to boot. He married her, I understand, and she's now the darling of Roman society, living in a plush palazzo with fountains and gardens and servants galore. Things didn't go so well for Gordon and young Robbie in Virginia. They were penniless, of course. Robbie apprenticed himself to a blacksmith, and Gordon eventually became chief foreman on a tobacco plantation."

The maid had finished dusting the rug. She started back toward the house. One of the footmen pinched her backside. The other pulled her into his arms and gave her a lusty kiss. The girl made a token struggle, then melted against him as the other man fondled that portion of her anatomy he had so recently pinched. The three of them finally went inside, abandoning the rug on the back steps, and I imagined they would spend a delightful hour or two in one of the roomy closets belowstairs. I felt a pang of something very like envy.

"Behave yourself, Brandy! You know Miranda doesn't allow you to chew on her sofa cushions. Why can't you take a nap like Pepe? Anyway," she continued in a weary voice, "Gordon soon realized he could never really succeed in America without capital. He returned to France a year ago and joined a band of men who have a tremendously profitable and extremely dangerous trade."

Marcelon paused for dramatic effect, waiting for me to respond. After a few moments of silence I turned away from the window and gave her an impatient look. She smiled.

"Thought that would hook you," she said.

"Well?"

"He's become a smuggler, my dear! Working off the coast of Cornwall, bringing goods in from France in the dead of night. The band he belongs to is notorious, a bloodthirsty crew, it seems, little better than pirates. The poor people of Cornwall are in league with them, of course, and the countryside is thronging with the King's agents whose job it is to capture the smugglers and stop the nefarious trade which is cheating the throne of a great deal of revenue. A whole army of redcoats patrols the coast, a ruthless band of the King's toughest men, and quite a number of them have been found with their throats slit."

I made no comment. Marcelon stood up and brushed her skirts.

"Gordon is apparently making money left and right as a smuggler, and he'll soon have enough to return to America and set himself up in style—if he isn't butchered by redcoats, that is. I always *knew* the man was criminal—all that violence in his novels. You're well out of it, Miranda."

"What does Dick think of all this?" I asked.

"Oh, he's appalled, of course, says Gordon's a damn fool,

but there's nothing Dick can do. He can't even get in touch with Gordon—Gordon's never given him an address. His letters have been arriving periodically at the rate of one every three months or so."

"I see."

"I felt you should know, my dear," she said, concerned now. "I do hope I haven't upset you."

"Not at all," I replied. "I—I'm glad you told me, Marcie."

"Forget him, my dear," she said quietly.

I've been trying to for three years, I said silently. I squeezed her hand and walked back to the carriage with her, poodles prancing around us, and I promised to think over all she'd said and stop brooding and go out more often. Marcie leaned out the carriage window to kiss my cheek, and then the carriage drove away and I returned to Dower House and thought about him and felt the old grief, the old pain. He was a smuggler, part of a notorious band, and he was often in Cornwall, risking his life every time he stepped foot on English soil. Hundreds of redcoats infested the coast, looking for the smugglers. . . . He was going to get himself killed.

Damn him. Damn him! Hotheaded, impetuous, foolhardy. He couldn't do something sensible, could he? No, no, he couldn't find some safe, respectable work, couldn't be content with anything as mundane as that. He had to become a bloody smuggler, landing on the Cornish coast in the dead of night, clambering over the treacherous rocks in darkness with a case of illegal merchandise on his shoulder, dealing with criminals, slitting the throat of any redcoat he happened to chance upon. The books he had written with such facility had been classic male fantasy, and he had vicariously savored each bloodthristy adventure. Now, by God, he was actually living out one of those fantasies. The fool. The bloody, idiotic fool! One of these nights he was going to stumble into a nest of redcoats and get himself captured and. . . . To hell with him!

Marcie was right. I was still young. I had my whole life before me, and I needed to start living it again. I was content, true, and my work gave me great satisfaction and a sense of fulfillment, but I was alone far too much and in danger of becoming a total recluse, growing more eccentric by the day. Social life held no appeal for me, but when an elaborate gold-encrusted invitation arrived the next day from Lady Julia Copeland, requesting my presence at a reception for the Dean of Southwark, I accepted by return message. Lady Julia was a voracious lion hunter, ever athirst for new celebrities to adorn her salon, and I had been turning down her invitations for months. There was bound to be a crush at her reception and it was bound to be a dreadful evening, but I convinced myself it would be good for me.

And when, the following Sunday, Davy Garrick appeared on my doorstep and begged me to take lunch with him at the park, I accepted his invitation, too, changing into the gorgeous new cream silk with its tiny floral print and thin pink and orange stripes. He stood up when I reentered the drawing room, and the look in his eyes told me that the gown was every bit as stunning as I thought it was. I had hastily brushed my hair and wore it loose and flowing. Davy gazed at me for several long moments, then assumed a pained expression and shook his head.

"Something wrong?" I inquired.

"I'm consumed with regret," he told me.

"Regret?"

"Regret that I'm a decent fellow. Were I the rake I've often been painted as being, I'd ravish you on the spot. Your beauty, I fear, has driven me quite mad, and I'm using the utmost restraint, I assure you."

"Which play is that from?" I asked.

"I'm sin*cere*, Miranda."

"You've never been sincere a day in your life, David Garrick. You've used that same bit of dialogue dozens of times before, I'm sure."

"It usually works," he complained. "You're a cold, heartless woman, Miss James. Hundreds of lovely, amoral women throwing themselves at my head, longing to sleep with the great David Garrick, and I have to fall in love with the only virtuous woman in London."

"Poor darling," I said.

"Heartless, utterly heartless. You don't know what all this rejection has done to me."

"I seriously doubt your self-esteem is in any real danger. You have enough opinion of yourself for half a dozen men."

"That hurt," he said, looking quite wounded.

I smiled. He grinned that marvelous grin and squeezed my hands and led me out to the splendid open carriage upholstered in pale tan velvet, driver perched up front in smart tan and gold livery, two muscular roans stamping in harness. It was a glorious day, brilliant silvery-white sunlight gilding the treetops, the sky a lovely blue white. Davy chatted amiably as we drove to the park, his wit and warmth wonderfully engaging. He looked unusually handsome in a dark blue velvet frock coat and breeches and a dashing white satin waistcoat embroidered with blue and silver fleurs-de-lis. Dark blond hair pulled back and tied loosely with a blue velvet ribbon, features animated, he radiated vivacity and that incredible charm that made him the idol of the English stage.

"They're staring at us," he said as we drove down the Mall where the elms spread shadows over the drive.

"You're very famous," I said. "They always stare."

"It's not me they're looking at. It's you. You're one of the Great Beauties."

"You mustn't believe everything you read in the papers, Davy."

"We make a striking couple—the famous actor and the scandalous lady writer. Everyone assumes we're sleeping together—if they but knew! Davy Garrick having a *platonic* relationship with a beautiful woman? My image would be irreparably shattered."

I smiled and he looked at me with crestfallen eyes that soon twinkled once more. The Mall was thronged with fashionable men and women in sumptuous attire, the leading lights of London society rubbing elbows with the most stylish courtesans. Strolling along the promenade or riding in open carriages as were we, they made a glittering assemblage, and it was hard for me to realize that I was part of the parade, gawked at by onlookers as I had gawked three years ago when I had first seen Lady Arabella.

"How—how does it feel to be so famous?" I asked Davy.

"You want to know the truth?"

"Of course."

"It means nothing to me. There's this dazzling fellow, David Garrick, and he's something to behold, a glamorous chap who plays his part and does what the public expects of him, but he doesn't have anything to do with Davy. Davy works hard and sweats a lot and wears shabby old clothes and wonders what all the fuss is about. He's actually quite serious, often melancholy, although he takes great pains to conceal it."

"I think I might like him," I said.

"I'll introduce you to him sometime," he promised.

The driver stopped the carriage and we climbed out and Davy took my hand, leading me away from the Mall with its stylish throng and into the park itself where humbler folk enjoyed themselves this lovely Sunday afternoon. We passed packs of noisy children romping on the lawns, laborers and their lasses sitting under the trees, middle class families picnicking by the ponds. The grass was a deep emerald, burnished with sunlight and spread with shadows from the trees. Swans glided elegantly on the ponds and ducks squawked near the banks. All the flowerbeds were in full bloom. A friendly, festive atmosphere prevailed, and I felt much more at ease than I had on the Mall.

"We'll buy sausage rolls and ale from one of the stalls," Davy informed me, "and if you're very good, you can have lemon ice for dessert. It's going to be a very cheap lunch, I fear."

"I adore sausage rolls. I'll skip the ale, though."

"Not good enough for you, is it? You expect champagne like all the other spoiled beauties. I detest the stuff. I have very common tastes—I'm just a working man, you know, toiling at my profession like a stevedore or fishmonger or shipping clerk, and, alas, I'm usually short of cash."

"I'd be delighted to pay for lunch," I teased.

"I may be poor, but I have my pride. I'll pay, thank you very much. Like a twist of chips to go with your sausage roll?"

"That would be lovely."

Davy purchased the food and led me over to a secluded spot beside one of the ponds. Willow trees sheltered us, and a family of brown and black ducks splashed about near the water's edge. The grassy bank was soft, and there was a strong smell of moss and mud. Davy parted the curtain of willow fronds, indicating the ground as though it were a plush sofa. I sat down and spread out my silken skirts. Handing me my sausage roll and the greasy paper twist of chips, he plopped down beside me and took a hearty swig of ale.

"Ah, pure bliss," he declared. "What better way to spend a Sunday? Who needs the admiring hoards? How's your sausage roll?"

"Delicious. Lots of mustard."

I felt wonderfully relaxed and content as we ate our food there by the water with the ducks cavorting and the pale jade green willow fronds catching the sunlight as they dangled all around us. We were both absurdly overdressed for such an outing, but that was part of its charm. I ate all my chips and half of Davy's, finished my sausage roll and wiped my hands on the grass. Davy lounged back with hands behind his head, staring up at the willows and savoring the contentment that filled him. Water lapped against the mossy bank. Leaves rustled. We could hear the noisy cries of children in the distance.

"Simple pleasures are always the best," he said lazily.

"I agree."

"We look like a Watteau painting, me in my fine velvet, you in your silks, enjoying the simple life."

"I should be making a garland of flowers."

"And I should be looking at you with smoldering eyes, contemplating your firm young bosom with a lascivious smile."

"Watteau was always a bit gamy."

"Elegant pornography. As a matter of fact, I often *do* contemplate your firm young bosom."

"Do you?"

"I long to possess you, have ever since I first saw you there in Marcie's studio, a beautiful, mysterious mute."

"Poor Davy," I teased.

"I'm serious," he protested.

"You're an incorrigible flirt who's been deplorably spoiled by far too much attention from far too many women. A list of your conquests would fill volumes. I prefer to be remembered as the one woman who didn't sleep with David Garrick. It's quite a distinction."

He propped himself up on one elbow and gave me a disgruntled look. Lounging there on the grass in his splendid attire, he looked like a handsome, indolent pasha. I plucked a blade of grass and stroked his cheek with it, and Davy sighed. I felt a great affection for him, great admiration, too, for he was indeed a very hard worker and absolutely dedicated to his craft. If I allowed myself, could I feel something more as well? I wasn't immune to his immense sexual allure, but I staunchly refused to think of him in that way.

"Would it be so unappetizing?" he asked. "Sleeping with me, I mean."

"It—it would probably be appetizing indeed. I've no doubt you're every bit as accomplished as they say you are, but—"

I hesitated, gazing at the mossy bank and the water beyond. The pale green willow fronds swayed gently in the breeze, shimmering in the sunlight. Davy sat up and curled his arms around his knees.

"But you're still in love with Gordon," he said.

"It isn't that, Davy. I—I'm just not emotionally equipped

for a casual, frivolous affair. It would be diverting, yes, and it would probably be a lot of fun, but I—I'd much rather treasure your friendship."

"Is that what you think I want? A casual, frivolous affair?"

"Isn't it?"

Davy frowned. Picking up a small, flat rock, he skimmed it across the water. The ducks squawked, paddling away indignantly. It was several moments before he finally replied.

"I suppose it was," he confessed, "in the beginning. You were just another beautiful woman, and I wanted to add you to that list you were speaking of. I found you titillating, intriguing, a challenge, and then—" Now it was his turn to hesitate.

"And then?" I prompted.

"I'm not very good at this," he told me. "I'm just a humble player, and without a writer to give me the words, a director to give me the movements, I'm as inept as any bumpkin."

"You exaggerate."

"And then—then I got to know you," he continued. "I discovered your intelligence, your strength, your compassion. I grew to admire you, and that initial yen to possess you developed into something—something far more disturbing. You treasure your independence. I treasure mine, too, and up until now I've been as unwilling to make a real commitment as you are. How am I doing?"

"You're doing very well."

"I grew to respect you, too, and I respected you far too much to resort to a cheap seduction—I've no doubt I *could* have seduced you, my beauty. You're not that strong, and I can be very persuasive."

"So I've heard."

"I—I'm not getting any younger, Miranda," he said glumly.

"I know. You'll start creaking any day now," I teased.

Davy ignored my quip. I brushed a stray leaf from my skirt and pushed back an auburn tendril that had fallen across my temple.

"I've enjoyed my freedom, Miranda. I've enjoyed being adored by all the ladies, plucking them like so many rosebuds, but now I'm ready to settle down. I'm ready to put dashing Davy out to pasture and devote the rest of my life to one woman."

"I see."

"That fellow I was talking about earlier—the chap who works hard and sweats a lot, who's serious at heart and is often

~435~

melancholy—I'm introducing you to him now, Miranda."

He looked at me with grave, dark eyes, and I knew that I was indeed seeing another Davy, a warm, serious-minded man nearing middle-age who longed for the domestic stability that would provide the balance he was beginning to need more and more as the years passed. The glamorous, dazzling personality he wore like some splendid garment had been temporarily put aside, and I saw a basically simple man, good-hearted, dedicated to his work, willing to work ten times as hard as anyone else in order to excel in his profession. His face was attractively lined and stamped with character, and the shabby old clothes suited this Davy far better than the fine velvet suit and embroidered satin waistcoat.

"Few people have met him," he said. "I fear he's rather a bore."

"I like him a great deal."

"Do you think you could love him?"

"Davy, I—"

"I love you, Miranda. I want you to become my wife. No, no—don't give me an answer just yet. Think about it. Davy is a scamp, a flashy scoundrel full of nonsense, unworthy of you, but the other chap—the other chap would do everything in his power to make you the happiest woman in London."

I was touched, and I was flattered, too. When I told him so, Davy sighed and shook his head, looking for all the world like a little boy who has just been let out of the classroom by a particularly stern schoolmaster. He climbed to his feet and, taking my hand, pulled me to mine, the old Davy now, all vitality and jaunty charm.

"That's the hardest speech I've ever given," he confided. "I hope I didn't muck it up too badly. I felt dreadfully awkward without a script to follow. The mighty David Garrick stuttering and stumbling about like a moonstruck adolescent—wouldn't my rivals love it!"

"You didn't need a script," I said.

"Bit of rehearsal wouldn't have hurt. I believe I promised you a lemon ice. Still want one?"

"Desperately."

"Something a bit stronger would suit me, but—lemon ice it shall be."

Davy led me through the curtain of willow fronds and across the lawn, holding my elbow in a loose grip. A burly laborer and his buxom lass were embracing passionately beneath one

~436~

of the trees while a jolly family enjoyed their picnic nearby. A little boy with shaggy blond hair raced exuberantly past us, chasing a small black and white dog who yapped blissfully. Davy strolled over to one of the stalls, purchased our ices and handed one to me.

"Took the last penny I had," he complained. "All this high living's going to bankrupt me."

"It's delicious."

"You—uh—you don't think me a bumbling fool, do you?"

"I think you're probably the nicest man I've ever met in my life."

"And?"

"I feel very honored, but—"

"Don't say anything now!" he said hastily, cutting me short. "I don't want an answer yet. Just—just promise me you'll think about it."

I told him I would, and Davy looked vastly relieved as we sauntered back toward the Mall. His step was light, his manner teasing and attentive, and I felt another rush of fondness. He was the most famous man in London, already a legend in his mid-thirties. Radiantly handsome, generous, kind, he was everything a woman could want. I would be a fool to turn him down, yet . . . I would think about it. That was the least I could do.

32

A LINE OF GLEAMING CARRIAGES INCHED SLOWLY along Berkeley Square, each stopping in front of the majestic white marble facade of Lady Julia Copeland's imposing, ostentatious town house. Passengers alighted with great dignity, and footmen in powdered wigs, blue satin frock coats and white satin breeches held torches aloft on either side of the narrow walk leading to the portico which resembled a Greek temple. Orange flames waved against the darkness, casting shadows over the faces of guests moving in a steady procession up the walk. Every window in the house was ablaze with light, and a babble of voices spilled into the night as I climbed out of Lord Markham's finest carriage and moved past those rows of silent, immobile footmen.

Why did I *ever* agree to come? It was going to be abysmally boring. I was going to be utterly miserable. One of the wealthiest women in London, Lady J. flaunted the fact with astounding vulgarity. The house was preposterous, dominating the square with its size and splendor and looking all the more ludicrous when compared to the simple, elegant houses surrounding it. Gold gilt and mirrors blinded the eye as I stepped into the foyer, three opulent crystal chandeliers spilling floods of brilliant light, pendants glittering like waterfalls of diamonds. A mob of chattering, sumptuously attired people filled the place like so much cattle, moving slowly toward the ornate doors of the drawing room where our hostess and her mousy, intimidated husband greeted each guest.

I hadn't wanted to come, had fretted all the while as Millie carefully did my hair, fastening coppery waves on top of my head, arranging the long ringlets that fell in back. She had selected my gown, a rich black brocade with narrow stripes of gold, pink and silver, the full puffed sleeves worn off-the-shoulder, the snug bodice leaving half my bosom bare. The very full skirt belled out from the narrow waist, spreading over half a dozen black gauze underskirts. *Ever* so glamorous, Millie had assured me. She just knew I'd be the most stunnin' woman there, and she could hardly wait to hear all about it when I got home.

A mistake, Miranda, I told myself. You'd better make your escape while you can. Two hours in this suffocating mob and you'll be ready to swoon. I turned around, fully intending to leave. A strong, ink-stained hand gripped my arm, restraining me.

"No you don't!" a gruff voice warned. "If I'm going to endure this abomination, you are, too."

A grumpy, puffy, pockmarked face scowled at me, dark, intelligent eyes daring me to protest.

"Johnson!" I exclaimed. "I never expected to see you here."

"I'm a certifiable lion," he grumbled. "I've come to eat my regular quota of Christians."

"I suppose I'm the first one on the menu," I retorted.

"You're a colleague," he countered, "loath though I am to admit it. I've always contended that a woman writing a book is like a dog walking on hind legs. It's not done well, but you're surprised to find it done at all."

"Typical of you, Johnson."

"Don't know what the world's coming to," he complained, shaking his large, shaggy head. "Women writing books, writing them damned well, too. Next thing you know, men will be banished to the kitchen."

"That might not be a bad idea. It would leave women free to accomplish all those things they're fully capable of accomplishing. There'd be fewer wars, far less corruption."

"And sheer havoc in the kitchen," he added. "I must confess I found *Duchess Annie* damnably readable. I actually shed a tear or two."

"I didn't know you were capable of such a thing," I taunted.

Johnson grimaced. "Behind this surly, formidable, offensive-to-the-eye exterior there beats, I fear, the heart of a blubbering sentimentalist. When I'm not snarling and snapping at fools, I'm a shameless softie. The world, alas, is filled with fools, most of whom seem to be here tonight."

"Let's sneak out," I pleaded.

"Sniveling coward, are you? Can't face the fire? Typical of your sex, of course, but I expected more from the notorious M.J. It won't be so bad," he told me. "The old bag packs the place with idiots and gibbers like a chimpanzee in heat, but she serves the finest victuals and the best wine in London. I fully intend to stuff myself like a pig, then drink myself into oblivion. I always do at these affairs."

Johnson grumbled ominously as we were shoved forward by the crowd in back of us. In this glittering throng he was an odd spectacle indeed in his poorly mended white stockings, crumpled brown knee breeches and shabby, oversized brown coat with its bulging pockets and frayed cuffs. His long gray wig was far from clean, set slightly crooked atop his head, and his great size and lumbering gait augmented one's impression of a sullen, ponderous bear in human guise.

"I've no idea why I'm here," I complained as we inched toward the drawing room doors. "I don't even know who the Dean of Southwark *is*, and I feel certain I'll detest him."

"What!" Johnson cried. "You've never heard of the swank Dean Jordon? He is the most fashionable clergyman in London, pampered and adored by the stylish ladies who flock to hear his rosy platitudes and pathetic homilies. Sleek popinjay, red-haired, the darling of the salons. A worldly cleric is always somehow reassuring. Bloke's written a book of sermons. It's selling out all over the city, third and fourth printings already snapped up, a fifth and sixth already on the way."

"Have you read it?" I inquired.

"Gave me acute indigestion," he retorted. "Felt like I'd just eaten an enormous box of bonbons. Precisely the sort of pap the ladies devour, all sugar, no substance. Bloke's musical, too, I fear. Plays the organ with a string accompaniment."

"Not tonight, surely?"

"Lady J. installed an organ in the music room last week, I understand. A monstrous affair, big as a behemoth—gold-plated pipes, of course."

"Jesus," I whispered.

Little by little we were pushed toward the drawing room doors and a few moments later found ourselves face to face with Lady Julia and her husband, a tiny little man in brown who seemed to fade to total invisibility beside his outlandish spouse. Lady J. was extremely tall and seemed even taller with three towering white egret feathers affixed to the side of her powdered coiffure with a diamond and emerald clasp. Skinny to the point of emaciation, she had a beaky nose, a great pink slash of mouth and pale, protruding blue eyes that brought to mind a startled giraffe. Never had I seen so many diamonds, so many emeralds—all needing a good cleaning, I noted.

"Miss James!" she cried, grabbing my hand. "What an *honor* this is! We've been *dying* to have you, haven't we, James? I just adored your novel, so naughty, so true to *life*!"

"Thank you for your invitation," I said sweetly.

"We must find a few minutes alone together, my child. I'm ever so interested in writing—I'm thinking of writing a book *myself*! You must tell me how it's done."

I made polite noises and she looked past me and saw Johnson and, letting go of my hand, clutched his and began to gush over him. Johnson made a fierce face, jerked his hand free and asked her where the food was. Lady J. tittered, delighted by his rudeness. What a marvelous eccentric he was! How wonderful of him to snap and snarl like that! She just *knew* his dictionary was going to be an enormous success when it was finally finished, and she fully intended to *buy* a copy.

"Buy ten," he growled. "You can use 'em for doorstops."

"Isn't he *divine*!" she shrieked.

"Wretched woman," Johnson muttered irritably as we moved on into the drawing room. "Always clattering like a cockatoo, not a thought in her silly head. Did you happen to smell her breath?"

"I'm sure she means well," I said.

Johnson made another face, adjusted his greasy gray wig and brushed at the lapels of his shabby brown coat, glaring peevishly at fellow guests. I strongly suspected that his gruff, boorish manner was merely a smoke screen to hide an innate shyness. Davy swore that, in private, he was the kindest, most charitable of men, a cuddly old bear who was the softest touch in town, forever emptying his pockets for some needy friend.

"Every charlatan and fraud in the city must be here tonight," he grumbled. "There's the food over there. Come along, Miss James, let's hit those tables before this mob eats everything up."

The drawing room was as large as a ballroom, the molded ceiling gilded with gold leaf and dripping with chandeliers, the walls covered with pale pink brocade and hung with enormous paintings. Gigantic plants abounded, and there were quite a few Greek statues standing in niches. Because of the size of the room, the mob didn't seem nearly as large. Johnson led me over to the three linen-covered tables where a marvelous array of food dazzled the eye. Although I protested that I wasn't hungry, Johnson insisted on filling a plate for me.

"Prawns, aspic, a slice of that lamb, some asparagus—we'll try those pastries later on. So you're determined to break my friend Davy's heart?" he said, thrusting a plate at me.

"What gives you that idea?" I inquired, taking the plate. "Really, I can't possibly eat all—"

"I'll help you," he grumbled. "Here, take this plate, too. I'll grab one of those preposterously garbed footmen who're circulating with trays of drinks. Champagne?"

"I—"

"You'd better have some. You're going to need it. Find us a place by the wall. I'll join you as soon as I get our drinks."

Johnson ambled off toward one of the footmen, and I stood there balancing the two plates and feeling extremely foolish. There must have been seventy-five people in the room, and all of them seemed to be staring at me as I finally made my way toward one of the huge Greek statues. Setting the plates on the edge of the waist-high black marble pedestal, I contemplated making a quick escape before Johnson returned. The din was deafening, voices babbling, china clattering, music playing loudly in an adjoining room. Bach. Although a row of French windows stood open, leading to the gardens beyond, the air inside was fetid, heavily laden with the odors of sweat, stale powder and cloying perfumes.

"Here's your champagne," Johnson said. "Glass of port for me. Where's my plate?"

"There on the edge of the pedestal."

Johnson took his plate, set down his port and glanced up at the naked, armless, decapitated marble statue that loomed above us.

"Abominable taste," he muttered. "Not even genuine, nor are any of those Van Dyck's festooning the walls. The Lelys of Nell Gwynn and Barbara Castlemaine are real enough but decidedly second rate. Now, what's all this nonsense about your marrying my friend Davy?"

His eyes were accusatory, his tone harsh, almost hostile. Taken aback, I gazed at him for a moment in silence, and when I spoke my voice was cold enough to cause frostbite.

"Davy asked me to marry him, Mr. Johnson, but I really don't think that's any of your business."

"'Course it is. Davy's like a brother to me. These prawns are superlative, by the way. You're not going to eat yours? He's ready to settle down and longs for a quiet, well ordered domestic life—exactly what he needs. If he's going to keep on working in the theater, he needs a calm, serene home atmosphere, someone to cook his meals and keep his clothes in order and pay his bills and watch out for his health and protect him from the public, someone, in short, willing to devote the rest of her life to the care and feeding of Davy Garrick."

"I agree," I said crisply. "That's precisely what he needs."

Johnson finished his plate of food, indicated mine, gave me an inquisitive look and, when I shook my head, began to empty it as well. I took a sip of my champagne. I could feel spots of color on my cheeks and was finding it extremely difficult to maintain my temper. Genius he might be, London's First Gentleman of Letters, currently engaged in a titanic undertaking that would revolutionize the language, but I found his well-known bluntness quite offensive.

"What he does *not* need is another artist," Johnson continued, "and you are indeed an artist, Miss James, as excellent in your way as he is in his, I suspect. *Duchess Annie* genuinely moved me, moved me to tears, and it made a perfectly valid statement about the human condition. I understand your new book is even better. You must send me a copy as soon as it's out."

"Mr. Johnson—"

"Call me Sam. All my real friends do, and I feel quite friendly toward you, child. Two strong, creative personalities dwelling under the same roof—" Johnson paused, took a gulp of port and shook his head. "An impossible situation, as I'm sure you'll agree."

"I don't see what that—"

"Of course you do," he snapped. "You're an extremely intelligent young woman—and that's one of the problems, too. Davy doesn't need an *intel*ligent woman. He needs a dull, devoted woman who will be content to sit at his feet and look up at him with loving eyes and nurture him, not someone who thinks for herself, has her own creative endeavors. Every word I say is true, and you know it, child."

He was right, and that's what made it so irritating. I had given Davy's proposal a great deal of thought, and I had reached the same conclusions myself. The shabby, shaggy old bear of a man beside me was merely verbalizing them. I sipped my champagne. Johnson finished the food, looking up occasionally to glare menacingly at fellow guests who came too near.

"Delicious!" he declared. "Must have some more of that lamb, another helping of that aspic. He's in love with you, child, genuinely in love for the first time in his life, and that's bad. Love's a marvelous, maddening distraction, but it's deadly for a true artist, saps his strength, drains his creative energy. It takes him away from the important thing—his work."

I finished my champagne and, beckoning one of the footmen, put the glass on his tray and took another one filled to the brim with the sparkling amber beverage. Johnson straightened his wig again and brushed bread crumbs from the lapels of his coat.

"Marriage would be disastrous for both of you," he told me. "Davy's work would suffer. So would yours. Instead of sewing his shirts and polishing his boots and cooking hot meals, you'd be writing another book, and he would resent that. Instead of being supportive and understanding when you hit a bad patch in your book, he'd wring his hands and moan about the problems with his new production, the wretched actress he'd been saddled with, the inept stagehands and the damnable second act speech that just doesn't work."

Right again, you crafty old sod, I thought. I took a large swallow of the champagne.

"I suppose you have the ideal wife picked out for him," I said acidly.

"I have, indeed. Mademoiselle Violette, that plump Austrian dancer who's so hot to have him. She's in the theater, yes, but she has no dedication and would dump it all in a minute to become Davy's wife. She's sweet and dull and utterly undemanding, and she happens to worship Davy. Eva Maria, to give her her real name, is a stolid German hausfrau at heart. She'd be perfect for him. He doesn't *love* her, but he's quite fond of her, and I've no doubt that in time he would be utterly devoted."

"You—you've thought everything out, haven't you?"

Johnson nodded. "I love Davy like a brother. I want the best for him. He has a great deal to contribute to the world, and so, my dear, do you. I'd like you both to be happy."

His voice was strangely gentle, and those eyes that could be so fierce and formidable were full of compassion now, the eyes of a kindly man who was genuinely concerned about his fellow man. He gave my arm a pat and said he was sorry he had been so blunt, hoped he hadn't hurt my feelings too badly, and for a moment I glimpsed the Sam Johnson that Davy and dozens of others loved so well. My irritation vanished entirely.

"I haven't given Davy my answer," I said quietly.

"As I said, you're an extremely intelligent young woman— I feel sure your answer will be the right one."

"It will be," I replied.

"I've been monopolizing you far too long, child," he said amiably. "It's time for me to go gobble up some Christians— Lady J. would feel horribly cheated if I didn't insult at least half her guests. Sure I can't bring you another plate of food?"

I shook my head. Johnson patted his wig, straightened his lapels and, assuming his curmudgeon character, shambled off to perform his social duties. He was soon surrounded by a group of fluttering females who recoiled in delighted horror at his remarks. Leaving the Greek statue, I got another glass of champagne and was soon surrounded myself. I smiled politely and answered the innane questions and forced myself to be civil. Yes, writing books was a difficult job. No, I didn't find it at all unfeminine. Yes, I had just completed another novel. No, it wasn't autobiographical. It was about whores.

A plump matron in blue velvet gasped. A stodgy gentleman with a monocle blanched. An actress tittered. A suave French painter grinned a lewd grin and asked me if I'd consider sitting for him *au naturel*. I asked him if he'd like a knee in the groin. All this while I had felt someone staring at me, an unmistakable sensation that was almost physical. I could feel the eyes boring into my back, and when I turned around, the tall, muscular soldier in his tight white breeches and scarlet jacket continued to stare, openly, arrogantly, with a hostility that was undeniable.

Lady Julia swooped upon me and fluttered her beringed hands and blinked her protruding eyes and told me again how thrilled she was I'd come and continued to gush for a good five minutes, a tall, breathless giraffe of a woman in soiled white satin and dusty diamonds and emeralds, harmless enough but, at the moment, extremely irritating. I had accepted her invitation, though, and gave her all my attention, as charming as I could possibly be. Lady J. asked me the usual questions and was convinced we were kindred souls.

"I must see to my other guests now, alas—being a good hostess is *such* a dreary chore, I'd much rather be doing something *crea*tive. We must get together for a *real* talk soon, without all these worrisome distractions."

"We really must," I said.

"I'm ever so eager for you to meet Dean Jordon—he's a writer, too, you know. His book of sermons is so in*spir*ing, so *elevating*! He's not the least bit prudish, either—so comforting to see him tease and flirt and drink his wine just like a *normal* person."

"I look forward to meeting him. Incidently, who—who is that tall soldier standing over there in front of the pink sofa? He looks remarkably like a—an old friend of mine."

Lady J. peered across the room, her eyesight obviously bad. "Oh! That's Captain Ramsey—Captain Jon Ramsey, a fascinating man. One of the king's most trusted agents, utterly ruthless, they say, stationed somewhere in the country, doing a very important job—I forget the details. He's on leave now. A stern, handsome soldier is always an asset at a gathering like this."

"Definitely."

"I strive for variety. It's terribly taxing to always come up with just the right combination!"

Lady J. fluttered off to pounce upon a prominent historian, and I drank the rest of my champagne. It was going to my head. The room seemed stuffier. The noise seemed louder. The dazzling lights, the brilliant colors, the noxious odors were beginning to get to me, and I felt as though I'd stepped into the middle of a garish kaleidoscope. Moving over to the row of French windows, I stood there savoring the cool night air and wondering if it would be possible to slip through the gardens, climb over the wall and flee.

"How are you, Miss James?"

The voice was cultivated, distinctly upper class with an underlying hardness both harsh and commanding. I turned. Captain Jon Ramsey stood not three feet away, staring at me with brilliant blue eyes as cold as ice, his straight blond brows lowered, a deep crease between them. At least six feet tall, his superbly conditioned body shown off to advantage in the tight-fitting uniform, he had strong, even features that might have been sculpted from granite, hard and ruthless. The lips were thin, the Roman nose perfect, the cheekbones flat and broad. Tight, short blond curls covered his head like a close-fitting cap, reminding me of the head of Apollo. His was a cruel, handsome face that would intimidate his men and fascinate a number of women.

"I don't believe we've been introduced," I said stiffly.

"Captain Jon Ramsey, at your service. I know who you are, of course. Everyone knows the famous Miranda James."

"Are you interested in literature, Captain Ramsey?"

"I'm interested in writers—one in particular."

"Oh?"

Those brilliant, icy blue eyes stared at me with open hostility, the lowered brows a straight, sullen line above them. Rarely had I been stared at so intensely. Captain Ramsey made no effort to conceal his opinion of me, those eyes judging, condemning me. I wished my brocade gown weren't cut quite so low, wished I could control the flush tinting my cheeks.

"Which writer would that be?" I inquired.

"Cam Gordon. I understand you were his woman."

I made no reply. I could feel the anger beginning to boil.

"He's still wanted," Ramsey said.

"I'm fully aware of that."

"Have you been in touch with him?"

"I don't think I care to answer that, Captain Ramsey."

"The latest report is that he's involved with a gang of smugglers working off the Cornish coast. He's been seen, identified as one of them. The reward for his capture has been doubled."

"I fail to see that that has anything to do with me."

"On the contrary," he said, eyes glaring, "I suspect it might have quite a lot to do with you."

If I hadn't been a lady now, if I hadn't been a guest in a stranger's home, I would have slapped his face so hard his ears would ring for hours, but I was no longer a fierce little street urchin. I was a dignified adult now, so I merely looked at him with level eyes, one brow faintly arched. Captain Ramsey curled his thin lips, his eyes holding mine while, in the room behind us, voices chattered and china rattled and laughter rang out, drowning the music that was still being played in another room.

"I repeat, have you been in touch with him?"

"I have a suggestion, Captain Ramsey," I said. My voice was extremely polite.

"What's that?" he sneered.

"I suggest you take your questions and shove them up your ass."

Ramsey didn't flinch. The thin lips tightened, and his hands curled up into hard fists. He would have loved to have knocked me down, beaten me black and blue, and he would have liked to do something else, too. I could see it in his eyes. I knew very well how his kind treated any poor woman unfortunate enough to find herself in his power. He would enjoy inflicting pain, and only the most brutal rape would appease his particular appetite.

"You may be a famous writer, Miss James, you may be protected by wealth and powerful friends, but in my eyes you're still the whore of a wanted man, and you haven't seen the last of me."

"I'll be listening for your rattle," I said. "In the meantime, why don't you just sod off."

Captain Ramsey glared at me for perhaps thirty seconds longer, and then he whirled around and marched off, the fringed gold epaulettes on his broad shoulders shimmering and swaying. The encounter had shaken me far more than I cared to admit, and I longed for another glass of champagne, although I knew it would be a disastrous mistake. I remembered all those questions they had bombarded me with three years ago. Dear

God, wasn't it over yet? Several minutes passed in a blur, the kaleidoscope shifting, colors whirling, and I was surprised to find myself staring into Lady Julia's face, her eyes protruding, her mouth flapping open and shutting like some great pink trap.

"—know you'll adore it," she was saying. "It's his favorite piece. No Bach for Dean Jordon, just this Albi—Albay—just this Venetian composer over and over again. Have you met him yet? No? The ladies have been monopolizing him, I fear. I'll see that you're introduced to him after the music."

"I—really, Lady Julia, I don't think I—"

"Come along, my child," she said gaily. "You'll want to get a good seat, I know."

I found myself following her as though in a trance. We left the vast drawing room and moved into another almost as large. The ornately molded ceiling was pale pink-beige with circular designs in gold leaf, three enormous chandeliers spilling tiers of crystal pendants. The walls were pale powder blue with pink-beige panels painted with delicate green leaves and garlands of roses and plump cherubs playing various musical instruments. Fifty delicate gilt chairs were lined up ten to a row, and at the end of the room, on a low rosewood stage, a huge organ loomed up, the great, golden pipes gleaming in the light. A dozen men in black were tuning up their string instruments, and a spry, red-haired man with a clerical collar bustled about, giving them last-minute instructions.

Quite a number of guests had been more fortunate than I, making their escape before the performance began. Only half the chairs were taken, and I was one of the last to enter the music room. Captain Ramsey was nowhere in sight. Music would hardly be his pleasure, I thought, still a bit dazed. Sam Johnson had not been among those to make a hasty exit. Seeing me standing there inside the doorway, he leaped out of his chair and moved ponderously over to me.

"Thought maybe you'd been able to slip off," he mumbled. "Damned women I was talking to bustled me in here by force, one pulling my left arm, one pulling my right, another powdered hussy pushing me from behind, all of 'em tittering like demented magpies. Come, child, we'll take seats in the back row."

I sat down on one of the gilt chairs, my striped brocade skirt spreading out with a crisp, silken rustle. Johnson sat beside me, the fragile chair making ominous creaks as he shifted his bulk into a comfortable position. People talked quietly, the women toying with fans, many of the gentlemen taking snuff from the small bejeweled boxes no fashionable male was without. The musicians were tuning up, violins making twangy, cricketlike noises. Lady Julia skittered about, speaking to various guests, the tall feathers affixed to her hair bobbing like bizarre tentacles.

"I hate to admit it," Johnson remarked, "but Jordon's really quite good, could have been a professional musician had he not taken the cloth. Invariably plays the same music, though, Adagio in G minor by Albinoni—it's his showpiece, don't think he knows anything else. Sentimental claptrap, no intellectual content like you find in Bach, but I suppose it's a pretty enough tune. I like something a bit more cerebral."

I hardly heard him. The encounter with Captain Jon Ramsey had distrubed me a great deal, but not for the obvious reasons. The man himself, his open hostility bothered me not at all— I'd encountered far too much hostility in my lifetime to be bothered by that—but his questions had brought it all back again. Would I never be free? Would Cam Gordon haunt me the rest of my life? Would I feel this sadness, this loss every time I . . . every time I remembered that tall, slender body, that mouth, those piercing blue eyes, the heavy black wave flopping over his brow? Damn him. Damn him. Why must I remember, why must I long for him still with every fiber of my being?

Dean Jordon was still bustling about on the stage, speaking to the musicians, occasionally jotting a note on the sheet music in front of them on elegant rosewood stands. Lithe and agile, a bit below medium height, he wore his dark red hair pulled back sleekly and tied at the nape of his neck with a thin black velvet ribbon. Although soberly dressed all in black with the white collar around his throat, he nevertheless had a dandified look. The black breeches, vest and frock coat had the dashing cut only the best tailor could provide, and the cloth was much finer than one would have expected to find on a clergyman. Southwark was, of course, a plush, fashionable parish, I thought, trying to distract myself. Dean Jordon was certainly no longer a youth—he must be at least forty, I reasoned—but he somehow reminded me of a merry, mischievous lad inordinately pleased to be able to show off in front of such a swank, affluent crowd.

He was taking his seat at the organ now. A hush fell over the people sitting on the gilt chairs. I rarely had an opportunity to hear good music. Perhaps it would help drive those memories away. It began, lovely and lilting, a wave of melody swelling, swelling, ebbing, swelling again, music that was indescribably poignant, as though . . . as though the most intimate human emotions had been magically transformed into melody . . . as though the sadness and longing inside me had been captured in sound. The organ swelled. Violins sang softly, sweetly, sad, so sad, lovely, so lovely, over and over again until heartbreak itself washed over one in waves of music. Cam. Cam. There in front of me, his eyes gleaming. Holding me now, caressing me, making love to me . . . disappearing, my arms reaching out, emptiness, longing, love replaced by anguish as the music ebbed for a final time and the last notes were played. Silence at last, sadness still wafting on air.

There were tears on my lashes. I brushed them away. Johnson grumbled at my side, dabbing at his own eyes, as moved as I had been but not about to admit it.

"Sentimental claptrap," he muttered, "cheap emotional effects, not an ounce of real content." He added that he seemed to have gotten a speck of dust in his eye.

Dean Jordon was standing now, bowing humbly in acknowledgment of the polite applause. People were getting up, chattering again, a magical spell broken. "More champagne!" Lady Julia cried. "Everyone must have more champagne!" Johnson stood up, gave me his hand. I felt weak, emotionally depleated.

"I—I'm really not feeling well," I said. "I must—must get home."

"Come with me," he said gruffly.

He gripped my arm and led me out of the music room and through the enormous drawing room, snarling viciously at all those who approached us, trying to stop our progress with questions or effusive comments. He led me into the empty foyer and told me to wait, he'd have my carriage brought around front, it'd probably take five minutes or so, take deep breaths. Was I going to swoon? I shook my head. He gave me a worried look and shambled out, glaring menacingly at the two bewigged footmen stationed on either side of the door. I stood beneath one of the chandeliers, a tall, pale woman reflected in the mirrors, her rich coppery red hair worn in sculpted waves, long ringlets spilling down in back, her black brocade gown with its thin gold, pink and silver stripes rich and sumptuous. Who was she? What was she doing here?

"Honora?"

I turned. Dean Jordon was standing several yards away, staring at me with incredulous brown eyes. He shook his head, blinked, looked at me again and put a palm to his brow.

"You—you must forgive me," he said. "It couldn't be, of course. For a moment—" He cut himself short, shook his head again as though to clear it of some disturbing image. "Forgive me," he repeated.

"You—you called me Honora."

"You reminded me—you look so much like a lady I once knew, many years ago, a very lovely lady. Your hair is a different color, your eyes, too, but the features—the features are amazingly alike. You might be her twin. She would have been about your age when I last saw her. I played the organ at her wedding, Albinoni, in fact, the piece you just heard. I was a mere lad at the time—it must have been twenty-three, twenty-four years ago."

Dean Jordon came closer, still studying my face as though he couldn't believe what he saw. The two footmen stationed by the door were immobile, looking at us with indifferent eyes. Close to, the Dean still resembled a mischievous lad, only the fine lines about his eyes and mouth betraying his true age. It was a good-natured face, the mouth generous, the eyes amiable, a scattering of freckles across his nose and cheekbones.

"Her name was Honora?" My voice was barely a whisper.

"Honora James. Married Jeffrey Mowrey. Never saw a young couple so much in love. Like a fairy tale, it was, their story, with, alas, a very sad ending. He died right after the wedding, and she—"

"I am Miranda James," I said.

Dean Jordon took a step backward, shaken. His eyes grew even wider with disbelief.

"No. No, it—it's too—you couldn't be the child who—" He placed a palm over his brow again as though to check for fever. "She disappeared, vanished into thin air, it seemed. My uncle, Reverend Williams, came to London as soon as he received Honora's manuscript and read it. She had already died. The child had run off. He spent almost three weeks in St. Giles trying to locate her."

"My mother died," I said. "They were going to send me to the parish workhouse. I ran away. I—I had a friend. She hid me from the authorities."

My voice seemed to come from a very long way off. It seemed to belong to someone else. The sparkling crystal chandeliers, the gold gilt, the footmen in their white satin breeches and blue satin coats and powdered wigs, the sound of laughter and chatter drifting into the foyer, the woman in the mirror, the redhaired man in black—none of it had reality. Dean Jordon took my hands in his, holding them in a strong grip.

"My child, you're pale. Probably am myself. I never thought—the fate of that child has haunted me for over two decades, and now—" He hesitated, squeezing my hands tightly. "I still have the manuscript your mother wrote. She sent it to my uncle in Cornwall, and it was with his things when he died."

Johnson came through the door, looking extremely belligerent when he saw the Dean gripping my hands.

"You couldn't really call it a letter," Dean Jordon continued. "She wanted to—she wanted my uncle to know the full story so that he could explain things to you when were you were old enough—"

"What's this!" Johnson barked. "Miss James isn't feeling well. She's in no condition to listen to you chatter about some—"

"I'll bring it to you tomorrow," the Dean said. "Four o'clock in the afternoon? Will that be convenient?"

I nodded. "Grosvenor Square. Lord Markham's place, the Dower House in back of Markham House."

"My child, this is amazing. I still can't believe—"

Johnson led me away and helped me into the waiting carriage and insisted on riding back with me. I vaguely remember saying good-bye to him when we got home, sending him off to his own house in the carriage. Millie had come over and was waiting up for me, eager to hear all the details of my glamorous evening out. I shook my head, unable to speak. She helped me undress, helped me into bed. The champagne, the encounter with Ramsey, the music, the memories, the amazing meeting with Dean Jordon had all taken their toll, and I sank into a heavy sleep immediately, one blessedly free of dreams.

I slept until ten the next morning and awoke in a stupor. Millie brought a pot of hot coffee and some buttered croissant rolls up on a tray, hovering over me like a broody hen. My head was splitting. I sent her away. The coffee was very strong. It helped. By eleven I was feeling somewhat better. By twelve I had bathed, washed my hair, brushed it and put on a simply cut but elegant yellow silk frock. When Dean Jordon arrived at four, I was waiting for him in the drawing room, calm, composed, in complete control of myself.

"I must apologize for last night," I said when Millie showed him into the room. "I'm afraid I wasn't myself."

"Nor was I," he admitted. "The shock of it all quite discombobulated me. After all these years—it's amazing, child, absolutely amazing."

He carried a thick parcel covered in heavy brown paper. He handed it to me, and I placed it on my desk. The Dean was wearing clothes identical to the ones he had worn last night, sober but expensive, exquisitely cut, a fresh white clerical collar around his throat. Sober or no, there was a glossy patina about him, an indefinable glamor, and one sensed exuberant high spirits carefully repressed, boyish merriment just beneath the surface.

"Could I pour you a glass of wine?" I asked.

"I'd be delighted. You have a lovely place, Miss James. That Hogarth—I know I've seen it before."

"Prints of it were sold all over London," I said, pouring sparkling white wine into a crystal glass.

"I know who you are, of course. Miranda James—M.J. I didn't make the connection last night. I read *Duchess Annie*, of course. I suspect much of it is autobiographical—an orphan who grows up on the streets, becomes a pickpocket, meets an artist who takes her into his home."

"I—I used some of my own experiences, yes."

"I've also read your stories. You're a very gifted young woman."

"Thank you."

"You're not joining me?" he inquired when I handed him the glass.

"I'm afraid I couldn't. I'm not accustomed to drinking, and I had far too much champagne last night. It was the only way I could endure the evening."

"Things do tend to get rather hectic at Lady Julia's, but she's a dear lady, actually. Means well, even if she's a mite overbearing at times. Extremely charitable, too. That's very important in my line of work."

"It was very kind of you to come today, Dean Jordon. I know you must have a terribly crowded schedule."

"There *are* an awful lot of demands," he confessed, "but it's all for the Lord. I reread your mother's manuscript last

~453~

night—it's a remarkable document. It's all there, my own small part included. She caught me to the life, I fear. You came by your literary talents quite naturally."

"I'm eager to—to read it."

Dean Jordon took a final sip of wine and set the glass down. His thick red hair gleamed in the sunlight streaming through the windows. His freckles were a light golden brown, adding a piquant touch to that boyish middle-aged face. He took my hands as he had done the night before, holding them in a surprisingly strong grip. He smiled a gentle smile and nodded and squeezed my hands tightly, releasing them a moment later.

"Of course you are," he said quietly, "and I shan't detain you. I'm delighted to have found you at last, my child, and I hope you will come to see me soon. We have much to talk about."

"I will," I promised.

I showed him out. A carriage was waiting for him on the drive. I waited until it had driven away, standing there on the doorstep with the sunshine making silver yellow patterns on the lawn, and then I went inside. I told Millie I did not wish to be disturbed. I went into the drawing room, sat down at the desk and unwrapped the parcel Dean Jordon had brought. The pages were old and brittle, beginning to brown slightly with age, and the ink was faded, but the words were quite legible. I hesitated, a strange, tremulous feeling welling up inside, and then I began to read:

There is so much to say and so little time. There is so much Miranda must know, so much she must understand, and one day she will, I trust. One day she will be old enough to understand and forgive. I'd like to take her into my arms right now and explain it all to her in my own voice and let her see my eyes and what is in my heart, but I dare not....

33

THE SKY STRETCHED OVERHEAD, ENDLESS AND AIRY, white, with the vaguest suggestion of blue, while below the land was rugged and rocky, bleak, gray and brown and gray green with patches of tarry black. There were touches of pale, faded purple as well as the stark white sunlight washed over the short gray-tan grass and the enormous gray boulders. Gulls soared against the sky, cawing angrily as my private coach forged ahead, the four sturdy horses plodding steadily, the coach itself shaking and rocking as the wheels moved over the rough ground. I had hired it in London. The horses had been changed a number of times, and it seemed I had been on the road forever, staying the nights in rustic inns. My journey was almost over now. I should reach Mowrey House before noon.

The coach windows were open, and I marveled at the clean, invigorating air in Cornwall. It was laced with a salty tang and laden with pungent, earthy smells I seemed to recognize instinctively. That was peat, yes, and that had to be lichen. That was the smell of sun-washed grass, and that was mossy rock, damp sand, seaweed. I hadn't seen the sea yet, but I could feel its presence just beyond the horizon to my left, a vast body of water that gave this part of the country its unique character, dominating the land, alternately providing sustenance or wreaking havoc. Bleak though it might be, Cornwall had its own kind of beauty, I thought, stark and clean and uncluttered. There was a curious grandeur as well, something sensed, not seen, a feeling of centuries past, of ancient rituals, of violence, unheaval and survival, as though the land retained invisible impressions of all that had gone before.

Leaning back against the shabby leather cushion, shaken about as the coach rumbled over a particularly bad rut, I tried to hold back the tension that had been mounting ever since I had left the inn this morning. I had dressed very carefully, selecting a sapphire blue silk frock with narrow black stripes. I wore long black velvet gloves and a wide-brimmed black velvet hat with a large sapphire silk bow on the left side of the crown, a cascade of sapphire plumes sweeping over the right side of the brim. Expensive, elegant, restrained without being sober. When I finally came face to face with my uncle I wanted him to see a strong, composed, self-sufficient woman who was fully capable of holding her own. When I met the man who had destroyed my mother's life I wanted him to know he was not dealing with a timorous girl he could intimidate as he had intimidated that gentle young governess who had trembled before his cold stare almost twenty-five years ago.

I had no idea what I was going to say, no idea what I was going to do. I only knew I had to see him and confront him with what I knew, yet I had closed up the house in London and put all my personal things in storage, and the bags strapped on top of the coach in three weighty heaps contained all the clothes I owned. Would I leave in three or four days? Would I stay in Cornwall indefinitely to fight my uncle for a portion of the inheritance I neither wanted nor needed? I didn't know, yet I had made my farewells to Marcelon, Bancroft, and Sheppard as though I expected to be gone for quite some time, and I had written a long, painful letter to Davy, giving him the answer I had known I must give, even before my talk with Johnson, wishing him the best life had to offer and adding that I hoped we would always remain friends. That letter had undoubtedly hurt him when he read it, but Davy would recover soon enough, and he would eventually come to see why such a match would have been disastrous for both of us.

How startling it had been to learn that I had known Davy Garrick when I was a saucy, mishievous little girl in Lichfield, feeding bread crumbs to the ducks and "skittering around Lichfield like a ray of sunlight, romping with the other children, spurring them on." Young Davy had called me the prettiest little minx he had ever seen and, at four, I had announced that I was going to marry him when I grew up. The ironies of life, I thought as the coach bounced over a series of ruts. I had known Sam Johnson, too, tagging after the gawky, ungainly bookseller's son and taunting him quite cruelly along with the other children. What changes the years had brought into the lives of all three of us, and now my life had changed dramatically once again.

I gazed out the window of the coach, thinking about that

remarkable document my mother had written with the very last strength in her body. How different my life would have been had she been able to finish it and mail it off two or three weeks earlier, had Reverend Williams arrived in St. Giles a few days sooner. . . . How I had wept when I read that sad, heartbreaking story. Like a magical key, it had unlocked the doors of memory, and hundreds of long-forgotten incidents came flooding back. I remembered Lichfield, remembered the pond, the cathedral, saw that bright, rowdy little girl, that sad, beautiful, loving woman who was so patient and tender, who spoke so softly. I remembered those early years in London when, a happy child, I had rarely been aware of the horrible struggle to survive that plagued each day for my mother until we finally ended up in St. Giles, utterly destitute. I knew now all that had gone before, and, at last, I knew who I was.

Before leaving London I had gone to visit Dean Jordon in his swank parish and we had talked for hours. He had told me all he could about my mother, my father, my uncle and that great gray stone house with leaded windows where the tragedy occurred. An intelligent, compassionate man with a sincere dedication to his work despite the fripperies and his stylish facade, Dean Jordon agreed that I must journey to Cornwall to discover my roots, but he had added that I must not go for the wrong reasons. I must put all hatred out of my mind, must realize that my uncle had endured a terrible punishment all these years. His life had been utterly destroyed when he lost his brother, my father, the only person on earth he had ever loved. I mustn't hate him, Dean Jordon told me. I must pity him, and I must try to understand.

I could see the cliffs now, and as the road curved I had my first glimpse of the sea, steel gray waves surging turbulently, capped with foamy white, not a touch of blue in evidence today. Over the plodding of horse hooves and the skimming of wheels I could hear a swooshing, sweeping sound and the splattering explosions as waves crashed against the rocks below. Gulls squawked overhead, swirling in the air like flapping scraps of white paper. The smell of salt was much stronger now, a sharp, zesty tang. I could smell wet rock and sand, moss and gull droppings, too, and it was all somehow exhilarating. The air here in Cornwall had a brisk, bracing quality, such a contrast to London and the noxious odors one learned to live with.

The road turned inland again. A few minutes later I saw the clay pits, great, gaping excavations, dusty gray, adorned with a flimsy network of rotten brown wooden ramps. The pits were deserted, empty, ugly eyesores. The factory beyond was deserted, too, a squat, hideous structure, several windows broken out, the tall black smokestacks streaked with rust. The out buildings were in pitiful shape, several of the sheds tumbling down. Sprawling there in the brilliant sunlight, the place looked as though it had been abandoned a dozen years ago. So the Mowrey pottery works had closed down? What were the villagers doing for a livelihood now?

Very little, it seemed, for when the coach entered it a short while later, the village had a depressed, impoverished appearance, everything unkempt, run-down. A grim atmosphere seemed to hang over the whole place, and the people I saw through the coach windows had a defeated air, as though they had given up all hope of a better life. Almost a quarter of a century had passed since my mother first arrived here, spending her first night in that now desolate-looking inn with its wooden sign hanging ajar, colors long since faded. Many changes had obviously taken place during the past twenty-five years, none for the better.

The driver stopped at the inn to ask directions to Mowrey House. I waited in the coach, the object of many curious— hostile?—stares. Who is this woman with all those bags strapped on top of her coach, those stern, weather-beaten men seemed to ask. The women with their worn garments and lined faces clearly wondered what such an outlandishly attired creature was doing in this part of Cornwall. I sensed their resentment, and I couldn't help feeling relieved when the driver climbed back up on his seat and we drove on.

Half a mile or so from the village we passed four soldiers on sturdy black horses who were riding back toward town. They were tough, fierce-looking men in their polished black boots, tight white breeches and scarlet tunics, faces tan, wary, eyes hard. One of them tugged on the reins and stopped, turning around to stare suspiciously as the coach moved on around the curving road. Looking out the window, I could see him behind us, motionless, watching, growing smaller and smaller as the distance between us increased. Did he imagine I had come here on some nefarious mission? Sod the bastard. I'd give him the finger if he weren't too far away now to appreciate the gesture. Cornwall certainly wasn't a *friendly* place, I thought, but then I hadn't come here to make new friends.

Five minutes passed, cliffs to our left again, waves crashing below, rugged terrain to our right, and then the road curved once more. I saw Mowrey House for the first time. It was exactly as my mother had described it, a great, sprawling place with leaded windows, the gray stone bleached by the elements. The gardens had gone wild, vivid—multicolored flowers choked by tangled underbrush, trees wind-twisted. The place looked ominous indeed, and as we drew nearer I saw that several of the windows were broken. The roof badly needed repairs. Was Mowrey House deserted, too? It certainly looked so. Had I come all this way for nothing? The coach moved up the drive. The driver stopped in front of that massive portico. My throat felt suddenly dry.

I climbed out. The enormous, weighty bulk of the house seemed to loom over me, threatening to crush me. The dark, leaded windows seemed to stare like hostile eyes. Although the sunlight was still brilliant, there was none here, the huge house casting deep shadows over the drive. I gazed up at it, trying not to shiver. All right, Miranda, I told myself. You're here now. Let's get on with it. You're not going to be intimidated. I straightened my hat and brushed dust from my skirt and turned to the driver with cool composure.

"Wait here," I told him. "I don't know how long I'll be."

The driver nodded. I moved up the flat gray steps and under the heavy portico and knocked on the large dark-oak door. Several moments passed. I knocked again. Sure, I had a lot of courage, and yes, my chin was held high, but I felt a nervous tremor inside just the same. What was I going to say to him? What was I going to do? Why had I come in the first place? Frowning, I knocked yet again, impatiently this time. No one was home. I was almost relieved. No, wait, those were footsteps, barely audible out here. There was the loud, metallic click of a bolt being shoved back. The door swung open, creaking badly.

A tall, solidly-built man in his early forties stared at me with wary brown eyes. His brown hair fell in a thick, monklike fringe over his broad, low forehead. He had strong, rugged features and might even have been considered attractive had his nose not been broken at least twice. Tough, muscular, with enormous hands and very broad shoulders, he looked like a retired pugilist who longed to get back into the ring. Wearing a thin black leather apron over a coarsely woven white shirt and worn brown breeches, he smelled of garlic and furniture polish. There was a sooty smudge on his left cheek. He glared at me as though I had come to rob the place.

"Yeah?" he asked sullenly.

"I wish to see Lord Mowrey," I said.

"Yeah? What for?"

"That's none of your soddin' business," I snapped.

You could carry this being well-bred just so far. It didn't extend to taking impudence from a surly menial who looked like he'd spent most of his life in a boxing ring. He scowled. His hands curled into fists. Was he going to strike me? I stared at him with imperious blue eyes, daring him to try. Was that the suggestion of a grin on those wide pink lips?

"Guess you ain't a bill collector," he said.

"Are you going to fetch Lord Mowrey, or shall I go find him myself?"

"You'd have to get past me first."

"That wouldn't be difficult, I assure you."

It *was* a grin. The dark brown eyes were amused. The brute was obviously a watchdog, and from the looks of the place he'd probably glared down his share of bill collectors. The Mowrey wealth had clearly vanished. The great front hall was in a deplorable state, and the drawing room the man led me into was in even worse shape. The faded white and yellow brocade covering the walls was in tatters. The floor was bare of rugs. Any object of the slightest value had been removed, and the furniture that remained was battered and worn. Dust was everywhere. Ancient gray ashes filled the fireplace, spilling out onto the hearth. Lord Robert Mowrey had fallen onto hard times indeed.

"Wait here," the watchdog said. "I'll get him. Who shall I say is calling?"

"I prefer not to give my name. Let me surprise him."

"Oh, he's gonna be surprised, all right. Don't steal any of the silver," he warned.

I just managed to hold back a tart, graphic rejoinder as the man sauntered casually out of the room. I could hear him moving heavily up the staircase in the hallway beyond. What had happened to the family fortune? Why had the factory been shut down? The house was a ruin. Would Lord Robert Mowrey be a ruin, too, or would he still be thin and harsh and icy, dressed all in black? I heard footsteps on the staircase again, coming down this time, lighter footsteps that seemed to *bound* down the stairs. I turned. A perfectly dazzling young man in threadbare white silk shirt and old gray breeches swung jauntily into the room, coming to an abrupt halt when he saw me standing there near the fireplace.

"Jesus!" he exclaimed. "Ned was right! You *are* a stunning piece."

"You—you must be Douglas," I said. My voice was strangely tight.

He grinned and gave me a mocking bow. He was tall and extremely thin, a loose, lanky youth with merry gray eyes and a gorgeous mop of thick blond hair that tumbled over his brow in unruly waves. His virile, wonderfully handsome features were those of an amiable but distinctly mischievous angel. He would be twenty-eight years old now, but he looked younger. My brother. I stared at him, unable to speak, emotions I'd never felt before sweeping over me. My brother. All grown up now. Not at all perturbed by my rude stare, he gazed back at me with one dark arched brow cocked.

"I—I came to see Lord *Robert* Mowrey," I finally stammered.

"I'm afraid you're a bit late."

"Late?"

"My uncle died five years ago."

"He—he's *dead*?"

"I'm almost positive," he said.

"And—and you're all alone?"

"The place looks spooky, I know, but I've got Ned to protect me."

"I—I see."

I wasn't making good sense. I realized that. He must think me a complete idiot. I stared at him, my nerves all atremble. I wanted to cry. I felt suddenly very shy, afraid to tell him who I was. Douglas moved closer and studied me intently, a frown beginning to make a crease between the fine arched brows. The gray eyes filled with recognition, and his face became that of a bewildered little boy, lips parting, frown deepening. Without being asked, I removed the hat with its wide brim and spilling plumes and set it aside so that my brother could have an unobstructed view.

"It—it isn't *pos*sible," he whispered.

"Douglas—"

"It's just not possible!"

He took hold of my wrist then and led me roughly out of

the room and up the stairs. Too startled to protest, I tripped along behind him, his fingers digging into my wrist like iron bands. I stumbled. He didn't notice. Caught up in his own excitement, Douglas dragged me along, up the stairs, down another hall and, finally, flung open a door and pulled me into a long room with windows looking out over the side gardens and the land beyond, the sea just barely visible through the wind-twisted trees. Dust was so thick it rose in clouds as we entered. Cobwebs festooned the walls in silky patterns and dangled from the ceiling.

Douglas released my wrist, an intent, determined look in his eyes now as he began to open cupboard doors. I recognized the nursery from my mother's descriptions. There was the old worktable, there the bookcase with its clutter of dusty volumes. There was the globe she had used, and there on the wall were the pictures my brother had done for her—a lopsided tree, a horse that looked more like a buffalo, a gigantic red apple. The paper was yellow, brittle with age, but the colors were still vivid. He emitted a curse, slammed a cupboard door, yanked open another.

"I know it's here somewhere! I always treasured—I haven't been in here for years, but I know I couldn't have thrown it—"

He gave a cry of triumph then and took out a piece of paper and blew on it to remove the dust. He gazed down at it tenderly and then turned to show it to me. It was a small, beautifully colored cutout of a young woman with sad gray eyes and auburn hair. She was wearing a blue gown. I might have posed for it. The resemblance was startling.

"She's—you're exactly—" Douglas cut himself short. "No, your hair's redder than hers was, and her eyes were gray, not blue, but—you're—other than that you're—you might be her twin."

"She was my mother," I said quietly.

"Honora was your—"

I nodded, and a tear trickled slowly down my cheek as I gazed at the lovely paper figure.

"Miranda," I whispered.

"How did you know her name was—"

"My name's Miranda, too."

Douglas put the cutout back into the cupboard, placing it carefully beside a dusty cardboard replica of the Globe Theater. He closed the cupboard door and looked at me for a long moment, a new kind of recognition in those beautiful gray eyes. Sunlight filtered through the dirty windows, creating a soft yellow haze that filled the old nursery. The past was here with us, both of us thinking of the rowdy, sensitive little boy, the lovely, demure young woman who had been his governess.

"You're my sister," he said.

I nodded again, not trusting myself to speak.

"I—that day she—she was gone for such a long time. I loved her so very much, you see, and when she didn't come back and didn't come back—" He paused, remembering. "When she finally got home I was here in the nursery, looking at the paper doll of Miranda. She—Honora told me she had a surprise for me, and later on, after I had eaten, she told me we were going on a trip together and my father would be coming, too, and then—"

He cut himself short, his eyes full of remembered grief.

"Then your father got into a terrible argument with your uncle," I continued. "There was an accident. He—the banister broke and he fell to the floor and—. He and my mother had gone to the village that afternoon. They were married in the church. Reverend Williams performed the ceremony. That's what they were quarreling about. I—my mother was already expecting me when—"

I couldn't go on. Douglas took my hands and squeezed them so tightly I almost gasped.

"I always wondered," he said. "I lost my father and lost Honora, and I always suspected there was something—something I didn't know. My uncle wouldn't tell me anything, you see, and he had forbidden the servants to mention her name. All these years I've—and now, now I have a *sis*ter."

We looked at each other, silent, and the bond was there between us, drawing us together already. Both of us felt it and all restraint vanished and my brother gave me an exuberant hug that nearly snapped my spine. He was not one to hide his emotions, my brother, and he clearly didn't know his own strength. If things went on like this, I'd be bruised all over and battered beyond repair. I pulled myself away from him and straightened my hair and tried to maintain a modicum of dignity.

"You may be my brother," I said testily, "but that—that doesn't give you the right to *maul* me."

"No?"

"We don't even *know* each other yet."

Douglas grinned. "Seems my sister has a temper."

"I do, indeed."

"Marvelous! Brothers and sisters are supposed to fight a lot, I understand. It's tradition."

"I wouldn't know about that."

"Come on!" he cried. "We'll go back down and I'll have Ned make us a pot of tea and you can tell me all about yourself and I'll tell you all about *me* and we can make plans! You're staying here, of course. The place is tumbling down on my head and I'm afraid it's not horribly comfortable but now that I've found you I'm not letting you out of my sight."

"I—my coach is outside. The driver is waiting. My bags are—maybe I'd better go to the inn and—"

He propelled me back downstairs, manhandling me with rough affection. He thrust me down onto a sofa in the yellow and white drawing room and raced back into the hall to shout for his servant. I heard him barking amiable orders in a deep, merry voice and then there were noises and more voices and all my bags were brought in and carried upstairs. Douglas appeared to inform me that everything was being taken care of. He ordered me to sit still. I did so gladly, dazed, unable to think clearly.

"Never seen so many bags," my brother said, coming back into the room a few minutes later. "I sent your driver away. He said he'd already been paid, which is a good thing, I might add."

"It seems I'm to stay here."

"Of course you are."

"I might have other plans. I might—"

"Let's not get into a really *big* fight yet, at least not until we've had our tea."

I gave him a peevish look. Douglas grinned and rested one shoulder against the mantelpiece, slouching there like a lanky, virile imp. I tried to be angry. I couldn't. He was altogether too engaging.

"Ned's making the tea now," he informed me, "and then he's going to get your room ready."

"You—just have the one servant?"

My brother nodded, rubbing a smudge of dust from his cheek. The threadbare white silk shirt was slightly moist from all his exertions, tucked loosely into the waistband of the snug gray breeches. He really was quite dazzlingly good-looking, I

~464~

thought, but he was much too lean and lanky. I wondered if he got enough to eat.

"Ned's stuck by me through thick and thin—and it's been mostly thin for a long time. He practically raised me, Ned did. He was a footman here and he was the only one who could handle me when Mrs. Rawson left to marry her blacksmith— you don't know who she was, of course—"

I did, but I didn't interrupt him.

"Anyway, after she left, Ned brought me up—saw to all my needs, took me fishing, taught me how to box—he'd done some boxing when he was in his teens, amateur champion of Cornwall, he was, got his nose broken just the same. I had tutors, of course, and there were all sorts of servants, but Ned was the one who paddled my bottom when I misbehaved and sat by my bedside when I had fever. My uncle raised his wages and turned me over to him. He—my uncle didn't have a great deal of time for me himself, you see. Nor any interest in me," he added quietly.

The burly servant with the broken nose came in with the tea things—cups, teapot, creamer and sugar bowl on a tarnished silver tray. Although the china was very fine, both cups were chipped. There was no bread and butter, no tiny cakes, just tea and that quite weak. Douglas slouched down into a yellow silk chair and watched as I poured.

"Now," he said as I handed him the cup, "I want you to tell me everything—how you've lived, why you've never tried to contact me before."

"I didn't know of your existence until two weeks ago. I found out—quite by accident."

"So *tell* me," he insisted.

Tell him I did, speaking quietly in a carefully unemotional voice. I told him all I had learned from my mother's document, of my years in St. Giles as a street urchin roaming wild, picking pockets for a living. He was clearly horrified, fascinated, too, listening intently, rarely interrupting. I told him of my year with Cam Gordon, and he accepted that without even elevating an eyebrow, passing no judgments. I described my apprenticeship as a writer and the publication of the first stories and, ultimately, *Duchess Annie*. I described the reception I had gone to at Lady Julia's, my encounter with Dean Jordon and what I had learned from him.

"When I finished reading my mother's pages, I—I knew I

had to come here. I didn't know exactly why, but—I had to come. I thought I would meet my uncle. I thought—I wanted to see—"

I fell silent then, my careful composure beginning to slip. Douglas was silent, too, those lovely gray eyes thoughtful again. He had been deeply moved by my story. I could see that. Jaunty, ebullient, high-spirited he might be, but there was a deep sensitivity as well. The little boy my mother had written about had grown up to become a virile, engaging man, but much of the little boy remained. Douglas was not afraid of emotions, not afraid of showing them. He looked at me now and slowly shook his head.

"It—it's an incredible story."

"I suppose some people might think so."

"I feel we've both been cheated," he said, another deep frown creasing his brow. "If I'd been there, none of those things would have happened to you—I'd have protected you. If you'd been here, I wouldn't—I'd have had someone besides Ned. I wouldn't have felt so lonely, so lost, so unwanted."

He was silent again, sad, resentful, still amazed by this sudden appearance of a sister he had never known. He stretched his long legs out, gazing into the sooty white marble fireplace filled with heaps of cold gray ash. A ray of misty sunlight played across his face, touched that thick blond hair. He sighed deeply after a few moments and, shaking his head once more, brought himself back to the present.

"More tea?" I asked. "Mine's quite cold."

"So's mine," he replied, "but I'm afraid there isn't any more. I'll send Ned down to the village and have him try to cajole the shopkeeper into extending us a bit more credit. If that doesn't work, Ned'll probably get him in a stranglehold and *choke* credit out of him."

"Ned sounds quite resourceful."

"He is. I couldn't get along without him."

"You—you're not very well off, are you?"

"That's putting it mildly," he admitted. "My uncle made some very unwise investments in his later years. He'd lost interest in the factory, finally shut it down. When he died— well, let's put it this way, I have an abandoned pottery factory and I have Mowrey House. You can see the shape it's in. Anything worth selling was sold a piece at a time—the good furniture, the paintings and plate, the carpets—it's a long, dreary story. I'll tell you later. Right now I'm going to take you up to your room and let you catch your breath."

"I *would* like to freshen up a bit."

"I thought so. Come along."

The room my brother had assigned me was on the second floor, the only bedroom besides his kept in livable condition. Large, with windows looking over the front drive, it had a bed, a dressing table and wardrobe of golden oak polished to a dark honey sheen. Counterpane and curtains were faded yellow brocade embroidered with tiny white silk flowers. The hardwood floor was bare, the wood black brown with age. The room smelled of polish, lemon and camphor and, though clean, had obviously not been used for quite some time. My bags were stacked up beside the wardrobe.

"Keep the place up for guests," Douglas told me. "Haven't had many recently. Hungry?"

"Not at all."

"Good. I'll tell Ned to forget lunch. Never eat it myself. There's water and a ewer and such behind that big white screen over there. I'll be knocking about downstairs—if you need anything, just shout and Ned or I'll come running to do your bidding."

He grinned and sauntered breezily out of the room. Two hours later, rested and refreshed, having unpacked one bag and changed into a frock of pale tan muslin sprigged with tiny pink and brown flowers, I went back downstairs to join my brother. Unable to find him, I took the opportunity to explore some of the huge rooms. Denuded of their finery, filled with dust and cobwebs for the most part, they still retained their sound structure and grand proportions. In my mind's eye I could see them as they must have been twenty-four years ago when my mother had given lessons to the boisterous young Doug and given her heart to his father.

Leaving the library, crossing the hall, I opened a door and stepped into my uncle's old office. There was the crudely executed painting of the Mowrey pottery works hanging over the fireplace. There was the shelf of cheap blue cups, saucers and plates, the set of more expensive dishes, milky white china adorned with pale orange flowers outlined in gold. There was the desk where Lord Robert Mowrey had poured over his accounts. It was littered with papers now, and a big leather-bound ledger lay open. Though messy—wads of paper on the floor.

a pair of muddy boots in one corner, an apple core and a small chunk of dried cheese on a chipped plate beside the ledger— the office was free of dust. No silken cobwebs festooned the ceiling.

"Have a nice rest?"

I gave a little cry and whirled around. My brother grinned at me. He had been in the smaller office adjoining this one. The connecting door stood open. I hadn't heard him come into the room.

"Did I startle you?"

"I—I was thinking about the past."

"Lovely frock you're wearing."

"Thank you. I—I came downstairs half an hour ago. I called. There was no answer."

"I sent Ned down to the village to see if he could harass, cajole or bully the grocer into giving us a few provisions on credit. I've been in Parks' old office, fantasizing."

"Fantasizing?"

"Indulging myself in foolish dreams. Come, I'll show you."

He took my hand and led me into the smaller office. It had been cleared of all furniture but an enormous battered worktable covered with a wild jumble of large white sheets. They were drawings, I saw—some of them in pencil, some in charcoal, some of them colored. A box of watercolors and a cup of dirty water set on the edge of the table, two wet brushes dripping onto the floor. Douglas picked up a still damp sheet and handed it to me.

"My fantasy," he said.

It was the design for a plate, the most beautiful plate I had ever seen, exquisitely done in watercolors. Garlands of tiny, pale-blue flowers and delicate jade leaves were worked around the rich pink rim outlined in gold. The center of the plate was white, scattered lightly with the same flowers and leaves as though one of the garlands had been shaken loose. I gazed at it with something like awe, amazed at the superb detail, the incredible craftsmanship.

"You—you did this?"

"Afraid so. I've got designs for cups, too, saucers, side dishes, teapots, platters, you name it—all the same pattern. There are other patterns, too, but this is my favorite. I've also designed some new pottery. It's not nearly so fancy, of course, but it's much nicer than that drab blue stuff Uncle Robert used to produce."

He handed me sheet after sheet, each design as beautifully done as the first I had seen, and my sense of wonder grew. There were wonderful soup tureens, covered vegetable dishes, coffee urns, soup bowls—an endless array of fine china executed in marvelous detail.

"But—these are amazing," I said. "I've never seen anything like them."

"You write books. I design china. It keeps me occupied."

"You're incredibly gifted."

"I was always interested in the factory," he confessed, "even as a little boy. My uncle could hardly keep me away from the place. I learned everything I could about the business, worked alongside the men when my uncle wasn't looking, and later on, instead of going to Oxford, I went to France and spent four years as an apprentice to the masters there."

"Why France?" I inquired.

"The factory at Vincennes produces the best china in the world, better than Dresden, finer than Meissen. It's a favorite of Madame de Pompadour's—she intends to move the factory to Sèvres, the village just below her estate at Bellevue, so she can personally supervise things. They've created new colors— *Rose Pompadour*, *Bleu du Roi*, apple green. They've intented highly original shapes, too—fluted spouts, scalloped edges, porcelain filigree reminiscent of silver. The things I learned there—"

Douglas sighed, and there was a sad, defeated look in his eyes as he began to stack the sheets neatly together on the table.

"I dreamed of turning our own factory into—into something similar, on a much smaller scale, of course. Why can't English pottery be as fine as French? I asked myself. I planned to make a great many changes when I took over. When he was about the age I was then, my father had drawn up a set of plans for renovating the factory, modernizing it, making it safer, healthier to work in. He made a list of proposals, too, that would alleviate the hardships of the workers, give them more incentive. I found them one day in my uncle's bottom desk drawer, all curling and yellow with age."

"He had a dream, too," I said quietly.

"And I hoped to make it come true. I hoped to renovate the factory, make all those changes as—as a sort of tribute to him—and realize my own dream at the same time."

Doug shoved the stacks away from him and turned to me with a wry smile on his lips.

~469~

"It wasn't to be," he said. "When I returned from France Uncle Robert had already given up on the pottery works. He— things had been going downhill ever since my father died. Uncle Robert immersed himself in work, but he had lost all interest, all initiative. He just didn't care any longer. Things went from bad to worse and—well, he finally shut it down. All those people out of work—"

I could tell from his expression that the fate of those men and women who lost their jobs bothered him a great deal. Douglas clearly had Jeffrey Mowrey's compassionate nature and concern for his fellow man. He emitted another heavy sigh and pushed the mop of blond waves from his brow.

"It's stuffy in here," he said. "Let's go for a walk."

"I'd love to see the moors."

"See them you shall."

Douglas led me down the hall, past the staircase and through a narrow door and into the great back hall where former generations of Mowreys had exercised their horses on inclement days. It was like a vast, chilly cavern, I thought, the ancient rushes on the stone floor exuding a sour smell. I almost expected to see bats hanging from the ceiling. After the eerie gloom of the back hall, the sunshine seemed all the brighter, although it was paler now, the brilliant silver faded to a thin yellow-white.

"What happened after that?" I asked as we moved through the gardens.

"After my uncle closed the factory? He died a few months later. I think he was glad to go. He—I had a feeling he had just been marking time ever since my father's death. He was a very unhappy man, my uncle, strangely twisted."

We had cleared the back gardens now, and the moors stretched out before us in all their stark splendor, rising slowly to the hills where the Roman legions once had their camps. The sky was a pale gray-white now, watery with sunlight, arching high over that rugged expanse of uneven ground covered with brown gray grass that had a faint purple tinge, patches of tarry black bog making a sharp contrast. There were enormous gray boulders streaked with rust and dried green moss. As we walked over that spongy earth, a light breeze caused my skirts to billow, caused silky tendrils of coppery red hair to blow across my cheeks. My brother moved in a loose, bouncy stride, loping along with his hands thrust into the pockets of his breeches.

"There was no money," he continued. "I had the factory, I had the house and barely enough to buy food. I—I held on. I began to sell things, paintings and furniture and ormolu clocks, anything I could get a few pounds for. I kept believing that someday, somehow, I'd be able to reopen the factory. I've received several offers for it—the clay here is superb, some of the best in England. Other factory owners have toured the place, seen the potential and made generous offers, hoping to expand, but—"

"You refused to sell," I said.

"Guess I'll have to eventually. Ned and I have been scratching along for the past few years, but I realize it can't go on much longer. Besides, now I have you to consider."

The land had begun to slope upward now, gradually rising, and we stopped beside a large, flat gray rock. I sat down on it, spreading my muslin skirts out, and Douglas stood there gazing pensively at the land around us, his hands still in his pockets. A large brown bird—was it some kind of hawk?—circled slowly against the sky, growing smaller and smaller. Mowrey House looked like a child's toy house in the distance, an ugly gray block set among those tangled gardens. I thought of my parents, remembering that picnic on the moors my mother had written about when young Douglas had scampered about looking for colored stones and my father had told her of his dream.

I felt a curious serenity, being here with my brother. It seemed so right, so natural for us to be together, intimate already, as though all the years separating us had never been, and I could tell that Douglas felt the same way. The bond between us had been recognized immediately, immediately accepted by both of us. He turned to me now, his handsome face serious, his lovely eyes grave as he looked at me.

"You've been cheated of everything, Miranda," he told me. "I—I intend to make it up to you. I don't know just how, but—I'll do it. I'm going to take care of you from now on."

"I've always managed to take care of myself," I said.

"Maybe so, but you've got me now."

His voice was filled with resolution, his expression grim. I was touched, and I was secretly amused, too. I had told Douglas about my writing, but I hadn't told him the extent of my success. This handsome young man who didn't know where his next meal was coming from had no idea that his new-found sister was a very wealthy woman with the prospects of being

~471~

even wealthier when the new book came out. I smiled to myself. Douglas took my hand and pulled me to my feet, blond waves flopping over his borw.

"We'd better start back. Ned will have returned from the village—and not empty-handed, if I know Ned. He'll prepare our meal. You're bound to be hungry."

"A little," I admitted.

"There'll probably be stew and coarse brown bread, maybe even a bottle of cheap wine."

"It sounds delicious."

"You're not going back to London," he told me as we started back toward the house. "I'm not going to let you. You belong here, with me. I'll find some kind of work. I—I'll sell the factory if I have to, but I'm going to take care of you."

"Douglas, there's something I—"

"No arguments," he said sternly. "I've just made your decision for you. That's what older brothers are for. We're together now, Miranda. Things have been rough for both of us and they're likely to be rougher still, but we'll see them through."

I didn't argue. It would have been futile. My brother intended for me to stay, and stay I would. Both of us were silent as we strolled slowly back over those bleak, curiously beautiful moors, moving toward the distant house. Douglas guided me around a gigantic boulder, past a tarry patch of bog, deeply immersed in his own thoughts. I felt a wonderful sense of kinship, and I felt a sense of purpose, too. A plan was beginning to take shape in my mind. I would write Bancroft first thing tomorrow morning.

34

BANCROFT FLATLY REFUSED TO LET ME INVEST ALL my money in the pottery works. He journeyed down to Cornwall as soon as he received my letter and toured the factory and had several long conferences with Douglas and a blazing argument with me. I adamantly informed him that it was my own bloody money and I could do as I bloody well pleased with it, and Bancroft stoutly declared that he had worked his arse off making me a rich woman and he wasn't about to let me make a pauper of myself in one fell swoop. Douglas sat on the sidelines, an amused smile on his lips, for he and Bancroft had already reached a decision as to how the business should be handled. The factory was, indeed, a potential money maker, particularly if my father's plans were used for renovations, his proposals adopted and Douglas' designs used, along with the new techniques he had learned at Vincennes, but such an undertaking would not only take every penny I had but would also deplete all the profits I stood to make from *Betty's Girls*.

"I don't care! It's my money. I'm going to use it."

"Over my dead body!"

"Goddamn you, Dick Bancroft, that can be *arranged*! If I had a blunderbuss in my hand right now, I'd blow your bloody head off!"

"Charming sister you have," Bancroft said to Douglas.

"I'm beginning to find that out."

"You said yourself the factory could be the best in England, could make a fortune for its investors! If that's the case, I don't see why—"

"Investors. Plural. That's the key word. If you'd stop shrieking like a fishwife and let me get a *word* in, I'd ex*plain* things to you. Your brother and I have already worked out a plan. Your money will be used to cover approximately one half the costs, and you and Douglas here will own fifty-one percent of the business. The rest of the money will be provided by individual investors, each of whom will buy so many of the remaining shares."

"You know I don't understand all—all these technical details, Bancroft. We *own* the factory, and now you say we're supposed to—"

"Do you think we could gag her?" Bancroft asked.

"Might not be a bad idea," Douglas replied.

"Sod both of you!"

"I intend to buy ten percent of the remaining forty-nine shares myself," Dick continued, ignoring my condemnation. "Actually, there'll be more than a hundred shares—there'll be thousands, each share costing so much—but I'm trying to keep my explanation simple so as not to confuse you. You and Douglas will have controlling interest, will—"

"Details!"

"Everything has been worked out. Your brother, incidentally, is a very astute businessman—that's one of the reasons I'm willing to invest some of my own money. In short, my dear muddle-head, the factory will be reopened as planned, but only half your money will be used. The rest will be safe and secure."

"Do you think I might possibly have a few pounds to have this house done over and refurnished?"

"I suppose that could be arranged."

"You're bloody generous, Dick Bancroft!"

"I intend to keep a very close watch over every single expenditure, mind you."

I glared at him and Bancroft grinned and Douglas did, too, and I stamped out of the room. Bancroft returned to London two days later, and the following weeks were sheer chaos as work got underway at the factory and the house was invaded by crews of cleaning people and workmen, the majority of them from the village. The rooms were cleaned, aired, the floors and woodwork polished by a team of chattering village women who couldn't believe their good luck, and walls were painted or recovered by their husbands and sons. The roof was repaired and the broken windows replaced, ceilings replastered. The dim, decrepit old house took on a bright new sparkle inside and out, for the gardens were cleaned out as well, lawns trimmed, flower beds replanted, new trellises installed.

Sunlight filled the dark rooms. It wasn't easy to turn Mowrey House into a cheery place, but I made a valiant effort, using hundreds of gallons of white paint, selecting pale lemon and linen white wall coverings. Salesmen from London trooped down with samples and catalogs, and I selected draperies and rugs and ordered new furniture, most of the latter from the workshop of Thomas Chippendale, whose furniture was every bit as elegant as Mrs. Wooden had told me it was. Bancroft did indeed keep an eye on my expenditures, making occasional rude noises via the mail, but the rapidly depleting coffers were just as rapidly refilled when, two months after my arrival in Cornwall, Thomas Sheppard & Company brought out *Betty's Girls*.

While I was engaged with the house and hiring a staff of

servants from the village, Douglas and a team of experts he had brought in were busily renovating the factory and installing all the new equipment. When the work was well under way and it was possible for him to leave, Douglas made a hurried trip to France where, with his charm, his promises and his pockets full of money, he persuaded three of the major craftsmen at Vincennes to defect to Cornwall, bringing them back with an air of jaunty triumph. This treacherous act was said to have put La Pompadour to bed for days with an excruciating migraine.

Work was almost finished on the house and I had just hired a full staff of servants when, one afternoon, I had an unexpected visitor. Burly delivery men were unloading a lorry of furniture just arrived from London, bringing the elegant pieces into the hall, and I was wearing an old blue cotton dress that was the worse for wear, for I had been working in it all day. My hair was damp and atumble, a mess, and my face was probably streaked. I was telling the delivery men where to place the furniture, footmen, maids and my new houskeeper bustled about and I was totally unprepared to receive a guest. Miss Morrison knocked on the open door. In the confusion no one heard her. Directing the men to carry the gorgeous new desk into my sitting room in back, telling one of the footmen to accompany them, I sighed and looked up and saw her standing there in the doorway, cool and poised and lovely indeed in a pink and gray striped frock.

"I'm afraid I've come at a bad time," she said. "I should have driven on when I saw the lorry in front."

"I--how do you do?" I stammered. "You must forgive me. I—things have been rather frantic today and—"

"I understand perfectly," she replied. Her voice was cool and lovely too, undeniably patrician. "I'll call again at a more convenient time."

"You—"

"I'm Linda Morrison. My family lives in the next county. I've known your brother since we were children."

"Don't—don't leave, Miss Morrison. You must at least let me give you a cup of tea after you've come all this way."

"It isn't that far, Lady Mowrey, and I quite enjoy gadding about the countryside in my cart. There's not all that much to do."

The delivery men came back up the hall, sweaty from their exertions. Only one piece of furniture remained to be brought in. I told them to take it into the library, told one of the maids to see that they had something to drink before they left and asked the housekeeper to have tea brought into the drawing room for Miss Morrison and me.

"I really mustn't intrude," Miss Morrison protested. "You're busy, and I can easily come back another time."

"No, no—to tell the truth I'll welcome a cup of tea myself. Please do stay and visit for a while."

She hesitated, undecided, then nodded and followed me into the drawing room. I had never encountered a young woman so beautifully composed. She was extremely reserved, almost stiff, yet I could sense an innate friendliness behind that ultra well-bred facade. Her long raven hair was neatly brushed, her clear blue eyes full of intelligence. Tall and slender, with cool, lovely features, she wasn't quite as young as I had first judged her to be. The bloom of early youth had given way to an unmistakable maturity.

"You've done an incredible job with this old house," she remarked, glancing about the newly refurbished room.

"It hasn't been easy."

"I understand the place was practically a ruin. I haven't been inside Mowrey House for years. Your uncle was still alive then. My mother and I came to call on him."

"You know my brother well?" I inquired.

"Not well. To be frank, I haven't seen him in over ten years. He was in France, and by the time he returned I was already in Brussels, teaching English in a girls' school there. Your brother and I knew each other casually when we were children."

"Please sit down, Miss Morrison."

Linda Morrison sat down on the sofa and folded her hands in her lap. She sat very straight, proper and demure, shoulders squared, back stiff. I sat on a chair facing her, slightly ill at ease and trying not to show it.

"To be even franker," she continued, "I used my tenuous acquaintanceship with your brother as a pretext to call. I'm afraid my motives were not entirely admirable. I was eager to meet the notorious Miranda James."

"I—I see."

"You're quite the talk of the countryside, Lady Mowrey. Everyone knows the whole story by now—you can't keep anything secret in these parts, and a few of us get the London papers, albeit late. They made a great to-do about your finding your brother after all these years."

Damn Thomas Sheppard, I thought, and not for the first time. He had leaked the story to the gentlemen of Fleet Street just a day or so before *Betty's Girls* came out, and they had indeed made a great to-do of it, dubbing me "Lady Miranda" and exploiting it for all it was worth. A few of the more prosperous papers had sent journalists all the way to Cornwall to interview me, and I had been forced to treat them politely, answering their questions begrudgingly. I could understand Sheppard's motives—*Betty's Girls* was selling like wildfire as a result, seven printings already and the book just out a month and a half—but I felt a few things should be private.

"So everyone knows who I am?" I said. "I suppose all the local gentry are scandalized."

"They're a rather narrow-minded group, Lady Mowrey, good-natured as a whole but bigoted to the core. They're consumed with curiosity about you, of course, but they wouldn't dream of calling on you. They're far too respectable to call on a woman who has openly lived with a man without the benefit of marriage, who once picked pockets for a living."

"And you, Miss Morrison? Why did *you* call?"

My voice was much crisper than I had intended. Linda Morrison looked at me, and the faintest suggestion of a smile played on her lips. One of the maids came in with the tea tray then, setting it down on the table in front of the sofa, and my guest waited until the girl had left the room before she replied to my question.

"Unlike most of my gossiping neighbors, I've actually read your novel, and I admired it very much. I thought it was a brave and beautiful book. I don't happen to share the prejudices of my neighbors, Lady Mowrey."

I got up to pour the tea. Miss Morrison took hers with a polite nod of thanks. I sat down on the sofa beside her, and she turned slightly so that we were facing. That long raven hair so neatly brushed was soft and gleamed a rich blue-black, and the patrician features were beautifully molded, the cheekbones high, the nose straight, the mouth a soft, pale pink. The clear blue eyes looked at me frankly, totally without guile.

"I've read your stories, too," she said. "I think you're a remarkable woman, Lady Mowrey. To have risen from your environment, to have achieved all that you've achieved, is almost incredible, particularly for a woman. We aren't supposed to achieve. It makes men terribly uneasy."

"It does, indeed," I replied.

"I was as curious about you as everyone else, of course, but I wanted to call on you and personally thank you for writing such moving and compassionate works."

"I—I don't know what to say."

"I also wanted to welcome you to Cornwall."

"That's very kind of you, Miss Morrison."

"If you should ever care to get away from Mowrey House for a few hours, my father and I would be delighted to have you call on us. Morrison Place is not very grand, I'm afraid, but we have lovely gardens."

Her voice was cool, but I could tell that the invitation was sincere. I sensed that it had taken considerable courage for her to come here this afternoon. She might not share the prejudices of her neighbors, but Linda Morrison was clearly a very respectable young woman, and the local gentry were going to be appalled to learn that she had called on me. Seeing that self-assured demeanor, looking into those intelligent blue eyes, I doubted she would let that bother her too much. Though bound by the conventions of her class, Miss Morrison had something of the rebel about her.

I offered her more tea, and she hesitated a moment before accepting. I suddenly realized that she had been ill at ease herself and uncertain of her welcome.

"Please stay a while longer," I said kindly. "You're my first visitor, and I shall feel dreadful if you rush off too soon."

She looked at me as though to determine my sincerity. I smiled. Linda Morrison returned the smile with one of her own, and I glimpsed the charming young woman who hid behind that rather too prim facade. We had more tea, and I began to ask her questions about herself, hoping to draw her out. She relaxed a bit then, and I began to discover the warmth and humor that accompanied that keen intelligence.

Her family, I learned, was one of the oldest and most respected in Cornwall, landed gentry since the days of Good Queen Bess. The land, alas, had been sadly depleted by her grandfather who had sold yet another parcel every time his gambling debts became unmanageable. Linda's father was left with a half-dozen poor tenant farms, the income they brought in barely enough to enable him to maintain Morrison Place and support his wife and three daughters. Linda, the eldest, had had her season in London, had been bored by the monotonous round of parties and balls and disdainful of the foppish and empty-headed young men who vied for her attention.

"The idea, you see, was that I should snare a wealthy husband whose fortune would save the family from destitution. My mother staked everything we had on that season in town—it was terribly expensive to rent a house and a carriage, pay for my gowns, give the obligatory dance. When we came back to Cornwall I was husbandless and every penny we had was gone."

Miss Morrison smiled a wry smile and took another sip of tea. Her younger sisters had been crushed, knowing full well that Linda's failure meant they would not have the same chance. It was then that she had decided to earn her own living, scandalizing everyone by taking the position at the girls' school in Brussels. Well-bred young women from good families simply didn't *do* such things—far better to subsist in genteel but respectable poverty—and Miss Morrison's unconventional behavior was deemed a betrayal of her class.

"I was able to send half my wages home," she continued, "and eventually both my sisters had their seasons in London. Millicent married a vicar in Kent, and Lucinda managed to snare the son of an earl—the second son, alas. They're currently in Bombay where he's trying to make a fortune with the East India Company."

Linda's mother had passed away six months ago, finally succumbing to the consumption that had plagued her for the past three years, and Linda had come home to nurse her through those final sad days, remaining in Cornwall to take care of her father, whose own health was rapidly deteriorating. She was also managing the remaining tenant farms, further scandalizing the gentry by going to the farms in her cart several days a week to supervise work. *Some*one had to do it, and her father was no longer capable. It was difficult for me to visualize this lovely, demure young woman ordering fertilizer, having barns repaired and overseeing the shearing of sheep, but as she talked my admiration for her increased by bounds.

"I—I'm afraid I've bored you quite enough," she said, placing her cup on the tray. "I don't usually talk about myself this way. Please forgive me for running on so."

She stood up and brushed the skirt of her pink and gray striped frock, a soft, lovely garment that, from its cut, was clearly several years old. Probably her best, I thought, getting to my feet.

"I've enjoyed your visit a great deal, Miss Morrison," I said. "I hope you'll call again—often."

"And I hope you'll come to Morrison Place. My father reads quite a lot. There's not much else for him to do. He's an admirer of yours, too."

"I look forward to meeting—"

I cut myself short as the front door banged open noisily and clattering footsteps echoed in the hall. "Miranda!" my brother shouted. "Where's my sister!" he barked. A maid told him I was in the drawing room, and a moment later he burst in, boots dirty, snug tan breeches dirty, too, his white silk shirt bagging loosely over the waistband, threatening to come untucked. He stopped short when he saw the two of us standing in front of the sofa, his handsome face registering acute surprise.

"Jesus!" he exclaimed. "I didn't expect you to have a *guest*!"

Linda Morrison bristled at my side. Appalled by my brother's rudeness, I was momentarily unable to speak. Douglas shoved a heavy blond wave out of his eyes and peered at Miss Morrison with intense scrutiny, a frown digging a deep furrow above the bridge of his nose.

"I know you," he said. "I'm *sure* I do."

"Linda Morrison," she said crisply. "It's been a long time."

"Linda? *Linda?* The skinny little girl I used to run into on the moors all those years ago."

"The skinny little girl you used to torment quite cruelly," she retorted.

"Always had a book with you, I remember. Always sitting on a rock, gazing dreamily up at the sky. What happened to those long pigtails? What happened to those freckles?"

"The same thing that happened to your short pants and slingshot. I grew out of them."

"Seems like I did have a slingshot. Seems like I used to—" He hesitated, then grinned. "I guess I wasn't exactly an angel in those days."

"Far from it," she assured him.

Her voice was decidedly icy, her manner just short of hostile. The grin that continued to play on his lips didn't help matters a bit.

"Thought you were still in Brussels," he said.

"I've been back half a year."

"Really? Didn't know that. I've been out of touch with everything for a long time. Did you know we're reopening the factory? We just finished installing the conveyor belts—that's what I wanted to tell you, Miranda. You ought to see them! These great long belts—they're attached to pulleys, you see, and they'll bring the clay up in buckets and—it's fantastic! I was in the pits myself, helping the men install 'em, and—"

I gave him a severe look. Douglas managed to contain his enthusiasm.

"You'll have to forgive me," he told Linda. "I'm afraid I get carried away sometimes. It's all so exciting. So you're back in Cornwall? I guess you got tired of teaching English to bored young misses. Must have been terribly dreary. Never could understand why you'd want to do such a crazy thing in the first place."

"You wouldn't," she said dryly. "I really must go now, Lady Mowrey."

"We're having the opening ceremonies in two weeks," Doug said casually. "It's going to be quite a bash—food and ale for all the villagers, a puppet show for the children, investors coming in from all over England, lots of festivity. Miranda's going to cut the ribbon to officially open it, and I'm going to light a furnace. You might want to come."

Linda Morrison didn't reply, but the look she gave my brother was answer enough. He shrugged and sauntered nonchalantly over to the fireplace. I accompanied her out to her small, spanking neat cart, a handsome gray standing in harness. He whinnied. Linda stroked his neck and told me that she had enjoyed her visit and hoped she hadn't imposed. I assured her the pleasure had all been mine. She climbed into the cart, took up the reins and clicked them smartly. I watched her drive away and then went back inside to give my brother hell.

"I've never *seen* such rudeness!" I cried. "It's inexcusable!"

"Rude? *Me?* You're imagining things."

"You come charging in here like a madman, covered with dirt, looking like a—a crazed ruffian, and then you stare at her and act like she was some kind of intruder and—"

"You must be talking about someone else," he protested.

"Then you start *teas*ing her! You're—I swear, Douglas Mowrey, sometimes you're an absolute oaf!"

"I resent that!"

"I wouldn't blame her if she never spoke to you again!"

"Wouldn't bother me in the least," he replied. "Brainy women make me uneasy, never could abide 'em. What's it matter to me if a twenty-eight-year-old spinster got her feathers ruff—"

"Douglas!"

"All right, all right—I'm *sor*ry!"

~481~

I glared at him and he gave me an exasperated look that clearly conveyed he didn't know what I was making such a fuss about. I longed to hurl something at him, preferably something heavy.

"It's beneath you to make such remarks," I continued. "I happen to be a spinster myself, if you must use such a denigrating term, and most people would call me brainy as well. Do *I* make you uneasy?"

"At the moment—very."

"Damn you, Douglas! That pixie charm of yours wears very thin! Linda Morrison happens to be an absolutely charming young woman and she's had an extremely difficult time. If I weren't a lady, I'd *shake* you for treating her in such a shabby, cavalier—"

"All *right*, Miranda. What do you want me to do?"

"I want you to apologize to her. I want you to go upstairs and scrub yourself and put on those new clothes I had you buy in London when you stopped there on your way to France. I want you to brush your hair and pick a bunch of flowers from the garden and drive to Morrison Place and—"

"Jesus!"

"I mean it, Douglas!"

"Can't today," he replied. "I have to go back to the factory. I'll probably be there till—oh, it'll be after dark, I'm sure. I'll do it tomorrow afternoon."

"You'd better," I warned.

And so, the following afternoon, he came dragging downstairs looking marvelously handsome in tan breeches and frock coat, beige satin waistcoat and a yellow silk neckcloth. His unruly blond waves were temporarily subdued. His gray eyes were repentant, his expression suitably grave, though I suspected that was mostly for my benefit. He had the new groom bring his horse around, sulkily plucked a bunch of flowers and rode off. He was gone an inordinately long time, barely returning in time for dinner. When I questioned him, he grudgingly admitted that Miss Morrison was indeed charming, if somewhat snappish, and she had grown up into a fine figure of a woman. She was a rose, all right, if you liked 'em thorny, but he wasn't at all interested.

"Women like that want to take you in *hand*," he grumbled.

"In your case, brother, dear, it's high time someone did."

"Women! Never give you a moment's peace!"

Nevertheless, he rode over to Morrison Place twice during

the following week and professed amazement that a woman could do so much, be so efficient. The Morrison tenant farms were the best in the county, the cleanest, the most productive, and Linda supervised everything herself, driving out in that cart of hers, looking lovely and feminine and never raising her voice. The farmers worshiped her, too, worked like the devil for her, didn't seem to mind at all taking orders from a woman. You had to admire her, even if she *was* cool and reserved and much too brainy for a man to feel really comfortable with her.

Bancroft arrived the week after that, looking spruce and prosperous and optimistic. He hugged me exuberantly and gave Douglas a hearty handshake and told us things looked bright indeed. Word of Mowrey pottery works and its big potential had already gotten out, and he was having to turn *down* investors, shrewd businessmen who smelled a good thing and wanted to get in on it. If he cared to, he could sell his ten percent interest in the business for double, maybe triple the money he had put into it, but he wasn't about to. Douglas took him on a final tour of the factory before its official opening the next morning, and that evening Bancroft told me that, from the looks of things, I stood to be an even richer woman a few years from now.

"It's going to be a great success, Miranda. That brother of yours might be whimsical about a lot of things, but when it comes to business he knows what he's doing."

"I'm fully aware of that."

"Shrewd, intelligent—incredibly gifted, too. You're going to be extremely proud of him."

"I already am, Dick."

I was especially proud of him the next morning during the opening ceremonies and the festivity that followed. Handsome in gray breeches and frock coat, dark blue brocade waistcoat and a sky blue neckcloth, he was amiable but subdued, very much the man of business. There was an enormous crowd. Almost everyone from the village turned up, for the factory had already transformed their lives and would provide a healthy livelihood for the majority of them. Their bright, smiling faces were far different from the grim visages I had seen four months ago when I arrived in Cornwall. Several of the investors had come down for the occasion, staying at the inn, and a number of the local gentry arrived in their best carriages, their curiosity about Lord Mowrey's refurbished factory momentarily stronger than their prejudice against his scandalous sister.

Linda came in her cart, cool and elegant in a lovely pink silk frock and a wide-brimmed white straw hat trimmed with pink velvet ribbons. The crowd cheered when I cut the blue satin ribbon stretched across the main door and cheered again when Douglas lighted the first furnace, almost burning his fingers in the process. The kegs of ale were rolled out. The tables were spread with food. Noisy merriment ensued. Children consumed lemonade and shrieked over the antics of the puppets. Douglas and I were toasted repeatedly, Bancroft, too, and the three Frenchmen from the factory at Vincennes were robustly embraced, even if they *were* bloody foreigners who didn't speak a word of English. Rowdy bonhomie prevailed under the clear blue-gray Cornish sky, and things grew even rowdier when later on an amateur boxing match was set up with Ned officiating.

Wearing a rust and cream striped satin gown, my coppery red hair tumbling to my shoulders in loose, natural waves, I smiled and shook hands with the villagers and accepted their thanks for "savin' us all, an' that's a fact." I rescued the Frenchmen, saw that they had white wine and chatted pleasantly with the investors, stout, rather dour men who were blatantly out of place amidst all this noisy provincial festivity. I noticed in passing that Douglas was devoting a great deal of attention to Linda Morrison, personally showing her around and explaining points of interest. The gentry, I observed, were the first to attack the tables of food. They stared at me, the women passing judgment behind their fans. I nodded politely to one and all, so well-bred it almost hurt.

I sipped champagne with the investors. I drank a mug of ale with the villagers. I spent over half an hour with the children, watching the puppet show set up under a brightly colored striped awning. Three hours passed, four, five. My feet were beginning to hurt. My back ached. Being charming and well-bred every single minute was bloody difficult, I thought, longing to sit down in a quiet place. I smiled. I shook more hands. I chatted with Linda for a few minutes until Douglas whisked her away to show her his designs. It was after three o'clock in the afternoon when Bancroft finally came to my rescue.

"You're looking a bit ragged, lass," he said.

"You always did know how to give a girl confidence, Bancroft. If you want to know the truth, I *feel* ragged."

"Why don't you let me take you back to Mowrey House," he said. "It looks as though this is going to last till nightfall—

and tomorrow's the first working day at the factory," he added. "I'm not so sure all that ale was a good idea."

"Always thinking of your investments, aren't you?"

"That's why I'm a wealthy man."

"Do you really think it would be all right for me to leave?"

"Your brother already has. He and that fetching brunette in pink rode off in her cart over an hour ago. Something brewing there, I suspect. Come along, Miranda. Much more of this and you'll start snipping and snapping and showing your true character. I know you, lass."

"Being a lady definitely has its drawbacks."

"Hard work, isn't it?"

"You've no idea," I said.

He took my hand and led me through the crowd toward the area reserved for the carriages. The fine open vehicle we had come in stood with the others, a flaxen-haired lad with freckles watching the horses. Bancroft tossed him a coin, helped me up onto the plushly upholstered seat and, climbing up beside me, took the reins. In a few minutes we had left the noise and confusion behind and were moving slowly along the winding road that led through the village. It was virtually empty this afternoon and was already beginning to show signs of prosperity. The inn had been refurbished, the front whitewashed, a brightly painted new sign swinging invitingly over the door. The horses' hooves tapped on the cobbled street. The sound echoed eerily through the village.

"Pleased?" Bancroft asked.

"Very," I replied. "Mostly for my brother's sake. It's a dream come true for him. I'm glad I was able to help him see it come true."

"Your father's dream as well," Bancroft said.

"That, too."

"Your parents would have been very proud of both of you, Miranda. You've already done so much good for so many. Look at this village. Look at those people back there."

"I wish I could feel noble about it. At the moment I merely feel exhausted. These past four months have been so—so incredibly busy."

"You've accomplished wonders."

"I suppose we have."

We had left the village now and were moving along the road where I had seen the redcoats. It was a lovely afternoon. Sunlight sparkled on the water, making silvery patterns on the blue. Waves washed quietly over the sands below, and the gulls circled lazily overhead. We were silent for a while, Bancroft clicking the reins lightly. I could see Mowrey House in the distance, wearing its new splendor proudly. The lawns were neatly trimmed, the gardens abloom. It was hard to believe it had been so grim and forbidding such a short time ago.

"Do you miss London?" Bancroft asked.

"I—I'm not sure, Dick."

"Oh?"

"I love my brother very much, but—he has his own life to live, and I'm not sure I can—" I hesitated. "I'm not sure I can fit into it. I've discovered who I am at last, it's true, but—"

"You're not sure it's who you want to be," he said.

"You do know me, Bancroft. All too well. I think perhaps I've scrapped and struggled to survive for too many years to settle for being the gracious lady of Mowrey House. It's my heritage, but—I'm not sure it's in my blood. Am I making sense?"

"Perfect sense," he told me.

"I suppose I sound ungrateful for all that has happened to me. I'm not. It isn't that at all."

"I know, lass."

The carriage was moving down the drive now. The rhododendron shrubs growing in front of the house, on either side of the portico, were in full bloom now, the pale purple-blue blossoms making a soft contrast to the weathered gray stone. I could smell their subtle fragrance as Dick tugged gently on the reins, bringing the horses to a halt in front of the wide stone steps. He climbed down and gave me his hand, helping me alight, and we stood there on the steps for a few moments. He had to go back to confer with the investors, but he would be returning to dine and spend the night. I hated to think of his leaving for London tomorrow morning. This tall, hefty, attractive blond with his strength, his warmth and wisdom meant a great deal to me, and I would miss him dreadfully. He probably knew me better than anyone else, and he knew what I was feeling now. He knew the reasons why as well.

"You've come a very long way, Miranda," he said.

"I suppose I have."

"Hard to believe you were once a dirty-faced little urchin with a voice like a squawking duck."

"My voice was never that bad, you bastard."

"It was worse. Never will forget that morning at Tyburn

when you picked my pocket. Crafty little minx, you were. Not quite crafty enough as it turned out. Filthy, foul-mouthed, wild as could be—and look at you now."

Remembering, I made no reply. I could feel the sadness growing inside, and I tried my best to stem it. This should be one of the happiest days in my life. I should be filled with elation over all we had accomplished. Bancroft took my hand and squeezed it. His warm brown eyes were understanding and full of affection.

"Cheer up, lass," he said. "Everything is going to work out."

"It already has. That may be the problem."

"This isn't an ending, Miranda. This is merely a beginning. Things happen to you—you're that kind of person—and I have the feeling they're going to go right on happening. The journalists claim your life has been like a fairy tale. I suppose it has in a way, but the tale isn't over yet, lass."

"What would I do without you?" I asked quietly.

Bancroft allowed himself a grin. "Go to debtor's prison, more than likely, the way you've been spending money of late. Go on inside, lass. Get some rest. Things will look brighter tomorrow."

He gave me a hug and climbed back into the carriage and drove off. I stood on the steps, watching the carriage grow smaller and smaller as it moved down the drive, and the old sadness swept over me anew, stronger now than it had been for a long time. I had everything . . . and I had nothing. Damn, I thought. Damn, damn, damn. Why can't you be happy? Why must you still long for . . . I wasn't going to think of him. I wasn't. I was Lady Miranda now, and I didn't need anyone, certainly not a moody, volatile Scot who . . . Silently I damned him, and then I went inside to get on with my life.

35

I WAS IN THE LIBRARY THREE WEEKS LATER, BUSILY
sorting out books and putting them into stacks. They had all
been dusted, the fine leather bindings properly oiled, but they
had been jammed onto the shelves in hodgepodge fashion, with
no respect to author or subject matter. Greek histories stood
alongside Elizabethan journals. Books on botany leaned chum-
mily alongside Restoration memoirs. Putting them all into some
semblance of order was a gigantic task, further complicated by
the fact that all my own books had recently come from London.
I had been devoting several hours a day to the job and, in truth,
I was quite grateful to have it. Douglas spent most of the day
at the factory, most of his evenings at Morrison Place, and I
saw little of him. Work on the house had been completed. The
staff I had employed was wonderfully efficient, everything was
running smoothly and there was not much for me to do.

Day followed day, serene and peaceful, lovely, sunny days
that were perfect for long walks, but one could take just so
many walks. I was thoroughly familiar with the moors now—
I had even taken a pilgrimage to the old Roman ruins—and I
had walked along the cliffs and climbed down the rocks to
stroll on the beach below. Restless, vaguely discontented, I
seemed to be in a state of suspension, waiting for something
to happen—I knew not what. Working on the library helped.
I lined the books on geology on an empty shelf and placed the
books on tin mining beside them. It was after three now, bright
afternoon sunlight slanting through the windows, making silver
yellow pools on the fine parquet floor. I pulled the bell cord
and a plump, pleasant maid came scurrying into the room a
few moments later, her pink cheeks flushed, her jet black hair
untidy beneath a hastily donned white mobcap.

"Hello, Polly," I said. "Do you think I might have a cup
of tea?"

"Oh, yes'um!" she exclaimed. "I'll bring one right away. You shouldn't be workin' in 'ere so 'ard. Me an' Nan 'ud be more'n 'appy to put all of them books back up."

"I'm sure you would, Polly. I appreciate your offer, but I prefer to do it myself."

"Ain't fittin', th' mistress of th' 'ouse luggin' all them books around, gettin' 'erself all perspiry."

"The tea, Polly."

"Cook's just made some scones, they're still 'ot. Want I should get you some with fresh butter an' strawberry jam? Bring 'em with your tea? You didn't 'ave any lunch, Lady M."

"I'm really not hungry. Just tea will be fine."

Polly gave me a disapproving look and left the room. The servants I had hired were as concerned with my welfare as Lord Markham's had been and longed to spoil me as they spoiled Douglas. He, of course, adored the attention and treated them with a casual amiability that inspired near-worship from one and all. I was a puzzle to them, neither stern and dictatorial nor helpless and incompetent. I was polite and friendly and kept an efficient eye on things, but I left the running of Mowrey House to Ned who, with a full staff at his command, was in his element and did a superb job, though I suspected he was something of a tyrant belowstairs.

Stepping around several piles of books, I sat down in one of the comfortable leather chairs near the fireplace. A half-emptied crate set beside the chair, and I began to take books out of it, fondly examining the volumes of *Tom Jones* and the copy of *An Account of the Life of Mr. Richard Savage* that Sam Johnson had personally inscribed to me. Setting them on the small table on the other side of the chair, I pulled out the plays Marcelon had given me and a battered but beloved copy of *Moll Flanders*. I took three more books out of the crate, and my heart seemed to turn over. *The Curse of Hesketh. Gentleman James. The Stranger From Japan.* Why had I kept them? Oh, Dear God, why hadn't I disposed of them? There was a hollow sensation in the pit of my stomach, a dry tightness at the back of my throat. The three volumes acted as a kind of catalyst, and it all came flooding back, the pain as strong, as real as it had been three and a half years ago when Cam Gordon marched out of my life.

The Curse of Hesketh . . . I had been reading it that day in the dilapidated flat on Holywell Street and Bancroft and Cam had come in and Bancroft had expressed amazement that I could read and I had launched into a criticism of the works of Roderick Cane and Cam had grown chillier and chillier as I passed judgment. I remembered his anger and my own dismay when I discovered that Roderick Cane and the surly Scot who held my article of indenture were one and the same. *Gentleman James* . . . how happy I had been during the time he was writing that, totally, passionately in love for the first and only time in my life, discovering all those exquisite new sensations, elated, enraptured, moving in a golden haze of happiness, waiting on him hand and foot and delighted to be able to do so. *The Stranger From Japan* . . . I had started my own writing and he was heavily involved with his cousin and Robbie and the other rebels and moodier than ever and there was constant tension and quarrels and he finished the book just before that dreadful night when. . . . I set the books aside and closed my eyes for a moment, fighting the emotions that possessed me.

You're not going to cry, damn you. You're not! He isn't worth it. He isn't *worth* it. No man is worth this kind of anguish. You loved the son of a bitch with all your heart and soul and *gave* him your heart and soul and he rejected that gift, he abandoned you without a moment's hesitation and he'll never, never, never find anyone else who'll love him like that. He'll be miserable and alone and one day he'll realize what he tossed aside and . . . and you're better off without him. You survived. You made a new life for yourself. Pull yourself to*geth*er, Miranda. It's over.

"Your tea, Your Ladyship," Polly said.

"Oh, I—I didn't hear you come in."

"I took th' liberty of bringin' you some of them scones I was tellin' you about, some butter an' a pot of strawberry jam, too. Thought you just might be tempted, even if you said you didn't want 'em."

"Thank you very much, Polly."

"*An'* a surprise. A letter. Came all th' way from London, it did. Chap from th' village brought it up just a few minutes ago. Addressed to you, it was, not Lord Mowrey. I thought you'd want to see it right away."

She set the tea tray down beside me and handed me the letter, filled with ardent curiosity she could scarcely conceal. That a letter could come all the way from London was still amazing to a girl like Polly. I thanked her again in a dismissive voice, and she reluctantly left the room. I poured a cup of tea. I drank it slowly. It was very hot, very strong. It helped. I put the three Roderick Cane books back into the crate and put Cam Gordon out of my mind and, pouring another cup of tea, opened Marcelon's latest missive.

My dear!

I have so much to tell you and, as usual, I'm rushed, rushed, rushed and, frankly, not much good at letters to begin with! The past few weeks have been absolutely *frant*ic, what with the new production getting under-way—Wycherley, my dear, at the Haymarket, a Restoration romp, and you should *see* my costumes, maybe you'll get up to London sometime during the run. *Also*, and this is the really important news, Thomas and I have *done* it! We got married!

The dear man almost got cold feet—I had to *drag* him to the altar at the last minute—but everything's been bliss ever since! He's *so* patient and so tolerant and he *adores* the dogs, takes them for walks in the park every morning. I had to give up the house on Greenbriar Court, alas, it simply wouldn't do, and we've moved into *his* place, which is large and comfortable and which I'm currently redecorating like mad. Thomas grumbles a lot and he has a lot of fussy little habits I'm gradually breaking him of, but we're so happy. (*Entre nous*, there's not a great deal of *romance* in our marriage, if you know what I mean, but we've both reached the age when companionship is far more important.)

Thomas struts around like a peacock, he's so proud of himself for bringing out *Betty's Girls*. The book is *still* selling wildly, my dear, and making tons of money which, if I understand correctly, you get a hefty share of. Johnson has declared it the most important book of the year, as you probably know—I did send you all the newspaper clippings, didn't I?—but he added that it should be kept under lock and key lest it fall into the hands of impressionable innocents. That, of course, caused sales to soar even more! The really interesting thing is that *Betty's Girls* has stirred up a number of public-spirited souls who are appalled at the conditions those unfortunate creatures live under, and they're forming committees to see what can be done to help them and also to prevent other girls from slipping into the same

~491~

plight. Dean Jordon is heading one of the committees, and I've lent my *name*, although I'm much too busy with Wycherley to be of any real help.

I assume you've heard about Davy. He finally married his Austrian dancer, who has retired from the stage and is devoting herself to the care and feeding of D. Garrick. He was *des*olate when you left London, Miranda, and Mademoiselle Violette or Eva Maria or whatever was there to hold his hand and comfort him and move *in* on him. Never liked her much myself, too cold, too Germanic, but apparently she's exactly what Davy needs and, if it's not a particularly blissful match, its an eminently sensible one for both of them. Davy's already become a placid, domestic creature, staying at home with his slippers and hot toddy, no more gadding about London, no more late hours at the coffeehouses. He's conserving all his energy for his work, which, though dull, is wise indeed.

So . . . I hope things are going well with you, Miranda, dear. Bancroft told me all about the opening of the pottery factory when he returned from Cornwall. (He gave me *away*, incidentally, at the wedding, I mean. A bit too *eager*ly, I might add.) He's done nothing but rave about your brother. Lord Mowrey, he says, is sharp as a tack, bright and businesslike and a wonderfully gifted designer as well. He's going to make a raging success of things, Dick declares. How incredible it is, your finding each other after all these years! (I gave my husband *hell* for leaking the story to the press, my dear, even if it *has* generated incredible sales. Anyway, you're "Lady Miranda" now and more famous than ever. They're *still* writing articles about it.)

I must dash now. All three dogs are barking and Thomas is patiently waiting to take me out to dinner and the new maid has made an absolute *chaos* of my wardrobe! Do write, my dear, and do try to get to London soon—bring that fascinating brother of yours with you. We all love you very much, Miranda, and we miss you dreadfully. Ta ta for now, luv.

Marcelon might well have been there in the room with me, so completely did that bright flow of words capture her shining, eccentric personality. I missed her, too, and I finally admitted

~492~

to myself that I missed London as well, missed the excitement and stimulation only that crowded, noisy, filthy city could provide. Cornwall had its own special grandeur, true—the moors mysterious, the seacoast rugged and magnificent—but the tang of salt and the screech of gulls couldn't take the place of those noxious smells and the brawling din that gave London its boisterous character.

I was still thinking of Marcie's letter late the next afternoon as I returned from a long walk on the moors. It was a dreary day, the sky the color of old pewter, what sunshine there was falling in thin white rays. The stiff, tarnish-gray grass that covered the moors had a pale purple cast and the rusty streaks on the boulders reminded me of dried blood. It was turning cooler. A brisk wind tossed my hair about and caused the skirt of my violet blue frock to whip about my legs. The heavy blue cloak I was wearing lifted in the wind and flapped behind me like indigo wings.

Marcie had sounded so happy, bursting with verve and vitality, more zestful than ever. I was very pleased for her, pleased for Thomas, too, for both, for all their success, had been essentially lonely people. Now they had each other, and their autumn years would be bright with color and warm with companionship. Marcie would undoubtedly lead him a merry chase and Thomas would undoubtedly grumble and fret, but both would enjoy every rocky, riotous moment. Thomas needed a few fireworks in his life, and Marcie needed a bit of sobriety. They would complement each other beautifully, I felt, and I wished I were there to hug them both and give them a splendid party.

The sky was growing darker, a distinct purple hue tinting the pewter gray, and clouds were roiling about, casting moving shadows over the moor. Although it couldn't be much later than four, the sunlight was fading fast, even thinner now. It was going to storm, I thought, shoving a silken skein of hair from my cheek. The brooding, ominous weather was a welcome relief after all the weeks of dazzling clarity. I walked slowly over the spongy ground, moving around the ancient gray boulders and skirting the patches of bog that gleamed tarry black in the ghostly white light. Mowrey House stood in the distance, a solid gray block surrounded by the green of lawns and shrubbery.

I was also pleased for Davy, for he had married the woman who was apparently right for him, who would provide the stable background he needed in order to concentrate on the most important thing—his work. Davy had loved me, I knew, and he had been hurt by my letter turning down his proposal, but in hurting him I had spared him a much greater harm. I would always be fond of him, but I could never have loved him as he deserved to be loved, nor could I have given him the home life the new Mrs. Garrick could give him. Davy was a genius, and a man with his complex nature required total devotion, constant attention. That, to all appearances, was precisely what his wife was giving him, and he would ultimately be much happier than he could ever have been with me.

The cloak whipped behind me as I left the moor and moved across the lawn in back of the house, passing the new trellises covered with dark green leaves that rattled noisily in the wind. I opened the back door and stepped into the enormous hall where Mowreys used to exercise their horses. Although it had been thoroughly cleaned and new rush matting laid on the cold stone floor, it was still dim and ugly and faintly sinister. No way to cheer up a great, grim cavern of a hall like this, I thought. Shadows shrouded the walls, and the damp, sour smell hadn't been entirely banished. Still gave me the shivers, it did, this gigantic hall, and it was with relief that I opened the narrow wooden door and stepped into the hallway that ran alongside the main staircase, moving past the spot where my father had crashed to his death almost a quarter of a century ago.

"*There* you are, mum!" Polly exclaimed, hurrying toward me. "We've all of us been in a terrible tizzy, we 'ave. No one knew *where* you were. I told Mrs. Clemson you'd probably gone for a walk, but she was upset just the same, flutterin' about like a nervous 'en—I know I shouldn't be sayin' that, 'er bein' 'ead 'ousekeeper an' all, but it's true!"

Her dark eyes were bright with excitement, her manner extremely agitated, and I felt a tremor of alarm.

"What is it, Polly? What's wrong? My brother—has something happened to—"

"'E's at the factory," she said quickly. "Mrs. Clemson thought maybe we should send for 'im, but it's you the soldier wants to see. 'E specifically said 'Lady Miranda Mowrey,' and Ned—" Polly blushed and nervously twisted the hem of her apron.

"Yes?" I prompted.

"*Brown* said you wudn't in," she continued, "an' th' soldier said 'e'd wait. 'E's in th' drawing room right now, still waitin'. 'E's been 'ere an 'our already."

"In that case it won't hurt him to wait a bit longer," I said. "I'll go upstairs and change. You may tell him I'll be down shortly."

Polly skittered off down the hall, in agony over her careless slip, and I smiled ruefully as I went up to my bedroom. Our Ned Brown was quite the Lothario, I reflected, removing my cloak, taking off the violet blue frock. I knew he was topping Mary, the buxom blonde who did the laundry, and I had once happened upon him in the pantry, hotly embracing Coral, one of the kitchen maids, but I hadn't known he was servicing Polly as well. Had his own harem, it would seem, but as long as he continued to run things with such stern efficiency, his sexual exploits were not my concern.

Ten minutes later, wearing a rich garnet silk gown, my hair neatly brushed and gleaming with coppery highlights, I went back downstairs and stepped into the drawing room to greet my mysterious guest. He was standing at the window, staring out at the gray sky, his back to me. He was tall and superbly built, the scarlet tunic accentuating his broad shoulders and slender waist, the snug white breeches covering long, muscular legs like a second skin. His black knee boots were polished to a high gloss, and his head was covered with short, tight blond curls. I cleared my throat. He turned.

"We meet again," Captain Jon Ramsey said.

Those brilliant blue eyes were as hard and icy as they had been when I had encountered him at Lady Julia's reception, the cruel, handsome face as hostile. During the intervening months I had almost forgotten that disturbing encounter, but it all came rushing back to me now as he stood there in front of the window with his legs spread wide, fists resting on his thighs. I stared at him, and a totally unreasonable alarm stirred inside. Several moments passed before I was able to control it.

"Captain Ramsey," I said. "How—how unexpected."

"Is it?" he asked.

It was an accusation, not a question. His voice was like a saber slashing the air.

"Won't you sit down, Captain Ramsey? I'll have one of the servants bring some tea. Or perhaps you'd prefer something stronger?"

"This isn't a social call, Miss James."

~495~

"It's no longer 'Miss James,'" I told him.

"I read about that in the papers. It seems you're a lady now."

"I'll thank you to remember it," I said tartly.

He smiled a thin, sarcastic smile, pleased to have riled me, and I damned myself for rising so quickly to the bait. Captain Jon Ramsey was undeniably a commanding figure in his gleaming black boots and snug white breeches and that impeccably tailored scarlet tunic with its shiny gold epaulettes and swirls of gold braid. Hard, harsh, arrogant, he undoubtedly inspired terror in his men, but I wasn't about to be intimidated. I moved over to the sofa and rested my hand on the curved back, but I didn't sit down.

"I knew you'd come to Cornwall," he said.

"I've hardly made a secret of it, Captain Ramsey."

"I made it my business to know. I've kept very close track of your every move."

"Indeed?"

"I knew when you left London. I knew when you got here, to the very hour. One of my men spotted your carriage and reported to me immediately. We've been watching you. We've been watching the house."

"How very dreary for you," I replied.

"You didn't know it, of course. No one did. I've had two of my best men on the job. Naturally they weren't in uniform. Blended right into the scenery, they did."

"How clever," I observed.

"One of them even applied for a position as footman here, but unfortunately your man Brown turned him down."

Thank God for that, I thought. While I had hired Mrs. Clemson and all of the maids, I had let Ned hire the footmen and grooms. I was shaken, far more so than I cared to admit, but Captain Jon Ramsey wasn't going to know that if I could possibly help it. I gazed at him haughtily, very much the Great Lady of the Manor.

"You know why I'm here," he said.

"On the contrary, I haven't the faintest idea."

"You're lying."

"How dare you—"

"I'm the King's agent, Miss James. The Duke of Cumberland personally appointed me for this particular job. He hasn't forgotten that assassination attempt three and a half years ago—

far from it. He's more determined than ever to round up every single man involved."

I didn't deign to respond. Jon Ramsey moved toward me, seething with hostility, wanting me to cower, but I had nothing whatsoever to hide. He stopped a few feet away from me and folded his arms across his chest, the fringe on his epaulettes swaying to and fro, glittering brightly. His blue eyes were no longer icy. They burned now with murderous hatred. I stood my ground, desperately trying to control my alarm. I had encountered dangerous men in my day, but Captain Ramsey made Black Jack Stewart and crew seem almost amiable.

"I want Cam Gordon," he said.

"I'm afraid I don't have him."

"You know very well he's part of a band of smugglers working off the Cornish coast."

"I'd heard that, yes."

"And I suppose you expect me to believe your coming to Cornwall was merely a coincidence?"

"I know this will probably come as a terrible shock to you, Captain Ramsey, but I couldn't possibly care less what you believe."

He didn't like that. He didn't like it at all. He moved a step closer, unfolding his arms and spreading his legs again, planting his fists on his thighs. My throat had gone dry and my heart was beginning to beat much too rapidly, but I gazed at him with cool hauteur nevertheless, staunchly refusing to show the least sign of intimidation.

"They've been working off the coast some thirty miles from here," he told me. "Naturally our main force has been concentrated in that area, although I've kept an eye on all the villages in this part of Cornwall."

"Very wise of you, I'm sure."

"You've both been very clever," he said.

"Clever?"

"You haven't fooled me, though, not for a minute. You've been in Cornwall four and a half months. Cam Gordon has been slipping in and out of the country all during that time, just thirty miles away. Are you going to tell me the two of you haven't been in touch?"

"I'm not going to tell you anything."

"I don't know how you've managed it—we've been watching you, watching the house—but I know you've been secretly communicating somehow or other. I don't believe in coincidences, Miss James. I find it very peculiar that a young aristocrat without a penny to his name should suddenly have the money to open a pottery factory that's been closed for years and completely do over the family mansion."

"My brother's financial affairs are no concern of—"

"I'm sure many a man would gladly have a whore in his home for that kind of money, pass her off as his long-lost sister. Your little charade may have taken in a lot of people, but it hasn't taken me in."

Calmly, as calmly as possible, I moved over to the fireplace and pulled the long yellow cord that hung beside it.

"I'm going to ignore what you just said, Captain Ramsey," I said, turning to face him again. "I'm not going to slap your face. I'm not going to have my menservants throw you out of the house. I'm going to let you leave peacefully. This minute."

"Your charade's almost over," he informed me. "Abetting a wanted man is a criminal offense. I shouldn't be surprised to see you hang right alongside your lover."

I pulled the bell cord again, rather too violently. I wasn't going to lose control. I wasn't. I wasn't going to give him that satisfaction.

"We had a little skirmish with the smugglers two nights ago," Ramsey continued. "Walked right into a trap we'd set, all of them. It was a very dark night, lots of confusion and shouting, knives flashing, blood spurting, gunfire, smoke. Never knew what hit them. Three captured. Seven killed."

He watched intently to observe my reaction to this piece of news. I showed none whatsoever, gazing at him with a cool composure that completely belied the turmoil inside. Not Cam, I told myself. Not Cam. If Cam had been one of them, Ramsey wouldn't be here. Please, Dear God, not Cam. Ramsey's thin lips lifted at one corner in a cruel half-smile, his blue eyes gleaming darkly.

"Killed two of the bastards myself," he said. "Most satisfying. Unfortunately, neither of them was Cam Gordon. Gordon and one other man got away during the confusion."

I said nothing. Ramsey moved toward me.

"We captured his companion this morning, not five miles from here. He was sneaking toward a farmhouse, planning to steal food. Apparently he and Gordon were hiding out in one of the caves or tunnels that riddle the coastline around here. I had the man brought to me, determined to make him talk and reveal Gordon's whereabouts, but I fear I was a bit too zealous in my interrogation. He won't be in any condition to talk again for at least twenty-four hours."

He was standing in front of me now, so close I could have reached out and touched that cruel, attractive face with its cap of tight blond curls. I tilted my head back, looking up into the blue eyes that smoldered now with a perverse lust. The skin across his cheekbones was taut, his thin lips tight, and I repressed a shudder. I knew all about men like this. They used to flock to Mother Redcoat's in St. Giles to satisfy their brutal appetites.

"I have fifty men in the area, searching for Gordon," he said. "Five of them are waiting outside right now. It occurred to me he might possibly have slipped past my men somehow and gotten into the house. I intend to search it from top to bottom."

"Like hell you will!"

My composure was gone. Lady Miranda had vanished in an instant and Duchess Randy was ready to kick and claw and do as much damage as possible. Ramsey sensed this. He smiled again, pleased to have cracked my cool facade at last. I glared at him, the wildcat of old.

"I suggest you cooperate, Miss James."

"And I suggest you get your arse out of this house this instant!"

"Once a whore, always a whore. I look forward to dealing with you personally when this is all over with. It's going to—"

I slammed my palm across his face with such force that he lost his balance, reeling, stumbling backward. I grabbed one of the silver candlesticks standing on the mantelpiece and gripped it as I would grip a club, fully prepared to smash his skull in. Ramsey was stunned, a vivid pink handprint burning on the side of his face.

"You little bitch! I'm going to—"

"Trouble, Lady M.?" Ned inquired.

He strolled casually into the room, looking more than ever like a pugilist in the tight black uniform that emphasized his tough, muscular build. A silky white neckcloth was folded neatly into the top of his black vest, and his black frock coat swung open, flapping slightly as he moved. That rugged face with its broken nose and monklike fringe of thick brown hair was unperturbed, brown eyes bovine, as though there was nothing at all remarkable about finding the mistress of the house clutching a candlestick, ready to swing at a visitor.

"Captain Ramsey was just leaving," I said crisply.

"Want I should show him out?"

"Please do."

"I'm not leaving! Not until I've searched this house! I'm going to call my men in right now, and—"

"Seems we have a bit of a problem," Ned interrupted.

His voice was a lethargic drawl, his manner utterly nonchalant, yet he exuded brute strength and an undeniable menace. Ramsey hesitated, eyes flashing blue fire, and then he drew himself up, assuming an air of steely authority.

"If I were you, I wouldn't interfere, Brown. I'm the King's agent, answerable directly to the Duke of Cumberland. I have five men outside. They're fully armed. Get in my way and you'll find yourself in serious trouble."

Ned grinned a broad grin, his brown eyes full of lazy amusement as he contemplated the smartly dressed officer with the tight blond curls. Ramsey was disconcerted and not a little uneasy. Ned didn't answer at once. He gave the grin full play, and then he shook his head.

"Don't know what kind of authority you might have," he said lazily, "but I feel pretty sure it doesn't extend to searching the home of a lord without his permission. If I were *you*, I'd leave at once—while you can still walk."

"Are you threatening me?"

"Guess you might say that. It'd give me considerable pleasure to break your neck and leave them little tin soldiers out there without a leader. Start walking, Captain."

Ramsey hesitated, sizing the man up, taking in the powerful build, the broken nose, the dark brown eyes that seemed to be anticipating that pleasure he had just mentioned. He paled, the burning pink handprint standing out even more vividly. Like so many other petty tyrants, Ramsey was accustomed to bullying those weaker than he or, as with his men, those in no position to fight back. Confronted with someone like Ned, his true cowardice showed through.

"You'll regret this, Brown!"

"I'm gonna be patient. I'm gonna count to ten."

Ramsey whirled around and glared at me. He didn't say anything. He didn't have to. That tight mouth, those murderous blue eyes said everything, and I repressed another shudder as he twisted his lips and stalked out of the room. Ned ambled after him. I heard the front door open, close, heard loud voices and, a few moments later, the sound of horses galloping down the drive. I set the candlestick back on the mantel and took a deep breath, desperately striving to compose myself. Ned came back into the room, frock coat flapping.

"Are you all right, Lady M.?"

"I'm fine, Ned. They—they left?"

"Rode right off. They're going to be watching the house closely. There'll be at least a dozen men watching it, maybe more."

"I—perhaps I'd better explain, Ned."

"You don't need to explain anything, Lady M. Reckon I know what it's about. This fellow Gordon, the one Ramsey's so eager to capture, he's the chap you used to live with. He was working with the smugglers."

"Two nights ago there was—"

"I know all about that. Gordon and a man called Hawkins got away. Hawkins was captured this morning. Gordon's still on the loose, and Ramsey thinks maybe you're hiding him."

"I haven't seen him in years, Ned. I haven't heard from him. He—he doesn't even know I'm in Cornwall. Ramsey—"

"You're not to worry, Lady M.," he told me.

His voice was calm and reassuring, his dark brown eyes full of concern, and I felt much better having him on my side. Ned might look like a brute, might be wry and cocky on occasion, but he had devoted most of his adult life to my brother, watching after him with a loyal devotion that could only be called paternal. He had a quiet strength that had nothing to do with his size. I felt it now. I seemed to draw from it.

"I don't want my brother to know about this," I said. "I don't want him to be bothered."

"No need for it," Ned agreed.

"If he sees the soldiers, if he finds out that Ramsey was here, we'll merely say they're looking for a—for one of the smugglers who is believed to be in the area."

"Right," he replied. "None of the servants will tell him anything, I promise you."

"Thank you, Ned. I don't know what I would have done if you hadn't come in when you did."

Ned grinned again. "Bashed his head in, probably. You wield a wicked candlestick, Lady M. *I* sure wouldn't want to get you riled."

~501~

He gave me an admiring look, still grinning, then made a mock-servile bow and left the room. I went upstairs and took a long, hot bath and washed my hair, trying my best to put the incident out of my mind. Putting on a thin cream petticoat with half a dozen gauzy skirts aswirl with ruffles, I dried my hair thoroughly and sat down at my dressing table. I brushed my hair until it fell to my shoulders in loose, flowing waves shiny with red gold highlights. My cheeks were pale. I carefully applied a subtle pink rouge, applied a touch of pink lip rouge as well, gazing at the stranger in the glass with dark sapphire eyes that seemed haunted, lids etched with blue gray shadow.

The wind howled, whipping around the house as though trying to break in. The windows shook in their frames, rattling furiously, and thunder rolled in the distance like cannon fire. That didn't help my nerves at all. I frowned and put the lip rouge aside. You aren't going to think about it, I told myself sternly. Cam Gordon may be in the area, but it isn't because of *you*. He doesn't even know you're here. Getting involved with smugglers, risking his bloody neck . . . the son of a bitch hasn't changed one bloody bit. It would serve him right if they caught him. The idiot. The bloody idiot! Dear God, let him get away. Please let him get away. I closed my eyes, gripping the edge of the dressing table as the emotions swept over me.

Half an hour later, wearing a rich cream satin gown with thin gold stripes, I greeted Douglas with a serene smile and accompanied him into the dining room. My nerves were still ajangle and I was emotionally depleted, yet, determined he not suspect anything, I somehow managed to present a poised facade for Douglas. He was very excited about the new pink the craftsmen from France had perfected, *such* a pink, dark and rich, unlike any pink you've ever seen. Things were going fantastically at the factory, fantastically, the first set of new china would be ready to show in a day or two and orders were *already* pouring in from major distributors whom Bancroft had contacted. All the best shops in London were going to carry it, shops in Bath, and the inexpensive pottery was going to be sold all over England! He seriously doubted they could even *fill* all the orders.

He chatted exuberantly throughout the meal, so carried away with enthusiasm he probably wouldn't have noticed had my hair suddenly turned white. He talked about the various processes they were using, going into technical details above my head, zestfully describing exactly what was done and why and how important it was to have just the right degree of heat for baking in the colors and how you had to be careful when you were using gold, the kilns had to be . . . I listened and nodded and longed to hurl the salt shaker at his head. Douglas sensed this eventually and grinned a sheepish grin.

"Guess I can be a galloping bore at times," he admitted.

"You?" I arched a brow. "Surely not."

"I feel kind of guilty, going to the factory every day, having all the fun, leaving you alone here. Must be dreadfully boring for you."

"Rarely that."

"You're looking unusually gorgeous tonight in that cream and gold gown," he told me. "Bit daring, isn't it?"

"They're wearing them this way. Dessert?" I inquired. "I believe Cook has made a chocolate cake."

"Tempting," Doug said, "but I really must hurry. I promised Linda's father I'd stop by for a chat tonight."

"Oh. So it's Linda's *father* you're courting."

"He's a very interesting chap!" Doug protested. "Drops off to sleep quite early."

"And then?"

"Linda's very interesting, too. A bit too cool and snippy to suit my taste, but she's warming to me."

I smiled. Doug grinned again and we went into the hall, my satin skirt making a soft, rustling music. He had changed into his best outfit before dinner and looked dashing indeed. I straightened his lapels, fussed with his silk neckcloth and brushed errant blond locks from his brow. Douglas grimaced, impatient with my ministrations, eager to be gone. The wind was still howling fiercely, and thunder rumbled constantly.

"Do be careful," I said. "It's going to storm."

"I'm not a *baby*, Miranda. Besides, it could keep this up for hours before we get a drop of rain. I'll probably be late."

"You usually are. Give Linda my love."

He left, and I wandered into the library. The candles were lighted, casting a warm amber glow over the rich leather bindings. One of the footmen came in and asked if I would like him to light the fire. I nodded, for the room was rather cold, and he soon had a nice blaze going. I looked in despair at the stacks of books on the floor and the two crates of my own books that hadn't yet been opened. Sighing, I set to work, though I was hardly dressed for it. Best to keep busy, as busy as possible. My nerves were near the snapping point, and I knew that if I allowed myself to dwell on what had happened I would crack completely. Work. Don't think. Work until you're ready to drop with exhaustion.

I did just that. The clock struck eight. I separated books, arranged them on the shelves, put them in order. Eight-thirty. Nine. I started on another pile of books. The thunder was growing louder. The house seemed to shake. Douglas should never have gone out on a night like this, I thought, carrying an armload of leather-bound volumes over to a shelf. Virgil, Livy, Suetonius. I'd put the three volumes of Josephus with them. Nine-fifteen. Nine-thirty. The wind stopped abruptly, howling one moment, still the next. An eerie silence followed, as though the earth itself were holding its breath. There was a deafening crash of thunder then, and the deluge began, rain pouring, pounding, lashing the house in furious sheets.

I continued to work, ignoring the furor of the storm, and by eleven o'clock I had put away all the books stacked on the floor and emptied the crate I had already opened, putting the Roderick Cane novels on a bottom shelf alongside the other novels. The storm hadn't let up at all. It was, if anything, worse than ever, sheets of rain slashing against the windows like angry waves. Douglas would never be able to get home in this. He would have to spend the night at Morrison Place. I was exhausted now, and I knew I hadn't the strength to open the two remaining crates from London. The fire had burned down, a heap of glowing coals. The candles were beginning to splutter. I arched my back and brushed a heavy wave from my temple. Maybe I could sleep now.

Saving one candle in a small pewter holder to light my way upstairs, I put out all the rest and stepped into the hall. It was very dark, walls covered with shadows that seemed to waver and float like ghostly black clouds, the flickering flame I carried providing the only illumination. The rain pounded and lashed in a frenzy, filling the house with rattling, echoing noises, as though a band of demons charged through it. It was cold. There was a draft. My candle blew out. I hesitated for a moment in total darkness, emitting a very unladylike word, and then there was an earsplitting crash, a shrieking noise like a scream, and the hall was filled with a silver-blue flash that lasted only an instant.

Lightning. One of the trees in back had been hit. Moving past the staircase, I headed toward the narrow door that led into the huge back hall. I wondered how the servants could possibly sleep in this din. They had all retired hours ago, no doubt, and were snug in their beds. Setting the candlestick down on a small table, I opened the door and moved into the cavernous back hall. The long row of windows that looked out over the back were uncurtained, rain pouring down the panes in torrents, and constant flashes of lightning created a bizarre lighting effect, silver-blue, black, silver-blue again, flickering wildly. I stepped over to a window and peered out, and after a moment I saw the tree in the distance, split in two, visible for only an instant in the lightning. Seeing that there was no fire, no apparent danger, I turned to go back, and it was then that the lightning stopped and I was in pitch black darkness.

"Damn!" I exclaimed.

It was icy cold back here and so dark I could barely see two feet in front of me. I'd probably stumble on the rush matting and break my neck. Clever, Miranda, I told myself, very clever, prowling around in the dark in the middle of the worst storm in years. I moved cautiously toward the narrow door I had left open, not at all sure of my direction. Icy air caressed my cheeks and stroked my bare arms and shoulders. Had to wear one of your lowest cut gowns tonight, didn't you? You'll probably catch your death of cold. Layers of darkness seemed to part in front of me, and then I stopped, paralyzed. A dark form stood some ten feet away from me, solid and unmoving.

"Who is it?"

My voice was a hoarse whisper. I could feel his presence now, feel his eyes on me. My throat tightened. I couldn't breathe. I couldn't move. I could only stare at that tall, dark form, black against black, unmistakably human. Never in my life had I known such stark terror. Furious gusts of wind sent sheets of rain slamming against the windows. The back door flew open, banging against the wall. It had been locked. Someone had forced it open, hadn't closed it properly. Rain swept through the opening, splattering on the floor. There was another flash of lightning, and in the brief, blinding explosion of silver blue light I saw the intruder. I cried out. He rushed toward me. I stumbled. He seized my arms and I struggled violently and lightning exploded again and I saw his face.

"Hello, Miranda," he said.

36

I DREW MY FOOT BACK AND KICKED HIS SHIN AS HARD
as I could. He grunted in surprise and pain. I pulled my arms
free and doubled up my fists and slammed them into his chest
and he stumbled back. Lightning flashed constantly now like
some bizarre silver-blue light flickering on and off, on and off,
and his face showed amazement and alarm as I kicked him
again. He doubled over. I seized his hair, pulling it with all
my strength. He cried out. He decided to fight back then. He
grabbed hold of my wrists and twisted them. I let go of his
hair. He swung me around, slamming me up against him, my
back crashing into his chest. Flinging his arms around my waist,
trapping my own at my sides, he held me so tightly I gasped.
I lifted my left foot, stomping on his as hard as I could, and
he yelped with pain.

"Have you lost your bloody mind! It's *me!*"

I stomped on his foot again. He let go of me promptly. I
whirled around. His eyes were full of agony. I slapped his face
even harder than I had slapped Ramsey. My wrist almost broke.
Cam Gordon backed away from me, hobbling. The rain pounded
against the windows, swept through the open door. Thunder
boomed. Lightning struck another tree. There was a brilliant
silver-orange flash.

"You son of a bitch!" I cried. "You bloody son of a *bitch!*
You haven't got the brains of a peahen! The whole goddamn
countryside is swarming with redcoats, there must be at least
twenty watching this house!"

"Yeah," he said, "I saw 'em."

"God*damn* you, Cam Gordon!"

"Still the same Miranda," he said. "I thought maybe you'd
changed. I was afraid maybe you'd become that cool, elegant
lady you always wanted to be."

"I *am* a lady, you bastard!"

He arched an eyebrow. "Oh? You certainly fooled me."

"I'm going to kill you. I'm going to *kill* you!"

"Jesus! You really *do* bear a grudge, don't you? Back off. Back off! I'm convinced!"

Then, to my utter humiliation, I started to cry. Tears streamed profusely down my cheeks. I sobbed. He moved toward me and placed his hand on my arm. I slapped him again. He caught me to him and held me and I continued to sob, resting my head on his shoulder. He rocked me gently, and the splendor of the moment made me cry all the more, that strong body pressed against mine, those arms holding me tightly. So long. So long. It had been so long. I had been half alive. I reveled in the bliss of his nearness, and after a while I lifted my head, looking up at that lean, beloved face.

"Feel better?" he asked.

"You're wringing wet," I said, pulling away from him. "Your hair is plastered all over your head. Your clothes are soaked."

"A good, solid rainstorm'll do that."

"You're a goddamned fool, Cam Gordon. I meant every word I said."

"I believe you."

"Ramsey knows you're in the area. He thinks you—he believes the two of us have been in communication. He thinks that's why I came to Cornwall—because of you. He—"

"Let's not worry about Ramsey for the moment."

"How did you know I was here?"

"I didn't, not until two weeks ago. Thought I was going to have to go back to London for you, and then I happened to see a London paper—I was in France at the time—and decided to make one last jaunt with the smugglers."

"You must leave at once."

"In this storm?"

"In this storm," I retorted.

"The whole goddamn countryside is swarming with red-coats, there must be at least twenty watching this house."

"Don't mock me, you sod!"

"You *are* feeling better."

I squared my shoulders and brushed hair from my cheeks and assumed the dignity I had momentarily lost. I might have been in a torpor the past three and a half years, part of me completely numb, and I was fully, gloriously alive again, every fiber of my being singing with life. I acknowledged it freely, but I wasn't about to let Cam Gordon suspect how I felt. I gazed at him cooly in the constant flashes of lightning, regal and imperious.

"Why did you come?" I asked.

"I think you know."

"You want money. You want help."

"I want you."

"Like hell you do. You turned your back on me three and a half years ago. You broke my heart, you son of a bitch. I'll give you money. I'll do all I can to help you get away, for old times' sake, but you don't have to cozen me into it. You don't have to pretend—"

"Must we really discuss it here?" he asked. "I am, as you observed earlier, wringing wet. I'm starving to death. I'm dropping with exhaustion, and I'm also sore all over from your tender ministrations."

"Don't expect sympathy from me, you sod."

"I mean it, Miranda. If I don't have something to eat, I'm likely to faint. I haven't had a bite of food in two days. Do you think you could possibly stop acting like a tight-assed countess and give me a little aid?"

The lightning stopped then. We were in total darkness. The rain was still lashing against the windows and sweeping through the open door, but some of the furor seemed to have gone out of the storm. Several moments passed without either of us speaking, and my eyes gradually grew accustomed to the dark and I began to make out vague shapes and outlines. Cam was shivering.

"I don't suppose I have any choice," I said. "I suppose I'll have to help you. No one must know you're here. I'll take you upstairs to my room."

"That's terribly kind of you."

"I've had just about enough of your sarcasm, Cam Gordon. Watch your mouth. Understand?"

"I understand," he said.

"Had to break the bloody door, didn't you? Rain pouring in like mad."

"I didn't break it. I merely picked the lock. Guess I didn't shut it properly."

"Close it," I ordered. "We can't leave it open like that."

"I'm too weak," he protested. "I'll get drenched again. I—"

"If you think *I'm* going to get drenched and ruin this satin gown, you're out of your bloody mind."

"All right!" he snapped.

He stumbled over to the door and caught hold of it, and waves of rain lashed him and drenched him anew. He slammed the door and snapped the lock and cursed loudly as he slipped on the floor, almost falling. He groped his way back over to where I stood, and I took his hand and led him toward the narrow door opening into the front hall. We moved alongside the staircase in the darkness, Cam tottering behind me, and I prayed the servants were all still in bed. Gripping his hand firmly, I led him upstairs and along the upper hallway to my bedroom. Several candles burned in wall sconces, their flames protected by glass globes, and the pale yellow light sent shadows scurrying over the walls.

"In here," I said, opening the door to my bedroom.

I pulled him inside. Candles were burning. There was a fire in the fireplace, burning low now, and my bedcovers had been turned back. I felt jubilant, full of strength now, spunky as could be. He really did look weak and pathetic, I thought. He had no coat. His thin white shirt was plastered to his body, his tight black breeches clinging wetly. He was still shivering, and I thought his skin had a faint bluish cast. Letting go of his hand, I put another log on the fire, poked at it until it began to blaze and then turned to face him, all cool efficiency.

"Come stand by the fire," I said crisply. "Take off those wet clothes at once. I'll go to my brother's room and fetch one of his robes."

"Food," he whispered.

"I'll bring you some food," I retorted. "Do as I say."

"Jesus, you've become a bossy little bitch, haven't you? If I weren't half dead, I'd—"

"Shut up," I said. "Drink this."

I had poured a glass of brandy from the crystal decanter on my night table. I handed it to him. He gave me an inquisitive look.

"You've become a sot as well as a bossy bitch?"

I didn't answer him. I lighted the candle that stood in a silver holder on the mantel and, carrying it with me, moved briskly back down the hall toward my brother's bedroom, which was located on the other side of the house. Rain splattered against the windowpanes and there were still distant rolls of thunder, but the fury had diminished considerably. Douglas' room was dark. My candle cast a wavering yellow-orange pool of light that gradually widened, banishing layers of black. Opening the wardrobe door, I pulled down the first dressing robe I saw, a sumptuous navy-blue brocade embroidered with black silk leaves and lined with black satin. I draped it over my arm, picked up the candleholder and departed, closing the door quietly behind me.

My blood seemed to tingle. My whole body seemed to glow. I might have had a whole magnum of the finest champagne. I was giddy with elation I couldn't control, a marvelous music inside guiding my steps as I walked back down the hall. He was here. He was waiting in my bedroom. I could hardly believe it. He was a reckless, foolhardy idiot, and I was going to give him hell for taking such an insane risk, but . . . I stopped abruptly. Someone was moving up the stairs. I saw the circle of candlelight grow brighter and brighter as the footsteps neared the top.

Ned stepped into the hall. He saw me standing there with the dressing robe draped over my arm, the candleholder in my hand, and I must have looked terribly guilty. If so, he didn't acknowledge it. His face was expressionless as he gave me a polite nod.

"Everything all right, Lady M.?" he inquired.

"Everything's—just fine, Ned. I was—my brother asked me to—to mend a tear in this robe and the storm was keeping me awake so—so I thought I'd do it tonight. You—you haven't been asleep?"

He shook his head. "Storm's been pretty bad. I figured I'd better have a look around before I went to bed. Everything secure up here?"

"Secure as can be," I said shakily.

"Will you be requiring anything else?" he asked.

"I—as a matter of fact, Ned, I—I'm ravenously hungry. I wasn't able to eat much at the dinner table tonight. I wonder if you could bring a tray up?"

"Certainly."

"I'm *very* hungry, Ned. Brings lots of food."

He nodded and turned back down the staircase. I heaved a sigh of relief, shaken. I didn't handle that well at all, I thought as I returned to the bedroom, but at least food was on the way. I opened the door and stepped inside. Cam was standing in front of the fireplace, tall and tan and lean and completely naked. He had draped his clothes over the firescreen. They were beginning to steam. His boots stood beside the hearth, tilting crazily, crusted with mud. He had dried his hair and brushed it, and the thick, straight locks gleamed jet black in the firelight. I handed him the rich brocade robe without a word. He slipped it on, drawing the silky folds around his naked body, fastening the satin sash around his waist.

"What about my food?" he demanded.

"You'll get your bleedin' food!" I snapped.

"Temper hasn't improved a bit, I see. You may be the elegant Lady Miranda like they say, with all the posh trappings, but the feisty little street urchin still lurks beneath the surface. You just dropped your final 'g.'"

"Go to hell," I said.

"I've been there for the past three and a half years."

"What's that supposed to mean?"

"I think you know."

He looked even leaner, I thought, the planes and angles of his face sharper than ever, severely handsome. That heavy black wave was slanting down over his forehead again like a lopsided "V" with the point above his right eyebrow, and the blue eyes looked at me with lazy detachment. The brocade robe rustled with a silken sound as he reached up to smooth back a lock of hair, the sumptuous navy-blue folds shimmering, black silk leaves seeming to ripple. I felt a tightness in my throat and an ache inside that spread through my body like fever.

"You've done well for yourself," he said.

"I have, indeed."

"You're even more beautiful than I remembered. I've never seen you in a gown like that. Your brother buy it for you?"

"I bought it myself. I happen to be an extremely wealthy woman."

"I've read about your success," he told me. "Every time I had an opportunity I read the London papers. They always seemed to be full of M.J. I read *Duchess Annie*—chap in Brittany had a copy, I borrowed it. Norman Lloyd was obviously patterned after me—and you weren't particularly kind. He was an utter bastard."

"Drawn straight from life."

"He was also a goddamned fool, deserting Anne as he did, turning his back on the one good thing that ever happened to him. The book cut a bit too close to the bone. I resented it bitterly."

"I'm not surprised."

"I resented it because I knew I could never hope to write anything half as good, because it made the bloody melodramas I wrote look like the claptrap they always were. I resented its success, the fame and fortune it brought you, and I knew I was every bit as big a fool as your Norman Lloyd, a miserable son of a bitch who didn't deserve anyone as rare, as special as Anne."

"Ned will be bringing the food up," I said coldly. "I'd better meet him in the hall and take the tray from him. He mustn't find you here."

Those clear blue eyes studied me closely, peering into my soul, and I felt a flutter of panic.

"My confession upsets you?" he asked.

"Your 'confession' doesn't mean a bloody thing to me. You *are* a miserable son of a bitch, Cam Gordon, and my only concern is to get you fed and out of my house as soon as possible."

I turned then and left the room. You're not going to fall for that line of malarky, I told myself. You're not! The bastard tore your heart out and threw it back at you, and you're not going to let him do it again. You're going to be cold and remote and...and you're going to ignore all these feelings stirring inside. You're going to fight them with all your strength. You want him, yes. Just looking at him makes you weak all over, makes you trembly, and you ache to touch that lean cheek and feel those arms around you again, but you're going to *fight* it.

Ned was coming down the hall with the tray of food, a fine white linen napkin covering it. I took it from him and thanked him in a shaky voice and told him that would be all. He gave me a curious look and hesitated a moment before nodding and heading back toward the staircase. The tray was very heavy. I carried it back to the bedroom, pushing the door open with my foot, kicking it shut behind me. Cam relieved me of the tray and took it over to the rug in front of the fireplace and set it down, then sat down beside it, the folds of the dressing robe spilling back, leaving his legs and most of his chest bare.

"Hmmm," he said, whipping off the napkin. "Cold chicken. Slices of ham. Slices of roast. Bread. Butter. A wedge of cheese. A pot of tea—hot, too. And what are these? Fried apricot tarts, looks like, sprinkled with sugar. A veritable feast."

He began to eat then, ignoring me completely, and I stood nervously across the room, watching him, watching the way the loose sleeves of the robe slipped back over his forearms, the way his thick, sleek hair gleamed blue black in the firelight, the way his teeth sank into the piece of chicken, tearing meat away from the bone. The candles were burning down, spluttering quietly, filling the room with a misty gold light that grew dimmer and dimmer as first one, then another went out with a soft splutter of wax. It all seemed like a dream, the dying light, the man in front of the fireplace, the steady patter of rain, but the ache inside was real enough, mounting by the moment.

Cam finished the piece of chicken, picked up another. "Delicious," he remarked. "Want some?"

"No, thank you."

"A cup of tea?"

I didn't bother to answer him. I moved over to one of the windows and held the curtain back and stared out at the night. The rain was slackening now. The clouds were disappearing, the moon almost visible. What was I going to do? How could I send him back out into the night, knowing the property was probably overrun with soldiers? He had slipped past them earlier in the thick of the storm, but they would be far more alert now. He was weak and worn down, thoroughly exhausted. I would put him in one of the guest rooms and let him sleep there tonight and . . . and worry about the rest of it tomorrow. I had to get him out of the house, yes, but first I had to get him out of this room with the quietly crackling fire and the pale golden haze and the large bed with its covers turned down invitingly, beckoning, waiting.

I remembered another bed and the lean, hard body and the mouth that covered mine in the darkness, the weight, the warmth of skin, the musky smell, the furor of emotions that mounted as that body pressed and pinioned me and my hands moved over the muscular curve of back and firm, tight buttocks. Clutching the curtain so tightly it almost ripped, I remembered the hard, throbbing entry and the sensations that exploded as thrust followed thrust and wells of bliss brimmed over, bursting into fountains that showered us with splendor. I gnawed my lower lip, trying to force the memory out of my mind. The curtain tore with a soft, shredding noise. I let go of it, damning myself for such folly.

"You're frightfully tense," he observed.

I turned. He had spread the napkin back over the tray and pushed it aside, and he was drinking a cup of tea, his thumb hooked in the handle, strong fingers curved loosely around the blue porcelain bowl. He lifted it to his lips, taking a long sip, his eyes watching me. I moved restlessly over to the bed and tucked the covers back up over the pillows, smoothing them down.

"That supposed to tell me something?" he asked.

"Have you finished eating?"

"For now. I'll probably have more later."

He took another sip of tea, emptying the cup. He toyed with it for a while, caressing the smooth porcelain, and then he smiled an enigmatic smile and set it down beside the tray. The heavy wave dipped over his brow. His eyes were dark, almost blue black in the dim light, and his face was brushed with shadows as the flames crackled behind the screen, tiny yellow-orange tongues avidly licking the log. The sash had come undone. The robe spilled behind him, one fold carelessly thrown over his thighs. I was so tense now I thought I might scream. I poured myself a glass of brandy, decided against it, set it down so smartly the liquor splashed over the brim.

"Why did you come here, Cam? *Why?*"

"I came for you, Miranda."

"After all this time? You expect me to believe that?"

He climbed slowly to his feet and the smooth black satin lining slipped and slid and he almost lost the robe. He gathered it around him again and tied the sash, ignoring my question, concentrating on the sash, and then he looked at me, cool and self-possessed. When he finally spoke, his voice was flat.

"Abandoning you was the gravest mistake of my life. I realized that immediately. I cursed myself. I damned myself for the world's biggest fool. I was a rebel, a wanted man, and I was damn near penniless—"

"You needn't have been. You needn't have taken that money and made arrangements with Bancroft to provide for me. I could have—"

"This is difficult enough as is, Miranda. I'll thank you not to interrupt me."

"You don't have to tell me anything. I just—I just want to get you out of here."

"I blamed you for that night. I convinced myself it was your fault things went wrong. I told myself that if you hadn't given me that drugged wine, if I had been there with the others, I could have—" He hesitated a moment, remembering, and then he continued in the same flat voice. "A few weeks in the court of the Bonnie Prince convinced me what bloody, idiotic fools we'd been in the first place, what mad folly our intrigues. I realized that if it hadn't been for you, I would probably have died a fool's death, to no cause. In short, I came to my senses."

I maintained an icy silence, gazing at him without expression.

"I missed you. I wanted you. My life was empty without you. I finally admitted to myself that I loved you, and I resented that, resented you for disrupting my life. I went to America, hoping to forget you. It didn't work. I knew I had to have you back, and I knew I had to make something of myself in order to be worthy of you—"

"So you became a smuggler," I said acidly.

"America is a wonderful country, but a man needs to have a solid stake if he wants to succeed there, really succeed. I returned to France, I looked around, I saw that smuggling goods over to England would be the quickest way for me to make the kind of money I needed. I've made a great deal, and it's all been transferred to a bank in Philadelphia."

Another candle spluttered out. Only three were left burning now, and shadows danced over the walls as the flames leaped and spluttered, wax popping. Cam moved across the room toward me, the robe swaying, rustling. My heart was beating rapidly. My wrists felt weak, as though the weight of my hands were too much for them, and my knees were weak as well. I couldn't go on standing much longer. I was going to collapse any moment now.

"I had originally thought of purchasing a tobacco plantation," he continued, "but a few months ago I met a gentleman from Philadelphia who owns a newspaper and wants to sell it. I've made arrangements to buy it."

"You—you're going to run a newspaper?"

"Far more fitting than raising tobacco. America—the spirit there is young and fresh and vigorous. No one cares who you are, where you come from. They're fiercely independent, and they're already beginning to resent the yoke imposed on them by a distant monarch. The life there, the people—it's a remarkable place, Miranda, constantly growing. I want to be part of that growth. I want to make a new start in a new country, and I want you at my side."

"I have my own life now, Cam."

~515~

"I'm fully aware of that."

"I have a home, a brother, a—a profession I intend to continue. I'm going to keep on writing books. I—"

"They publish books in America, too."

"You've got a—a hell of a nerve, thinking I'd give up all I've worked for to go traipsing—you're out of your bleedin' mind! You left me. You damn near wrecked my life! I loved you, you sod, and—"

"You love me still."

"I detest you!"

"You're lying, Miranda."

He took hold of my shoulders. I tried to pull away. His fingers tightened, squeezing my flesh so forcefully I gasped. I wanted to fight him again, hit him, hurt him, but I was too weak, too weak. Cam looked into my eyes, his own full of cool determination.

"I made my money. I made arrangements to purchase the newspaper. I intended to come to London for you, and then I happened to see the London paper and discovered you were in Cornwall. I decided to make one last crossing with the smugglers, since they'd be landing not thirty miles from here—"

"Risking your bloody neck!"

"I was fully aware of the risk."

"And came charging ahead! You're a bloody fool, Cam Gordon!"

"I well may be, probably am, but I happen to love you, Miranda. There, I've said it, and it hurt like hell, but I'll say it again—I love you."

I caught my breath. The weakness vanished, and I was filled with exultation and glorious new strength. I pulled away from him. I rubbed my shoulders where his fingers had squeezed so tightly.

"It took you bloody long enough," I snapped.

He scowled, ire destroying his cool self-possession. His eyes flashed with the old anger. His nostrils flared. I backed away, elated.

"Goddammit, Miranda!" he roared. "I risk my fool life getting to you! I stumble into a trap, barely getting out of it with my skin intact! I spend two days roaming the countryside without food, I hide in a foul, damp cave and slip past a battalion of soldiers in the middle of a raging storm and then I pour my heart out to you and you make a snippy little— god*damn* you!"

"I didn't ask you to do any of those things."

"You aggravating, exasperating, infuriating little *bitch*! I must be out of my mind!"

"I've often said so."

I had gone too far. Fury possessed him. He lunged for me, the robe flying behind him. I cried out. He seized me and I felt sure he was going to strangle me and then he slammed his mouth over mine and crushed me to him and devoured my lips with his own. I struggled viciously, playing the old game, and he subdued me savagely and I caught his hair in my hands and pulled and then let go and ran my palms over his shoulders and down his back and finally clasped him to me as a thousand sensations shattered inside. He kissed me again, again, his lips moving to my throat, the curve of my shoulder, the swell of my bosom, and I held on, a captive now to those sensations that had been dormant so long, so long, sensations he alone could summon. Leaning back against the arm curled tightly around my waist, I caressed the back of his neck and ran my fingers through that thick silky black hair, lost, lost, spinning in a shimmering void of ecstacy.

My Scot, my savage Scot, mine again, here in my arms, not in my dreams, his body solid and strong and charged with energy, his lips firm and warm and burning my skin, covering mine again, parting them, his tongue thrusting, my senses reeling, reeling, reality receding, nothing real but the bliss of the moment and the splendor spreading through my veins. He let go of me and I staggered and almost fell and he took my shoulders and turned me around and began to fumble with the tiny hooks in back of my gown, impatient, all thumbs, unable to get them unfastened, finally succeeding, peeling the bodice down, my breasts swelling, nipples straining against their prison of cloth, satin rustling as he tugged at the gown, pulling it down over my waist. I moved my hands down, helping him, stepping out of the circle of satin, wearing only the frail petticoat now, the gauzy skirts billowing, ruffles aflutter as he whirled me back around and gathered me into his arms again and kissed me anew.

Splendor spread, melting into an urgent ache that grew and grew until the torment was beyond endurance, swelling inside, sending me into a delirium that would surely shatter me to pieces if it weren't soon assuaged. He caught both thin straps of my petticoat and jerked them down sharply and my breasts burst free of their final restraint. I writhed in his arms as he tugged and pulled at the petticoat, the cloth tearing. He sank to his knees, bringing the gauzy layers with him, tearing at them until they finally fell away and I was naked, trembling, tormented. He clasped the back of my calves and began to move his hands upward, kissing my legs, clasping my buttocks now, squeezing them tightly, his lips moving higher, burning. I swayed and caught his hair and tugged violently, slowly drawing him up, up, and he kissed my stomach, my navel, each breast. I parted my lips and threw my head back, hair spilling behind me, and he kissed the side of my throat and lifted me up into his arms and carried me to the bed and stretched me across it, the pillows to my right, the footboard to my left.

The last candle spluttered out and there was only firelight as he stood at the side of the bed, looking down at me. I arched my back, the satin counterpane smooth and slippery beneath me. He shrugged his shoulders. The robe fell to the floor with a soft crumpling noise and he stood naked, erect, as lost as I, caught up in a private furor that demanded immediate release. His mouth was tight, his cheekbones taut. His eyes gleamed darkly. The log in the fireplace glowed hot orange-pink, crackling, breaking in two. Fiery sparks showered as he fell atop me and caught my wrists and spread them and plunged into my body with a mighty thrust that caused me to cry out. I threw my legs up and locked them around his buttocks as the mattress sagged and the springs squeaked in a wild, shrieking symphony and he thrust again, again, and the counterpane began to slip and our bodies began to slide and we spilled to the floor, locked together, entangled in folds of satin, barely noticing as senses shredded and wave after wave swept over us and sent us crashing onto that blissful shore of completion.

Later, much later, he sat in front of the fireplace again, contentedly devouring the last of the apricot tarts, a fresh log burning brightly and filling the room with cozy warmth. Wearing my brother's now sadly rumpled robe, he was totally absorbed and didn't notice when I came back in from my dressing room in a thin white cotton nightgown. Ablutions performed, I lighted a few candles and picked up my gown and petticoat and put them away in the wardrobe. Cam finished the tart, licked his fingers one by one and then looked up, lazy and lethargic.

"You ruined my petticoat," I informed him.

"You're a rich woman," he drawled. "You can afford a new one."

"I see you've eaten the rest of the food."

"Yeah. I could sure use another cup of tea. There's some left, but it's stone cold."

"I suppose you expect me to traipse downstairs and make a fresh pot."

"Wouldn't hurt you," he replied.

"I'm no longer your servant, Mr. Gordon. People wait on *me* now."

"La de dah," he mocked. "Who'd have thought it? I pick up a dirty-faced, foul-mouthed little urchin and bring her into my home and she turns out to have blood bluer than mine."

"Considerably bluer, you sod."

Moving over to the dressing table, I sat down in front of the glass, picked up my brush and began to brush my hair. I felt bruised and battered, aching all over with that wonderful ache of afterglow, but sanity had returned and, with it, calm resolution. I ran the brush through the long coppery red waves that glistened with dark gold in the candlelight. It had stopped raining some time ago, but rain still dripped from the eaves with a steady, monotonous patter. He drew his knees up and folded his arms around them, watching me. I could see his reflection in the glass, firelight behind him.

"I've missed that," he said idly, nodding toward the bed.

"It's been three and a half years, Cam. Don't try to tell me there haven't been other women."

"I won't. None of them were like you."

"How many?"

"One or two."

"You lying bastard."

"Five or six, then. Bored me terribly. You've spoiled me for any other woman, you minx."

I set the brush down and placed my hands behind my neck and lifted the heavy waves up, the silky weight soft in my palms. Sighing, I let them fall to my shoulders, dark gold gleaming. My eyes were a dark sapphire in the glass, lids coated with mauve gray shadows, and my skin seemed to glow, cheeks tinted a soft pink. How was I going to send him away? I had to be strong. I had to be very strong ... but where was the strength to come from?

"What about you?" he inquired. "You must have been very

~519~

much in demand after the book came out—young, beautiful, wealthy, famous overnight. I suppose the men flocked around you in droves."

"They did, indeed."

"That sod Garrick in particular."

"Davy in particular," I said. "He wanted to marry me."

"Bloody sod. Wish I'd flattened him when I had the chance."

"There've been no other men, Cam," I said quietly. "I can't give myself unless—unless there's deep feeling."

"And I've spoiled you for any other man."

He stood up. Folds of heavy navy-blue brocade rustled as he moved over to stand directly behind me, our eyes meeting in the glass. He placed his hands on my bare shoulders and began to gently rub my flesh.

"You're coming to America with me," he said.

"No, Cam."

"I've already booked passage on *Le Dauphine*—it sails from Cherbourg two weeks from now. I booked passage for both of us, Miranda."

"You assumed a great deal."

His thumbs pressed against the back of my neck, his fingers kneading the flesh on either side. His eyes in the glass were tender, filled with emotions I had never seen there before. Was it possible that he had really changed? I arched my back as his thumbs slid down to press against my spine, stirring the ashes of aftermath, causing them to glow warmer. A honey-sweet languor filled me, spreading slowly, building.

"I couldn't leave without you, Miranda."

"You'll have to, Cam. I have a new life, and—and I'm very pleased with it. I'm not going to—" I closed my eyes, praying for strength. "I'm not going to throw it away for—for folly—"

He was leaning over me now, his lips brushing my earlobe, his knuckles running up and down my spine.

"Stop, Cam. Please stop."

"I've missed you. God, I've missed you."

He curled an arm around my throat, resting his lean cheek against mine. I smelled his hair, his skin. I trembled with longing, and I knew I must resist. I must. I must.

"I'm not going to be hurt again, Cam."

"I'd never hurt you," he murmured.

"I—I survived it once. Somehow I managed to get over

what you did to me and put the pieces back together and get on with my life, but I—I couldn't do it again."

"Words. Mere words. You love me."

Taking hold of my shoulders, he turned me around so that I was facing him. Candlelight flickered. The fire crackled. He pulled me to my feet and held me loosely.

"You love me," he repeated.

"I don't deny it. I'm not pleased about it, but—yes, I love you, and I wish to hell I didn't. It would be much easier that way."

The arm around my waist drew me closer, my thighs against his. I felt his manhood, swollen, throbbing, pressing against me. He kissed my temple, cupping my chin in his free hand and tilting my head back so that I was forced to look into his eyes.

"I'll run the newspaper, and it will be the best newspaper in America and I will be a solid, respectable citizen, Mr. James Ingram—that's the name I've been using—and we'll have a fine house and you can go on writing your novels and I'll write brilliant editorials and—"

"No, Cam."

"And you will be the beautiful Mrs. James Ingram and I the envy of every man in Philadelphia."

I didn't answer. I looked away from him, visualizing it, knowing it was a dream that couldn't be. He hadn't changed. He was still a rebel at heart, athirst for adventure, and he would meet like kind in America and they would conspire against the distant monarch and there would be trouble and I couldn't survive another heartbreak.

"I've just asked you to marry me, Miranda."

"It would never work, Cam."

He kissed me then, a long, lazy kiss, gathering me closer, and I felt my bones ache and my blood tingle as the splendor spread anew. I made a valiant effort to fight it, trembling inside, and he lifted his head and looked into my eyes and smiled. I shook my head as he took my shoulders and slowly backed me toward the bed.

"Guess I'll have to persuade you," he crooned.

"It—it's almost dawn—" My voice was barely audible. "You—you must get dressed and—"

The back of my knees touched the mattress, gave way, and he gently shoved me down until I was stretched on the bed,

~521~

my breasts swelling against the beribboned white bodice. He stood back, silhouetted against the candlelight, my tormentor, my fate. He reached up, catching the lapels of the robe and parting them. The robe slipped from his shoulders and dropped softly to the floor.

"I love you," he said huskily, "and you love me. There's no other woman in the world for me—no other man for you. I think we established that rather conclusively a while ago. Guess we'll have to establish it anew."

"No, Cam—" I pleaded.

He blew out the candles and moved back over to the bed in the light of the fire and sat down beside me and pulled me up into his arms and brushed his lips lightly over my brow.

"Once more," he murmured.

"It won't make any dif—"

"Once more, Miranda."

37

A DIM GRAY LIGHT FILLED THE HOUSE, COLORS NOT yet distinct, as I moved upstairs with the coffee I had prepared in the kitchen. None of the servants were up at this early hour, and the house was very still, so silent my footsteps seemed to bang loudly, though I moved almost stealthily, and the rustle of my silk skirts was like the crackle of dry leaves. Pale white rays slanted in through the windows at the end of the hall upstairs, wavering white spokes swirling with motes of dust. Darkness had melted away, but the sun hadn't yet appeared to dissolve the predawn gray. I moved slowly down the hall, balancing the tray carefully, walls a dark gray, almost black, floor ashy gray, bright gray-white where pools of light spilled and spread. Reality is gray, and this is reality, I thought. Last night was fury and fireworks and splendor, but night is over now and now I must face the gray reality.

Reality was fifty soldiers scouring the countryside, at least half a dozen watching the house. Reality was Captain Jon Ramsey, determined to capture the man in my bedroom. I had put him off yesterday, but I had no doubt he would be back, perhaps this morning. Somehow I had to get Cam out of the house and safely on his way to France. At the moment I had no idea how I was going to do it, but I had no doubt I would manage it. I had saved him once before, and I would save him now, doing whatever I must, whatever the risk, whatever the cost. Cam wasn't going to be captured. No. I would save him somehow, and he would leave the country and I would never see him again. I had made my decision, and that was reality, too. The madness and magic and marvel of the night had stolen my senses, had transported me into a realm of quivering emotions, but emotion was contained now, under tight control, and I was able to use my head.

Cam had fallen into a heavy sleep soon after our second tryst, arms wrapped around me, one leg thrown over mine as of old, and I had lain awake listening to his breathing, smelling his skin, his sweat, savoring the warmth of his body and the discomfort as he stirred in his sleep and bones dug into my flesh and weight crushed down. I made no effort to disentangle myself. I stared at the darkness and wept silently and made the only decision I could sensibly make, and after a while, as black gradually faded to gray, I finally got up and put another log on the fire and heated water and bathed and brushed my hair and put on this low-cut bronze silk gown with its off-the-shoulder puffed sleeves and tight waist, skirt spreading out over layers of bronze underskirts, vain enough to want to look my best during our last hours together, and then I had gone downstairs to make the coffee.

I stepped into the bedroom, closed the door behind me and set the tray down on the dressing table. The fire was burning low. Wavering spokes of hazy white light slanted in through the windows with just the faintest touch of orange pink now, a bare suggestion of color. Cam was still sleeping heavily, his legs twisted in the bedcovers, his head buried in a pillow he clutched tightly, as though it were a wrestling partner he had vanquished after great exertion. His naked back glistened with a thin layer of moisture, and his hair was damp, too, darker, the heavy locks like black, black ink spilling over his brow and clinging damply to the back of his neck. I poured myself a cup of coffee. He moaned in his sleep and scowled, shifting position, clinging to the pillow and kicking the bedcovers off his legs.

The room was warm. I opened a window. A bird warbled in the distance. The sun was beginning to rise, pale red and gold banners spreading on the horizon. I went back to the dressing table and sat on the stool and sipped my coffee, watching him sleep. I was calm and composed and filled with resolve, but that resolve wavered as I remembered the second time and the lazy deliberation of his lovemaking and the incredible tenderness that was a marvel of restraint. Intent only on my own pleasure, he had given as he had never given before, murmuring lovely words all the while, and it had gone on and on until rapture became blissful agony that sent me into a shuddering oblivion of ecstacy. He did love me, yes. He had convinced me of that, but it didn't change things. I mustn't let it. I must listen to my head and heed not my heart.

The slanting rays were pale pink-orange now, no longer white, and gray began to vanish. I set my cup down in the saucer. It rattled loudly. Cam snorted and scowled and opened his eyes. He pulled himself into a sitting position and rested his back against the headboard and blinked, shoving damp locks from his brow. The light was growing stronger by the moment, bright pink-orange changing to misty gold, gold fading to silver. Cam looked at me sleepily and blinked again and smiled. He patted the mattress beside him. I shook my head. He frowned. Pouring a cup of coffee, I took it to him and then sat back down on the stool as the light grew brighter still. He took a sip of coffee.

"Delicious," he said. "Strong, too, just like I like it. You remembered, didn't you?"

"Hurry up and finish it. You have to get dressed. We have to get you out of here."

"Your voice is terribly crisp."

"I'm sorry. Drink your coffee."

"No eggs? No toast? No kippered herring?"

"There isn't time."

"You look cool and calm and frightfully efficient this morning," he told me. "You also look incredibly lovely. Your hair's like copper fire in this light, and that bronze gown—I'll never be able to afford to buy you dresses like that when we get to America. You'll have to pay for your own clothes."

I said nothing. He drank his coffee, looking at me with fond eyes. I felt a sharp pang and got up and bustled about, picking up my brother's navy blue robe, tossing it onto the bed, straightening things, fussing. I folded his clothes and placed them in a chair and picked up his boots. Flecks of dried mud scattered onto the hearth. I put the boots down and turned and Cam held out his empty coffee cup.

"One more cup," I snapped. "You'll have to drink it quickly."

"You angry about something?"

I refilled his cup, handed it to him. "No, Cam, I'm not angry."

"Why the brisk manner? Why the clipped voice?"

"I'm trying to be sensible. One of us has to be. You seem completely oblivious to the fact that you're a wanted man, condemned to a certain painful death if captured. You seem indifferent to the fact that Cumberland's personal agent is on your trail and is very likely to show up here with a band of soldiers. Forgive me if I'm not up to breezy chatter."

"There's something else," he said.

He set the cup of coffee on the night table and got up and pulled the dressing robe around him, his eyes never leaving mine as he fastened the sash. His expression was grave, and I could sense anger beneath the surface. I wasn't up to a scene. I couldn't handle one. I silently pleaded with him to let it drop, but he was determined to bring it out into the open.

"You've made your decision, haven't you?"

"Yes, Cam." My voice was weary.

"I'm not leaving without you, Miranda."

"You'll have to."

"But—" His eyes were puzzled. "Last night—I thought we settled—"

"We settled nothing, Cam. Last night was—was nothing but wild, extravagant emotion. It always was with us. There's more to life than that. I can't live on my nerves. I can't live in—in a constant turmoil of emotion, and that's the way it would be, the way it always was."

"You love me, Miranda."

"Yes—yes, I do, and I probably always will, but I have my own identity now. It took me a very long time to establish that identity, Cam, to be able to live my *own* life, not—not a life wrapped up entirely in you. I can't turn back now. I can't throw away everything I've worked so hard to build."

The anger was there beneath the surface, and he was trying hard to control it. His jaw was tight. A vein throbbed at his temple. His eyes were dark, a line between his brows. He hadn't understood a word I said, hadn't even tried to understand, was instead prepared for another explosive scene, and that in itself was proof of what I had said earlier. Life with Cam would be ever tumultuous, filled with exhilarating highs and shattering lows, as before, and I hadn't the strength to endure it.

"There's a bowl of warm water in my dressing room," I said. "There's soap, towels and a razor as well. You—you probably want to wash up and shave before you leave."

"Miranda—"

"I'm not going to argue, Cam." My voice was calm now, cold. "I suggest you save your strength."

"Last night meant nothing to you then?"

I steeled myself. "I had a lovely time," I said.

He looked at me for a long moment, wounded, wanting to strike back, and then he moved past me without a word and stepped into the dressing room and closed the door. Silver yellow light flooded the room now. I stood very still, willing the emotions away, refusing to let them take hold. There was a commotion downstairs. I frowned, listening. A few minutes passed and then there were footsteps in the hall outside and a knock on my bedroom door. I opened it. Ned stood in the hall in neatly brushed black uniform and white silk neckcloth. His expression was unperturbed, but I could sense a contained excitement.

"What—what is it, Ned?"

"I'm afraid it's Ramsey, Lady M. He's waiting on the front steps with seven men, determined to search the house. The house, incidentally, is completely surrounded. His whole force is out there."

"I see."

"I've put him off for a while. I told him Lord M. would have to grant permission, that he would be returning within the hour. Ramsey agreed to wait, most reluctantly, I might add. I've taken the liberty of sending a carriage for Lord M."

"Douglas has his horse. He won't need—"

"I'm fully aware of that," Ned said. "I have a plan, Lady M."

"You—you know?"

"I saw you bringing him upstairs last night. I have no great love for redcoats, Lady M., no great love for the Hanovers, either, for that matter, Cumberland, in particular. If you'll allow me, I—uh—I think I might arrange things to your satisfaction."

"Ned—"

"There's a tunnel, Lady M., a secret tunnel. Lord M. doesn't even know about it. It came in very handy during the late civil conflict. The Mowreys were ardent loyalists, you know, and Cornwall was overrun with Roundheads. There's also a priest's hole behind a secret panel in the east wing, but I don't believe we'll be needing that. Better to get him out of the house as soon as possible."

There was a faint spark of excitement in those dark brown eyes, but his voice was perfectly flat. He might have been discussing the breakfast menu. Once again his strength gave strength to me, and his calm helped me to remain calm. I took a deep breath and forced back the panic.

"The tunnel is in the wine cellar, behind a rack. It's quite long, leads to an abandoned tin mine half a mile from here. The carriage will be waiting there. Mr. Gordon and I will drive to a fishing village fifteen miles up the coast where I have a good friend. He has a big boat, certainly big enough to cross the Channel. I believe he's done it quite a number of times, in fact, not always legally, I fear."

"Thank God for you, Ned. Thank God for you."

"I thought we might plan a—uh—little diversion for Captain Ramsey to put him off the scent. You know young Tim, of course."

"The new footman you hired last week?"

"An able lad—a second cousin of mine, I may as well confess it, but he needed a job and I've always had a soft spot for his mother. The important point is—he's a stranger to these parts, hasn't even been down to the village yet, and he's extremely tall and lean and has an unruly mop of pitch black hair. He's only nineteen, but he looks older."

"Surely you're not suggesting we—" I shook my head. "I couldn't permit you to expose him to—"

"There'll be no danger involved. As you know, a coach leaves the inn at nine o'clock. Young Tim will leave the house on an errand, wearing his uniform, everything above suspicion. He'll walk right past the soldiers, and once he's clear of the house he'll remove his uniform, under which he'll be wearing Gordon's clothes. He'll continue to the village, purchase a ticket to Dover and, at the proper time, Ramsey will receive word that a tall black-haired chap fitting Gordon's description has taken the coach to Dover and they'll be off in hot pursuit."

"And when they overtake it?"

"They won't. It's a very fast coach. My man in the village won't bring word for at least four hours. Ramsey'll go to the inn, confirm the report and take off at a fast gallop, taking his men with him. Young Tim will idle away a day in Dover, an innocent country youth, and return in his own good time."

"I don't know, Ned. It's—"

"I suggest you leave everything to me, Lady M.," he said, and his voice was firm. "I've had a—uh—certain amount of experience in these things. If you'll give me the gentleman's clothes, I'll take them down to Tim and bring some of Lord M.'s garments for your friend."

I hesitated only a moment, then picked up Cam's clothes and gave them to Ned. He nodded politely and ambled non-chalantly down the hall. I closed the door, turning to find Cam standing in the doorway of the dressing room, freshly shaven, hair neatly brushed, as cool and unperturbed as Ned had been.

"You heard?" I asked.

"I heard."

"The house is surrounded, Cam. The soldiers—"

"I heard, Miranda," he said sharply. "Hysterics aren't going to help."

"I'm not hysterical. Not in the least. Oh, God, I knew this was going to happen. We've got to get you out of here, Cam. Oh, God. You should never have come. You should never have risked it."

"How trustworthy is this servant of yours?"

"I'd trust him with my life."

"Then I suppose I'll have to trust him with mine," he said calmly.

Standing there in the brilliant silver-yellow sunlight in my brother's dressing robe, the light burnishing his sleek black hair, he looked at me without emotion, his manner icy and remote. He had been deeply hurt and he had retreated behind that invisible wall and it was just as well, I thought, just as well. There was so much more I wanted to say, but words would be futile now. Cam went back into the dressing room, and Ned returned a few minutes later with my brother's maroon frock coat and breeches and other garments. I was so tense I couldn't stand still, couldn't sit down, couldn't bear another moment of inactivity. I took Cam's dirty boots and carried them downstairs and cleaned and polished them myself, scandalizing the footman who brought me brush and polish.

Polly intercepted me on the stairs as I was going back up with boots in hand. Her eyes were wide with excitement as she breathlessly informed me that a dangerous criminal was on the loose and that Captain who was 'ere yesterday thought 'e might've snuck into the 'ouse last night durin' th' storm an' all them soldiers were goin' to search th' 'ouse just as soon as Lord M. got back an' gave 'em permission an' it was so upsettin' she just didn't know what to *do* with 'erself.

"They're outside right now, waitin' for Lord M., an' a restless lot of brutes they are, too, ma'am. That captain's pacin' up an' down, slappin' th' side of 'is boot with 'is ridin' crop. I do wish Lord M.'d 'urry! A murderin' smuggler might be lurkin' in th' attics this very minute!"

"I seriously doubt that, Polly."

"Oh, Lady M., what're we goin' to *do*?"

"We're going to cooperate with the soldiers," I informed her. "Tell Cook to make several pots of coffee, and when it's ready I want you and Nan to take it out and serve it to the soldiers. It's a chilly morning."

"Nan'd *love* that!" Polly exclaimed. "She's been peekin' out th' windows all this time, sayin' 'ow 'andsome some of them redcoats are. Me, now, I find all of 'em upsettin', even that red'aired chap with th' broad shoulders an' wicked brown eyes, but if I 'ave to go out there an' talk to 'em and serve 'em coffee an' all I guess I *will*."

She scurried back down the stairs, more excited than ever, and I returned to the bedroom and found Cam fully dressed except for his boots, cool and wonderfully handsome in the maroon frock coat and breeches, the white satin waistcoat embroidered with black and maroon silk flowers and the creamy white silk neckcloth. The clothes fit remarkably well, although the coat was a bit loose. Silently, I handed him the boots. He sat down on the dressing stool and pulled them on, the heavy black wave spilling over his brow as he leaned down.

"Do you have any money?" I asked quietly.

"Not a cent."

"I'll give you some."

"No, Miranda."

"Don't be so goddamned stubborn!" I snapped.

He stood up and shoved the wave from his brow. I stepped

over to the bureau and took out the flat leather purse I kept in the top drawer, remembering the ginger jar we had kept on the mantel in the old days. The purse was thick with folded notes, at least a hundred pounds, probably more, I didn't bother to look. Cam took it without a word and put it in his inside coat pocket. I could hear a horse galloping up the drive, the sound muted, barely audible. Several moments passed. Neither of us spoke, the invisible wall high between us.

"I'll return the money," he said finally. His voice was clipped.

"You needn't bother."

"I'll send it to Bancroft, he can forward it to you. I'll send enough to pay your brother for these clothes as well."

"You *are* a cold son of a bitch, Cam Gordon."

"You made your decision, Miranda. I suppose you have your reasons for making the decision you did, but don't expect me to reciprocate with tender avowals of eternal love. Don't expect me to plead."

"I don't expect a bloody thing from you."

"If you should happen to change your mind, I'll be sailing from Cherbourg in two weeks on *Le Dauphine*, as I informed you last night. Passage has been booked for you already."

His voice was dry, indifferent. It might have been a knife blade, each word stabbing my heart, but I showed no reaction whatsoever. My expression was as icy as his own. We might have been strangers, cold and aloof, scarcely able to tolerate the other's presence, and only last night we. . . . I mustn't think about last night. There was a smudge of black boot polish on my thumb. I wiped it off, and Cam stepped over to the mirror to adjust the folds of the creamy white silk neckcloth. I was going to scream. I couldn't help myself.

There was an urgent knock on the door. I hurried to open it, and when I did I heard loud voices in the hall downstairs and the sound of many footsteps. The noise rose up the stairwell and reverberated against the walls. I could feel my cheeks turn pale. Ramsey was barking orders. I recognized his voice. The footsteps stamped and shuffled and banged. I was weak, dizzy. I was going to faint. Cam stepped behind me and gripped the back of my elbow tightly and looked over my head at Ned.

"They're in the house," Ned said. "We'll have to hurry."

"Right," Cam said.

"Oh, God," I whispered. "Oh, God."

"Pull yourself together, Miranda!"

~530~

"No need for alarm, Lady M. We'll take the back stairs."

Cam pulled me aside and stepped into the hall with Ned. "Stay here in your room," he said curtly, "and try not to give us away. One look at your face——" He cut himself short as heavy footsteps pounded up the stairs.

"I'm afraid she'll have to come with us to the wine cellar," Ned told him. "Someone will have to swing the wine rack back into place after we've gone into the tunnel."

Cam seized my hand. "Come along, then, and be quick about it!"

My heart was beating rapidly and I was dizzier than ever as Cam squeezed my hand and jerked it and we hurried down the hall with Ned leading the way. Footsteps grew louder, louder, banging on the stairs. There must be at least three soldiers. They would burst into the hall any second now. They would see us! I gasped, stumbled, almost lost my footing. Cam jerked my hand again, pulling me along behind him. My bronze skirt swirled, rustling with a noisy crackle. The back stairs were at the very end of the hall, to the left, wide stone steps that led down into the enormous back hall below. We'd never make it! I heard their voices now, the gruff, excited voices of hunters eager for prey. Ned darted to the left and Cam gave my wrist a mighty tug and we were standing in the shadows at the top of the stairs and the soldiers were tromping down the hall.

"Stay here," Ned whispered. "Stay quiet."

Cam flattened himself against the far wall and pulled me beside him as Ned ambled casually back into the hall to intercept the soldiers who were moving in our direction, footsteps tromping heavily. My breath came in short gasps. My bosom rose and fell. I was shivering. Cam scowled and curled an arm around my shoulder, holding me firmly. He might have been made of stone.

"You there!" a voice barked. It was frightfully near.

"I'm the butler, sir, Brown's my name. I've just come up the back stairs. Lord Mowrey has asked me to assist you gentlemen any way I can. I imagine you're looking for the staircase leading to the attics."

"Skulking around, appearing out of nowhere, I don't like the looks of him one bit!" another voice boomed. "Looks like he's hiding something!"

"Oh, no, sir," Ned protested. His voice was exceedingly

servile, full of injured innocence. "I've just been comforting
one of the maids. Scared out of her wits, she is, said she heard
something in the attics as she was bringing up the linen. I told
her there was nothing to worry about now that you gentlemen
were here."

"Heard something in the attic, did she?" the first voice
inquired.

"Claims she did, but the girl's a nonsensical sort, always
seeing ghosts on the staircase, hearing chains rattling. Me, I'm
certain no one could be in the attics, no way he could have
gotten up there without someone—"

"He's hiding something!" the second voice roared.

"Come off it, Kemp," a third soldier said. "Chap's just a
butler. You're as bloody-minded as Ramsey, wasting our time
like this. Gordon's probably halfway to France by now."

Gordon was no more than ten yards away, leaning against
the wall at the top of the stairs, stony-faced, tense. My heart
was pounding, pounding so loudly I felt sure they would hear.
I caught my breath, and Cam's arm tightened brutally around
my shoulder. He clamped a hand over my mouth. I couldn't
breathe at all then. Panic possessed me. Everything began to
grow black.

"Where are these famous attics?" the first soldier asked.
"How do we get up to 'em?"

"The staircase is at the other end of the hall, a narrow
wooden staircase, you can't miss it. I'd be happy to go up with
you, sir. Make me something of a hero to the maids, it would,
if someone *was* up there and I was with—"

"That won't be necessary!" he snapped. "Come on, Rogers.
Come on, Kemp. Let's get on with it. Ramsey says we're to
go over every bleeding inch of the place. We'll probably be
here all day!"

"I still think he's—"

"Come along, Kemp! That's an order!"

The hand clamped relentlessly against my mouth, the edge
of the index finger blocking my nostrils, cutting off air, the
ball of the thumb pressing painfully against the side of my
nose. A black fog enveloped me, growing denser and darker,
swallowing me up. My limbs were numb. My lungs were afire.
I was going to die here and now if he didn't remove his hand.
I tried to struggle, but I couldn't move. I was becoming part
of the fog now, drifting, drifting off into blackness, and far,

~532~

far away, as in the haziest dream, I heard footsteps receding and saw a misty black shape moving toward me.

"Pardon, sir, but I believe you're suffocating her," Ned observed.

"Oh?" Cam said.

He removed his hand from my mouth. I gulped precious air and my knees gave way and I slumped forward and he caught me and held me as my head whirled and the fog still swirled black around me. Several moments passed as I gulped and panted, limp in his arms, unable to stand. My head gradually cleared and blood began to course through my veins and the numbness wore off. I pulled myself away from him, stumbling. Ned gripped my arm, supporting me. We could hear the redcoats tromping off down the hall, footsteps far away now.

"Careless of me," Cam remarked.

"You're bleedin' right it was!" I hissed viciously. "I've 'alf a mind to turn you over to 'em, you wretched sod!"

Ned arched his brow, surprised by my language and startled by the St. Giles accent to which I had unconsciously reverted. Cam's face was as stony as it had been before, and I longed to cover it with bloody claw marks. I panted, regaining my strength little by little as air filled my lungs. I finally pulled free of Ned's grip and shoved a heavy wave from my temple.

"I'm all right now," I said in patrician tones. "I suggest we move on. I want to get this son of a bitch out of the house as soon as possible."

"Very well, milady."

Ned led the way down the wide stone steps. The staircase was enclosed, and there was very little light, dark gray shadows filling the well, a dim square of light at the bottom. We descended slowly, cautiously, Cam at my side, Ned moving in front of us. The house was full of soldiers. I could hear them calling to one another, opening doors, moving from room to room. The narrow door leading to the front hall was opened. Ned threw up his arm. We froze, perhaps ten steps from the bottom. Footsteps crunched on the rush matting below, and I could see three pair of legs, all that was visible from this angle, two clad in white breeches, boots gleaming, the other in blue breeches, white silk stockings, and elegant black pumps.

"Just a big, empty hall," my brother said. "Couldn't see anyone trying to hide back here, but you're free to search."

"We intend to!"

~533~

"I say, do you really think this chap might be in the house? Hope my sister's not too upset. I imagine she's still in her room—it's frightfully early."

"Ain't no one back here, Peters."

"Look behind that big chest over there, Barnes. A man could easily crouch back there."

"Disconcerting, this, arriving home to find a troop of soldiers camping on my front steps, hearing a dangerous criminal might be lurking inside. Gave me quite a turn."

"He ain't behind th' chest, Peters."

"Look inside it!" Peters ordered.

"Sure, Andy, I'll do that. Maybe he's a bloomin' midget."

"Well, you mates search to your heart's content," Douglas said. "I'll go back to the drawing room and see if I can charm your Captain Ramsey. Uncommunicative chap, that one, just said he needed permission to search the house and he wasn't going to take no for an answer. Why should I refuse him permission? If a dangerous criminal's crouching in the cupboard, I'd *want* you to find him."

"Ain't *in* the chest either, Andy."

Douglas sauntered back into the front hall and the two soldiers continued to prowl around the hall and we stood on the steps, half hidden in the shadows. Cam and Ned were both tense, prepared to fight it out if necessary. An eternity seemed to pass before the legs were visible again at the foot of the stairs. Ned and Cam exchanged glances. Cam hooked his arm in front of him and drew it back sharply, silently suggesting a possible maneuver. Ned hesitated, then nodded, and they prepared to creep down and take the soldiers by surprise.

"You stand guard here, Barnes," Peters ordered. "He might try to slip out this way. I'll go back up front and see if they need any help searching the pantries."

"Sure, Andy, you do that, and give that plump little brunette a kiss for me, you hear?"

"None of your lip, Barnes! I'm your senior, and don't you forget it!"

"One bloody stripe and he's a bleedin' tyrant. Shove it, mate."

Peters stalked out, slamming the narrow door behind him, and Barnes stood at the foot of the stairs with his back to us, humming to himself and tapping a toe restlessly. Ned started to move down. I grabbed his arm, restraining him. Cam shot me a furious look.

"I'll distract him," I whispered. "When I have his attention, you two can slip on down to the wine cellar. I'll join you there."

"Don't be a fool!" Cam hissed.

"Sod you," I retorted.

I marched noisily on down the steps, and the poor soldier was so startled he dropped his rifle. He fumbled to retrieve it, terrified, certain his throat was going to be slit. I stepped into the hall and gave him a questioning look as he pointed the rifle at me. He had very broad shoulders, bright red hair and brown eyes that were wide with alarm and not at all wicked. Barnes was obviously the soldier who had caught Polly's fancy when she and Nan had been tittering behind the window curtains.

"Surely you're not going to shoot me?" I said.

"Uh—Jesus! No—no, ma'am, I wouldn't think of it, it's just you gave me a terrible fright. You—you must be—"

"I'm Lady Miranda."

"Beg your pardon, I'm sure," he said, lowering his rifle. "There's nothing to worry about, ma'am. We have everything under control. If he's here, we'll flush him out for sure."

He couldn't be more than twenty-one or -two, I thought, and he clearly had no idea I was supposed to be in league with the wanted man. He tried to look stern and reassuring as I glanced apprehensively around the hall. I told him I thought I had heard the back door banging last night during the storm and asked him if he would help me check the lock. He leaped at the chance, following me as I led the way to the other end of the hall. Leaning over the lock, he tested the doorknob and made a great show of male efficiency, and I saw Cam and Ned slip down the remaining stairs and disappear around a distant corner.

"Looks all right to me," Barnes said, giving the knob a tug. "Lock's a bit loose, but it's holding."

Playing the vulnerable female, I managed to look both confused and relieved, and Barnes grinned, extremely pleased with himself. I gave him a gracious smile and thanked him profusely and then looked helpless and disturbed and said I had left my book on the seat under the far trellis yesterday afternoon and hoped it hadn't been ruined in the storm and, oh, dear, I'd like to go fetch it but I was afraid the ground might be muddy and ruin my shoes. Barnes responded promptly, predictably, gallantly offering to retrieve the book, and I was overwhelmed and thanked him again, even more profusely, and he opened the door and headed toward the trellis I had pointed out to him.

Hurrying down the hall, I felt a great relief. Barnes wouldn't find a book, of course, and he was likely to find himself in trouble for leaving his post, but my little ruse had probably saved his life. Cam and Ned had been fully prepared to kill him and hide the body, and I shuddered at the thought as I turned a corner and started down the steep, narrow flight of steps that led to the wine cellar. It was separate from the basements, with separate access, and I prayed Ramsey and his men would search the basements before they came here. The steps led down deeper, deeper, the stone walls on either side damp and clammy. The air was clammy, too, and icy cold. A torch was burning in a wall bracket at the bottom. The flickering orange glow washed over the gray stone walls and a heavy oak door blackened with age. It creaked loudly as I pushed it open.

Cam and Ned were waiting just inside. Ned held a pewter candlestick in his hand. The thin flame of the candle revealed their faces and cast dancing shadows over the labyrinth of tall racks filled with dusty bottles. Cobwebs waved in the icy air. Cam's face was still stony, but I could sense the tension that crackled beneath the surface. Ned greeted me with his usual polite nod.

"Everything all right, Lady M.?"

I nodded, shivering in the cold air.

"He see you come down here?" Cam asked.

"Credit me with *some* sense, at least," I retorted. "I sent him out to the garden to look for a book. No one saw me come down here."

"We'd best hurry," Ned said.

Our footsteps rang loudly on the cold stone floor as we wound our way through the labyrinth of racks. I hadn't realized the cellar was so extensive, thousands of bottles resting on the racks with the corks tilting upward, several huge wooden kegs standing against the walls. Ned led us to a rack against the west wall and, setting the candlestick down, removed a dusty brown bottle and thrust his arm into the opening. There was a soft click. The rack swung outward, rusty hinges creaking with a shrill, metallic noise that echoed eerily in the close confines of the cellar. The gray stone wall behind it was moist, streaked brown with mildew, and the stone door was so cleverly concealed as to be barely visible to the naked eye. Ned leaned his shoulder against it and pushed. Currents of icy air swept over us as the door swung inward and revealed the tunnel beyond.

"I'll close the door from inside, Lady M.," Ned explained, "and all you've got to do is swing the wine rack back against the wall, make sure it clicks into place and then put the bottle back."

"I understand."

"If you'll hand me that candlestick, sir."

Cam gave him the candlestick, and Ned used the flame to light a torch he had removed from a niche inside the tunnel. There was an acrid smell as the material caught fire. Smoke billowed. Ned handed me the candlestick and stood waiting inside the tunnel for Cam to join him. My hand trembled slightly, the flame leaping at the end of the candle. Cam looked at me, and I forced myself to meet his gaze with level eyes. I couldn't bear it. I couldn't. My heart was going to be torn out of my body all over again.

"Cherbourg," he said. *"Le Dauphine*. It sails in two weeks."

"Good-bye, Cam."

"I love you, Miranda. Remember that."

His voice was flat, that harsh, handsome face without expression. He hesitated a moment longer, looking into my eyes, and then he turned and stepped into the tunnel and Ned shut the door and the light of my candle washed over the damp stone wall. Tomorrow, I told myself. Tomorrow I will cry. Tomorrow I will grieve. I couldn't afford that luxury now. I pushed the wine rack back. It was surprisingly heavy. There was a soft click as it locked into place, and I slipped the dusty brown bottle back into its slot and started back through the labyrinth, the pain a vital force inside, destroying me from within.

He was safe now. That was all that mattered. With Ned's help he would get to the fishing village and take the boat and safely cross the Channel and be out of harm's way. I moved slowly past the racks of wine, cobwebs waving in the air, brushing my face and hair. I wiped them away. He was safe now and the soldiers would continue to search the house and later Ramsey would get word from the village and they would all be on their way to Dover. I stopped a few feet from the door and forced back a sob as the pain swept over me. I closed my eyes and sent up a silent prayer for strength. Several agonizing moments went by before I finally left the cellar and went upstairs to join my brother.

38

WHY MUST THE SKY BE A PURE PALE BLUE UNFURLING overhead like fine blue silk and shimmering with silver sunlight? Why must the air be clear and sharp and clean, silver-stained and marvelously invigorating? The sunlight gilded the gray rocks with silver sheen and made rippling sunbursts on the water. The water was calm, waves washing gently over the shore below, a darker blue than the sky and tinted a deep purple on the horizon. The gulls were silver-winged today, and they circled and soared high against the blue as though in celebration of a rare and radiant day. Why, when my soul was bleak, must the beauty of the afternoon spread out before me as though in mockery? I strolled along the edge of the cliffs, my heart numb with grief as the gentle breeze tossed tendrils of auburn hair across my cheeks and caused my dusty rose skirt to billow over the ruffled white petticoats beneath.

I paused for a moment to gaze across the water at that misty line where sea met sky in a blur of blues and purple. Three days had passed, and Cam was safely in France now, awaiting his departure for a new land, a new life. Ned had returned late that afternoon to inform me that all had gone well, without a single mishap. They had followed the tunnel to the abandoned tin mine and the carriage had been waiting. Even as Ramsey and his men continued to search the house, they had reached the fishing village and made arrangements with Ned's smuggler friend who had readily agreed to "help out a colleague" and "put one over on them bleedin' redcoats." He and Cam had departed immediately in his sturdy boat on waters smooth and becalmed after the previous night's storm, Ned watching from the pier until the boat was a mere speck on the horizon. Shortly after one in the afternoon Ramsey had received word from a concerned villager that a man fitting Cam's description had purchased a ticket to Dover and taken the nine o'clock coach and he and his men had hastened to the village to confirm the report before charging off after the coach.

They hadn't overtaken it. Young Tim had come back home yesterday afternoon to regale his uncle with amusing tales of the chaos in Dover as the redcoats ran through the town, turning it upside down in their anxiety to find the wanted man. Ramsey had been in a panic, Tim reported. The lad had audaciously volunteered to help the soldiers search the docks, laughing to himself as the ashen-faced Ramsey barked orders and deployed his men in all directions. Ramsey knew full well that if he failed to deliver the rebel Gordon, Cumberland's wrath would know no bounds. It gave me great satisfaction to visualize that meeting when the nervous captain made his report to the livid, apoplectic prince. Instant demotion was going to be the least of his worries.

It was over now. In eleven days that ship would sail from Cherbourg, taking Mr. James Ingram to his new position as owner of a newspaper in Philadelphia, and the rebel Cam Gordon would no longer exist except in my heart. Leaving the sun-drenched cliffs, I walked slowly toward the trees separating them from the grounds of Mowrey House. He would make a brilliant editor, I reflected. All the fire and fury that had gone into his novels would go into his paper now, and it would crackle with controversy. How exciting it was all going to be for him, how challenging and stimulating. James Ingram would soon make a name for himself, and I felt sure he would be enormously successful, a firebrand in a country of firebrands, a rebel in a country where rebellion was the norm. There would be constant crises, but it would never be dull.

Sunlight slanted through the tree limbs, spreading deep blue-gray shadows over the ground. A bird warbled gleefully over-head. I touched a tree trunk, gray bark dotted with rusty flecks, knobbed with dark gold lichen. And me? No more crises, no more confusion, no more exhilarating highs and shattering lows. I would write another book, then another, and . . . and my work would sustain me. I would continue to play the chatelaine of Mowrey House and life would be calm and peaceful, each day serene and . . . and duller than the one before. I had my own identity now, it was true, but now, as I rubbed the rough bark and listened to the bird, I realized that that hard-won identity was a hollow thing and had little to do with the woman within.

I was a Mowrey by birth, Lady Miranda by right, but Duch-ess Randy had grown up on the streets of St. Giles, tough and fearless and living off her wits, often hungry, always on the alert for danger, and the education she had received on the streets was an integral part of the woman. M.J. had toiled endlessly to perfect her craft, to achieve a goal, and the need for work was deeply ingrained now, the need for achievement as well. While I had been renovating the house and helping my brother to realize our father's dream, I had been able to play the role of Lady Miranda with relative ease, but now . . . now I realized I could never be the refined, elegant creature I would have become had my father not died, had my uncle not sent my mother away. I may have been born a Mowrey, but fate had decreed I become the woman I was today.

And that woman was only half alive. Part of her had died when that stone door swung to and locked into place. A vital, invigorating force had suddenly ceased being, a flame snuffed out, for fate had decreed I love Cam Gordon, too. Without him I was incomplete, a part of me—perhaps the most important part—simply unable to function. I had survived for three and a half years, and during that time I had accomplished much, but I had been living in a state of suspension, that vital part of me numb. Four nights ago, in the black hall, while the storm raged furiously, I had sprung to life again, wildly, gloriously, passionately alive, every fiber of my being alert and aglow. As the sunlight streamed through the trees in wavering silver columns, as the blue-gray shadows spread beneath them, I faced that truth. I had used my head, yes, and I had condemned myself to a life in limbo.

Leaving the shelter of the trees, I walked slowly toward Mowrey House, passing through the gardens. The house stood bleak and gray, yet clothed in its own rugged grandeur. Behind it the moors stretched out, gray and tan, brown and mossy green, brushed with a hazy patina of silver this afternoon, rocks gleaming, patches of bog a flat silver-black. I could see the old Roman ruins atop the hill, mere specks in the distance, and I thought of my mother and that stormy afternoon when she had become a woman in the arms of Jeffrey Mowrey. There had been but one man for Honora, too, but . . . she hadn't been given a second chance.

"Miranda!"

I turned to see my brother tearing out of the house and racing toward me, that unruly mop of blond hair flopping over his brow. The tail of his light tan frock coat flopped, too, bouncing behind him, and he was swinging a flat leather case by the handle. Dashing past a row of rhododendrons, he knocked against them with one shoulder and scattered pale lilac and lilac-pink blossoms onto the path. His lean, lanky body lent itself superbly to the sprint, loose and nimble if not precisely a portrait of grace in motion.

"I've been looking all *over* for you," he said irritably, drawing up in front of me.

"I decided to take a walk. Why aren't you at the factory?"

"I left early. I have something to show you."

The irritation was merely a pose. Exuberant, bursting with high spirits, he grinned, his gray eyes aglow with excitement. I felt a wonderful rush of affection for this exasperating and engaging creature who seemed so much younger than I. Smiling, I reached up to adjust the folds of his yellow silk neckcloth, tucking it back into the top of his wheat-colored waistcoat. Douglas grimaced, eager to spring his surprise.

"I have something to show you."

"You said that already."

"You might show a little *int*erest."

"I'm wildly interested, Douglas."

"Moping around these past three days, going for long walks, silent and sad, not even *spat*ting with me—I've been worried about you, Miranda."

"You needn't be."

"I'm not as dense and unobservant as you think I am. What's a brother for if you can't talk to him and let him comfort you and give you advice and—"

"You said you have something to show me," I said, cutting him short.

"We really ought to make an occasion of it. We ought to open a bottle of champagne and be real festive, but I was so eager to show you I couldn't wait. I looked all over the house and couldn't find you anywhere and I ran into Polly and she told me you'd gone for another of your moody walks and I rushed out to find you. This is a very auspicious moment, Miranda."

"Indeed?"

"It bloody well is!"

Genuinely irritated now, he gave me an exasperated look, prepared to sulk. I smiled again and touched his cheek and told him I was sorry, and after a moment he grinned, his sunny disposition shining anew. He opened the flat leather case with considerable flourish and held the top back so I could see what it contained. Inside, resting on a nest of heavy cream velvet, was the plate I had first seen in watercolor the day I arrived. It gleamed against the velvet like some priceless treasure, incredibly beautiful, and I gazed at it for several moments, unable to speak.

"Well?" Douglas inquired.

"It—Douglas, it's even more beautiful than I imagined it would be."

It was indeed. Outlined in gold, the pink rim was a rich, dark pink unlike any I had ever seen, a sumptuous pink glowing with warmth, and the tiny garlands of pale blue flowers and jade leaves were done in exquisite detail, colors delicate and distinct, and the flowers and leaves scattered lightly over the smooth white center of the plate looked as though they had fallen there by accident, so superbly had they been done. Touched by the afternoon sunlight, gold glittering and colors aglow, it was so lovely I felt tears welling in my eyes.

"The rest of the service is finished, too—our first complete set—but I just brought the one plate."

"It's going to make you famous, Douglas."

My brother beamed, full of pride. "We did do rather a nice job," he admitted. "It's going to make you famous, too, Miranda—or more so, I should say."

"What do you mean?"

Douglas grinned again as he closed the case very carefully and made sure it was secure, and then he held it at his side by the thick leather handle, beaming even more.

"As you know, I hadn't settled on a name for this pattern. I have one now. I've decided to call it the 'Lady Miranda.' You're responsible for it, Miranda. If it hadn't been for you, none of this would have been possible."

I was touched, so touched the tears brimmed over my lashes. Douglas looked at me with lovely gray eyes, pleased with the honor he had just bestowed, and he looked startled when I shook my head. I couldn't accept the honor. No. It belonged to someone else, the person who was truly responsible for it all. It belonged to the woman who had come to Mowrey House so many years ago, who had tended him with such care, who had given herself to our father that afternoon in the Roman ruins, who had brought me into the world, a product of that love which had sustained her even unto death.

I wiped the tears away, and it seemed she was here in the

gardens with us, a loving, invisible presence watching over us both. Douglas felt it, too, and he turned his head to follow my gaze, looking with me at the ruins atop the distant hills. He understood. He took my hand in his and squeezed it tightly, remembering, perhaps, a quiet afternoon in the nursery, a five-year-old boy and a gentle young governess who patiently colored the tiny cutout of a figure who so resembled the sister who stood beside him now.

"She was responsible, Douglas," I said quietly. "It should be called 'Honora.'"

He nodded in silent agreement, and we stood there for a few moments as the bird warbled again in a tree behind us and the light breeze stirred the rhododendron blossoms, scenting the air with their fragrance. My brother sighed and gave my hand another squeeze, then released it. A ray of sunlight touched his thick blond hair, giving those unruly locks a silver gold sheen. His gray eyes were thoughtful.

"It's strange, isn't it? She came here almost a quarter of a century ago, and she fell in love with my father, and because—because of her, his dream has finally come true. Mine, too."

"She would have been very proud of you, Douglas," I said. "Both of them would have been proud."

He brushed errant locks from his brow and sighed again, clutching the handle of the case. My dusty rose skirt billowed in the breeze, the silk settling back over the petticoats with a soft rustle. There was a hesitant look in his eyes now, and he seemed suddenly ill at ease. I gave him a questioning glance. He frowned.

"I—uh—I have something else to tell you," he confessed.

"I rather imagined you did."

"It's about Linda."

"I rather imagined it was."

"Dammit, Miranda, I have something very important to say, and I'd be grateful if you wouldn't make fun of me!"

"I couldn't help it, darling. You look so very grave."

"Something happened the other night—the night of the storm. As you know, I was forced to spend the night at Morrison Place and—well, I'm afraid I made a bloody fool of myself."

"Oh?"

"Her father retired early. We'd been discussing Shakespeare and some chap called Marlowe and he had two full glasses of port and started nodding—I was terribly relieved, Shakespeare's not my best subject—and, well, anyway, after a few more minutes he went on up to bed and left Linda and me alone there in the parlor."

"I see."

"There was a fire in the fireplace and the rain was pouring and it was all cozy and romantic and she was wearing a pink dress—not the one she wore to the factory opening, another one. It left her shoulders bare and part of her bosom and she looked so lovely I—well, I made a bloody fool of myself."

"What did you do?"

"I lunged. I grabbed her and kissed her quite savagely— I'd never kissed her before. I'd *wanted* to, of course, but I always managed to restrain myself. Linda—Linda's not the sort of girl you grab and kiss."

"I shouldn't think so."

"You have to play it very cautious with a girl like Linda. You don't want to go too fast. She's a thoroughbred, you see, and they shy easily."

I repressed a smile. For all his experience—and I suspected that it had been extensive, primarily with barmaids and the like—my brother knew very little about women. In that respect, he was no different from most other men.

"And what did the thoroughbred do?" I prompted.

"She kissed me back." He shook his head, still amazed. "She asked me what took me so bloody long. You could have knocked me flat with a feather."

"And then?"

"Then I put my hand on her breast and gave it a squeeze. She slapped me so hard my ears rang for a full ten minutes. She said there'd be none of that sort of thing until we were properly married."

"Smart girl," I said.

"So like a bloody fool I asked her to marry me and she said yes and I spent the night in the guest room feeling trapped and miserable. Jesus! One kiss and she expects me to *marry* her!"

He looked utterly abject, exactly like a little boy who was being punished for reasons unknown, and I allowed the smile to play full on my lips. He saw it and scowled, ready to explode. I gave him a hug. He stood stiff and unresponsive, mouth pouty, the scowl digging a deep furrow above the bridge of his nose. I stepped back, smiling still.

"It's all very well for you to smile!" he snapped. "You're not the one in a trap!"

~544~

"She loves you, Douglas."

He gave me a doubtful look. "You really think so?"

"You're extremely lovable, you silly ass. Of course she loves you, and you love her."

He thought about that for a moment, and then he nodded. "I—I guess maybe I do," he said. "I haven't been able to think straight ever since that day she first came to visit in her bloody cart, so cool and snippy and self-possessed. I wanted to put her in her place. I wanted to—"

He cut himself short, and a mild pink blush actually suffused his cheeks. I had a rather good idea how he would have ended the sentence. He emitted a heavy sigh and tugged at his neck-cloth, getting accustomed to the feelings he had felt all along and refused to acknowledge.

"I'm very happy for you, Douglas. Happy for you both."

"It's just the shock of it all. I mean—I never figured to *marry* her!"

"Men rarely do."

"I—I know this is going to sound idiotic," he said, "but I just couldn't see living the rest of my life without her. Nothing would have any real meaning if Linda weren't there to share it with me."

"It doesn't sound idiotic at all," I told him. "It—it makes perfect sense. Perfect sense," I repeated.

And the numbness wore away and the sadness disappeared and a glorious elation began to stir inside, growing by the moment, sparkling and spreading until I wanted to shout with joy. What a fool I had been! What a bloody fool! My mother had not been given a second chance, but I had . . . and I had almost thrown it away! I knew exactly what Douglas meant. I couldn't see living the rest of my life without Cam Gordon— bloody, infuriating Scot that he was—and nothing would have any real meaning without him. Damn his eyes! I loved the son of a bitch and life would be tumultuous and I would live on my nerves but at least I would be *alive*. The elation continued to sparkle and spread, that vibrant, vital, magnificent life force coursing through my veins like the finest of wine. My brother gave me a puzzled look. I smiled at him. He frowned.

"Is something wrong, Miranda?"

"No—no, everything's right. Everything's wonderfully right! I almost—I was a bleedin' ninny, so smart, so sensible, so soddin' sensible—"

Douglas was genuinely concerned now. He took hold of my

arm, looking at me with alarmed gray eyes.

"I think maybe we'd better go inside."

"Yes!" I said. "There's not a moment to lose."

"You're not upset about Linda, are you? It's true she'll be the lady of the house, but—she won't be sup*plant*ing you. There'll always be a place for you at Mowrey House, Miranda. Linda likes you and you like her and—"

I smiled and shook my head, impatient now, eager to be gone. There was packing to do and I would have to stop off in London for a day to see Marcie and Thomas and make business arrangements with Bancroft, but if I left tomorrow morning I would have ample time for that. Douglas was still chattering away, but I didn't hear a word he was saying. I knew who I was now, at last I knew. I was Cam Gordon's woman, that was my true identity, and he was my man and life with him would rarely be serene but the bastard would get as good as he gave, I'd see to that.

"—no reason at all why we can't all live happily and comfortably together. Linda wants six weeks to make all the preparations, she insists on having a gigantic wedding with all the trimmings and she has to get a trousseau together—women are always thinking about clothes! You'll be the maid of honor, of course, Linda has already mentioned it to me, and—"

"I won't be here, Douglas."

"What? What do you mean?"

"I'm leaving Mowrey House. I'm leaving first thing in the morning. My work here is done, Douglas. Now that you have Linda there's nothing—there's nothing to keep me. I'm thrilled for both of you, believe me. Linda's exactly what you need, and she'll be the perfect mistress of Mowrey House, something I could never be. I have my own life to—"

"Have you lost your *senses*!"

"Not at all. I've come to them at last. I really can't dally out here any longer, Douglas. I have to start packing and—"

"It's that bloody Scot, isn't it?"

I nodded and started moving rapidly up the path to Mowrey House. My brother trotted along beside me, seizing my arm, forcing me to stop alongside the rhododendrons. I gave him an impatient look, hardly noticing him, my mind on other things now. His fingers clasped my arm in a bruising grip, restraining me when I tried to move on.

"Don't think I don't know he was here the other night. I'm not nearly as naive as you think I am, sister dear. Soldiers all over the place, my best suit of clothes missing, Ned gone all day—I can put two and two together. I didn't say anything because I thought the least said the better, but if you think I'm going to let you run off and wreck your life over a—"

"I love him, Douglas. He loves me. He wanted me to go with him, but I sent him away—like an idiot I sent him away—"

"God*damn*, Miranda, the chap's a bloody—"

"He's going to America. His ship sails from Cherbourg in eleven days. I've got to spend a day in London, there's business to take care of, and—"

"You're going to *America* with him!"

"You can't stop me, Douglas."

"Jesus!" he exclaimed. "Are you *sure* about this?"

"I've never been surer about anything."

"All right, then, but I'm not going to let you go tearing off by yourself. I intend to go to London with you and then on to Cherbourg. I intend to meet this man and let him know he'll have me to contend with if—"

He let go of my arm. I hurried on up the path, knocking against the rhododendrons, scattering blossoms in my wake. Douglas scurried after me, trotting to catch up.

"And I'll tell you another thing!" he shouted. "You may not be here for *my* wedding but I'm bloody well going to be there for yours! If that bastard thinks he's going to sweep you off to America without marrying you first, he's in for a big surprise! I'll use a gun if I have to, but—"

I wasn't listening to him. I was listening to the music inside me, a joyous music that filled my soul with splendor. Skirts flying behind me, my hair flying too, I raced toward the house with my brother in hot pursuit, still shouting at me as I hurried up the steps and into the arms of the future.

About the Author

JENNIFER WILDE lives in Texas in a three-storey, octagon-shaped red brick house filled with books, paintings, antiques, and an old manual typewriter on which another bestseller is currently being written.